VAMPIRE MASTER

Vampire Queen Series: Club Atlantis

JOEY W. HILL

Vampire Master

Vampire Queen Series: Club Atlantis

A Vampire Queen Series Novel - Book #16

Cover design by W. Scott Hill

SWP Digital & Print Edition publication December 2019 by Story Witch Press, 452 Mattamushkeet Dr., Little River, South Carolina 29566, USA

Digital ISBN: 978-1-942122-99-9

Print ISBN: 978-1-951544-00-3

Big and bad enough to be any girl's nightmare—or her best dream ever...

Beyond your grasp. Those are the three words that come to mind, every time Ella sees Wolf at Club Atlantis. He earns the term Master, in and out of scene, yet there is something deeper and darker about him. She wants to dive into that abyss.

Wolf sees the yearning. But the submissive he ultimately claims will become his servant, soul-bound to him for all eternity. Ella is a natural submissive, with an endless desire to please. She's perfect for the role, really. Except Ella is a gift he doesn't deserve.

However, vampires are wired one way—to take what they want. Even Wolf isn't strong enough to resist his nature...

Non-Series Titles

Chance of a Lifetime

Choice of Masters

If Wishes Were Horses

Medusa's Heart

Make Her Dreams Come True

Snow Angel (short story)

Submissive Angel

Threads of Faith

Unrestrained

Virtual Reality

www.ingramcontent.com/pod-product-compliance
Lightning Source LLC
Chambersburg PA
CBHW051931020726
47501CB00001B/80

* 9 7 8 1 9 5 1 5 4 4 0 0 3 *

ACKNOWLEDGMENTS

Authors find inspiration in so many places. The conversations and revelations of others often enrich our work, providing us direction. This is the case with Ella's view on a life of abundance. I send a tremendous thank you to LK for opening my mind to that viewpoint, so Ella could express her core identity in such a powerful way.

Also, gratitude to the Muse, who I do not thank as often and fervently as She deserves. Thank you for taking me down the paths of all these stories, introducing me to unforgettable characters, and helping me share them with readers. If there are any shortcomings in the telling, the fault is mine, because you certainly give me treasure. No matter when this current life journey ends, you have offered me something tangible to leave behind, each book intended to be a celebration of the many ways love can be expressed.

Author's Note: In my mind, my Muse is a She, though I expect creative AND divine energy are far beyond our understanding of gender or species. Thank heavens for that, because the mystery and wonder of it all make for many, many amazing stories.

CHAPTER ONE

She'd made herself a promise that she'd stop getting these obsessions. They were too painful, and embarrassing. But she kept coming back to this one. To him.

He scared her like walking the narrow ledge collaring a tall building. That thrilling fear of being so close to the line between the known and unknown.

She wanted to walk that path all the way around, see the view from every angle. Then, opening her hands and letting go of fear, she'd stand at one corner, position her toes over the edge. She'd raise her arms above her head, and tip her face up to the wind and moonlight. Totally trusting, she'd feel joy when he laid his palm in the center of her back, giving her the heat of his touch before he gently pushed her into space.

He'd do it, knowing she could fly.

At that moment she would finally *know* what life was supposed to be, not simply long for the frustratingly nebulous sense of it. She was sure it was there, just past a boundary she needed to step across. The point of no return.

She'd stepped across a lot of lines, looking for it. While that worried people who cared about her, it wasn't the jump she sought, but what lay beyond it. She didn't know how to explain that.

Any more than she knew how to explain her feelings about Wolf, since the sum total of their meaningful interactions was less than the time it took to tell a child a favorite bedtime story.

She grimaced. If she was at home in *her* bed, she might argue the whole "time is a relative construct" thing with herself, but fortunately she was at Club Atlantis. Too much good stuff was happening tonight. Time to lock the obsessive part of her mind in a closet and focus on the here and now.

"When the Lights Go Out" by Five was pummeling the air, giving it a heated edge and sparkle, for those with the eyes to see it. It was just before midnight, the best time to wander through the club. People were settling into their scenes, and those who couldn't lock into anything had left, so that swirling, heavy energy could permeate every corner of the club without disruption.

Entering the club from the outside world at this time of night was like stepping into a fairy circle. She'd dance until her heart was exploding, but she wouldn't want to stop. Even if, when the night ended, she found a hundred years had passed, everything she once knew as her life left behind.

That would be okay, because the people she loved best in the whole world were here, in the place where she felt most at home.

Ella let the music take hold of her, twisting and rolling her body, dropping her head back so her long hair brushed her backside. The blood red waist cincher she wore tightened its hold. The white gauze shirt beneath the laced garment had a scoop neck and flowing sleeves, looking like something a pirate woman would wear. The thin fabric revealed and caressed the soft smudge of her nipples, and strained over her full breasts.

Her staff sub service collar and a pair of black latex shorts completed the look, the points of the shirt loose and fluttering over her hips and backside. A temporary ink tattoo of a flight of birds crossed her sternum, a few fluttering up the side of her throat.

As she danced, she threaded her way through the groups of people milling in the social areas, sometimes rubbing up against the ones she knew. She was rewarded with smiles, an affectionate touch in return.

Mistress Chantal was leaning against the divider between two booths, twirling a gleaming red carbon cane deftly over her scarlet painted fingernails. She wore a black form-fitting dress printed with a gold and red dragon. The whiskered creature wound its way over her breasts, waist and hips, enhancing those curves and making her even more enthralling than usual. Her hair was swept up and held with gold pins tipped with scarlet porcelain flowers. The look accentuated her delicate features and sharp eyes.

Ella had seen physically powerful men stay at Chantal's feet in whatever position she demanded, no restraints necessary, for impossibly long stretches of time. Cocks stiff with agonizing levels of need, bulging muscles straining, but heads bowed. As if they'd wait for her command until hell froze over. When she finally let them come, the experience was so overwhelming that some of them blacked out.

It was hugely arousing to watch, but Ella's favorite part was the aftermath. Chantal might kneel, cradle the male in her arms, his head against her breast and her arm around his wide, rounded shoulders. She'd ground him with sips of water and soothing words, as gentle then as she'd been ruthless before.

The dress looked fabulous with her glossy black knee-high boots. When Ella reached her, the Mistress looped her toned arm around Ella's waist, the two of them moving into a playful bump and grind. The music had moved on to the primal drumbeat sounds of Gloria Estefan's "Don't Let This Moment End," the Hex Hector club mix.

Don't let this moment end...

Ella felt that way every night here. She never wanted the sun to rise. When she worked at Atlantis, morning was her least favorite time of day.

They adjusted the steps of their fluid dance as needed to protect the male Chantal had stretched out on the floor. His arms were out to his sides, his chin lifted and body frozen. Since he wore belted jeans and nothing else, a woman could appreciate the broad shoulders, the cut abs, the arousal straining against denim. He had a beard and a mane of coarse dark hair, a few strands scattered over the gleaming hair on his broad chest.

He had an intimate view of the two women dancing over him, because Chantal hadn't commanded him to close his eyes. Ella noticed his avid blue-gray gaze tracked the Mistress like a tiger ready to hunt for his dinner.

As the music segued into "Dancing Machine" by the Jackson 5, Chantal laughed, her white teeth flashing. On the horn section, she and Ella raised their arms above their heads and bumped hips, this way, that way, stepping left and right over the male, precise and graceful. As they kept it going, others joined in around them.

Using a flourish of the cane, Chantal moved everyone back, cutting a wider swathe around her captive. With a provocative serpent-like roll of her upper body to her hips, she spun down to a seated position on her submissive's chest.

She arched, rubbing her ass in slow circles against that furred terrain. Ella watched his eyes course up her body, following the upward tilt of her breasts. Chantal reversed direction, curving forward to press a kiss to his forehead. Her command for stillness meant he couldn't reach for anything, with mouth or hands. His lips parted as if he had muttered a curse, while hers curved against his flesh in response.

The Mistress stood again, one foot planted by his elbow, the other heeled boot propped on his chest. She reached under the stretched fabric of her dress, bringing a pair of black lace panties into view. With admirable balance, she worked them off, shifting her stance, then draped them over the edge of the carbon cane.

"Open your mouth," she said, gesturing to her own since she didn't care to shout over the noise. He read the command, his lips parting.

She brought the panties down, dropping them on the lower half of his face. His chest expanded as he inhaled deep. Chantal's eyes glowed at his response. Using the tip of the cane, she pushed the panties into his open mouth, balling them up.

Ella had seen her do the same maneuver with a violet wand. Chantal would never activate it while it was near a sub's mouth, but the suggested threat added to the sub's experience for that night's scene. As the cane did for this male.

Chantal had one boot sole pressed against his sizeable erection. As she rocked toe to heel and back, applying a quelling pressure, she touched his arms with her cane. "My legs," she said, loudly enough to be heard by him this time. "No higher than my knees."

His large hands left the floor. Ella gave him credit for not grabbing Chantal like a sailor seizing a mermaid. He molded his palms over her calves, just above her ankles, slowly, each finger pressing into the thin layer of boot so she would feel the strength in his hands.

Chantal's eyes glittered, her lips parting. An expression that said

Nicely done. This man was focused on giving her as much pleasure as she was giving him.

The spontaneous scene space the Mistress had created had drawn a watching crowd. Ella didn't think he was aware of that, even if his subconscious was feeding on the wave of voyeuristic energy.

When Chantal glanced at Ella, Ella fanned herself and did a little "go girl" spin with fist pump that had Chantal's lips curving. Then Ella leaned close enough to speak in her ear.

"You didn't tell me you'd caught Aquaman."

Chantal shot her a wicked look. Combing her fingers through Ella's thick locks, she wrapped the strands up in her fist and gave them a firm tug. "Looks a lot like him, doesn't he? There's no fish I can't hook, little one. You know that."

After a few more pleasant moments, Ella left her to it, moving onward. Next stop was the largest public play area in the club. She stopped in the wide archway, hugging the right side to stay out of the flow of foot traffic.

Point Blank's rock and roll "Great White Line" had started up. *Never going home...* Ella recalled the scene from Pink Floyd's *The Wall*, where the fan girls overran band security. The age of metal bands and their groupies. Latex and body glitter, long hair and hungry eyes.

She should propose a Rock Star night to Anwyn, Club Atlantis's owner, and see how that played out in their world. While she expected most of the Doms would go the rock star route and the subs would take a groupie or roadie role, she could imagine some who would flip it. A rock star wanting to be under the command of a devoted Dominant fan. Or maybe a Dom roadie punishing his rock star boss for acting like a spoiled diva.

She grinned. Anwyn called Ella her official Minion of Play. Gideon, who belonged to Anwyn and was part of the club's executive management staff, had nicknamed Ella "Julie," after *The Love Boat* cruise director. Ella wore both names with pride.

The first time she'd approached Anwyn with her ideas, she'd been so nervous. But Madelyn and Chantal, both Mistresses on staff, had encouraged her to do it. They'd told her to pitch it to Anwyn the same way she'd pitched it to them, spoken straight out of her well of love for the club.

"New members or guests might want to play, but at first they're not sure. They want to watch, get into the flow gradually. We also have a lot of people who come *just* to watch, because that's all they need or can do. We're already doing demos, which are great, but theme nights would show the application in a fun, interactive way. Then the more self-conscious people start to feel comfortable."

"Like getting people out on the dance floor, so the more bashful ones can join in," Anwyn had said.

"Exactly. And the bigger the voyeur crowd, the more energy it gives the public scenes."

Bringing in guest DJs had been another of Ella's ideas. She visited the clubs and raves where the DJs showed their stuff, listened to what they put together, and brought her recommendations back to Anwyn for vetting.

Ella's attention landed on her latest find, surrounded by sound equipment, stationed on a raised platform. Ed was an unassuming-looking guy, with curly brown hair, golden-brown eyes, and a shy smile. He was putting together some unusual and ambiance-creating pieces, perfect for the mood of the club. That was part of the fun of having the DJ; seeing how the moods he evoked altered whatever might happen, spontaneously or planned.

If he wasn't totally freaked out by what he was seeing inside the exclusive Club Atlantis, he'd hopefully become a regular. Since he was laughing in a relaxed kind of way at something a couple dressed in nothing but cuffs and chains were calling up to him, the signs were encouraging.

He was back to Gloria Estefan, the hot fast Latin rhythm of *Oye,* a duet with Pablo Cortez. Ella glanced back to see even more people crowding onto the dance floor, a mix of writhing bodies, glinting metal and rippling, colorful fabrics.

Hey boy, I see you looking, I know you're watching...

But you won't make that move.

The line fit Chantal and her Aquaman. Except for the "boy" thing. That sub was a hundred percent knee-weakening grown man, head to toe. She bet Chantal had moved him to a private room, the preliminaries over. The overflow area around the dance floor perimeter was getting too crowded to safely keep him there.

While the DJ was piling them onto the dance floor, he was also boosting the vibe in the public play space. Ella had seen every emotion happen here. Tears and laughter, as well as revelations, from small epiphanies to life-changing ones. Sometimes someone experienced a total breakdown of who they thought they were. Or laid a new foundation for someone they'd never thought they could be. People could fall in love here or in lust, only for the moment or forever.

Usually when she wandered through this section, she would take her time, absorbing all those different possibilities. But now that she was here, her steps quickened, taking her toward the session happening in the back corner.

If she was being honest with herself, it had been her destination all along. Though when it came to Wolf, she didn't always believe in being honest. Comforting lies kept her from making a fool of herself.

Most of her intense crushes landed on people out of her reach. In this case, that was the world's biggest understatement. Compared to those earlier obsessions, Wolf was another solar system.

Yet here she was.

People had sunk to the floor around him in a semi-circle, just outside the marked boundary of the session space. The marking was something the staff Doms had suggested a while ago. Now the more popular scenes didn't result in lookers-on pressing too close, disrupting the connection between the top and bottom, or causing safety issues if the Dom was throwing a whip or doing anything that needed more elbow room. This corner was also set up with an elevated dais, which helped reinforce that barrier.

She eased herself into a small opening close to the wall. Wolf had a naked female submissive restrained on a black wooden frame. The silver of the chains clipped to her cuffs gleamed like her perspiring henna-colored skin.

She was in her forties, and her stretch marks said she'd had children. She was wide-hipped, with a large, heart-shaped backside and full breasts. *Selena* and *Mario* were tattooed on one shoulder, surrounded by a spray of flowers. Her children, Ella deduced. Her long dark hair had been bound up in a strap and pinned to the cross, holding it out of the way and increasing her immobility.

It was rare to see Wolf with a woman. Initially, Ella had thought men were his dedicated preference. However, the first time she'd seen him do a public scene with a female, his absorption and sexual interest had been no less intense. There'd been a different tone to the pause and transition moments, though. Softer. Once or twice he'd paced away, taken a seat to stare at her as he sipped from a bottle of water. Something about the straight set of his body, a tension in his shoulders, had made Ella wonder if women were more difficult for him, more emotionally draining.

In addition to regular sessions like this, he did BDSM therapy. Not just for their members, but for guests from other clubs, since his reputation had gotten around. Those sessions were always private room scenes.

She would have dearly loved to watch one, and not merely because of the professional interest. He was so contained on the public floor, yet there was an energy behind his gaze that hinted of a storm of limitless magnitude. The kind that came with thunder and lightning which split the heavens, and brought torrential rains. Rains that could put out the fires that roared through the heart, leaving loss and never-ending pain in their wake. Was she being fanciful, or could he really do that for others? Would she want him to do it for her?

She'd only have to ask. She could book his time like anyone else, and receive a hefty employee discount.

Yet she didn't ask. It wasn't what that obsessive side of her wanted, and she was smart enough to contain it, mostly. Taking only a bite didn't do anything but increase the craving for something she likely couldn't have.

In a futile attempt to prove she had some self-control, she'd made herself look at the female sub first. When she did glance his way, she forced herself to do a slow drift, rather than snapping her gaze to him like a rubber band fired from a pointed finger. Her reward was absorbing his impact in a gradual way, a slow fill of her lower extremities with the sweetness of building desire.

No offense to the entity who had created him, but whoever had released Wolf to walk among mortals had been freaking insane to let him go.

Six foot five. Skin like charred bronze. Eyes like silver lightning. A stern mouth that went with the prominent sloped cheekbones and set jaw. His shoulders were broad. Tonight, Wolf wore metallic coated black denim jeans over laced boots, no shirt, exposing a lot of gleaming brown muscle. He was a giant, a sharply sculpted one, every shape chiseled. One part ancient warrior king, one part sensual demon lord, comprised of black smoke and fire.

She'd looked at prime male specimens before, but Club Atlantis attracted all body types. Different ages and sizes engaged in the artful give and take of Domination and submission. When done right, it erased physical boundaries and took them into far more spiritual and emotional areas. That was why she knew it wasn't merely his physical side that held her attention.

When she gazed at him, she saw the endless darkness surrounding that building ledge, far up in the clouds. She couldn't see what was in it, but it was waiting. Pulling at her to leap. When he pushed her, he would be pushing her into the abyss of himself.

Time to get a grip. No matter how strong the pull she felt toward him, they had a nonexistent relationship, really. He never invited her to do a session with him, though he occasionally accepted Ella's assistance to help him clean up after a scene, or provide backup aftercare. Whatever his thing was, she wasn't it. Which hurt, but that was okay. In their world, the only appropriate response to courteous rejection was gracious acceptance. Even when a childish temper tantrum or cathartic cry would be far preferable.

He was aware of everyone, grasping details that made anyone in his sphere feel exceptionally noticed. Which meant his notice of her wasn't exceptional at all.

But what should be and what was, weren't always on the same page in her mind. When his gaze flickered in her direction now, marking her, her arms tightened against herself. She had them folded against her upper torso, her fingers wrapped over her hip bones as she leaned against the wall. A protective posture, or perhaps self-restraint, so she didn't fling herself at his feet.

He turned his attention back to his submissive, putting his hand on the woman. Her spine was curved, every vulnerable vertebra visible. Her backside was stained red, handprints blotched beneath the sharp stripes of a switch.

He could be extreme, or he could handle a newbie. He evaluated what every sub needed and took them to their limits to give them the experience they'd hoped for, with a thrilling, sometimes terrifying, glimpse of even deeper possibilities. A reevaluation of those limits, or a reinforcement of why they were there.

The woman let out a cry as he dug his fingers into the switch marks. He pushed his knee between her legs, rubbed, a move that made his body flex from back to hip and buttock. "You going to come for me?"

"It hurts," she gasped. "So much..."

"Yeah, it does. You're still going to come for me. Pain doesn't exceed obedience. Does it?" He had a deep voice with a rasping edge. Another erotic rough texture to tease the senses.

She shook her head, but she was shaking, tears running down her face. "Lift your left foot," he said. As he slid his other arm around her waist, holding her securely, he kept moving her against his knee. The coated jeans would provide friction to aroused tissues.

She raised her foot, trembling. He'd changed out the switch for a riding crop and teased the looped end across her sole. He rolled it in his hand, flick, flick, trail. Flick.

Slap!

The sting of the blow wrenched a cry from her throat and had the crowd flinching, even as they remained wide-eyed, leaning forward.

"Work yourself against me as I tickle your feet, *mamacita*," he crooned.

She shuddered, but twitched her hips on him. He moved the hand on her waist up to cup her breast, enjoy a squeezing massage of the curve. His grip showed flesh like rising bread dough between his fingers, and he tugged her nipple between his knuckles. He continued to move his leg back and forth, manipulating her on it as that crop kept falling, as he kept fondling her breasts. His coordination and rhythm were almost inhuman.

With every strike, her cries kept rising, short, clipped wails, pleas. "Please...no more...*no más*..." Then the words gave way to screams of pleasure, as the orgasm overtook the pain, his will demanding compliance from hers.

Ella was quivering, using the embrace of her wrapped arms and tight fingers to stay together and not shatter with the woman. Rapt attention held the crowd around Wolf and the sub, the Doms projecting an additional level of critical attention, learning from his technique.

Ella glimpsed one or two people who looked a little uncertain, newbies unsure about the sub's pleas for no more. Ella knew the woman could safeword and end the scene whenever she wished, but even if she didn't, Wolf was closely monitoring her. If he thought she was too lost in subspace to protect herself, he would act upon that even faster than she could safeword. But Ella made a note to search out those couple of folks after this was over and talk it out with them, be sure they understood. Every staff member was trained to help with education and awareness, and look for the cues of members and guests who needed it.

See? She could stay professional and tuned into her job, even if ninety percent of the rest of her was engrossed by the scene happening before her—or rather, the Master orchestrating it.

Wolf's stern mouth had curved as the woman lost herself to the orgasm. He took her all the way down that slide, until she was at the bottom, slowing down, hips jerking, body shuddering. Now she was talking again, mumbling. "Thank you, *Dios*, thank you..."

She was panting, her hands fisted around the chains, the fine hairs on her nape soaked.

Ella slipped across the session boundary. He hadn't asked for her help, but the staff stayed alert to when a Dom needed more hands, particularly at the end of a strenuous session.

She knelt, reaching out and accepting the crop Wolf handed her without looking, as if he'd expected her to be there. "Water," he said.

She rose to put the crop in the open bag of tools he had left a few feet away. Then she withdrew a bottle of water from a small fridge concealed by a curtain.

He'd released the woman's hands, and eased her down to the floor, her legs too weak to hold her. Wolf dropped to one knee and braced her against it as he chafed her wrists. When Ella handed him the water, he fed it to the sub himself, one hand holding the bottle, the other cupping her face. His attention was on her and her alone. It was painful and glorious to watch. Glorious because that absolute attention was a drug to any submissive. Painful because Ella craved it like air.

"Small sips," Wolf told the woman. She nodded dazedly, her hands cupping his around the bottle. Then, without looking at her, he said, "Thank you, Ella. Stay here."

He didn't say why, but a Dom didn't need to do so. She'd knelt when he'd squatted, because she'd had two options—move back to a respectful distance, or assume a position where she wasn't standing over him, but could still remain close.

No brainer there.

She gazed at his wide back, the long valley of his spine that led to the rise of his taut buttocks covered by the jeans. The back center loop of the jeans stretched against his belt, and she could see the twin depressions marking his pelvic bones. Her eyes returned to the dip of his shaved head as he bent attentively over his charge. The dark bronze skin gleamed under the club lighting. He had no visible tattoos, which was strange for anyone these days, especially in their world. She'd never seen him fully naked, though when he was aroused, there was no doubt he was mouthwateringly equipped.

She imagined trailing her fingers along the curve of his smooth skull, down to his nape, following the track of his spine. Resting her fingers on his waistband, she'd hook them there to hold onto him as she knelt. She thought of putting her mouth on all the places she imagined her fingers touching. What would he taste like? She knew his scent, a mix of spice and damp rain in the forest.

Wolf rose, lifting the woman as if she weighed nothing. He navigated the two steps of the dais with a sure stride, but he moved slowly, head bent over his charge, still talking to her. It gave the clustered people time to ease out of the way.

Kevin was already sitting on a couch close by, waiting on him. The alpha submissive handled most of Wolf's aftercare for him. A fireman in his daily life, he projected the steady confidence that made him excel at both roles. He had red hair and freckles, and rich brown eyes that transformed ordinary features into exceptionally appealing ones.

Many staff Doms chose to delegate aftercare to a trusted sub or fellow Dom. If someone paying for a session confused the emotional intensity of a D/s scene with an invitation for a continued relationship, the incredible intimacy of aftercare could exacerbate that misunderstanding. Handing it over to someone else was a firm demarcation line and grounding step, helping the sub to pull her or himself together, and keep things in perspective.

Wolf put her in Kevin's arms, kissed the woman's hand, touched her face, and then pivoted, striding back toward the platform. His expression while looking upon the submissive had been stern but caring. When he turned away, Ella saw his expression return to its usual unreadable mien.

Everyone had their story for why they embraced a Dom or sub side, even those for whom it was simply a natural evolution of their sexual interests. But he had never revealed his motivations or how he'd reached this level of expertise. That he enjoyed his sessions, she had no doubt. But she'd not yet figured out the more complicated layers to it, except for her belief that men were easier for him.

After he'd left the platform, Ella had stood up and moved to the rack holding sanitary cloths. When he returned, she was wiping down the play area, getting it ready for whoever used it next. She expected clean-up help was why he'd asked her to remain. As he watched her, he withdrew another bottle of water from the fridge and took a swallow.

The audience viewing the session was dispersing. Sometimes he was approached afterwards with questions, but since he kept his attention fixed on Ella, he projected an unmistakable "not right now" vibe that the inquisitive respected.

He remained silent, though. Her skin was tingling under his intent regard. When she finished and disposed of the wipes, he nodded.

"Follow me."

She was surprised when he took her hand, guiding her down the two steps off the dais. But she wasn't objecting. The few times he'd touched her, she'd noted a suppressed power to his grip. His fingers were warm and the right kind of smooth and strong.

Regrettably, he released her after the functional touch and proceeded, her trailing him, until he reached a quiet corner with an unoccupied deep easy chair. He took a seat in it, but sat on the edge, and pointed between his spread knees. It meant he was curved over her as she sank down between his feet. A tremor ran through her as she wondered what this was. She kept her gaze on the floor, though she had the pleasure of it traveling over some tempting terrain before it landed there.

"I want to see your face."

He wasn't typically much for caressing or casual gestures of intimacy. Most of his gestures were very purposed, like now, where he deliberately placed his hand against her face, his forefinger against her cheek bone, his thumb pressed beneath her chin so she had to lift it.

"What were you thinking when you were kneeling behind me, Ella?"

Well, shit. It was far easier for her to lie to herself than to a Dom. No way could she hold back while a Master like Wolf was staring right into her face.

"Don't think of lying to me," he said in a casual, not-at-all-casual voice.

And definitely not when he did that.

She complied, but kept her gaze on the wall just beyond his right ear. He hadn't told her to look him in the eye. In her peripheral vision, she was aware of him studying her so intently, it was like a touch on her face. She had to remind herself of the question.

"I was thinking I'd like to be her," she said. "And I was thinking of touching you."

"Touching me how?"

"Touching your spine." She reached behind herself to run her finger up the mentioned area on her own body. The trail of her fingers on her lower back below the cincher caused gooseflesh, as if it was his hand touching her instead. She blamed his stare for that transference effect.

It wasn't calculated, but the motion thrust her breasts out. His eyes rested there briefly, with enjoyment, then went back to her face.

"And?"

How did he know there was more? He could be guessing, but the best Doms excelled at tormenting a sub this way, pulling way more out of them than they wanted to say.

"Um. Your head. I was thinking of touching your head, feeling the smoothness." She colored a little over that one. His expression remained unreadable. She fought not to squirm.

"What have you done to earn such a privilege?"

The answer to such a question was "Nothing," since a few minutes cleaning his scene space hardly qualified for such a gift. However, other things surged forth, wanting her to offer a different answer. She even boldly looked him in the eye. Well, for a split second. It would have been undetectable by the human eye, but sometimes there were things about Wolf that seemed other than human.

"I could earn it, sir."

He leaned forward until there seemed to be less than a breath between them, though Ella couldn't test that theory since she'd stopped breathing. Wolf curled his fingers around her wrist.

He tugged on it, so she stood up on her knees and inched closer between his, her breasts brushing his bare chest. The thin fabric did nothing to lessen the jolt of sensation that sparked through her body and arrowed downward.

She had to tip her head back to keep her face in his view, as ordered. Those piercing eyes and unsmiling mouth, his scent and heat, were so close, overwhelming her. It was almost a bittersweet relief when his gaze shifted downward.

His free hand lifted. She strangled on a soft sound as he brushed a curved knuckle over one taut peak.

"These beautiful, beautiful tits," he said quietly. "Just out there, begging to be touched."

He fanned his fingers like a bird wing to caress the full mound of one. Then he curled those long, strong digits, and two of his knuckles closed over the nipple, a firm clamp like a hawk's beak. She swallowed, noisily.

He guided her captive hand past his waist, to his back. The heat in the small space between their bodies intensified. "You can touch me as you imagined," he said, that deep, rough voice tagged with a growl. "As long as you can bear the pain. If you ask me to stop, then you have to stop."

"Yes, sir."

He let her wrist go. As soon as she started to slide her liberated hand toward his spine, his knuckles began to tighten.

She knew how to take a lot of discomfort, but an enticement like this made it harder to focus on pain management. She thought of how he'd brought the woman to climax while beating the soles of her feet. It wasn't the first time he'd demonstrated his mastery at bringing a sub right to the threshold where pain and pleasure had to go their separate ways. When he did that, she saw the sadist in him. One who would push a sub past that threshold, feeding on how much she would be willing to take for him.

She wanted to give him that, almost as much as she wanted to touch him. So she was doubly motivated. But hellfire, he *was* going to make her earn it. The pressure of that clamp continued to grow, the pain lancing through her breast as she reached the center of his back.

Her middle and index fingers settled in the valley of his spine, the other three alighting around it. His skin was warm, with an amazing solidity, the skin merely thin gift wrap over muscle. She started low, just above the tempting dip between his buttocks. The hard bones of his pelvis were briefly under the heel of her hand as she trailed upward.

A gasp escaped her as he added a slow twist to the pincer grip. She'd dampened when he took her hand at the dais, so it was no surprise that she was fully wet between her legs. She was incapable of concealing her strong reaction to honoring a Master's will, earning his approval, all while enjoying the pleasures he gave her as a reward.

When she reached the base of his neck, he twisted harder. She cried out, and her fingers jerked, but then she dug them into his flesh. Hell, it hurt so much. Her body was contorted in a rigid curve around that central pain point, trying to ease what couldn't be eased.

"You just have to say stop," he reminded her in a throaty rumble.

Which meant she'd have to stop touching him. She shook her head, a quick snap, and pressed into his punishing touch so she could slide her fingertips along the slope of his ear, headed to his skull. She tipped her face up, gazing at the strong line of his cheek and jaw, his ear, the movement of her arm. She could feel his total focus on her reactions.

He was tall, even sitting. He slid his other arm around her waist, hand over her hip and buttock to give her the extra lift needed to touch the crown of his head. She had a round ass, but his hand was nearly large enough to span the whole cheek he gripped. He scattered her mind when he tightened that hold, kneading. Supporting her needs while he took what he desired. It was a powerful combination, one that could break open dangerous yearnings in her.

He increased the compression on her nipple. She was beyond true agony, but if she wanted to touch him the way she'd described, this was the price.

How badly do you want it? That question always stood guard between a person and any goal worth having. But there was more to this, and that, as much as her own desires, kept her enduring. What was she doing to him? What pleasure was he receiving from her pain, her willingness to bear it simply for the right to touch him?

She passed her fingertips over his crown. Her hand was shaking, but she fought through the pain rocketing through her to make it a caress, to convey how much she liked the feel of him.

Abruptly, the compression stopped, which yanked a moan of relief from her. She sagged against his shoulder and upper arm before she could catch herself, but he had her. He was still holding her up, letting her touch him. She'd stopped moving her hand, though, anticipating what he might command next.

Instead, he dipped his head down, making her heart beat faster and giving her more access. An unspoken permission to continue.

She breathed out a sigh as she touched his skull. A man who shaved his head had to care for it, to keep it gleaming and smooth like this. She wouldn't mind helping with that, rubbing in whatever after-shave products he used to keep it pleasurable to the touch.

She imagined how this felt to him, the tiny tracks each of her fingertips were making over his bare skin, a skimming, easy caress. Down to the nape, behind the ear, back up. The head, nape and occipital bone were all erogenous zones. His breath heated the base of her throat, and she realized his head had dropped further.

He closed his hand fully over her breast, massaging her throbbing nipple in the nest of his palm, soothing while he explored the fullness of the curve. Her breath caught again as he put his mouth on the top of her breast.

Now she had both hands on him, one stroking his nape, measuring the width of his shoulders. The other continued to caress and explore his head, the shape of ears, the creases at the base of his skull, then around to the temple and up to that crest again.

He moved his touch up her back, wound his fingers into her hair, and drew her head back farther, way farther. He arched her over his arm as he nuzzled her collar bones, used his tongue to tease her temporary tattoo, all the little birds fluttering up her throat. She could hear the artery pounding harder beneath his mouth and he paused, his fingers tightening on her. When his teeth scraped her, she moaned, and he muttered something that reminded her of Aquaman, the way he'd cursed against the demand for self-restraint. But she was the sub. Wolf could do as he liked. She wanted him to do whatever he wished.

After a charged moment, he moved downward, lips playing over the birds on her sternum. Then he placed his mouth fully over her nipple. An even more needy sound escaped her throat as he suckled her through the cloth, rubbed the folds of it wetly against her. She swayed in his hold, her hands dropping to grab his shoulders. They felt wide enough to carry the world.

Most of the things she did at Club Atlantis had a very defined structure. Beginning of session, end of session. Wolf hadn't set any parameters. Just brought her here, asked her a question, made clear his price for the answer. She didn't have any context or meaning for what he was doing. She was adrift on a heavy tide of feeling. Her sex was throbbing, making her want to rub herself against him.

He lifted his head, and cupped hers in one hand. She was bent back over his arm, still on her knees but almost parallel to the floor as he leaned over her. He'd left the chair and dropped onto one knee to hold her like this, suckle her nipple. Her hair was brushing the floor while his fingers remained buried in it, his palm supporting her skull.

He looked down at her breasts, straining against the gauzy cloth. "Show me the one I hurt," he said.

She fumbled her way to her chest, found the loose elastic of the scoop neckline. Lifting it over the nipple and pulling the fabric down, she exposed the breast to him. Her whole body quivered at his look, the silver-touched-with-fire irises getting more iridescent.

"You've pleased me, Ella," he said.

"Thank you, sir." Her voice was barely a breath.

"There will be bruising around it. If you do a session, you'll tell the Dom to avoid that area." He lifted his gaze to her, and if he'd driven a spike through a collar around her throat, locking it permanently, he couldn't have her attention more completely. "No one touches that nipple but me, until I say so. The rest of you is fine, but that one belongs to my mouth and my hand. You understand?"

She found her voice again, somewhere, somehow. "Yes, sir."

He lifted her hand from his shoulder and examined it, his fingers spreading hers, his thumb running over her palm. Tingles shot through her arm, to her upper torso, flushing her neck and making her exposed nipple harder.

"Curious," he murmured. He brought her hand back up to his scalp and placed it against the broadest part of his skull. As he pressed her palm against the heat of flesh and resilience of bone, his gaze pinned hers. "That's a place only you have touched, like this, in a very long time."

He straightened and brought her up out of the arched position, lifting her to her feet as if she weighed nothing, even though he stayed on one knee. Once she was upright, he adjusted the neckline of her shirt. She wasn't much taller than him, even while he was kneeling.

For a minute, she felt like a little girl, her daddy straightening her clothes. The impression was enhanced by the stern way he was looking at her. Because of what he said next, she wondered if he'd intended that.

"I'm doing a workshop on Daddy Dom/little girl play at Friday's early evening orientation session. I need an assistant. You'll be there at seven."

Though it wasn't the primary form of BDSM expression for either of them, they'd both had plenty of experience with guests and members who did enjoy Daddy Dom play. That was why he was asking for her assistance, she told herself. There was nothing unusual about it.

Except he'd never asked her to assist him before, despite the wealth of expertise she had, in a variety of areas.

Sorting quickly through her complicated schedule, she was relieved to find she could make that work. Saying she couldn't do it would have caused her far worse pain than what he'd done to her nipple. Now that he'd taken his soothing hand and mouth away, the throbbing was back. But she wondered if the thumping pulse of blood she felt in the abused area had more to do with the awareness he'd planted in her mind than the physical trauma.

No one would touch that part of her but him. It was his, until he said otherwise. What was happening here? This wasn't a session. What was he doing?

She knew the boundaries and negotiations that went into healthy Dominant and submissive relationships. She could ask for permission to ask questions, request definitions, structure, to whatever this was. She wasn't weak-minded or desperate, unwilling to ask or say no for fear of rejection. That kind of mindset was born of insecurity, a poor self-image. Anwyn and the other Dominants were quick to detect it when it came through the doors. They either educated the sub to bring them up to speed, or regretfully denied them membership until they could get to a healthier place.

So it wasn't that which kept her silent. Something about him had always been...more, when it came to the Dom thing. As if his Dominance went beyond a sexual orientation, which was an odd thought, since an orientation was part of a person's core identity. Regardless, she couldn't find it in herself to question him now. Instead, she was drifting in a haze of instant recall, remembering the way he'd bent his head to let her touch his neck and head. His skull had been so close to her mouth she could have pressed her lips to his flesh, as she wound her arms around his broad shoulders.

The music had changed radically. The DJ had dialed it down with "Danny Boy," sung by a female vocalist.

I will sleep in peace until you come to me...

She didn't know about that, but peace wasn't always peaceful. Sometimes it rode the current of something overflowing with possibilities, right over a waterfall and down beneath it. The pounding strength could drive her to her knees, keeping her exactly where she wanted to be. In over her head.

"Yes, sir," she said. "Seven o'clock." *I'll be there.*

She didn't say that part, because there was no need. His expression said no other answer was possible.

CHAPTER TWO

Grenadine had been his last session of the evening. Usually, Wolf stayed longer, helped monitor the floor, maybe picked up an additional walk-in scene, but tonight, after what had happened with Ella, he finished up and headed out. There was plenty of night left, but he needed to think, so he drove to the place he currently used for his daylight sleep. He'd owned the building since the nineties, renting out the top space for income while he lived in the basement. Beneath the basement was a bomb shelter only he and the City of Atlanta records office knew about. It had been constructed by the original builder, back in the Cold War fifties.

A management company handled the property, so the tenants didn't know he was the landlord. He was just the shadowy renter who lived in the basement apartment but was rarely seen coming or going.

He'd outfitted the apartment to be a comfortable living space when he wanted to use it that way. Once in the bedroom, he punched in the code that opened up the insulated back panel of the bedroom closet—no hollow sounds if someone tapped on it. That gave him access to the stairs leading down to the bomb shelter, an area with a bedroom, kitchen and living room.

It was the perfect hideaway for a vampire—or a person assuming they could outlive the apocalypse.

He'd changed clothes at the club and wore comfortable jeans and a button-down shirt. He removed his shoes and socks before he sank down in his large easy chair. As he picked up the pack of cigarettes on the side table and shook one out to light it, he tried to figure out what the fuck he'd been thinking tonight.

But he knew. Over the past several weeks, his path had crossed with Ella on two different occasions, outside the club walls. He didn't engage with a submissive like her, beyond the basic courtesies that working in the same club involved. But one night, he'd been out near a bookstore she frequented, something he hadn't known until he'd seen her go into it. He'd followed her in there, talked to her a few minutes, then left. Well, after dropping a bag containing her favorite local deli sandwich in her bike basket. She'd looked pale and tired when he'd talked to her. It had bothered him.

But he wouldn't have followed her into that bookstore if it hadn't been for the first outside-of-the-club experience they'd shared. Which had occurred when he'd been helping Gideon with security needs. As he drew in and released the smoke, watching it curl toward the ceiling, he went back in his head to review that night, even knowing reliving it wasn't going to help the situation.

It was far more likely to make this need growing in his gut worse.

~

A few weeks ago...

Wolf paused in the doorway of Club Atlantis's security office. Stan, rocking back on the axis of a creaky black chair, glanced his way.

"She left the alley about ten minutes ago," the guard said. He pointed to one of the screens he was monitoring. "Stopped by before she headed out there. Told me not to worry if she wandered out of camera range, that she'd be fine. Soon as she did, I stepped out, but I didn't see her. I radioed Gideon, and he said he'd handle it. I guess you're how he's handling it."

Wolf didn't smile. "Yeah. I'll handle it."

Despite extra precautions to make the club and its surroundings safe, there were always those who would insensibly push the boundaries. Like meandering aimlessly in and around the neighboring warehouses after dark.

Truth, on a normal night, there weren't a lot of problems. This section of Atlanta's industrial district wasn't the same crime magnet as other places in the city. However, it was Wolf's experience that predators were always drawn to prey.

He should know. He was one of the predators.

He stepped out into the alley, letting the door close behind him. Stan hadn't known which direction she'd gone, but he didn't have Wolf's vampire senses. Ella's scent was a distinct combination of cinnamon and caramel. Wolf left the alley, turned north and found her, sitting on a stack of empty pallets on a loading dock.

A hollow metallic sound drew his gaze to a mobile made of Pepsi cans. They hung from the tin roof overhang. Probably the result of a moment of idleness, a whimsy an indulgent manager had allowed to remain.

Ella was reaching up, trailing her fingers along the bottom trio of cans, creating that music.

James, the normal head of security, was on an unprecedented vacation to New Orleans. Anwyn, the owner of Club Atlantis, had bullied him into it, since he hadn't taken time off since he started working for the club. In James's absence, Gideon was taking care of security.

Gideon was Anwyn's servant, a marking that had happened very soon after she'd been turned into a vampire. Since then, Gideon's responsibilities at the club had been increasing. Therefore, with his hands full, he'd called for Wolf's help on this one.

Like the rest of the human world, most of the staff at Club Atlantis didn't know about the existence of vampires, much less that their employer and a staff Dom were one. However, since Gideon did, he'd known who to call as his most effective tracker.

And once you find her, you can help me hold her down to inject a GPS chip in her ass.

Wolf's lips quirked at the memory. It wasn't a problem for him; he didn't have a session for another hour, so he could handle this task while Gideon juggled other ones.

Ella's hand drifted back to her lap, settled. Her hair was down, miles of dark curls. As he approached, he saw she'd been using her other hand to comb one thick curtain of it alongside her face in a meditative way.

"I know it's you," she said, without looking his way. "Wolf, who moves so silent. The absence of sound still makes a noise, have you noticed?" She turned the side of her face hidden behind her hair toward him, then tilted her head to reveal a half smile. "Look, I'm Cousin It."

Her Southern accent couldn't be mistaken for anything but small-town Deep South. For him, it resurrected images of lemonade on the porch in summer. Grandma fanning herself with the cardboard fan she'd kept from the latest revival.

Boy, you're a big, handsome one. You'll make something of yourself, if you don't let that go to your head. Don't ever let your head get ahead of God.

"You're too young to know who Cousin It is," he said.

"I watch that channel with the old black and white stuff," she responded. "Life sometimes looks better in black and white."

As he sat down next to her, bracing his longer legs next to her dangling ones, she laid her hand on his arm. Unexpected, since even outside the club she usually observed protocols between Doms and subs. She studied the contrast with her pale skin. He was the dark-skinned end of the color spectrum. He'd also grown up in Gulf-side Florida, where he'd spent most of his nearly thirty years of human life outdoors in the sun. Back then, he'd known swamps and fishing. Being drafted for Vietnam was the first time he'd been more than a hundred miles from home.

"See," she whispered. "Black, white. Everything looks better with those two colors in it."

He clasped her fingers, a reproving squeeze. "No one gave you permission to touch me," he said mildly.

"I know. I like that about you. You're a Master all the time. You don't switch it off. It's comforting. It tells me you're real, all the way through. It's not a fantasy. It's *not*." She added that last part with a touch of fierceness.

Ella was one of the most sought-after female submissives they had on staff, not only for the unattached Doms, but for those who needed another player with their own submissive. Within what was permitted inside the club walls, she had no limits at all, seemingly, and a lot was permitted.

Except she didn't top. Ella wouldn't have the first clue of how to do that.

Otherwise, she could be whatever they wanted. A brat, a service sub, a slave, or whatever grade was needed in between. She could get off on hardcore pain or a satin ribbon flogger. She would serve Master or Mistress, because what drove her, fed her need, her ultimate aphrodisiac, was the pleasure of the Dom. If the Dom needed her to get worked up over feathers, wanted to hear her sobs, or have her giggle like a schoolgirl, she would. She could be the unattainable queen, brought to her knees by a forceful conqueror, or the prison inmate forced to satisfy a guard's pleasure. She could be the naughty teenage schoolgirl, frisked thoroughly by a police officer.

She could be anything, apparently, but something someone wanted to take home and keep. There were times when she reminded him uncomfortably of the dog at the shelter who gave two hundred percent to everyone who came in looking, but was always the one left behind in favor of the dog who played more morose or hard to get.

Maybe because those looking wanted to know that what the dog would give to them, she wouldn't just as willingly give to anyone else. If all she wanted was love, the one providing it must be irrelevant to her.

Or maybe they couldn't believe someone was that giving and loving. There must be a catch. People were inevitably selfish and perversely conditional.

So were vampires.

Yes, she gave every scene, every Dom who engaged her, her full energy. Yet she was intriguingly hard to break down to the marrow. For many Dominants, that was fine, especially when doing a session with someone who wasn't their collared sub.

Not for him.

Other Doms might not need that, but he was different. For him, the treasure he was after was what a submissive wasn't willing to give, but needed desperately to relinquish.

It was also something a vampire craved. He'd stayed away from doing it with Ella, telling himself he couldn't exactly explain why.

Which was bullshit. He knew exactly why. He stayed away from the ones he might want to keep.

Despite his admonishment not to touch him, he'd kept her hand. With his other one, he pushed her hair back from where it covered her face, a practical stroke. That fabulous, curling mane fell to her hips, bouncing and moving like playful cat's paws on a dark sea. Her eyes were different all the time, because she had several types of colored contacts. Today her irises were violet, with a silver ring around the outside, her pupil dark and striking in the center.

But what caught his attention, more than their beauty, were the emotions there. She'd been using the hair to conceal the fact she'd been crying. The tears had dried, but her eyes had that tired look to them she'd tried to pass off with the smile. It would have worked on most men, because a beautiful woman's smile could blur the details of what was going on behind it.

He wasn't most men, though.

"I knew deep down it was a pointless crush," she said abruptly. "I just didn't realize how much it would hurt, knowing for sure James didn't want me that way. He's meant for someone else. Someone he's met in New Orleans."

Almost everyone but James had been aware of Ella's infatuation, but from the beginning most of them, including Ella, had known it was one-sided. Her acceptance of that wasn't new, as her own acknowledgment of it now told him, but the information about him meeting someone in New Orleans was.

Part of what made Ella such an exceptional sub was her uncanny intuition. She also picked up on changes in energy. Though Anwyn hadn't known it until later, the night she was attacked and turned by rogue vampires, Ella had arrived at the club only moments after it happened, nearly hysterical, because she was sure Anwyn was dead.

"And I'm fully capable of caring for myself, by the way. I've been doing it my whole life."

The switch from fierceness to sadness and back to fierceness again, bordering on anger, told him something had set her off. He was getting pieces of things, not the full story. James meeting someone was just a final straw thing. However, from the way she was throwing rocks around the subject, she wasn't ready to talk about it, which worked, since he didn't want to encourage too much familiarity.

Still... Because she was obviously hurting and feeling alone, a question came to mind he couldn't stop himself from asking. There was a whole building of people nearby who loved her as much as she loved them, and yet she hadn't wanted to be around them for...whatever this was.

"Ella, do you have family?"

She blinked at him. Suddenly the mask of the contacts irritated him. He wanted the real color of her eyes. He wouldn't order her to remove them, though. Not here. She didn't have anywhere to put them.

She'd been smart enough to don a black hoodie. Beneath it, she wore a black corset that laced her in tight and set her C-cup breasts up high, though they were currently shadowed in the folds of the partially zipped coat. Slick black leggings and a gold and green gauzy skirt over them finished the look. Earlier, on the dance floor, she'd been sashaying around in just the leggings, corset and four-inch stilettos that gave her fine ass a tempting swing-and-twitch motion. Now she wore ratty canvas sneakers for walking.

He was used to seeing her inside the club, where everything about her fit. It made her an expected part of the scenery, the fixtures, as unkind as that thought sounded. He noticed her in the safe way he noticed any of the female subs.

Here, the contrast of her surroundings made all the details of her appearance seem new and different. More of an impact to his senses.

Despite the sneakers and hoodie, she was astonishingly beautiful. When she was made up, like now, her lips wet and full with crimson color, her skin creamy and smooth, she looked like a vintage pin-up. When she wasn't wearing makeup, she was girl-next-door irresistible.

He realized she was still gazing at him, and hadn't responded to his question. "Ella," he said.

"You were looking at me so oddly," she said. "I wasn't sure if you wanted me to answer yet."

He touched her chin. "I do. Now."

She dipped her head, her lips brushing his hand. She was overwhelming, how much she was willing to give, so immediately. He'd never known her to be this forward with him. The reserve he maintained with her, that kept her at arms' length, wasn't working tonight. Maybe it was her mood, but he was concerned he was projecting something that he shouldn't be.

"I'm this close to putting you over my knee," he admonished her, sharpening his tone. She drew back, telling him he'd been right. It was him. *Shit.* "Ella. Last time. Where is your family?"

"They're all phoenixes."

Her gaze lifted and held his again. Even with the contacts, there was so much there. That look, all the inexplicable things it could mean, fell deep inside him. Without thought, he gripped her upper arms, as if he thought the rest of her was about to follow.

"Whoosh," she said quietly. "They went away in flame. I was there, but they didn't take me with them, because I was trapped in my room. I sat in a corner and watched the fire come closer, but I could still hear them. My mother screaming for me, my father shouting. My brother and sister just screaming, then...just silent. A fireman came out of the wall of fire. He took me outside, held me in his lap, and pointed to the flame. He said 'Look. There's your family, their spirits, dancing in the fire, dancing up to Heaven. It hurt at first, but now it doesn't hurt them at all.'"

A light smile played on her lips, but something very different was in her gaze. An unexpected sense of danger ran up his spine as he saw something wild and savage and angry, something he'd never known was inside Ella. Then it was gone, replaced by her usual open expression.

"I think my nightmares would have been far worse if he hadn't told me that," she said thoughtfully. "I hear them screaming still, but when the dream gets too unbearable, the screams die away. Like they were the ones having the nightmare, but they've woken up and now they're dancing in the flames.

"Wouldn't it be nice, to be able to do that? I've danced in the wind, and the rain, and even in the mud." Her tone became teasing. "Remember that night we celebrated the anniversary of *Stripes*, recreating the mud fight, all topless? But I've never danced in the fire. Maybe one day. It scares me too much now."

She looked away and started combing her fingers through her hair, covering that one side of her face again.

Did Anwyn know any of this? He didn't engage in a lot of chitchat, but he kept his ears open around the staff. As far as he knew, Ella never talked about her past. Had she ended up in the foster care system? Had she ever had a family again, before Atlantis?

"Okay, enough pathetic wallowing." As if a switch had flipped, she turned back to him, all those shadows abruptly gone. She tossed her hair back and shone a smile upon him. It was genuine, fully in the moment. "The carnival's in town. Want to go ride the rides, eat bad food, get sick? Flirt with trashy carny women while I tease the men? Or vice versa?"

"I have a session in an hour," he said. And was surprised to find he regretted that. On a normal night, he wouldn't seek out the overwhelming noise and light of a carnival, but she projected a calmness that was contagious, even when reliving one of her most horrible memories.

Maybe he could reschedule the session. But Ella had already acknowledged his response with a nod of respect, and hopped down from her perch.

"Oh, of course. I should have remembered that. Anyway, it's here for another week or so, so you can go another time, if you like. I need to get back."

"Ella."

She stopped, already across the dock and headed down the steps. She didn't look at him, but she glanced over her shoulder, her gaze on the wall of the building behind him. "It's okay, sir. I'm okay. I'm always okay."

"Yeah," he said. "You are."

She dimpled at him for that, then cocked her head. "You know those scenes in books when the main characters have been separated, and they finally find one another after going through so much apart?"

"Chick stories."

"You sound like Gideon." Her smile deepened. "In those scenes, when the people come back together after so much horrible stuff, they're crying and their hearts are breaking, but they're so very happy, because they're together again and it's all okay. That's how I think it will be when I see my parents again, my brother and sister. I know it's going to roll out just that way. I'd live in a library if I could, full of stories like that."

She was down the steps, striding away briskly. It was unusual for her to take her leave of a Dom that abruptly, but he could feel her need for space.

She wasn't the only one needing that.

~

Wolf scowled, returning to the present and his dark apartment. He'd wanted to go after her, soothe her. Do other things. But he hadn't. He didn't get involved in the lives of the others, not that deeply.

Especially not mortals.

He said that, but after that night, he'd told Gideon he'd keep track of Ella on an ongoing basis. He'd told himself he was merely taking on a few responsibilities to share the load with Gideon in James's absence.

And yet, tonight, he'd invited her to be his assistant at a workshop.

He took a drag on the cigarette, felt the burn. Fuck, it was one class. It didn't have to be a mistake. She'd done plenty of assisting for other Doms. He'd treat it just like that, then cut her loose.

Yeah, right. If the assistant thing had been all there was to it, that might work. But he'd laid a full-on claim on her when he'd put her between his knees, gripped that full, firm breast. He'd done an Evel Knievel leap across the chasm he maintained between himself and most humans. Particularly a female sub like her.

Apropos of nothing, she would have no idea who Evel Knievel was. His lips twisted at the random thought, but his eyes half closed as he remembered how her nipple shaped itself into such a delectable point beneath his touch. Her lips had parted, her eyes glinting with unshed tears as she struggled through the pain to earn the right to touch him. Those fingers, so astoundingly gentle, trailing over his shoulders, his neck, his head, sending a shiver down his spine that tightened his ass and hardened his cock.

He'd smelled her arousal. He'd wanted to push her down, lift her spread legs to his shoulders and lick every bit of that honey, knowing she'd only gush more. Which would work out fine when he shoved his cock into that sweet stickiness and spurted himself deep inside her.

She was curvy but small. He'd curl her up in his lap and baby her afterward, right before he went after her again, keeping her in a constant state of sore and soothed.

His lips curved, dangerous. *Think you know insatiable, baby girl? Think again.* There was a reason that vampires had third marked servants. A normal human could be fucked to death. Literally.

He shook his head at himself. A pussy was a pussy, just like a cock was a cock. His fixation on her was because of other things, dangerous things she made him feel and want. The packaging just made it even more tempting.

If he was smart, he'd get someone to step in for him on that workshop. He'd shoot Ella a message on the club forum, tell her he'd had something else come up, but she could assist whoever was doing the lecture. They'd be glad for her help.

If he withdrew now, sending a clear message that, whatever he'd done tonight, what he wanted their relationship to be was what it had always been, she'd respect that. He'd rein himself in better, because she was as sweet, decadent and fresh as warm pralines.

She didn't deserve to be hurt by yet another asshole who didn't want to be with her.

Or couldn't be.

CHAPTER THREE

"Do you ever look at a man and feel like he walked out of every fantasy you ever had?"

"Yeah. Except in the case of who you're thinking about, it's more like your fantasy landed on the workbench of some cranky goddess, who scoffed and said, 'Bitch, let me show you what a fantasy *really* looks like.'"

"Or the workbench of a god. One who wanted to ram his divine cock into an ass that perfect."

Madelyn and Chantal had made the first two observations, but it was Lars who threw in the third. He was stretched out on his stomach on the bar, reading a textbook. An unfinished Mai-Tai was next to him. He was twirling the purple paper umbrella that had garnished it in his fingers as he studied the page. He wore only a pair of loose cotton trousers that molded his own not unworthy-of-notice backside.

From the table where the two Mistresses sat, Chantal tossed an amused look at him. "You think a goddess couldn't conjure a cock to enjoy that same pleasure? She is a goddess, after all."

"I defer to a Mistress's perspective on it," the bartender noted. "Since she is as close to a goddess on earth as one can get."

Chantal shook her head at Madelyn. "Save us from the silver tongue of a switch who taunts us with his beauty, while bestowing it only on the less fair sex."

Lars sent her a grin, but then he returned to his textbook. He was working toward a Masters in English. He lived with four rowdy roommates, so often came to the club before opening to study. Anwyn encouraged her trusted staff members to see Club Atlantis as a place of retreat during the off hours, which was why she had workout facilities and other amenities to support their needs.

Accordingly, Chantal and Madelyn had met with her earlier to review current membership applications, but now that they were done with that, they'd decided to share a glass of wine in the cozy second level bar area.

For her part, on her nights at Atlantis, Ella always tried to arrive as early as she could to assist wherever setup help was needed, but at the moment everything seemed well in hand. So Chantal had pulled her down into a chair, put her silk stockinged feet in Ella's lap, and teasingly demanded a foot rub.

Ella was glad to oblige. And not just because it kept her close to where Wolf was, without seeming like that was what she was doing. This second level held a smaller dance floor and a couple of alcoves for equipment, and he was in one of those alcoves, working on a mechanical problem.

When their paths had crossed a half hour ago, he'd offered her only a short nod. His fixed expression had given her a sinking feeling. She was sure he was going to tell her he'd changed his mind and didn't want her help at the workshop. However, he strode away without further discussion, obviously focused on whatever he'd arrived early at the club to do.

While that had relieved her, his behavior had left her feeling on uncertain footing with him. Any other Dom, she might have asked straight out if everything was okay, but something held her tongue. Maybe fear that she would give him an out, which she knew was stupid, but there it was.

So for now, she settled for being quietly nearby and trying not to look at him, an exercise in self-restraint.

She did catch enough of what was happening to know Wolf had arrived early to meet Fred. Fred, full name Frederica, was a mechanic at a nearby garage. The thirty-something woman's mechanical skills weren't limited just to cars. When she'd discovered that, Anwyn had invited her to handle their occasional repair issues for extra cash.

The two pieces of custom equipment in the alcove drew a lot of spectators when either or both were in use. One was a bondage wheel that looked like a spider web made out of steel pipe, with a cushioned board bolted to the center and four cuffs on the outer edges that could be adjusted closer or further, depending on the height of the submissive upon it.

The other was a horizontal wooden X-cross with a holding cage as the base. Wolf had shut it down earlier in the week when he'd noticed the cross had too much wiggle in its movements.

Chantal was studying Ella with a thoughtful look. It was likely she had picked up the betrayals of body language; a slight tension to Ella's shoulders, the tilt of her head in Wolf's direction while they were discussing him. In a roomful of Doms, it wasn't likely that anything was going to escape their radar.

The Mistress might or might not say anything to her about it. Ella didn't know if that would be a good or a bad thing. When she'd had her crush on James, Chantal had been the first to tell her he wasn't the right choice for her. Not unkindly.

Ella thought of the forty-something man with gray eyes and close-cropped brown hair, his broad shoulders, and the protective streak a mile wide. He had a striking alertness that never flagged, his prior work in law enforcement a natural fit for his club security role. He'd accepted the Club Atlantis world in a way that had raised Ella's hopes, but Chantal had pointed out the flaws early on.

"Acceptance is not the same as active participation. Have you ever seen him seek out a scene with someone?"

He'd watched plenty when he remained at the club to do paperwork or have an afterwork drink, but Chantal believed any Dominant leanings he had were dormant. If they were ever triggered, it would be by a woman with a similar level of interest, but whose personalities and needs overlapped the far more vanilla side of his conservative personality. Ella was the deep end of the pool for someone like James.

"It's a Daddy's girl crush, Chantal had told her firmly. *"Don't fall too far."*

As Ella's nimble fingers worked the muscles of Chantal's overworked arches, Chantal let out a pleased hum, dropping her head back on her shoulders. Her black dress fit her body snugly. An ornate cross was henna tattooed between her shoulder blades, revealed by the low back. Her strappy heels lay in a tumble on the floor next to her.

"You remember the badass alpha primal that Wolf had here a couple months ago?" Lars turned a page without looking up. "Private session. A mat and a spanking bench were the only things Wolf wanted in the room with him. That bench was bolted to the floor. Word was, the alpha nearly ripped it out. Wolf still managed to take him down."

"You said that just to tease us. I do know how to apply a Taser to testicles with maximum pain but minimal damage," Madelyn told him.

Lars chuckled. "Have to catch me, Maddie."

"Fate is a wondrous thing," Chantal observed. "Wolf was referred to Anwyn by a club owner up in Colorado. He was looking for a change of scenery. Lucky us."

It must have been a powerful referral, Ella thought, because it hadn't taken long for Wolf to become a trusted member of the staff. But Anwyn had excellent judgment when it came to her people.

He also brought in a good income, since he had a continuous waiting list of people who wanted a session with him, and he was generous with his time. Session approval was exclusively up to the staff Dom or sub in question. Anwyn understood that sessions, even paid ones, worked better when everyone wanted to be there.

After a Dom like Wolf or a sub like Ella approved an applicant, the requester paid an after-session fee to the club, fifty percent of which went to the Dom or sub. If the client wanted actual sex to happen, and the Dom or sub was agreeable, no payment was collected, since that would break prostitution laws.

In her outside-Atlantis life, Madelyn was an attorney. Chantal was always trying to get her to take on a case where she could legally challenge why a person's right to reproductive decisions for their own body didn't extend to willingly offering that same body for paid sex. While she didn't disagree, Madelyn routinely reminded Chantal, with dry humor, that she was a real estate attorney. Chantal just as routinely bounced back with brash retorts.

Branch out, bitch. I want to see a selfie of you at the Supreme Court.

Wolf had never done a public session where sex had happened. If he ever did, Ella expected Atlantis would have record attendance that night.

"So what do you think of our Wolf, Ella?" Chantal asked, her eyes half-closed.

Yeah, she'd noticed. Ella suppressed a sigh and tried not to shoot her a narrow look. Madelyn flicked a glance toward her fellow Mistress, a smile pressed between her full lips. People-study was a passion of every Dominant Ella knew. Though she was their friend, they analyzed her the way they did all submissives under their care.

What did she think? Every time her attention moved back toward him, her nipple would twinge. She wasn't going to tell them that, though. Ella pressed her upper arm discreetly against it, containing the feeling.

"He's not looking this way," Madelyn said helpfully. "You can stare all you want."

"Oh my." Chantal's dark green eyes went to ecstatic slits. "I'd recommend it. That will feed my personal fantasy calendar for a month."

Ella turned around in time to see Wolf putting himself on the cross. He was barefoot, the hems of the camo pants he was wearing brushing the tops of his feet. He'd removed his socks and black work shoes, placing them out of the way. The socks were folded precisely over the toes. As he hiked himself onto the X-cross, he spread his legs to align them with the frame. The movement stretched the fabric over his groin and powerful upper thighs.

While reaching up to thread his hands through the handlebars at the top, he was directing Frederica to bind him with the straps over his legs and torso. She was having trouble. While she'd long ago overcome her initial *holy shit* reaction to the club's eye-opening interior, all six foot plus of Wolf stretched out on the cross was obviously causing her some issues. She was scarlet from her neck to her hairline.

Wolf said something else quietly to her. Kindly. She offered a deprecating half chuckle, and stepped back. Then Wolf turned his head toward their small table.

"Ella."

Her hands jerked on Chantal's feet. He'd spoken briskly. He just needed her help, was all. *Stop being an idiot.*

"She's working on Chantal's feet," Madelyn said quickly. "Can I assist?"

"Opportunistic bitch," Chantal said under her breath, and Madelyn grinned at her.

Doms always seemed to fantasize about topping other Doms. Ella understood enough about the way a Master or Mistress thought that she understood the drive, but it didn't make sense to her as a submissive. The last thing she'd ever want to see was someone topping Wolf, male or female. It wouldn't feel like the natural order of things.

A faint look of amusement crossed Wolf's gaze. "As much as I appreciate your 'generosity,' Mistress, it's Ella I require."

Chantal nudged Ella with her toe. "Go help him," she said. "Try to act like you'd prefer tending my tired feet."

Ella dimpled at her. "Giving you ease is my only desire in life, Mistress."

Chantal rolled her gaze toward Madelyn. "Between Lars and her, we need to line them all up for flogging. Bunch of wiseasses here."

"The Taser idea is better," Madelyn said. "A flogger excites them like a bunch of puppies let out to play."

Ella moved Chantal's feet to the seat of the chair she vacated, mindful not to drop them like a sack of potatoes and bolt to Wolf's side. Excessive eagerness was often prized in a session. If she acted like that right now, she'd seem too much like the puppy Madelyn described. But she didn't dally, moving efficiently to his side.

He nodded to the restraints. "I need to test that the base won't loosen again if there's an enthusiastic male my size on it. Strap me in tight."

"It may end up needing nightly adjustments," Fred noted. "Sometimes these things have to build in some give, so the parts don't get too much stress on them. Your maintenance staff could add it to their checklist."

"Good idea," Wolf said.

Ella moved down to his feet to fix the leg straps over his ankles, across his shins, and just above his knees. As her fingers slid over the camo cloth, she felt the rigid power of the man beneath. With the barest shift of her gaze, she'd get a close view of the heavy fabric curving over his groin.

She imagined him stretched out on his bed, his erection hard and stiff, her mouth wet and wanting to taste. She kept her gaze lowered with effort, efficiently handling the straps, pulling them as tight as they needed to be. Then she moved to handle the upper body.

The straps across the chest required her to lean down upon him to gather up the two ends, bundle them together, adjust their length. His chest needed the maximum reach, no surprise.

The scents that clung to him brought to mind fresh mown grass on a summer morning, the humid salt air off an ocean, a fire on a winter night. It had to be some kind of cologne or aftershave, and the heat of his body gave it a richer, more erotic scent. She imagined his skin dewed with perspiration during a powerful fucking, his large hands on her backside, holding her with a bruising grip to make that deep rutting happen. Her nipple kept twinging, even as her buttock tingled, remembering the grip of his hand there.

His eyes never left her, though he was talking to Fred. Fred was back to her usual self, now that Ella had taken over this part.

It wasn't common to have a Dom like Wolf in such a provocative position. Ella was half afraid that, once she had him bound, Chantal and Maddie might pounce on him like cats. Though she expected they'd exercise restraint, she wouldn't be surprised if a very rich fantasy scenario was unfolding in their minds. Well, she couldn't throw any stones on that one, could she?

She checked the straps, running her fingers under them as professionally as possible while being very aware of the resilience of his body beneath her touch. The man was built like a tank.

"Ready," she said.

"Are you claustrophobic, Ella?"

"No sir."

Wolf touched her chin, cupped it, brought her face up. He'd kept one arm stretched along the upper limb of the cross, his fingers wrapped around the handlebar. He wore an Army green T-shirt untucked that stretched over his chest and biceps, a good workout for the cotton fibers.

He put his thumb against her mouth. The pressure made her part her lips, and he teased the moist edge of her teeth and tongue. Staying still was difficult, but he'd tell her if she could move. His relentless expression said so.

He rarely smiled in a spontaneous, genuine way. But sometimes his eyes smiled when his mouth didn't, and that felt real. She wished his eyes would smile now.

"Good," he said at last. "I want you in the cage beneath this so you can see what the screws attaching the cross to the base do when I start fighting the restraints. All right?"

"Yes, sir."

She saw the flicker in Fred's gaze. Even if the mechanic wasn't part of this world, watching the elements of it play out in front of her was probably like sitting in a dark theater, getting pulled into the story on stage.

Close enough to touch, even if you wouldn't.

Ella opened the cage door, and folded herself into the space. It could accommodate a tall man in extremely cramped conditions, knees to chest. Everyone would see the crease of his ass, his balls resting against it. She had to bring her knees up, too, but she could brace her sneakers against one side, her back against the other.

When she closed the door, shutting herself in, Wolf reached down and wrapped his fingers over the bars near her shoulder.

"Okay?" he asked.

"Yes, sir."

"Touch my hand."

She did so, but not with the hands she had curled against her chest. Instead, she leaned forward and rested her forehead against his overlapping fingertips, then turned her head, a slow movement that brushed her temple, her cheek, against his knuckles.

She didn't forget herself to the point she dragged her lips across his skin, but it was a close thing. "Why did you ask me if I was claustrophobic?" she asked. "You've seen me in enclosed spaces in sessions."

"I don't know if you told those Masters or Mistresses the truth. You know how to power through discomfort to please them."

"How do you know I told you the truth?"

"Are you sassing me, Ella?"

It was such a sweet, old fashioned word, it made her toes curl. "No, sir," she said. "Truly. I just wondered."

His finger tapped her forehead, once. "Would you lie to me, Ella? Ever?"

No matter what tone he used, he always sounded like a Dom.

Whether it was to her or Lars, Chantal or Anwyn, he spoke with a direct assurance that suggested being a Dominant was what came easiest to him. People weren't only one thing, not ever, but she'd had yet to see any other side to him than this.

He was the only Dom on staff she could say that about. Chantal and Madelyn, even Anwyn, had different layers to who they were. With his voice alone he held her in place, telling her she would give him the truth.

He traced a deliberate line from her cheek to her mouth with his index finger, reminding her she hadn't answered.

"No. No sir. I wouldn't lie to you."

"That's what I thought."

He flattened his palm against the bars, and she mirrored his, on the other side, not touching. He shifted so his forefinger passed that barrier, found a section of her creased palm and traced it. Because he didn't forbid it, and because she was in a cage, where higher reasoning started to flee, leaving only the desire to feel, and touch, she let her fingers curl, grazing his.

When she wasn't physically bound, a Master's command would keep her still. But the more she was restrained, the more most Doms appreciated her attempts to take advantage of the smallest ability to touch.

"I'm going to pull against the frame now," he said at last, taking his hand away. "Remember, watch the bolts above you."

Without further delay, he threw his weight against his bonds. The force of it knocked her out of her fugue state. Not surprisingly, his struggles shook the cage, made it groan and creak in protest, the cross likewise making clanking noises against the base. She wished there was a mirror where she could see the flex and stretch of his body. The rapt expressions she saw on Lars, Chantal and Maddie's faces said she was missing something more impressive than her imaginings, if that was possible.

He stopped. The force of his struggles had been impressive, but he didn't sound even winded. "Anything?"

She cleared her throat and pointed for Fred, who was bent over to follow her gestures. "The bolt on this corner loosened. The others stayed in place. The platform holding the cross also seems to be shifting some."

"Okay. Come on out."

She pushed open the barred door and crawled forth. As she pulled herself to her feet, her fingertips briefly brushed his thigh. His glance went to her, held.

"Seems to me it needs a true test, Wolf," Maddie called. "It's not really genuine unless the big animal strapped on it is being teased to mindless response. Adrenaline and all that."

"A fair point," Wolf said, but his gaze didn't leave Ella. "Draw the curtain."

The chorus of complaints from the bar area made his lips twitch and Ella smile, despite the butterflies in her stomach. She was as locked in place by his unrelenting gaze as she'd been in the cage beneath him. Wolf spoke to Fred next. "Go check on the bartender's issue with the beer dispenser. I'll call you back in a few moments, after I do a true stress test on this."

"You got it." As Fred retrieved her toolbox, Ella noted an amusing reluctance to her movements. She might not be a BDSM person, but no hetero woman in her right mind would pass up the chance to see what was about to unfold here.

Last month, a Mistress Lyda, visiting from Tampa, had come and used this piece of equipment with her two subs, one male, one female. She'd put the male on the cross part, and tucked her female in the cage beneath. As Lyda had tormented her sub, Noah, in various ways, Gen's hand had snuck through the bars, caressed his hip. Lyda had made her hold out her hand and smacked her palm with a ruler, like a schoolteacher. Then she'd bound Gen's hands behind her, making the cage even more confining and movement within it more awkward.

When Lyda at last freed Noah from the cross, she rewarded him by letting him drop to his knees, feed his cock to Gen through the bars. The Mistress ordered her to suck him off while Lyda fucked him with a strap on. It had been memorable.

No matter what was about to happen here, Ella suspected it might eclipse that memory entirely. Wolf's gaze moved back up to her face. "No, don't look down. Hold my gaze, Ella. Too much goes on in your head. A Dom can miss a whole novel if he doesn't see your eyes. Would you give me your mouth if I demand it?"

She'd give him pretty much any part of her body, including her mouth, but he didn't like gushy subs. She'd seen him tense up when they got too over-the-top like that. So she simply nodded. "Yes, sir."

"Does a good sub pout when denied, or does she channel it toward a stronger response when a Dom has need of her?"

She thought about that. "A good sub wants to focus on what her Dom wants, not what she wants. She knows she pleases him with her obedience. But I don't think a Dom would want her not to feel disappointed when denied. He just wants her to mask it appropriately, so that he can feed off the energy of the denial, not deal with the attitude."

"Well spoken." His eyes glittered, his mouth set. His expression was that unreadable mask again. "You may go. Tell Lars I want him and his smart mouth in here now. I'll see you at the workshop tonight."

He'd set the trap so neatly, she felt like a mouse choking on the cheese set on the metal plate. But she'd swallowed more challenging reactions.

"Yes, sir."

If Fred's work shoes had been dragging, then Ella's feet were encased in lead blocks, as she left behind the male spread on the cross and ready to test it with a display of rippling, straining muscle. But she found the strength to nod demurely and take her leave without a single shuffle.

Fortunately, the scream of frustration that could have shattered eardrums stayed locked in her head.

CHAPTER FOUR

A half-hour before the Daddy Dom workshop began, she opened the door to the meeting space, intending to confirm everything was set up as Wolf had specified.

Club Atlantis offered these classes about the many facets of D/s play for new and existing members. They occurred early in the evening, so that those attending wouldn't miss the sessions on the club floor that increased in number and variation after nine o'clock.

She snapped on the switch and jumped as light flooded the windowless space.

Wolf stood at the front, hips propped against the six-foot table placed there. He didn't blink the way a person did when a light flooded darkness. His gaze was on her, as if he'd been looking at her when she opened the door. She noted his irises glinted translucent, like an animal's eyes when passing headlights reflected off them. Then they went back to their normal unusual pale gray.

He had his arms crossed over his chest. He'd changed into a Club Atlantis black staff T-shirt and blue jeans. Like the earlier Army green shirt, this one stretched with impressive elasticity over his broad shoulders and massive biceps. His blue jeans were broken in distractingly well.

"I'm sorry," she ventured. "I didn't mean to interrupt you."

"You didn't. I was just going over the discussion points in my mind, and I prefer the darkness. Turn off the light and come here."

Unexpected. She glanced at the route between her and him, logging what obstacles she might face. The room had been set up auditorium style with thirty-six chairs, an aisle down the middle.

She switched the light off again. The curtain of darkness fell, but now the darkness ahead felt less like a void, because he was waiting in it. She'd intended to take a left, use the back row of chairs to guide her, then turn right and follow the middle aisle to him.

"Come straight toward my voice," he said instead. "I won't let you run into anything."

She moved forward, a little unsure, but he fixed that in a heartbeat. "One step left. Now forward. Ten steps in a straight line and you'll be standing right in front of me."

When she complied, on step ten her thigh brushed his knee. She came to an abrupt halt, but his hands closed over her waist.

"Good." He eased her to his side, guiding her to a seated position on the table. As he settled back next to her again, her waist tingled from the contact of his hand, her abdomen from the caressing pressure of his thumbs.

"Sir, may I ask you a question?"

"It will be quid pro quo. I answer, you answer me."

She was pleased he'd want to ask her a question, so fair enough. "Why don't you have any tattoos?" she asked.

"How do you know I don't? You haven't seen me completely without clothes."

"No, sir." Though, gods and goddesses, she might donate a limb for the pleasure of it. "I just...I don't think you do."

He paused. "It's a good guess. There are a couple reasons. The main one is that a tattoo is a story about the person wearing it. If I want someone to know my stories, I'll tell them, in my own time and way."

She opened her mouth, but he cut across her. "One question, asked and answered. The night I found you on the loading docks. What happened to send you there?"

Her question hadn't been very personal, she thought, though she suspected his answer had a soul-deep reasoning behind it. Whereas his question went straight to her core like a jagged-edged knife and twisted. She'd rather he asked anything else.

"Ella." His voice sharpened. For a submissive like her, it was as effective as truth serum. She couldn't not respond to an injection of that authoritative tone.

"Do I have any choices other than telling you?"

"Yes," he said after a moment. "You can tell me no, and accept a punishment for not telling me."

"You won't let me help you tonight." She tried to bite back the despair in her voice. To be denied this first official chance to be helpful to him made everything feel worse. But the reason she'd been on the loading dock was too personal and pathetic. It made her feel stupid, which frustrated her with herself.

"Ella." He placed a hand on her shoulder, against her neck. The firm hold snapped her out of her head. "You'll still help me. But you'll accept another punishment from me if you can't answer my question."

"Okay," she said.

"Don't sound so relieved. You're not likely to enjoy my punishment any better."

His hand was still on her throat, but now it moved upward. She was wearing a light wrap over her outfit, because the meeting room could be chilly when mostly empty. Once restless, aroused human bodies filled it, it would get warmer.

His thumb hooked the slim collar she was wearing and twisted in it, tightening the strap and increasing her heart rate. The collar had a silver tag fastened to it.

Daddy's girl.

She'd sent him a note on the club forum earlier in the week, asking him what he wanted her to wear for the class.

"Wear what you think would please your Daddy, Ella."

She understood the context. The session was going to be about Daddy Dom play. But she'd wondered if he meant something appropriate for a typical Daddy scene—if the word typical could be applied to any D/s scene of any stripe, once the people involved were deep into it—or him specifically.

She'd followed her heart on it, and here she was.

"Take off the robe," Wolf said. "I want to know what you're wearing."

There was only one way he could determine that with the lights off. Her heart pounded a little harder. She slipped off the table, untied the sash of the robe and took off the garment, folding it over and laying it on the table.

She wore a backless halter in a gauzy fabric. The garment was held in place with slim ribbon ties at her neck, under her arms and waist, three simple tied bows down her back. All of it was a dreamy lavender color, the ribbons a slightly deeper purple. Other than that and the collar, she wore only a pair of white silky underwear. Her breasts pressed against the thin fabric of the halter top, nipples visible through the sheer weave. He'd seemed to like that about the pirate shirt she'd worn, so that was one big reason she'd chosen it.

She had her hair up in a banana comb to keep it off her neck. It was still long enough to fall down her back to brush her shoulder blades.

His other hand joined the first at her throat, measuring the slim column in the collar of his fingers. She drew in a shaky breath, swallowing against his grip, and he stroked that area, registering the movement. He found the ribbon tie at the neck, followed it down to the one under her shoulder blades, traced it back to the front of the halter. He outlined the curves of her breasts, teased her nipples, drawing them tighter against the fabric. Back around to touch the bow in the middle of her back. He caressed her bared spine, drawing her between his knees so he could more easily follow that valley down to the waist tie and below, to her backside and the silky panties.

"Is this what you normally wear when you agree to a Daddy scene with our guests and members?"

"It depends on what they want. But I haven't worn anything I'm wearing tonight for anyone else."

She probably shouldn't have said that. She'd told herself she wasn't going to do anything that suggested she was making a play for his affections or attention. But she also knew that was a way to protect herself. Under his touch, she could only tell him the truth.

She lifted her chin. "I wore what I thought would please Daddy."

"Daddy is pleased," he murmured.

She flushed. She suspected he was gauging how the scene would work, how they would fit together for it, so it was okay for her to have a genuine reaction. It worked better that way. The most effective workshops included real-life demos to drive in the points. He was weighing how that was going to play out, getting her in the right headspace. She'd go there, happily skipping, no little girl puns intended.

He took his hand away. "Stay here. I'm going to go turn on the lights."

When he switched them on, he stood at the door, looking right at her. His gaze coursed over her the way his hands had. Thoroughly. He had such an intense gaze. Whenever she was under it, desire and yearning swamped her, as well as a little bit of fear. As if she couldn't depend on him being entirely civilized, following all the rules.

She admonished herself to stay on track. Be what was needed for the moment, and stop mooning over him. Since it was going to be a Daddy Dom workshop, and she liked getting into the mood of things, she laced her fingers behind her and rocked forward and back, heel-to-toe, in proper little girl fashion, her hair swinging along her back.

His lips twitched, and he nodded to the wall to their left. "The carnival's still in town."

The knot of tension dissipated, replaced by delight. Nearly two dozen stuffed animals were arranged on the table. They were multiple sizes, from a giant teddy bear to life-sized kittens. Displayed in an attractive semi-circle around the animals were Daddy Dom books from the club library, and handouts on the same subject. Several staff members, including Anwyn, handled educational resources for these short seminars, so Ella knew those and the swag would have come from one of them. That included a box of inexpensive, fun little collars with metal plaques on them, echoing the sentiments on her own decorative one.

She noted the stuffed animals were good quality nursery toys, soft and plush, not thin stretched fabric over foam. "Those aren't carnival stuffed animals."

"No. But the carnival is, in fact, still in town."

Staying in character, she gave him a hopeful look. "Can we go? Please?"

His serious eyes gleamed. She thought he was enjoying her impromptu play to get in the right frame of mind. She wouldn't mind him putting on some Daddy airs to do the same. He obliged.

"We'll see. Depends on how good you are."

She shot him a smile, and then the door opened, the first arrivals entering.

"Daddy Dom play is a 'safe' way to act out your persistent pedophile fantasies. On the sub side, it's a chance to enact your secret desire to fuck your father. Or avoid being a capable adult, letting someone run your life rather than handling it yourself."

As Wolf opened the workshop with the brusque statement, rustlings in the room stilled. They'd run out of chairs, so people were sitting on the floor in front and standing along the wall in back. Nearly fifty people. As word spread that one of Atlantis's most mysterious and charismatic Doms was leading the class, more had flocked to it.

"If you agreed with any of those statements," Wolf continued dryly, "get the fuck out of here and find a really good therapist. Because none of those things is what Daddy Dom/little girl play is supposed to be about."

The sudden tension dissipated into nervous laughter from newer members, more relaxed chuckles from existing ones.

Ella liked how he opened right into the heart of it, not droning on with vague introductions, or drawn out summaries of what was about to be taught. Another reason people liked it when Wolf taught a class. Every minute was instructional, no time lost.

"As you probably know," he said, "Mistress Madelyn is going to do Part Two of this workshop next week, addressing the Mommy Dom/little boy side of things, but you'll hear us both cover some of the same principles, starting with this next one, equally important."

He preferred to orate in the pose he'd had when she'd entered the room, his hips braced casually against the table, ankles crossed. He braced his hands on either side of him, fingers curved over the table edge as he swept the group with his piercing look.

"A cake and a cup of coffee both use sugar. At least the way I drink mine." His eyes glinted with brief humor. "Same ingredient, two very different things. In Daddy Dom play you might be offering—and your sub might be wanting—safety, authority, expectations, strictness, connection. Those are things that happen in a parent-child relationship, too, but between two adults in a Dom/sub relationship, the focus is very different.

"But keep in mind Daddy Dom/little girl play is hard to define in absolutes. Which basically makes it the same as most of D/s play," he added with a tight smile. "Sex may be part of Daddy Dom play all the time, or only at specific times, or not at all. For example, if it includes the Little wearing ruffled dresses, playing with toys, and taking time out to have a tea party, that's often about providing a safe 'down time' space for her, not sex. For another couple, the sub might be wearing a kitten collar and nothing else, and sex is very much part of the play."

He adjusted his stance to look toward Ella. She was stretched out on her hip on another six-foot long table, pushed flush to his. He'd unrolled an exercise mat on hers to cushion her, and she was making use of a couple of key props, a coloring book and crayons. She was diligently filling in a spray of irises in vibrant yellow. At his attention, she lifted it so he could see, and offered him a crayon to join her. "You can color the leaves," she said.

The group chuckled, whereas her nerves rippled at his stern, tender expression. They were good at this, the two of them. She loved role play, but this felt natural to her, especially with him. He was completely in control, much as a strict father would be. Or a totalitarian dictator.

"Maybe in a moment," he said with a mild touch of reproof. "Daddy's talking to other adults right now. Don't interrupt."

She nodded, hiding a smile at her thoughts, and returned to her coloring.

"Ella asked me what she should wear for tonight's session," Wolf said. "I told her to wear what she thought her Daddy would like. There was a lot going on there. She asked because she wants to be sure she wears what pleases Daddy, but I wanted to see what she thought would please me. It provides me information and tests her."

She tipped her head up to give him a genuine, little girl smile, no artifice, just pure adoration. Something not difficult for her to do naturally, when it was directed toward him. His gaze flickered, and he gestured to the stuffed animals at the table. "Go choose the one you want," he said. "But only one. You have to share."

"Thank you, Daddy." She took his hand to sit up, slip off the table. Since he gave her a caressing pat on her silk clad backside as she moved away, she had to fight not to stumble at the sensation that spread out through her upper thighs. Definitely not the reaction of a child to a father's touch, but she expected that was part of why he'd done it. She was embracing the inner child to be innocently flirtatious, but he was reminding her who he was, and not to get too cutesy.

She already knew which one she wanted, but that didn't keep her from touching them all. The animals were soft as downy pillows, meant to be hugged. She tried that on several of them, thought about taking one, started to turn, then changed her mind, put it down and picked up another, petting and playing. The audience members were tittering as Wolf crossed his arms over his massive chest and eyed her with increasing paternal impatience.

"All right then, that's enough. You can't have them all. Pick one and get back here."

She began to reach for the one she intended to pick, and something odd happened. She realized she couldn't. Thoughts crowded in. He'd likely put it there specifically for her to choose it, though he hadn't told her that. With his attention fixed upon her, picking the one she really wanted felt too stupid and obvious. So she picked the one next to it, a gray bunny with floppy ears that framed his serious face. She turned to face Wolf, the rabbit folded against her.

He pushed himself up to a standing position. "Come here," he said.

All that looming height and strength was waiting for her five steps away, and his flat expression told her what to expect, even before his words did.

"You already know you're in trouble. If I have to come over there to get you, it will be three times worse."

She came to him, though the threat wasn't what compelled her. Unless the tight yearning of her body that grew more excruciating with every syllable he uttered counted.

"Daddy isn't pleased. You didn't choose the one you wanted." He lifted a finger, tapped her face. "We discussed you lying to me."

She flushed. He was just acting out the scene with her. There was no way he could know that she truly hadn't chosen the one she wanted.

He removed the rabbit from her arms and set it aside. Gripping her wrist, he made her face the table, her back to the audience, and pushed her down, her cheek to the cool surface. "Look at the one you really wanted," he said.

She had to turn her head toward the side of the room holding all the carnival stuffed animals. As she did that, he molded his palm over her ass. He pushed his fingers beneath the panties, drawing up the elastic edge to expose one fleshy cheek.

"Keep looking at it," he said.

He knew how to hit the widest part of the buttock, down low, the sweet spot. He also knew how to build the sting, so within three or four swats she was starting to hurt, to quiver, want to wiggle. But that was okay, expected. It was another reaction that disturbed her.

Shit. This was Wolf, and she kept some walls up between them because she wanted him more than she should. Yet the tears were welling up, aching in her throat, making her chest hurt, making it more difficult to breathe, with every swat. He was hitting her harder, as if sensing it. Of course he sensed it. He was a damned Dom.

She'd willingly relinquished her dignity in scenes with Masters and Mistresses who demanded it, letting the emotions ebb and flow as they would, because that was part of the pleasure for both of them. The personal reward, satisfying their demands, was worth any perceived embarrassment. It also showed those watching this was a safe space to explore every corner of their needs.

But this was different. She normally made that choice, and this hadn't felt like a conscious decision. She fought it, and started strangling on the reaction.

"Let it go, little one," he said firmly. "You're safe, and I'm going to look after you."

He was going to break her heart. No, he was going to stomp it into nothingness. She had her fist pressed against her lips and teeth, trying not to go there, but it didn't matter. The tears overflowed, the sobs burst forth.

It wasn't an ugly cathartic cry, thank the gods, but as soon as she let it go, she knew what it was and why it had happened. So did he.

"All right then. Sshh." He'd spanked her through the worst of it, but as the sobs started to diminish, he eased her up, gripping her elbow, and brought her to him. He shifted so his back was to the group, her shielded in front of him. Every person in the packed room was silent, their hushed presence a warm cocoon reinforcing his arms around her. They would see her hands which came around, gripped his back, clung, as she tried to get her emotions under control. "It's all right. Daddy's here," he said. "All is forgiven. You only have to be yourself to be loved."

That one hurt worse than anything else, such that she shuddered on one last hard sob. He tightened his grip. He adjusted a few inches, the amount necessary to turn slightly toward the group and address them, but still kept her shielded from their view.

"Before the session started tonight, I asked Ella a difficult question about herself. She asked for the right to refuse to answer, and I granted it, with the condition that a punishment would be meted out instead. This was not that punishment, so don't get too relieved, little one," he said dryly, squeezing her. She snuffled a sheepish chuckle against him, responding to the tentative laughter of the group.

"But when I punished her for choosing the wrong stuffed animal," he continued, "her submissive reaction to hiding her true desires and lying to her Daddy, her Dom, came to the surface. Such a reaction usually connects to a lot of things. Every day we have the chance to succeed or fail, connect to others or drive them away. Say the right thing or wrong thing. Feel like we've accomplished something, or that we've wasted another day of the life given to us. It builds up in our subconscious, and especially for a submissive, it can lead to a sense of failure hard to shake, when she doesn't think she's met her own expectations, which are far higher than any her Dom will ever set.

"That's an important note about Daddy/little girl play," he added. "Your little girl gets the chance to let go of that. She can be playful, unselfconscious, knowing Daddy will tell her if she does something wrong and needs to correct her behavior. And he decides the punishment for that. Once that's been done, there's no fallout or collateral damage. It's simply done and she can move on."

He turned his attention back to Ella. He plucked a tissue out of a box on the table, a staple in most rooms. He eased her back onto the table and dabbed at her eyes, wiping away the tears, wiping her nose. Her hands were on his wrists, holding onto him as she trembled, still shaken.

"Good girl." He brushed a loose lock of her hair back from her face. "That's my very good girl. Now, go pick the one you really wanted, and remember you always tell Daddy the truth, whether in action or word."

"Yes sir." The genuine approval in his eyes steadied her. That, as well as muscle memory from a thousand scenes put her back on track for their audience. She returned to the table, put the gray bunny back. Then she closed her hand on the wolf. While the other stuffed animals had the soft colors and benign expressions expected for a children's toy, the wolf was black, with defiant amber eyes. No open mouth, so it gave the stuffed animal a serious look. The silky fur and floppy limbs fit against her bosom just right, though. She could rest her chin on top of the toy's head as she slept, its presence against her a comfort. It was a good size, about eighteen inches high.

There was a ripple of laughter through the room, responding to her choosing the "wolf." She could be embarrassed by that, but she knew one thing for certain. She wasn't returning it or offering it up to the attendees when they chose their own stuffed animal. She'd reimburse the club for it if needed.

"I don't believe in overanalyzing," Wolf said to the group as she returned to his side. Back in character, she hopped up onto the table once more, letting her legs swing free as she cradled the wolf beneath her breasts. "I think we have instincts far smarter than our conscious thoughts. Daddy Dom/little girl play provides an opportunity to reinforce the desires you have on both sides, to need and be needed."

He swept the room with his gaze, touching on attentive couples. "Maybe your woman needs the reminder that she can rely on you to take care of her. Maybe your man needs the validation of knowing you trust him to care for you. Women often think relinquishing power to the man they love is weakness, a betrayal of feminist principles. Men are told being protective and territorial is Neanderthal-ish. We face that issue in many Master/sub relationships, and sometimes it takes some serious work to get past it, really embrace the relationship you want with one another. Daddy Dom/little girl dynamics give us a playful option, which might help loosen up those expectations more quickly."

He glanced toward Ella, giving her a thoughtful look that made her heart skip a beat. "Whether you embrace a Daddy Dom/little girl relationship fully, or it's another aspect of your Master/sub relationship, the main thing is to do what works for the two of you. That's how you find what you're really wanting, deep inside."

~

From there they went into specific elements of the Daddy Dom/little girl relationship. The workshop ran over, not surprisingly. Wolf answered a bunch of questions, as did Ella.

"Yes, you can do subtle things in public," she told one woman. The redhead with gold rimmed glasses and the earnest look of a Type A personality had started the workshop looking far more nervous than she did now.

"It's actually a lot of fun, sending 'secret messages' to Daddy when you're around others. Like for instance, you're out for a walk together. Maybe your Daddy has a rule that you have to hold his hand to cross the street." Ella looked at the woman's fingers, laced with her Dom's. The dark-haired young man with a bushy beard and knit cap had kept her hand in his, resting on his knee, throughout the workshop. "So, at every traffic crossing, you take his hand. Nobody would think anything about a couple holding hands, right?"

She sidled up to Wolf as she spoke, slipped her hand into his. When she stepped away from him so she could swing their arms between them, just like a little girl, the audience laughed. His grip held her fast, his palm and fingers warm against hers. When she met his gaze, he was looking at her in that steady, stomach-jumping way, as if in his mind, he was responding to her in a far different manner. She cleared her throat, earning a glint of male satisfaction.

"Getting piggy-back rides from your Daddy is another thing that passes as flirtatious love play between adults," she continued. "Even vanilla lovers who aren't aware of the nuances of Daddy Dom/little girl play are getting in touch with that dynamic when they do things like that. The nice thing about vanilla is it can blend with so many other flavors. Between partners who are loving and open with one another, there's a delightful D/s language playing out between us all the time, whether we know it or not."

"Can't think of a better note to end this on," Wolf said, glancing at the wall clock. "If you have further questions, both Ella and I are on the Club Atlantis message board..."

As he concluded the workshop, the attendees applauded and began to rise, moving to the side table to pick up their literature, look at the books, and take their free stuffed animal. Ella hiked herself back up on the table, feet swinging, watching. She expected Wolf to slip out, because usually the presenter's assistant oversaw this part of things, and he did so, giving her a nod.

Having her remain behind served a dual purpose. The Dom tended to draw more hangers-on at the end of a class, so it cleared people out more quickly in his absence. It also gave the Dom the opportunity to go to his next commitment, if he couldn't linger. She didn't know Wolf's schedule tonight, but wouldn't be surprised if he had a couple sessions pending.

It took about ten minutes for everyone to drift out. All the animals had been taken, except the wolf she'd kept with her, no matter that more than one person had looked longingly at it. She was usually very generous. She didn't collect possessions, even giving away most of her precious dog-eared books after she read them, so someone else could discover the stories. She wasn't ready to let go of the wolf, though.

"You're very good at this."

She jumped. Wolf was back, leaning in the doorway, his arms crossed. "Sorry, I wasn't expecting you there," she said. "Thanks. I think it was a really good class. You teach it well."

"Yeah. We set the bar pretty high for Madelyn. She'll have to up her game."

Ella chuckled. "I'll be sure and tell her. She'll take it as a personal challenge from one of those 'damn Doms.'" What she and Chantal routinely called all the Masters.

His gaze gleamed with humor, but then his expression changed in a way that had her pulse fluttering. "You owe me a punishment."

"Yes. Yes, sir."

He moved from the door, but he didn't seem in any hurry, sauntering up the aisle, straightening a couple chairs, bending to pick up a half empty water bottle someone had left. He fired it toward the trashcan in the far corner of the room. It bounced off the wall above the can and fell into it.

Doms technically never had to lift a finger when subs were around, relying on them to handle cleanup at events. Wolf often did things like this, showing he understood the line between reinforcing the submissive craving and providing free labor to lazy-assed Doms. That quote came from Anwyn, when she'd taken a Domme to task for leaving tissues and other debris from her scenes lying around the public play areas.

Now he stopped in the middle of the aisle, and tilted his head at her. "Do you remember your father?" he asked.

He knew how to keep her off balance. It was another loaded question, but this one she could handle. "Just a photo album in my head. Pictures with feelings. He's raking leaves. I 'helped,'" a difficult smile curved her lips, "which meant he stopped and played in the leaf piles with me until he had to get back to it. He told me to sit on the stoop and read to him from the book I was holding. Can't remember what the title was, and I wish I could."

It was about a horse, she thought. An old book from the school library, with a worn greenish-gray cover and stamped gold lettering on the spine. "Then it sort of fades out, probably because I was reading and lost in the story, but the picture comes back sharp when he's done raking. He sat on the upper step, me just below him. He wrapped his arms around me and rested his chin on the top of my head for a second. Then he let me stay there, him leaning back on his elbows, drinking a beer and gazing up into the trees while I read. I stayed in this cocoon of his arms and legs. Maybe for twenty minutes. Maybe for a month. It felt like the best place to be."

Wolf turned, went to the back and drew a wooden footstool from beneath the back table, an aid to shorter presenters when raising the mobile projector screen on its tripod. He placed the stool before a chair in the front row, and took a seat in that chair. He pointed to the stool. "Come sit here, facing away from me."

When she obeyed, she closed her eyes as he leaned forward, wrapped both arms around her. He caressed her upper arms as his breath stirred her hair. Her hands curled against his denim-clad shins.

"Did it feel like this?" he asked.

"Yes and no. It feels really good. Safe. But I have some reactions to you doing it that I definitely didn't have with my father."

He laughed, a deep, body-stroking sound. "Well, remember what I said at the beginning of the workshop. It's all about the sugar, baby. All about the sugar."

She smiled, rested her cheek against his biceps. He stroked her hair, bent, pressed a kiss to it. "You're such a little thing, but so strong."

The compliment surprised and warmed her. "Thank you." She lifted her face to look at him.

"Are you ready for your punishment now?" he said.

"I think so."

His expression sharpened. The involuntary leap in her stomach, the straightening of her spine, were the reactions that kicked in, full force, when a Dom gave her that look.

"Yes, sir."

"Okay, then." He rose, swinging his leg over her, and moved toward the rear wall. Once there, he cut the lights.

She was in the dark again. She stared at the blackness, listening to her pulse thud. She didn't hear him move, didn't hear him breathe, but as she sat there, her senses open, she knew when he was beside her again. Her heart rate increased when his fingertips trailed over her shoulder.

"Give me your hand."

She obliged and he brought her to her feet. He guided her forward several steps and stopped her.

"Can you see in the dark?" she asked, her voice little over a whisper. It was meant to be subtly teasing. She assumed he had an uncanny ability to measure and calculate distance between objects with only a brief look.

"Yes." He'd shifted behind her and slid his hand up her hip, to her waist, to cup her breast, stroke. He didn't sound like he was joking.

She swayed into his touch, ripples of sensation moving all over her skin. "Thank you, Master," she whispered softly. Unplanned, just fervently felt.

"Take a breath."

She did, and his knuckles closed over her other nipple, through the gauzy cloth. Now she knew what he intended, and there was nothing for it but to endure. He wasn't giving her a tempting incentive as he'd done last time. Her hands remained at her sides because she knew that was where he wanted them. He began that slow compression that became progressively worse and worse, and then he started to twist.

A groan escaped her, but she held, her hips pressing back into him as she reacted to the pain. "Please..." tore from her lips.

"You need me to stop?"

She didn't want to tell him to stop. She didn't want to deny him anything, but Goddess, it hurt. "Please...mercy."

It wasn't her safe word, but he understood. She didn't want to safe word out, but she could take no more. She would if she had to, but she begged him for compassion instead.

He eased off, massaged around the throbbing nipple. Turned her slowly in the dark, untying the ribbon at her neck and around her back so the gauzy fabric fell to her waist. Then he knelt before her, a position she was beginning to realize he liked for the proximity it gave him to her breasts. As he began to suckle the abused one, she swayed, but was held firmly in the cradle of his arms.

He moved to the other one. Desire was spiraling through her, up and up. He lifted and moved her, sitting her on the presenter's table. His mouth went to her throat. She clutched his shoulders, a cry tearing from her as he bit. Pain lanced through her like twin injections of fire. She'd had her nipples pierced at one time, and it had felt like this, the pain excruciating but yet somehow welcome. She shifted her grip to his nape, the back of his head, the smooth, heated skin.

He didn't let go of her, kept that clamp in her throat while he stroked and soothed her breasts. But after awhile, he eased back. Her body felt made of liquid fire.

"Now that one belongs to me, too. No one touches your nipples, Ella. Not unless I give permission. Tell me you understand."

"I understand, sir."

But did she? Was he laying claim to her, one body part at a time? What was going on?

Did she have the courage to ask, or would she take the bliss of his attention as long as it lasted?

For now, she knew the answer to that. Wolf caressed her face, ran a calming hand over her back and shoulders, brushed a kiss across her forehead. Then he withdrew. A moment later, the light snapped on. He was in the doorway and gave her a nod.

"You did well, Ella. Thank you for your help. I'll see you later."

"Okay. Um, yes, sir."

But he was already gone.

CHAPTER FIVE

Being a grown-up was far better than being a kid. It baffled her, people who wanted to return to those early days. Everything learned as a kid, felt as a kid, could be indulged fully as an adult. And you could have way more fun with it.

For instance, you couldn't be a kid and stand in the middle of a BDSM club. Couldn't plunge in the middle of a pack of human puppies—members who embraced puppy play—and roll and play like a puppy yourself, rubbing against firm, warm bodies with intimate affection.

It was male Puppy Night at Club Atlantis. The converted and padded dance floor was currently populated with tennis balls and soft toys instead of dancers. Many of the participants wore head masks, complete with ears and long snouts. Ella always thought the ones with floppy ears had a happy-looking demeanor, whereas the ones with pricked ears projected a more aggressive attitude. Alpha dogs. Some wore the full puppy body, with big cloth paws. Others wore the head mask with only jeans, or nothing at all.

Roughhousing could sometimes pave the way to a joyous puppy fuck, but they didn't often do it in the public play space. Though with the "puppies" tangling with one another, occasionally a more dominant "puppy" dry humped a more submissive one, a hint of what might happen behind closed doors later.

At the moment, however, it was all play. She bounded in among the playful canines, tackling Toby.

Toby was one of those who wore the German shepherd style head mask with a pair of jeans. Calling himself an old dog, he was a senior among the "puppies." He was about thirty-five, but a lot of those on the floor tonight were in their twenties.

He'd seen her coming and caught her, rolling them over and over. He'd taken care to wrap his arms around her and cushion the tumble, but when he let her go, he was all dog, cavorting around her, growling and darting in for ticklish nips at her breast, hips, stomach and legs that had her laughing and rolling away. Which only took her into the middle of another group who were happy to have her sit up on her knees, pet them, toss the tennis balls across the ballroom so they could chase them as a group, wrestle and tumble one another.

She wasn't the only one taking advantage of the chance to play with puppies, but she did it with such enthusiastic abandon, the number of human playmates increased exponentially. So when she was out of breath, she moved to the edge of the converted dance floor.

Once there, she met the gaze of Arthur, assigned Dungeon Master over the puppy gathering in this section, and therefore renamed Master of the Hounds for the night. She gave him a slight nod. When he returned the gesture, telling her he was ready, too, she stepped behind the wall around the dance floor and into the shadows. She stripped off the tunic, revealing the black body suit and laced bustier she wore beneath. A ribbon had kept the loose end of her "tail" attached to her hip, but now she removed it so the tail could twitch freely with the movements of her body. The base was sewn underneath the bottom of her bustier, fitted just above the seam of her buttocks. From practice, she knew it swished quite jauntily, particularly when she gave her hips that extra swing that could draw male eyes.

An alert staff member at the nearby drink station came by with a secret smile and a tray of drinks, slipping her the headband with tufted ears. Ella winked at him, then positioned it, digging the comb-tipped ends securely into her thick hair, which she loosened from its overtaxed barrette, so the dark curls spilled down her back. Then she removed the black mask tucked in her bustier. It covered her face, giving her whiskers and the illusion of tilted feline eyes, while leaving her mouth and chin visible.

That was okay. She wasn't attempting to present herself as all cat. Instead, she was going for the fantasy, a mix of the feline and feminine. Providing elusive, teasing prey to a pack who were a mix of canine and human male.

The pièce de résistance was the gloves. They fit her like a second skin and had claws embedded in the fingertips. Not too sharp, but they could do damage. She liked imagining the sensual uses, raking them up the back of a strong Dom, plowing himself between her legs. A Dom with a wide, bronze back...

Stop it. Time to get in the right headspace. If she gave herself to whatever the moment required, it was easy to assume any role she wanted to play. At so many different points of her life, the skill had come in handy. It also offered the perfect escape from all sorts of pain and regrets that time didn't heal.

Still in the shadows, she dropped to her haunches and then all fours, her eyes closed. She thought of cats. The way they moved, the way they looked at the world. They liked to taunt, to live on the edge. To encourage danger to come close, meet it with an indifferent languor and then slip away like a flash of light.

She'd practiced this a lot before tonight, preparing, so it wasn't hard to shift. She liked that word, shift. Like the books with wolf shifters, only she was shifting to a cat. She rubbed against the wall, using her chin, her face, the way a cat would, marking it with her scent. She rubbed her whole side against it, liking the feel of the hard surface stroking her side. Taking her time, indulging the pleasure, because that was exactly what a cat would do. No schedule except what revolved around her.

At length, she rose and moved into the opening.

Toby noticed her first. His head came up, his mask nose quivering, as if he were sniffing the air. His body went stiff and alert, all the muscles along shoulders and arms rippling.

Demonstrating a kitten's guileless indifference, she sashayed along the wall's inside perimeter. Only a few feet, though. She needed to keep close to that egress point. She kneaded the floor, letting her claws lightly scrape it before she straightened, moved toward that opening with a saunter and swish of the tail. She rubbed her hip against one side of the threshold, rotating her backside in their direction. She was wearing the kind of slippers professional ballet dancers wore to give her good, non-slip footing.

More canine heads were up, eyes fixing on her. Play had stopped, and several of the dogs were advancing, at a slow, stalking pace. There were over two dozen of them.

People sitting at the tables outside the dance floor, enjoying the puppy play, conversation, and their drinks, had noticed the change in the program. Anticipation was spreading, quieting conversation.

She lifted her chin, letting her lips tip up. The dogs were at rigid attention, waiting for a signal, knowing one was coming. They were human males, but just like herself, they were mixed with the animal in a way that had her heartrate increasing, her breath shortening.

"Meow," she said.

The chase was on.

~

The dogs erupted into movement, surging toward her, voices lifted in a chorus of baying, yips, urgent barks.

She took off through the club, careful to avoid the semi-private alcoves with active scenes. She cut through the public areas with abandon, though, looking like a cat in truth, lithely jumping from one table to another, an army of the joyous, barking dogs in pursuit.

Since it was hard for a human to gain any speed on all fours like the dogs they emulated, most went with the two-legged approach, like her, and several of the males behind those masks were athletic and swift. Like Toby.

When she reached the smaller bar and sprang up on it, her first safe zone, she turned, hissed, batted at Toby's nose when he shoved it at her. They gathered around, and she sat down on her haunches, catching her breath. One of the dogs made a grab at her, and she was away again.

She dashed down the bar, neatly missing any drinks not abruptly pulled from her path. The puppies were slowed by the need to navigate, to not topple or destroy anything in their path. The pound would be a picnic next to Mistress Anwyn's wrath.

She dodged, leaped, feinted. Laughing faces, sparkling eyes flashed by, a wave of ebullient energy. The club visitors and regulars were loving the unexpected drama, puppy and non-puppy alike. She should be delighted, because this mini-event to kick off the evening had been her idea. Compliments of Julie, your cruise director.

But something was off. She'd looked forward to immersing herself in child's play, because she couldn't figure out what kind of mindfuck Wolf was doing on her. He acted like he didn't want to pursue anything with her, but he kept engaging her. He'd bitten her, and not just a love bite. He'd broken skin, left two puncture marks from his canines that were still healing. She'd run her fingers over those marks a million times, trembling a little over the obvious sign of possession. A sign Wolf wanted her.

She was running from the dogs, but she was also running from frustration, anger, a little fear of herself and her life, the loneliness that never seemed to abate.

She went over a spanking bench, doubled around the sub strapped on it. The dogs swarmed around him and the Mistress tending him. Everyone had been warned of the planned drama, and how it might momentarily disrupt a public scene, to add to the realism of the chase. The Mistress stepped closer to her bound male, her hand on his back, and made a menacing gesture with her cane, applying it liberally on the dogs who came too close—probably on purpose, since she managed to land fairly targeted strikes on hindquarters. One floppy-eared one in a thin body suit even stopped and lifted his hindquarters for an extra smack, giving her a lolling tongue look of pleasure that made the Mistress's lips twitch before the dog was on his way again.

Ella shot for a different section of the club. It was thrilling, really. The dogs were closing in, because there was only so much space, and so many of them. It was a little scary, but primal play could be like that.

A table toppled with a crashing noise. A pup caught and rolled her, so she stumbled and hit the ground pretty hard. The inner cat came forth, and she didn't hold back. "Rrowr!" She squirmed, snarled, struck him with her claws, and got away, though she felt his hands grab at her ankle. Not just his. There were two other "dogs," and they piled on.

She screeched, used the claws liberally to shred the forearm of the one holding her the tightest. He let go with a whimper, followed by another snarl, but she'd wiggled free then and scrambled away. Someone caught her hair.

When a BDSM scene evolved into something else, it could be amazing, a high like nothing else. But there were times devolution happened, too. Sometimes shit could get real.

She was a cat and a woman, scrambling free and bolting for safety with no thought in mind but getting beyond their reach. The dogs—and men—were in fierce pursuit. As one rolled her again, he spoke against her ear. His laughter didn't sound quite right.

"Run, little pussy. Try to run."

Her heart was triple hammering, her breath rasping in her chest. She could use her safe gesture. All she had to do was rip the tail loose and wave it like a flag. But she didn't. No, it was just a weird moment. Things would settle down. She was safe here. Always safe at Atlantis.

Another crash. She wrestled free and headed for her end goal.

There was a tree in Atlantis. Not a live tree, but one constructed of wood and fabric, commissioned by Anwyn from a company that did upscale private playgrounds.

See? For kids, yet adults had even more fun with them. The reminder brought her back to herself, helped steady her. She leaped for a grip on the lower branches and scrambled up. She kept going, until she was well above the heads of the tallest dog.

They had to behave like dogs, so they couldn't climb after her, but they had her well and truly treed. She hissed and growled, and they barked and growled back. She saw their dancing eyes, the sparkle, predator pursuing prey.

That shiver-inducing side was still there, the humans behind the masks channeling what they would be driven by instinct to do. Acting as a pack had brought to life a savage drive that stayed dormant when they were individual, far more socialized pets.

Thinking of that, it wasn't hard for her to summon the kitten response, the meow this time far more plaintive, a little fearful.

The perfect note. It was okay. Everything was all right.

There was a social area near the tree playground, with another small bar area, the round tables populated with Doms and subs watching the entertainment. It helped remind her. This was a show. That was all.

"Well, *that* was exciting, wasn't it?" Madelyn had picked up a megaphone behind the bar and spoke forcefully into it.

The jarring sound seemed to break the spell. Some of the dogs looked a little dazed. Ella didn't know which of them had whispered that menacing threat in her ear, and she wasn't sure she ever wanted to know. She couldn't reconcile it with the playful men who'd romped with her on the dance floor only a few minutes before.

She briefly met Madelyn's gaze. It hadn't taken the Mistress more than a second to figure out things needed to be taken down a notch. She mouthed *Okay?* at Ella.

Ella managed a nod. She was fine. She needed to be better than fine, though, so whatever weird thing had just happened didn't become a big deal. Maddie's expression was caught between "what the fuck" and "Anwyn's going to want to discuss this."

Ella shoved the big bundle of nerves in her stomach aside and went into full performance mode. Cocking her head, she peered down her nose at the dogs and summoned a disdainful hiss, a bat of her paw in their direction, the cat equivalent of *up yours*, inciting laughter. Good. The audience was on board. Now she just needed to calm her shaking, which was ridiculous anyway. Everything was fine.

"Our kitten needs a rescuer," said Madelyn. "But our sexy emergency responder requires compensation for his services. Tonight is Charity Tuesday, so our kitten will donate a free two-hour session, good for a year, to the first person who makes a donation to our local animal rescue. Minimum $300."

"Three hundred and fifty, right here."

Master Charley called out the bid in her musical, throaty voice. She went by the title of Master instead of Mistress, because she didn't like the historic connotations of the word mistress, a paid woman kept in style to do the dirty things a man couldn't or wouldn't do with his wife. Charley's preference was male subs, but she sometimes used female subs to help her. She was always creative and fun, and Ella liked working with her. She had a straightforward brusqueness, and could give male subs a hell of a workout.

"Well done, Master Charley," Madelyn tipped her head to her. She raised her hand, a signal, and spoke loudly in the microphone, angling it toward the public area around the corner, out of Ella's line of sight. "Our kitten may now be rescued."

"Or you can shake that tree and let the dogs have their way with her," one of the Doms called out.

The suggestion set off a chorus of loud, piercing howls from the pack as they danced and jumped. Ella flinched, shrank back.

The Dom was teasing. It was a sexual suggestion, not a threatening one. *The puppies are just playing now. It's okay.*

But as she looked down into their eyes, something went wrong in her head. She didn't want to come down out of that tree. Not until they were gone. They blurred before her, and it wasn't the dogs leaping and jumping, howling. It was flame, leaping, grabbing, roaring. Telling her there was no escape.

Oh, hell no. She wasn't the type of person who fell into that kind of vat. She desperately grasped for logic. She could remove the mask, speak normally to all of them, and everything would be fine. But that would break scene. Just knowing she *could* do that should be enough for her to regain balance.

With the exception of Madelyn, the audience seemed to be enjoying themselves, no evidence that they thought anything was off. If she could hold it together, there'd be nothing but compliments for the drama.

She just needed them to stop the howling and barking. *Please, please stop.* Despite all her logical thoughts, she could feel the heat closing in on her skin, the smoke filling her lungs...

The tree shook and she yelped, clutching the rope wrapped around her branch. Several of the dogs were standing on hind legs, pushing against the trunk. A playful shaking. Just playful.

"That's *enough*."

Lars was supposed to be her "rescuer," but the command that vibrated through the air like rolling thunder didn't belong to him.

Wolf strode past the bar, between the assembled tables. He didn't slow his pace when he reached the pack, and they scrambled to get out of his way. It was as if they'd suddenly, forcefully been reminded that they were subs, and there was a Dom in their midst who was in an ass-kicking kind of mood.

She had always loved thunderstorms, but never more than at this moment.

When he reached the base of her tree, the only one who didn't back away was Toby. Toby had some of the switch vibe that Lars had, and he stood up, almost as tall as Wolf. For one tense moment, they locked gazes.

"You better re-think that, boy." Wolf's expression was hot and cold at once, containing all the elements of *back off or you will be fucked up*.

Toby held his ground. He might just be playing the part, but since that pivotal moment in the chase, the scene seemed to have taken on a life of its own.

Ella held her breath as a deadly tension swept Wolf's body. Was she just imagining the glitter of savage malevolence as he shifted forward? Barely an inch, but the movement contained the dense power of a face punch.

Toby dropped to his haunches, reverting to proper dog behavior. Not even a sullen whine. He simply backed off, head bowed. The other dogs took an additional pace in retreat, following his lead.

Ella wasn't entirely sure that Wolf wasn't going to go after Toby anyway. To do what, she wasn't sure, but his fingers were half curled at his sides and his vibrating energy had everyone within its range on full alert, like a herd of antelope suddenly aware there was a predator in their midst, way too close to outrun.

A movement at the bar caught her attention. Anwyn had appeared. Ella bit back an oath, but the club owner's attention was latched onto Wolf, not her. Gideon was at her side. He wasn't as big as Wolf, but he was still impressively built, at six feet and broad shouldered, with a lined, rugged face and dark hair to his shoulders. His midnight-blue eyes reflected an equal alertness.

They were worried about what Wolf was going to do, she realized.

Just like that, she shifted away from her worry and toward what a submissive most desired. The ability to serve her Master, give him what he needed. It steadied her like nothing else.

"Wolf," Ella said softly. Following instinct, she added another word to it. "Master."

Slowly, Wolf's gaze pulled away from Toby, came to her. Ella held his look with an entreating one of her own. She needed him to help her out of this tree, get them both away from this. Whatever this was.

The energy changed, called back. She could almost feel a collective breath drawn as Wolf became the formidable—but very in control—Dominant they all knew. "Time to return to your owners," Wolf said brusquely to the pack. "Get. All of you. Dog park is closed for the night."

The puppies slunk away under his hard eye, some rejoining their Doms, others headed to different parts of the club. Some took a seat together at the tables, stripping off head masks and paws to get a drink. There was a murmuring undercurrent of conversation, a half laugh, strained, but things were hesitantly moving back toward normal. Ella could breathe again. As soon as her heart stopped choking her with its manic pounding.

Wolf looked up at her. All she wanted was to drop into his grip. But the audience was still too uncertain. She needed to do her part to show that everything was fine.

Plus, Anwyn was watching. Damage control now could make this a much better conversation later.

"Come on down, kitten," Wolf said, raising his voice. "I won't let the dogs get you."

She made herself waffle, prance. Channeling her feline side, she lifted a paw and licked it, as if casually taking a bath. Laughter rippled through the bar. Wolf's face creased in a mock scowl and he shook the tree, lightly. She meowed piteously, went up another two feet.

"If I have to come up there to get you, you won't like it a bit," he promised.

"Maybe she's a little concerned, a cat trusting herself to a wolf," one of the older Doms called out. Master Dorian had been part of the lifestyle since the Leatherman movement. His way with submissives of all ages, his colorful stories and confidence made him a club favorite.

Wolf cocked a challenging brow in his direction. "You want to come get her down?"

No. As much as she liked the other Dom, she wanted Wolf to bring her down. Fortunately, Dorian's response aligned with her wish.

"I'll add to the donation. Double it, in fact." Dorian grinned through the whistles of appreciation and applause that swept the area, taking a little bow. "But I'll leave the honor to you. She has claws, and you have younger knees."

"Pussy," Madelyn said through the megaphone, which she'd turned toward him. Since she was only three feet away, Dorian made an exaggerated wince at the noise, but shrugged, spreading his hands out wide in acceptance of the good-natured censure. "It'll happen to you, too, hot mama," he told her. "Just wait a couple decades."

Wolf returned his gaze to Ella. "Come here, kitty." His voice dropped to a gentle rumble. She had to dig in her claws, literally and figuratively, to keep herself from melting out of the tree into his grasp.

Shit could get real, yes. In a scary way, but in other kinds of ways as well. Wolf had a faint smile on his lips to play to the crowd, but the expression he had locked upon her contained something different. A Master's look. His lips straightened into that serious, firm set.

"Come to me," he repeated, low. He raised a hand, fingers spread. Not reaching. Waiting.

She had a knee hooked over one branch, and was holding onto another with one suddenly less sure hand. She tightened her core to lower her upper body toward him. Just like a cat, she nuzzled his knuckles, then dipped her head to rub it against his fingers. Very lightly at first, not too close, but as his hand turned, stroked, she leaned more into the touch, rubbing her whiskered face against him.

Play. Role play, kitten play, it was all about play. Everyone here knew play was an avenue to the deeper, real heart of this. The sudden quiet in the bar area told her she'd brought them into that space again.

She reached for his shoulders, letting go, and dropped into the cradle of his arms. The relief that flooded her was absurdly immense.

More applause, and Madelyn said something in the microphone, thanking Charley and Dorian for their donations. Ella missed most of it. Wolf carried her through it all, skirting the bar. She thought he nodded to Anwyn, a wordless reassurance, but he didn't pause.

He didn't let her down when they were clear. He took them through the main public play area, but used a staff door to access a cut-through. It brought them back into the club at the wax gallery.

The wax gallery was a section of the club that had three long tables arranged in an open horseshoe shape around a counter. The counter was where paraffin could be heated in crock pots. None were plugged in right now, since the area was vacant, but the sweet smell lingered. A multi-colored wax sculpture the size of a school volcano project covered one end of the prep space. It consisted of softened bits of wax broken off of the subs who'd been decorated here.

Wolf put her down in a sitting position on one of the tables. Ella did her best not to cling, but she didn't have to worry that he was moving away. He stood between her knees, and braced his hands on either side of her hips, dominating her personal space.

"I should strap your ass black and blue."

"I'm good," she said. "You didn't need to carry me all the way here."

"You're still shaking," he said darkly.

"Just adrenaline. Everything's fine. It went great."

She licked her lips. Apparently, she was channeling nervous cat gestures. She had her hands in her lap, his arms caging her so closely, his forearms brushed her elbows. She wanted to lift her hands and curl her fingers around those solid biceps, but his expression told her that doing anything without his permission would be even less advisable than normal.

"We discussed lying to me. I always wear a belt, Ella. Keeps it close to hand for when it's needed."

His formidable tone brought the words out of her she'd told herself she wouldn't say, so she could pass it off to Anwyn the same way she'd just attempted with him.

"It got a little too real," she said.

"You think?" He surveyed her with exasperation. "And you would be a black cat."

What did that mean? That she was bad luck? Then he was back to pinning her with a look that told her to brace for a lecture.

"A group can become a mob faster than a fired shot. If you set up the right situation to see the wrong side of human instincts, you will. Primal play works pretty good when it's structured, and directly supervised by the Doms in charge of those submissives. But it should never, ever be let loose like that in a pack. And Christ, particularly not a group channeling their inner canine. That made those instincts come to the top way faster. Especially with a trigger like chasing live prey."

With a low curse, he shoved himself from the table and paced away from her. The vehemence shook her, but it gave her a little more breathing room to marshal her thoughts. All staff Doms got worked up if they thought a sub was in danger, because they were wonderful that way. It was a reminder to her that she'd never been in any danger, and she needed to assure him of the same.

"It didn't get that out of hand because it *did* happen in a supervised setting. Madelyn was there, you, Dorian. I just let that weird energy get into my head, and you and Madelyn picked up on me being unsettled by it. Everyone else seemed okay, like they were having fun. I mean, our mantra is risk-aware consensual kink. It's like jumping out of an airplane. Scary at times, but mostly exhilarating and positive. I'll bet a lot of people are considering puppy play who hadn't before."

He pivoted and stared at her, making her swallow what else she'd been intending to say. "You're a smart woman. Which is why I can't figure out why you act so oblivious about certain things. I don't know if it's a cry for attention, a lack of common sense, or I've overestimated your intelligence."

Before he could see her stung reaction, he bent and retrieved a bottle of water from the small fridge under the counter. Bringing it back to the table where she was sitting, he put it down next to her with an abrupt movement. "Drink that before you get up off the table. You're done for the night."

"Oh. I have two appointments with members. And I told Lars I'd help in the bar after—"

"I'm not in the habit of repeating myself," he said, with a hard look that made her stomach quake. "Reschedule. I'll tell Lars he needs to get someone else's help tonight, since he couldn't be bothered to be there when he said he would."

"He couldn't help getting caught behind the bar. It's busy tonight. And..." She made a helpless gesture. She hated to argue with him, didn't want to disobey. This was the part of being a sub that could be so difficult, especially when it involved a Dom who made her feel the way Wolf did. She wanted to please him, wanted to obey his every word without question. But she couldn't.

He crossed his arms and leveled a stare on her that she expected could make grown men quake. But she knew beneath the intimidating exterior, he was trying to take care of her. That gave her the courage to speak.

"I really can't break an appointment, sir. It's unprofessional, and there's no reason for me to do so. Both of them are Doms I've worked with before, and I'm helping them, participating in the scene as a facilitating third party. Neither one is edge play."

As he continued to give her that stony look, she dropped her gaze. "Please, Wolf. Anwyn probably already thinks I screwed up tonight. I can't have her thinking I'd skip out on appointments, too. I want her to know she can count on me."

He moved toward her. She heard the firm tread, saw him stop in front of her knees. They were still spread from when he'd stood between them, because she'd stayed that way, remaining open to what he wanted from her.

"Look at me."

She did. He framed her face with one hand, his thumb sweeping her chin and the upper part of her throat, then stopping there, applying a firm pressure. He had one of the most intense expressions she'd ever encountered in a Dom, almost inhuman sometimes. It was capable of capturing her gaze in the lock of his, or snapping it downward with no more than a one-word command. He was leaned in so close, her nervously curling hands ended up resting on his abdomen and that belt he'd threatened to use on her.

"What if I forbid it anyway?" he said. "What would you say to that?"

Her stomach jumped. "I'd want to obey, so very much. It would tear me up inside not to, because..." She moistened her lips. "I don't belong to you, sir, but when you talk to me like this, it makes me feel like I do. It messes me up, but I have to honor my promises."

He studied her a long moment. He'd begun a slow glide over her throat with his thumb, forward, then back, pressing on the pulse, stroking it.

A massage of the carotid artery. It made her slightly dizzy, particularly when he put his head and mouth down there, breathing on the racing pulse. She felt the sharp scrape of his teeth, and realized he was putting his mouth on the area he'd bitten. She tightened her hold on his belt, feeling the intimate strip of his flesh beneath it. Pumping heat, rock hard muscle.

Abruptly he straightened and stepped back, but he held onto her until her pulse leveled out and the fog cleared. "I'll be talking to those two Doms on your schedule tonight, to ensure you're not pushed further than you should be. If what they're planning crosses the line of what I know you can handle, they'll find a substitute. Take it or leave it."

She didn't have to ask him for the consequences. If she refused to accept his dictate, he'd likely take his concerns to Anwyn, adding to the weight of that post-event briefing she had coming. She wondered if the range of concerns about the event would only involve her actions, however. She remembered the tension in Anwyn's face, in Gideon's body language, when they'd watched Wolf face off with Toby.

He moved toward the archway leading out of the wax room. That was it, he was leaving. He hadn't responded to her assertion about him acting like he was her Dom. He'd just continued to do so, and nothing about his behavior said he was ready to have a discussion about that.

She was clinging to a precariously spinning top, and everyone knew how that ended. Her best course of action, for her head and heart, was to assume status quo. Not because that was entirely true, but because he hadn't officially offered anything more. He was a staff Dom looking out for a staff sub. End of story.

Just like that time, a little while back, where he'd unexpectedly shown up at a bookstore she was at. He'd left her a sandwich in her basket. She'd wanted to make more of it than it was, then. But it all fit under the umbrella of a staff Dom caring for a staff sub. Mostly.

"Um, thank you, Wolf. For taking on the rescue bid part of things. I really do think Lars got held up at the bar. He's very dependable usually."

Wolf paused, glanced at her, offered a spare nod. Then he was gone. He let the curtain at the entry fall back in place as he departed. It gave her another few minutes of privacy, though it wouldn't be for long. By midnight, all rooms would be full. They'd done the puppy skit early.

So. She took a breath. She needed to get on with things, never mind that he'd left her aching. When his arms had been around her, and he'd carried her away from the pack, she'd felt rescued, in all the right ways. But the shaking in her lower belly returned in the immediate wake of emotions following his absence. Okay, so he might be right that she'd been a little freaked out by tonight, in ways that could be brought back out if she engaged in a demanding session.

I don't know if it's a cry for attention, a lack of common sense, or I've misinterpreted your intelligence.

But he'd also said she was a smart woman.

She pushed that away. "He thinks of you as a child." She said it aloud, no matter that it hurt. It hurt a lot less than a heart pummeled by the disappointment of wishful thinking.

She should label him patronizing, judgmental, and adopt a "who cares if you don't approve of who I am" attitude about it. But that wasn't who she was.

It was hellishly hard, pushing herself off the edge of the table, but she did it. After she drank the water he told her to drink.

Life went on, even after knee-weakening moments with mysterious Doms. Particularly one who seemed to want something even more mystifying from her.

CHAPTER SIX

For the next two days her other jobs took priority. She spent one morning at the salon, doing manicures, and the other waitressing. The afternoons and early evenings were filled with bike courier work for the neighborhood gourmet grocery store.

But on day three she was back at the club, and had the unpleasant but rare experience of dreading the first part of her night there. Anwyn had scheduled a meeting to discuss future "social events," which included a review and discussion of how the puppy play event had unfolded.

Fortunately, Ella had gone over it in her head enough to feel somewhat prepared and secure in her own evaluation. It didn't keep her stomach from being a little unsettled as she took a seat in Anwyn's office.

It wasn't overly large, since Anwyn didn't spend much time here, but she had a backlit picture of Tiffany glass mounted behind her desk. It featured muted red poppies interspersed with shades of purple, blue and green, drawing the eye. A floor lamp made of intertwined bronze poles had sensual curves and a tulip shaped ivory glass shade. The walls were painted a soft blue and the floor was polished wood. There were two matching guest chairs whose upholstery picked up that same blue.

The desk had the usual debris of a busy business owner—computer, bills, paperwork—but the surroundings were in keeping with the Mistress of Atlantis's appreciation for lovely, unique things. A bouquet of fresh, blood-colored roses in a cut crystal vase was on a side table, next to a dish of chocolate candies.

Fresh roses had been there as long as Ella could remember. Even before Gideon's arrival. As soon as they began to fade, they were replaced, though Anwyn wasn't the one who replaced them. An ongoing mystery to the staff.

"Security suggested a pre-event review of the puppy play event," the Mistress of Club Atlantis said. "Was that done?"

Ella perched on the edge of the chair, trying to look relaxed, her hands folded in her lap. "Yes, ma'am. Stan and I went over it. We also went over the rules with the participating puppies, particularly about not letting things get so out of hand that club facilities were damaged. At the time, we believed that would keep everyone mindful that it was play. I apologize. It's difficult, when things are in the moment, not to get lost in it, and think it's something it's not. I've thought a lot about how to address that, without taking the life and energy out of it."

Anwyn remained silent, her blue-green gaze fixed on Ella. The woman's sable hair was clipped on her nape, the waves framing her precise features. Her delicate beauty didn't fool anyone who knew her. Ella needed to be honest. Anwyn couldn't be bullshitted.

"For the most part, the participants had a good time. We lost important elements of control during the chase. I'm not sure how we could have anticipated that, having taken the other precautions, but I think it gave us important info on how to make the next one or similar events go even better. We can adjust the prep talk accordingly, to make everyone more mindful of that risk. Sometimes to do it right, we have to have a few rehearsals where things go a bit wrong."

Anwyn digested that. She hadn't moved, maintaining a stillness that sometimes seemed eerie, as if she'd become a statue, though the sensual energy that vibrated off of her said she was very much alive. That dense, tingling field around her reminded Ella of Wolf. Particularly when Wolf had locked gazes with Toby and backed him down. Or when he leveled his intense look upon Ella.

That expression said she wouldn't be making a move without his say so, because he considered her entirely his.

She immediately relegated the latter part of that thought to the

"Ella's private fantasy" part of her head, since it wasn't based in any reality whatsoever.

"I really like being the Minion of Play," Ella said, looking down at her folded hands. "I apologize if I did something to abuse that role, and I hope you'll continue to let me do it. If you need me to do something differently, I'm more than willing to do that. I never want to cause you problems, though I know I do, way more than I should."

"That's the damn truth."

That came from Gideon, as he slid into the office. Rather than sitting in the guest chair next to Ella, he moved to stand against the wall behind Anwyn's left shoulder. Not an unusual position for a submissive to take, except Gideon didn't give off a sub vibe. But service and protection? Those vibrated off him in spades.

Her stomach tightened in a hard knot over his words, but then he winked at her. She relaxed a little, realizing he'd made the remark with his usual fond, big brother-style exasperation. A big brother in name only, thank goodness, which allowed her to flirt with and tease him, the way most of the staff at Club Atlantis did. His heart and soul belonged to Anwyn, but he had an out-front sexuality and dry humor that made him an irresistible target.

He also had several unusual brands, two that braceleted his wrists and one around his throat. The two on his wrists had a letter stamped in the brand, A on one wrist, D on the other. The A was easy to figure, but the D had puzzled more than one staff member. The one on the throat had a trio of what looked like tears or drops of blood, arranged in a circle. He had the same design, only larger, on his chest. That one was an unusual mix of brand and tattoo, the raised drops deep crimson, suggesting they represented blood, not tears. But Ella sometimes thought they meant both.

Though it was obvious to the staff they were signs of ownership, Gideon didn't discuss them. As he crossed his arms over his broad chest, unconsciously emphasizing the ones on his wrists, Anwyn glanced at him. Sometimes there were pauses between them, as if they could communicate without words. This seemed to be one of those moments.

Anwyn turned her attention back to Ella. "I agree with your analysis," she said. "There's a reason for the term Risk Aware Consensual Kink."

Ella wished Wolf was here to hear Anwyn echo her own sentiment, word for word. She wondered if she could get the club owner to repeat it to him. Probably not. Doms tended to cover each other's asses so subs couldn't get the upper hand on them. Darn it.

"Our play isn't always safe, though we do our best to make sure it is," Anwyn continued. "When it isn't, there are safety nets to prevent too much harm from being done. I believe you took those precautions, and I thank you for being diligent. I agree with your suggestions to improve the next similar event. So, what's next on our social schedule?"

Ella let out a breath, unclasping her hands that were clutching her knees. "Thank you, ma'am. Burlesque night. I think that's going to be a lot of fun..."

She proceeded to go over the details with Anwyn, growing more enthusiastic as she left behind the nerves that had driven the first part of the discussion. Gideon was called away to check on something with Stan, leaving the two women alone to their planning.

Several times during the conversation, Ella sensed Anwyn's gaze on her, as if the woman had something else on her mind. But one didn't question a Mistress. If she had something to say, it wouldn't need to be coaxed out of her. So when the meeting was concluded and Ella was headed toward the door, she wasn't surprised that Anwyn arrested her at the threshold with a question.

"How do you feel about Wolf, Ella?"

Ella turned. The Mistress of Atlantis had her arms crossed on the desk as she leaned forward on her elbows. "Ma'am?"

"Your honest answer, as always, Ella."

Ella tightened her grip on the notebook of event notes she had hugged to her chest. "Way too much, as usual. It's okay. It will pass." She attempted a smile. "You know I get too caught up in the Doms who have the really protective vibe. I'm learning to manage it so I don't embarrass myself. And there are Masters with that vibe who already do sessions with me. I've got an outlet for it."

"But they don't capture your attention the way he does."

"Well enough. None of the ones who are a good fit for me have offered an exclusive relationship."

Sometimes it puzzled her. She did everything needed in the scene. Everyone went home happy. But she never went home with anyone.

The couple offers she'd had just hadn't felt...right. The Doms in question were totally okay when she politely declined, suggesting the proposition had been a nice-to-have rather than a must-have for them, too.

"I think you haven't found the right one for yourself, and they sense that." At Ella's baffled expression, Anwyn's lips curved. "You've never watched any of the videotaped sessions you've done, have you?"

"No, ma'am." She knew other subs did, but she wasn't one of them. She was in the moment in those scenes. Seeing them secondhand wouldn't seem right, somehow.

"You are a delightful play partner, and an even better third-party assistant to scenes. You project the professionalism of a staff member, and the enthusiasm of a genuine submissive, performing a hundred percent for the pleasure of the guest. You obviously enjoy yourself. But you don't get lost in it. You are always in control."

If Anwyn had told her she was a Domme in sub's clothing, she couldn't have startled Ella more. "What?"

Anwyn folded her hands. She wore a bracelet with a centerpiece of glittering topaz surrounded by a quartet of teal stones. Both hues picked up her intent eye color. "It isn't a criticism, Ella. I'm not implying you try to top from the bottom. Not at all. You project a hard-to-miss message: 'I belong to Club Atlantis.' I believe that's because it's the relationship you trust above all others. That no one has been able to match. Because I feel I *am* Club Atlantis, I take that for the gift it truly is."

Anwyn's voice had softened, flooding Ella with warmth in every corner of her heart. Setting aside the notebook, she moved around the desk, sinking to her knees at the Mistress's feet. "Thank you," she said.

Anwyn leaned forward, touching Ella's bowed head, stroking her hair a moment before touching her chin, bidding Ella look up at her.

"I've only seen that message slip twice. On Puppy Night, when Wolf took you out of the tree. And in the Daddy Dom workshop, when he spanked you. I reviewed the tape."

Ella's cheeks heated, though she wasn't sure why she was embarrassed. Not just Anwyn, but plenty other people, had seen her spanked in scenes. She did a lot of public play.

"I...I guess I hadn't really thought about it. The message thing.

But as far as Wolf goes...he's totally out of my league, and not really interested in me like that."

"Hmm. It's always best not to assume too much about what a Dom thinks," Anwyn said. "especially one like Wolf. But he has my respect and regard. As do you, Ella. You are both important to me."

"Then that's all I need in the world," Ella said. And she meant it. Ignoring the treasure one had for what one thought they wanted or needed was a recipe for unhappiness. Once that lesson was learned, happiness could always be found close to home.

"That may be. But I hope that you will eventually receive far more." Anwyn touched her face once more, then sat back. "I believe you have a ten o'clock. Unless you have anything else to tell me, I'll let you get to it."

"Yes, Mistress."

She loved being in Anwyn's presence, but Ella was relieved to slip out of the office. Despite the bolstering effect that her boss's compliment had given her, the overall conversation had started a low-level ache below her breastbone.

As such, she didn't linger, hurrying through the club, avoiding the areas where she might get caught up in staff conversations. She didn't stop until she'd reached the relative sanctuary of her destination.

The two rooms on this short hallway had once been maintenance closets, until their contents had been relocated to the basement, and the closets transformed into two cozy massage rooms for guests who'd enjoy that service.

Brownie, a club staff member, was a certified massage therapist, and Ella had learned everything under her mentorship. She had over three hundred hours of experience to date, enough to earn her the second assigned space. To her delight, she'd been permitted to decorate it according to her desires.

She'd painted the walls a warm ivory, and hung small pictures on the wall in asymmetric arrangements. Ocean scenes, sensual women dancing, a bolt of lightning across a night sky. A closeup of green leaves in the woods, spattered by rain drops. Two small tables held candles, the electronic ones that put out a flickering small light, ambiance rather than illumination. One wall was draped with a transparent sheer that moved in slow ripples, with the help of an artfully placed tabletop fan that made a whispering breeze noise.

She could do Swedish massage, hot rocks, and deep tissue massage. She could also do sensual massage, where it incorporated sexual play.

Her ten o'clock appointment was with a man named Leroy D, who wanted "a mix." Ella frowned. She liked to know in advance what the client specifically was anticipating so she could prepare, but sometimes reception was in a hurry and didn't ask all the questions she would.

Brownie was folding towels when Ella entered her massage space to see if she knew more about the appointment. "I saw it," the short, stocky woman said, before Ella could broach the subject. She wore her usual massage outfit of loose pants and a thin, soft T-shirt. The hands folding the towels were impossibly strong, thanks to her many years as a masseuse. "Don't worry. If you need any help or he asks for anything you're not as familiar doing, give me a yell. My next appointment isn't until eleven. I'm working on my taxes here since my son is practicing with his rock band in our garage. I was afraid the kitchen light fixture was going to vibrate right out of the ceiling and crash down on my paperwork."

Ella grinned. "None of that will matter when he's earning millions of dollars and saying 'Hi Mom' on TV."

"Which is why I'm here and not at home, screaming at him to stop before I decide to have an extremely late term abortion. Oh, and your ten o'clock gets the staff discount, but he said he'd pay the full amount."

"Well, that was nice of him, but for a staff member, I'll do it for free. Everyone here works so hard."

"Hey, don't show me up too badly. I need the money for Freddie Mercury's music lessons," Brownie said.

"Is he someone new?" Ella asked. "I don't know a Leroy on the staff."

Brownie gave her a bouncing eyebrow look. "Wolf. And he requested you specifically, you lucky thing."

"What?" Ella had been smoothing the stack of towels she'd folded to help Brownie, but now she clutched the top one, creating a tent of wrinkles.

"Yeah, I was surprised. He's never used the massage service at the club before. Thank God he wasn't requesting a deep tissue massage, because he's made out of iron. We'd have to tag team him to get through that." Brownie grinned. "Not that the effort wouldn't be worth it. There's my accountant calling now." She returned to her small desk and laptop, littered with paper, and sent Ella a relaxed wave as she picked up the phone. "Hey, Tom. I appreciate you calling me afterhours like this..."

Ella moved back across the hall in a fog. First Anwyn's unsettling question, now this. She glanced down at herself. She wore a thin V-necked T-shirt much like Brownie, and a pair of snug, stretchy shorts that were high on the thigh. Her flip-flops could be kicked off. Massage work was physically demanding, and the room was kept warm since the subject was undressed, though under a warm bath sheet.

If he wanted her to wear something different, she expected he'd tell her. Forcing herself to be calm and not think too much, she checked to make sure the sheets and hot rocks were properly warm. By the time she did her supply check, she'd settled her nerves, but they jumped to attention when she heard his long, ground-eating stride in the hallway. He was such a big man, her walls vibrated as he came up the narrow hallway.

She turned toward the door, a light smile pasted on her face. He wore a gold-colored T-shirt and blue jeans. Though the shirt was untucked, she had no doubt he was wearing a belt. He'd pretty much branded that fashion accessory in her brain for the rest of her life. His shaved head gleamed in the soft light, adding shadows to the chiseled features and sparks to the silver gaze.

It slid over her, head to toe. "I need to know your boundaries," he said, before she could say anything. "Are you a sub in here?"

With you, I'm always a sub. She didn't say it, but she suspected it was obvious on her face, from the flicker in his eyes, the flex in his jaw. But she found her words.

"Yes, if that's what you want. If you don't, I'm just a massage therapist, helping you with problem areas. You can treat me the same way you'd treat a normal masseuse. Or you can treat me as both at once. It's up to you."

"Both sounds good." He stepped over the threshold. In the cozy little space, he seemed even bigger. She normally maintained a respectful distance from him, which gave her room to gauge what he was wanting. In these close quarters, she had to tip her face up to look at him. Much as she'd done when he'd moved between her knees in the candle wax room.

She didn't often look up into a Dom's face until given permission, but in this situation, she felt like he wanted her to do it. He wanted her to feel that difference in size and strength, how much bigger he was than her.

She wet her lips. "Is what I'm wearing acceptable, sir?"

"For the moment. I'd like you to lose the shorts, though. Wear just the shirt and panties. No bra." He glanced at himself. "How about me? What do you need me to wear to do this right?"

Despite a BDSM club being less modest than other venues, she usually gave clients a little speech that Brownie had recommended, to put them at ease about their weight or any other perceived physical flaws. It went something like "There's no need for any embarrassment or self-consciousness. During a massage, I don't see the body; I see muscles."

There was no way she could say that to Wolf with a straight face, so she redacted that line in her head before it made it anywhere close to her lips.

"You've never had a massage?"

"No."

That knowledge helped her click back into her role, pull together some of the focus that his presence had scattered so effectively. "Well, it's up to you. Most guests prefer to be completely unclothed so there's no impediment to the massage, but if you prefer to leave on underwear, I can work with that, no problem. I put a heated sheet over you as a cover, and I only fold it back from the area I'm working on."

"I tend to run hot. Is having the cover a requirement?"

"Not really. You'll be lying on a heated pad, which helps with the muscle relaxation, but I can take the heated blanket off the top entirely after a couple minutes, if you prefer that."

"Okay, then." He pulled off his T-shirt, the stretch of his muscled upper torso capturing her gaze and not letting it go. The arch of his body was exaggerated because, in the small space, he had to straighten his arms more than normally would be necessary, to keep from rapping her with his elbows. Her palms itched to press against the ripple of chest and abdomen muscles, the sides of his waist. All well within reach.

Just as she'd known, he was wearing a belt. When he started to unbuckle the plain silver buckle, she turned to busy herself elsewhere.

"Look at me, Ella. You have my permission."

Treat it like a session, she thought. A session that any Dom could request from her, that she could approve or not. Though the wisdom of not engaging with him was starting to become painfully clear, she knew she wouldn't refuse him. No matter the plea echoing in her mind, her heart.

Don't let me get pulled so deeply into him. Don't let me get trapped in that same lonely sea of finding everything I want there, but nothing that wants me back.

She'd turned back around to face him, but she'd closed her eyes, her hands fisted in the table sheet. His grip closed over one of them. "Ella."

She raised her lids, stared at the expanse of his chest. It was bare, the bronze muscles limned with a gleam of dim light. He stood behind the table, but she glimpsed bare hip bone and knew he'd fully undressed. It surprised her, since she thought it should have taken more time, at least to take off his shoes and socks before he removed the jeans.

Maybe the jeans were merely pushed down to his knees, and he was attending to her state of mind before finishing, though she couldn't imagine Wolf in such wardrobe limbo. "Yes," she said. "Sorry. If you want to lie down on the table on your back, we can get started. If you're ready."

Instead, he caressed her fingers with his, traced her palm. He came around the end of the table, still holding onto her. She wasn't shy about nudity, but her gaze stayed fastened on a straight line to his chest, which came much closer as he tugged her to him. When her bare feet encountered his, she confirmed he was naked. He drew her full against him, guided her arms around his torso. He closed his arms around her, tucked her head against his chest. "Breathe, little girl," he murmured.

His body, chest to upper thigh, was against her. Even through the clothing she'd not yet shed according to his orders, she could feel the heat of him. That scent that was uniquely Wolf—rainwater, male flesh, spice—was enhanced.

His cock was pressed against her abdomen, his thighs against hers. If she stood on her toes, she could nestle her sex against the heavy weight of his testicles, feel their pressure against her clit. She let herself be held and held him back. He'd put her hands low on his back, just above his waist. While he stroked her nape and the valley of her spine with strong hands, he played under the thick weight of her hair. She had it clipped up high on her neck.

She needed to ask him what he thought of her, why he was seeking her out like this. But maybe she didn't really want those answers, not right now. Instead, once she'd steadied, she lifted her head to give him the effort of an easy smile. "You are so tall."

"No. You're just so petite. I could carry you in one hand." He returned the smile with a faint one of his own. It made her toes curl against the inside of his feet framing hers.

"Leroy D," she said. "Is the *D* your last name initial?"

"Middle name."

"What does it stand for?"

"Something God Himself will not pry out of me."

She smiled again, and he glanced toward the massage table. "There, you said?"

She nodded and he let her go, shifting a hip onto the table and stretching out. The cot shuddered under his weight. Moving to the end, she adjusted the extension for a seven-foot length so his heels could rest on the cushioned surface.

"Thank you, Ella. Let's start with the therapeutic massage. I'll decide how I want to enjoy you as that unfolds."

Focusing on the requirements of the therapeutic massage while anticipating what the second part of his desires might be wasn't going to be easy. She expected he didn't intend it to be.

"Yes, sir. I'll cover you for a few minutes with the heated blanket, then remove it and we'll get started. I recommend clients simply relax in silence during those few minutes. Get into the right headspace to turn themselves over to my hands and care."

His gaze coursed over her in the T-shirt and shorts. "I can do that. Soon as you move back up here and do what I told you to do."

She moved to the side of the table, well within his view and reach.

The shorts were easiest to remove first, so she did that, shimmying out of them. As she did, the snug fabric pulled on her panties, taking them halfway off her hips. His gaze tracked the exposed flesh and he reached out.

She stilled as he slid his fingertips over the upper curve of her buttock, around to the hip bone in front. The expansive caress rippled nerve endings all the way to her labia. Then he drew his hand back and gestured to her to proceed.

She eased the panties back into place after she'd dropped the shorts, stepped out of them and put them aside. Reaching under the back of her shirt, she unclipped the bra and pulled the straps off through the short shirt sleeves before easing the whole garment off by pulling it free of one sleeve. All required clothes now set aside, she waited, so he could gaze at her, top to toe.

The more time she spent with a Dom, the more time she spent cataloging his reactions, so she could learn his unique nonverbal language. The set of Wolf's face, the flicker in his gaze, the rigidity of his limbs, told her he approved. Deeply and dangerously.

Closing his eyes, he shifted so his hands were folded on his upper abdomen, his face turned square to the ceiling again.

She pulled out the heated sheet and laid it over him, from his shoulders to tucked over his feet. As she'd explained, she could do a normal massage, where she kept a person mainly under the cover, only revealing the area she was handling. When it was a sensual massage, the person usually liked to be slowly revealed, particularly a woman. Ella would gradually tug a sheet below the breasts or above a leg, across a groin, at a key moment.

Wolf wanted the blanket removed once she deemed his muscles were sufficiently warmed, so she'd be dealing with him completely nude. If he did want things to turn in a sexual direction, he might want her proportionately smaller hand wrapped firmly around his thick length. She imagined his growl if she teased him with featherlike touches along that impressive shaft. The idea made her smile and her inner muscles tighten.

It wasn't the first time she'd done a massage while aroused. But her hands and stomach were a little shakier than usual. That feeling only increased as she obeyed his wishes and folded the blanket back in segments until she reached his feet and removed it completely.

Seeing him stretched out before her in such a display of virile male beauty required a moment's pause to savor. So as she returned to his head, adding the oil to her hands she would use, she let her gaze rest upon him. He'd said she could look, after all.

She noticed his cock first, because well, it was in the center of things. It lay at rest against his thigh, but even in that state, it was an impressive length and girth, just as his arousal under his jeans had suggested plenty of times while doing a session. He was smooth down there, no hint of any razor stubble. She wondered if he lasered, because he didn't seem the type.

He was utterly beautiful, but in a rough-cut way, as if every muscle in his arms, chest, shoulders, back and legs had come from hard use. With barely a change in his expression, he could go from impassive unreadability to looking like he was ready to break whatever crossed him into bits.

She thought about him a lot, but in relation to how he made her feel. Now she put that aside, because he was here for a massage. It was time to think about the man, separate from his significant impact on her. Normally she took these meditative few minutes to really look at the person on her table, and feel what they might need. Who they were, before she laid hands on the person and learned even more about who he or she was, beneath the skin.

"This is a very peaceful space," he said, his eyes still closed. "I like the fan on the curtains. Reminds me of being in the mountains, taking a nap with the windows open."

"What mountains?"

"I've been in a lot of them. I remember terrain more than I do location. Sometimes it's nice, not to have to worry about where you are in the world. No address. No need to put it in context of anything else. Kind of like the earliest explorers. It was just one big park or garden."

"I like that," she said, smiling a little.

His eyes opened, held hers. He lifted a hand, brushed his knuckles over her breast, just beneath the bump of her nipple, prominent in the thin T-shirt. "Anyone else been touching these?"

She shook her head. "No sir." Her breath caught as he kept stroking, watching the nipple respond to his touch, harden and lengthen. As he touched her, his cock did the same, but eventually he took his hand away.

"Good. You can get started."

She'd contemplated too long, rubbing the oil too deeply into her skin. Grimacing at herself, she refreshed it, and then she was ready.

She began with his hands and arms. People were used to touch in those areas, so it helped them relax faster. Starting at the armpit and biceps and moving down the limb, she worked the oil in, massaging the muscles, noting any tension spots. When she reached his thick wrists and then his hands, she interlaced fingers with him and rotated hers, taking his along for the spin.

It was an intimate, slightly playful part of the process. When she glanced up, she found him watching her through half-closed eyes, his lips curved. "What does that do?"

"It loosens the muscles between the fingers."

"Hmm." He didn't say anything else for awhile. She did her best to do as she was supposed to do, see each part of the body as a group of muscles, not a part of Wolf she was getting to intimately touch.

She wasn't successful in that, but as she continued to work on him, and he stayed quiet, time slowed. When she returned to the head of the table and eased her hand beneath his shoulders to work his scapula, she found tension. It was a common area for it. She pushed her fingers into the hard masses of muscle, working out the kinks to give him ease. She knew he was a big man, broad shouldered, but having them under her hands told her she'd underestimated their size and strength. Brownie had been right. It was like massaging iron.

She felt the burn in her arms and back. Sometimes she and Brownie gave one another a quick massage at the end of a grueling session to ensure they didn't kink up themselves. This appointment might call for that.

She moved back down his side, began to work on his left leg. She often closed her eyes when she massaged, to increase the reception in her fingertips. As she worked up to the thigh, she felt something curious, explored around it. "You have scar tissue here, beneath the skin."

She opened her eyes as he folded an arm beneath his head and looked down toward her, an unconscious yet very distracting Michael Stokes calendar pose. "Yeah," he said. "It goes across to here." He used his finger to draw a line over hers on his upper thigh.

He moved it across his body, directly over his groin area, and curved up to his rib cage on the opposite side. If the scar tissue along the track was as deep as what she felt on his upper thigh, she couldn't imagine how he'd survived with his reproductive organs intact—or survived at all.

When her hand tightened in reaction on his leg, Wolf, returned his hand to hers to caress her suddenly tense knuckles.

"No worries, little girl. It happened years ago. It doesn't hurt anymore."

There was the slightest of pauses before he said the last part, as if he meant only one kind of pain, the least important kind.

"You can talk about it if you want," she ventured. "I'm not asking because I'm curious, though I am. This is a good place to speak words to the silence, if that makes sense. I won't say anything. I'll just keep doing what I'm doing."

He grunted in acknowledgement, but said nothing more. She continued her work. As she rubbed from the taut buttock to the heel, she felt a new level of tension. So when she worked on his foot and he twitched, she feathered her fingers over the long sole and earned another jerk.

"Ticklish?" She shot him an impish look. The shadows disappeared from his gaze, that stiffness under her fingers easing some.

He snorted. "I will spank you, little girl. And it won't be pleasant."

If he used the heated flat of his hand, she didn't care how much it hurt, she'd enjoy every moment of it. But she tucked in a smile and returned to her massage.

She moved to the front of the leg and worked back to the top, going laterally from the groin area to the outside of the hip, learning and exploring every muscle group. Then she switched legs to do the same process over again.

When at last she was done with everything she did while her client was on his back, she was pleased to see he was sunk more deeply into the cushioning of the massage table, evidence that the muscles had released.

"Now you need to turn over on your stomach."

He complied with a reluctant grumble that made her smile. It satisfied her deeply, that she was giving him ease. What stresses did he face? Who was he, outside of Club Atlantis? Some staff members, like

Madelyn and Lars, became comfortable enough to reveal some pieces about who they were outside the club walls. Wolf never spoke of it.

She returned to the head of the table and began to work on his neck, shoulders, upper back. As she did, Wolf curved his hands around her upper thighs, holding her. His palms sent heat tingling over her backside, her lower back. His thumbs swept the curve of her buttocks and tucked themselves into the crease between cheek and thigh.

"They say if a woman can carry a pencil in that area, she needs to work on her glutes," Ella managed.

"If I had my way, they'd all be able to carry a jumbo magic marker," he rumbled. "Nothing so nice as a round, soft ass. It's the way nature intended women to be."

"Oh, that so? You have a direct line to management about that?"

He cupped her buttocks fully, squeezed. It pulled her against the edge of the table, and she shuddered as the cushion of her clit pressed against the padded edge, a friction that increased because of her massage movements. He rubbed her ass in idle circles, building the arousal in her lower regions.

"You have to ask?" he said. "Doms are the closest things to God you can experience on earth. It's why our subs are always calling us that. At certain key moments."

Ella chuckled, though her brow furrowed as she detected more scar tissue between his shoulder blades. "That's where my wings were," he said, his voice muffled as he kept his head in the depression that allowed a client to lie face down comfortably.

"A fallen angel. That I can believe."

She earned a pinch for that remark, but not a hard one. Then he withdrew his touch to allow her to move to his side. She leaned down to place her elbow against his back. Since the position put her very close to him, she had to resist the desire to put her mouth on the muscle group she was manipulating.

He showed no such restraint. Now as she worked around him, he took every opportunity to caress her hips, her thighs, her buttocks. His hands were moving over her the way hers moved over him, a flow. They became one creature; he touched and she moved with him, fluid and perfect and nothing needing to be said.

When she completed the last muscle group, she'd sweated through her T-shirt in the warm space. It was sticking to her skin. Since he'd said no bra, it was as effective as a wet T-shirt contest.

He'd turned his head and was looking his fill. Her nipples were stiff and large. When he adjusted his hips, she suspected he was getting aroused again.

She was more than willing to massage that part of him if he so desired it. Her thigh muscles were tight thanks to the throbbing between her legs.

He was well aware of all that. It was in the lazy way his eyes rested upon her, sure of his hold on her senses. Yet he said nothing, expecting her to complete the massage as promised. Denial only increased the ache.

She was tempted to pitch the stones at his head, so was proud that her voice came out a soothing murmur. "Next I'll do hot rocks," she said. "They won't burn you, don't worry. I'll move them off you quickly."

She went to the container that held them, picked up one in tongs and came back, dropping it where it needed to go. She rolled it quickly over his skin with the flat of her palms before removing it and doing it several more times with different rocks. He stayed relaxed under her touch, just as he should when she was doing it right.

Even with her muscles worn out from the strenuous exercise, she would have done it all over again for the chance to keep her hands on him. Instead, she made herself step back and pick up a towel, wiping her hands.

"I'm finished, but I recommend you lie there a few more minutes. Just come back to earth at your own pace, so to speak."

He shifted, turning to his back again. With effort, she kept her attention on his face, which became easier when he extended a hand to her. She put hers in his grasp, watched it disappear as his long fingers closed over it. "You took good care of me, Ella. Thank you."

His steady gaze made her flush, which seemed silly, given how much time she spent indulging in sexually explicit behavior. But his look flustered her, so intent, penetrating. He noticed her in a way no one else did.

Talk about an alarm flag. *Don't do the "no one else makes me feel this way" thing. There's nothing down that road.* Except the illusion there was something there that wasn't. She knew she had exceptional intuition about a lot of things, but whether a person was meant for her specifically or not wasn't one of them. Maybe the Powers That Be did it deliberately, ensuring even an intuitive soul couldn't locate their deepest wish so easily.

Still, she had no desire for him to release her hand. So she set the unsettling thoughts aside. She could absorb a safe amount of what she was feeling from him. She could give herself just enough of the fantasy to feed her soul, without getting lost in it.

Hadn't she said she preferred not to be honest with herself around Wolf?

Her gaze slid to the center of the table. During the massage, when he'd been on his back, he'd been semi-aroused at times, his cock like a restive animal, twitching against his thigh. Now he was fully erect. Her heart thumped into her throat and the tissues between her legs contracted, like they had when he'd been fondling her ass. She could feel the moisture collected along her labia as she shifted.

"Do you want that?" Wolf said in an even tone.

"Yes, sir."

"Go lock the door and put your back to it. Hands behind you."

She let her hand slip from his loosened grip. It seemed a long three steps to the door, but she made it on trembling legs. She flipped the lock. When she turned, he'd sat up and put his feet on the floor. He rose, a tall, erect, dark-skinned god with piercing eyes, targeting her.

He sidestepped to the electric candles, met her gaze and switched them off, a full blackout except for the strip of light under the door, coming from the hallway.

In the darkness, there was nothing but him and her. Without being able to see his face, there was nothing for her to measure or judge, calculate. She wondered what the darkness brought him, why he preferred it. Then she decided she didn't want to probe too deeply, in case she came up with ideas about that which would hurt her, take away from this moment.

If he could see in the dark, a fanciful notion, was it like blindfolding her, where he could see her every reaction, and she could see none of his? She wanted to see that look in his eyes he had when he looked at her. But he had other ideas.

As she waited, she realized she couldn't hear him. She could feel his presence, filling the small space, but she heard nothing. No shifts of his body, no breathing.

But the heat increased, the warmth, the sense of being surrounded. She trembled, knowing a moment before it happened that he was close enough to touch her. His fingers slid along her arm, so slow and easy. Up across her breasts, knuckles brushing her nipples, grazing the tips, back and forth, back and forth. She shuddered, bit back a whimper of need, her hips jerking a little as more moisture touched her inner thigh.

"A few minutes ago, when I was holding your hand, you went away from me, Ella." His voice was a molasses-rich murmur. "Where did you go? Did you protect yourself from me?"

"No sir. From myself. From wanting more than I'm allowed to have."

"Do you think I'm kind, Ella?"

"You...um. Yes. You're kind to me."

"I need to show you a different side of myself, then."

She gasped as he lifted her in one swift movement. Pushing her back against the door, he dropped to one knee and draped her legs over his shoulders. He held her suspended, one palm flat on her chest, fingers spread over her cleavage, the other arm around her hips. His mouth settled on her pussy, tongue stabbing through silky cloth.

"I've wanted my mouth on your cunt from the moment I saw these panties," he muttered.

He was the strongest man who'd ever handled her. She couldn't move, not even to wriggle in sensual abandon. He kept her still with the strength of his hands alone, and one uttered command.

"Be quiet, little one. Silent as a mouse."

She felt the scrape of one of those canines that had bitten through her skin only a few days before. She heard a soft, prolonged *scrich* noise, and realized he'd used that tooth to split the crotch of the panties. Not torn with the rough tug of motion she'd expect, but a slit of almost surgical precision. The man knew how to use those sharper teeth in diabolical ways. When his tongue stabbed through the rip he'd made, the firm, heated curl of it penetrating her convulsing tissues, she couldn't stop herself.

The climax rolled through her, and she nearly bit through her tongue, trying not to wail or whimper. She lost that battle, though the sounds she made were strangled cries, showing she was trying to honor his command, even if it was beyond human capacity to do with his clever mouth moving over her flesh.

With that one command, he'd made her want to do the impossible, no matter what minor price it cost her. Like sanity.

He kept eating her, even as her body shuddered into aftershocks. Her climax was a side effect of his main goal, to taste her pussy to his fill. She bit back more whimpers, kept herself as still as possible, though with every curl of his tongue, suction of his lips and scrape of his teeth, it was clear he wanted her fighting a hard, sweaty battle not to wiggle, squirm, scream.

When he finally drew back, it wasn't to give her a break. It was only to guide her weak legs to the floor before he banded his arm around her waist and lifted her. Her arms fell around his shoulders as he took one stride back to the table and lay on it again, swinging his legs up. His stomach muscles contracted against her core as he took her with him, making her straddle him and sit up. Her backside was on his stiff cock, the length of it nestled in the crease between her buttocks, against the fabric of the panties she still wore.

One hand was on her hip, the other on her shoulder and throat. Those fingers on her throat flexed as he spoke, a rough command. "Hands behind your back, Ella. I don't need your help to use your body the way I want to."

He shifted then, began playing with her breasts, squeezing the nipples, twisting them, reinforcing the message he'd first left on each one. They belonged to him, and no one else. When her body bucked, his response was swift, ruthless.

"Hold still." The warning in his tone ensured he only had to tell her once.

Once again, he took his time with it. He was as thorough as she'd been with her massage. Her body built back up toward orgasm, little pleas caught in her throat that made him chuckle with a demon's pleasure.

"I want you hurting for it, baby girl. Hurting bad."

She was there and then some. Her whole body was convulsing and twitching, involuntary movements. Everything was focused on his hands, pinching, twisting, brushing, flicking, teasing. At one point, he lifted her under the arms like a doll, bringing her forward so he could put his mouth over one nipple, suckle her through the T-shirt. She cried out, a long, plaintive sound that she couldn't contain. He bit her, a sharp reproof, and she choked it back. When he moved to the other nipple, the feeling just intensified, making it even more difficult to stay quiet.

He put her down at last, standing her on her knees so he could reach between her legs. He ripped that slit in the panties wider with his fingers, so there was no barrier to his entry. Three fingers pushed inside her wetness, curled forward. He had her throat in his other hand, guiding her up and down on his hand. Slow, as he moved those fingers, rubbed them along that thick spot in her channel wall. His cock brushed the inside of her thigh, the wetness a promise held just out of reach.

He was right. He was showing her just how pitiless he could be. She needed release, but she also wanted more. She wanted to give him everything he demanded, as long as he demanded it, no matter how much it took from her. She didn't mind being a husk when it was all over, as long as she'd nourished him with everything inside she had to offer.

His fingers slipped free, and he put the head of his cock there instead. A shuddering sob of relief broke from her lips. He paused, and she could feel blood pulsing in the swollen tissues of her labia, as if her cunt was trying to grip him, pull him in.

"I'm clean, and I can't get you pregnant," he said. "I want you without anything between us."

She wondered if that harrowing beneath-the-skin scar was why he couldn't get her pregnant, but now was not the time for such questions. "How do you know I'm clean?" she said in a hoarse voice.

"Because you take care of others, Ella. You always put them first."

The sudden tender note, contrasted with the physical evidence of hard male lust, brought that ache to her throat again. It couldn't distract her, though, not from the urgent throb between her legs as he teased her with the tip of that substantial organ. He lay back, his hands on her hips, holding her in place for long, excruciating seconds.

She tried to stay still because she knew that was what he demanded. But oh, it was so difficult, her breath coming quick, that never-ending moan humming in her throat.

His implacable tone took over once more. "Take care of me, Ella. I want my cock inside you, all the way to the balls. Do it slow. I don't want you hurting yourself, and I'll enjoy seeing and feeling you work for it. Once you're all the way in, you can put your hands on me to brace yourself."

She trembled every second she worked herself over him, hips adjusting forward and back, bathing him with the honey from her wet cunt. Every stroke sent sensation rocketing through her. Her fingers twisted and curled in a knot behind her back. She took him in, inch by inch, slick and deep, breath leaving her in a gasp as he stretched her. The ridges of his cock, his girth and size, all of it sent sensation spiraling up tight through her core.

"That's my girl. So good for her Master."

Submitting fully because the male holding her was caring for her, watching over her, building her a castle made of his rules and words, his stern looks and desired approval. That was when she felt most like herself, the submissive she truly was.

Who was he? Why did he make her feel this way? Damn it, he *was* different, so much so she was afraid everything she'd felt before now had been wishful thinking in comparison.

Which should scare her to death, because knowing that down to her soul didn't change anything in terms of their future. To Wolf, it likely didn't feel anything like that. He was just another extraordinary Dom in a club full of them. Pleasure was a fluid thing they all enjoyed. Voyeurism, exhibitionism, an atmosphere saturated with sexual promise and acceptance? Of course it led to situations like this.

But she wasn't going to let this go due to fears of a day-after drop. A moment of utter care and pleasure could fuel her for weeks.

He had lifted his upper body and now had his mouth on her throat. When she felt the scrape of his very sharp teeth, she expelled a breath, clutched him, inside and out. "Wolf..."

He bit. His teeth were in her flesh again, deep enough to hold her. Her body responded to the dual penetration with a violent surge of arousal. There seemed something even more powerful about his bite this time, a tingling that went straight to her heart, made it beat even faster.

She clutched his shoulders, pressed against his mouth, telling him with her whole body he could have what he wanted and needed. He took over the thrusting, working inside her as she rose and fell, her body moving with his. The table was bolted down, and she was glad of it. Her body was rippling, shuddering, rising toward that peak, and he was taking her with him, his strokes getting more powerful, on the edge of discomfort. But she wouldn't ask him to ease up. She wanted to be battered by desire, his need. Wanted to make herself believe it was for her, and not just the drive of lust.

"Sir...I'm close..."

"Hold on," he said against her throat, her pounding pulse. "Not until I say. You know that, don't you?"

She nodded against his shoulder. It was wet with her tears. Not bad tears. Just tears.

"Good." His hand was in her hair now, winding it around his knuckles. She was ready when he pulled her head back, a forceful, controlled move that curved her spine back the same way. It changed the angle and depth, her knees clamped close to his hips, her body completely open for and taken by him.

"Now," he said, and began to release inside her. The jet of his seed took her over, her tissues rippling over him. He'd told her to be quiet, but while her mind and soul were willing, she couldn't stop the scream that tore from her.

He tightened his hold, drove deeper, and she was lost, in all the right ways. Everything was a response, nothing was a thought, and she was flying...flying...just gone.

When she finally shuddered to a slower rhythm, it seemed the room was still echoing with the sounds of her release. He kept her moving on him, and she felt the heat of his attention on her face, her throat and breasts, dipping down to perhaps look at where they were joined, his dark hand still clasping her hip. She was beginning to believe he could see in the dark in ways no one she knew could.

He let her tip her head forward, but he didn't let go of her hair, holding her straight. Now it felt like he was looking at her to assess every part, from her open lips and glazed eyes, to her quivering breasts.

He lifted the hand from her hip and toyed with a nipple, still swollen and sore, hypersensitive. He was gentle, though, his fingertips light.

"All mine," he said.

He eased her off of him and sat up, dropping his feet to the floor and turning her so she was cradled between his thighs, his damp cock against her hip, her legs draped over his knee. It didn't seem like his strength had flagged at all. The arm around her back, keeping her leaning against his shoulder, still held her just as tightly.

He leaned over, still holding her. If he couldn't see in the dark, he had an exceptional recall for details, because he didn't hesitate, picking up something and settling back in one smooth motion.

He pressed what he'd retrieved against her. As she curled her fingers into the soft, plush fur of the wolf she'd kept from their workshop, a smile crossed her face. Reassuring warmth filled the pit of her belly, where emptiness had been about to take over, anticipating the end of this time together in the dark.

She put her head down on his shoulder, with a little sigh when his arms wound securely around her. A cue, letting her know she could treat him like a Daddy Dom for the moment.

But a Daddy Dom had one prime directive. To care for his little girl. Unfortunately, his interpretation of that took him in a direction she would have preferred he wouldn't go.

"It's time for you to tell me," he said quietly. "Why were you crying on the loading dock, that night I came to find you?"

She played with the wolf's silky fur, felt her breath rebound to her against Wolf's strong throat. "Why is it so important to you to know?"

"Talking back?"

She shook her head. "I'm afraid you'll hear why, and you'll agree with the person who made me go there that night. I'm tired of being judged. I know people who judge have no power that you don't give them, but resisting that can drain the energy from you, you know?"

"Do you trust me, Ella?"

"Right now?" she chuckled weakly, no humor to it. "In this moment, in this state of mind, I'd trust you with everything I am, but I'm not stupid."

"No, you're not. You're incredibly honest." He tightened his arms around her. "So I will give you the same. I don't know how I'm going to react to the story, but I find you a remarkable, fascinating person. Trust me with your story, in the darkness."

She pressed her face to the wolf, while her body did the same, pressing against the bigger, more animate Wolf. "Did you ask Anwyn to put a wolf in among the swag to direct the scene?"

"No. She provided the other toys, and I brought that one. I wanted to see if you'd want to choose it. I don't believe in contriving situations, Ella. The demo works best if it's natural, and honest. Just like our conversation here."

He had such a deep voice. In the dark, it was like thunder inside a mountain. She thought about lying against the mountain's side, feeling the vibrations of the earth beneath the surface. It was stable. Safe.

The dark would make it easier.

She sighed. "All right. I'll tell you."

CHAPTER SEVEN

A few weeks ago...

After putting on a hoodie over her bustier and leggings under her fairy skirt, Ella left the locker room, mulling over what to do next. She had no more sessions, and she was off shift now. She was tired, but not really ready to go home.

She thought about reading the current book she had stashed in her locker, and at the same time considered how glad she'd be when James was back from New Orleans. He liked books too; he usually wanted to know what she was reading and why.

Even though she'd reconciled herself to the idea that he wasn't for her, he was always warm and kind. Her innocent flirting could get him to smile, sometimes even flush a little, which charmed her, because he was so temptingly in charge most of the time.

Sometimes she'd curl up under the security desk near his feet, read one of her books. He might ask her about it, but often he'd simply let her be there near him, his calmness relaxing her nerves. He was quiet. She liked quiet.

It brought back a memory. Being in the garage, wood shavings falling from a workbench, her curled beneath it, reading a book. Her father had been teasing her about sitting on the dog bed intended for their eighty-pound German shepherd mix. Robie was in the house, his black and tan body sprawled on the couch with her brother, his hopeful nose likely inches from his open bag of Cheetos.

Her attraction to James really had been that simple, hadn't it?

Chantal had hinted at it, but with her recollection of the childhood memory, Ella accepted the full truth of it. Her feelings for James weren't even a Daddy Dom/little girl crush thing. He reminded her of what it had felt like to have an actual father.

That revelation came with a nice silver lining. James cared a lot about her, and would continue to encourage her to think of him that way. She didn't get a Dom, but she did get a fatherly friend. What he'd always been.

Somewhat bolstered, she reached the door of the admin security office and found Stan, watching the monitors. "How are things going? Do you need me to grab you a coffee from the break room?"

Stan offered a smile, though he kept his eyes trained on his task. "Naw, I'm good. I think we'll all be glad when James gets back, though it sounds like he's having a really good time in New Orleans."

Maybe it was the sudden shift in her thinking about him, but hearing the two words, *New Orleans*, opened up something inside her, one of those odd feelings she got. For just a flash she saw James and a dark-haired woman. And a sliver of light finding its way through a crack in the empty sadness of James' widowed soul.

Good. That was good. She took a breath. Even if it still pricked her soul a bit. Maybe it showed on her face, because Stan's expression softened as he glanced her way. "I'm sure he misses us here."

"Oh heavens, he's in New Orleans. Why would he?"

The cheerful half-scoff came from Naomi. Ella hadn't seen her approach, but this corridor provided several staff short cuts to the deeper recesses of the club. Naomi laid a friendly hand on Ella's shoulder.

Naomi was another sub with no committed Dom, though she had a few regulars she enjoyed. She had a perky cheerleader personality in sub mode, but was a controlled, self-designated "real world" pragmatist when she wasn't. Sometimes she rubbed Ella the wrong way, because she could be judgmental toward submissives like Ella, who felt that who they were inside Club Atlantis was far closer to the truth than who they were outside it.

Most the time, Ella could let that roll off. Naomi's attitude had more to do with the young woman's conflicting feelings about compartmentalizing this part of her life, rather than Ella's view of it.

So Ella pasted a smile on her face. "Even if he misses us, he more than deserves the break," she said in a light tone. She looked toward Stan. "Let us know if we can help with anything, Stan. You have big shoes to fill."

"Not me," Stan chuckled. "Gideon's the one standing in for James while he's gone. Since James eats, sleeps and breathes this place, you might see if *Gideon* needs anything. Oh, but I do have one thing he gave me..."

Stan reached beneath the desk and produced a clipboard, looking through the top two pages. "I went over your summary for the puppy play thing. We might need to hit on a few details a couple days ahead of time. People in groups sometimes forget how to behave themselves."

"I'll touch base with you about it, no worries."

"What would we do without Ella around to shake things up?" Naomi observed. "James isn't the only one who lives here 24/7, even when he's not here. Not me, though. And in a couple months, not at all."

Her tone changed to one of barely suppressed excitement and she waved a flashing hand at Ella. "I'm getting married."

"Whoa, wow. Oh, Naomi that's wonderful." In a heartbeat, any irritation Ella felt toward her disappeared. She saw the woman's genuine happiness. With a beaming smile, Ella enveloped Naomi in a big hug.

Stan gave them both an indulgent look, obviously already the recipient of Naomi's big news. Since another security staff member was approaching the office to talk to Stan, Ella drew Naomi off into the hallway to gaze at the ring. "This is the man you've been seeing for the past few months, right?"

Naomi nodded. "Frank. He operates a chain of furniture stores, and his passion is jogging. He runs marathons."

"Good stamina then." Ella grinned. "I'm so happy for you. Is he a member at another club, or have you introduced him to your sub side at home?"

Naomi shook her head. "God, no. He's vanilla. And going to stay that way forever."

Ella's brow creased. "He doesn't know about you being a submissive?"

"Doesn't need to," Naomi said, withdrawing her hand. "Our

engagement became official a few weeks ago. I'm letting Anwyn know I'll help out until the end of the month, on the non-session side of things, but then I'll be gone. I work in sales when I'm not doing this, and I'm good at it. I'll be an asset to him, because he runs six furniture stores in this state alone. We're going to do a cruise to Europe for our honeymoon."

Ella remembered the last scene Naomi had done. The Dom had been a suspension artist, tying her up in a web of crimson rope before applying a violet wand on her in ways that had her climaxing several times. He'd pushed Naomi to surrender herself completely into his hands, a level Ella had rarely seen her pushed to give. But when she'd achieved obvious, true bliss, it had been a beautiful thing to witness. Naomi had relinquished all control to him, and he'd sent her soaring on that subspace cloud.

Ella remembered Naomi had seemed unbalanced by the intensity of the experience, not reappearing at the club for a week. But when she did, she acted like her normal self, except she claimed not to remember much about the session when Ella invited her to talk about it. That had been a month ago. Around the time she expected all this had started to come to fruition. "Naomi, I really am happy for you. But are you sure you can be content leaving this side of yourself behind?"

"Of course." Naomi's tone took on a slight edge of irritation. "I love being here, Ella, but this world is a fantasy, you know? It works because it's insular, but it's time for me to leave the carnival and grow up."

"Maybe he would—"

"No. He wouldn't. I pretended I'd stumbled onto a couple BDSM sites while he was around, just to gauge his reaction." A shadow crossed Naomi's gaze. "He scoffed at the people in them, said they were a bunch of freaks. 'Takes all kinds in this world, but maybe not that kind.' Quote, unquote."

Ella blinked. "Maybe he just needs a better understanding of what it's about."

"No. Even if he did understand it better, he wouldn't ever want to be a part of it. Don't look like that. He's a good guy."

Ella spread out her hands, a placating gesture. "No, I'm not trying to—"

Naomi shook her head, cutting across Ella's words. "Just because he has the same opinion about this as ninety percent of everyone else doesn't make him bad. This isn't about him. It's about all of us. Why do you think James doesn't see you the way you want him to? He's a vanilla guy who found a good-paying job helping out at a BDSM club. He views it like doing security at the circus. He's part of the real world going on around it, the world that sees us all as deviants or bored people spicing up our sex lives."

"James doesn't see us that way," Ella said, stung.

"Not consciously." Naomi shrugged. "He's a 'not my thing, but as long as you don't shove it in my face, we're cool' kind of guy. But he shows his preferences in the choices he makes. When James finds someone, it's going to be like my Frank, only in girl form. Frank is a good and loving man. I've had enough time to sow those wild oats. I'm in my thirties. I'm ready to have kids. You're not getting any younger yourself, Ella. You should think about that."

Ella was still in her twenties. Maybe her expression was making her look older. Even though she told herself not to do it, Naomi's defensive goad made it impossible for Ella not to ask the question. "Why would you want someone who doesn't love you for who you are? Someone you can't tell everything about yourself."

"Because nobody loves you for *everything* you are," Naomi said impatiently. "They love certain parts of you, and they accept the others, or learn to work around them, because they love the most important things about you. I didn't make the decision lightly, Ella. I even talked to my therapist about it. She said people grow and change all the time. It happens subconsciously, responding to environmental influences, but they have many different faces during their lives, and most are content with them. This is just that. I've enjoyed being Naomi the sub. Now I'll enjoy being Naomi, Frank's wife who sells furniture, works with him, has kids, and a great life together."

Ella didn't know what to say to that. But Naomi reached out and closed a hand on hers. "This feels really normal to all of us, because we're here, in this closed box. But take it outside and shine a light on it, that light's not really kind. We *are* freaks, Ella."

No, we're not. But Ella found her tongue frozen as Naomi continued, still holding her hand in that co-conspirator kind of way, her expression earnest.

"He's kind. I need kind in my life. A lot of kind. If getting that requires staying inside prescribed boundaries, that's what I'm going to do. I'm going to be happy that way. I know you all might judge me, and not think so, but we're all different. I've had enough time to explore this side of myself, and I can move on with no regrets. Can you be okay with that?"

While Ella's kneejerk reaction was to wonder why Naomi was asking not to be judged when she was throwing judgment on those around her like a suffocating blanket, she stopped herself, thought it through. She didn't understand Naomi's choice, didn't agree with it, but Naomi was right. They were two different people. Everything Naomi was saying might be absolutely true—for Naomi.

Naomi interpreted her silence in the wrong way, because she frowned. "Do you remember when you went to that other club and got into trouble? How Anwyn ordered you not to go anywhere but Club Atlantis from then on?"

Ella stiffened. She wasn't aware that the other subs knew about that, but she guessed it made sense. While the Atlantis staff could be trusted with their members' deepest secrets, among their inner circle, everything was known.

A guest Dom had told Ella his normal club was bringing in a new piece of equipment on their Saturday demo night. It was an Inquisition-style stretcher wheel kind of thing. The sales rep would pay a sub a couple hundred dollars to work the booth, explain the equipment's workings, and demo it. It was the club's busiest night of the month, partially because from nine to midnight the public play sections and demos were open to lightly vetted guests.

At first it went fine. She demo'ed it for two Masters and one Mistress who wanted to see the way it worked, but who didn't have a sub with them. Each live demonstration attracted an audience, so when the demos evolved into mini sessions, increasing interest in the product, the sales rep was pretty happy. Ella enjoyed the three Doms who put her through the equipment's paces, and drummed up some potential business for Atlantis, because they were all three interested in Anwyn's more exclusive club.

Then Ella had a Mistress ask her if she was okay with sensory deprivation on the wheel. They went over some parameters, and since she was here as a visiting sub, just showing off the equipment like a game show hostess, she wasn't expecting a problem.

She'd been gagged, hooked up to the device, hooded. She and the Mistress had worked out a safe word signal. All reasonable precautions. But the Mistress was easily distracted, and became involved with the audience, more into performing for them than focusing on her submissive. She didn't notice when Ella signaled. Not the first time, second time, or when she was doing it frantically.

A sharp-eyed Dungeon Master patrolling the area noted her distress. However, before she was pulled off of the wheel, she'd gotten nauseous, thrown up inside the hood and nearly choked. Plus the Mistress's overenthusiastic turning of the stretcher control had wrenched Ella's shoulder badly, something the adrenaline spike of panic masked until the next day. Ella ended up at an Urgent Care, needing an X-ray and then meds and some PT to remedy the injury.

Ella had been shaken, but all was well that ended well. The sales rep, likely worried about how she would talk about the incident, had paid her four hundred dollars for her time. Most of it went to the treatment she'd needed for the shoulder. But Ella accepted it as an honest mistake on the Mistress's part, one that the truly chagrined woman would use as an important lesson to avoid future incidents.

However, word had gotten back to Anwyn. The Mistress of Atlantis was a strong, self-sufficient woman, and treated the women on her staff, Doms or subs, with a similar respect. But she had another side, a protective streak closely linked to her Mistress identity. Ella was a sub under her protection, and unfortunately it wasn't the first time Ella had gotten in over her head by trusting a Dominant too much.

"You play here exclusively, or you don't play here at all, Ella. You'll give me your word."

"You were ashamed you didn't have the judgment to take care of yourself. I remember that," Naomi said, bringing Ella out of her head and back to their conversation. "Have you ever asked yourself if things like that happen to you because you embrace this side of yourself too much? Eventually you've got to abandon this romantic fantasy that you can surrender all of yourself to someone, and face the reality. You can't trust anyone a hundred percent to watch after you. That's too much to put on them, and there's no one in the world you can trust that much anyway."

Ella shook her head. "I don't ask someone to do that for me. It's not like that, Naomi. You don't understand why—"

"Oh my God, Naomi, Leann told me he gave you a rock. Let me see..."

The unwitting disruption of their conversation had come from Mavis, Club Atlantis's gift store manager. She ran the shop several nights a week and ran her own erotica store in town during the off days. Seeing Ella and Naomi talking, she'd stopped to join in on what she'd perceived to be a social chat.

Ella knew she could take the out, simply nod, smile and walk away. However, though she'd sent Mavis a half-smile, Naomi was still holding Ella's gaze. Ella saw a mix of things there, but expectation was one of them. She was waiting for an answer from Ella. A blessing of sorts.

Wow. "You're right," Ella said, stopping Mavis mid-enthusiastic sentence. "We're responsible for our own decisions and the consequences of them. Someone like me, my okay doesn't count for much, does it? I do wish you happiness, though. I would always wish that."

She walked away from the two women with a forced pleasant expression for Mavis. She paused at the security office, where Stan had finished his conversation with Wendy, the other security guard. "I'm headed out into the alley to be with the cats. I might take a walk after that. Don't worry if I go out of camera range."

She knew he might object to that, but she didn't wait for his response. She escaped out the side door. Being around Anwyn's feral colony was calming, some of the cats friendly enough to approach. There was no judgment here.

For a moment, she stood where she was, taking deep breaths, settling the emotions in her gut. She knew when she was in dangerous territory and sure enough, here it came, the sudden surge of temper, strong enough to make her lightheaded. She shut her eyes, kept breathing. Working back toward who she was. Who she wanted to be.

Anwyn's disappointment and worry for her *had* shamed Ella to the core. It had taken her a while to get over it. Even though she suspected Anwyn letting her plan theme nights might have been due to some regret at coming down so hard on Ella, she had valued every step toward winning Anwyn's respect and trust again.

She didn't want Naomi's words to make her doubt that, but she still felt as if she'd taken a body blow. She needed time to regroup, meditate, before she re-entered the club, and she didn't want to be where she was under anyone's watchful eye.

So she headed to the place near Atlantis she went when she needed to be alone.

~

Ella lifted a shoulder, coming back to the present. "That's all of it. That was why I was on the loading dock."

Wolf stayed silent, holding her, stroking her hair. So she kept talking, even though she told herself to stop.

"My first real experience as a sub was being a rope bunny. I was nineteen. The top wanted to believe I was twenty-one, like him, and I let him. He needed a date for a play party, and I was game. I'd never seen anything like it and yet, while we were there, and he was tying me up, I felt centered and at peace, in a way I'd never felt before. It didn't take me long after to realize this was a world that could keep me balanced, no matter what else was happening in my life or what I had to face."

She shook her head. "Hearing Naomi say what she said, it wasn't different from what others say about it; it's just normally people on the outside who say things like that. Not someone inside, who knows how it's different. It threw me off. And I guess I was still more raw from the set down by Anwyn than I should have been. That had happened months before, after all. But what she thinks of me matters so much. Probably too much."

She wasn't asking for confirmation from him. It was a legitimate question she asked herself. "Naomi had no clue that I've been taking care of myself most of my life. I do hair and nails, and waitress. I work as a courier. I'm good at those things, but I don't have an interest in making a career of anything. I do jobs that give me the freedom and flexibility to live the life I want to live. Club Atlantis and being a submissive are at the center of it."

He spoke against her ear, a low vibration. "'*I'm fully capable of caring for myself. I've been doing it my whole life.*' I remember how you said it, that night. With the fierceness of a bobcat."

"Yes." She lay in his arms, was content to be there forever, and that was the other side of it. The two sides of who she was. "Even though she upset me, afterward, thinking about it, I knew why Naomi thought that about me. What I want is supposed to be wrong."

"What do you want, Ella? Tell me here, in the darkness."

She wanted to tell him. At least for right now, he'd taken away a lot of her shields, built to address her worries that someone might think what she wanted was an obligation she intended to pin on someone, make their responsibility. Like him.

"I want to belong to a Master, be owned by him. I want to know, all the way down to my soul, that he watches over my every move. I want to give him everything, and take care of him, like no one else. I want that totally out of control, over the top kind of relationship, and I want it to last forever."

She lifted a shoulder against his solid chest. "Might as well wish big if you're wishing for the impossible. If that makes me a disappointment to womankind, I'm sorry, but I think I'd feel that way if I was a guy, too. I've never thought about it as a gender thing. I just want to be owned, totally, and feel safe with my Master."

She took a breath. "So she's right. That *is* a fantasy, a wish I carry around every day. But she's wrong, thinking that I don't know that there aren't a lot of people you can trust with that much of yourself. That want that level of responsibility. I get it. I do."

"You've thought about it a lot since then."

"Of course. Incessant self-analysis is the road to enlightenment. Or a great way to drive yourself batshit."

He smiled, his jaw shifting against her temple. He passed a hand over her hair, to her neck and shoulder, thumb caressing her collar bone. "It helps stop the screaming, doesn't it? When you're in session."

He'd remembered what she'd told him on the loading dock. Perhaps a little too well. When she stiffened, he made a noise, part reproof, part gentling.

"Yes. I like having lots of jobs when I'm not here," she admitted.

"Because when I'm busy, I don't have this anxious feeling that I'm as alone now as I was then, in that corner, watching the flames close in. I know I'm not," she said quickly, before he could point it out. "I know I have a family here. But I can't get that message to penetrate all the way, if that makes sense."

"It doesn't sink in soul deep," he said slowly.

"Yes," she said, surprised he understood. "Probably because I'm not connected to anyone to that level. But maybe no one is. After considering what Naomi said, I thought, okay, if James *had* been interested in me, maybe I could have made just loving and taking care of him be enough, without the overt Master stuff, because of my strong service side. But I don't think it would have stopped the screaming. The only one who can do that is someone who can be down at the bottom of my soul, in that darkness with me."

Her cheeks heated as she realized he might construe that as a deliberate hint, drawing his attention to the two of them together, in the darkness of her massage room. "I didn't tell you any of this because..."

"I know that. I told you to tell me, Ella. You did as I required. Be still now. I'm pleased with you, in every way."

He said it with such assurance, she believed him. A relief.

He moved from her hair to stroke her face, her mouth, and she pressed her cheek to his palm. She was still weak. He'd been brutally demanding, as much as he was gentle with her now. His fingers slipped up to bracket her neck and ear, the side of her head, and he tucked her under his chin again, letting her rest her head against his thudding heart. It had an odd beat, slow. Then he made hers speed up.

"Ella, as of tonight, I consider myself your Master. Within these walls. Do you understand and accept that?"

"W-What?" Despite being unable to see him, she lifted her face, and felt like she was meeting those piercing eyes.

"I don't think I need to repeat myself."

"No, sir. But...you do? Consider yourself my Master?"

"Yes. Within these walls." His touch eased, fingertips stroking her jaw, a light caress.

"I think I missed a turn, or a step."

He chuckled. "I don't think you did. I suspect you already wondered why I kept seeking you out recently. You were being respectful, trying not to assume until I stated my intentions. My offer isn't motivated by what you've told me tonight. Only reinforced."

Each time she'd wondered what his intentions were, if she should ask him to clarify, yes, there'd been that feeling inside her. But it was an additional relief to hear him acknowledge it, confirm that he wasn't offering out of obligation.

A confirmation which made her toes curl.

"I...I've never really had a relationship here. Nothing committed like that."

"First things first." He gripped her chin. "Do you have a problem with me being your Master at Club Atlantis?"

"Not at all." Even if he didn't mean it in the all-encompassing way she would want it. "If I won't be a disappointment to you," she said.

"That's not possible."

"If I want too much, I will be." She made herself say it, face it. "I tend to want too much."

"We all do, Ella. That's just the nature of our hearts."

As he lifted her chin, her eyes closed. She anticipated and then experienced his mouth on hers, the demand that she open to him. He had a strong mouth, a demanding, teasing tongue. She trembled as his touch upon her transformed, becoming something noticeably different. Now he was holding something that he perceived as his, that he wanted to be his. It made the pressure and heat of his grip feel so very different to her.

"I should have told you my intentions before the Puppy Night event," he said at length, lifting his head. "A retroactive punishment is going to happen for that one."

"Retroactive spankings aren't recommended in the childcare books. It only confuses the child," she said primly.

His hands tightened on her and she heard an anticipatory growl in his voice that tingled through her. "Don't worry. It will make a very clear impression. On every level."

"I need... Can you tell me your expectations, sir? So I can do my best to meet or exceed them?"

"It isn't complicated. Within these walls, I'll take care of you, but I expect you to take care of yourself, too. When you don't, it will be my responsibility to address that."

Within these walls. He kept saying that, enough that it gave her a little sinking feeling, but she pushed that away in favor of a better thought. Sure, the other staff watched out for one another. Gideon, James and especially Anwyn watched over them all, but to have a person considering it his responsibility to watch out specifically for her...that was new.

He brushed his lips lightly over hers, tugged her hair. "I'm taking you to the carnival next week."

"Really?" The starburst his words lit inside her banished any lingering shadows.

"Really." There was a smile in his voice. "Does Tuesday night work?"

"I have to work at one of my other jobs Tuesday night. But I could do Wednesday or Thursday night."

With a disappointed feeling, she braced for Tuesday being the only night he could do it, but he nodded against her, reviving that pleasurable fireworks feeling in her breast.

"Thursday night, then. Tell me where you live, and I'll pick you up at seven."

"I'll meet you here, because I told Mavis I'd help her check in new stock for the gift shop that afternoon," she said. "When I do that, she lets me pick one item out for free from the old stock. Under fifty dollars, of course."

"The woman is not a fool." There was amusement in his tone. "All right. I'll pick you up here. Now, much as I'd prefer to stay in this nest of yours all night, I better get to the set up for my twelve-thirty."

"Oh. Of course." She set the plush wolf aside and scrambled up, wobbly legs and all. She would have staggered if he hadn't caught her.

"Stand here," he said. "I'll turn on the lights."

His hands slipped off her with a nice lingering heat, and then the light came on. The switch activated a lamp on one of her low tables, filtered by a sheer red scarf she had wrapped over the shade. It gave everything in the room a nice, sensual wash of soft color, including him, and his bronze skin.

He picked a robe off the door hook and brought it to her, leaving himself distractingly naked. Whoever thought men couldn't pull off walking naked in a sexy way hadn't seen Wolf do it. His slow, powerful saunter made the most of every inch of revealed flesh, the ripples of muscle, shift of limb, the slide of his cock over his thighs.

He slipped her arms into the robe as she looked up into his face, searched it. He looked calm, hard-to-read, but not unpleasant. Wolf-like.

He didn't tie the robe right away, instead putting his hands beneath it, on her waist and hips. He brought her close, lifting her onto her toes and then off of them to hold her firmly against him, flesh to flesh. She wrapped her legs around him, laid her head on his shoulder as he put his arms around her. She shivered as he kissed her nape, her bare shoulder where the oversized robe slipped off.

"What's your schedule the rest of the night?" he said.

"Just working the floor, seeing who needs help where. I work until two."

He wrapped his hands in her hair to turn her face where she could see his frown. "You work tomorrow at another job?"

"Mm-hmm." She didn't elaborate, because he'd said "within these walls." She wasn't going to pull him into anything else. Apparently, he had other ideas.

"When does that one start?" he prodded.

"Six. I do the breakfast shift at Joe's diner. I'm off at noon, and I don't start my courier work until three p.m. I finish that at seven and will be off tomorrow night. I have a couple days of that, then I'm back to Atlantis. I only have three days a week when I work three jobs. The other three days it's just the two. I alternate days between the salon and the diner.

"You work six days a week."

"Usually."

He let her slide down to her feet and propped her against the table. "Leave the robe open. Back straight, and keep those lovely tits out."

She obeyed, her body doing a little throb of reaction. He reached for his clothes. As he pulled on his jeans and T-shirt, his socks and shoes, he kept glancing at her. At her round breasts and smooth sex, all her pale flesh. When he finally finished getting dressed, putting on the T-shirt last with that nice ripple of upper body movement, she was warm inside and out again.

He came to her, tied her robe around her himself, though he kept the ends of the sash wrapped around his hands. He was still frowning, so she felt the need to reassure.

"I like the work I do," she said. "And like you said, you're my Master within these walls, right? You don't have to worry about anything outside of them for me. I'm all good."

She knew she brought out the damsel-in-distress mode in certain types of guys. But she'd also learned that could backfire, become toxic, so she avoided the trap for both of them whenever possible.

"As I said, I can stand on my own when I need to do so," she said, meeting his gaze. She laid a hand on his arm, hoping it was okay and would be taken as a gesture between equals. "I'm really happy about what you've offered me."

His grip loosened, his brow furrowing. His eyes stayed on her, but flickering, as if he was mulling her words.

Show him you understand and accept what he's willing to give. She slipped around him to unlock and open the door. It changed the environment of the room, made it less intense, easier to shift into a more casual mode with him.

Fortunately, Brownie helped out, coming to the threshold of her room. "So how'd your massage go?" she asked Wolf.

"I couldn't have asked for a better experience," he said after a moment, loosening the knot in Ella's lower belly. She didn't want him to change his mind, chalk it up to a bad idea before they could even give it a shot. And she really, really wanted to give this a shot.

His gaze went to her. "I'll see you Thursday," he said.

In front of a slack-jawed Brownie, he bent and captured Ella's mouth with his own. He gave her a thorough kiss he combined with a firm hand on her backside, pressing her against his body. Her sore tissues, stretched by his formidable size, contracted, wanting him there again. At the thought, her settled stomach flipped over, and her head swam as he stroked her face with his other hand, cupped the side of her neck so she was far more aware of her pounding pulse.

When he straightened, his mouth had a more stern-looking set than usual. "We'll talk more then."

"Y-yes, sir."

He nodded and left them. As he strode down the hall, Ella stared after him, the set of the broad shoulders, the gleam of his dark head from the hallway lights. The strong thighs and firm shift of his incomparable ass.

All those things were capable of increasing the heat he'd left burning inside her, but there was one thing that made the flame leap a little higher.

A carnival was definitely not "within these walls."

CHAPTER EIGHT

Now there was no doubt about it. He'd lost his fucking mind. Tonight, he'd given her the first mark, a geographical locator. Not prohibited, especially if the human wasn't aware of it. These days, a lover biting into flesh was considered kinky, exciting—not evidence he was a vampire. Hell, in their BDSM world, the sharpness of his canines would merely suggest he'd had them purposefully filed. It wouldn't be until he fully unsheathed them that they would cause comment.

Her blood had been sweet, though, so hard to resist taking more than a few drops. But he'd given her the mark that would let him find her. It would help him do the job he'd told Gideon he'd do.

But that wasn't why he'd done it. And now he knew what it felt like to be inside her, to have her ride him. To touch the full breasts and generous backside, both of which spilled over the limits of his large hands with endless soft temptation. He knew how her eyes flashed when he buried his fingers in her hair and yanked, to keep her mind on his demands. He knew her cries of pleasure and sighs of needy desire. He could still feel the dig of those surprisingly strong fingers into his muscles, begging for more.

But the sex wasn't the problem. Sex for vampires was like morning coffee for humans. A daily occurrence, always a pleasure and admittedly close to a vital need for his kind, but not something that stayed on his mind like this after consumption. There was always plenty more of it in the pantry, in a variety of blends.

When he first started at Club Atlantis, he'd been curious why Anwyn kept particular tabs on the young woman. Ella seemed capable and independent enough. But then he'd realized she tended to ignore common sense and do as her heart led her, like sitting on the loading dock by herself in the middle of the night. And often she was too trusting. Like the other night. Inciting a group of young males in dog pack mode to chase her, for God's sake.

As he'd told her, not nearly as forcefully as he'd wished, the only thing that kept people from crossing that white line in the center of the road was a mindset of cooperation and structure. When the right set of inflammatory circumstances occurred, civilized behavior was the first thing abandoned.

He hadn't needed to become a vampire to know that. He'd learned the lesson as a soldier in Vietnam. Which, in a real kick-in-the-teeth irony, had better prepared him to be a vampire than most turned humans.

He could say the same for Anwyn herself, one of many reasons he'd clicked with the Mistress of Club Atlantis. She'd been the human owner of the successful Atlanta club when she'd been attacked by a pack of rogue vampires and forcibly turned. Vampires were driven by blood and sex, and they preferred to enjoy both as a Dominant. So Anwyn, as a Mistress, had been pretty set up for that outlook, though Wolf would never have wished such a traumatic experience on anyone, let alone Mistress Anwyn.

Unfortunately, her turning had left her with a unique and perilous handicap in the power-driven vampire world. Thanks to the diseased blood of her sire, she suffered violent seizures, but she managed them admirably, with the help of two males. He hadn't known about the seizure part at first, not until he'd gained the gift of her trust. But he had met the two males at his job interview with her.

The first was Gideon, her servant and, remarkably, a former vampire hunter. Not just any vampire hunter, either. Gideon Green had been the most successful hunter known to the vampire world. How he'd escaped execution from the Council was obviously a need-to-know thing that only the Council needed to know, but Wolf was sure his permanent binding to Anwyn was part of the reason Gideon was still breathing.

The binding wasn't forced, though. Gideon was as devoted to her as an army of pit bulls, and ten times as dangerous, though to most at the club he was simply Anwyn's lover and a welcome addition to the security staff and management. He had a cynical sense of humor and liked yanking the chain of anyone capable of killing him, which only increased the awe factor of his continued existence. Until Wolf found out about the other male responsible for Anwyn's survival.

Before coming to the club, he'd been working as a Dom at a club out in Colorado, doing paid sessions as well as his therapy sessions with PTSD-stricken service members. The work was satisfying, but the darkness in him needed a change. Allan and Fort had been getting on his nerves with their not-too-veiled observations about therapists using therapy for others as a way to ignore the need for it themselves.

When he'd heard that a vampire was in charge of a BDSM club in Atlanta, he'd gone through the proper channels to express his interest in visiting and seeking possible employment. He'd tied in Lord Richard, the Region Master of the Atlanta area, to ensure if he did find work there, it would be okay for him to switch territories. Wolf knew how to navigate the vampire protocols pretty well, and had enough money to pay the necessary relocation fee.

At his initial interview with Anwyn, Gideon had stood against the wall behind her, his gaze trained on Wolf as if he expected him to leap on her over the desk. Wolf had ignored him, as was appropriate, since the male was just a servant. He wanted the position enough to be far more tolerant than he normally would be of a human servant eyeballing him with such attitude.

However, during the interview, he'd had to suppress the urge to keep turning around. There was a large mirror behind him, and he was pretty sure it was two-way. He was also sure there was someone behind it. When Anwyn started asking him questions about his background as a vampire, he knew why the hairs were rising on the back of his neck. The one watching had to be a vampire; otherwise she wouldn't be talking about that part of things. While he couldn't sense the identity of a vampire, he normally could sense the presence of one...and if there was more than one. Yet he only detected Anwyn. But he knew he wasn't wrong.

"Would you like your partner to come in and join us?" he asked, at a courteous pause in the conversation.

She raised a brow, showing she was surprised he'd realized another vampire was present—also curious—but she shook her head with only a brief hitch. "He will make himself known to you in time. Suffice it to say, there is another vampire in residence here."

The steady look in her vivid blue-green gaze sent an important message. *If you think you can take over here, you're outnumbered.*

He'd address that up front. He rested his fingertips on the edge of the desk she sat behind.

"I know you're a fledgling," he said evenly. "Which means I'm stronger and faster than you. In our world, that means I outrank you."

He noted the servant tensed, but Wolf kept his attention on Anwyn. "If you treat me fairly, and are as good at running this club as your reputation says you are, you don't have to worry about me taking advantage. I'll be an ally you can count on if others try. I need a job, and a place to do what I do. Being a professional Dominant in a place run by a vampire has all kinds of advantages for me, as I'm sure you can imagine. I'm not looking to fuck that up."

She pursed glossy lips, cocking her head. "Gorham recommended you to me. He confirmed your bloodlust impulses have settled. He said you have exceptional self-discipline and an even temperament. Since you have an excellent track record at your former clubs, experience seems to bear that out."

"I don't feed where I work," he said. "I can keep it separate. If I let my temper loose, it's because I've realized that it's needed and unhooked the chain, not because it breaks."

Not entirely true, of course. Any of them could be goaded to bloodlust, but she was right. He had exceptional control of it, more than most made vampires his age.

Her gaze shifted slightly, a disconnect. He knew the signs of someone speaking to someone else in their head, and so waited patiently, though the wheels of his mind were moving. Since vampires could speak to their marked servants that way, it could be she and Gideon were exchanging information. The flicker in Gideon's gaze suggested it, but then, when both of them looked toward the door, he realized that the vampire behind the mirror could speak to both of them. Which meant Anwyn had trusted this other vampire enough to let him in her head with a blood gift, or Gideon was a shared servant. Dual-marked full servants were rare, because that level of trust between vampires was even rarer.

As the door opened, Wolf immediately came to his feet. It was the instinct of a soldier, because the power signature that preceded this vampire was a hell of a lot older than him or Anwyn. It made his inability to detect the other male even more unsettling. He'd never known a vampire who could cloak himself from other vampires, and reveal that side of himself whenever he wished, like now, for maximum effect. But for all that the guy's aura was unsettling, meeting his gaze was even more so.

Jesus Christ.

He'd met the type during his missions in Vietnam. He was facing a killer. All vampires killed of course, but he meant one who did it for a living. An assassin. An assassin worked for someone, and in the vampire world there was really only one body that might employ one with this kind of power and age. Now he knew exactly why the male's identity was so closely guarded by Anwyn and Gideon. There were whispers among the middle echelon of vampires, about how Council handled vampires who stepped too far over the line. If they weren't or couldn't be called before Council to be punished and atone for their misconduct, then they sent someone to deal with it. Maybe several someones.

Looking at him, Wolf suspected they only needed the one.

Lean, dark-eyed, with dark hair, the male vampire wore *gi* pants and a black T-shirt. He was barefoot, as if he'd been working out. It didn't dilute his authority at all. Wolf inclined his head and the upper half of his body in a slight bow. He wasn't an idiot. He already knew what title this guy probably carried.

"My lord," he said, by way of greeting.

The male glanced toward Anwyn and Gideon. "He can be trusted," he said, his voice deep and sure. "His soul is true."

The other two visibly relaxed. Anwyn met Wolf's bemused gaze. "This is Daegan," she said. "And while the title is technically correct, he prefers you not to use it. His existence is a closely guarded secret in the vampire world, though it's gotten out a bit more in recent years. He's an enforcer for the Council."

An enforcer was sent to reinforce rules. This guy was sent to eliminate the issue. But Wolf didn't argue. He extended a hand, just to prove to himself and this male that, though he knew his ass could be toast if this one was of a mind to go that way, Wolf wasn't in the habit of cringing in front of anyone.

"If Mistress Anwyn does me the honor of hiring me, her wellbeing will be the top bullet on my job description," Wolf said.

"Nicely spoken," Daegan said, accepting the hand clasp. The dark irises and pupils seemed to take up more room in the eye space than was typical, increasing the intensity of his gaze. "And though your soul is true, our minds at times take us down the wrong path. Your life depends on staying on the right one. If you do not keep her wellbeing at the top of that list, you will wish you had."

Threats didn't scare Wolf, but he could tell Daegan issued the ultimatum as simple fact. When a person loved someone enough to safeguard them with such certainty, Wolf respected that.

"Not a problem," he said.

~

"What are you doing?" Gideon asked.

Returning to the present, Wolf realized that Gideon had joined him. Wolf was leaning on the mezzanine rail, blindly watching the dance floor. The servant was braced next to him. Good thing Gideon wasn't a vampire hunter anymore, or Wolf would have been shish kebab.

He'd have expected Gideon to point that out himself, because he never missed an opportunity for a smartass remark. Except the stiff way he stood next to Wolf wasn't companionable. And the question wasn't spoken in a friendly tone.

Since that first meeting, he'd confirmed Gideon was a fully marked servant to both vampires. Which had kind of blown his mind. While Wolf knew that the issue of sexual preference didn't matter much to vampires—the only consistent thing about their sexuality was that they were all active Dominants—a servant had to be willing to become a servant, and that meant the whole package, especially the sexual submission. If anyone had a straight, alpha, not-submissive vibe, it was Gideon.

Yet he remembered a joke Gideon had made about vampires once.

"They'll fuck anything that puts up a fight." He'd said it with a glint in his eye that Wolf had realized was meant to tease someone in addition to Anwyn. What had been in his voice, his manner, had told Wolf the world's most successful, now retired, vampire hunter, was equally devoted to both Daegan and Anwyn. Life was always stranger than fiction.

Well, in life there were no absolutes. Hell, maybe behind closed doors, there was a submissive vampire. True submissive, that is. Vampires had a hierarchy, and if another vampire was stronger than you and compelled submission, you submitted. Sometimes that was a distasteful necessity, sometimes something else.

From the energy between Anwyn and this other vampire, it had been clear he topped the formidable Mistress of Atlantis. But her submission had been won and earned.

Wolf expected nothing less of the woman who never gave an inch with him, even outmatched in strength and age. It wasn't just because she had the muscle to back her up. It took that kind of will to have a man as her servant who didn't act like a proper one most of the time. Like right now.

Wolf straightened. "I'm on my way to a session. I have a full schedule until two."

"Yeah. You usually do. But you're exceeding expectations in time management tonight. According to breakroom gossip, you managed to find time to fuck with Ella's head. As well as the rest of her."

Wolf turned to square off with the other male. He'd been a vampire longer than he'd been a mortal now. Which was three times longer than necessary for him not to respond well to being questioned by a human. Particularly not another vampire's servant.

"I expect that's none of your business."

"I expect it is." Gideon met him toe to toe, his midnight blue eyes hard and mouth set. "She doesn't know what you are. And what was that on Puppy Night? You about lost your shit with Toby."

"I already had that conversation with your Mistress," Wolf said evenly. "You should back the hell up before you get hurt."

Gideon's lip curled in a half smile that wasn't a smile at all. He started to say something else, but he was interrupted.

"Gideon." Anwyn had materialized out of the shadows, with a tantalizing waft of perfume and femininity. She put her hand on her servant's shoulder. "I need to speak to Wolf. Please go make the rounds."

When she gave Gideon a direct look, a thought that was obviously on the heavy side of *I mean it*, his jaw flexed. At length, he inclined his head. Wolf wondered what had been said and answered in their minds, because Gideon wasn't easily ordered around, even by his Mistress, though she was one of the few who could do it effectively. As he left, Gideon shot him a passing "Don't make me kick your ass look." On another day, that would have made Wolf smile in violent invitation, but then Anwyn was in his field of vision.

Anwyn clasped her hands and leaned an elbow against the railing. It turned her body into an attractive sinuous S, garbed as it was in latex leggings and a gossamer dark purple top drifting down to her upper thighs. Her hair was swept up so her silver dangling earrings caressed the swan-like column of her throat.

In this section of the club, there were clear panels and curtains placed strategically to filter noise. So she didn't have to raise her voice, a melodious purr with an attention-grabbing mix of female softness and implacable steel. The dark eyeliner she wore enhanced the laser sharpness of her gaze.

"He's rough-mannered, Wolf, you know that. But he cares about her, as do I. And while yes, we addressed the bloodlust you called back on Puppy Night, I did not discuss then what motivated it. I think the time has come for that question."

He was aware that his possessiveness toward Ella that night had been way out of proportion with the normal professional protectiveness he exercised toward any submissive within the club walls. In the aftermath, he'd said the right things to Anwyn to smooth out the situation. She'd listened to him, accepted it with a short nod and surprisingly little commentary. However, she'd watched him talk as if she was hearing the things he wasn't saying, things he hadn't sorted out for himself. He shouldn't be surprised that she'd returned to the subject, far more directly.

"I'm asking you, as a peer, your intentions toward her."

"You're a fledgling, not a peer," he said shortly, turning back to the rail. Yeah, he was being an ass, but he wasn't in the mood to be questioned, not when he couldn't figure this out himself.

"Okay." Her voice hardened. "I'm also the one who owns and runs this place. I can throw you out on your ass if you don't drop the attitude. I have the resources to make that happen with a simple toss, or by shoving you through a meat grinder first."

Fair enough. Still, he had to let her know he wasn't going to fall in line at a snap of her fingers. That was the Master and vampire in *him*. "Calling in reinforcements? Calling Daddy?"

She laughed, a sharp sound. "You know that's not the shape of my relationship with him. But my ego isn't so big that I won't put it aside to protect a girl I care about deeply. Her scent is on you. You've had her. You're arrogant as hell and you don't like to be questioned, but you're a good man. So stop making me want to hurt you, and tell me what's going on."

Her expression altered subtly, and she laid her hand on his arm, reinforcing the change of tone. "I'm a far better friend than enemy, Wolf. I care about both of you."

"I know that." He dropped his head down, shoulders lifting in an impatient sigh. "The impression I got from you and Gideon was if Ella had someone pick up the reins on her, at least here at the club, it would help her be happier, safer. A sweet, fucked-up little girl looking for a Daddy."

"Hmm." Anwyn produced her phone and tapped into it. "Shortly before you came here, Ella was in a CNC session. Consensual non-consent. She only had one hard limit. The Dom didn't respect it, didn't respond to her safe word."

"I hope you threw his or her ass into the street."

"We would have, but he required medical attention first." She paused, scrolled. Wolf saw she was going through archived video footage. He knew most sessions in the private rooms were recorded, but the sessions without incident were deleted after a prescribed period of time. The ones with incidents were kept indefinitely.

"James or one of his guys taught him a lesson."

"No. Not them." She offered him the phone, reached over his thicker wrist to press the play button. "I fast forwarded it to the relevant part."

An unearthly, hoarse shrieking blasted from the phone. He'd been picking up most of the buffered club sounds with his vampire hearing, but suddenly all other noise disappeared for him.

Ella had been strapped to a chair for the CNC session. As the tape began, she was surging up from it with an adrenaline-fueled show of strength. The chair had I-bolts to hold cuffs. While it was a secure enough hold for someone her size, she popped them loose from the wood like they were nothing. A side table with implements the Dom had been using crashed over on its side, scattering them.

She leaped onto the guy, driving him back. He was a tall male in his thirties, not overly muscular, but likely stronger than Ella. Normally.

He stumbled and went down. She was all over him, screaming, punching. Wolf had seen Ella irritated, but he'd never seen her angry like this, in a way he recognized far too personally. This was rage, called from a bottomless, boiling well of it. When blood bloomed on the Dom's arms, held up defensively before him, he realized she'd grabbed one of the items on the floor. A scalpel.

"Christ." Wolf sharpened his attention, realizing those hoarse screams were words.

"I said no. No. One thing. No."

Anwyn reached over, clicked stop and darkened the screen, so he wasn't looking at Ella's frozen, fury-distorted features.

"She knows how to take care of herself, Wolf," Anwyn said. "If she makes a decision, she makes it. She doesn't let it be made for her. It took me a while to realize it, too, because she is such a natural submissive, and there is a true fragility to her that calls to the protective side of our nature. She loves to serve, and will do anything to take care of others, give them pleasure. But she does have her lines in the sand. She's also not looking for just any Dom willing to have her. Three Doms have wanted to collar her. She's turned all three down, told them she's not what they're looking for." An amused look crossed Anwyn's lovely face. "Then she found each one of them exactly the kind of submissive they needed. She could be a matchmaker.

"In terms of endurance and stamina, she's physically tougher than a lot of our male subs, and more emotionally resilient than most submissives I've seen here." She took the phone back. "So going back to your fucked-up little girl comment, any Dom who spends more than ten minutes with her knows there's a lot more than that going on with her. Including you. What's been happening between the two of you is making you defensive."

Anwyn said it as a quiet observation, making it hard for his hackles to rise. Especially when he knew she was right. "I may not want to argue those points, but it doesn't change the fact I don't want anything outside this structure. I've been upfront and honest with her about that, Anwyn. I promise. There are plenty of relationships that happen only within these walls. They're satisfying, intense." Manageable.

"That's true." Anwyn's tone was neutral, her eyes doing that thoughtful thing, as if she was weighing the additional, invisible weight his words carried. He hated how women did that.

"Eventually, you'll need a servant."

He blinked. "Did we just take a left at the Grand Canyon and jump? That was quite a segue."

Her full lips pursed. She was wearing some kind of wet lipstick on them tonight the color of plums. He could even detect the scent. "Not really. Surely you knew this day would come, when you'd choose one."

"That is *not* what's going on here," he said, straightening from the rail once more to face her. Realizing he'd spoken more forcefully than intended, he dialed it back, continued more steadily. "This is the twenty-first century. With the Internet and twenty-four hour open everything, particularly in cities, there are plenty of ways to handle our needs. Blood is as plentiful as fast food restaurants. Grab a person, pull them into an alley, dinner is served. Use some compulsion on them, they're fuzzy about the whole thing. Or I can mask it as rough consensual sex play, no muss, no fuss. There's some risk in random blood donors, but not if you take precautions to make sure it's not a vampire hunter plant."

"There are other, deeper reasons a vampire takes a servant. You'd do better to tell me the truth; that it's those reasons you're avoiding, not some bullshit about convenience. No offense."

She said the last with a mild amusement that didn't reach her eyes, reminding him that, no matter the tone of this conversation, she hadn't forgotten what it was about. Who it was about.

"As far as those other, deeper reasons," she continued, "Ella is a better choice than most. She is a strong service submissive, obedient to a fault, but with the intelligence to stand up for herself in charming, inoffensive but entirely effective ways. Those qualities make her versatile, adaptable. She keeps her wits about her, even when she's rattled. She's not going to balk at the sexual games that happen between vampires. If she has a Master guiding her, the more violent and political encounters won't get the better of her."

"Maybe I just don't want someone up in my space all the time."

"Interesting." Her sable hair tumbled over her shoulder as she tilted her head, considering him. "That's a male reaction to a committed *human* relationship. Your servant is there for you. If you want to see her five minutes a day for blood, if you want her to kneel in a corner for hours waiting on your needs, that is what she does."

"Why, Mistress Anwyn. That sounds pretty damn cruel." He shifted. It was time to bring this conversation to a close.

"I'm making a point." She ignored his poised-for-exit body language. "For a servant truly dedicated to their Master or Mistress, it isn't cruel at all. Not that way. You've seen subs who are that devoted to service, who are fulfilled as long as they know they're doing whatever their Master wants them to do. Ella has a great deal of that in her, and something more."

Anwyn sobered. "I haven't been a vampire long, Wolf, but even I've realized there's something...different, about the humans who embrace the life of a vampire's servant. There are 24/7 subs within these walls who don't have that something. Gideon has it, the most unlikely candidate ever to embrace the role."

"Embrace is a strong word." Wolf snorted. "It doesn't have anything to do with him being suitable to be a servant, and everything to do with you. What he'll do for you."

"Yes. Exactly." She met his gaze. "And that's the root of it."

The riposte speared his gut, right on target, because yeah, he'd seen that in Ella. Felt it. He wanted to say it wasn't anything unique, that she showed it with all different kinds of Doms. But he remembered her words, modified for their meaning in his head.

I need someone who can find me in that darkness at the bottom of my soul.

He sighed, scowled. "If I eventually choose a servant, it will be a man."

"Someone you don't have to feel so protective about, being the old-fashioned guy that you are." Anwyn tossed him a grimly amused look. "You were born in 1946. You don't have to act like it. Women aren't nearly as helpless as you want to think we are. And not to get too repetitious, but having a servant is more than that. It's about what you need, too. Emotionally. "

"Do you know why there aren't any Daddy Doms among vampires?" he asked. Time to turn the tables here.

From the flicker of her gaze, the shadowing in her face, he knew she knew the answer. Same as he did. But he spoke it anyway.

"First rule of being a Daddy Dom is take care of your sub. Servants are the property of a vampire, subject to whatever they want from them, and want to do to them, regardless of how the servant feels about it."

Anwyn nodded. "No argument. I'm not saying there isn't a little girl side to Ella's submission, but that's only one component to it. You're a Master first and foremost, so it's not the Daddy side alone drawing her to you. But it does still exist inside you. Here's a prime example."

She laid a hand on his arm again, drawing his gaze, and spoke firmly. "I've known Ella far longer than you. If I told you to back off this thing with her, because I don't think it's a good idea, would you listen to me?'

He looked out at the dance floor. This late, most people were in scenes in private rooms or the public play areas, but there were a few couples dancing, in manners from primal to graceful, to outright sexual. Different ways of expressing what they wanted from one another. "Is that what you're doing?"

"Interesting again. Not a yes or no." She turned so they were shoulder to shoulder. At length, she spoke. "Tell me the truth, Wolf. What can you give me on this?"

He thought it through, and she waited on him. At length he looked toward her again, met her gaze squarely. "I can be a cruel and ruthless bastard when the moment calls for it. But I'm not so far from being human that I've forgotten how to be kind. I'll have a care for her feelings."

She straightened, gave him a nod. "See that you do. Cleaning that meat grinder is very time consuming."

~

Wolf gave her a tight smile. Then he picked up her hand and brushed a kiss over it, a courtly gesture that bemused Anwyn. As he strode away, the mantle of a Master was as evident as a cloak thrown over his wide shoulders. Billowing outward, it affected the very air around him. Eyes followed him from all corners.

When he'd joined her staff, and Daegan had confirmed they could trust him, Wolf had solved several problems. First, he eased Daegan's concerns, and her own, about not having vampire backup on her seizures when Council work took Daegan away from the club. Gideon was vital to helping her manage them, but if one came on her full blown, she could cause her servant a great deal of damage while in the throes of her convulsions and mindless rage. Possibly even kill him. Not having to worry about harming one of the two men she loved best in the world significantly reduced one of the stressors that could ironically bring on the seizures.

Though he'd initially balked on it for her sake, having Wolf here had also given Gideon the chance to join Daegan on his more difficult assignments, something that put her and Gideon's minds both more at ease. While Daegan might think he was invincible, he meant too much to both of them. She liked knowing Gideon had his Master's back on jobs that were more challenging than the norm.

Finally, least important but still a nice perk to her businesswoman side, she'd acquired a staff member who brought in a lucrative income. Wolf's paid session times stayed routinely booked because the male was an incomparable Dom. He did his therapy sessions for free, and she fully agreed with that, allowing him to do them whenever they worked best for those clients, even if during his work hours.

Vampires didn't experience trauma the way humans did, one beneficial side effect to the personality changes that came with the transformation. But as a human, and during her turning, she'd had a front row seat with trauma. If her club could help victims of violence deal with what they'd seen, endured and done, maybe it would balance some of the violent acts she herself had to perpetuate in this strange world she now inhabited.

Wolf stayed to himself, speaking little of his past, always deflecting to get others to talk about themselves. He gave generously of his time and knowledge to anyone on staff who needed it. She didn't know where he went when he left the club before dawn. She was sure

Daegan did, but she'd respected Wolf's privacy and hadn't asked Daegan to tell her, unless it was something that endangered her club. It wasn't. She'd been speaking the truth. She'd grown to like the big male and care a great deal for him. He was a member of her Atlantis family.

"So, he likes her." Gideon was back at her elbow, scowling. "And he doesn't realize how much. Which means he might trample her heart."

Anwyn curled her arm through the crook of his as he leaned against the rail with her. She rested her chin on the point of his broad shoulder. "You don't have to protect everyone in the whole world," she reminded him. "We have to get our hearts broken to live and love. It's part of the deal."

"A part that sucks." Gideon shook his head. "I know she's tough. But she's also fragile. It's the way you girls work."

"It's the way we all work," she said, with a soft smile. She feathered his dark hair back from his strong face.

"He might break her heart. But just maybe, he'll mend it with the broken pieces of his own."

CHAPTER NINE

Autumn in Atlanta could alternate between temps in the eighties and the more traditional coolness. Tonight cooperatively went with the latter. It was a crisp fall night, the kind that made blood and hope stir in a nebulous but not unpleasant way. After his conversation with Anwyn, Wolf had thought about cancelling the carnival trip, but in the end, he hadn't. So here he was, approaching the front doors of Club Atlantis an hour after dark on Thursday.

Ella was waiting for him. The club wasn't open until eight, so no one was at the front security desk, though he knew the one on the admin corridor was staffed twenty-four seven. Ella flipped the locks to come out to him. As she moved away from the doors, he saw Mavis emerge from the recesses of the lobby to lock them after her.

He returned Mavis's wave, but her secretive smile made him want to scowl. It felt uncomfortably like, "you kids have a good time." A reminder that this could be construed all kinds of wrong ways, and not just by Ella, Anwyn, Gideon or whoever the hell else at the club was going to weigh in on it.

Still, as Ella came skipping toward him, her enthusiasm made it hard for him to stick with those storm clouds. She wore a pale turquoise shirt with white birds printed across it, and a black knit skirt whose hemline was just above her knees. She had on white ankle socks with her turquoise-colored canvas sneakers. She wore a Wiccan pentagram and long earrings, a few rings. To match the shirt and shoes, she'd painted a turquoise streak in her hair, which was loose and tangled around her shoulders and elbows, except for one thin braid wrapped in silver that hung parallel to that turquoise streak.

She was a beautiful, enchanting young woman, girlishly excited about being taken to the carnival. Her eyes, which hadn't left him yet, were sparkling. Everything about her, head to toe, appealed to him, made him feel good.

He should be discouraging this at every level.

Yet Anwyn was right. Her eyes might be shining, but Ella wasn't starry-eyed. She was the type of person who tended to embrace the unknown and see where it would go, because she wasn't afraid to fall on her ass. She'd just dust herself off, wipe her own tears, and get on with it.

He wouldn't mind being the one to wipe her tears, or even keep her from falling on her ass.

He'd enjoyed the Daddy-little girl workshop with her. With a fierceness that reminded him the protective Master side of him had been a part of his makeup before he'd been turned. He hadn't known what to call it back then. Too young and stupid, not enough time to know what it meant.

But Ella's personality reminded him, brought it back to life, and let him explore it. Hell, even gave him the chance to be playful with it in a way he hadn't expected, letting loose things in him he'd had buried for a hell of a long time.

Yeah, this was a total mistake. Still, as she skipped the last two steps to him and did an enthusiastic little hop, he caught her so she wrapped her arms around his neck, her legs around his waist.

Ella pressed her very not-little-girl body warmly against his. That knit shirt was getting a workout over her full breasts, making him wonder what kind of underwear was beneath it and the skirt, and whether he'd make her take it off before they reached the carnival.

"I'm so looking forward to this," Ella said, her cheeks flushed. She started to get down, perhaps thinking that was what he wanted, greeting done, but he tightened his hold on her waist, telling her he wanted her right where she was. He dropped one hand down and put it under the skirt. Christ, she was wearing only a lacy thong. If a good breeze hit the fairway, a lot of teenage boys would be nursing hard-ons. And maybe a few not-teenage boys, present company included.

He cupped the exposed buttock, nice and soft, and took a healthy squeeze that had her lips parting.

"Me, too," he said honestly. He let her down, though he kept her hand as he guided her to the parking lot. Her smile stayed in place, and had him grinning at her like an idiot. Jesus.

As he reached the vehicle, her widened eyes and thoughtful expression told him she hadn't known what he drove. The restored 1968 Ford Ranger Styleside pickup was painted in black on the upper body, gray on the lower panels.

"It suits you," she said. "Older and kind of scary."

He snorted. "How old do you think I am?"

"Maybe thirty-five," she said. "Unless you look into your eyes, or watch how you act around everyone, the things you know, how calm you stay about most things. Then I'd say you're about eighty years old."

She said it with a mischievous grin. Though she was teasing him, she'd come within a handful of years of being exactly right.

"Good guess." Opening the passenger door, he lifted her onto the high seat. Reaching over, he drew the seatbelt across her ample breasts.

Then, because he could, he dipped his head and put his mouth over one, cupping it through the cloth to make that even easier, and bit the nipple through her bra cup. She gripped his shoulder, but she didn't squirm away, his good girl, even as he increased the clamp.

She took the pain, held onto him, digging into his muscle as he flicked his tongue rapidly over the captive peak. The immediate moan that escaped her lips told him she'd come out the starting gate ready for him, thinking of him.

He'd jacked off twice in the shower before he left his place to come get her. Knowing her body was already prepped for him wasn't going to make the fit of his jeans any more comfortable tonight. He'd worn his button-down shirt loose over them. Good choice.

"You have really sharp canines," she managed when he drew back.

"I do." Too sharp. He noted something, not by sight, but by scent. They were alone in the parking lot and it was dark, so he didn't hesitate to draw up the hem of her shirt, deftly lowering the bra cup in almost the same motion.

Her breath drew in, raising the breast toward his mouth as he dipped his head once more, this time to put his mouth over the wound his piercing fang had made. He sucked it gently, using the clotting agents in his saliva to stop the flow before it could do more than leave the tiny stain inside the soft foam cup. The bra was a mix of turquoise lace and shimmering mesh, telling him what color the thong had to be.

He wondered if she'd look at the drop of blood later, pass her fingers over the puncture wound in her flesh, and remember this moment. Then he didn't have to wonder.

As he drew back, she was looking down, the hair falling along her cheek brushing his forehead. She studied the wound, passed her fingertips over it. Once, twice. She swallowed, looked up at him, touched his mouth, as if she knew he'd licked away the blood.

"Master," she said softly.

Anwyn was right about that, too. He might have some Daddy Dom in him, and Ella some little girl, but the word Ella uttered now was the umbrella over it all. Master. He was her Master. And she was his. Period.

"We're going to the carnival," he told her. Firmly. And shut the door.

When he came to the driver's side, Ella had that impish look on her face again. "Who are you trying to convince? You or me?"

"Misbehaving will not get you a funnel cake," he said.

"How about one with powdered sugar?"

"Definitely not. I'll tell them to sprinkle it with hot pepper and make you eat every bite."

"You're so mean," she said, a twinkle in her eye, and laughed, squealing and pressing herself to the side of the truck as he grabbed for her knee.

But then she slid over and wrapped her arms around his upper torso, her head on his chest, and pressed her lips to his heart. "Thank you for taking me to the carnival," she said.

He put his arm around her, holding her close, and looked down at her. She made him hurt. She fucking made him hurt in a way he didn't know how to handle. And he was smiling like an idiot again.

~

He bought her a funnel cake with powdered sugar. Later, when he tasted her skin, he knew he was going to taste the sugar, since that shit got all over everything, her fingers, her clothes, down the front of her shirt. He wanted to taste her there, right in front of everyone, but he restrained himself.

As expected, there was a lot of cheerful noise, bright lights and noisy people, but he could handle that in small doses. Working in clubs like Atlantis helped him maintain those coping skills. There were made vampires who got antsy around that much fresh blood, who couldn't handle it. He'd worked hard to make sure he could, knowing adaptability was key to survival.

It didn't help with his reaction to Ella, though. He was edgier around her than expected amid all that noise. He was far more aware of the heated course of her blood through her throat, her thighs, her wrists. Saliva gathered in his mouth as he imagined tasting her blood with the sugar. Drawing both into his mouth while she melted into his arms, allowing him to nourish himself upon her.

For a male who'd worked hard at avoiding triggers to bloodlust, he seemed to be hitting them all, like one of those guys trying to ring the bell with a really big hammer to impress their girls. He was fighting temptation while keeping it within arm's reach. And, even more precariously, within the reach of his fangs.

But he found a way to settle himself, doing what he suspected neither of them did too often. Having some good, clean family fun.

He rode the scrambler with her, the octopus, the bumper cars—where she clearly outdrove him and took far too much delight in that fact. Then there was the Ferris wheel, the merry-go-round, the caterpillar, the teacups...

He would have lost count, if he was keeping count. Instead, he was enjoying the way she grabbed his hand and pulled him toward each ride, a fistful of tickets in her other hand, fluttering against her forearm. It had been so long since he'd smiled this much, the muscles were going to hurt tomorrow from the workout.

When they finally took a break, they wandered through the arcade area. She had a huge purple ball of cotton candy on a stick, and offered pieces of it to him in fluffy bites. When he finally decided to have one mouthful, she turned toward him, teetered up on her tiptoes to taste the sugar on his lips, lick it off with easy abandon as she braced her hand on his chest.

He made a grab for her, and she was skipping away, tossing him a teasing look over her shoulder, sashaying that cute backside back and forth. The skirt swished enough from a passing breeze he was granted a nano-second view of those pale buttocks.

She didn't do it in a practiced way, knowing just what the hell she was doing to him, but as a girl enjoying showing her lover what was his. It made his chest tighten up again.

He didn't want it to happen, but it did. It was inevitable.

For a moment, just a moment, he didn't see Ella. He saw another woman, laughing at him over her shoulder like that. Her dark hair curled in a bob at her shoulders, her brown hand and warm dark eyes beckoning to him. *"Let's ride the roller coaster next..."*

Nobody had been able to take him all the way back there, not in a long time. He didn't mean back before he was a vampire. He meant a far more important *before*.

"Leroy?"

"Wolf?"

He snapped back to the present, to Ella's curious, concerned eyes, as she walked back to him, put her hand out to touch—

"Don't."

She froze in mid-motion, slowly withdrew, watching him closely. He took a breath he suddenly needed, no matter that vampires didn't. That wasn't entirely true, he'd found out. They didn't need to breathe to live. But they needed it to speak, or to sometimes do this. Draw a breath in, let it out, a rhythm that matched the pulse of the earth and helped center them on it. Maybe made vampires needed it more than born ones, since it was a memory of human life.

A staccato of sharp shots had him seizing her arm, putting her behind him as he spun toward the noise. His fangs snapped out. Just in time, he managed to cover them, swiping his free hand across his mouth, tucking his lips over them. Numerous times as a fledgling he'd had to conceal the reaction, because it took decades to control it, and that repetition helped him now.

But the loss of control rattled him. The people blurred, the colors swallowed by green, too damn much green. He drew humid jungle into his lungs, cigarette smoke.

He knew how to climb out of this. *Choose a focus.* And for once, that focus was easy.

Ella brought him back to the present, one sense at a time. Her thin wrist in his grip. Her scent. He reached out to the others around it, gathering them in. None of them belonged to that jungle, that time of his life. Cotton candy, popcorn, laughing children...not children in a village, but children at a carnival, with clothes from The Gap and sneakers from Nike. Carrying cell phones, taking selfies...

He closed his eyes. Ella's free hand lay on his lower back, a comforting pressure point. "I'm here," she said quietly. "It's okay."

The shooting gallery, he remembered. They'd passed it on the way to the teacup ride. She'd crowed over the little stuffed hedgehogs; how much she wanted one, and would he consider coming back to win one for her? The staccato sounds were the BB-like pings against the metal targets. They were a mere shadow of real gunfire. He wouldn't have even gone there without that other memory, overlapping Ella, making her disappear for that harrowing moment.

"Wolf," she said.

He registered the strain in her voice, and awareness snapped back fully. "Shit."

He loosened his grip and saw involuntary relief flood her pale features. As she swayed into him, he cradled the quivering wrist he'd squeezed so hard. Damn it, had he broken any of those little bones? He could have, way too easily.

"It's okay," she said. "It hurt, but I didn't hear anything break. You have such a strong grip."

Christ, baby girl, you have no idea. He could crush every bone in her wrist like crackers in a plastic bag. "Let's sit down. I'm sorry."

"It's okay," she repeated, placing her other hand on his face, drawing his eyes to her. "Seriously, it is. You're not the only one who's done the therapy sessions. I get it. Is whatever triggered it still happening? Do we need to get out of here? Or do you want to manage it a different way?"

So calm and steady. Not the least bit flustered. *Versatile, adaptable and she keeps her wits about her, even when she's rattled.*

If he'd ever had any doubt that Anwyn was a damnably good Mistress, he wouldn't anymore, because she was getting into *his* head. Annoying female.

He found a bench. It was occupied by a group of teenage boys, but he evacuated them with a thunderous look as he bore down on them, barely restraining the urge to carry Ella there. He realized she was under his arm, which he had wrapped around her like a protective hawk around his chick. Her arms were circling his chest and waist, providing him reassurance. They sank down together, and he didn't care how it looked. He scooped her up and put her in his lap. He needed to feel as much of her body against him as possible.

He grasped her wrist again for a closer inspection. No, he hadn't broken it, but he'd bruised the hell out of it. Getting her to move it up and down made her wince, her fingers twitching.

"There go my plans to win *you* a hedgehog," she said. "I was going to impress you with my marksmanship."

"Have you ever handled a gun?"

"Yes. Gideon took me to the gun range a couple times. I haven't practiced a bunch, but I know how to use one."

"Christ."

Wolf imagined the fortitude it must have required for the former vampire hunter to take her to the shooting range. He expected Gideon had to suppress then the feeling Wolf had now, an irrational desire to reach back in time and pluck something so lethal out of her hands almost the second she picked it up.

Women aren't nearly as helpless as you want to think we are.

Yes, definitely annoying.

Ella frowned at him, almost an echo of Anwyn's aggrieved expression. "You guys always seem to think I need protection. I know I get into trouble a lot, but I get out of it, too, so I don't know why you feel you need to protect me."

"Because you're precious, and precious things should be protected. You being not helpless—in fact, you being as strong and amazing as you are—that makes it worse. Because no matter how strong they are, precious things are vulnerable to the bad things in the world. They attract too damn much attention from them."

He'd said the first thing that came to his mind, something he didn't usually do, and she was staring at him like she had no idea what to say to that. Then her lips curved in a tremulous way and her eyes became soft. "Thank you," she said. "But we were talking about you. Are you okay?"

"Yes, I am." He was. He was holding her now, and sitting up straight, and not caught in a snare of the past where it felt like a noose had tightened around his throat. He'd fought off a Charlie who'd tried that, a little stringy guy who'd surprised him when he was clearing a house. The guy had slipped out of a vegetable bin of all things, and jumped him from behind. He had to give it to the little bastard, because though Wolf had been twice his size and weight, the Charlie had known the fragility of a windpipe. He'd damn near garroted Wolf.

"How did you know?" he asked her.

"Everything about you says former military," she said. "When I did your massage, the kind of scar tissue you have, the way you acted about it, I put it together. Plus, you looked at me just now like I was someone else, which told me you'd gone somewhere in your head, somewhere in the past. A painful memory, which can trigger other painful memories, especially when a shooting gallery lets loose that close by."

She gazed up at him. "You spun toward it like you thought you were on a battlefield. You wanted to protect me, shield me from harm."

"I did. I'm glad it was a memory, and not the real thing. I'd never want to see you actually in the middle of something like that." He cradled her, let her abused arm rest against her middle.

"Do you want to leave?"

He shook his head. "I was enjoying myself. If you give me a minute, I can enjoy myself again. It was just a flash, that was all. And I am going to win you something. Let's just do something other than the shooting gallery, okay?"

She smiled up at him, focused on him and only him. Tonight, she wore ocean blue colors on her irises. "They had the hedgehogs over at the ring toss, too. And these huge, huge bears. But I want the little hedgehog. They say the ring toss is a total scam, though. Almost no one ever wins it. That's why they put the biggest prizes there, knowing no one will get them."

"Is that so? We'll see about that." He grunted and rose to his feet, still holding her. Though he let her sneakered feet touch the ground, he gripped her hips, keeping her close. Her mouth was there, so he might as well indulge.

Time slowed.

He'd kissed her before, but while holding all the control, not letting her in, not seeing her as who she was. For some reason, when he brought his mouth to hers this time, he stopped when he made contact and held there. He waited to see what she was going to do.

She started soft, slowly, then with seductive promise. She picked up that he wanted her to prove something to him, to show him how much she wanted her Master.

She knew how to arouse with her velvet lips, heated tongue, the clever movements of her cinnamon-scented mouth, but just like when the skirt rippled over her mostly bare ass, it wasn't calculated skill. She simply gave everything to it, such that he literally felt it all the way to his toes.

He'd been a teenager when he'd had his first kiss, and that was different, a miasma of hormones. It had been nice, but there'd been other later kisses that were better, when he and the woman in question had known one another more deeply. As a result, he'd dismissed "the magic of the first kiss" stuff as romantic nonsense. Now he realized he might have to re-evaluate that.

The first kiss where the souls met one another? That was a true magic.

He tasted, dove, tongue teasing hers, so Ella leaned into him, both arms around his neck, body stretched up. It made it easy and almost a damn requirement that he run his hands up and down that luscious terrain. Nip of waist, outer swell of breast, to her shoulders and slim throat, and back down again, fingers overlapping her hips to rest on the swell of her backside, his thumbs on her hip bones. He'd never been so glad to have the reach that big hands afforded him.

"When we get somewhere private tonight," he growled against her lips, "I'm going to be so deep inside you that you'll cry for mercy."

Her eyes were so wide and deep, he felt an odd wave of vertigo, like leaning over the ledge of a tall building. When she spoke, the whisper resounded in his mind, in his cock. And even deeper places he didn't want to think about.

"Then I hope you're not in a merciful mood."

~

He took her to the ring toss. As she'd predicted, the carny didn't look the least bit worried about losing the trio of near life-sized stuffed bears dangling over his head. A beef-jerky strip of a man in his twenties, he dubbed himself BadBob as he strutted back and forth. "Two big old large Bs, if you get my meaning," he said with a wicked grin. He had stringy, longish hair Wolf expected teenage girls would find dreamy.

BadBob gestured with nicotine-stained fingers at Ella. "Three rings for five dollars. Give it a try. Some of the best prizes at the carnival, right here..."

Ella opened her mouth, probably to say something about wanting only one of the little square-shaped hedgehogs. They lined the top edge of the booth opening like furry molars. Wolf placed a hand on her shoulder, thumb caressing the base of her throat, a Master's touch that drew her attention and stopped whatever she'd been about to say. Giving her an approving look, he pulled fifteen out of his wallet and handed it over to the man. "I'll be doing nine," he said. "You're about to lose those three bears. But if you quit the crude jokes to my girl, you'll keep your teeth."

The carny blinked at him, a sneer lifting his lips, but he wisely said nothing further.

Until Wolf landed each toss precisely around three bottle necks. Vampire reflexes and coordination had never felt like such a perk. Ella's widened eyes and delighted smile made him want to puff out his chest like a rooster.

"Fucking hell. How'd you do that?" the carny demanded.

"I practice a lot at home." Wolf shot him a look. "Want to see me do it again?"

He did do it again. Twice. Ella danced on the balls of her feet and applauded. Her abundance of curves bounced in a way that made him glad she hadn't done it while he was tossing the rings. He might have sent them ricocheting into space orbit. His third round had attracted a scattering of onlookers, who cheered as the last ring landed neatly on the neck of a bottle.

As the grumbling carny picked up his hook and started to pull down the trio of giant bears, Wolf caught Ella's wistful look toward the little hedgehogs. It was gone in a flash, and she was nothing but beaming smiles and exclamations of pride. She almost made him chuckle as she executed her dance in and out of the onlookers, high-fiving a couple teenage girls. "Yep, that's my Mas—man."

She caught herself. When she glanced his way, flustered, he shot her a grin—yes, totally wolfish—and stretched out a hand.

She came to him immediately, ebulliently tossing her arms around his neck so he could lift her off her feet and give her a good squeeze. When he put her down, her arms slipped under his and she held him, her cheek on his chest as he kept one arm firmly wrapped over her back, hand spread on her hip, telling her that was where he wanted her.

"Your prizes, little girl."

When she'd jumped into his arms, she'd had eyes only for him, another thing that made him feel ridiculously pleased, but now he directed her attention to the three bears. They were almost as tall as she was, lined up in front of the ring toss stall.

"Oh, wow. Um, since I don't need three, is it okay if I..."

"Give all three away. To whoever you want."

Her shining eyes flitted up to his, to see if he meant it. "That's an order, Ella."

"Right now?"

"Whenever you want. If who you want to get one isn't here, we'll take it to them later."

She bit her lip, her mind reviewing the possibilities, then she shrugged. "Spontaneous feels like the best way to go."

She seized one of the furry mammals and bounded away, waving her hand at a mother and daughter pair, the daughter about ten years old. Just the right age to want to have a giant bear in her room.

Wolf left her to it and approached the counter and a now-sullen BadBob. He shook his head. "No way, dude. Don't know how you did it, but I don't have any other big ones. You're going to run me out of business."

"How about you give me one of the small hedgehogs and we'll consider it even? I won't even toss a ring." He pulled out an additional five. "I'll just give you the price of a ticket."

"Done," the male said, visibly relieved.

Wolf pointed to the hedgehog he'd seen her gaze light upon, then took it and turned away from the booth, not wanting to deprive himself of another second of watching Ella be Ella.

Her second giveaway went to a kid in a wheelchair. When she placed the bear in his arms and lap, the kid disappeared entirely, except for his two hands, clutching the brown fur with the fervor of new ownership. She offered the last one to another little boy, who reached for it with outstretched hands. He wore an Iron-Man T-shirt, and his wide smile was wreathed with a purple sticky ring from his cotton candy. She touched his hair, said something to his father, and then skipped over to Wolf, where he leaned against a sweet gum tree that likely provided good shade to BadBob during the daylight hours.

"You've made three kids really happy," she told him.

"How about you?"

She beamed at him. "Are you kidding? That was *so* much fun."

"So I guess you don't need this." He brought the hedgehog out from behind his back.

She blinked and then took it from his hand with both of hers, almost as if she expected it to be fragile. Or disappear. "You won me a hedgehog. Just like I wanted."

"Of course."

She looked up at him, her eyes suddenly serious and maybe even a little misty. "Thank you."

He touched her chin. "What is it, Ella?"

She shook her head, but he merely tightened his grip. "Tell me."

"Making my Master...a Master happy...it makes me happy. Really happy. But when you notice what makes me happy...I'm not talking about sex. I don't know, it does weird things to me inside."

He expected she knew exactly what "weird" meant, but was doing her best to keep it within the limits he had set. Never mind that the carnival was not within the walls of Atlantis. Ella was good at knowing what her Master needed to call boundaries, even if he was smashing the hell out of them all by himself.

She hugged the stuffed creature to her cheek, exclaiming at its softness, and extended it to let Wolf feel it as well. He cupped her hand instead, stroking the back of her knuckles, preferring the plush give of her silky skin.

She moved into his touch, looking up at him with an open, searching look that told him she would give him everything. And everything wasn't just a night of pleasure. There was so much more to her. So damn much more.

"Master?" she whispered. He had the world's best poker face, but Ella had a way of looking deeper, seeing more. The other Doms at Atlantis had mentioned that. A warning he knew damn well he should have heeded. But he hadn't believed it. "Do you need to be inside me?" she asked.

"Yeah. I want that. And I want to take it all, Ella. But tomorrow, I can't be that for you. It's a moment, so you can say no. You understand?"

A fleeting look of sorrow, sharp as a spike, crossed her face, then it was gone. As fast as the hedgehog look. But it was the equally quick but no less sharp expression of resignation that cut him deep. She was used to the "you're my right now, not Miss Right" speech, which made him no different from the others she'd pleased, cared for so generously, and been left behind by.

The only difference was, he'd won her a hedgehog.

The look was gone, buried somewhere deep as she met his gaze. "I understand. I want whatever you can give me, Master. Truly. Don't hold back. Right now is a hell of a lot better than never."

The use of the rougher language reminded him she was a woman. One who, by her own admission, had taken care of herself for a long time. She might wish for more, but she wasn't pretending or covering. She wanted him, every bit as much as he wanted her, and wouldn't let a moment of regret affect how either of them acted upon that desire.

Her voice was throaty, eyes yearning, and suddenly he wanted her so damn much he was afraid he'd get no further than the truck before he'd take her. But he wanted to do so much more than that.

He supposed everyone had the songs of their youth burned into their brains, ready to be called forth whenever strong feelings resurrected them. He remembered lying on the nose of a Jeep, taking a few minutes respite in the relative safety of the base before they'd be sent out in the jungle again. The radio had been playing "Angel of the Morning" by Merilee Rush and the Turnabouts. Gazing into Ella's face, he saw the spirit of the song reflected there, as strong and brutally as the heat of the sun he'd felt that day.

If the morning brought regrets, that was okay. It was what they wanted now. He wouldn't deny her...or himself.

"Time to go," he said.

CHAPTER TEN

He didn't take her to his place. Too intimate, too familiar. He wasn't going to be that unkind. Instead, he took her back to Atlantis. He used his key card to enter through the back door, which allowed them to reach the hall of private rooms without encountering anyone who might engage them in chitchat. He'd sent the booking for the private room he wanted through his phone, charging it as a credit against his next session fee. Anwyn likely wouldn't have charged him for it, since it was a weeknight and the private rooms were only half full, but he wanted to pay his way tonight. Take care of Ella with no shortcuts.

The room he'd chosen had a canopy bed with a frame sturdy enough to permit rope suspension. A Master could tie up his sub, stretch out beneath her and enjoy looking at his live mobile, play with her to his heart's content.

A nice feature, but that wasn't his intent tonight. He liked the bed because it was big enough for someone his size to have plenty of maneuvering room.

After he closed the door securely behind them, he moved her in front of him and combed his fingers through her hair, spreading it over her shoulders. As he toyed with the silver threaded braid, passing his touch over that turquoise streak, her lips parted, eyes half closing. She swayed into his touch, giving herself to it in a way he liked. He saw how much she enjoyed him stroking her. At length, he lifted the hem of her shirt but didn't remove it, revealing the lacy turquoise-colored bra beneath that cradled ripe curves. As he caressed them, a little sigh escaped her moist lips.

"You do nothing I don't tell you to do. Speak only when spoken to."

She nodded, her blue eyes opening to fasten on his face. "Take out the contacts. Leave your clothes the way they are."

She moved to obey, and he stayed where he was, watching. He'd pushed the knit skirt lower on her hips when he'd held her by the waist, his hands beneath the cloth so he could feel bare flesh, the edge of her thong. The movement of her hips was accentuated by the adjustment. Her shirt, gathered high under her arms, revealed the curves of her waist. Though as she moved, one side of the shirt tumbled to a creased fold high above her hip.

She'd brought her small purse in with them and left it on a table. She went to that, withdrawing a lens case. After she used drops to lubricate her eyes, she removed the lenses, tucked them away. Then she turned to face him again, her eyes reflecting the light in the room even more vibrantly. Her true eye color was light brown, close to hazel, but now they made him think of the lighter colored beach sand that became much darker and more opaque, the closer one drew toward the surf.

"Extraordinary," he said.

He stretched out a hand and she came to him in that way she had. Quickening her pace, showing her eagerness not just to please, but to be closer. He clasped her fingers briefly before scooping her up, lifting her onto the bed. It had a dark green coverlet under which he knew was a pad, so the mattress was never damaged by the intense behavior that happened here. At the end of a session, the pad was replaced, the coverlet sanitized in the clean light fragrance that permeated all the club rooms. This time, though, he might want to keep that blanket, take it home, rub himself against Ella's aroused scent like a dog.

Or a wolf.

She gazed up at him, trusting. He fixed the cuff chained to the bedpost to her unbruised wrist. Then he moved down and did both her ankles, taking up the slack on the chains so her legs were in the air, spread to shoulder width. They quivered as he opened her to him. His gaze slid down over the turquoise bra he'd revealed by pushing her shirt all the way up again. Then down to the skirt gathered at her thighs, the mound of her cunt barely contained by the satiny fabric of the thong.

He moved back up the bed, lifted the wrist he'd abused. He gave it a kiss, and used a soft velvet cuff to bind it, but didn't take up the slack on the chain. He put the wrist in an elevated, supported position on a pillow above her head. "You'll keep that there, no matter what," he ordered.

"Yes, sir," she said. Her eyes and mouth were soft, appreciating his care, and made him feel like a hero. At least for the second before he remembered he was the bastard who'd hurt her wrist in the first place. When he stepped back, he had her legs and one arm lifted and spread, held with bindings. The vampire predator and demanding Master took over his senses. In this room, he could take as much as he wanted and give her...enough.

More than enough, because Ella fed on serving a Master's desires. Tonight, he wasn't going to stop himself from wanting her with a savagery that could scare her.

Maybe that was a good thing.

~

His face had taken on that intimidating look, the one touched by darkness. Adrenaline spiked, because that look told her he was going to demand a lot from her. She wanted that. It was the drug that appeased everything.

However, she should have known Wolf would administer that drug in a manner that made her crave more, more and more. All while tempting her deepest needs to the surface. It was as if he was working for Lucifer himself.

He moved around the bed, studying her. As he did, he slid his fingertips down the curve of her shoulder, her collarbone, under the neckline of her gathered T-shirt, finding flesh. Slow, learning the shape of her, the terrain of her body.

She'd had Masters do all sorts of things to her. Some took their time in really pleasurable ways. But she'd never had one act as if he literally had all the time in the world, *and* her flesh was the most fascinating thing he'd ever touched.

He doubled back, and did that same exploration, more than once, not in a repetitive way. The nerves in every inch of skin he touched lifted to him, so her body did as well, even though he was doing nothing more than stroking her arms, her sternum, her shoulders, the curves and angles. He didn't remove her disheveled clothes, which gave her a contrast of textures and sensations. He tugged her sleeve, played under her gathered short skirt, traced the line of her thong.

When she dared a glance toward his face, she saw his eyes were closed as he touched her. As if he was absorbing her through his other senses.

That thrum between her legs increased, need building. She didn't care if he ever touched her there, though; it wasn't necessary. With his exploratory touch, he was arousing everything, focusing everything. Her breath was starting to accelerate.

"It's time to get these out of my way. Keep your legs up, but bring them together, knees bent at a right angle over your body." He unhooked her ankles so she could comply, and when she did, he slid off her skirt. "Spread your knees out again. Keep them there like the chains are still holding you up. Stay in that position until I say."

She had to tighten her stomach muscles to comply, and he adjusted her legs out, closer to how they'd been when cuffed and chained. Within seconds, her abdominal muscles were getting a severe workout.

She wasn't a huge fan of formal exercise. She danced, she rode her bike for miles for her job, she ran her sneakers off as a waitress, so her body was toned, her legs especially, but there were certain muscle groups that didn't get a workout that often. Her legs started to shake way too soon, but he ignored that, staring at her lower body in just the thong. Oh, fuck. Her pussy was throbbing under the mere touch of his gaze, but those muscles were burning, warning her they weren't going to hold for as long as he wanted her to stay this way. She couldn't disappoint him. Couldn't.

The muscles cramped, but the second her body jerked, no longer able to obey her mind's plea to stay in the position he required, his hands were under her knees, pushing them back together and toward her chest, easing that cramping ache in her abdomen. He shifted, one hand holding her legs folded down, his other behind her head and upper back, folding her into an egg shape to relieve the burning pressure.

She was sorry, so sorry, but she managed to bite it back. No talking unless spoken to.

"You'll start doing some core exercises three times a week," he said, almost conversationally. "I'll give a list of them to you and check on your progress. Have Brownie give you a massage for the soreness you'll initially get from doing them. It's important to have a strong core."

Now he removed her thong, sliding it off her legs and casting it aside before he hooked her ankle cuffs back up to the chains, giving her blissful support. He left her T-shirt and bra where they were and returned to gazing at her body in that maddening now-until-the-end-of-time way. She was shaking for different reasons, especially when his fingertip slid over her labia, lightly, so lightly, then over her clitoris and around, down, back up.

"Let's see if my girl is wet." His voice had that deep rumble that made her quake on so many levels. Though she liked the helplessness the bindings gave her, he didn't need to put restraints on her. He'd told her to stay as he put her, and she would—core strength failure notwithstanding. That tone pulled her to him in a way that she didn't want to resist or escape.

She drew in a breath as he dipped into her. Not far. Just a questing fingertip, a slow massage that went deeper on each circular motion.

"No more than my first knuckle is inside you, and feel how much you've given me," he said. "That's why a woman's cunt is a honey pot. You're overflowing, little girl. Thick and hot, making me want to taste. Let's see how far down that well goes."

He slid in deeper, still stirring. He was exploring, stroking, rubbing here and there, making her moans grow more guttural. A woman's channel wasn't smooth. There was a thickness to those aroused tissues that gave them contours. With his touch, he could register that shape, the thread-like veins in the swollen flesh, the slick layer of juice the pressure of his touch created.

With her legs up and spread in their vulnerable position, every response was even stronger. Violin string sensation plucked the nerves in her inner thighs, all the way to the tingling soles of her feet.

A whimper escaped her as he stilled, holding his finger curved inside her, another way to keep her pinned. He tunneled under her shirt with the other hand, grasped the joining point between the two cups and lifted them up and back, so her bra was folded above her breasts. The shirt was tucked beneath the tension of the bra. Her hard nipples jutted up, her breasts quivering beneath his gaze, her clothes pushed out of the way but not removed.

His hand moved to her throat, always a sensitive spot. He gripped her jaw, tightening his fingers, then using them to stroke her with hard purpose, with enough pressure that he had to be feeling the bone. "So fragile," he growled. "So easy to break."

As gentle as his hand was below, it made the contrast above more marked. Her heart thumped into her throat at the look in his eyes, a flash of feral awareness. Then he made her turn her head, cheek toward the mattress but chin slightly raised. He kept pressing down and up, that same powerful, not fast but impossible to resist strength, until her head was tilted back, her throat exposed. He slid his fingers down the beating artery, and he began to move his finger inside of her again, playing in that wetness. Her hips jerked, making the chains holding her ankles clink.

"Master," she whispered.

He stopped. She bit it back, but it was too late. When a straining quick glance captured the disapproval in his face, tears sprang to her eyes. She always got too emotional during these things. She wanted to apologize, but that would be more forbidden talking. He was staring at her with that hard look, she knew it, though she'd immediately lowered her gaze. Her cheeks were flushed, her mouth parted to allow rapid breaths.

Please don't stop. Please don't stop.

He was a harsh enough Master to do it, she knew. He'd told her no talking. For all his moments of tenderness with her as "Daddy," when Wolf the "Master" issued a command, he expected it to be followed, no excuses.

"There will be no more of that. Will there?"

She shook her head vehemently, flicking her eyes up in blatant apology. He gave her a long look that told her he would punish her for her forgetfulness. She just hoped it was later, not now. A futile hope.

"You've just lost the right to make any sound or move at all. No moans, no gasps, no squirming. Or I stop. Understood?"

She nodded, another tear squeezing out, because no way in hell could she obey what would come tearing from her throat when he touched her in certain ways, and he knew it. But maybe if she tried as hard as she could, it would count.

He resumed what he was doing. She bit back cry after cry, moan after moan, even though it was pure torture, trying to stay still and quiet as he played his fingers inside her, made her need so desperately to writhe that tears ran in flowing streams down her face.

There were no words to explain it to anyone who didn't already understand it, soul deep. Why it was that she wanted to try so hard for him, and he would get off on being so cruelly demanding, until the whole universe was just the two of them, a give and take that explained everything good or bad about life. The reason to exist at all.

At length, he put his knee on the bed, sat next to her, cupped her face. Leaned down slow, pressed his lips to a tear track. Then another. "Speak to me, baby," he murmured.

A sob broke from her, and he captured it with his mouth, his fingers sliding over her cheeks and jaw, around her throat, as she shuddered under the kiss, her body vibrating the bed. He used his thumbs on her chin to bring it back down to a more comfortable angle, the other digits massaging the back of her neck to ease the strain.

She spoke no actual words. Moans, whimpers, sobs, were what she could do. He hadn't told her to move, so she stayed still, hoping he noticed how well she followed direction, and he did.

"So good," he said against her flesh. "So very obedient."

Her body felt empty, wanting him much closer. She wanted to beg, but Wolf would tell her if he'd like that. He looked for obedience, and took the begging from her body language, her pleading eyes and soft mouth.

He caressed her face and left her, but only to stand next to the bed and take off his shirt, with that glorious ripple of dark muscle. He opened his jeans, toed off his shoes, all while studying her with that wonderful yet terrifying look that told her he was far from done with her.

He stood over her once more, now naked, his muscular thighs pressed against the side of the mattress. His cock was stiff and thick, ready, glossy at the tip. When she licked her lips, his lips curved.

"How does my obedient girl handle giving head?"

If he brought all of that close enough, she'd show him. She was good at it, but like with everything else, she expected Wolf would challenge her skills. He wanted to push her to where she was drowning. The only reason she'd keep floundering to the surface to take a breath was to serve his desires, not to protect any part of herself.

Because that was what he wanted from her.

He straddled her upper body, standing on his knees so he wasn't putting his weight on her chest. He curled his fingers around himself, and leaned forward, his other hand gripping the headboard as he brought the head of his cock to her open mouth. "There you go," he said. "Take all of me, Ella. I want to feel your sweet bottom lip against my balls."

There was no way. He was too thick and long. But she knew how to relax her throat and did so, taking him as far as she could. She started to gag two-thirds the way there, and she cursed the involuntary reflexes of her body, fighting them, trying to take him anyway, so she could at least say she'd reached his thick base, if only for a second.

Instead, he eased off, his hand once again on her jaw and throat, rubbing, soothing. "A good try, baby girl. Better than most. We'll keep working on it, won't we?"

She nodded vigorously. "Good. Now I want you to look at me while I fuck your mouth. I like seeing your eyes with your mouth stretched by my cock."

He started working in and out, slow, pleasing himself with watching her face, her lips work him. He spoke encouragement, lust suffusing his features. He reached behind him to fondle her breast, then gripped it. She sucked in a scant breath as he tightened his grip, pulling upwards on the full curve, pinching the nipple in rhythm as she gasped and sucked, licked.

"Do you remember who is allowed to touch your nipples?"

She nodded, her mouth full of him. His gaze burned heat into her face.

"Only me. Right?"

She nodded again, and he pushed harder, gagging her and then easing off, though he balanced it with a hard pinch of her other nipple. A keening note was in the back of her throat.

Her cunt was throbbing. If she was touched at all she would climax, which meant she was glad, in a perverse sort of way, that he wasn't touching her there, since she knew coming before him or without his permission would be the ultimate disappointment.

He'd eased off again, was shuttling his cock in and out of her mouth in shallow thrusts. She made up for her lack of ability to deep throat him with the movements of her tongue on his glans, under the shaft, everywhere she knew a man enjoyed the touch of a woman's heated mouth.

She pleasured him every way she knew how, and in instinctive ways that were beyond thought. She loved every reaction in his face, the fire in his vibrant eyes, the tightening of the jaw, flexing of the cords of the throat and muscles in the chest and shoulders.

"You're doing so well, baby girl," he said, a strained note to his voice. "Keep working me."

She did, until she lost time and space and realized he was holding himself back, testing her stamina. Her jaw was screaming, her breath was rasping, and still she kept going, her body wet and willing, and then, at last, his cock convulsed in her mouth.

She closed her eyes, in bliss. He jetted into her mouth, his harsh groans shuddering through her body. His convulsive grip on her breast was painful, but in the most demanding, lovely way possible. She'd given him pleasure to the point he'd lost himself in her.

There was no greater gift a sub could give.

He'd flooded her mouth and throat, and yet he had more to give. He pulled out of her mouth, worked his hand over himself, so she watched the last spurts land on her breasts, her abdomen. Finally, with a flash of fierce possessiveness in his gaze, he positioned himself between her legs and pushed deep inside, all the way to the balls. She cried out, body lifting to the penetration, and he gripped her hips, working her in short, hard thrusts that had her breasts quivering and her body spasming.

"Master..."

"Come, Ella."

She did, body bowing up, head tipped back to let out a raw scream of reaction. The climax swept over her like an avalanche, so out of control, her body not her own.

~

Wolf couldn't take his eyes from her. He was thrusting full into her, still hard, and he suspected he'd be hard as long as he was inside her. No matter how many times he came, his cock could never be less than steel in the willing grip of her wet pussy, even if it drained every ounce of blood from the rest of him.

He was okay with that.

But he'd worked her hard. She wasn't a servant, he reminded himself. Still a human woman, with human limitations. Like the core muscles she'd fought to keep holding her legs up, long beyond their capacity. A reminder that the stubbornness of her submissive will would far outlast the limitations of her body, which meant a Master had to watch out for her.

He was reluctant as hell to pull out, but he wanted to care for her as much as he wanted to keep fucking her mindless. Both were a deep pleasure. When she came down at last, he released her bonds, massaged her limp legs and arms. He retrieved a wet washcloth from the small bathroom and cleaned her up, because she was too exhausted to care for herself. He liked that, liked her depending on him. He also liked the way she leaned against him, nuzzled his jaw, as she rested her head on his chest.

He removed her T-shirt and bra, all her jewelry, so she was fully naked. Then he gathered her up, left the room and took her to a private shower chamber in the club locker rooms.

He passed a few people, but paid them no attention beyond his automatic placement of who they were and their reaction to him. He was carrying a well-used, beloved naked sub, his to care for. Their gazes lingered in soft appreciation and understanding as they parted, letting him through without interruption.

That innate understanding was what made Atlantis home for so many of them. Even for him, at least right now.

Once in the shower, he sat her down on a bench and turned on the jets. Dropping to a knee, he washed her off with another soft washcloth. Shampooed her hair, cleaned every crevice. She watched him with wide, dazed eyes, still floating around in subspace, her small hand on his shoulder, holding onto him.

He let her keep that touch there as he washed himself, working around her hold until he had to stand and rinse. Her hand fell to his thigh, rested there, fingers half curled. She watched him, wanting to look at him, and he didn't deny her. Truth, he probably couldn't deny her anything at the moment. She'd given him everything a Master could want and then some. And then she gave him more.

Still drifting, so he wouldn't call it an infraction, she leaned forward and pressed her lips against his cock. It twitched at the contact, but arousal wasn't her intent. She pressed multiple soft kisses on it. Random, all over, the base, the shaft, the head. She didn't use her hand, but nuzzled against it to reach the underside, pressed her face full against it, the weight of his testicles.

She was paying homage to him, worshipping her Master, his maleness. His hand had fallen on her head, fingers in her wet hair, a light hold, as he stared down at her. When at length he tightened that grip, she lifted her head, gazed at him. He'd heard of priestesses in ancient days who had found the sacred, soul-deep connections that could be accessed through sex, put into a trance as they channeled the power of such magic. If he believed in such things, he would think he was looking down at one of its precious acolytes, given into his care, her subspace connecting her to that moment in a previous life.

He swallowed hard. He was apparently having some kind of Domspace moment himself, losing his mind to...whatever this was. Time to focus. His girl needed care.

He took her out and dried her. She moved however he needed her to move, loose, relaxed, her brown-green-gold eyes never leaving him. He bundled her in a soft robe. Because the room was intended for aftercare sessions, there was a comfortable reclining chair. He carried her to it. When he sank into the generous cushioning, holding her in his lap, he rested his head against the back of the chair. As she nestled deeper into his hold, releasing a little sigh, he felt an unusual and rare feeling.

Contentment. He was content, the two of them just being here, together. Nothing else required except holding onto one another.

Wolf had played with a lot of subs. Even done things with them like he was doing right now. So it was unexpected to feel the same act differently. Even more unexpected to get a memory flash. Particularly one of his freaking grandmother.

Grandma in her kitchen, her apron dusted with flour, telling him she could bake a cake with the same ingredients every time, and yet sometimes it would turn out better than other times, even if it was always good.

"Something about that time makes it memorable, boy. Maybe it's the taste, maybe it's what's happening when you eat it, a good memory. Something you wish could last forever, even as you can't help downing that last bite and licking all the crumbs off the plate like a hound dog."

Then she'd winked and told him, "That's why you always want to bake another. See if you can make it happen again. But that kind of goodness is up to God, not you."

Other subs had been willing to give him all of themselves. It was the intensity of the moment, something to be expected if things came together as they should.

It didn't mean that they understood one another far deeper than that, a level that stuck with him long after the session was over. Made him want to take that sub home, put her in his bed, wrap himself around her and keep her with him, because something about her had bonded with something deep in him.

Somehow, without knowing anything important about him, Ella had recognized who he was at his core in a way he couldn't deny, to her or himself. It didn't change anything, but it was a sweet, heart-breaking gift. Another punishment for his unforgivable sins.

He'd learned a long time ago that words couldn't describe the human condition, what drove them down the paths they walked. Attempts to do so only fell short. But when it was felt, no words were needed.

He couldn't have this one. Didn't deserve her. But in this moment, he wasn't going to think about that, because he wanted her too damn much to deal with the self-flagellation bullshit that he truly wished was bullshit.

He'd chosen being a vampire over being with the family who needed him, and the consequences of that had been severe.

There was no therapy that made that okay—or forgivable.

CHAPTER ELEVEN

"*Tomorrow, I can't be that for you.*"

He'd made it clear. Made sure she understood and accepted. She'd been in that position before.

Well, not exactly in that position. She'd realized something deeply frightening the night she and Wolf parted ways, just before dawn.

She'd never felt this way about any man. Worse, she was certain he felt just as strongly about her. But for whatever reason, he wouldn't let himself have her. No matter that she'd offer all of herself to him again in a moment.

One thing love didn't have was pride. But it sure as hell required self-respect.

Over the next week Ella held to that mantra, even when it felt like it was shredding her insides. She respected his space as she always did. She didn't reach out, didn't try to contact him on the club forum, though she checked her own messages way too many times. She wouldn't approach him without invitation, and he didn't invite.

Their schedules overlapped at Atlantis on Monday. When he arrived and passed through the second level bar area—the first time she'd seen him since the carnival—she offered a warm smile when his eyes met hers. She didn't let it falter, at least not on the outside, when he didn't smile back.

But he did stop, consider her from head to toe, an unreadable appraisal that nevertheless filled her with longing and warmth. At some point, he had left that list of exercises in her locker. She was doing them. She wondered if he could tell already. She certainly could, the first morning after she'd done them.

If anything proved she felt differently for him than any other Master she'd served, it was her willingness to do abdominal crunches at his command.

She held onto the wry humor, needing it. After that one lingering moment, he readjusted his hold on his tool bag and disappeared. Probably to the private room where he'd be doing one of his BDSM therapy sessions tonight. She made herself turn away, back to the glasses she was helping Lars dry. He said the dishwasher didn't clean off the spots, and they needed to sparkle when drinks were poured in them.

Anwyn hired people with the same motto about running a successful business as she did. Every detail mattered.

There were times that personality trait was a pain in the ass. Like when it had her thinking over that look Wolf gave her, every possible meaning it could have, until her brain was tired.

"Wolf's going to have a rough one tonight," Stan said. He was sitting on a bar stool, swiping through his evening notes on his tablet. "I remember the guest from last time. Pretty much demolished the room."

"Wolf didn't ask for reinforcements?" Lars asked, with a smirk that said he already knew the answer.

"He never does." Stan grimaced. "Doesn't need them. The guy's a tank. Client's a class act, though. Set up a payment plan so he could reimburse the club for the damage."

"Oh, yeah. Don. Damn." Lars shook his head, continued drying. "So that's why Buddy in Maintenance was replacing what's normally in that room with some cheap secondhand stuff. Boss lady ain't no fool."

"She sure isn't. But that was Wolf's doing," Stan said dryly. "He might be a tank, but he has a healthy respect for her. Remember a few months back, when she took a plug out of him for that guest who pulled a spanking bench out of the floorboards of the Velvet Room? The oak floor had to be repaired and the bench had to be replaced, because the base cracked. Guy he strapped down on that had to be an animal."

Ella remembered that "animal." Rand. She didn't know if it had been a scene name or his real name, but he was the alpha male primal Lars had mentioned, only a few days ago. She recalled long brown hair, jeans that fit just right and peculiar eyes, blue with flecks of gold. The male's physique had been as formidable as Wolf's. Like all the staff, she would have donated a limb to be a fly on the wall for that session, but if it had been recorded, Anwyn hadn't been willing to share, as she sometimes did to instruct the staff on a technique or safety point.

The guest coming tonight elicited different feelings. Sadness. Don was a compact male with restless eyes and a tiredness to his movements, as if his body was a ponderous prison. He had no obvious injuries, but he'd been honorably discharged after returning from service in the Middle East. His PTSD symptoms apparently had been too severe to approve him for continued military service.

He lived in a one-room dive since his divorce. The night of his destructive visit, his wife had been awarded full custody of the kids, because neither she nor the courts felt the children were safe around him anymore.

While every guest's privacy was respected to the utmost degree outside of Atlantis, the staff usually knew a great deal about everyone who spent time within these walls. Part of it was intentional and driven by safety. The staff had been made aware of Don's situation, because if he decided to exercise a guest's right to wander the public floors before or after his session, they needed to be watchful for any flags in his behavior and get ahead of it.

When Wolf initially vetted him, he did a risk assessment with Anwyn that resulted in her standing direction to the staff about Don. "When he's not under Wolf's direct supervision, we all need to keep an eye on him," she'd said. "If his stress level appears to be escalating, get security involved. They've been trained and advised how to best help Don, without exacerbating the situation or endangering other guests. Otherwise, treat him as you would treat anyone else. This needs to be a safe space for him, as much as we can manage it without endangering anyone else."

Ella had sat next to Don at the bar one night, chatted with him. He watched a lot of TV now, finding it hard to get off the couch, so they discussed a couple series she liked and had binge-watched. One of them was one he also liked, *Veronica Mars*. Since then, she was one of the few staff members he acknowledged when he came in, and sometimes sat with afterward. Wolf required that he stick around a half hour after aftercare, to ensure he was in the right headspace to go home. Sometimes he wasn't, and Wolf took him.

She made a mental note to be around after they were done if Don wanted to hang out. It gave her something to anticipate, and distracted her from the overwhelming urge to seek Wolf out, hop into his arms to see if he'd hold her, or let her help, or do anything to allow her to be near him.

She shouldn't have gone there, even in her head, damn it. The feeling swamped her, and she closed her eyes, hunching tighter over the glass so no one would see the hurt that clogged her throat, the tears in her eyes. Damn it, damn it. She needed to get out of here tonight, not stick around. She was way too aware of the other session Wolf had scheduled tonight, after Don's. A woman who wanted a public session, not a therapy thing.

For a male who so rarely did scenes with women, here he was, having two in a month. Murphy's law sucked. Ella resolved she'd be gone before then. She was strong, but even she had her limits.

It wasn't jealousy. If Wolf could be with Ella, she would delight in watching him exercise his remarkable skills with paid clients and even those members he scened with on the house, just because he embraced his Dominant side and enjoyed whatever appealing challenge they presented to him. She understood the difference between a club session and the kind of sub a Dom wanted to take home with him.

She surely did.

Why did she still smell him on her skin, days later? She could hear his voice in her head, feel his touch. Her heart was going to explode out of her chest, and her throat was tight.

"Ella."

Lars touched her hand, but she wouldn't look up. A bar napkin came under her field of vision. "Getting new water spots on my glass, honey," he said gently. "Did your heart get broken again?"

She took the napkin. "It mends," she said.

"Ain't that the truth. Mine probably looks like a jigsaw puzzle by now." He stroked her hair, and she let herself accept the comfort, even as she thought of another hand, a much larger one, the heat and strength of it. "Hey, a group of us are going to play cards tonight in the break room, after closing. Join us and then crash at my place tonight. It's closest."

"Okay. Maybe I will. Thanks."

It frustrated her, when she couldn't work herself out of a funk. Unfortunately, it only worsened as the evening progressed. Don arrived, gave her a nod. He didn't look in the best of shape, which should have given her a kick in the ass, a reminder that her pining for a male who'd made her no promises he couldn't keep was not the world's biggest problem. She wasn't even sure if Don had changed his clothes or showered recently. He headed for the back with barely a wave. Hopefully Wolf would talk him into using the club facilities to take a shower after his session.

She wondered how it played out between them. She'd assisted in a couple therapy sessions, talked to Dominants who did them, and had read up on it online, but like anything else in their world, it could fluidly take a lot of forms. Re-creation of the stressor, restraints or pain to let go, other psychological mindfucks that were intended to help with healing or confronting emotional wounds. The one in therapy might be a top or a bottom; sometimes that didn't matter to how the therapy rolled out, though the therapist retained control of the direction of the session, no matter the roles played.

Wolf always blocked off a couple hours for Don. Ella intended to avoid the private room hallway like a plague until well after he was done. But, proving again that Murphy was her fucking arch nemesis tonight, at the end of hour one, Sabrina radioed the bar to ask if Ella was there. She wanted to know if Ella would watch the concierge desk while she took a thirty-minute break to eat a late dinner and handle some family stuff.

Every private room was well stocked with essentials—towels, bottled water, soap—but a Dom could press a call button if he or she discovered a need for an extra pair of hands, or a supply that wasn't in there. With the concierge desk centrally located in the hallway, they could get those things without breaking scene, or leaving their sub personally unattended. It was also a one-push method to summon emergency help if needed.

When the rooms were occupied by more experienced Doms, there was usually little to do at the desk, since they usually came prepared or were less likely to have a situation get out of hand. Sabrina confirmed it when Ella arrived. "It's been quiet. We only have four rooms occupied tonight, and they're all regulars. Though there was a moment where I was a little concerned about Wolf's. It sounded like they were coming through the wall once or twice, but it's settled down."

Ella nodded. "Don's sessions can get loud, even with the sound buffering."

"So I'd heard. I just hadn't experienced it directly." Sabrina gave her a quick smile. "I'll be back soon. I just need to check in with my son. I have to confirm he's done his homework before he can start his pre-bedtime marathon of video games. We have a rule that he has to wait for my call."

"Are you sure you're a sub? That sounds like some serious Dom sadist stuff."

"You'd think so, from hearing him complain about it." Sabrina grinned. "Why do you think I look forward to my sessions with my Master here? A blissful two hours where I don't have to be in charge of a twelve-year-old boy, which I'm pretty sure is harder than controlling the universe."

Ella chuckled and waved her off. "If you run longer than thirty minutes, don't worry about it. I have nothing scheduled tonight."

"Thanks, Ella."

After Sabrina departed, Ella sat down at the desk and took out her dog-eared paperback. The call signals had a loud tone, so she could read and not be concerned that she would miss one. The desk didn't have monitor access to the rooms, something only Anwyn or the security team were allowed. Though situations like what Sabrina described about Wolf's room could heighten concerns, they all had faith that security knew their job. If Wolf was in trouble, they'd have already been here. If Don was in distress he couldn't handle, Wolf would call for assistance even faster.

Ella propped her sneakered feet on the edge of the desk, putting herself in her favored U-shape where her knees could become the book prop. As she'd told Sabrina, she didn't have any sessions planned, so she was in casual wear tonight, intending only to be waitstaff and do things like this. Tonight in particular, she was sincerely glad Anwyn never pushed her Doms or subs to pick up walk-in paid sessions when things didn't feel right.

She'd read two chapters, and was getting pleasantly immersed in the book, a welcome distraction, when the desk panel beeped. Between her toes, she saw it was Room Three.

Of course it was Room Three. Wolf's room.

If Murphy had been present for her to send him a really dirty look, she would have seared him down to his Fate-induced hypothetical essence. "Yes, sir?"

"I need—"

A howl drowned out whatever Wolf had been about to say, followed by a crash that came through the mic like static. She heard a scream, then a grunt of pain. The connection went silent.

The scream had been Don, uncontrolled and full of rage. The pain was Wolf's.

She was out of the chair and headed down the hall before she thought, but she recalled herself enough to spin, run back to the desk and hit the button for security. The longest two seconds of her life happened before Stan answered.

"What—"

"Room Three. Wolf's in trouble, or the guest is." Then she was running down the hall. She could hear Don still screaming, though it was heavily muffled through the insulated walls.

She reached the door, just as it vibrated from a heavy impact. She skidded to a halt, knowing that she needed to stop, listen, get some cues. Interrupting a session without the Dom's specific invitation was extremely bad etiquette in a normal situation, and could be catastrophic for a therapy session. But she heard that grunt of pain in her mind again, and decided she was damn well taking it as an invitation.

She reached for the latch, at the same moment the door was yanked open. Don charged through, wild-eyed, face streaked with tears. His surprisingly hard-muscled body was stripped down to his boxers. His arm whipped forward, and she saw a heavy wooden paddle coming toward her face.

She ducked and rolled, the wood glancing her cheek and shooting pain through her head. Don had moved with her, and they fell together. She realized in a heartbeat she was fighting a man who knew how to fight. From his crazed eyes, it was clear he was seeing an enemy, not her. He lifted the paddle again. She grabbed at his arm with both hands, knowing she didn't have the strength to stop him, but maybe she could slow him down. And she still had her voice.

"Don, it's me. It's Ella. *Veronica. Veronica Mars*."

Maybe it was a kneejerk safeword reaction, but she'd blurted out whatever short combination of words would seem familiar, sane, as far as possible from this moment. His knee was planted in her stomach, hurting like hell, but adrenaline compensated.

Then she realized, with a surge of relief, the deadly blunt instrument was no longer a threat. A powerful dark hand was wrapped around Don's wrist, another arm over his chest. Wolf was braced behind him. His face was bleeding but he looked as steady and in control as he always did, which helped her be the same.

"Easy, Don. Easy."

She knew immobilizing a person with PTSD, like this, wasn't always a good idea, but Wolf had done it to protect her. The least she could do was help diffuse things, especially since it looked like she'd found a way to do it.

After her blurted words, Don was looking less ferocious and even more dazed. He was staring at her as if from a huge distance, but his lips were moving. *Veronica.*

"Yes, Veronica. Remember, we were going to talk about Season 2, next time you were here? About her and Logan, and Weevil?

Now he mouthed that. *Logan. Weevil.* The paddle fell out of his fingers. It thunked to the floor. His gaze turned to her hands, holding tight to his arm, and Wolf's sure grip higher, on his wrist. His face creased, crumpled.

"Oh no," he said, and the rage in his voice was gone, replaced by defeat. "Oh no..."

"No, no, Don, it's totally okay," she said, wanting to soothe. She didn't know if that was the right thing, but he suddenly looked so... broken. He wanted to pull away, but as she released his arm, she reached toward his jaw. Wolf's gaze burned into hers over his shoulder, but he gave an imperceptible nod. She was female, something not part of the demons he was fighting in that room. She could help ground him.

This she knew how to do.

"Let me go," Don said. Wolf shook his head, his much more massive body still flush against his back.

"Take a break. Let her help. You can't do anything at this moment but accept her comfort."

"I almost—"

"No, you didn't," Ella said. "Wolf was here, every step of the way. Do I look the least bit scared?" There'd been no time to be, which was helpful, because at some point she'd realize just how close he'd come to splitting open her skull. But what that would have done to Don worried her more than anything, particularly since she was safe and sound.

Thanks to Wolf. She had no fear while he was here, and it showed in the steadiness of her voice, her touch on Don's face, guiding his eyes back to her. She noticed something now she hadn't at the beginning. There were abrasions on his throat, as if he'd had something cinched around it that had cut, rubbed. It didn't look fresh enough to have happened in this session.

Her heart tightened into a fist. At her very worst moment, she'd never contemplated...but Don had. He'd been in a well of despair that deep, thinking there was no way out of it.

She let it all go away. Everything about their immediate surroundings, the three of them lying halfway out in the hall. Don poised over her in his underwear, Wolf holding him in an obvious restrained position, security on their way. All of that disappeared as she focused on everything Don was revealing to her in his eyes, his body language.

It was terrible, how lost people could get. How much life could take from them and yet they endured, half a person, broken into so many pieces. She'd learned as long as all those pieces were still inside them, they could be put back together. Maybe not the same way, maybe not as perfect and new, but perfect and new were overrated.

"No thinking," she said softly. "Just rest. It's okay."

"No," Don said. "It's not. It doesn't make sense. It's not the way it's supposed to be. It's just not. Someone needs to fix it, so it makes sense."

His voice was breaking. He was fully back in the moment with them, but in the moment meant facing his reality, which he obviously saw as bleak as endless rain. He was headed back down into that deep well.

"Come to me," she said quietly. "Hold me. I need you to hold me, Don. Can you do that?"

His gaze flickered at the word "need," so she repeated it. "I need you, Don. Please."

In her peripheral vision she sensed movement. Security. Wolf shook his head, a short, sharp movement. Whoever it was stopped. They were still there, she expected, but he'd kept them out of Don's field of vision.

Don seemed to be processing what she'd said. She repeated it a couple times, moving her hands to his neck and shoulders, to his chest and around to his sides, gentle pressure, urging him to come down to her. A whole conversation made up of cues was likewise happening between her and Wolf. Eye contact, small gestures. Two of Club Atlantis's most experienced staff members, helping a guest find his way.

Wolf's arms loosened, encouraging Don to respond to her pressure. In an abrupt move, he did. Don wrapped his arms tight around her waist, buried his face in her breasts. When he hunched his body in a peculiar way, Ella realized he was trying to curl around her. Or inside her.

Back to the safety of the womb was an instinct older than conscious thought. She struggled to move, to turn herself, and Wolf fortunately recognized the same thing she had. He helped her sit up, adjust Don so the shaking veteran was in her arms, in her lap, turned toward her so his legs bent and pressed into her hip. It coiled him around her as much as possible.

"You're right," she whispered, rocking him gently. "It's not okay, none of it, but this is. You're loved, you're forgiven, you're safe here. You can be weak and still be strong. You're not alone."

There was no message more important in the whole universe. She knew that firsthand. When she said it to someone like Don, he knew she understood. She could do this, make him feel for a little while he wasn't alone with it.

As she held him, her gaze went up to Wolf. He was crouched on his heels, his arm under hers around Don's back, helping her hold his heavier weight, his other hand on Don's shoulder. It was a posture of additional reassurance, but it also put him where he could intervene on her behalf if Don's mood changed.

She wanted to lift her hand, touch the bloody spot on his face, make sure he was okay. Tend to him. Because though the cut was bothersome, she worried more about other things she saw in his eyes now, particularly as he watched her hold Don. She saw shadows, and an odd echo of some of what she'd seen in Don's eyes. Old, unhealed rage and grief, the despair of the lost.

She couldn't risk touching Wolf in comfort. She was rubbing Don's upper arm and back in soothing circles, and stopping that for even a moment might change things for the worse. She settled for mouthing *Are you okay?*

Wolf nodded. He glanced toward the end of the hall where security likely waited. That was fine, but she didn't think whoever had arrived was needed anymore. Don's sobs were muffled against her breasts, his breath hot and shaky, his body heavy with exhaustion.

He was okay for the moment. Except for the cut on his face, Wolf was fine, too.

He gestured, and now Wendy came into Ella's field of vision. Unplanned but fortunate, that a woman agent had responded. Don was winding down, getting himself back together, and didn't seem to have a problem with Wendy helping him to his feet with Wolf. Ella got up, her legs only a little wobbly, and squeezed Don's arm.

"If you're not up for it tonight, we'll talk later about Veronica. Otherwise, I'll be in my usual spot."

He gave her a nod, a weak smile. Then Wolf and Wendy were guiding him back into the room.

Ella expected Wolf would wind down the session now, do aftercare. She picked up the paddle, the weight of the half-inch thick wood heavier than normal in her hands, especially as she imagined it connecting to her face. When she turned to head back to the desk, a dark hand closed over her arm. Wolf had returned to the hallway.

"Ella."

"Yes, sir." She made herself face him, but kept her gaze to the floor. He touched her chin.

"Look at me."

She did, studying his eyebrow intently as he brushed his fingertips lightly over the spot where the paddle had made contact. Her cheek was sore. Tomorrow she expected there'd be a bruise there, but it could have been a lot worse. "I'm fine," she said, anticipating him. "Please go help him. He really needs you."

She needed to get clear, otherwise she would have her hands on his face, then be checking him all over for any other injuries, acting like a complete idiot.

"So does my sub. Or did you forget I'm your Master?"

In these walls. No, she hadn't. "No, sir. But I'm good, really. This isn't the first time that I've helped calm a situation. The puppy play thing, the way I reacted to that, that wasn't my normal crisis mode. I'm usually pretty good with them."

"Well, being hunted by a pack of wild dogs, even the human kind, isn't a daily thing for you. I assume."

She managed a half smile and looked down. "No sir."

"The cut on my face is superficial, Ella. When I clean up the blood, you won't be able to see it." He touched her chin again, reminding her to look at him. It was just difficult. She wanted to touch. She closed her hands harder on the paddle.

"Thank you, Ella," he said. "Even though I was only calling you for towels."

She blinked. "Oh. I thought...I heard the yelling."

"Yeah. I thought he was at a lull point. I was wrong."

"So I caused the problem."

"No." He grazed a knuckle along her cheek. "Wendy trusted your judgment. As she should. And though you exercised your usual propensity for finding trouble, in this case, I think you helped, despite that."

Her cheeks heated at the reproof, despite the dry tone of amusement. "Will he be all right?" she asked.

"He will be for tonight." Wolf's gaze hooded. "Sometimes all you can do is day by day."

"Yeah. That's true."

She knew that. But as he gave her another nod and then disappeared inside the room, she wondered how he did.

~

She heard that Wolf took Don home after the session. Dieter, a security guy who was also a veteran, went with them. He was going to stay with Don until Wolf finished his second session of the night.

She thought of how Wolf had addressed his own issues at the carnival, and was glad Don had someone like Wolf to help him. But when Wolf returned to the club, and she glimpsed his face, she saw that despairing echo underneath the impassivity. Such a session took its own toll on the therapist. The compressed energy around Wolf said he wasn't in the best headspace himself.

Confirming it, he didn't engage in conversation with anyone, and disappeared during the down time before his next session. She was working the bar at the time, surrounded by members, so she didn't know if he'd even seen her. Or wanted to see her. She wanted to go find him, offer him comfort, but she wasn't sure if that would be construed correctly, and...

Damn it, it was what a friend would do. But were they friends? The kind where she could casually go to him, offer help, without ulterior motives being assigned to it.

Oh, fuck it all. Was she really second-guessing herself like a damn teenager? Enough of this.

Once she wasn't needed at the bar, she went to look for him, the Master she cared about, to see how she could help. She was responsible for her own feelings; they were hers to risk. She wasn't going to alter who she was to protect herself or deny him the care he might need. Even the most invincible Dom could use a hand on the shoulder, a hug, or simply a quiet, caring presence after a rough session. She could sit near him, just be there.

The problem was, she couldn't find him. The truck was still in the parking lot, so he was here. Maybe he was with Anwyn, talking something through. Then she thought about the alley. Though not a heavy smoker, Wolf usually went out there once a night to indulge a cigarette.

As she moved through the back hallways, headed for the side door, she ran into Gus, who had a panful of scraps for the feral cats. Since he looked harassed and busy, Ella put out her hands. "I'll take the food to them, unless you need the break."

Gus gladly turned the tray over to her. "Honestly, I usually need the laugh the little furballs provide, but I'm up to my ass in marinating mushrooms. Providing top end snacks here instead of just peanuts on the bar can sometimes be a pain. Our hors d'oeuvres are getting way too popular."

"Because the chef makes them too tasty." Ella grinned. "Throw in a couple of cockroaches, and the demand will go down."

"Yeah, right. I'd be looking for a job."

"No, you wouldn't." Gideon was striding by, looking as if he was five minutes late to his destination, but he still took the time to yank Ella's ponytail in his usual obnoxious big-brother-like way. He fended off her punch, catching her smaller fist and giving it a kiss. "Anwyn doesn't believe in firing her employees. She believes in concrete shoes and watery graves."

"Comforting," Gus said dryly, and nodded his thanks to Ella, retracing his steps back toward the kitchen.

"Where are you headed?" Ella asked Gideon. He grimaced.

"Quarterly risk assessment with the rest of the security team. I think James specifically extended his New Orleans vacation into a sabbatical with his new lady friend to avoid it. Heard you all had some excitement." He touched the spot on her face, like Wolf had, but Gideon's touch had a whole different feel to it. A hundred percent friendly concern and sexy protective guy comfort, but nothing complicated that could tie her heart in knots.

"Did Wolf get you into trouble?" he asked. "Want me to beat him up for you?"

The visual of a sparring match between Gideon and Wolf, both shirtless and in jeans, might just carry her through her next masturbation fantasy. Letting the trickle of humor bolster her, Ella smiled. "I'm good, truly. It's just so sad, what someone like Don is going through."

"Yeah, it is. Come here. You still look like you need a hug."

"Maybe you need one, but since you're a tough guy, you're just using me as an excuse."

"Busted. Risk assessment meetings totally trigger me. I may need ice cream and a high body count action flick afterward to recover, but I'll take the hug now."

He removed the tray from her hands, set it aside, then pulled her close to hug her tight. Ella let herself enjoy those strong male arms, and tried not to wish so hard they were someone else's. She'd take what she could get, and Gideon was definitely not sloppy seconds.

Gideon cupped the back of her head. "You're the best thing about this place, after Anwyn herself," he murmured, surprising her. "Don't let anyone drag you down, or I will seriously fuck them up. You keep things sparkling."

The praise warmed her. She tipped her head back enough to give him an amused look. "Sparkling?" she asked.

"Yeah. You keep us seeing the shine on things. Oh, shit, I'm really late now. Are you..."

"Totally good," she promised, squeezing his hands on her waist and stepping back. "You helped. Thank you."

He snorted, his gaze on her face. "I'm putting you at the top of the risk assessment list. Risk of breaking all our hearts with those big eyes of yours."

"You're so goofy," she said.

"Yeah, I am." He touched her cheek. "Find me later. I hear there's going to be a card game. You know Chantal always cheats."

"I'm going to tell her you said that."

"Counting on it." He was headed onward and called it over his shoulder, making her smile.

It was really okay. She had a family here. She'd find Wolf and help him feel better, give him a hug if he wanted one, and ask for nothing more than that.

She retrieved the pan and exited the side alley door. She waved at the camera, an acknowledgement to whoever was monitoring it.

As she moved out into the alley, calling "kitty kitty," feline silhouettes materialized out of the shelters and maze of crate towers Anwyn had arranged for them. They offered a mix of sunning spots and places to get out of the rain.

Ella's thoughts about having a family at Atlantis made her remember what had happened to Anwyn out here, but not in a dark way.

There were cultures that believed cats were good luck, or spirits that warded off evil. Since, remarkably, the Mistress of Atlantis still came out here regularly to feed the cats, refusing to let the horror of her attack define this spot for her, Ella didn't have a hard time believing it.

Ella hadn't been here when it had happened, but had woken up in the middle of the night, thrown a hoodie over her pajamas and borrowed her landlord's car to race to the club. Her gut had told her something terrible had happened.

After that, Anwyn had changed in some hard to define but impossible to miss way, and Gideon had come to stay with them. But not just him.

Well, that wasn't exactly accurate. The other man in Anwyn's life had been there for some time. But before that, Ella caught only brief glimpses of the unsmiling, dark-haired male who ghosted the staff hallways in the depths of night. To the inner circle of about a dozen staff members—that Club Atlantis family—James had indicated he was a particular friend of Mistress Anwyn's and shouldn't be approached or discussed without invitation. Not even among themselves. Since Anwyn saw the value in the staff keeping one another informed, if she ruled something specific was not to be discussed, even between each other, they took it seriously.

After that terrible night, he'd become a more permanent fixture. Still not seen all that frequently, and he didn't encourage conversation when he did, but once Ella had come face to face with him in the hallways. Or face to chest, as was the case with her and any male six feet tall or higher.

He'd been dressed all in black. A duster had swirled around him like a movie prop, covering matching jeans, T-shirt, shoes. It wasn't a fashion statement as much as it was camouflage. When he stepped out into the night, she imagined he instantly became part of the shadows.

His eyes had been black as well, and he'd briefly met her gaze, an assessment. Then he was moving onward, the duster brushing her hand as he passed. She'd felt dizzy, and a little like a person did when they found out later they'd exchanged a cordial nod with Jack the Ripper in the local Starbucks.

Sort of. The danger waves coming off him had been intense, but they hadn't been targeted at her. It was a general sense of who or what the male was. Lethal, but in a way that Ella had decided meant good things for Anwyn. Protective things. When she'd reviewed that chance meeting in her mind later, she'd remembered a trace of warmth in the male's gaze when she met it, a slight curve to his mouth. He'd dipped his head to her, showing her courtesy, as if he knew her. As if she had his regard, because she cared for and belonged to Anwyn.

When their boss was finally able to get around, her appearances during open hours were initially very limited. She seemed more intense, incredibly focused. There was a stillness to her that hadn't been there before. She'd been an amazing Mistress, incredibly gentle and inexorable at once, even ruthless and intimidating when the moment called for it. Those qualities seemed even more potent now, yet she no longer conducted any sessions one-on-one. She supervised, provided guidance, helped plan sessions with the staff Doms as needed, but she herself did not solo with any guests or members.

None of them ever saw evidence of her injuries, but something fundamental, emotionally, physically, had changed for her. Ella understood one component of it, and so did Chantal. Ella because she sometimes just knew these things, and Chantal because she'd worked with victims of sexual assault and recognized the signs.

Ella remembered the first day Anwyn had been able to spend most the evening on the floor. James had told them when it was going to happen, and what was needed. It was vital they act as if today was no different from any other day, instead of the great leap back toward normalcy it seemed to be. Even being overly celebratory would be hard on her. She needed things to be smooth, routine. They'd proceeded under those rules without complaint or question, only asking him if they could do more.

Ella had truly, really meant to behave as required. But an hour before opening, she'd come face to face with Anwyn and felt that energy hit her. Violence, fear. Like Don, but different, something broken that would never be the same again. It didn't show in Anwyn's face, her still body, but Ella felt it, the maelstrom beneath the flesh, as if the storm swirled around them both.

Her Mistress, tall and strong before her, had been torn apart and remade in a way that had irreparably changed her.

Without thought or calculation, she'd dropped to her knees at Anwyn's feet, pressed her lips to her shin. She hadn't touched her otherwise, not until Anwyn bent and lifted Ella's face, which had been streaming with tears.

Anwyn's expression had altered, her blue-green eyes shimmering with so many emotions that twisted that knife in Ella's heart, made her cry harder. She wasn't pitying Anwyn. She was crying for her, for what she'd endured, while being so glad she was alive, okay.

Anwyn had sunk to her knees, wrapping her arms around Ella. That was when those other staff members, the ones trying to act like everything was the same as always, but keeping Anwyn in sight, because they'd all missed her presence so much, closed in from every direction. They'd knelt in a protective circle around her, leaving a buffer of space but reaching out with a look, a murmured word, or a brush of light fingertips. Chantal had taken Anwyn's hand in a hard grip.

"Anything," Chantal said for all of them. "Anything you need, Mistress. We're all yours."

Ella remembered Gideon standing, watching. They hadn't known him all that well then, but his grim expression held many of those same emotions they were all feeling. That was when she noticed the other male, blending into the shadows of the wall so well she might have been the only one who saw him. He'd met Ella's gaze, and said his first words to her, mouthing them silently.

Thank you.

Both men loved Anwyn, permanently, irrevocably. The way every person in the world needed to be loved.

So, yeah. Ella was part of a remarkable family here. She'd survive falling in love with a gorgeous Dom who was everything she'd ever wanted, who felt he couldn't have her, even if he wanted her, too.

It would be nice to know why, but she'd learned to recognize a certain look in someone's eye, when they were like a firmly planted tree. She could fight the person on it, but usually that just succeeded in driving him away and increasing her sense of rejection and failure. If change came, it would come from the root of that resolve, not from her trying to pull it from the soil.

She went to the assortment of bowls, and squatted so she could start spooning the contents of the tray into them. As she did, six of the cats came closer, talking to her and twining around one another. A couple were friendly enough to rub against her hips and ankles as she crouched there. Pausing to scratch a few heads, she glanced up at the black and white cat perched on the closest tower of crates. Barnaby had his own code. The short-haired feline only allowed Anwyn to pet him, though he gave Ella a regal, benign look as she spoke kindly to him.

It was a nice night, some stars visible in the sky, despite Atlanta's intense city lights keeping the bulk of them invisible. Ella thought about taking a trip to the beach where she could see way more of the night sky. Maybe she'd borrow Krista's car and go down for a couple days. Her landlord would be okay with that, she was sure.

Life went on, as it did. It might seem silly that she cared so much for Wolf after such a short time of receiving his attention, but time really didn't matter when it came to those things. At least not for her. If the heart and soul had been waiting for a certain kind of person to come along, then their presence triggered a well of love that had been a lifetime in the making.

She knew that, but she also knew something else, with equal certainty. What she'd told Lars had been truth, not empty bravado. Her heart broke, but it healed. She was strong that way. Everything would be all right.

CHAPTER TWELVE

As Wolf drove back from Don's place, he wanted to turn his fucking head off, but he needed to think about some things.

Like the abrasions on Don's neck. The guy had admitted to trying to strangle himself to death, earlier in the day. The closet door hook where he'd looped the belt, leaning against it, trying to let the pressure do the trick, had pulled free from the cheap plywood and the belt thankfully had loosened. He'd woken up on the floor of his seedy motel to the sounds of a couple screaming at each other next door, and a hooker working her John upstairs with rhythmic squeaks.

He'd lain on the floor and laughed hysterically. After that, he'd stayed on that stained, thin carpet for seven hours. Then he'd gotten up, rethreaded the belt through his pants, and come to Atlantis for his session.

He'd spent months in a hellhole after being taken captive on patrol. The bastard who'd been in charge of him had been a twisted fuck, mostly interested in breaking a white bread capitalist American mind. He'd succeeded.

Wolf had restrained Don, giving him the sense of helplessness and stress that could put him back in touch with his emotions, the bonds ironically helping to free him.

They'd choked him in the prison, jerked him in the air by his neck, and he'd connected to that in his choice of self-imposed suicide. So Wolf looped a belt around Don's neck, depriving him of air for short periods without causing him harm. He'd used the additional stimulus to walk him through death scenarios and how they connected to his stress. He'd pushed him until Don broke down and cried, letting the rage loose.

Wolf had been prepared for that. He'd trained with a Dom who specialized in auto-erotic asphyxiation, carotid massage, because they were two of the most dangerous BDSM practices out there. Maybe for a second, he'd been remembering how Ella had responded to that massage of her neck, the way she'd leaned into him, her eyelashes fluttering.

A Dom never, ever let himself get distracted. Especially during a therapy session. Even in the aftermath, for Christ sake. Don had been on his knees, head bowed, eyes closed, chest rising and falling as he tried to get his breath. In hindsight, Wolf knew he wasn't getting his breath; he was ramping up again, his mind seized by his demons.

Wolf had reached for a towel to hand him, and realized it was the last clean one. When he pressed the call button and began to speak, Don erupted from the floor and flung himself at him, screaming.

Wolf blocked him, but he gave Don points for getting under a vampire's guard. He'd clocked Wolf with the belt he'd left wrapped around Don's hand. The buckle had cut Wolf's face. It hadn't been superficial, like he'd told Ella, but since it was already fully healed, thanks to that perk of being a vampire, he had to make sure she didn't expect anything different.

Don had rushed for the door. In his head, he was escaping the prison, and anyone he met would be the enemy, to be struck down. Cursing, Wolf had shot after him with a vampire's speed, the cameras be damned. If there was anyone in the hallway, they'd be in danger.

He hadn't expected someone to be standing in front of the door, ready to come in. But that was his girl. As he'd said, if there was trouble to be found, she responded to it like a homing beacon.

His heart had nearly choked him in that second when Don was raising the paddle, something that could strike her skull with the force of a baseball bat.

Ella was quick on her feet, ducking and rolling away. If Don hadn't lost his footing, she would have been clear, instead of getting tangled with him. Then she'd held his arm at bay with every straining muscle, kept her wits about her and used their common interests to bring him back to himself. *Veronica Mars.* Of all the unlikely things...

Wolf shook his head. Another good thing about her timing—it had scared Don, how close he'd come to harming her. Wolf had him almost talked into voluntarily checking into the VA hospital again. He'd left him under Dieter's care while Wolf handled his next session, but when he went back to Don tonight, Wolf was pretty sure he'd manage it. If he didn't, he was moving in with Don and would work out the daylight stuff somehow. He wasn't giving up on him. Never mind the hypocrisy of it.

Which turned his mind to the other thing roiling in his gut. He kept seeing Ella's face, hearing her voice, as she spoke to Don. Telling him things that weren't bullshit platitudes but simple, difficult truths, laced with a genuine line of hope, acceptance and love.

As he'd watched Ella hold Don, a lump had grown in his own throat. What she'd said to the distressed man, she'd meant from the part of her soul that connected to... Wolf wasn't inclined to say something Bigger, though that was true.

It was a river. The river carrying all of them, that washed them clean, moved them forward, so they could see the great wide sea ahead. That river was made up of tears, one drop falling in amid all the others.

Tears even he had felt, pushing up into his throat, turning into jagged bits of glass. He wondered what would have happened if those tears had spilled out where Ella could see them, but he knew.

She would have looked up and seen the tears. The concern and compassion in her eyes, the softening of her mouth, they would have drawn him in.

When she'd lifted her hand to Don, she would have brought Wolf into a three-way embrace. He would have closed his arms around them, because he was big enough to hold them both, but he would have felt like he was the one being held.

Christ. He realized he'd reached Atlantis and had parked, without any idea how he'd arrived there. He slid out of the truck, slammed the door a little harder than intended, making the body rock. He marched into the service entrance. He vaguely recalled passing some people, but they moved past without engaging. D/s lifestylers picked up on social cues better than most people.

He stopped at the breakroom, snagged a bottle of water. Taking the admin hall, he passed the security hub, and sent the guards there a curt wave. He had forty-five minutes until the next session. He needed to clear his head, or he'd have to cancel it. No way could he handle a sub well with this kind of mental state.

He emerged into the alley. The black and white steely eyed tom sat beside a bowl, washing his feet. The tom and several other cats, lazing in defensible crevices or on lookout perches, watched him. They had a picnic bench out here, because a lot of staff members enjoyed spending a break around the cats. Pet therapy, Anwyn style.

As he reached the table, the cat sprawled on it gave way with a baleful stare. Wolf grunted at him and sat down on the tabletop, propping his feet on the bench, his knees splayed.

He fished out his cigarettes, and shook one loose. He dipped his head to the metal lighter he withdrew from his pants' pocket. One of the advantages of being a vampire was smoking wasn't addictive or a health risk, and it was a habit he'd enjoyed when he was a human. He saw no reason to deprive himself.

Well, aside from the expense. He'd been tempted more than once to snag some, using vampire speed, save himself some dough. Plenty of vampires without the means of the born vampire elite had no problem stealing what they wanted from humans. They didn't see it any different from humans taking eggs from chickens.

He wasn't there yet. Didn't matter that decades had passed since he'd been human; somebody worked to put every item on a store shelf, and stealing it without paying for it...that wasn't him.

He thought about Don, the way he'd raged against the things inside himself he couldn't seem to heal or accept. The nerves and darkness had formed an impenetrable wall between him and his wife and children.

"I broke her heart," he'd said, his voice as raw as his insides. "How do you figure your way back, Wolf? And when you know you can't, that it's way too late, how do you live after that? With that? How do you find a way to *want* to live?"

Shit, Don. It's easy. You become a fucking vampire, change your entire physiology so it rewrites your brain map. You become a different being, with just enough of the human you were to make you feel the guilt of it for the rest of your immortal life. But you no longer want to kill yourself, because vampires are too predator-centered to be self-destructive. See? Problem solved.

Wolf put the lighter back in his pocket, exhaled smoke. He'd changed into a loose linen shirt and a worn pair of jeans after the session. The fabric felt soft and easy against his flesh, a light breeze keeping things pleasantly cool.

He recognized the small rustlings of other cats moving on and off the crates, pattering over the top of the closed dumpster. The adjacent warehouse piled excess garbage next to it when it was full. The cats sometimes formed nests on the bags with softer materials in them.

Homeless people occasionally used them for that as well, burrowing themselves among the bags for the night. They were pretty much harmless, and the whole area was under a camera monitored 24/7. Logically, he knew it was a decently safe spot. Instinctively, it wasn't a place he liked a woman hanging out by herself. Particularly one.

He drew on the cigarette again and dangled his hands between his spread knees, smoke curling up from his fingers. "You know, you really shouldn't be out here alone."

He'd known she was here the moment he stepped out. He detected her breath, her blood, her haunting scent. She was sitting in an alcove provided between two stacks of crates, her hands looped over her knees as the cats twined around her. She was as unobtrusive as she'd been for the past few days, making sure she didn't impose any demands on him. She'd done nothing to contradict her apparent acceptance of the limitations he'd placed on their relationship.

He was the one who'd fallen short there. He'd told her he'd be her Master, within these walls. Yet he'd pulled back from that faster than a snapped rubber band, because one evening at a freaking carnival and he'd been thrown off balance inside the grip of her arms and legs, under that soft, shining smile and those far-too-understanding warm brown eyes.

He still had every intention of honoring his promise, to watch over and care for her, but he had to figure out how to do that from a safer distance, one that wouldn't give her—or himself—the wrong idea about their relationship. When he figured it out, he'd tell her how it changed the structure of the promise, and apologize if needed. Being a Master didn't mean getting to be a total dick, not without being sorry.

Especially when she was doing everything she could to respect him. Damn, she was good at self-control. The few times he'd checked on her, she'd been flirting, playing, laughing, helping. All the things she normally did. Yet he detected the tension in her shoulders, the forced levity in her voice, and knew it was an act. She was trying hard, for him. For herself.

Which made him want her ten times more, and it already felt like he'd been missing a limb since the carnival. When he took her body, he'd let himself entertain the idea of Ella being really, truly his. Her body his to enjoy, her special smile just for him, her attentiveness, as they worked at Atlantis, knowing they had a bond above and beyond that.

"There's a camera," she said in defense of her solitude. Her voice was muffled. "Is Don okay?"

"He's with Dieter. I'll stay at his place tonight." It wasn't an answer, but he didn't trust himself to respond to the question. Too much might spill out of him.

"I can take a few hours with him so you can get some sleep. He and I can watch DVDs together. Order a pizza."

If he couldn't get Don to check into the VA, he'd intended to have Dieter stay with him during daylight hours. But Wolf thought of how well Don had responded to Ella. He'd also watched them sit at the bar and talk on previous occasions, and Don did respond to Ella favorably. Particularly when every trigger hadn't been intentionally tripped by a rough therapy session.

During sunny daylight, watching TV with Ella, Don was more likely to stay on an even keel, partly because he'd be as protective of Ella as Wolf himself.

"Yeah. Maybe. Do you work tomorrow?"

"No. I can give my whole day to him if you need me to."

~

Not just because she cared about Don, but because she'd probably do anything Wolf asked of her. *Please go back inside*, she thought. *Please, please, please, because I can't keep acting like everything's fine.* She wanted to get up, run across the alley and throw herself in his arms, because she loved the way it felt when he held her, smiled. How he made that stern face while his eyes were so warm and inviting...

She'd stayed so quiet, not because she was hiding, not really, but because the chance to simply watch him was a need she couldn't deny herself. She didn't find herself surprised that he knew she was there all along, though. He noticed everything.

He would have made a hell of a cop. As she thought of him in a police uniform, her blood tingled, pretty much everywhere. Yeah, she'd convert to rabid badge bunny in about two blinks.

"Do you think...what do you think will help him? What will it take to fix him?" She remembered what Don had said. *Someone needs to fix it, so it makes sense.*

"You can't fix structural failure." Wolf spoke after a long pause. The words held a startling bitterness. "A bridge breaks, it takes everything down with it."

"I don't understand."

Rising from the table, he pinched out the cigarette, pocketed the butt. Because the streetlight was behind him, she only saw his silhouette, not the details of his expression.

"A lot of therapy is about coping, not cure. We call it accepting, moving on, making the most of your life. But for the worst of the worst, it can only help you anesthetize yourself. When you've failed everyone who counted on you, and there's no going back, there's no fixing it...a smart man knows that. Won't be bullshitted or anesthetized. There's no way to stop the pain. You've created hell for yourself while you're still breathing, and you deserve every minute of it."

The words were a rusty knife blade, tearing into hope, shredding it. The vehemence behind them chilled her.

"You think Don deserves what he's experiencing?"

"I'm telling you what he feels, that's his truth. It's tough as hell to fix the truth."

She thought it through. One of the usually more shy cats sniffed her toes, rubbed against the tips of her fingers when she extended them. Sauntering several steps away, he took a seat, giving her a cat stare. The tentative act of trust warmed her, pointing her toward a response.

"No. I'm not buying it."

Wolf turned, so she saw the outline of his shoulder, the cock of his head. He was dark as the night itself, but she could see him, feel his heat, even at this distance.

"If you thought he was this total shit not worth helping, you wouldn't. Which means he's a good guy who got messed up, lost his way. You're trying to help, and you're not the only one. He's coming to see you, so he's trying to help himself. He hasn't failed. He's still trying to figure it out, even if he can't see that. The bridge may be in bad shape, but it's still standing. You're not at the finish line until it's done."

He moved forward a couple steps. The light over the alley door had a cloud of nighttime insects dancing and swirling in it. Ella was glad for the illumination because she could see his face. She saw the tiredness, knew his spirit was sick from helping Don. She could help with that.

"May I give you ease, Master?" she asked softly. "You can take me to my massage room and have me do whatever you like. If you just want to lie in there and rest, with me close by, I can do that, too. I can watch over you."

"Isn't that my job?" he asked after a moment.

"Yes. After you use me how you desire. Then you take care of me. What do you want, Master?"

In a blink his expression changed, become a little dark and scary. A tremor went through her.

"I want to bury myself in you, Ella. I need to tear every cry from your throat, hear you beg me for everything I give you. I want to be the big, bad wolf."

Then the light died from his eyes, and his mouth tightened. "What I want from you isn't fair to your heart and soul, little girl."

"I am a woman, Master," she reminded him. "My heart and soul are mine to give, and they are yours. However you need and want them."

Shadows suffused his face, and he started to say something else. Instead, his attention swiveled sharply at the same moment Barnaby's ears flickered toward the pile of garbage bags next to the dumpster.

Ella was going to reassure Wolf, tell him it was likely just one of the cats burrowed down in the nest the bags formed, but then the movement became too disruptive to be made by a cat. She heard a groan, like someone waking up, followed by a raw smoker's cough. Immediately she relaxed.

"Perry," she mouthed to Wolf, and the tension left his stance as well.

Wolf had never met Perry, but she was sure he'd heard other Atlantis staff members talk about him. One of the homeless regulars in the area, Perry wasn't old, maybe forty, though a life on the streets had given him an extra decade in appearance. As he moved out of the cocoon the bags had provided him, Ella had to discreetly breathe out of her mouth. Even from this distance his odor reached her, and he smelled particularly foul tonight, a mix of old urine and food trash. Plus an acrid scent that suggested he'd been sprayed by one of the cats while he slept off his latest drunk. There was stale alcohol in the mix, confirming it. In comparison, Don was as fresh smelling as one of those mountain breeze detergents.

She wondered if Perry had overheard their conversation, and suspected not, since he often seemed in his own head, and looked as if he'd just woken up. Just as well. Not that she was ashamed of anything she'd said, but it had been private, meant for one man's ears. A man who, once he'd sized Perry up, was now back to giving her a look that said as soon as they had the opportunity, he was going to do exactly as he'd implied to her.

Which gave her every incentive to handle this as quickly as possible. "Good evening, Perry," she said. "You want some food? I can go into the kitchen and get you some."

"That'd be kind, honey," he said, coughing the gravel out of his voice as he shuffled away from the dumpster. "If you find a few bottles half finished, you could bring them out. Man's gotta have something to drink with his meal."

She shook her head at him, but gave him a smile to take the sting out of her response. "You know I can't do that. But I'll bring you food."

As Wolf studied the male, she saw he'd noticed the dog tags clinking against Perry's chest. Anwyn always showed compassion to homeless people, helping them with food, shower facilities, changes of clothing, and a trip to the local shelter if she could talk them into it. If not, she'd let them sleep in the alley under the relative safety of the security cameras, as long as they were kind to the cats and didn't repay her kindness by loitering around the front during open hours, begging her patrons for money.

Ella saw the brief flash of compassion and painful understanding in Wolf's eyes. Perry turned his gaze to him, a little wary, as most people were at Wolf's size and demeanor. Wolf shook his head.

"I'm not going to cause you any problems, man. A friend of Ella's is a friend of mine."

"She's a good girl," Perry responded. He swiped his hand across his nose, eyeing Wolf. "You got another of the cancer sticks?"

Yeah, she was definitely heading in. Even before she'd learned Wolf was an occasional smoker, she'd sometimes detected the tobacco scent on him. Fortunately, it wasn't a frequent enough habit that it detracted from his overall good smell, since she wasn't overly fond of cigarette odor. The smoke gave her headaches. If the two of them were lighting up, the food was a good excuse to absent herself.

She suspected Wolf would enjoy talking to Perry awhile anyway. He could come find her after his second session if he still wanted... what he'd described. She hoped he did, but she'd put it aside if needed.

"Sure." At Perry's request for a cigarette, Wolf drew out two and put them to his lips. As he did, he dug into his pocket for his lighter.

The homeless man eagerly moved his way. Ella sighed and rose.

Her intention was to cross between them, the shortest route to the door, and give them both a friendly nod before she disappeared.

Instead, a sharp feeling of foreboding bloomed in her chest, halting her in her tracks. Her head snapped toward Perry. Wolf still had his head down, lighting the cigarette. Ten steps away, Perry's eyes had gone needle sharp, back straightening like steel pipe as he reached inside his clothes with a practiced smoothness.

"*Wolf.*"

She ran at Perry as she shouted it, not sure what she knew, only that something was suddenly really, really wrong. The instinct to protect flooded her mind, leaving only time for action. And not enough even for that.

Wolf's head came up so fast, it looked like someone had hit the fast forward button on reality. She didn't see him move, but she was between him and Perry, and then suddenly she wasn't. She was surrounded by hard muscle, and the world exploded.

The roar of noise that hit her ears lanced through them, into her brain, the pain overwhelming. She was airborne. Thunder vibrated through her bones like a struck gong. Startled cats squalled. Metal, wood, and other, terrible, fleshy wet things struck her skin. She screamed when fire licked close, but then it was gone with a blast of terrible heat, a wind carrying them away from it.

She landed on the pavement with a grunt of pain and another frightened cry, snatched away when the breath was driven out of her. Wolf was on top of her, two hundred plus pounds of muscle forcing her into the unyielding surface. Yet she heard his expulsion of breath, and felt something she'd never forget – the twisting and shuddering of his body as things tore into his flesh. Things that would have torn into hers, if he hadn't been wrapped around her as tightly as a caterpillar's cocoon.

She cried out his name, or tried, but she couldn't breathe or move, a terrible, helpless feeling. They skidded, rolled, and then came to a stop. Wolf's arms were still locked around her, tight, too tight. Self-preservation had her pulling on him, to tell him she couldn't breathe, she needed to breathe. His grip at last loosened, and she was able to wriggle free of the weight of his limp body on her.

Everything was muffled, hard to hear, as if it were far away, but that heat and the choking smoke, laden with dust, told her otherwise. She put her shirt up to her mouth, which helped a little.

Wolf. Oh my God... The words were there but now couldn't make it past her clogged throat. He was on his face and not conscious, his nose and mouth mashed to the concrete. His back. Oh Goddess...he had no back, just a mass of blood. Already feeling weak and close to passing out, she came even closer to oblivion as she thought she saw his spine, glistening among raw, bleeding flesh.

He was dead. He had protected her with his life.

"Son of a bitch." When the walls of the club shuddered like an earthquake had hit Atlanta, Gideon was up and out the door of the meeting room, the rest of the executive security team, including Stan, on his heels.

"What was that? A fucking earthquake?" Stan demanded.

Gideon already knew what it was. It wasn't a natural disaster. He wished it was.

As they emerged into the hallway, they could already see the rubble ahead, the smoke. Fuck, the security offices and the accounting area, both of which had people in them. He snatched his radio from his belt to reach the front security desk, and got Rick.

"Don't evacuate until we know what we're dealing with," Gideon said sharply. "Don't let a single fucking person leave. Tell them this may not be over and they're safer inside. If they insist, make sure you log who they are. Otherwise, get everybody into the main bar area."

The main bar was in the center of the building, farthest from the danger of any other external explosions. It also had several exit options, once they knew which exits were clear.

Gideon wouldn't automatically assume this was vampire-related, but he would react to it like it was. Vampire hunters had the same M.O. as any other group trained to kill for a cause. Maximum body count in the smallest amount of time.

"You got it," Rick responded. "Nine one one's been called. Front entrance is clear and I had Tony go take a look. Looks like whatever happened originated in the alley."

The alley. Ella was in the alley. Plus all those cats Anwyn loved. If they hadn't all scattered before the blast, with that sixth sense for danger some animals had. But some didn't.

"Call the mobile vet Anwyn uses," Gideon barked. "We may need them."

"Already on it, boss," Rick responded. They'd gone over that in risk assessment, because the cats were part of Atlantis's family, too.

"Was Ella still in the alley?"

"Yeah. Not just her." Rick's voice was tight, making Gideon's heart clutch with dread. "Wolf and a homeless guy. Perry, I think. It happened pretty quick after he showed up."

Gideon exchanged a glance with Stan. They skidded to a halt with Stan's two other guys when they hit the wall of smoke and dust. Building materials were piled at their feet, wiring hanging and sparking from the torn ceiling.

Well, at least they knew the side door wasn't booby trapped for any responders, since the door wasn't fucking there anymore. Then Gideon felt Anwyn's touch, a riffling of air from her passing, and knew she'd joined them, heading out into the alleyway at faster-than-the-human-eye speed. Which meant there must be a hole blown in the wall, concealed by the smoke, big enough for her to use.

She'd heard Rick's report in Gideon's head. She knew they couldn't let anyone get to Wolf before them. If Wolf was alive. Blowing a vampire into pieces was pretty much as effective as a stake through the heart.

"Get to the front," he told Stan. "Help keep everyone contained in the main bar, guard that front door. Have someone ready to direct the first responders. Leave Jonas and Nevin here to check the offices for wounded. They can radio you with a status to send back the responders and fire guys, for whatever they need to get the wounded clear. I'll get to the alley from this side."

Stan gave him a measured look, but nodded, sparing Gideon any of the sensible precautions about waiting for the first responders to clear the scene. He knew better than to waste his time. Plus, Gideon was counting on the police needing to do that before letting anyone into the alley. That would give him and Anwyn time to do what they needed to do for Wolf. With any luck.

Ella...Christ. He could get to Ella faster this way, too. He waited only as long as needed for Stan to head away from him, Nevin and Jonas proceeding toward the accounting and security offices. Then Gideon plunged into the smoke.

He used his speed, strength and enhanced third mark senses to avoid hazards and find the same hole Anwyn had. He couldn't move faster than a vampire, but he could move far quicker than an unmarked human.

He hated this fucking alley, especially at this moment, because the scent of blood that reached his nose recalled the night he and Daegan had found Anwyn here. Her body ravaged by rogue vamps, her skin already feverish and hot because they'd turned her even as they raped her.

He forced himself to focus on what was happening right now. The bomb had been a powerful one, taking out most of the alley wall of Atlantis, and blowing the dumpster into the wall of the vending machine distributor who was their immediate neighbor. Fortunately, it appeared to have damaged the outer wall, but not made it all the way through.

Gideon. Anwyn's voice in his mind, urgent. He headed toward her. He stepped over several body parts, just bloody meat, but he didn't look close. If he recognized anything of Ella, he might lose it. His toe hooked on a set of crimson-stained dog tags, and his heart stopped, until he remembered Wolf never wore any.

He found Anwyn on her knees, her face hard and set, hands on a bloody slab he realized with a sharp jab to the gut was Wolf. Next to him in a crumpled heap was Ella, her dark hair coated with a dampness that had turned the dust to mud. He worried that the wetness was her blood, but at least she was awake, and alive. Her clothes were filthy, torn, exposed skin coated with a white-gray film, making her unsettlingly ghost-like.

Then her eyes jerked to him, wild and wide. She'd worn green contacts today, the brilliant color jarringly out of place in this smoky, dust-choked world.

She mouthed Gideon's name, and the words came out as an unintelligible croak, either because her throat was choked with smoke and dust, or because it was burned. But she was sitting up and alive, so they had a bigger priority.

"He needs blood, now," Anwyn said. "Before we move him. He's still alive, but it's a close thing. Nothing fatal seems to have penetrated his heart, but it's vulnerable."

Yeah, hard to blast the skin and muscle away and not jostle the internal organs. Gideon forced his stomach not to turn at the sight and jerked up the sleeve of his shirt. Daegan might have something to say about it, because they all knew giving blood to a vamp who wasn't your Master or Mistress could cause some problems. However, Anwyn's expression was more Club Atlantis boss than vampire. She wanted Wolf protected, and truth, so did Gideon.

Ella made a noise and Anwyn looked down. Wolf was moving, reaching blindly, body shifting, shuddering. Ella had propped herself on one arm, and it was near his head. Blood was running from a cut in her upper arm. Wolf's hand closed over her wrist.

"Hey man, no. She's hurt." Gideon moved to separate them, as gingerly as possible, but Anwyn stopped him.

"He shielded her from the worst of it," she said. "She's got a few cuts. I think mostly she's suffering mild shock."

In her former life, Anwyn had been an emergency room nurse, so her "I think" held more weight than his layperson first aid training. Still, Gideon shot her a sharp glance. Anwyn met it with one that contained more than one message. There was no time.

Muttering a curse, he pulled off the Henley he'd donned over his T-shirt, since the club air in the offices was cold. He draped it over Ella's shoulders, shifting behind her to hold her trembling body, give her warmth. Wolf had his mouth on that rivulet of blood, sucking on it, licking it.

"Ella." Anwyn put her hand on Ella's face, drew those pupil-dominated her eyes to her. "Wolf needs some of your blood to live. Will you give it to him, here and now?"

Ella blinked. Her voice came out with sound this time, but a little off-rhythm, like she still couldn't hear herself. "Does he need a transfusion, or..."

She wasn't connecting why he was licking her arm like his namesake recognizing the proximity of a raw steak. But her willingness was real. Gideon didn't doubt that. If they'd been in a hospital, Ella would have donated blood to keep Wolf alive in a heartbeat. But no doctor would have allowed it until she was checked out.

This was the shit he hated, when it came to vampires. But even in this condition, there was no guarantee Wolf would take Gideon's blood as easily, and they had only a spare few moments before the EMTs would be on top of them.

"Just follow his lead," Anwyn said. They could hear the sirens, confirming Gideon's concerns, but she kept her voice even.

Wolf grunted, trying to lift himself up on arms that didn't really work. Ella, always the anticipatory sub, suddenly figured it out. Again, Gideon attributed it to shock, how she didn't seem to question that this blood transfusion was going to be administered orally. She stretched out, not too hard since she seemed like she needed to melt into a horizontal position. Curling herself like a shrimp around Wolf's head and shoulders, she brought her arm closer to his mouth.

She let out a startled cry when he struck at her forearm like a snake, piercing the vein with unsheathed fangs.

Hold, Gideon. It's okay. Anwyn put her hand on him to reinforce it, before he could jerk Ella back.

Gideon was leaning over Ella, so close to Anwyn leaning over Wolf that they formed a protective arch over the two injured. Her calm hand and order, along with his knowledge of how vampires worked, were the only things that overrode his instinctive response. Even then, he had to clamp down on it, because he'd seen too many vampires kill innocents before.

"Ella, place your hand on Wolf's face, speak to him," Anwyn said. "So he knows he doesn't have to be savage. He knows you're offering your blood willingly to him."

Ella's obedience was so ingrained that she followed direction, no matter that she was shaking from shock, and her pupils stayed dilated like saucers.

"I'm here," she said hoarsely. "I'm here, Master. It's okay. I have what you need."

Gideon tightened his grip on the girl. Anwyn's hand rested on one area of Wolf's round shoulder that hadn't been shredded. Now her fingers also curled inward, a stroke of reassurance. She dipped her head further to speak into Wolf's ear. A Mistress, totally in control, reaching out to a peer, another Dom.

"You are feeding from Ella, Wolf. Your little girl. Do not cause her harm. Ease up."

"Mine," he muttered, an animal growl that sent chills down Gideon's spine. Wolf was older than Anwyn and normally a lot stronger. Not so much at the moment, but he was also combat trained. Gideon didn't doubt he could still do serious damage, even unintentional.

"Don't...touch," Wolf said, a raspy snarl.

"I'm helping you," Anwyn said smoothly. "I'm not touching her, but you are. You need to have a care with her."

"Not...you. Him."

He shifted his gaze to Gideon, pinned him with that lethal stare. Just in time, Gideon curbed the instinctive reaction, to curl his lip and match him snarl for snarl. At Anwyn's glance, he instead lifted his hands off of Ella, albeit reluctantly. He stayed close.

Anwyn continued speaking. "It's Gideon. He is helping to steady and protect her. He's helping you protect her. Do you hear me? It's Anwyn. Do you know you're feeding on Ella? Wolf, do you know Ella?"

"Ella...Ella." By slow degrees, his grip on her forearm eased, and his drinking from her became less gulping and manic. But she wasn't going to be able to give him enough for them to move him. Not and survive it. Gideon was watching the girl's face closely, and she was already pale as a sheet. She could have internal injuries.

A vampire's life was often a violent one. Gideon had witnessed plenty of situations where a badly wounded vampire fed from a servant without endangering him or her, but they'd taken blood from a fully marked servant, not...

"Second mark, Wolf," Anwyn said. "I know you've given her the first. Give her the second mark so you don't kill her. Do it."

Wolf stiffened, his eyes rolling up, wild, uncertain. "She's yours, isn't she?" Anwyn demanded. "Or does she belong to someone else?"

His fangs, already out, bared in threat.

They were surrounded by plenty of wood shards that could double as a stake. Gideon's fingers itched to grab one. Just as a precaution.

Hold, Gideon.

Stop fucking baiting him.

Wolf might be only eighty something years old, but he was a scary-looking bastard, even this wounded. His pale gray eyes got that fierce white light look to them, promising death and destruction. The muscles of his face had altered so the predator was out front and center.

Gideon needed to get in there and offer his arm to Wolf, just like they'd intended from the beginning. He might resist, but he could die or drink. Gideon was betting he'd drink. He liked Wolf fine, but his Mistress was a foot away from that snarling visage. Nothing trumped that.

Except herself. Her expression was as cool and calm as the night she'd faced Gideon down for the first time. She didn't flinch. It was something he loved about her as much as it gave him *and* Daegan ulcers. Well, the equivalent of ulcers, since human servants probably couldn't get those, and a vampire definitely couldn't.

She'd been human and way more fragile that first night he'd met her, and he'd been just as much of a beast as Wolf was now. It had turned out okay.

The thought didn't do much to calm him, but at least they took up time. Fortunately, all of it happened in a blink, before Gideon's protective instincts would override even Anwyn's command.

Wolf surged up, just enough to drag his body halfway over Ella's arm and side, because her body was still curled around his head and shoulders. His arm moved stiffly, but he tunneled under her cheek, and turned her head. He might not have managed it on his own, but Ella accommodated what he needed. She lifted her chin, averted her face.

Even though Wolf hadn't revealed what he was to Ella, during sex almost all vampires liked to bite and mark that area, even when they weren't formally marking it. If they'd been sexual with each other—no brainer there—some part of Ella would know what he was wanting.

In the next breath, he'd found her throat.

When his fangs struck the artery, Gideon saw Ella stiffen from the pain, but he also saw her manage it. Her quivering hand moved to rest on Wolf's blood-stained head, his shoulder, an unspoken consent and welcome. Gideon saw her body ripple, her lips parting as Wolf gave her that shot of something more, not just a taking but a giving. The second mark.

There was no time for what-the-fucks or moral debate, he knew that, but hell...there was going to be fallout from this. A second mark would put Ella firmly inside the circle of the vampire world. And Wolf would be able to read her thoughts, speak to her in her head.

Shit and fuck.

Ella's eyes rolled back, and she fainted. It wasn't the standard reaction to a second mark, but since she'd just been through a major explosion, that last body stress had sent her into oblivion. Maybe by the time she woke, they'd have all this under control so she'd think it was a hallucination.

Wolf was drinking hard and fast now, as if he knew he could, but it was time to call it. Fortunately, neither Gideon nor Anwyn would have to be in the firing line to try and break that connection.

"He's had enough."

Gideon felt that gut-loosening relief he preferred not to admit to, but was undeniably there, when Daegan arrived on the scene of something that was far-beyond-bad shit. The male vampire squatted next to him, his hand on Gideon's shoulder, his other reaching out to brush a knuckle down Anwyn's face. Her gratitude and relief were far more evident, but she was a girl. It was allowed.

The Mistress of Atlantis shot him a look that told Gideon he'd pay for that thought later. He was okay with that. "We need to get him moved," he told Daegan. "Like, now."

"Before then. The first responders are here. We'll take him to Anwyn's rooms below, and Ella, too. She's safe for now and we can get her to the hospital later if needed."

"Wolf," Daegan said firmly, dropping his hand to Wolf's shoulder. "You've had enough. Don't drain your servant. Ella needs your care."

Apparently hearing it said by a vampire old enough to have clear authority over him did the trick. Wolf released Ella. In the next second, Daegan had gathered up the large male like he was no heavier than a life-sized balloon animal and was gone.

Anwyn quickly bent and put pressure on the wounds in Ella's throat. There'd been no time for Wolf to close them on his own, with the coagulants in his tongue. "I'll take her," she whispered to Gideon. "I can move faster. Stay here and handle whatever needs handling."

They could already hear the voices of the police and EMTs, coming through the smoke, calling out to survivors. Gideon needed to ensure they didn't see the security feed that had Ella, Perry and Wolf on it. Since they'd probably already learned there were people in the alley at the time of the blast, he needed to cover that story. All sorts of shit to manage.

The rest...well they'd just handle that later. Including Wolf's reaction when he woke up. The guy who refused to bind himself to anyone was going to find out he'd given Ella a second mark. And that Anwyn had made that happen, even when her servant had been right there, able and willing to offer blood.

Wouldn't that be a fun conversation?

CHAPTER THIRTEEN

She was in a jungle. It was oppressively hot, mosquitos whining around her ears so continuously it could drive her mad. His...his? His palms were sweaty on the gun, not because he was nervous, but because it was just that damn hot.

He had that feeling in his gut that today wasn't going to be a good day. Not that any day in this cesspool corner of the world should be considered good. He knew some people said when the weather was nice, it was pretty, all the green, the rice paddy fields, the cries of the birds. He'd let Eden itself fall off the edge of the earth for five minutes at home, even at the height of a humid Florida summer, his mother's iced tea wetting his throat, the sound of his dad cranking the ice cream maker.

There it was. Shit. That feeling, like some demon was drawing in a breath. He was yelling at his men, telling them to get down, get away, as thunder rolled and the jungle exploded in blood and fire...

This was the past. Yeah. It wasn't a jungle. The explosion had been in the alley. The alley next to Atlantis. Perry shuffling toward him, hand out for the cigarette, a grateful look on his face that twisted in Wolf's gut—*sleeping in cat piss behind a dumpster and not caring. I've been there.* Then came the change on Perry's face, suddenly not like a homeless person at all. A direct look, full of deadly intent, his other hand reaching into his clothes...

And the world exploded into blood and fire.

Ella. God, fucking hell...where was his girl? She'd run between them. She'd known a split second before he had, and she'd run between them. He thanked all the gods he was a vampire, because he'd been able to snatch her back, turn and run a critical three steps before the detonation. But was she okay? He'd landed on her.

He remembered blood.

"I'm fine. I'm here. It's okay."

He felt her hand on his face, those slim, impossibly small fingers. So delicate. All of her, so delicate. "Ella." He gripped her wrist with a fumbling hand, and had to bite back a vile curse at the pain that lanced through his back.

He was on his stomach on a mattress. Cool strips of something were across his back.

"It's healing, Wolf," Ella told him. "Don't move if you can help it."

He remembered blood again, but not the kind associated with injuries and explosions. Her blood on his tongue, in his throat, sweet, so sweet and rich, coursing through him, pulling him back from the edge. Christ, he could have taken too much, killed her. He needed to open his eyes, see her, make sure she was fine, but so much of his body wasn't listening to him. That was also too much like another memory that he didn't fucking like. Waking up in a hospital bed, surviving the unsurvivable, when death would have been so much easier.

"I need to move." He had to fight to stay in control of himself, not lose his shit. His words clogged in his throat like a shower of gravel mixed with sawdust.

"Your back is laid open like a can of tuna," said a brusque male voice he knew well. "The skin's knitting, but it's taking time. She could only give you so much. She's not a third mark."

No. Ella wasn't a servant at all. That geographical locator she didn't know about didn't make her a servant. She still didn't know what he was.

Though, considering he'd just revitalized himself on her blood, that might have changed. Time to get his mind unscrambled and figure out what the fuck was going on.

He doesn't look so good, but they say he'll be all right. Why won't they take him to a hospital? You know why. Just nobody has said it straight out, because they're hoping you didn't notice and won't say anything. Which, maybe you should do. Maybe it will make it more comfortable for him.

What the...?

"Ella." Anwyn's voice. "Go lie down for a bit. He'll be fine. I'll watch over him."

"Oh, I really don't think I should leave him. I mean, in case you need..."

"'S'okay," Wolf rasped. He opened his eyes, a major accomplishment without the help of a pry bar, and discovered Ella was sitting on a pillow next to the mattress. She had her fingers overlapping his. He saw bruises, a torn and bloody shirt. It looked like her face had been cleaned, since it wasn't coated with building dust like her arms and clothing. Her expression was creased with concern and stress, but since it all appeared to be focused on him, that meant she was likely okay. It filled him with a relief so strong it burned in his chest like acid. "I'm good. Go get some rest. That's an order. You look... pale."

"So do you. Of the two of us, I think that's a more alarming symptom for you."

He couldn't help it, she knew how to make him smile, even right now. "Go lie down," he said, as sternly as he could manage. "I'll come find you."

She seemed dubious about the idea of him getting up anytime soon, but when he spoke in a semblance of his normal no-nonsense voice, different emotions filled her face. She was wearing her green contacts. He was going to tell her never to wear contacts around him again. He wanted to see her real eyes, always. But the different color didn't mask the tears that filled them, spilled forth with honest relief. She put her hand on his jaw. "I should have known ordering someone around would be the first thing you'd be able to do."

He detected a snort of laughter. Gideon. He managed to look past Ella and see the male, standing beside his Mistress. The laughter had been grim, though, and the male's blue eyes weren't laughing.

Wolf's mind was working better now, and other things were coming back. While it was a relief to push back the nightmares of his past resurrected by this explosion, they were being replaced by disturbing, present-day nightmarish possibilities.

He held those thoughts to himself, though, as Ella made it to her feet with Gideon's help, the man supporting her underneath the arm. Ella kept one hand on Wolf until the last possible moment, slipping from his jaw to his neck, to the point of his shoulder. She didn't say anything further, but her eyes said plenty.

"Go take care of yourself," he said. "I'm good."

"Okay." But she looked at him for an extra moment or two, some puzzlement in her gaze, as if she was picking up two different messages from him. Then he realized he still had her other hand.

He needed to see her clean, so he made himself let her go. "Stay nearby," he said. "But care for yourself."

"All right, Master," she said softly. Then she turned away with quiet dignity. She looked up at Gideon and gave him a reassuring nod, but she pushed away from him enough to walk on her own. The effort obviously cost her. He'd seen spryer eighty-year-olds. Humans, that is.

"He prefers to be the only male touching me," she told Gideon. "Especially right now."

Memory flashed, him baring his fangs, wanting Gideon to get his hands off of Ella, a completely unexpected thought. Gideon had no designs on Ella. And Ella wasn't Wolf's, not like that. Though his gut called him a fucking liar.

Gideon's jaw flexed, but he respected her request. Though he stayed close and followed her, obviously picking up the same thing Wolf had. That she might not make it to wherever Anwyn was sending her without help.

"Did she get medical attention?" Wolf asked. He didn't like this, stuck on his belly like a legless crab, but the pain of his healing torso and upper thighs was starting to make itself known, promising him exponentially more agony if he so much as twitched. It would be a lot harder to remain in control if it escalated from a dull roar to a full storm.

"Yes. She's been tended. Right by your side." Anwyn wore what he'd seen her in last, jeans and a T-shirt, but they were dirty and blood-stained, too, her hair scraped back from her face and held with a clip. It emphasized the tense harshness of her features, even as she gave him a steady response, what he needed.

"She refused to leave you until you regained consciousness. Apparently, there is only one Master who can order her around when she's determined to have her way."

He managed a grimace. "Not always. She's a lot more stubborn than she seems."

Anwyn offered him a tight smile. "Noticed that, have you? Over time, I've learned that Ella is like a river."

Was it odd that Anwyn had used the same image he'd applied to Don's pain? But it was a good one. He told his BDSM therapy patients to have a visualization go-to, to help calm them, center them. His was running water, in forests. Creeks, rivers, streams. Not the ocean. Too loud and big. But a creek meandering through a quiet forest, that was different.

He remembered the creeks he and Newt played in, growing up. Building dams, rival forts for their toy soldiers, built on opposite banks so they could fire rocks at one another with small catapults made of sticks, string and old spoons. To distract him from trauma episodes, he'd rebuild those forts and mock battles in his head.

Unfortunately, as the pain built in renewed waves, his grip on the image slipped. Then he made the mistake of closing his eyes. The quaking in his belly spread along the fault line of his memories, and widened quick. He heard the high-pitched whining in his ears. No, damn it.

"How is she like a river?" he demanded. He needed something to pull him away from where his mind wanted to drag him. Explosions, screams...blood. Staring eyes. Eyes that promised him hell because of who he was, what he'd done to those he'd loved, to himself. He'd failed his grandmother utterly. Thank God she'd died before Vietnam, no matter how much he'd grieved for her loss.

Don't ever let your head get ahead of God.

Thankfully, Anwyn seemed to understand what he needed, even if it might be too late. "A river will flow up, under and around anything," she said. "Alter its shape, size, even location, no matter how large or immovable the shape seems. With all its rain, a big thunderstorm only adds to a river's strength and determination."

"Thunderstorm." Good metaphor for an explosion. Jesus... "Anwyn."

He had his eyes shut again, couldn't open them. He needed to open them. He sensed her reaching out, the movement of air before she'd make contact.

"Don't touch me," he said sharply. Fuck, he had to move, even though he knew he shouldn't. His arms tensed, hands bracing to push himself up, and pain detonated everywhere. But if he couldn't move, he'd fucking—

"Wolf, reach out to Ella's mind. Do it now."

He was too caught up in his head to question it. He did, and found her, right there. The calm place inside a storm.

~

Anwyn lived at Club Atlantis. The glassed-in penthouse on the top of the building, as well as part of the basement area, comprised her private lodgings. An elevator with a security code known only to a few provided access.

It was to the basement apartment that she'd taken Ella. By the time Gideon had arrived, after handling whatever needed to be managed above, Anwyn had helped her clean up some, checked her over for more severe injuries. Daegan had put Wolf on his stomach on the bed in the same room, tending to him while Anwyn checked on her. Ella was like a zombie doll, though her gaze clung to Wolf the entire time, her mind not capable of anything much.

Until she started to see those jungle images. It didn't make sense. It wasn't her who was the soldier...it was Wolf. But why did it seem so clear in her mind?

Not all of the strange, whirling thoughts seemed like hers. Maybe she had a concussion. But when Gideon guided her to a spacious bathroom with the gateway to bliss—a shower—she didn't care if she had a brain bleed. She wanted to be clean first. Suddenly she was way too aware of what was crusted on her body, embedded in her torn clothes.

"I've got it from here," she told Gideon. "Would you go back to Wolf and Anwyn, so I'll know he has all the help he needs?"

"Anwyn's got it," Gideon told her, his hand at the small of her back, a steadying touch Ella needed more than she wanted to admit. "Best for me to stay nearby in case you need some help. Traumatic events have a way of doing a loop-de-loop and coming back to hit you when the adrenaline wears off."

She opened her mouth to assure him she'd be fine and careful, and the thought got caught in a wave of...she couldn't describe it. She clutched the doorframe of the bathroom as Gideon shifted quickly to grab her. Her mouth opened on a rough snarl that was nothing like her.

"Don't touch me." Not because she didn't want to be touched... what was going on? It was like the jungle, the gun in her hands, but not her.

Gideon had steadied her anyway, but with a much lighter touch than she expected he would have used. He spoke with a calm authority that grabbed her attention.

"Ella, you're feeling what Wolf is feeling. Give him something else to think about. Nice, normal things. Push past it and focus on the bath. Think Ella-type thoughts. Help him find his way out of that pit. They're not your thoughts. They're his."

Yes, he was right. She had a way of intuiting what people thought or were feeling, but this was like she was standing inside Wolf's head, getting hammered by overwhelming feelings of fear, anxiety, rage, the need to act, to move, to kill. He was in pain. Goddess, so much pain.

"No, you need to stay here." Gideon blocked her way as she tried to spin and return to her Master. "You don't need to be beside him to help him, Ella. Your Master needs your help. In his head. In your head."

There was a sharpness to Gideon's tone that somehow reminded her of Anwyn. She could almost feel the Mistress's gaze on her, demanding she push past her own personal reaction and obey.

She took a deep breath, slowed things down. Calm. His thoughts, not hers. None of it made sense, but at the moment she'd take it all at face value, respond rather than analyze.

She'd never been in a jungle like the one she was seeing, feeling. What a terrible place, full of fear, fire and blood. Oppressive heat. She drew herself out of there, into the bathroom, squatting down to put both palms on the cool white and blue tile. Clean, like cold water. Following instinct, she drew her shirt off and then stretched out, putting her upper torso against all those chilly, clean tiles. She was still wearing her bra, but the tile felt so good against her upper abdomen, her arms, that she laid them above her head, elbows bent.

She toed off her sneakers, let the sides of her feet enjoy the same coolness. This bathroom, with all its tones of blue, white and silver, they were as far from that humid, violent jungle as anything, right?

That feeling that wasn't hers was evening out, receding.

Shirt. What was on your shirt?

Somehow, she knew he meant the pattern, not the other things she wouldn't think about. *Palm trees. A seagull. It was a Veronica Mars Investigations T-shirt. I wore it for Don.*

She fanned out her fingers on the tile. *Master... Am I talking in your head, or are you talking in mine?*

A long pause. *Both.*

Take your bath. Wolf closed his mind slowly, like a doorway shutting gently between them, so he wasn't giving Ella any more of his fucking nightmares. But she'd pulled him out of them, with nothing more than a visual of bathroom tile. It would have made him smile if he wasn't ready to kill someone. Someone sitting on a stool near him, eyeballing him with a blue-green gaze that could bring men to their knees. Most men.

He remembered now. *"Give her the second mark. Do it."*

"You had no right to do that," he said between gritted teeth.

"I didn't," Anwyn said calmly. "It's not possible for me to second mark someone for you."

He showed his fangs. "Don't be a fucking smartass."

"You'd be wise to watch your tone. It would not take much to finish what the bomb started."

His gaze snapped toward the shadows, saw nothing. That didn't mean anything. He should have realized there was another vampire in the room, but his radar was a little scrambled. He was just about done lying down for this shit, but then Anwyn leaned forward, her hands clasped before her, and what was in her expression gave him pause.

Some regret, along with firm resolve, tension, and a great deal of caring.

"We had no time. You needed blood, and you'd fight taking anyone's but hers. I didn't want you to kill her by accident. She still doesn't know what you are. If you don't want her to know, then don't utilize the second mark. Keep your mind closed to her, now that you have your wits about you."

"Well, that horse is kind of out of the barn, isn't it?"

Anwyn shrugged. "Ella is very open to the non-mundane. She

would accept that it was caused by concussion. One of you temporarily had more access to the parts of the brain that permit telepathy."

"That sounds like total horseshit."

"More than you being a vampire? One who has second marked her, such that you can now read her thoughts and give her access to yours when you permit it, so that you can speak to one another without opening your mouths?" She cocked her head. "It makes kissing and talking much easier."

"Did you catch being a total wiseass from Gideon?" he said. "Respectfully."

He tossed that word out to the air, to wherever in the room Daegan was. He wanted him in his field of vision, but realized making demands wasn't likely to go well. And they were pointless. Even if Wolf was at top strength, Daegan had the strength to dice him up anyway.

He didn't think Anwyn was lying to him, but he also thought she'd had her own reasons for having him second mark Ella. He'd address that later, when he wasn't helpless on this mattress.

"Wolf."

He realized he'd drifted off. "Hell. Sorry. What?"

"It's okay." Pissing match over. Anwyn's concerned face was in his vision. "Here, drink some of this. You keep licking your lips, and they look dry."

Cold water tasted better than anything, other than Ella's blood. Anwyn had provided him a straw so he didn't have to lift his head. He drained the glass, rattling the ice at the bottom. Anwyn fished out a piece and ran it over his cracked lips. The intimate act was done with maternal kindness. Hell, he really must look like shit.

"What do you remember?" she asked. Suddenly he recalled there was a vital reason Daegan was in the room. Intel. Atlantis had been attacked.

That helped, because it gave him a focus, a way to help, to defend what was important to him. They needed his memory, every detail of what had happened.

He went back to the alley again in his head. He realized he'd recognized it a second before it happened. Just like in Vietnam, that sudden inhalation, like the bomb sucked in a breath before it detonated, but that pause gave you nothing, because by the time you heard it, it was already too late.

Like a lot of things about that time, the gunfire, the bombs, they were things he never wanted to experience again, that he actively avoided if he could. Not because the noise alone disturbed him, but because of what came with it. The screams, the blood. The death of friends, comrades.

Newt.

All the parts of him scattered. Because yeah, there *was* time to do one thing, if you were the one who'd accidentally triggered the damn thing. Throw yourself down on it so your last act on earth was a noble sacrifice, not a fuckup.

Then came the pointlessness, as the best friend who'd watched you die, who'd carried your blood and flesh on his fatigues until the end of the op, pulled it all together and moved onward to kill people he didn't know, in a country he hated because it wasn't home.

Newt should have gotten married, had kids. He deserved to get old. Since the little bastard had loved his fried foods, Wolf liked to think of him indulging that love for decades, then dying of a quick and painless heart attack while sitting on his porch, watching his grandkids.

Wolf was getting pulled off track, back toward that dark, whining fiery place. So he thought of cool tile. Went back to the bathroom in his head. Though he kept that door between him and Ella closed this time, he could see, hear and feel her and her thoughts, without her being aware of his presence.

"Give me a moment." He spoke with stiff lips.

"Take your time." Anwyn's voice, in the distance.

Ella had removed the rest of her clothes and was in the shower. There was a seat in either corner of it, and she sat on one, being pummeled by the spray. She had her head tipped back, her dark hair sleek over her shoulders, down her back, and over one breast. Her generous bottom flattened against the smooth fiberglass, her fingers pressed against the edge on either side of her thighs as she let the water wash away dirt and blood.

She was humming, he realized, humming to be sure nothing filled her head about the explosion. She had a variety of techniques for keeping stress at bay, which told him just how much stress she routinely handled.

Multiple jobs. And she lived...where the hell did she live? In a retrofitted garden shed with two rooms, a bathroom and a bedroom, with a standing clothes rack and small chest of drawers for Ella's belongings.

The renovated shed had a window A/C unit and a space heater for winter. Ella loved the place. It was in a friend's backyard, a garden of trees, shrubs and flowers. There was a small vegetable plot that Ella helped maintain, so she shared the fresh veggies with her friend.

A scattering of wind catchers throughout the landscaping made music in the middle of the night. Whimsical sculptures created graceful shapes that she imagined came to life in the full moonlight and danced. Especially the big concrete pig with floppy ears and a silly face by the stoop at Ella's front door. A pot of pansies was next to it right now. Pansy the pig. He'd bet good money that's what she called the lawn art.

He'd told her he'd look out for her within the walls of the club, but the club had always been her haven, where she was safest. It was outside those walls where she really needed someone in her corner.

He could know a lot about her now, with barely any effort. But not everything. A third mark would give him everything, down to her soul.

He closed that door firmly, and then closed the door to her mind. Well, cracked it. He let the song filter through, to keep the sounds of battle and fire at bay, and finally managed to answer Anwyn's question.

"Perry. He was wired with the bomb. And he wasn't a homeless guy. Before he detonated it, the whole act fell away. He was focused, steady. On mission."

"You're awake again."

The deep timbre had him stiffening, and he realized Anwyn was gone. Shit, he'd phased out again. How long ago had she asked her question? Told him to take his time?

"Anwyn had to return to the upper level, to answer more questions from the police and fire departments."

"What is she telling them?" Wolf couldn't figure out where Daegan was in the room. The Invisible Man thing was getting on his nerves.

"The part of the truth that works. A man posing as a homeless person blew himself up. She doesn't know why, though she assumes he was a tragically unstable person with a moral objection to the club's purpose."

"Could that be the truth?"

"You or Gideon are in the best position to know. You because you were there; Gideon because he knows how vampire hunters attempt to kill their prey. What do you think?"

His back was feeling better. Snarling pain instead of screeching pain. "I think I want to sit up."

"Not stopping you."

He assumed that was the male's way of saying his back had healed enough for that to work. Or that he didn't give a shit what Wolf did, as long as he answered the question. Either way, Wolf would take it. He levered himself up with a grimace, biting back a groan, and made it to a seated position, though he broke into a sweat doing it and felt lightheaded, more than a little nauseous. "Shit—"

The plastic bin was shoved under his mouth as a mix of blood and bile came up, and some other stuff he had no idea how to classify. Vampires didn't throw up much.

His back caught fire as he heaved, and it took everything he had not to faceplant when he was done. After he managed it, hung steady, he heard a tab being popped. A six ounce can of ginger ale was brought into his vision as the bin was taken away.

"Thanks."

"Don't mention it."

A chair was moved, and creaked as Daegan sat down in it. A pair of long legs in dark slacks adjusted, ankles crossed. Wolf looked up carefully, even the movement of his eyeballs hurting.

Daegan wore a fitted black T-shirt over the slacks, and the definition in his arms showed the elegant musculature of the warrior Wolf remembered from the first and only meeting until now.

"You still prefer Daegan, right?" he asked. "It's been awhile, but I remember you don't like the lord title."

"He actually prefers Mr. X. Cancer Guy. Deep Throat. Sometimes Princess Nefertiti, but that's only when we're role-playing and he wins the toss to wear the cute outfit with the tutu."

Gideon had returned. Daegan shot him an unfathomable look. Pretty much every other word Gideon spoke was a wise crack, so Wolf wasn't surprised to see that the male had come up with that one by rote, not a desire to be funny. There was still no humor in his gaze, his jaw set.

"Anwyn?" Daegan asked.

"She's okay. I'm keeping my mind in touch with hers. No warning signs yet. She's majorly pissed off, but I don't think the full impact has hit her yet."

As Gideon turned his gaze to Wolf, Wolf saw the hunter was out front, the Atlantis staff member taking a back seat. "So Perry was a plant from the get-go."

"Yeah," Wolf said.

"How was it missed?" Daegan asked, his far-too-still gaze on Gideon. Gideon didn't squirm under it. He didn't fear this male, not that way. They were brothers-in-arms, something Wolf also recognized. Gideon was sifting through just as much what-the-fuck-happened on this as Daegan.

"Since Perry's been around for over a year, this was a long-run mission," Gideon said. "I'd say there's a vampire hunter cell that's been scoping us for a while. Long enough to know how compassionate Anwyn is with those cats, and with the homeless people in the area. Perry infiltrated their community. He didn't come every night, but randomly every few days, enough to be seen as a regular. And yeah, we're not stupid. We ran his name."

Gideon's lip curled. "The truth is always the best cover. He *was* a vet, honorably discharged, some PTSD and TBI history. Fell off the map with his family a couple of years back. I'm betting if we look, we'll find out a family member or a friend got taken as some vampire's annual kill and he figured it out. Or a hunter saw him living close enough to the edge to make him a good recruit. Gave him a new purpose. To silence the crazy voices inside."

Wolf knew about those crazy voices and the need to find a purpose, anything, to quiet them. "Sometimes when you get back, all you want is to find something to fight. He found something."

A shadow passed over Gideon's gaze. "Yeah. But he and whoever he's working with couldn't figure out a way inside. Our security was too good for that, and they wouldn't risk Perry being outed by raising suspicion."

Gideon looked at Wolf. "How often did you go into that alley for a cigarette?"

"About every other time I'm here."

"Yeah. I suspect what they decided is that they'd at least get one vampire and take out some of the building, with the primary intent being to send a message to the vampire owner. They want to drive her out before this becomes more of an enclave for vampires."

His lips tightened. The flash through his midnight blue eyes revealed a churning inferno of cold rage, the helpless mix of fear and fury that came from knowing how close they'd come to an even worse scenario. "Anwyn feeds those cats, too," Gideon said. "If they could have gotten you both out there, with the right timing..."

Daegan's face was stone. "They did not. But we will address it."

The cold tone told Wolf someone's world was about to be burned down, and no one better stand in the way. He had to admit, he was right there with Daegan and Gideon on that.

He hadn't wanted to be blown up, but if the alternative had been Anwyn, or Ella being hurt worse, he'd rather be smeared across the alley like peanut butter now. But since he wasn't, he was all for being part of the plan to eradicate future threats.

"It takes a lot of effort and planning to take out just one vampire," Gideon said thoughtfully. "Everything can go wrong and get fucked up pretty fast. Vampire reflexes and instincts are just that touchy. He couldn't take the risk of wearing the explosives every night, just on the off chance that Anwyn and Wolf might be out there at the same time. Whereas Wolf was easier to predict. And there are so few vampires, relatively speaking, that taking out one at a time is still considering winning a major battle in the war.

"We learned...the vampire hunters learned," he corrected himself, with only a slight tightening of his jaw, "from the attack on the Council Gathering. Too many hunters were lost that night. One by one is the better strategy."

Daegan nodded, his expression now thoughtful. "Still, it does feel..."

"Like a piece is missing," Gideon finished. "That's what my gut says, too. These guys might not be done. There may be an even longer game in process. But we've got another immediate problem. Their M.O."

Wolf's brow furrowed. "What do you mean?"

"When I was with them, there was one rule hunters followed

above all others. Never where an innocent could be hurt. Innocent being defined as a human unaware of vampires. Servants of any mark level were guilty by association, because they knew. But now someone has decided they don't give a shit."

"Which means they might keep coming at Atlantis," Wolf said slowly. "Or maybe Atlantis is just the first. They might target other businesses where they know a vampire is involved. Places where a vampire's attention would be more distracted."

There were plenty of made vampires out there who ran businesses, or worked in them. Fuck, Wolf knew a vampire who taught at the community college, night classes. Another who loved kids, despite the inability to have her own, and ran an evening daycare.

He shared that, and Gideon shook his head. "The community college is a risk, but I'm thinking the daycare is safe. As bad as this is...what I'm thinking..."

"Is that Atlantis was targeted because of what it is. They realized public opinion wouldn't be as easily roused over a hit on this kind of business," Daegan said.

"People aren't going to worry about their own safety if the target appears to be some kind of sex club," Gideon agreed. "Or they were just able to more easily rationalize hitting us, but either way, yeah. I don't think it's a coincidence they went after the place that had top notch security, instead of one of the more unguarded places you just mentioned. Fuck. There's too much we don't know. We're guessing."

Gideon turned away, rubbing his hand over his face, the back of his neck. "Damn it, Daegan."

"I know," the male said. "We need to locate the cell and eradicate them. Until we do, Atlantis needs to close, for the safety of the patrons and the staff."

Now Wolf better understood the nature of Gideon's frustration and anger, the way he and Daegan kept exchanging the significant looks. They were worried about Anwyn. Because they knew what Atlantis was to her.

And losing that could conceivably lose Anwyn everything. Because of her seizures.

Vampires did not trust easily. Made ones probably trusted each other more quickly than born ones, but even made ones took their time about it. So when Anwyn had asked for a sit down with Wolf in her office months ago, he'd been wary. Until he realized she'd decided to trust him with something almost no vampire would.

~

A few months ago...

"Wolf, I need to ask your help."

"Anything," he responded, and meant it. The time he'd spent at Atlantis had only increased his regard for her.

She gave him a tight-lipped smile.

"Beware of empty platitudes. They can get you in trouble." She took a breath, tapped her fingers on the desk, as if giving herself a key few seconds to decide for certain this was a conversation she wanted to have. Or needed to have. "I wasn't turned willingly, Wolf. It was a group of rogues, and my sire was a schizophrenic psychopath. Literally."

Her expression remained steady, only the stiffness of her posture and mouth hinting at the cost of saying the words without inflection.

"Jesus." It didn't take much to imagine how that had gone. Sex and violence rode hand in hand for vampires. That helpless rage an honorable male felt, the desire to tear to pieces any of his gender who thought that was okay behavior, rose, but he tamped it back down. She didn't need that right now. But he couldn't keep some of it out of his voice. "Anwyn. I'm so sorry. Tell me they're dead, in the most painful way possible."

"They are dead." She nodded, a precise, controlled movement. "Thank you. As a result, I have seizures. Gideon helps me manage them. The mental part, he can of course manage that from a distance. When he's physically present, that helps me channel the physical response, mitigate it enough that he can help with it, get me down to our apartments below so I don't hurt anyone."

Her tone remained businesslike, brisk. As a fellow Dom, he knew how hard it was for any of them to admit weakness. For vampires, it was ten times as hard as that, so he kept his expression blank, attentive.

"Gideon will not say so, but I know he would very much like to join Daegan on his...business trips, on occasion, particularly the more challenging ones where he might need backup. To make that happen, I need to find someone else I can trust to help me keep my seizures under control, physically, when they happen in his absence. It would also be...reassuring, to have someone here who can match my strength, when Gideon is present and Daegan is not."

He was flattered, but he was also protective. She was a fledgling. "It's the height of foolishness to tell another vampire what you just told me."

She didn't flinch. "Any other vampire, yes. I don't think I've misjudged you. Have I?"

A reminder; fledgling she might be, foolish never. She'd be happy to hand him his ass, at least verbally, if he tried to patronize her. Another reason he liked her.

"No, you haven't." A slow smile slid over his face, but he also straightened. "I'm honored to have your trust." He paused. "I assume that another reason you're giving it to me is if I betray that trust, your, ah, silent partner...?"

"Will eviscerate you in ways that will make you long for the tender mercies of Hell."

She also said that part without blinking, even-toned. She wasn't given to hyperbole, so he took her at her word, though that wasn't why he'd tested that ground.

"Good."

She sent him a wry look. "Why am I always surrounded by overprotective males?"

"Because you are a female beyond compare, Lady Anwyn."

Since then, when Daegan was gone, Wolf was at the club or in the basement quarters guest room during most of the evening hours. When Gideon and Daegan were both gone, Wolf stayed at the club 24/7.

Though Wolf didn't dwell on the significance, he did now. She'd trusted him enough to let him see her at her most vulnerable. In the vampire world, there was only one interpretation for that. Gideon and Daegan, having this conversation with him in the room, only underscored it.

Someone trusted you that much when they thought of you as family.

He loved her. If the seizures got so bad she lost even more control over herself, it would not be good. But beyond that, the idea of this kicking the foundation out from under her...no. Just hell no.

"No. That's not right."

At his emphatic declaration, Gideon and Daegan brought their attention back to him. Wolf shifted, quelling the desire to wince at the screech of protest from his healing skin. "We don't give into these guys. No closing the doors."

"I don't disagree with you, man," Gideon said. "But we can't endanger people here, either."

"He has something in mind," Daegan said, watching him with those still eyes.

Wolf set his jaw. "I do. And if they *are* running a longer game, it will help. We call in reinforcements they won't expect."

He went over it with them. After their initial surprise, and him addressing a myriad of legitimate concerns, they had a consensus. He asked Gideon to find him a phone he could use, since his own had been demolished. Though he still felt like shit, Wolf wanted to get this done. It felt good to do something other than feel blown up, his head a mess, his soul scrambled between the traumas of the past and present.

He made a couple of calls, set some things in motion. While he did, he kept that door cracked, listened to Ella breathe, hum. Live. He thought of her soft flesh and cool tile. When he finished this, he was going to her. But for now, he would sit inside the remarkable calmness of her mind, checking on her, even if he wouldn't give in to letting her know he was there. Maybe he would do what Anwyn suggested, tell her the ability was some weird mind opening shit that had been induced by the blast, and wasn't there anymore. Then he'd close the door, never to open it again.

Maybe.

CHAPTER FOURTEEN

Anwyn stood in the alley. Dawn was coming. The firemen had gone, the police as well. The full security team had been called in, and James was on his way back from New Orleans, because the story had made national news. No surprise there, with the salacious mix of a bombing and a sex club.

Even if it hadn't made the news, James would have known quickly, because most BDSM clubs would have been alerted through the strong networking in their insular community. One of the places he'd intended to visit in New Orleans was Club Progeny, to check out their security setup. It was where he'd surprisingly met someone, special enough to extend his visit there from a vacation to a temporary work sabbatical he'd more than earned.

She knew when she finally checked her messages tonight, she'd have all sorts of communications from club owners across the country. While they'd sensibly want details, in case the threat was specifically targeted against BDSM clubs, they'd primarily be offering help. Their world was a very supportive one, especially in times of crisis.

She wanted to be strengthened by that thought, but the reality was setting in. With all the media exposure that was only going to build in the coming days, no member whose identity needed to remain private would be coming anywhere close to the club. Not until he or she was certain a reporter wouldn't be at the front door, shoving a microphone in their face.

But that wasn't the primary problem. She knew it, because of the ache in her lower belly, because of the way it goaded those gremlins in her head, threatening to send them into a full, screaming fit. She knew Gideon was staying close, tapped into her mind, ready for it if she had one of her violent seizures. Neither he nor Daegan had wanted her taking point with the police or firemen, adding to her stress. But it had helped distract her, focusing on their questions, deflecting without raising their suspicions.

Plus, she was the owner, damn it. This was her place. She'd built it. She'd made it happen, through unimaginable obstacles.

Then she'd been attacked, turned into a vampire. She'd thought she'd known what being helpless meant. She hadn't. But thanks to Daegan, Gideon, and her own will, far stronger than she'd ever realized, she'd persevered.

But now there was this. Pretty strong evidence that vampire hunters knew where she was and that there was at least one vampire in her employ. Hell, they might even know about Daegan's presence here, though she thought that less likely. Daegan had ways of blending and eluding detection, even from the heightened senses of other vampires.

She thought about Perry. She'd shared chuckles with him over the antics of her alley cats. He'd petted one of the friendlier ones, and she'd taken that as further proof he was okay, a good guy. Her heart had gone out to him, especially when he'd talked in faltering tones about losing his family, about being on the street, because he couldn't handle being in a house for longer than a few minutes.

The bitch of it was, Gideon had found all of that was true. Which made his duplicity all the more shattering and unnerving. A good man, willing to sacrifice himself because he considered her and Wolf something to be exterminated.

She'd watched the video, seen the benign but wary expression of a homeless man fall away, replaced by a determined suicide bomber. They hadn't turned the tape over to the police, saying that the camera in the alley had been out for the past week and they hadn't yet repaired it. She doubted the detective had bought that, but he had little choice to do otherwise.

She'd also seen the flash of relief in Perry's gaze a blink before the screen went dark, explaining why he'd chosen a method that guaranteed his own death as well. Unfortunately, Gideon thought that death wish had proved a useful tool. He didn't think Perry was a lone wolf. Neither did Daegan. Whoever was behind this wasn't done.

"Damn it." She picked up a chunk of asphalt, slung it away from her. It flew the length of the alley and hit the charred dumpster with a hard clang. She would have scared the cats, if any of them were here. Which they weren't. Would they come back? How could they? The alley was a mess, her shelters for them gone, demolished or scorched.

Cats being far more intuitive than humans, she hoped the majority of them had scattered when Perry rose from the trash. But she knew at least two or three hadn't been as clever. They'd learned to trust humans too much. The humans here at Atlantis.

She swallowed, remembering a portion of a black and white body, a tail, before Gideon had put his arm around her, cupped her head. She was strong. Strong as hell, but she'd pressed her face into his broad shoulder, taking the comfort, because the sorrow and rage were more than she could bear.

It hadn't been Barnaby, but one of the wild oats he'd sown before she got him fixed. His son, Tidwell.

"Barnaby's a survivor," Gideon had whispered to her. "He bugged out before the blast. I'm sure of it. He'll be back."

She wanted to believe that, but wouldn't feel at ease about his wellbeing until she saw him again.

Once the firemen had cleared the scene, she'd collected the parts of Tidwell and the other two cats into a box. Gideon had helped, and then given her a handkerchief to wipe away the tears that squeezed through her defenses. She'd take Tidwell and his brethren to a park she knew, and would bury them there, where there were birds and butterflies, whispering grasses and warm sunlight.

Goddamn it. She reached for her anger with both hands. It was preferable to the alternative. Why was life so goddamn uncertain? For animals, for people, for vampires. Yeah, it was important to live in the moment because one never knew how quickly life could change to shit, but knowing that didn't make it any better.

The gremlins' dull roar sharpened into individual voices. Her left arm twitched, made her body jerk. She couldn't get too angry, and even when she did, she couldn't try to block those gremlins. That made it worse. Resistance was a form of force, akin to violence, and they fed on anything like that.

She breathed deep, in, out, even as she wanted to rage and scream. Another form of helplessness, the inability to express her emotions the way she wished. But she knew how to control herself. That was a strength, a victory.

She turned her thoughts to other things. More positive ones. Ella and Wolf were alive. So were the three people injured in the accounting and security offices.

Anwyn recalled the section of the video tape when Wolf had grabbed Ella, surrounded her, run three steps before the blast had lifted them. If he'd been human, he'd have been knocked insensible instantly, his arms and legs flying open like a rag doll's, releasing his precious cargo. On the slow-motion replay, she saw his eyes were open, his mouth creased on a scream of pain as the bomb ripped into his back. But he never let Ella go. He landed and rolled with her still protected by that tank bulk of his body. One arm around her back, the other over her head, as much of his body curved around her as possible. Most of Ella's bruising had come from being landed on by the solid-muscled male who'd saved her life.

Good men were like that. Which was why Daegan and Gideon were with her now. Gideon had barely left her side since the explosion, though he'd given her space. Daegan had been in her mind through everything. As soon as all the responders left, he, too, had joined them, putting his arms around her and holding her close. She'd felt his wish, as well as Gideon's, to take any pain from her and, in the face of that impossibility, give her comfort however was needed.

After she threw the chunk of debris, they drew closer to her, though neither of them touched her. She was grateful for that. Simmering with so many things, she was likely to explode like that bomb with the trigger of a single touch.

"They know we're here now," she said dully. "No one is safe."

"This was a discussion I never wanted to have with you, *cher*," Daegan said quietly. "I have once again brought pain to your door."

"I should have dug deeper on Perry. I've gotten soft," Gideon said bitterly. "I saw a vet in pain, with a true sob story, and didn't remember that my story wasn't much different. It was what made me a vampire hunter, damn it all."

Anwyn rubbed her brow. "Stop it, both of you. Life sucks sometimes. Beginning and end of it. I don't have time to hold your hands and make you feel better about the situation, because I'm too pissed about it myself. If there were no bad guys, none of it would matter. But bad guys happen. I get it, and I'm going to be okay with it."

"We know that," Gideon said. "But we hate for you to hurt and not know how to make it better, which always makes it feel like our fault."

Her lips curved, despite herself, and she shook her head. "I know. I feel the same way when anyone I love is hurting."

"Like us?" Daegan's gentle tease helped, and she cast him an indifferent look, though it took effort.

"You two might be included in that group. Depending on the day. You're not trying to handle me too much through this, and I want to appreciate that. I'm not capable of it at the moment. I'd like to tear somebody's guts out with my bare hands."

She walked a few steps away, bowed her head to think. They let her do so. Daegan had marked Gideon directly, not long after she had, so he could talk to the other male directly in his head, rather than using her as a conduit. It allowed her to ponder things without the disruption of spoken conversation when she needed the silence.

As much silence as she could obtain when her head was inhabited by so many demons.

She took a breath made of sharp glass, tried to dial that surge of rage back, settling the cacophony. She hated when they giggled like schoolgirls. "So, we're going to shut it down. Hell, it will have to be closed anyway until we clean up this mess and do repairs. Once you find these guys and take care of them, we reopen."

She had to believe it was an isolated cell, as Gideon had projected to her. Most vampire hunters didn't believe in killing innocents. Unless the whole network had upgraded their strategy, in which case it would never end, and she and her club would never be safe.

"The Council has given me leave to hunt them down and dispatch them," Daegan said. "They will also alert all other vampires, not only in this area, and particularly the business owners, so that everyone will be on guard." He shifted his glance to Gideon.

"They'd like me to show my loyalty by giving you intel," Gideon guessed.

"Yes. But I will not ask for it. I will find them on my own."

Gideon stared at him. He'd been propping on a pile of rubble but now he straightened, though it was as if he bore the weight of the world on his shoulders. "No. This wasn't just an attack against vampires. It was against everyone here, so these are fanatics who don't care how many innocents get in their way. That's everyone's enemy. I'll help you hunt them."

"If you wish to provide me information, then that is your decision. But I will hunt them on my own."

Gideon's brow creased. "No."

Daegan held his gaze. "This is not up for debate. It will take a cost from your soul, vampire hunter, that I find unacceptable."

"You and Anwyn are my soul. I lost mine long ago."

"You didn't lose it at all. It found its home with us. Gideon." Daegan came to him, put a hand on his tense shoulder. "You may argue, we may fight about it, but my decision on this won't be swayed. I want you here, with Anwyn. This will be difficult for her."

"Don't use her to keep me on the sidelines." Gideon shrugged him off irritably. "That pisses her off as much as it does me."

"I am not using either of you. You are my family, and I will care for you as I know best." Daegan's voice became steel. Intractable. "I do not draw many lines in the sand between us. This is one of them."

Gideon looked toward Anwyn. She met Daegan's gaze, and he let her in his mind, let her see it. This wasn't a manipulation. This was how he felt, which meant it was how it was going to be. As he said, he didn't hold the Master card over both of them often, but when he did, no force in the world would change his mind.

So she turned to Gideon, who looked like he was deciding whether to go a second round with Daegan or not. To head that off, she took his callused hand. "I'm going to go with Daegan on this one," she said, surprising both men. "I need you here. Wolf is a good backup when the two of you hunt together, but this time...it's a little much. He's right. On both counts."

Gideon frowned, but she squeezed his hand. "You handle everything thrown at you, because you worry if you relax that vigilance, if you ever let anyone take any part of the load, you'll be less than you think you should be. I know that feeling. I knew that feeling. That was me, when all this started. I had to learn the hard way that there are people in my life I can trust to help carry me when I need it. Don't learn the hard way."

"It's the only way he learns," Daegan commented dryly. When Gideon looked toward him again, Daegan was close enough to brush a knuckle along Gideon's jaw. Though Anwyn knew the two men loved one another as fiercely as they loved her, it was a rare tender gesture between the two males, one that she could see unsettled Gideon.

"You are my family," Daegan repeated. "Give me the honor of doing this, knowing I can make one thing in your life easier."

"Well," Gideon said after a long moment. "Since I serve the two most demanding vampires in the history of fangdom, I guess I can take a day off."

But his expression remained pensive. "You know, when I made the decision to stop hunting, I met one last time with my guys, the ones who worked directly with me. Just felt like I owed them some type of closure, an understanding of what I was doing, even though at the time I wasn't all that sure myself. The conversation turned ugly, real quick. They said I was a traitor to my species."

He gave a half-laugh, looked away. "One of them told me I should just give it up, go be some vampire's fucktoy, since that's what I was going to end up being anyhow."

"Gideon," Daegan said. He put his hand on his face, his thumb on his throat, under his chin, lifting his face with the assertive touch of his Master. "Look at me."

Gideon did, but he also put his hand over Daegan's wrist, a strong grip. Anwyn stood beside them, her heart in her eyes. "I know what I am, Daegan," he said. "I don't agree with their assessment."

"Then why did you say it?"

"Because you're right. This would mess me up. Because at this point, we don't know what drew them here. It could be me. Maybe that was why they decided it was okay to kill 'innocents.'"

"That's too much to put on yourself," Anwyn said.

"Not if it's true." Gideon sighed and looked at Anwyn. "I get that you don't want to deal with us doing the guilt run, so don't take it like that. This is straight out something that I believe is my responsibility. The homeless guy in the alley is a technique I taught to my team, one that worked for me. I took three of my kills that way. Even if it's not my original group, it's someone who learned my tactics from them."

She pressed her lips together, not wanting to go there, even in her head, but fortunately Gideon turned his attention back to Daegan. "I know, even with that, they don't have a shot against you. But if they're good enough to see you coming, if you can manage it..." His hand tightened on Daegan's forearm. The vampire's eyes darkened, but he nodded.

"They will never feel a thing. And if they do see me coming, it will be as painless as I can make it."

"Thanks." Gideon dropped his grip and Daegan eased back, two warriors giving one another space. Gideon looked toward Anwyn. "They hurt Ella and Wolf, and your cats. The bomb could have killed even more people, so they didn't do the right thing. I'm bound to you two, and that's where I want to be. But it doesn't mean I stopped understanding the other side of it. And the fuck of it all is, it's all related, on both sides of the coin, isn't it?"

The anger in her wasn't willing to go down that road yet, but she understood what he meant, even as he said it aloud.

"When you see someone go after the people you love, or you feel like it's your job to protect people, and something other than 'people' are attacking them, that seems pretty straightforward. There's not always a lot of things that are straightforward, especially to a veteran like Perry."

Now he managed a wan grin. He picked up her hand, lifted it to his lips. She spread her fingers over his stubbled jaw and cheek as he nuzzled her palm. "Then someone like you comes in and mucks up the clearness," he murmured. "And a guy finds that's not always a bad thing."

She moved into his arms and held him. He held her back, just as tight. Daegan stood close by, his strong presence a reassurance, but she noted he was studying her with a brooding look, as if he had gone down another road in his head.

"It will be okay," she told him. "I will be okay."

"No, you won't."

She knew the tone. He was going to heap additional precautions on her, protect her further. She was not going to be handled with kid gloves. That was not the best way for her to get through this, and he should know it by now, they both should...

She opened her mouth to sharply tell him just that, but he'd already heard it. Her thoughts tended to project through Gideon when her gremlins were restless.

Daegan's hands landed on her shoulders. "Enough," he said mildly, in a way that wasn't mild at all. "Atlantis is your dream, and not just yours. Anwyn, I am very wealthy."

She blinked at the segue, arresting the forward motion of her frustration. "Okay. I've never asked to be your kept woman, but it's nice to know I won't be homeless anytime soon if my club goes under."

A tight smile touched his lips. "I suspect you will never capitulate to being anyone's kept woman. My point is, I don't need a great deal, but I have accumulated much."

"I'm so asking for a Ferrari for Christmas," Gideon said.

"Only if I can force it up your backside," Daegan said pleasantly. His fingers flexed on Anwyn before she could get impatient with them. She usually loved their banter, but it had been a superbly shitty day.

"Since I have precious little to use my money on," Daegan continued, "I am going to use it on this place. Bomb detectors, weapons scanners, more security. I can do whatever is necessary to secure Atlantis so it can be safe for you and your employees, while remaining operational. This will become the safest place in all of Georgia."

She stared at him. He was serious. "Setting aside all the discussions you and I will have on the allocation of your resources and my desire to be an independent businesswoman, even all that won't eliminate our biggest blind spot. Human security won't know exactly why this place is more at risk than others. The vampire angle gives the attackers an advantage."

"Yes and no." Daegan nodded to Gideon. "It was Wolf who started us down this path."

"Yeah." Gideon cleared his throat. "Wolf fully supports the idea of you reopening as soon as possible. He called several pals of his. Wolf was special ops when he was in the military, and apparently these buddies are, too. And they're vampires."

At Anwyn's widened eyes, Gideon smiled. "He suggested you bring them here to handle and train security on the upgrades while we get everything back up and running. With this new plan of Daegan's, they can take us to that next level. Wolf just needs you to give him the green light."

"Okay." She rubbed her forehead again, the wheels turning. "So I get word out to the membership. Keep them apprised of the clean-up and re-build, and assure them of the new security and privacy measures."

"Exactly. They will come back, because there is no club like this, Anwyn." Daegan tightened his hands on her shoulders. "You've made it a place they love to be and will want to support, especially when we assure them we are addressing all security problems."

She looked from one man to the other, then back. Slower. That ache in her gut, it was easing, and it allowed a flood of other things in. Because she was a practical woman, she could catalog every reason it would be a bad idea to re-open, especially with a target painted on their backs. As such, she'd been putting a lot of energy into reconciling herself to the end of her club for the indefinite future.

Finding out there was a damn good chance they could make it work unbalanced her enough it perversely almost launched her right into the vat of those gremlins. Even though they were receding with a dull buzz, the fuel for their fire gone.

But Gideon was there in her mind, steadying her, and she held onto that. With a sudden crumpling of her expression, she flung herself into Daegan's arms, and reached out to bring Gideon into the three-way embrace. "Thank you," she whispered. "Thank you so much."

But she lifted her head and pinned Daegan with a look. "I am paying you back. Or you're becoming a legal partner."

"I will have more than enough money left over, even helping you," Daegan said. "But you're correct, you will pay me back. Just not in money."

He could be a demanding lover, so he meant that, even if right now he said it to tease her, make her smile. She wasn't sure she could summon a real one right now, but she was far closer to it than she'd been only minutes ago.

"You know, you are wrong," she said, looking at both of her men. "Much as I love this place, you and Gideon are my heart. I couldn't bear the idea of someone hurting either of you."

"Unless it's you," Gideon said. "If I remember correctly, you wield a mean cane."

"She didn't think you needed intervention for those little taps that don't even leave bruises," Daegan said pointedly.

"They don't leave bruises because I'm a third mark and I heal," Gideon retorted. "That's like saying I can break your arm and it's okay because it mends in an hour. Give me your arm, let me prove it."

Daegan fended him off, shoved him back. But then he just as smoothly gripped Gideon's T-shirt and drew him close again with one arm, Anwyn with the other. Picking up on the change of tone, Gideon wrapped his arm around Anwyn's waist, the three of them linked. She put her head down on Daegan's chest, and Gideon pressed against her back.

"Neither of us will tolerate someone hurting you," Daegan said in her hair. "I will find this cell and deal with it. And after we reopen and things are on a good footing, the three of us will go somewhere to enjoy a real vacation. Kauai on a moonlit night is unforgettable. Particularly in an open-air bungalow with a wide hammock strung beneath the stars. And yes, there will be wi-fi so you can check in on things," he added to Anwyn. His expression tightened. "I wish you would go to Savannah for a few days, handle the repairs from there. This is going to be a media circus for the next week. It will help if the club owner is not available for comment."

She set her jaw. "I can't leave it this way. I'm with Wolf. I want those doors open again as soon as possible. I won't know how soon until I get started on the cleanup and get bids for the rebuild, but only the hallway was damaged, which means we lost the security annex and our accounting office, a storeroom or two. The main club doesn't need any repairs. Once Wolf's team is here, and you all deem it safe enough, we could conceivably re-open while the repairs are ongoing during the daylight hours."

She took a breath. "Ella had everything in place to do Burlesque night. I'm going to schedule that for the re-opening, make it a celebration, a club re-launch to help spur member confidence. Let those bastards know they didn't do anything to intimidate us. All right?"

Daegan was listening, studying her as she spoke. She knew the idea was sound, but also knew he was considering other things, things that delved into her state of mind, which might be masked under adrenaline and anger, so even she wasn't entirely sure what she could handle right now.

Which was the part she hated most. She was a Mistress, but she'd surrendered to Daegan, acknowledged him as her Master, and she gave him that respect. Which meant the final decision was his. If he didn't see it in the best interest of her welfare, he wouldn't agree, and nothing would dissuade him. Never mind he was almost always right when he disagreed with her. It was the principle of it, not being able to make the best judgment call for her wellbeing herself.

"It's merely proof of what a formidable woman you are, *cher*," he said with gentle reproof, picking it up from her head. "Not an indication of the opposite. You are the steel cable that doesn't realize it has a breaking point."

"Yeah, but if the shoe was on the other foot, and you didn't have full decision-making abilities, I doubt you'd take it any better."

"He'd just decapitate everyone who got near him and sit brooding among all the severed heads," Gideon said.

Daegan sent him a glance. "I'd prop my feet on yours, vampire hunter. It's big enough to be an excellent footstool."

Despite the teasing, when Daegan met Gideon's gaze, Anwyn could see what was going on, at least in Gideon's head. He was in her corner on this one, and that lessened some of the frustration. To this day, Gideon didn't fully understand the significance of it, how Daegan trusted his opinion, but Anwyn did, and was glad for the bond between them.

Because some days, dealing with these gremlins...it got so tiring.

Daegan's attention came back to her, his eyes darkening. They'd drawn apart during the discussion, so now he put out a hand and she came to him once more, letting herself be held. He put his lips to her forehead. "The gods only test the mighty, *cher*. You handle them well, you and Gideon, but if I could go in your head and slay them, I would."

"I know." She pressed her head to his shoulder, her fingers curled in his biceps, and felt Gideon behind her, covering her back once more. Always.

Daegan spoke against her skin. "Very well. I know you wouldn't be happy leaving the oversight to someone else. Plus, I'm certain you will have some design changes you want to implement, since they'll have to rebuild the wall anyway. I have a condition, however."

"Yes, I'll be careful. Yes, I'll keep Gideon close at all times."

"Do not presume too much about my directives." His dark eyes dwelled upon her, giving her a twinge of sensual trepidation. His mind reached out, covering the same terrain with a sensation that was a mental, intimate caress.

"My condition is that, when we do get to Kauai, I pick out the swimsuit you wear on the beach. Something with a great deal of string involved that barely holds your beautiful breasts. Gideon has to be blindfolded while you wear it, able to only imagine what you look like. Until I let him see you through my mind. Or use his hands and mouth to appreciate you while I take him from behind, with the beach breezes on our skin and the music of the ocean playing for us."

Both of her men responded to the idea, just as she did. Simple, clean physical desire was a good feeling at the end of a night like tonight. She caressed Daegan's jaw as Gideon's hands closed on her waist and hips. She leaned back against him, enjoying the heat and hardness pressing in on her.

"That's the kind of deal the Mistress of Atlantis can live with. Since it's close to dawn, I wouldn't mind if we continued the discussion in the place I most want to be with both of you right now. Our bed."

After she exhausted herself in the pleasure of taking and being taken, it would be easier to dream without nightmares.

She'd bank herself in the peace, knowing what she truly valued most in the world was as close as her heartbeat.

CHAPTER FIFTEEN

Ella moved through a quiet club. Atlantis was empty. Earlier, Anwyn had sent everyone home, telling them she'd send out a communication, letting them know what the plan was, after she determined it herself. The only personnel she saw was the occasional familiar face from security, ghosting through to do a check.

Gideon had told Ella that Anwyn preferred her to stay tonight. "So she can make sure you're a hundred percent," he'd said. "We'll make up the guestroom for you."

"No need to do that. I'll just bunk on one of the couches on the main floor. I'm comfortable up there."

She'd done that before, when closing had run late and Anwyn hadn't wanted her traveling home on her own at those hours. Gideon didn't try too hard to talk her out of it, and Ella understood why. Anwyn would need support tonight in ways that didn't really need a fourth wheel sharing their living quarters. Club Atlantis was Anwyn's soul, and someone had wounded it deeply. Ella didn't want to hamper Gideon or Scary Guy's intentions to care for her however was needed.

After everything that had happened, and dealing with all the unanswered questions still in her head, Ella was actually glad to have a little breathing space herself, in the place she felt most at home. She stood in her favorite spot, the second level dance floor. The first level had the biggest dance floor, and the more party-like atmosphere. The music pumped out with sultry beats, maintaining the right level of excitement and anticipation, which carried over into the adjacent public play space, where she'd watched Wolf do the scene with Grenadine.

But the second level was where the dancing and the play spaces were more intimate, even more intense. The kind of Dom/sub interaction that happened in these smaller spaces might be as exciting as watching grass grow, but only if the viewers didn't understand, didn't know the complicated language happening in the slightest give and take between Dom and sub.

The bar on this level was a piece of art, with gleaming curves of wood and mirrors that reflected interesting pieces of the people moving before it. The bottles lined up along the back were lit from behind, a dark rainbow of hues. Unlike the bar downstairs, this one only served non-alcoholic drinks, an acknowledgement of the type of scenes that happened here, and the audience it attracted. People who needed to be fully in command of all their senses so everything was experienced the way it was meant to be.

She loved being able to see Atlantis after closing hours, but then, she'd live here if she could. She liked her little place, a converted garden shed cottage in Krista's backyard, but this was where everything felt right, balanced. Krista ran the neighborhood grocery where Ella did bike deliveries, and had rented it out to Ella in exchange for Ella handling her yardwork and landscaping, as well as her house cleaning. Krista had health problems that made such physical work an almost insurmountable challenge. With her grocery store's small profit margin, she didn't have much left over to hire domestic help. So the arrangement was a good trade.

Ella went to the music system, made sure it was turned down to a reasonable, one-person level, and selected the playlist she wanted. Then she returned to the middle of the floor as "Feels Like Home" by Chantal Kreviazuk came on. Perfect, though the message was more about a person being home, rather than a place. As far as Ella was concerned, Atlantis was a person. Even if her uncooperative mind imagined an actual person as the lyrics filled the air.

Well, she'd kind of helped it in that direction, hadn't she? As she wrapped her arms around herself, she glanced down at what she was wearing.

She kept a couple changes of clothes in her locker here, including pajamas for the occasional overnights. Tonight she'd slipped on a pair of soft pink shorts, but she hadn't pulled out the tank top that went with it. Instead, she'd done something kind of bad.

The staff locker room was co-ed, though whoever preferred more gender privacy could go change in the spacious men or women's bathroom facilities. She'd gone to Wolf's locker and stood before it, debating, biting her lip. She wasn't trying to pry. She'd seen him open it before, knew all he kept in it were clothes, and he didn't lock it. Before she could doubt herself too much, she opened it.

If he'd only had one shirt in there, she wouldn't have done it, because she didn't know if he'd need the shirt tonight. She wasn't really sure where he was. Gideon had said he was fine and had the care he needed. At the time, he'd been up to his eyeballs in everything else, so she didn't push it, knowing her urgency was solely motivated by her need to be near her Master, assure herself of his wellbeing. The vision of his ruined back was too fresh in her mind.

He'd said he'd come find her. The message there was "Stay away until I call," which hurt, a little, that unspoken command. It meant a Dom didn't need her "right then," which should have been fine. But she couldn't help wondering what it would be like to be with someone who, even if they didn't actively need her for something, wanted to be sure she was close by, connected to him.

There were two T-shirts, one black and one white, in his locker. Since the white one was thinner and she never saw him wear something so lightweight, she suspected it was meant to go beneath more formal clothing.

She'd seen him dressed up once before. Christian Grey night. She grinned at the memory. There was a mix of reaction to the popular book among those in the D/s lifestyle, but they'd all had a lot of fun with it that night. Even those who had issues with the book had to admit that suggesting all the Doms show up in "Christian Grey costume" had been an extremely good idea.

The Dommes had been just as down with it. Chantal's severely fitted white shirt, slim black tie and pencil black skirt with heels and a bolero jacket had been memorable. But mostly Ella remembered Wolf, his charcoal gray suit jacket defining his broad shoulders, the tapering of the slacks over his taut ass and hips. The soft fabric of his silver-gray dress shirt had molded his upper body, coaxing a woman's fingertips. Particularly the couple times she'd seen him unbutton the jacket and slide a hand in his pocket, the movement folding the coat away from his upper body on that side. He hadn't worn a tie, leaving the shirt open at the throat. His cuff links had been shaped like handcuffs, and he'd worn a stick pin with three small porcelain red roses.

At one point he'd shrugged out of the jacket to handle a flogging. He'd removed the cuff links, put them in the pockets before taking off the coat. Then he'd carefully folded back his shirt sleeves. His fingers had flexed over the task, the shirt creasing over his arms. The whole look made Ella fully understand the term *suit porn*. He couldn't have riveted attention more if he'd stripped down to the skin.

Now she vividly remembered the faint outline of the undershirt beneath the dress shirt. It became more visible each time he threw the whip and the shirt fabric stretched over his powerful body.

She'd smelled a hint of Wolf's unique scent when she'd opened the locker. Now, as she ran her fingers along the cloth of the white T-shirt and lifted the garment to her nose, her eyes closed. She inhaled Wolf's aroma fully, and her decision was made.

She slipped the T-shirt off the hook and put it on. Most guys' shirts stretched tight over her ample breasts, but his chest was so broad, she had room, her nipples rubbing the fabric in a pleasant way as she moved. The shirt fell to mid-thigh. Because of that, she changed her mind and left the pink shorts and her underwear behind, folding them up neatly on the bottom of his locker to retrieve them when she brought the shirt back. She told herself she wouldn't wear the shirt all night, just a little while, to help her feel a little more... calm.

She'd kept it to the periphery of her mind, the unreal idea that someone had tried to blow her up. Her, Wolf, the club. She couldn't get Perry's face out of her mind, that last second of his life. He hadn't cared if the bomb killed them, a person she thought she knew...and liked. He had a dry sense of humor, a gentle touch with the cats that wasn't feigned. That was the part hardest to understand. His affection and friendliness had been genuine...until the moment it wasn't.

Those two, irreconcilable truths gave one an unsettled, bottom-falling-out-of-one's-world feeling. How could you trust anyone after something like that? A façade so good that it couldn't be fake was far scarier than anything she'd ever experienced.

She was trembling, she realized. Her arms had tightened around herself, as if she was holding herself up, and her knees were wobbly. Despite everything else he'd had on his mind, Gideon had obviously been worried that this would happen. He'd given her a steady look before letting her go upstairs. Touched her face and said firmly, "If you need me, call. You know the extension. I'll pick up. These things sometimes hit you worse later."

Everyone else had gone home because they had someone. A spouse, a mother or father. A sibling. She had friends she could crash with, but no one who would understand tonight in a helpful way. Gideon obviously did, but she would be damned if she'd take him away from Anwyn for even a second.

She wrapped her Master's scent around her, used it like she would Wolf's voice, his presence, to collect herself. "Iris" by the GooGoo Dolls came on, so she closed her eyes, swayed to it. And moved on to another unsettling puzzle.

She thought of the moment when she'd asked Wolf if she was in his mind or he was in hers.

Both.

In the basement apartment, two rooms away from Wolf, she'd heard that word in her head as if he'd spoken aloud to her. Bits and pieces of the alley aftermath were coming back to her, and most of it revolved around him. How he'd licked her arm, and then his teeth had sunk into her flesh. Canines she'd always thought were extra sharp when he teased her with them seemed even sharper when he'd bitten her, so savage. He'd gripped her in that brutal way that had bothered him so much the night he'd accidentally hurt her wrist.

It had hurt, but differently from the impact of the explosion. This was desperate need, and she'd laid her own trembling hands over his forearm, fingertips curling and uncurling against his corded flesh, letting him know it was fine, she was here, she had what he needed.

She went further back, to the changes she'd noted in Anwyn after she'd been assaulted in the alley, and she put them side by side with Wolf. The almost unnatural steadiness of their eyes, their erotic appeal, heady as a drug when you were close to them. Had she missed it because Anwyn was already an incomparable Mistress and beautiful woman? And Wolf was one of the most mesmerizing males Ella had ever met.

Throughout her life, Ella had cherished every forward step when she learned things she hadn't known before. No matter how bad things might seem, there was so much about how the world worked that she didn't know. Bad things happened. That was a given. What would be worse than that would be discovering that there was no mystery, no hope or anticipation for anything different.

Master. Where are you?

She stood still, as if concentrating was the trick to it, but a long moment later, she knew it wasn't. Whatever deliberation he'd been doing, about whether to answer her or not, once he made the decision, he appeared in her mind as easy as breathing. She could feel him. It sent a thrill through her, from her head to the tips of her toes.

I'm here.

She opened her eyes, and found that was true in more than one way. Standing at the edge of the dance floor, he was watching her. The GooGoo Dolls sang about a person being broken, and yet wanting to declare who they were. That was her interpretation of the lyric, at least in this significant moment.

He still wasn't a hundred percent. He stood with one hand braced on the back of a barstool. The way he held himself told her he was still in some pain.

Yet she'd seen the damage to his back. Anwyn had said he'd needed Ella's blood. Her blood had healed him. The fact he was standing, with no obvious blood or bandages wrapped around him, just confirmed what she was just now putting together.

He wore only a loose pair of cotton pants, Jamaican style, and it was a very good look for him. When his evening sessions were over and he lingered at the club to watch, this was often what he wore. Usually he put a loose, natural fiber shirt over the cotton pants, but he was shirtless now, and barefoot. The drawstring of the pants was loosely tied, keeping the garment low on his hips. She knew the intent wasn't provocation. It was to avoid putting anything against his tender back, but he was a beautiful male, so having more for the eye to appreciate was a bad thing, never.

Then she reached his eyes and she forgot about that. Those lightning-colored eyes were all over her in his T-shirt. She pressed her lips together on the apology, simply stood watching him.

"Dance for me some more," he said. "Like you're dancing for yourself."

She'd been swaying to the music. She closed her eyes again, because that was the way she preferred to dance for herself. She'd imagine whatever setting she wished. Tonight it was the here and now, the shadowy dance floor, bathed in the dim safety lights.

She could detect the lingering scents of the people who'd been here. Members were good about cleaning up after themselves, so it was rare the combination of scents was unpleasant. The cleaning staff came during the daytime to give it freshness, but she liked the aroma this time of night. Perfumes, sweat, arousal.

As she detected hints of candle wax, the crispness of liquid nitrogen, she realized the nuances of those scents were more distinct to her than usual. The effect of a near-death experience, she expected. She had to be imagining it, but there'd been at least one blood play scene, and she thought she picked up that faint metallic odor.

She heard him move, the pad of his feet over the dance floor. He was moving around her, watching her. She'd evolved from swaying to turning, twisting upward, reaching for the sky, arching back, liking the feel of her hair brushing against his shirt on her back. It was so soft. So soft against so much hardness, when it was stretched over his muscles and resilient form. He'd saved her. Formed a wall between her and destruction. Destruction had torn through him, and yet he'd held fast.

Kept her safe.

She was breathing faster, her chest aching, and she gave herself fully to his order, dancing for him. She turned, let her hair flow out. Leaped, crouched, spun. She was alive. Alive, because of him. She threaded her fingers through her hair, ran them over the contours of her face, paused on her throat, her fingers becoming his in her mind, then down, molding her shoulders, her upper arms. Her forearms brushed across her breasts as she spun again, and then she let her arms extend like ribbons from a spinning wand, a magic wand, where energy rippled out and turned death and darkness to starlight and eternity.

I'd give up forever to touch you... The first lyric of "Iris" lingered in her mind, and she gave thanks for the songwriters who knew how to put feelings to just the right words, to add to a moment like this, make it even more powerful.

She'd left the club. She was a bird now, soaring, dipping, landing on water, feeling the spray, watching the moonlight turn to fragmented ripples. In a blink she was a girl again, standing in that water lapping on shore, lifting her hands to the moon.

She stilled, because he was in front of her. His hands slid over her lifted ones, thumbs following the creases of her palms as he curled his fingers around her knuckles. He moved down to her wrists, so slim he could hold both in one hand, but he kept going, a slow glide down both her bare arms, down, down, down. Her arms trembled as she kept them up, staying as still as he wished her to do.

Slowly, she lifted her lashes, looked up at his face, so close to hers. The sensual lips, slash of cheekbones, those glittering, dangerous eyes. She saw it all, and knew her heightened senses weren't because of her almost dying. The energy pulsing from him had always been this, a creature of the shadows.

"I knew you were something marvelous," she whispered. And then she said it in her mind. What she knew had to be the truth.

Vampire.

His eyes darkened. Her hands lowered to his chest as he moved his to her shoulders. He gathered her hair with one hand, a slow twist that bared her neck. Tightening his grip, he made her tilt her head, exposing that area further. When he dipped his head, brought his lips to her flesh, he followed the pulsing artery up to her jaw. Every nerve focused on what he was doing. There was so much power in this kind of stillness; she thought it could shockwave the world out of existence with nothing more than a sigh.

His tongue teased her flesh, and she swayed, but it was all right. He had her now, his strength holding her, and it took so little, he had so much of it, even diminished from injury. His teeth grazed her. With them pressed against her, she felt the exceptional sharpness of his canines, felt them lengthen, thicken, as they unsheathed.

She felt his hunger, and knew she could feed him.

In the alley, it had been all adrenaline and survival, no pause for trepidation. She didn't feel trepidation now, exactly, but a rippling anxiety that she answered by tipping her head further away, toward the hand holding her opposite shoulder. She put her lips on his knuckles, an act of obedience, homage, and acceptance.

He growled, something that turned her to liquid, and then he bit down, that spike of pain followed by something in her that embraced the impalement. Only this time, her reaction was even stronger than what she'd felt in the alley.

The climax shuddered from deep within her womb and expanded outward, a rolling, undeniable tide that took her muscle by muscle with excruciating pleasure. A cry broke her lips and she bucked in his hands, trying to stay still but nothing was in her control. Her feet sought purchase against the tops of his, her fingers clenched on his shoulders. He dropped that hand she had her mouth against to her backside, bringing her full against him, lifting her one-handed against him, so her core was settled against his erection, firm and straining against the cotton trousers. She rubbed herself there, the climax increasing in intensity as he kept his fangs embedded in her neck.

He banded his arm around her waist, carrying her writhing body to a table. He sat her there, shifting his hold to her nape. When he withdrew his fangs, he licked the wounds with a sensual enjoyment that made her shudder with need. He let go of her waist only long enough to yank the cotton trousers out of his way. She already had her legs locked over his hips.

He sheathed himself in her damp, spasming cunt, which clamped down on him, making him utter a reverent curse against her flesh. She moaned in answer, her fingertips slipping down to dig into his chest like claws.

He withdrew and thrust back in, powerfully enough to push her back a foot. He returned the arm to her waist to keep her anchored and she held on, her glazed eyes resting on his face, taking in every flex of his jaw, the movement of his body, everything happening behind his eyes.

I want to know who you are. I want to know everything about you.

It was new to her, having someone in her head when she had these spontaneous, heartfelt feelings that she normally concealed.

She wanted so much to put her arms all the way around him, but enough of her brain cells were functioning to remind her that his back wasn't up to being scraped raw by her fingernails. Which would happen, because even though her climax was ebbing, every stroke of his cock inside her was creating intense aftershocks, wresting more cries from her throat.

"Love hearing you plead for more," he muttered.

She loved hearing the strain in his voice. She tightened down, lifting her hips to meet his every thrust.

More, more, more. Yes. She didn't want him to ever stop. Except she loved it just as much when, with a ripple of his muscles under her legs and hands, and a hard groan, he let himself release. He jetted inside her wet heat, making her cunt wetter and sending her into another incredible roll of sensation, just from the friction of his seed spurting inside her body.

He went on for awhile, as if he was trying to plow deeper and deeper into her. Sensing a change in what was happening inside him, she levered herself up. He helped, his arm immediately curving around her back, and she overlapped her arms high on his neck, palming his smooth skull with both hands. She pressed her upper torso fully against his, holding on, her face against his throat and shoulder.

I'm here, Master. I'm here. You saved me. You protected me.

His hand cupped her skull in return, and slowly, slowly, he stopped. He stayed within her, though, as they both drew deep breaths. The lore said vampires didn't breathe, but both he and Anwyn did. There were a lot of things she'd wonder about, maybe even ask about, if he was okay with that.

But later. Not now. Now, she didn't need to know anything. She just needed to be in his arms.

Right where she knew, deep in her heart, he needed her to be.

CHAPTER SIXTEEN

Wolf's phone call had been to Fortuitous Jones. Wolf and Fort shared the same sire, Robert Nolan, who'd been Fort's best mate in the trenches during WWII. Nolan had unfortunately died in an explosion when he did contract covert ops work during the Korean War, but he'd planted in Fort the idea of turning humans with intelligence and military backgrounds, whose human lives had reached a dead end.

He'd also taught Fort how to choose such people, in a manner that had resulted in less of the impulse control and stability problems that often plagued made vampires. A problem that routinely caused born vampires to look down on made ones, as an inferior strain of their race.

There were undeniable advantages to having vampires with intelligence and military training. Fort was one of the few vampires with almost carte blanche approval from the Council to turn humans, those who met his specifications and gut feel about how they could benefit the species overall.

He'd brought two of those vampires with him to Atlanta, a three-vampire team. They were onboard not only with providing transitional security to Atlantis, but restructuring and increasing it. Predictably, Daegan waited until they arrived before he left to pursue the other loose end—the cell who'd committed the attack. Just like with Wolf's interview, Daegan personally vetted the security team himself through Gideon and Anwyn's minds, the vampires who would be watching over his family in his absence. Wolf didn't take offense. In Daegan's stealthy shoes, he would have felt the same.

Fort lived up to the name. Built even more like a tank than Wolf, a gorilla might be the only beast with a fighting chance against the male hand to hand, and that was even before he became a vampire.

Allan Walker was an Army Ranger. He considered Fort his sire, though technically, that was another vampire, Clarence Wilson. Clarence had turned him for reasons of his own and then abandoned him. Allan would have likely stumbled into an early death, like many made vamps without a responsible sire, but Fort had found him and taken over the job.

Saturnia had been with the CIA before she became a vampire, and Fort was her actual sire.

When Wolf had met Allan and Saturnia, back when he was in Colorado, and learned of their skillsets, he'd told Fort he was obviously one of his rare mistakes. An observation that had earned him a narrow look and one of Fort's exceptionally loquacious responses.

"You aren't."

Allan had snorted and elbowed Wolf. "Yeah. But don't be too reassured by that. Fort believes he's pretty, too."

That was another unusual thing about Fort. As part of their predatory edge, all vampires had an undeniable sexual appeal and exceptional beauty. But Fort pointed out that was because the transition made the most of a person's best features.

"When you start out looking rough as a cob," he'd commented brusquely, "You can't do much with that, except throw it to the pigs."

His blunt features could easily blend into a crowd. At a glance, in the right clothes, he was the stereotype of the construction foreman, a plumber, a steelworker. A man who'd worked hard, dirty, manual labor long enough that it had stamped its mark on his weathered face.

"Dress him up in the right clothes, and he's got the physique of a demi-god," Saturnia had commented once. "But I can't get him away from the sales racks at the Goodwill."

"A Hershey bar wrapper is plain, because what's inside is pure bliss," Fort had retorted. "And everyone knows it. My mother named me Fortuitous for a reason. When you're born with this many gifts, the good Lord has to balance it, so as not to incur the jealous wrath of lesser men."

He preferred his oversized button-down shirts over loose jeans, so his physique looked burly, maybe running to extra pounds. Yet anyone who sparred with him knew his shape was the result of a chest shaped like a barrel, and muscled thighs thick as pilings.

Saturnia, in comparison, was so thin she could stand behind him and disappear, but her agile mind made her more deadly than most of the far more physically intimidating vampires Wolf had met. Her mind was four steps ahead of almost everyone else's, all the time. A mix of races, she had smooth fawn-colored skin, and gray-blue eyes that held a multitude of secrets. When Wolf had last seen Saturnia, she'd had her head shaved, a lightning bolt sculpted in the peach fuzz on the right side. Now she'd let her hair grow out in the front, silky strands covering her fine brows and long lashes, while she'd left it shaved in back. It made her striking eyes even more piercing. The look reminded Wolf of the badass mute girl fighter in the second John Wick film.

She had a servant, Holliman, nicknamed Hollow. Hollow had worked at the CIA as well, a level so deep she wouldn't even discuss it now. No matter that classified material from their human life wasn't relevant to the vampire species; some things were just ingrained. In her world, she only shared on a need to know basis.

Hollow still did some work for the Agency, which allowed him clearance to resources Saturnia might need for the team projects. As such, he arrived a day after the others, because he'd pulled together some info on the latest tech in security measures that she said would help their efforts at Atlantis.

Hollow was a guy no one with any sense would ever play poker with, because his face was so expressionless it made his nickname eerily appropriate. He spoke very little, but he was never far from Saturnia. He provided her blood, and the team technical support, on anything they needed. Saturnia said the male could lay his hands on any electronic information source in existence and get it to talk to him.

He could also blend into a crowd. Like Fort, in appearance Hollow was an anomaly for a servant. Most servants were as striking as their vampire counterparts. Hollow was strong but angular, almost awkward looking. He always looked like he needed a sandwich. His face was blotched with freckles and his brown eyes were sharp enough to pierce rock. He had a beautiful head of dark hair, his only attractive feature. He kept it pulled back in a tail on his shoulders.

Neither Fort nor Allan had a full servant. Allan had been a vampire less than a decade, so it wasn't unusual for a made vamp of that age not to have a full servant yet. Fort had had one until five or six years ago, when he'd lost her to a car accident. A truck carrying rebar had flipped. Eleven metals rods had speared through the windshield, and Gemma couldn't escape the law of averages. Two of them got her in the chest, metal through the heart, the one sure-fire way to kill a fully marked servant.

Wolf sat with Fort the night after it had happened. Fort had plowed his way through a case of Jack Daniels, trying to get drunk enough not to feel.

"What the fuck is that?" Fort had demanded, gesturing at him with the bottle. "Goddamn invincible most the time, they are. And then out of nowhere, a damn truck carrying a load of metal poles? Fucking hell. Why didn't she change lanes? Hell, if I was behind a truck carrying a load of survey stakes, she sure as shit would have told me to change lanes, right? Bossy little thing."

Vampires got close to their servants, though everyone knew they weren't supposed to admit to getting "too" close. Fort's situation was a little different. Gemma had been Fort's wife and submissive, before he was turned.

Fort had made her his servant, something that was now prohibited. Even then, it had been frowned upon. The Vampire Council felt a made vampire in particular was too vulnerable to human influence, which would make them resistant to putting the vampire species first. The physiological nature of a vampire that took over after the transition helped adjust that loyalty in the right direction, but the Council kept a close eye on factors that could make it less certain.

That said, if Fort ever did have a servant again, Wolf expected it would be decades from now, because the male still grieved, still missed the curly-haired woman who'd been inside his soul even before she'd been third marked.

Love could do that, right? He thought of Ella, of the ability to be in her mind. At dawn, after their memorable encounter on the second level of the club, he had to go to the basement apartment. He'd wanted her to stay with him. He could have ordered her to do that. She had already called into the diner and told them she couldn't work that morning.

But when he bit back the urge to offer, she'd given him the out to ease back, get some perspective. She told him she was going to go home, get a shower, sleep the morning away. She had to help the grocery owner in the afternoon, because they were having some kind of big sale. The work would be in the store, not on her bike, which was good. Though the second mark would help her recuperate from the bruises and sore muscles faster than if she'd been without it, it wouldn't have been an easy day to do that kind of exercise.

He'd told her he'd reach out to her, keep her in the loop. Kissed her thoroughly, held her, then let her slip out of his arms as he stepped into the elevator.

His last view of her when the doors closed was the brave smile slipping away from her face. His heart thudded hard in his chest, like a stone battering his lungs, but he didn't punch the button to reopen the doors.

Though he wanted to.

The night after the team arrived, Wolf arranged for them all to meet in Atlantis's small conference room. It was time to focus on the most important priority. Protecting Atlantis and its people, including Ella.

Allan had an errand to run upon rising—his preferred "morning" coffee brand—so arrived in the conference room after Saturnia and Fort were settled in. The former Ranger threw out his usual style of greeting.

"Hey, Fort. Put your head down here so I can knock the mud off my shoes with that butt-ugly buzz cut of yours."

Fort merely grunted in answer. He was already looking through the file that Wolf and Gideon had compiled for him on the current setup at Atlantis. Saturnia stood beside his chair, reading it over his shoulder. She gave Allan a succinct nod, her gaze glittering briefly with humor. Probably as much at Fort's ignoring of the jibe as the jibe itself.

Wolf hadn't seen any of them for nearly a year, but they usually picked up just like this, focusing on the task at hand, if there was one. If the purpose was social, they'd continue conversations they'd started last time they'd met, as if they'd never been apart.

Allan was the closest thing Wolf had to a best friend as a vampire, so the youngest vampire in the group went with the more traditional greeting with him. He clasped Wolf's hand and bumped shoulders in a man-style hug, balancing his coffee in his free grip. When Allan backed off, he gave Wolf an assessing look Wolf tried to ignore, since he'd already endured much of the same from Fort. "Found yourself some nice new digs here, man." Allan sipped his coffee. "Much better than that club out in Colorado."

"You still going?" Wolf asked.

"Sometimes. Club venue's not my preferred jam, you know. Now you're gone, it's even less of a draw. Don't have anyone to drink with."

Allan winked at Wolf. With a Ranger's physique, light green eyes and attractive features, he was well aware of his charm, though he could switch it off in a heartbeat, becoming as deadly as a snake. But for right now, he went with charm. He bent over Saturnia, blowing on her neck. She waved her hand at him, like she was shooing a fly. "Still annoying, I see."

"Still running your flower shop, I see. Or smell, rather. Soil, blooms and manure."

"Actually, the smell of bullshit is entirely you. Thank God you have vampire compulsion or you'd starve. The world's sexiest financial analyst, said no one ever."

Allan grinned at the reference to what he did when he wasn't helping Fort with one of his jobs. "Hey, say what you want, but I don't have to worry that I won't be comfortable in my old age."

"How quaint. You imagine someone as annoying as you will live that long."

Another grin and he took the tablet copy of the file from her offered hand. Hollow sat in the chair near Sat, working at his laptop. His thick brown hair was neatly combed, and he maintained a trim beard and moustache. As Allan secured a seat across from her at the table, he spared the servant a glance.

"Still dominating every conversation with your incessant chatter, Hollow?"

Hollow's reply to that was a lifted brow and a vague grunt. He didn't stop moving his fingers over the keys. Allan shot Wolf a wink.

Gideon and James slid into the room next. James had arrived hours after the bombing and taken command of the in-house security team again, freeing Gideon up to help Anwyn however needed. Introductions had already been made the previous night, so basic nods were exchanged.

Saturnia, now finished, sat down with her back to Hollow. She went into her odd phased-out Zen style state where she appeared to be looking at nothing and everything, all without moving a muscle.

Wolf wondered if she and Hollow were having a non-stop dialogue, but watching them, he somehow doubted it. They didn't have that kind of vampire-servant relationship. More of the approved kind; sexual, functional, not overly emotional.

Since the other night on the dance floor, he'd had a lot of really reasonable discussions with himself, about talking in his head to Ella. He told himself not to do it, not to make a habit of something that wasn't going to go in that direction. It didn't matter that she knew he was a vampire. She worked in a club under the direct supervision of a vampire, so as long as she worked here and Anwyn claimed her, no Council rules would be broached. He could keep his mind closed to her, discourage that level of intimacy.

But checking on her safety was a different matter.

She was at the little cottage she called home. She'd picked up an eggless egg salad and was sitting on the back stoop, eating her late dinner. As she licked her fingers, she watched the fireflies floating over a bank of dahlias. Since she wasn't wearing shoes, her toes curled in thick grass. Toes that wiggled as a grass spider skittered over them.

Second mark access gave him some sensory input. Not as much as third, but enough that he thought he could feel the brush of her thick hair along her neck, inhale the flowery soap she used. He thought of dancing with her, holding her, driving into her willing, supple body. So small and fragile, and yet so strong, holding onto him, digging into his chest, her mouth open and chin tipped back.

She'd had an orgasm when he'd bitten her. Christ. How in the hell did anyone resist that kind of temptation?

By reminding himself how much he liked her. By reminding

himself of the number one rule for a Dom, whether a Daddy or any other kind.

Take care of your sub.

Anwyn came in then. He noticed she looked tired, an unusual thing for a vampire, even when they *were* tired. Gideon's expression, though well-cloaked, showed concern.

She'd had a seizure, a bad one. Probably within the last hour. He exchanged a look with Gideon, who nodded imperceptibly. Things were okay. But Wolf suspected her servant was really wishing she was resting, rather than doing this, risking a seizure in front of three vampires.

But Wolf understood it was a fine balance. Give in too much to those demons she fought, and it would make it worse. She'd feel like she was losing the war. Being in this meeting, actively participating in the protection of all she'd built, might just help her beat them back.

She stopped by James, put a hand on his shoulder. He reached up and gripped the hand warmly. His shrewd gaze registered what Wolf had, but James was one of the few humans at Atlantis who knew what Anwyn was. She'd second marked him some time ago. Which meant he might see the same tiredness, but he wouldn't say a word about it. Especially not in front of other vampires.

"Glad to have you back," she said. "Though I'm sorry we had to cut your sabbatical short."

"That was my choice. If Atlantis is under attack, this is where I need to be."

She registered the tightness in his expression and shook her head. "You've already gone over everything, James. Your team did their job. None of us saw this coming. Perry was embedded well before you left. You didn't fail me."

"Respectfully, agree to disagree, ma'am. If the club was damaged and people were hurt, then I failed. I'll make sure it doesn't happen again."

Wolf knew Anwyn was right, but so was James. Anyone in charge of protecting others couldn't see it any other way. It was how they became the best at what they did, and James was one of the best. Plus, all of them were beating themselves up for missing Perry's duplicity, including Gideon and Anwyn.

"Sounds like the right note to get started on this." Fort looked up, pushed the file away from him. "There's no security plan in the world that's a hundred percent fool proof, something everyone here knows. But when you have a pretty hefty bank roll to fund it, and the right minds designing it—"

"Check, check," Allan interjected.

"—we can upgrade you so your security will reflect what they have at higher risk target sites. It may cause some discomfort among your guests, cause you to lose some memberships."

Anwyn lifted a shoulder. "That's marketing. I can repackage what we offer so the members realize the value of what they're getting, in exchange for the inconvenience. It will become routine to them over time, like security checks at the airport that weren't in place before 9/11."

"Good. So we don't have to anticipate any back pedaling on what you say you want."

Anwyn gave him her standard grab-them-by-the-balls Mistress look. "I'm paying you for your expertise. I'd be a fool to ignore it, wouldn't I? If I have a problem with anything you're proposing, then we review it and determine if we can still accomplish the objective with some modification acceptable to us both. If we can't, then safety is the number one priority. I won't go to a funeral because I was too busy protecting feelings or my bottom line."

Fort glanced at Wolf. "Glad to see my boy here never fails in his judgment of good people. Let's get down to the details then."

~

Fort, Saturnia, Hollow and Allan knew their business, and laid things out pretty straight. They'd get started with execution and have the whole job done in a couple of weeks, tops. It helped that James already had his men well-trained, because getting them up to speed was part of that timetable.

Anwyn laid out her plans for repairing the wall and they integrated the two efforts. When they were done, her expression was a little easier. Moving forward was always better than standing still and looking at the wreckage something had made of your life.

She rose to take her leave, Gideon at her side. "As we discussed, the plan is to re-open with Burlesque theme night. I'm giving the staff the interim time off with pay, but Wolf, I'd appreciate it if you would work with James, helping Fort and his team while I'm focused on the repairs. You'll know what impacts club operations and be able to troubleshoot. Bring me in as needed."

"Sure." Wolf met her gaze. "This place is invincible, Anwyn. Just like its Mistress."

Though the gesture was strained, her smile was genuine. "I hope so."

~

After she and Gideon left the room, Gideon's hand falling lightly on her back, Wolf and the team hammered out work division, rollout schedule. Then Allan gave him a nudge.

"Hey, let's get a drink. I want to talk to you about something."

Wolf glanced at Fort. His face was a blank wall, which tipped Wolf off. "What does Fort want?"

Allan grinned. "Come along and I'll tell you. What's the closest watering hole?"

Wolf snorted. "Right here. Selection is better from the main floor bar. You can choose your poison and we'll take it up to the second level. More private up there. We just have to leave money in the till to cover our consumption."

"What, free alcohol isn't covered on this job?"

"Were you in the meeting with the same smart business woman that I was?"

Allan laughed. "Point taken."

"You coming?" Wolf asked Fort. The team leader shook his head, jerked his thumb at Saturnia. "We have some groundwork and phone calls to do. You can help after."

So whatever this was, Fort considered it serious. Wolf took Allan out to the bar, snagged them both a couple bottles apiece of their preferred brew and guided him up the wide velvet-carpeted staircase to the second level. Allan whistled at the look of the more intimate area, brass and wood, deep blue carpets and shadowed booths. The chandelier that caught the dim lights sparkled like diamonds.

"This place is something else."

"Yeah." Wolf couldn't help looking toward the dance floor.

Remembering. Which made him want to touch Ella's mind again, make sure she was still okay. Fuck. It was too damn easy to rationalize being in her head.

Which didn't stop him from doing it.

She'd recently taken a shower, something he was sorry he'd missed, and was back on her porch, listening to the night sounds. Fucking hell, she was wearing his shirt again, and nothing else, her bare bottom on the smooth step. Her back hurt, her feet even worse. They'd had a million customers at the grocery, and she'd helped with everything; stock pulls, bagging, and hauling out more inventory.

Despite that, she'd noticed she was less tired than she'd normally be. Her clever mind had already put together that her sensory input had sharpened. She'd asked him nothing directly about the vampire stuff, though. Except for that remarkable statement on the dance floor, she'd made no direct reference to it since then, even more peculiar.

Or not. Ella had exceptional intuition. She'd realized the circumstances had required extreme measures, measures that might not have otherwise been taken. He would tell her what he wanted to tell her when the time was right.

Now she had her arms around herself, and was thinking about having his arms around her. *In the alley, giving him blood to help him survive, I don't remember that as clearly as I want to. But on the dance floor... he didn't take the blood just to help his wounds, I don't think. He was taking blood for reasons more than that. And...I loved it.*

Yeah, exceptional intuition. A reminder of why he shouldn't even be doing this, sitting silent in her mind, hearing her thoughts.

He tuned back into Allan, popping the cap off his beer. They sat at the bar, a couple stools apart so they could stretch out long legs, prop them on the adjacent chair legs between them.

"So what's up?" Wolf asked.

"I was at Lord Richard's place a month or so back. He had some work for our team, but it was a one-person job."

The Southern Region Master's home. If Region Masters were asking for their services, Fort's team was making strides in the vampire world. Wolf wondered what Lord Richard had needed them to do, but Allan would volunteer that if he could reveal it, or if it had to do with what he wanted to talk to Wolf about.

"I would have come to see you then," Allan continued, "but Fort had us on back-to-back jobs. When I finished what Lord Richard needed, I had to get back to Colorado. There's a second mark in Lord Richard's household. Been there ten years. He's looking to make a move, and Lord Richard is cool with it. Haru would really like to be someone's third mark. He's discreet, unobtrusive, intelligent as hell and can fight like a cross between a Samurai and a Viking berserker. He can give you blood when you need it."

Why in the hell was everyone obsessed with him getting a third mark? Though she was too fragile for him to get in her face about it, the more he'd thought about it, the more certain he'd been that Anwyn had prompted the second mark between him and Ella mostly because of her own opinion about his non-servant state.

He bit back a sharper retort, but the edge was in his voice. "I'm not looking for a third mark."

"Why not?" Allan pressed on, despite Wolf's answering frown. "You made an impression with the overlord and the Region Master out west, Wolf, and you know it. You're strong, serious and focused. It's not impossible that you might someday be considered for an overlord position yourself. You can say you don't want that, but you're a leader. You always have been. It keeps seeping out through the cracks."

"I'd prefer nothing to be seeping from me, thank you."

Allan's quick grin flashed. "Thank God for vampire immunity to STDs then. With our libidos, our dicks would rot off within the first year of our turning."

Wolf shook his head. "Why now? What's the push?"

Allan sobered. "You want to play dumb, fine by me. Not a lot of mades get the born elite's vote of confidence. Since the born numbers have been decreasing, the Council is paying a lot closer attention to mades with a track record of loyalty and strengths that augment the vampire race."

"Glad to know I've made the dean's list, but still clueless on why a servant figures into that."

Allan's brown eyes narrowed. "You're not that clueless. Everyone knows a vampire with a third mark servant is a stronger vampire. His management of the relationship proves he's reached a certain level of maturity."

"Maybe I don't want to go down that path."

Wolf put down the bottle, turned it on the surface of the bar. He imagined third marking someone, letting them in that deep. Yeah, he couldn't stop himself from seeing Ella's face the moment he had the thought, but he couldn't go that way. He wouldn't.

Allan hooked an arm around the back of his chair and pushed it back on two legs, studying Wolf. "Maybe you should march down to Savannah, into the heart of Council headquarters," he said at length. "Risk your ass to ask the oldest, most deadly vamps among us the question."

"What question?" Wolf frowned again.

"How many decades you have to live before you realize you can forgive yourself for being fucking human. For not being the superhero you believed you were, that nobody is, not a hundred percent of the time."

Temper surged, but before he could unleash it, they were joined by a third party.

"Wrong crowd to find human beings forgivable." Saturnia topped the stairs and drifted toward their table, carrying a bottle of wine and a glass. "Most of the Council were born vampires. Don't go down this road with him, Allan. It ends with broken furniture and you bleeding profusely. Been enough violence here this week."

Allan spread his hands out. "Okay, but let me say one more thing. How can you do the therapy thing, help others, and yet you don't believe in it for yourself?"

"Because they're humans, and their situation is different from mine. Time to move on, Allan."

"That's just my point. Sheila's dead, man. And Ross moved on a long fucking time ago. You—"

The two bottles were swept to the floor with a spew of liquid and the crash of broken glass. Wolf seized Allan's shirt front, lifted and slammed him down on the bar. Allan struck out immediately, but Wolf was faster and stronger, and had him down.

Saturnia was there though, her shoulder firmly wedged between Allan's chest and Wolf's bulk looming over him, her hands flat on Wolf's chest.

"Dial it back," she said sharply. "He's young and stupid, Wolf. He still thinks he's human half the time. He doesn't get it."

She stared up into his face, mostly blocking the view between him and Allan, though he could see Allan's expression. Allan hadn't seen this side of him up close and personal. The former Ranger looked startled by what he saw burning in Wolf's eyes, and felt through his death grip on him. Good.

Yeah, Allan was still young, for a vampire. He didn't know how some things burrowed into an immortal's soul and stayed there forever, like a wounded dragon always ready to rise up and kill when roused. That dragon only got stronger as the years passed.

"Yeah, she's dead, Allan," Wolf ground out. "You think I don't know that? And that I don't know why? I live with that, and I live with it my own fucking way. When you're there, you come talk to me. Until then, shut the fuck up and leave it alone."

Saturnia kept her eyes on Wolf, her hands on him, but she cocked her head toward Allan. "Message received, kid?"

"Loud and clear."

"He's got it, Wolf," Saturnia said. "Let him go. I want to drink my wine before it breathes its last breath."

Wolf released Allan and stepped back with an oath, pivoting to walk away, walk it off. He knew he needed better control over this particular trigger. That redness wouldn't go away, and his hands ached with the need to tear something apart. Not just his hands. He needed to use his whole body.

He'd go work out. He'd push himself past even a vampire's endurance, make sure he was a hundred percent again after the blast. Get this shit buried again, where it belonged.

But at the top of the stairs, he recalled himself enough to stop, take a breath. Two. Three. Then he turned.

Allan was standing, his eyes flashing, body tense. Wolf's behavior would have set off his own bloodlust. Now that he'd been released, he was trying to get a handle on it. Sat was at his side, her hand resting on his shoulder.

At Wolf's steady look, Allan lifted a shoulder. Managed to speak without snarling.

"I may be young and stupid still, but I care about you, man. And I fucking do know something about the road that took you...where it did. We all do."

"I know that. I know all of that." Wolf rubbed a hand over his face. He owed the man he knew was his friend an answer. Even if right now he still wanted to beat on him like a rug.

"I do the therapy to keep others from going so far down that road they can't find their way back. Some of them still get there, still burn their fucking bridges to ash, because some of us are too goddamned stupid to know what we have until it's too late. But if I can turn them back, I do. I'm not trying to save myself, Allan. Just trying to respect what I lost. Don't fuck with that again. All right?"

Allan nodded unhappily. Though he did add one more thing, a dog with a bone he wouldn't let go. "Fine, but Lord Richard might be coming here for Club Atlantis's reopening. A show of support for Anwyn. He'll likely bring Haru with him. If he does, I hope you'll at least consider the servant thing. He's a good-looking kid and strong. He was in the Navy before he moved into our world. Never saw combat, but he does understand something of that world." Allan gave him a tight smile. "I know you're not opposed to enjoying a male body."

"No, he's not," Saturnia interjected. "But I think he's hung up on the cute bit of fluff he second marked in the alley."

She patted Allan absently, like a puppy who had learned his lesson, for the moment, and returned to her chair and her wine. Allan shot her a narrow look. It almost made Wolf smile, since he was sure Sat had done it intentionally. She had no evident sense of humor, except in subtle moves like that. It helped him even out a little more.

"Anwyn says she's a hell of a service submissive," Allan said thoughtfully, telling Wolf they'd discussed Ella. His temper growled again, though he pushed it down, worked on keeping his expression impassive.

"She already knows you're a vampire," Allan pointed out. "And has taken it in stride. Two parts of the job description already handled, right?"

"She's not an option for that," Wolf said. He wanted to go downstairs, leave this discussion, but he needed to handle something first. The broken bottles and beer spilled on the floor.

Quelling a sigh, he moved behind the bar, retrieved mop, broom and dustpan, and pulled a bucket from beneath the sink. Allan, to his credit, took the dustpan and broom from him with a companionable nod and went to work on the broken glass. Wolf got the soapy water going to mop up the splattered liquid.

Watching them, Saturnia took a sip of her wine. "I get it. Look at Fort, how much of a wreck he was when he lost his wife. You and I weren't around for it, Allan, but Wolf was. Fort almost walked into the sun a couple times, it got so bad for him."

She pointed a finger at Wolf. "But most of the time, having a third mark isn't about that. It's practical, like having a car to get around. I didn't care two shits about having a servant, until Holliman showed up at my door. He'd tracked me down, the dysfunctional son of a bitch."

"That was because no one else knew how to work with him," Allan scoffed.

"He'd left the company," Saturnia demurred. "Or been encouraged to do so, with a generous pension and a consult upon demand requirement. More distance, better relationship for everyone involved. He's too socially awkward, even for a geekhead." Saturnia shrugged. "He couldn't perform for people he didn't click with. I'd always been his buffer, so the problem didn't become evident until I'd left. Once I was working with him again, they let him come back to do consult work, which has worked out nicely for us, the intel he can feed us that aligns with our interests and the jobs we take."

Wolf knew the bare bones of the story, but now he found himself reluctantly curious about more intimate details. "How did he handle finding out you were a vampire?"

"I didn't let him know, not at first. Honestly, I kind of resisted the servant idea, even when it started to make so much sense it was hard to ignore. Eventually, it happened, the way these things do. And when I marked him..."

She paused. Saturnia never looked relaxed. Fully wound up, focused, able to tear into a problem like a backhoe until she found the solution. That was her baseline. Yet as Wolf looked at her now, an emotion crossed her face that startled him, because he'd never seen it there. Contentment. "Sitting in his head is like getting in a swimming pool and sitting on the bottom," she said. "It's silent."

Her gaze met Wolf's. "Do you have any idea how blissful that silence is?"

He thought of Ella on the cool tile. He wouldn't say her mind was ever silent, but he didn't need that. He needed the swirling, drifting currents, something that took him from himself, helped steady him.

Yeah, he understood.

"He doesn't have moods or a bunch of emotional shit in his head," Saturnia said. "Everything there is ordered, planned, targeted. He's focused on the work or on the immediate moment. Anything I want or need—blood, sex, he'll deliver it how I want it, no drama or emotional shit. He doesn't even need to cuddle."

"Do you plug him into a charger at night?" Allan queried.

She made a face, but continued. "What he did for the CIA, it was all about the data, the target, the goal. Rinse, wash, repeat. He's kind of caught in the cycle. He's a little fucked up. So am I, right?"

She looked toward Wolf. "The point is, I have a high regard for him, but he doesn't have my heart. I won't break if I lose him. And his mind is so quiet, I don't need to listen in to find out if he's happy or not. He'll tell me if he needs something, but he's okay if I say no. He gets what our relationship is."

"You two could be a Hallmark movie." Allan said solemnly.

Sat shot him the bird. The former Army Ranger pantomimed catching it mid-air, kissed it and fanned out his fingers, as if flicking it back her way.

Now Wolf did smile. His gut was still churning, but he was remembering why he enjoyed being around people like Allan, Fort and Saturnia. An important part of their human life had been involved in a world they all understood. When push came to shove, they could fall back into the rhythm of dealing and maintain a balance together, despite the craziness of anything else going on.

"Did Fort ever tell you how Nolan, his and Wolf's sire, became a vampire?" Saturnia asked Allan. When he shook his head, Wolf grinned. They'd finished their clean up. After a moment of hesitation, Wolf decided to stick. He pulled the couple of spare beers out of the fridge where he'd stored them and slid one down the bar to Allan.

Saturnia tipped her head at him. "Tell our young'un the story, Wolfman."

"Going to start calling you old lady, you don't quit that young'un shit," Allan advised her. He pulled out a chair at her table and straddled it, taking a seat as she showed her fangs.

"Not sure I can do it justice," Wolf said dryly, "but Fort can tell it with all the voices and dramatic embellishments another time. I'll give you what I think were the actual facts. Nolan was taken on as the security detail of an archaeologist who was sure vampires existed. He told Nolan everything he thought he knew about them, then had Nolan accompany him on an expedition to the Amazon. The archaeologist was sure that they'd find vampires in these caves he'd located."

"Let me guess. The archaeologist left a memoir, and it became a movie, or TV series, or some shit like that." Allan tipped his chair back, bracing his feet on the side of Saturnia's chair. She gave his shoes a gimlet look but let them be, taking another swallow of her wine as she draped her hand over his shins. There was an easy affection between them, like siblings, an older sister, younger brother thing. Though Saturnia was the younger vampire, she'd been fifteen years older than Allan as a human, and she wasn't turned too many years after him.

"Wouldn't doubt it, but only if the archaeologist made his notes before the trip, because he didn't survive this one," Wolf continued. "They did find vampires in those caves. They were Trads. Vampires living away from human civilization, who viewed humans only as food. They killed the archaeologist, the four other geek squad members. One of the Trads wounded Nolan terminally, dragged him off to a private corner of his lair to enjoy his meal in peace, started drinking from him."

"No shit." Allan came down with a thump. "How the hell did he talk his way out of that?"

"Way Fort tells it, Nolan could keep his wits about him in the middle of the worst parts of Armageddon. As the vamp is feeding on him, Nolan paws weakly at the vamp, like he's sort of disoriented. Which was just to get his hands where he needed them to be. See, the other members of the team had thought the archaeologist was nuts, that there was no such thing as vampires, but Nolan had listened to all the archaeologist's theories and come prepared, just in case. He was wearing a pair of gauntlets loaded with wooden stakes."

"Fuck."

"Yeah. Shoots a stake into the vamp's heart. Problem is, blood's pumping out of Nolan from these gaping wounds, and he already knows it's a matter of minutes before he's decomposing in that cave for the next few decades. The archaeologist had told him how he thought humans became vampires. So Nolan finds the place behind the Trad's fangs that holds the turning serum. He puts the vamp's mouth back on his arm, knocks those fangs back into his flesh like you'd hit the top of a stapler to make it work—"

Allan chuckled.

"—and jets it into his blood stream. Now, Nolan had no idea if the vamp had drunk enough of his blood to make the turning happen or not. However, since he was pretty sure he was half a blink from stepping into his dead momma's arms—his quote—he figured it was as close a chance to surviving as he was going to get."

Allan's brow creased. "He became a vampire without a sire?"

"The archaeologist had given him some theories on how the sire part of things worked as well. In hindsight, he believes that the archaeologist must have stumbled on some direct source about vampires. No idea how that would have happened, but Nolan's alive because someone was loose-lipped with a human, or was stupid enough to write some of this stuff down where it was found."

Wolf shrugged. "Anyway, Nolan drained blood out of his sire, stored it in an underground spring where it would stay fresh as possible. It didn't last as long as he needed it, so it was a very difficult first few months of his vampire life, but the tough SOB did it. What saved him, ironically, were the other Trads. Once they saw how he'd turned himself, they were kind of impressed. They mentored and protected him until he got things going in the right direction."

"So I wonder why he did that, instead of stepping into his dear momma's arms?" Allan asked.

Wolf winked. "According to Fort, 'That tough old bastard wasn't going out any way other than how he wanted to go.'"

The three of them looked toward the staircase in unison, a blink before Hollow appeared at the top of it. The man never appeared disheveled, always in severely creased slacks, a crisp shirt open one button at the throat. He wore it over a white undershirt to absorb perspiration he never seemed to have.

Hollow seemed as generic as a Ken doll, until a person looked into his eyes. The workings of a complex machine were there, permanently in overdrive. Wolf wouldn't have suspected that there was a peaceful quiet inside the man's head like Saturnia had described. However, as he'd realized from his short time inside of Ella's, the mind was a far more complicated place than it seemed, with numerous chambers to explore.

In the time her eyes had met those of her servant's, Saturnia had received a full progress report. "First phase of the IT revamp on the security system is done. We'll pick it up tonight. Time to find a place to bed down. Dawn's coming in a couple hours."

"Anwyn offered her guest quarters downstairs," Wolf reminded her.

"Appreciated, but I prefer to select my own spots," she said, with a gracious nod. "Holliman found us a place."

"Undisclosed location," Allan intoned. Ignoring him, she rose and stood by Hollow.

"I was just singing your praises," she told her servant. "You and your blissfully quiet mind."

Hollow gazed at her as if she were the only person in the room worth noticing. Not a romantic thing, not exactly. As if literally, she was the only person that he would look at, acknowledge directly. "It's your haven to enjoy," he said.

It was the most intimate thing Wolf had ever heard him say. But he was glad Saturnia had found that. She needed it.

He knew her story from Allan, though hers had a lot less entertaining folklore embellishment than the one about Nolan.

She never turned her back to a door, never fully relaxed her guard. Not unusual for anyone with their training, but when she was with the CIA, she'd been burned at one point, outed to her enemies. Captured and held in some hole-in-the-ground prison, she'd been tortured badly enough that she never regained the composure to continue field work.

She'd continued to work for the CIA in intel and analysis, though. They paired her up with Hollow, not sure the match would work, but Hollow's inability to relate to others had one single exception. Saturnia.

However, five years after that, she was diagnosed with a rampant cancer, likely triggered by what she'd endured.

Allan had been part of the team who'd rescued her when he was a Ranger. Since he'd kept track of her, even after he was turned, he brought her to Fort's attention. Fort had offered her the vampire lottery ticket.

Though she indicated there wasn't anything emotional between her and Hollow, Wolf would call bullshit on that. It didn't present itself in a traditional way, but the bond between them was obvious.

Now she tipped her head to Wolf and Allan, a farewell, and left them, walking slightly ahead of Hollow as they headed back down the stairs.

Allan took the last swallow of his beer and tapped the bottle on the table thoughtfully. "The first time I saw her put Hollow through his sexual paces with other servants at an overlord gathering, it kind of freaked me out. They got into it full blown, but walking out to their car afterward, both of them looked deadpan as flat rock."

"You said she was raped, repeatedly and brutally, as a prisoner. It's probably easier for her to do it as an act."

"Yeah." The flash in Allan's gaze told Wolf he was remembering how he'd found Saturnia, in what condition. His next words revealed that lethal side of him, the side that Wolf would always welcome at his back in a fight.

"Never been so glad to take someone out of this world. Those fuckers are rotting in hell. Shitty world sometimes."

"Yeah. Good thing there's always more beer."

"You know it." Allan tipped his toward Wolf. "On that note, let's go again. Put more money in the till for your boss. It may not make us drunk, but it makes the dark dreams easier to sleep through. Right?"

"Right." Though they both knew that it was a lie.

CHAPTER SEVENTEEN

He and Allan spent a little more time shooting the shit, then Allan left Wolf to his thoughts. Wolf cut the lights and sat in the darkness. He had his back to the bar, his eyes resting on the dance floor. For probably the dozenth time tonight, he imagined his little girl turning there, her arms out, lovely ass shifting and sweet breasts quivering beneath his shirt, her hair swinging loose along her narrow back.

He didn't have to imagine those things. She was close, close as a thought. He'd denied himself long enough. When he closed his eyes, he was in her mind again. And where she was, what she was doing, had his body tightening.

She was in her bed, but she wasn't asleep. She lay on top of her covers and was looking up at a mobile of origami peace cranes, moving in the breeze from her open, screened windows. Atlanta had warmed up today, despite the fall season, so the tabletop fan facing the bed helped the paper flock spin and drift through the air. She had a window unit, but she apparently preferred the open windows tonight.

His shirt was gathered up on her stomach. Her hand rested on her soft abdomen, her fingertips loose and relaxed several inches above her mons. She'd bent her knees, her feet braced on the covers, and one knee rocked wide. So casual and relaxed in her nudity, letting the cool fan air reach all her sweet folds, slide along her inner thighs like the graze of fingertips.

On her back, her generous breasts were outlined against the fabric, her nipples tight points. She was imagining when he was inside her, thrusting hard, his hand on her shoulder, her throat. His mouth there. But she was taking it beyond where they had been, to other places, places she'd like to go. Him putting her over his knee and getting after her with his hand. Maybe a crop on the backs of her tender thighs.

He'd seen Ella embrace all manner of extreme BDSM scenarios, from spreader bars to suspension to forced orgasm towers or electric play. She'd participated with genuine enthusiasm and aroused pleasure, delighted to meet the needs of the Dom directing her. But none of them had the access he had now, to see the things that she truly fantasized about.

Her fantasies were sweet...almost gentle things. Because her fantasy was love. The love of a Dom who wanted to possess her, care for her, cherish her. And who would let her be and do everything she could to make him happy.

The kind of gift that he'd wasted and thrown away, so he didn't get to have it twice. The gods knew how to twist the blade, didn't they?

He'd told Anwyn this was a fucking mistake. He wished he could go back to that alley, reject the blood, take it from Gideon. Or even from one of those first responders, dull his mind, knock him out so he wouldn't remember a vampire using him for sustenance.

Why hadn't he gone that route? He knew logically he'd been out of it, and Anwyn was like Allan, probably thinking that the second mark, despite the circumstances, was a good idea. That Ella would be good for him. She was.

Which was why it pissed him off so badly.

Stop.

Ella froze. Damn it, he hadn't meant for her to hear that. He was used to having his headspace all to himself, so it was still a conscious decision to remember to keep the door between their thoughts one-way access only.

"I'm sorry, Master," she said out loud. *I didn't know you didn't want me to...*

The command had been aimed at himself. He'd been so into his own shit he hadn't realized her hand had been drifting down over her labia, light caresses, her hips starting to rise. His cock hardened to steel at the sight of her touching herself.

She was flushed, flustered, which was unexpected. Until he saw it her fumbling explanation to him, an appalled admonishment to herself.

I don't ever do that, self-pleasuring, without a Master or Mistress's permission. I was just...I forgot myself. I'm sorry.

He needed to get the hell out of her head, but the savage, pissed off part of him wasn't in the mood, and responded to her dismay with a good cleansing dose of lust. At least that was easy to understand.

Go back to your shower.

She obeyed and rose, padding the short distance over the boards to her bathroom. The shower was so small he wouldn't fit into it. The shower head detached on a long cord so that the person squeezed in there could thoroughly rinse.

Get in. Keep the shirt on.

She hesitated, then complied. *Wolf, are you—*

You'll only talk to me if I tell you to.

She pressed her lips together.

Turn on the water. Coldest setting, and douse yourself. Thoroughly. Look at yourself while you do it.

So he could see, too.

She liked his intent, but definitely not his method. She didn't like cold water, his girl. But she dutifully turned on the water, her body tensing and bracing when the first rush of water hit her, the shock of it shuddering through her. She groped for the nozzle, lifted it out of its bracket and started following his direction, rinsing the frigid water over her hair, the shirt, until it started to cling to her skin, allow the pink color to come through.

Just as he figured, her nipples, now taut, cold points, pushed beautifully against the fabric, which also clung to the curves, outlining them in mouthwatering display. Further down, the folds creased over her abdomen, the flare of her hips, and then the lengths of her upper thighs, drawing his eye to the crevice in between.

Now in between your legs. Full blast.

She did so, shivering and gasping as the jets hit her pussy.

Cools that hot little thing down, doesn't it?

She nodded, a quick jerk. She was following direction, wasn't directing that to him in think-speak, but he saw the rapid tumble flow of her thoughts about it. She was sorry, so sorry she'd touched herself without her Master's permission, but she hoped this would earn his forgiveness.

Keep it going until you can't bear any more. Show me how much you can take for your Master.

Much longer than he'd expected, but then he should have remembered how much she could take in far more extreme sessions. She was going numb, but even then, those jets of water were stroking her with ice cold fingers.

You're keeping your thighs too closed. Open them up as wide as you can get them in the shower.

She bit back a near sob as she complied, and then re-aimed the jets at her core. She cried out this time as the icy fingers reached new terrain. The rest of her was shivering in the cold air, water drops running down her throat, her breasts, over the tips of her nipples...

You're pleasing me, Ella. I am very proud of you.

God. He almost closed his eyes at what he felt from her. Near freezing, disliking this as intensely as a sub could, yet all it took was his approval to send a rush of resolve through her, a renewed determination to do this as long as he needed. She'd go on until the tank ran out of water, and then she could go get in her friend's swimming pool if he wanted, because it wasn't heated, though it probably wasn't as cold as this.

He had to smile at the rush of thoughts. *Turn off the water. No towel. Leave the shirt on and go stand in front of your mirror.*

When she complied, she moved stiffly, as one did when they were cold and had clothes uncomfortably sticking to them. He waited avidly for the full view he'd get through her eyes. It didn't disappoint him, especially since it came with the chance to direct her.

Back straight. No hunching. Show yourself to your Master.

She snapped into a display posture that lifted her breasts, angled her hips in an appealing way. She used her hands, pulled her hair back from her shoulders so there was no impediment to his view.

Good. Leave your hands up like that, holding your hair.

He drank his fill visually, her breasts pink mounds against the soaked white fabric, her thighs quivering columns that showed him more pale flesh.

Go lie on the bed on your back. Hands gripping the covers on either side of your head.

She moved back through the small space and lay down on her covers. No hesitation, no matter that she was dripping.

My good girl. My obedient girl.

She licked her lips, her hands clutching the blanket.

Close your eyes.

She did. He'd been on the move from the first moment he'd reached out to her mind, and at this late hour, Atlanta traffic hadn't been an impediment at all. So now, he entered her home with stealth. The screen door didn't squeak, aiding him. He took the two strides necessary to cover the entire space, still in silence.

He told himself to look his fill and then leave, continue to direct her in his head from a distance. Instead, he didn't move, his mouth dry, fangs and cock aching to penetrate what lay before his eyes.

His girl was cold. He couldn't leave her like that.

He shed his clothes, dropped his jeans to the floor. Her breath caught, her fingers tightened in the fabric and her nostrils flared, taking in his scent.

He stretched out over her, not touching her yet. The bed was not as long as he was, but he could put a knee up by her knee, fit the shadow of his body over hers. She shifted slightly, lifting, an unconscious yearning.

"Are you cold?"

"Yes." A whisper.

"Do you want me to get you a coat? Let you dry yourself and put on clothes?"

She shook her head vehemently, making him smile.

"So how can I make you warm?"

Her lips trembled, and he didn't make her answer. Instead he lowered himself upon her, absorbed her sigh of relief and the clasp of her arms and legs like the gift they were. He surrounded her with his heat, cupped her head and kissed her cold lips, cheeks, ears. He moved to her throat, but he didn't bite her. He did lick the area that he'd bitten earlier and noticed the way she writhed, a little moan coming from her lips at the stimulation.

You like feeding your Master.

Yes, sir.

Good.

He cupped her breasts through his T-shirt, squeezing so the nipples poked at the straining fabric even more, encouraging his heated mouth to seal over each one in turn, sucking and licking through the fabric. He ignited a fire that started to burn away the cold, her thighs shifting restlessly on either side of his hips. He had his lower body pressed into the mattress between her legs, a position that held her down. When she tried to rub her core against his abdomen, he growled his denial, making her still. A little frustrated breath puffed from her lips.

After spending lavish time on her gorgeous tits, murmuring his praise to her and them, he moved downward again. Kissing hip bones, raising the hem of the shirt, teasing tongue and lips over her navel, the piercing there. He paused. His girl had been shopping. She had a new piece of navel jewelry, a pewter wolf head. He tugged on it with his teeth, growling his approval. Then he moved further down.

Her thighs loosened under his mouth, and he found heaven. Her labia and clit were so cool, but the heated slickness within was a contrast that made his erection painfully thick. He wasn't going to deny himself her body, bastard that he was.

Take what you need, Master. Don't worry. I'm strong enough to handle it.

He had a long list of reasons to hate himself. What was the problem with one more?

The problem was it added to her list of disappointments, regrets and heartbreaks. His sins might not matter, but the one affected by them did. A whole hell of a lot. He might be a vampire now, but he'd never overlook that again.

I can't stop myself from taking what I want, Ella. But I'm here with you fully in this moment, and I cherish what you're giving me. Is it enough?

It wasn't in a vampire's nature to offer a choice. But maybe Allan wasn't the only one who had trouble letting go of being human at times.

Wolf shifted, braced himself on his arms over her, looking down into her face. She lay beneath him, so fragile and open, but her words had been true. *I'm strong enough to handle it.*

"No," she answered. *It's not enough. But I still want you inside me, need you to take what you want. Will you do that, even though I answered you honestly? I need you to be selfish enough to give me what I need right now, and ignore what might happen to me after.*

His attempted smile tore his heart, as if there were ropes between it and the muscles of his face. "Yeah. I can do that." A partial lie.

Satisfied, she closed her eyes. As she did, she lifted her slim hands, rested them on his shoulders.

I didn't give you permission to do that.

No, Master. May I keep my hands there?

Yes. I'll punish you later.

She embraced that idea fully, lifting her upper body, wrapping her arms around his back, fingers digging in, that needy, little girl/woman child "I want you to know I'm here" way. Her hips lifted, her legs opening further, and her gateway was there, that blissful slick heat.

He pushed in, feeling the contraction of her muscles, her jaw flex against his as she bit her lip in concentration. She took all of him, stretching, deeper. Her fingers pressed even more into his skin, giving him the bite of her nails. Her breasts touched his chest, those tight, lovely tips, the generous flesh. As he wrapped his arm around her curved back, he held them close together on one arm and both his knees as he thrust, worked his hips, felt her mouth on his neck.

She bit him, hard enough his fangs lengthened in predatory response. His thrusts became more demanding, the circle of his arm more possessive and binding. The human in him disappeared, the vampire taking over, saying what he knew, with every touch, every thrust, every moan and response he demanded from her.

You're mine.

Every lovely, sweet, sassy, complicated inch of her. And if he third marked her, he could have her soul.

Shit.

CHAPTER EIGHTEEN

The crickets chirped out in the garden, the frogs croaked. Occasionally, he heard a koi splash in her friend's pond. Because her bed was far too narrow, she lay on his chest, her hips and legs in the splayed cradle of his thighs, her soft stomach against his for-the-moment sated cock. He stroked her hair, the outer curve of her breast, her rib cage, the point of her hip, in a slow, endless circle.

She'd drifted in sleep for awhile. As he'd hoped, the second mark gave him some impression of her dreams, but not always clearly, since dreams came more from the third mark realm of the soul. However, they seemed content, peaceful. Hazy images of people and places that weren't angry, an interesting panorama of clouds and turning sky, as if she were a flying bird.

At length, he felt her wake, and was amused to watch the orientation of her thoughts. *Alone...not alone. Person in bed. Holy shit.* Wolf! *Okay, all right, it's Wolf.*

His laughter bounced her on his chest. "Holy shit, Wolf?" he asked. "What does that mean?"

"Don't vampires have some privacy clauses to keep from embarrassing people they mark?" she asked grumpily.

"None that I know of. But I tend not to read the fine print."

She sniffed, but he felt her smile against his flesh. "Well, up until a little while ago, you were *Wolf.* A totally unapproachable Master at

Club Atlantis, except by express invitation. For the day to day stuff, you were always courteous and business-like, but..."

"Are you saying I was intimidating?"

She nestled her cheek against him. "Lars says it's a bad idea to flatter Doms too much, because they're already overly full of themselves."

"I'll mention that to Clark, one of Lars' more sadistic regulars. He'll make sure to adjust that attitude."

She chuckled, fingertips tracing circles on the point of his rib cage, where the long scar beneath the skin ended. "No fair. I told you that in pillow talk confidence. You can't use that kind of information against Lars."

"Who says Doms are fair?"

"True enough." She wriggled as he ran his fingertips lightly down her back, tickling her. Her feet pressed against his shins, since his feet hung off the end of the bed. He propped one hand behind his head, keeping the other around her as she looked up at him, her lips soft and eyes quiet dark moons. "So, did you get Anwyn's email about giving everyone a few days off?" she asked.

"Yeah, she mentioned it during the security and renovation strategy meet. I'll be there, helping out at night."

"Good. Let me know if you all need any help. I'm working my other day jobs, but I should be available to help. All but one evening, possibly. Though if I can shift some things around, I hope to get that done in the morning."

"Hot breakfast date?"

"No. Not exactly."

He paused, sensing a shadow in her thoughts, a slight tension in her body, as she thought of whatever it was that would be occupying that evening.

"Going to tell me, or make me pull it out of your head?"

"Oh, don't do that," she said hastily. Her head became a confusion of thoughts, like a crowd of beach goers taking off because it had started to rain, a lot of blended colors as things spun and flapped, fluttered. "It's not...it's just old history. Personal business."

He had no right to demand. That was what his fair, far distant human self said. His vampire side had an entirely different view of it.

"You'll tell me, Ella."

She sighed, pressed her forehead to his chest, but relented. "It's nothing. This guy I used to be with a while back has something that belongs to me, and lately, I've decided I want it back. So I'm going to go get it."

He'd have let it go there, except he saw something in her head that made that a non-starter. She was calculating when the male in question most likely wouldn't be at home, because that was the best time for her to go. And how she should probably borrow Madelyn's Taser... just in case.

"This guy get rough with you in the past?" Another thing about being a vampire. With the right motivation, the idea of violence came very quickly to mind.

She sat up and slipped away before he anticipated it, because that beach scene was now as blank as if no beach goers had ever been on it. The sand pristine, wiped clean, only a few seagulls floating over the waves. He could almost smell the salt air, hear their cries.

Ella found a dry oversized shirt in her dresser and put it on. It was another man's shirt, but before his alpha instincts could growl, he detected only her scent on it. She'd likely picked it up from a second-hand shop, to use as a sleepshirt. It had a picture of Snoopy on it with his arms crossed, and one bold word printed beneath the famous beagle.

Nope.

He wondered if the shirt's attitude was indicative of her sudden cagey behavior. It was an unusual—and provocative—look for the usually forthcoming submissive.

Ella was figuring out how the mind-reading worked and countering it. Another thing third marking was good for, so he heard. No room of the servant's mind was off limits to a vampire then. When the vampire had the time, motivation and energy, a full light could be shone into every crevice.

Wolf had seen Ella meditate at the club, sitting on the bar in the lotus position, hands relaxed on her knees, back straight, as people moved around her. She'd "disappear," as Chantal put it, for fifteen or thirty minutes with seemingly little effort. But Madelyn had disagreed with that statement.

"On the contrary, a person learns to do it that well with a *lot* of practice *and* determination. Because what goes on in their heads, the things they carry with them—they have to be able to quiet all that down to keep it together day to day."

Thanks to the training he'd taken to do BDSM therapy effectively, he knew all kinds of treatments in the trauma realm included meditation, but it was a discipline very few embraced. Other forms of visualizations and thought re-direction worked better for most.

Ella had freed her hair from the neckline of the shirt and moved to the sink. She found a washcloth by rummaging in the cabinet.

"You haven't answered me, Ella. Has this guy gotten rough with you in the past?"

"Oh, sorry. No, nothing like that. Not exactly."

He'd handle this the same way he'd handle any sub trying to raise an unhealthy defense. Yes, she might have a right to privacy, but whatever argument there'd be for that was one his protective side discarded with annoyance.

"Ella. Look at me." When she complied, reluctantly, he gave her a no-bullshit look. "Explain what 'not exactly' means."

"It means he's nothing I can't handle." She set her chin. She was being stubborn with him?

"Was he a Dom?" he said, with deceptive calmness.

"No. Not even remotely." She waved her hands. "It wasn't that way. We sort of fell into being together, mainly because he offered to let me live with him when I didn't have a place. Having sex with him was part of the rent, if you know what I mean."

"Did he ever hit you?" He was going to get to the center of it one question at a time, if need be.

She sighed, and he saw her relent in her mind. Now that she'd put her foot in her mouth, she accepted that it was best to simply answer his questions.

Yes, it is. Did he ever hit you?

Her lips tightened, and she met his gaze. "Yes. But it was the world I lived in then. It happened. He might smack me in the face or shove me because of something I said or did. I'd yell at him and tell him not to do that, and throw something at him. Later that night we'd share a pizza in the living room, because it wasn't anything unusual. It was just the way it was."

She doused the washcloth, shut off the sink and started to wring the cloth out before she continued. "I wasn't some poor terrorized wife or girlfriend, Wolf. When I'd had enough, I told him to fuck off and that I was leaving. The problem was he shoved me out of the house, locked the door, told me he'd beat me bloody if I tried to come back in. There wasn't much in the house I had to have, but there was this one thing. I've told myself for a long time it didn't matter that I left it behind, but since we nearly got blown up, I've been thinking... you know, I really want that back. So I'm going to go get it."

She took a breath. "But as I said, other than when I do that, I can be available. If you see Anwyn needs my help but doesn't think she should ask, be sure and text me, let me know. Or you know, think at me."

A smile slipped across her face. "What range does the mind stuff have? Do we have to use cell phones?"

"No. We don't."

"Cool." She came back to the bed with the washcloth. "Would you like me to clean you, sir, or do you prefer to do it yourself?"

He closed his hand on her wrist, drawing it downward with the cloth. "You do it. I like to see your hands on me."

She wiped away the remains of his seed and her arousal from his cock and balls with intriguing thoroughness and a lingering touch. By the time she was done, he was semi-erect again. He noted her gaze on him, the way she bit her lip, and felt the stirring in his lower belly. He'd have her beneath him again before sunrise drove him back to his underground home base.

"Ella, when you visit his house, I'm going with you. Give me your word that you'll reach out to me and let me know. Don't make me divide my attention between securing the club and keeping track of you."

Her expression shuttered, that chin setting further. "I really don't need you to do that. I appreciate it—"

"You're acting like I'm offering you a favor. Listen to what I'm saying, Ella." He put enough reproof in the tone that her attention snapped to him like a taut fishing line. "Tell me what I'm saying."

Her lips pressed into a firm line. "If you're not going to be my Dom outside Club Atlantis, then why would you get involved in this?"

"Because I'm learning that, remarkable as it seems, you're even more prone to trouble outside the club. I will be the first vampire with post-turning gray hair."

That made her smile, but his serious tone meant business. "I'm expanding the geographical boundaries. For now, I'm your Dom, period."

She gazed upon him, and he held the look. "For now," she said quietly.

"For now."

Not surprisingly, he saw the leap of hope that it eventually might lead to more. But he didn't have to add any caveats to head that off, because almost immediately, she squelched it herself.

Don't make too much of it. Just accept it as it's offered. She nodded. "Okay. Yes, sir."

While he could tell himself such acceptance served her own interests, her desire to be around him, she wasn't a self-serving person. She knew he enjoyed being around her, and didn't want to take that from him by asking too much. Another way she could serve her Master.

She might just kill him with kindness. Fortunately, she still had that stubborn set to her pretty chin, a cue that she was going to think of other ways to dissuade him from joining her on this particular quest. Which just emphasized how much he needed to be there.

"As your Dom it's my decision how best to care for you. Even if you disagree," he reminded her. "But if you don't like the limitations I've put on our relationship, you have one choice. You can choose for me not to be your Dom."

In the vampire world, a servant has one choice. Whether or not to be a servant. After that, all choices belong to the vampire.

He really didn't want vampire canons popping up conveniently in his head right now. He squelched them.

If she didn't want him as her Dom, that was fine. He'd still be going to the old boyfriend's house as her friend. That was a given.

Trepidation flashed across her face. "You want...to give me a choice?"

"It's not my preference, no, but I'd like to hear your answer."

A tiny smile reappeared on her face at his irritable response. "I want you to be that," she said. "I just don't want to pull you into things that I can handle myself."

"Which is a very typical service sub reaction, but not always healthy, because you should be able to have expectations of others for yourself. Especially when you're as special as you are, to me, and lots of others."

That got her attention. She lifted her gaze to his. She wasn't wearing the contacts, so the brown pools drew him in. "So," he said, resisting the urge to be distracted. "You will let me know when you are going, and you'll go at night. I want to hear your promise, because I know you'll honor it. And then I'm going to make sure you remember it."

Her lips pressed together. This unexpected stubborn streak was making him harder. While his insistence wasn't sexually motivated, her reaction was turning it in that direction. Then a puzzled look crossed her face. "I'm not trying to question you—"

—which she totally was—

"But I was thinking of going in the morning, because he's usually hung over and less with it. Is there a reason you want me to go at night?"

"I'm sure if you think it through, you'll figure it out." He gave her a steady look while she sifted through her thoughts, then he saw the light bulb go off. The obviousness of it produced a sheepish smile on her face.

"*Oh.* I really haven't ever seen you during daylight, have I?"

"Not unless you remember seeing a ball of flame shaped like me."

"Yeah." She wrinkled her nose, a self-deprecation. "Sorry again. I was a little slow there. The whole nighttime thing for vampires. Check."

He shook his head. "Could you get any more adorable?"

She made a face at him, stuck out her tongue. He was going to spank her for that specifically. As well as a few other things. "I still haven't heard you promise," he reminded her.

"I promise," she said reluctantly.

"Why am I making you promise?"

"Because you want to look after me. Make sure I'm safe."

"Yes. Why?"

She got stuck there, but he gave it to her in his head, a hint and a reminder.

Because you are precious.

She pinkened, but then he grasped her wrist, taking the cloth away. "Open your mouth."

When she did, he rolled the washcloth into a bit shape and put it there, a temporary gag. He liked the idea of her inhaling the scent of his release, tasting the lingering essence of it. "Hold it there. I don't want your neighbor calling the cops, thinking you're being murdered in here. Hand me my belt."

Her eyes widened, but after only a brief hesitation, she complied. She lifted his jeans, gripped the belt and slid it out of the loopholes. When she brought it to him, she was all big eyes, lots of soft hair. Her lips were pressed into the terry cloth gag, shirt around her thighs over a body that wore nothing else. The picture she made tightened things inside and out of him, made him hurt, ache and want. The sub in her craved the punishment. She was already getting wet again. Yet he saw her recognize his determination, realize the next few moments might be memorable in a way that wouldn't be entirely pleasurable.

Good. It might impress upon her that, no matter how run-of-the-mill her words had been to her, to him, her being around a guy who thought it was okay to beat her, throw her out of his house and steal from her was not 'just the way things are.'

Well, beat her the wrong way, for the wrong reasons, that is.

Yeah, he was sure that was a sound bite that would go over like a lead balloon in most vanilla venues, but that wasn't the world that reigned in this room right now.

Clasping her wrist, he tugged and brought her down over his knees. He kept her elbows and upper torso on the bed while he centered her hips over his lap, her feet off the ground, dangling.

"No trying to hide thoughts, no lies by omission, no holding back any information from me. It's up to me to decide what's relevant to your wellbeing, not you. When I'm done, I'm going to ask you a question. If you respond to it correctly, I'll stop. If you don't, I will do it all over again, until you get it right."

Hell, he liked this, a lot more than he wanted to admit, being able to be inside his sub's head while he took care of her, disciplined her.

She was wondering if she should argue about it, point out that having a Dom in her head was new territory that maybe needed to be discussed, negotiated. She was absolutely right—if they were still in the human realm of things. The vampire in him had only one thing it wanted from her right now. Obedience.

He rubbed a hand over her round backside, pulling the shirt up to give him a clear view. He had already checked when he took her earlier, but he wanted to make sure he saw no lingering evidence of the explosion that would make this the wrong kind of pain.

The second mark had done its job. There were some hints of the bruises, but none in the area that would be receiving his attention. He ran his hand up and down her thighs, warming her up, registering every shiver as he trailed his fingers between her buttocks, close to the exposed lips of her cunt. When he was done, he was going to work his fingers in there, feel the soaking wetness. She responded strongly to discipline.

He was starting to get a picture of key portions of Ella's life. She'd never had anyone completely in charge of caring for her, not since the fire had taken her family. She had a hunger for it, so painful and deep that she'd shut off that avenue, barred the way with extreme danger signs, knowing it was a vulnerable place that the wrong person could take advantage of if she let them.

She was fiercely independent, something many might miss, because she so enjoyed revealing the vulnerable sub within. She yearned for a Dom's care, and she did such a good job of communicating that, people at the club did exactly what she'd pointed out. Treated her as if she were something fragile, in need of protection, watching after her before she did something foolish. All while depending on her to be there when they needed her, because she was. She anticipated what they needed, and supplied it, as a sub, as a staff member, as a person.

It wasn't an act. She was that vulnerable sub, a young woman with a remarkable combination of resilience and fragility. But he doubted she'd ever leaned on anyone a hundred percent in her life. She'd learned not to do that, and she'd learned why the hard way.

He'd brought her too close to that dangerous emotional edge. She did something very out of character for her usual behavior. She started to struggle off his lap, dropping the gag out of her mouth. "Wolf, I don't think we—"

He held her fast, leaned over her, retrieved the jeans or, more specifically, what was in the front right pocket. A length of cord. He sometimes worked on rope-tying knots at dawn, while waiting for sleep to claim him. Or at the club, while people-watching and not in session.

In the time she'd spoken those five words, he'd pulled out the cord, picked up the cloth, straightened and put it back between her parted lips, pushing it in securely. He ran the cord between them as well, tying it in place with a firm cinch that she felt pull at the corners of her mouth. Her eyes got wider, but he felt the little spike in her mind as he took control.

What about a safe word?

Her mind was still agile enough to figure out another way to talk to him. A sign of the right kind of emotional panic, trying to talk at all when he was so obviously done with that form of communication. He reminded her of it with an equally short response.

Vampires don't believe in them.

What question did he want answered? She'd been strapped with a belt before, loved it. It was her favorite Dom tool of punishment, but that was in-scene, with a Dom who was...temporary. Wolf was temporary. He'd made that clear from the get-go, yet she was reacting to him with an anxiety as if his expectations were going to matter to her well beyond this moment.

"We're not negotiating anything, Ella. This is punishment. I want to make sure you remember everything I've told you."

He ran his fingertips over her bare backside again, trailing along the seam, down to her exposed cunt. He pushed his thumb inside her, finding her heated and wet. He held her thighs closed so she couldn't spread them, and worked his thumb in there, sending spirals of sensation out through her buttocks and lower belly.

Then he withdrew his thumb slowly, painting the moisture on her labia with easy caresses. He touched her entirely for himself, for the pleasure of how she felt to him. As she became more aroused, she was giving him a gift that he himself had created, with his total attention upon her.

She couldn't afford this. While on the surface it didn't look much different from scenes she'd done at the club, every Dom and sub knew that the most powerful triggers were emotional ones. He was leaning on a door she kept closed. Truth, she was afraid he was already halfway over the threshold.

"Put your head down, sweet girl. Grip the covers. Both hands. Make fists, squeeze them tight. Don't let go. No matter what."

She obeyed. Through integrating her breathing and arousal, she knew how to manage pain, to make the experience more ecstatic for her. She focused on that, trying to leave the rest behind.

He started with a few light slaps, just warming up the skin, mixing it with rubs and squeezes, where he grunted his appreciation of having her ass in his possession.

Then he started striking her with more force. Breath left her, and her fists squeezed tighter, released. Her buttocks quivered, and she made a conscious effort not to tense them, to accept everything he wanted to give her. That was the gift to her, and she never wasted a second of it.

He kept strapping her, up, down. He had an excellent technique, never staying in one place too long. Then he gripped both buttocks in one broad hand, used pressure to pull the weight of them up, more toward her spine, exposing that tender valley where the thighs joined to them. Then he went after that area with the belt. Hard.

It was a different level of pain, one she thought she could take, but she'd never been strapped by Wolf. He cracked it down on her flesh, again, again. She started quivering, her fists clutching, unclutching. She had to move. Goddess, she needed to writhe or wriggle like a child trying to escape punishment. She didn't do that unless that was what the Dom wanted. Wolf wanted a question answered, one he hadn't even yet asked.

She bit down on the terrycloth gag, tried so hard to stay still. His hand was moving, pinching, squeezing, and the belt went back to the round part of her ass, which was a blissful relief, until he began startling her with an occasional crack back on that more sensitive part, and would stay there for three or four licks before moving back to the other.

She wasn't moving, but she was screaming against the gag, her fingers locked on the covers.

"Spread your legs."

No, no, no, no.

Do you think you can refuse me, Ella? Say no to me?

No, she wouldn't. Only in her head. She'd only ever say no in her head, but he was there, and he'd heard it. That rattled her. She struggled to part her thighs, though her sense of self-preservation fought her, asking her if she'd lost her fucking mind. He was scary, because he was setting and breaking all the rules as he deemed fit, all of it up to him. He was possessing her, saying she was his, totally.

Somehow, she managed to override her mind and spread her legs. He went back to work on her backside, but as he did, he pushed fingers inside her cunt. The feeling was indescribable. With the pain, he'd opened up a new well of feeling inside her. When he fucked her with his fingers, that well spilled over into her lower belly, flowed into her chest, her lower back.

Having his fingers inside her didn't change the force or direction of his blows. Maybe that was a vampire thing, excess agility and strength, no matter the awkward position of the throwing arm.

Then his hand withdrew, but he held her up easily, one palm flat on her lower belly and mound, holding her above his knees, in the air, legs dangling loose and open, and strapped her more.

Whap, whap, whap...crack.

She arched, breath hissing in between her teeth. He'd hit that one on the joining part of thighs to backside again, on flesh now already smarting and angry. He kept doing it, and it really, really hurt. She cried out against the terry cloth and let go of the blanket. She tried to get away, tried to fight him, and she couldn't. He was literally too strong. She was held down again, his elbow pressed into the middle of her back, her flailing feet held by his other forearm as he flexed it, worked the strap.

When she was sobbing against the gag, he finally stopped. Her body went limp, even as it throbbed. Her pussy had drenched her thighs, and she wanted...everything. Needed him inside her, his cock thrusting just as relentlessly as that belt fell. To remind her that he'd punished her because he cared about her.

He rubbed her throbbing buttocks, pinching a tender spot occasionally, making her flinch. Then he moved to her head, stroking her hair. As his strong palm and fingers moved under her chin, bringing it up to caress her, the tears that were already falling increased. He made a soothing noise before moving his palm to her sternum, spreading out his wide palm to lift her upper body, hold it arched in his lap.

"Yes, I do care about you, Ella. Very much. My girl. Reach back, grip your ass. Squeeze and rub yourself, digging your fingernails into the sorest points. Hard as you can, no holding back. When you're dug in as deep as you can go, stop and hold it there."

She complied, and fire lanced through those striped places. She kept squeezing, at his ruthless encouragement, until her arms shook with the effort. It was far easier to have him administer pain to herself than to have her do it. She knew that was why he did it.

"I have three questions for you to answer," he said abruptly. "'What can you expect of me? What do you expect of me? What do you want to expect from me?'"

Fuck. She couldn't form worms. Words. But she struggled for them in her head. Only one answer fit all three.

What you want to give me.

"A nice response. Straight from the heart. And a total lie."

CHAPTER NINETEEN

"You like pleasing Doms. Like telling them what they want to hear. For the right reasons, because it gives you pleasure to please them. It's a true response, but it's not an honest one. Honesty doesn't make anyone feel good. Not usually. It's why we bury it way down."

He paused, and ran his hand over her smarting buttocks. "You know, a second mark is not as resilient as a third mark. But those two marks do give you greater healing ability than none. Still, when I'm done, you won't be able to sit for about half a day. Riding that bike of yours is pretty much going to be torture. But the lesson needs to be reinforced. I want you thinking about how you can't sit, because of me. Guess that's a Dom thing, that sadistic pleasure in the pain a sub has endured just to please him. Makes me feel like fucking you all over again, because I know you'd come, even through the pain, and that mix of pain and pleasure, both coming from me? It's a fucking drug, Ella. You've had a taste, but I don't think you've ever gotten the full dose."

He turned her over in his arms, cupping her face. His silver eyes were glowing, his face set in that stern, uncompromising expression. Every word held her mesmerized. She was helpless, and it made her quake.

"Yeah, I want you scared. In the right way. I don't have to be fair,

Ella. I just have to be your Master, also in all the right ways. You want to know how I want to fuck you, baby girl?"

A wicked grin split his features, making him look demonic. If he'd ever showed her that expression before today, she'd have known he wasn't human.

"You should see how big your eyes are. I'd sit you down on the very edge of a wooden chair, making sure the edge was cutting into that place I've hurt so bad, between your thighs and ass. I like working that area over good when I'm punishing a sub, because I know how every step rubs the abraded skin in that fold, reminds you of the lesson. When it's happening, you think it's going to be too painful to come, but I'd prove you wrong. A full servant learns pretty fast just how much pain can be endured, while pleasure is still served its due. When they crave it all over again, when it's done, they know just how thoroughly a vampire has claimed everything they are. So I've heard. I've never had a full servant."

Those lightning eyes sparked. "When I finish fucking you on the chair, it will hurt so much that you're crying, those little fingernails leaving crescent marks all over my shoulders. But your clit will also be throbbing for friction, your nipples aching for attention. Hell, every inch of your skin will be begging for my mouth. That's when I'll turn you over. Use the sweet honey from between your thighs to lube myself up, and take your ass. I'll work myself down to the root, and give you the fucking of your life, girl. Every slam against your gorgeous backside will set those nerves on fire again.

"You'll think the pain is too much. You'll be so close to begging for mercy, wanting to give me the right answer to my question, if only it will stop me, make me stop hurting you. But that's not what I want. I want you to feel the pain, understand the lesson it's teaching you, so when I do hold you in my arms after, cradle my baby girl, the answers will float off your lips as easily as an expelled breath. You won't give me the words to stop the pain. You'll give them to me because you'll know whatever I demand from you is what you want to give.

"That's where we're going, Ella. So you get busy on all the smoke-screens you're going to try to sell me on instead of the truth. The more you do, the more it will please me, because of what I have planned for your stubborn backside."

He was pushing her past rational thought. Every word planted a startling seed of dread deep in her belly. But as he shifted around in that debris, it unearthed something else. A pale, sickly-looking plant, deprived of sunlight for a very long time. Yet it still had enough strength to lift its trembling face to the sun.

Hope.

The chasm that hope had to cross inside her reality was impossible. But she was going over it. He'd just made that clear. No safe words.

He turned her over again, even as she was protesting against the gag, still crying. This time, as if he knew her control wouldn't hold out, he produced another of those cords, wrapped her wrists in them and then dropped the tail end to the floor, stepping on it so she couldn't pull it free. She'd have to stay on his lap, bent over for his punishment, as long as he wished.

She didn't understand what he wanted from her. She thought she'd given him the right answer. Then he started over again, just as he'd promised.

He repeated every bit of it, until she was screaming, then whimpering against the gag. She knew her buttocks had to be bleeding, or at least in danger of blisters. When he stopped, he put his fingers in her again, stirred around, finding her just as wet, because...she had no idea why she was still that wet. But with every strap against her backside, different words jumped into her head, until only one held.

Why? What? Can he? Oh... Please... God, I can't... Wolf, please...Wolf. Wolf. Wolf.

When he stopped this time, she was panting. He traced very light fingertips over her backside. "Sweet darling. I'm a beast. A couple of those are going to welt up like a son of a bitch. I'll put some salve on them this week, keep you safe and well. But first you'll have to answer my question right, or there will be blood all over the floor this third time. Is that what you want?"

She shook her head vehemently. Saliva and phlegm had run into the terry cloth. She couldn't tell him, couldn't tell anyone, because she'd never told the truth of it to any Dom. Or to anyone. The words were scrambled, so far away across that chasm. Yet he'd catapulted her over to them, landing her on the unyielding stone of what her soul needed and wanted more than anything. It wasn't a soft, nurturing place, but cold and stark, because what lived there, lived alone. It expected to always do so, isolated from the rest of her mind, the way she lived her life.

He jerked the cord free and the terry cloth fell out of her mouth as she gasped through her erratic little sobs.

"Don't piss me off, Ella," he said quietly. "That's not a place you want to take me. Answer your Master honestly. Right now, no thinking, just the answer to the question."

He snapped the first one off in his mind, firing it straight into the turmoil of hers.

What can you expect from me?

"I don't know what I can expect from you," she sobbed.

What do you want to expect from me?

"Everything. I want to expect everything."

That was so awful. She should tell him she really didn't expect every—

What do you *expect of me?*

"Nothing."

It burst forth from her, a terrible, painful word. "Nothing."

She couldn't expect anything. Not from him, or anyone. She could value what they gave her, could keep her sanity, as long as they didn't put false expectations on it, things she knew they couldn't give. Sometimes she knew that before they did.

"I'm sorry. I didn't mean..."

"Shut up," he said gently. "Just be quiet."

Everything changed. The belt dropped to the floor, and he turned her over in his arms again, this time cradling her so close, holding her, rubbing her back and hip in soothing motions as she cried.

"You answered the questions correctly," he murmured. "Honestly, as you feel them in your heart. You don't have to spare my feelings. That's the good thing about me in your head. All you have to give me is honesty. Nothing more, nothing less."

He wasn't angry. Not even disappointed or dismayed. He held her curled up securely in his arms, one hand cupping the back of her head. He kept holding her, never easing up, not even a shift to disrupt the flow of tears, the little hiccups.

Not until she finally ran out of tears and lay in his possession, numb, quiet.

She thought of a sub she'd met at another club, one who gave a

Mistress everything. Any Mistress, whether for a night or whenever she wanted to cut him loose. No selectiveness, just a hungry desire to give away his free will. He carried his apartment key around his neck, his admission that if the Domme wanted him, he'd follow her willingly as she took possession of all his belongings, managed his life for him. In return, he'd give her everything, now just a member of her household.

She didn't want that, couldn't want that. She could love whoever and however she wanted. But full trust was something very few people earned. Naomi had been right about that. Ella wasn't even sure if she could live up to it herself, because in the end, people lived very much in their heads, the center of their own story.

Stop, stop, *stop*. This unleashed thinking was like running a needle through a piece of cloth, over and over. Over time, it just became a big ball of snarled lines, crossing, crisscrossing, no sense ever to be made of them.

Before the fire took her, her mom would read to her at bedtime, but she'd build on the story. Ella remembered a book with a picture of the earth, drawn in bright, brilliant blue and green colors.

"Do you know what the earth is, if you peel off the cover? A big, tangled ball of string. If you picked it up and threw it across the universe, that string would unravel forever, a trail of light like a burning star's tail..."

Wolf wiped her face with a fresh cloth, massaged the sore corners of her mouth with his strong fingertips.

"Stop thinking, Ella. Just be. Let yourself be."

He'd only second marked her, but he knew he'd dug that word out of her soul.

Nothing.

She lay limp in his arms. Emotionally drained. He hadn't intended to go this far with her, especially when he had to leave her before dawn. Because of his relatively young age, he pretty much had to be below ground before that first lick of sunlight turned the sky rose and gray, unless he liked feeling like a furnace.

He didn't want to leave her, though, and considered taking her back to his place. As if she was his full servant, someone he could command to be with him 24/7, if that was his preference. Who he could feed upon first upon rising, or have in his arms as he slipped into that daylight coma state.

When he'd first been turned, he'd fought that lethargy, but Nolan had told him to think of it like a teenager, needing more sleep for the growth of his bones.

As you get older, you'll be able to go to sleep later, sleep lighter, except at the very height of the day. For now, let nature take its course, boy. It will make you stronger. And if the lack of control keeps bothering you, pick up a full servant along the way who can keep tabs on you throughout the day.

"Can I see them?" she asked drowsily.

He'd been in his own head, not following her thoughts, so he had to catch up. "What?"

"Your fangs. I mean, I've felt them, when you fed, but I'd like to see them. They do some kind of lengthening thing when you use them. I figure that's why I've never really noticed how sharp your canines are. And you don't fully smile a lot. Do vampires learn to do that, keep them concealed by making sure they don't smile too big?"

"Yeah, pretty much. Why do you want to see them?"

"Well, why wouldn't I? It's like seeing a tiger in a sanctuary. There's some part of you that wants to squat down next to him and put your hand on top of his paw, because they are so enormous, and you just can't imagine having a foot that big. It's so different from what you are. Yet, when he studies you like you're just as odd to him, that's when you know there are things that make you not so different, too. It makes you curious. Want to touch, connect."

"Even if you know it's dangerous and probably not so smart."

"True." She didn't say anything further, but he saw that she'd deduced he didn't really want to "show" her his fangs. She'd respect that without further pressing.

Her words were slurred, her pupils large, so he knew she was drifting in subspace still. Some subs were silent in that state. Some slept. Others cried, little sniffles and sobs that went on for some time. Ella had demonstrated that here, but her tears had been because of a breakthrough. Her normal subspace state apparently was this, moving between drowsiness and streams of consciousness, charmingly innocent dialogues. It didn't surprise him a bit. It fit her.

What did surprise him was realizing he was self-conscious about showing her his fangs. He'd never been asked the question. Pretty much everyone who knew he was a vampire was a vampire or a full servant, so the question had never come up.

He closed his hand around her wrist, lifted her hand to his jaw. Realizing he was granting her request, her face tipped up quickly to see, interest and relaxed anticipation in her sleepy gaze. Whether she realized it or not, her curiosity and relative alertness were helping him resolve his aftercare concern. She was at home, in a familiar environment. Plus, he could touch her mind with his until he fell asleep. Her being a second mark would also help her recuperation time. She'd be okay.

He still gave himself a kick for going so intense with her, with such a limited window of time. It was evidence of being off his game with her. He'd work on that. For now, he guided her fingers into a closed curl, except for her forefinger. He parted his lips, put the pad of the straightened finger on the slick top of his right canine. "Don't move that finger," he warned her.

She giggled—giggled, for Christ's sake. She really was adorable, all big brown eyes and soft mouth. "You just beat the hell out of me," she said solemnly. "And you're worried about pricking my finger, like Sleeping Beauty."

"Behave," he told her, suppressing a smile. "It's not a sub's job to point out a Master's contradictions."

He consciously extended the fangs, and her eyes widened, lips parting in pleased delight as the slick enamel beneath her fingertip lengthened and broadened, until he was fully unsheathed. His fangs were almost an inch long extended, and they curved.

"Wow," she breathed, propping herself up on his chest to peer more closely at them. "Is it okay to move my fingers now?"

At his nod, she lightly explored both of them. He was surprised to find he could feel her touch, or maybe it was just a mental transference that made the pressure feel like a caress on even more sensitive nerve endings. When she reached the sharp end, she pressed on it lightly, her expression amazed anew at how little pressure it took to break the skin. He gripped her wrist, took the finger into his mouth and sucked the blood away, winning a distracted look from her as she trembled at the gesture.

"How do you keep from cutting yourself?"

"You really don't. Feel this?" He guided the punctured fingertip back to his lower lip and let her feel inside, the thickened area. "When you first become a made vampire, you cut this area, over and over. Either because of that, or because it's just part of our physiology, over time it thickens, forms a buffer, so to speak, and then you stop cutting the inside of your mouth. You can still slice up your lip pretty good at times. But we heal fast."

"That's good. Because canker sores suck."

"Yes, they do." As he retracted the fangs, she craned her head, like a thoughtful turtle keeping her head low while looking upward, watching that extra length disappear.

"So, do male vampires...compare them? Size?"

He couldn't remember the last time someone had compelled a full belly laugh out of him, but that did it. Her eyes were dancing as he held her until the chuckles subsided. "I'm not sure it's ever come up."

Her grin widened and he swatted her pretty ass. "Now you're doing it on purpose. Being cute."

"Hey, it was your phrasing, not mine. So Anwyn...are hers like that?"

"Female fangs do tend to be smaller, more dainty, but still just as wickedly sharp."

She put her head down on his chest. "They're very awesome. Thank you, Master."

He made a noncommittal grunt, but stroked her back, down to her hip, curled his fingers in the ends of her long hair. "I need to leave soon."

"I know. I'm going to try to go to sleep so I won't know when you leave. You'll just be in my dreams with me."

He didn't say anything to that, just kept stroking her as her breathing evened out, as she slipped into dreams as easily as an innocent child in truth. Yet she had one hand on his biceps, clasping them firmly enough to convey her desire for him to stay. When he reluctantly extricated himself, he curled her up in her bed. He put her covers over her bare body, bent down and put a kiss on her shoulder.

And then, because he could, he scraped a fang over that smooth, soft skin, pulling back enough to see the faint scratch he'd left, the tiny pinpoints of blood along the length. He touched his tongue to them, sweet, tart tastes of her. He thought of her words, her desire to take him into her dreams.

"I will be, little girl. Beautiful woman. I promise."

~

Ella knew a lot about serving Masters and Mistresses, and she took pride in doing it to the best of her ability. Sometimes that required homework. Though she had a busy schedule over the next couple days, she made time for one particular assignment.

When she arrived at Club Atlantis at midday, construction was in full swing. There was a small army of work trucks, a din of hammering and raised voices from the workers. Dust was billowing out from their efforts. Yellow hardhats moved purposefully to and fro, a dumpster loaded up with debris. They'd already cleared the alley and had scaffolding up to rebuild the wall.

It gave Ella a fist-pumping surge of "yeah" to see Anwyn mobilizing repair efforts so quickly. The Mistress's big "fuck you" to anyone who tried to take Atlantis down.

All Doms were control freaks, more or less. Anwyn wouldn't leave the construction staff unsupervised during her daylight sleep hours. So just as Ella had expected, she found Gideon keeping an eye on the work in process. He sat on the edge of the loading dock of the vending machine warehouse which shared the other side of the alley with them. Fortunately, they'd sustained only cosmetic damage, but Anwyn had already told Gary they'd fix it as part of her own repairs, a good neighbor gesture. The man had always had a really good relationship with Club Atlantis and Anwyn. She'd won his heart early on, overcoming his trepidations about having a "sex club" setting up next to his business.

Gideon's thick tread shoes dangled off the dock edge. He was drinking a Coke and eating a moon pie. There was a crate of similar snacks below his feet, along with a giant cooler of drinks.

As she approached, the question in her face, he nodded down to them. "Help yourself. Gary sent over a couple cases of moon pies and other snacks for the workers. Take a handful."

Ella selected a Diet Pepsi and a pack of trail mix that had cashews, walnuts, raisins and semi-sweet chocolate chips, and put them on the dock next to him. Obligingly, he leaned down, gripping her beneath the arms, and lifted her up next to him. Gideon was a very strong man, she knew that, but with her new perception on things, she realized he did it even more easily than a "normal" strong man would.

"So what's up?" he asked, giving her a shrewd look out of his midnight blue eyes.

"I've been picking up on some things," she said carefully. "Um... Anwyn. She's like Wolf, isn't she? And you're...her full servant."

Gideon studied her a long minute. Ella was ninety-nine percent sure of it, but when he inclined his head at last, she felt a surge of wonder, seeing it confirmed.

"Thank you. I'm not asking just out of curiosity."

"I figured that." His firm mouth quirked. "So now that you're part of the secret club, what's on your mind?"

She wanted to hug him, but she held back, staying on target. "I wanted to ask you about some things, if you're okay with that. If there's no rule against it."

"None that I've been told," he said.

"Which means maybe Wolf hasn't thought to tell you not to tell me anything, because he didn't anticipate me thinking to ask you."

"That's a mouthful." Gideon's blue eyes sparked with dry humor. "And you're smart enough to have figured out that coming here at the height of the day is the best time for your Dom not to be listening in."

She had the grace to blush and focus on opening the snack pack. "So, am I out of line?"

Gideon nudged her with his shoulder. "Do I look like a Dom to you?"

"Well, sometimes." She gave him a crooked grin. "But more alpha than anything else."

"Smart girl. Yeah, that's what I've been told. It's cool, Ella. Sometimes you work around them a bit, to figure out how best to take care of them."

That was a relief to hear. "Are you okay with me asking you questions that might get...personal?"

He pursed his lips. "Maybe. If you flash your tits at me."

She punched him in the arm and he chuckled. "Had to get you to loosen up. You looked too serious. Go ahead and ask your questions. Let's go down the rabbit hole."

She brought both her feet up, bending her knees against her chest, and rocked on the point of her buttocks. As she popped her soda top and took a sip, she jumped right in. "I've heard him and Anwyn say things like first mark, second mark, third mark, full servant. What does all that mean?"

"Easy, academic stuff first. They can bind a human to them with three different marks. The first is a geographical locator. It tells them where you are, within a certain range, and some of the older vamps can tell if you're in distress or danger, but it doesn't give them any other access to the marked human's mind."

Her brow furrowed. "Can they skip one? Do they have to do them in order?"

"Nope and yes." He nudged her. "My understanding from Anwyn is that he gave you the first mark a while back, to help us keep track of you. You tend to wander like one of Anwyn's stray cats."

She suddenly recalled, with great clarity, the several times he'd bitten her, but she remembered the time in the massage room the most, because it had felt...more tingly. She was willing to bet that was when he'd done it. She'd ask him.

"Second mark." Gideon continued. "They can read your mind and you can read theirs, if they let you. They can close down that link pretty easily, except when they're under attack or great physical distress."

"Like when Wolf was blown up."

"Yep. Again, a lot of this stuff can vary, depending on the age or maturity of the vampire. Some can see things through your eyes with the second mark, some can only hear your thoughts and put together the visuals through that."

"Do you know how old Wolf is?"

"Born 1946."

"Oh." She hadn't expected such a direct answer. "So his military experience..."

"Vietnam."

Amazing. And terrible. She thought of the scar tissue she'd felt during his massage, still existing beneath the skin, despite being a vampire.

"Anwyn became one after the alley thing, didn't she?"

He nodded, a shadow crossing his gaze. "She's what they call a fledgling. Wolf is still considered pretty young, but no longer a fledgling, mostly because he's a made vampire. It's a weird thing. Made vampires who are stable, they mature faster than born vampires in some ways, in the sense they gain control over their bloodlust faster. A born vampire is pretty much considered a 'teenager,' until they hit the first century mark, and then they're like a twenty-something until two hundred. But a big percentage of made vampires don't stabilize, which is why they're considered inferior stock next to born ones. Though some of that has less to do with reality than your typical elitism, same as humans who think their bloodlines make them better."

"Okay." She digested that. "That's two marks. Will you tell me about the third? I get the feeling it's really important."

"It is." He gave her a steady look. "It's the point of no return. A third mark is a full servant. That's when you're bound to that vampire in every conceivable way. Head, heart and soul. Supposedly you're even bound to him or her through eternity. That idea got started because if your vampire dies, you die, within minutes or even instantly."

"Whoa." She blinked. "Yeah, that would make you wonder about the afterlife, wouldn't it?"

Gideon lifted a shoulder. "Or it might be the result of some kind of chemical binding that happens during the third mark, reinforced by years of blood sharing. Lord Brian, he's the science guy for the vampires, is always quick to point out there are plenty of things which have been called the will of the gods, that eventually turned out to be simple science."

"So if either dies, they both die," she said thoughtfully.

"No," Gideon said. "The vampire doesn't die if the servant dies, but supposedly it feels like having a limb cut off, especially if the bond has been there awhile. But as extreme as that sounds, that's not the biggest thing about being a third mark that you need to understand."

He paused, as if looking for the right words. "They can be in your head like the second mark, but even deeper."

"Okay. I get it. I think."

He shook his head. "I'm not sure anyone really does, until they feel it. There's no way to keep them out, Ella. They can know whatever they want, even things you don't know about yourself, or want anyone else in the world to know."

His jaw flexed, his eyes hardening on hers. "If you resist it, it can be as invasive as rape. A vampire who third marks you could strip your mind, your soul. Hollow you out if he or she wanted to do so. Leave you nothing but a drooling vegetable. You are giving another being, a much more powerful one, total control over everything you are."

"You're trying to scare me."

"No trying about it. You're second marked now. Servants watch out for one another. We're kind of like an unspoken trade union, and us keeping each other informed sometimes prevents really bad things from happening." He tugged her hair, not teasingly, but to emphasize their bond, his care for her. "Vampires are a distinct species, with traits unique to them. Some are born, some are made. Even with a made vampire, the biology of being a vampire pretty quickly starts to override the human perspective. They're top of the world food chain when it comes to basic predator rules. They can't go out in daylight and they depend on human blood to live, and those two absolutes provide the only advantages we have over them."

On topics that mattered, Gideon was as serious and stern as Wolf. So when he paused to gather his thoughts, Ella stayed silent, waiting for more.

"At Atlantis, some people enjoy the whole Master/slave thing, or the *idea* that they totally belong to their Dom. A vampire-full servant relationship is the real deal. When you're deciding to become a vampire's full servant, you are making the ultimate leap of faith, believing in that vampire's regard for you, but you're also accepting that they will see you as their property. No matter how cherished, you're theirs. All vampires are sexual Dominants, Ella. Sexual Dominants on freaking steroids and then some."

He shook his head. "The only choice a human has is whether or not they want to be a full servant. After that, all choices belong to the vampire. I don't care how much a made vampire like Wolf, or even Anwyn, claims otherwise, that sense of the servant as fully owned property of that vampire is something a vampire can't unwrite from their DNA. Even the rewriting that happens to the made ones."

He pinned her with a flat stare. "In the vampire world, servants have zero rights. I mean zero. There are some moves happening away from that, and some instances where exceptions have been made due to the relationship a specific vamp has with their servant, but that's at the whim of the Council or the ruling vampire over the situation. What they do today can be changed tomorrow. Right now, if your vampire wants to torture you for three years running, he can. If he wants to kill you and get a new servant, he can. Up until recently, that's been the preferred way of handling a servant you don't want, because you can't let them go back to a regular human life with the knowledge he or she has. Can't even do that with a second mark."

"So if Wolf leaves and doesn't want me to go with him..."

"Then a case would have to be made to the Council that you're under Anwyn's direct supervision and therefore safe from being a danger of exposure to the human world. Fortunately, that's a pretty strong argument, so you don't have to worry about it."

"They don't have to kill me. Comforting"

He slanted her a grim smile. "Isn't it?"

"You're telling me all the bad stuff, and I get why you're doing that. But tell me something not so bad."

He paused, considering, then nodded. "As a third mark, there's nothing or no one you'll ever feel more connected to than your vampire. You'll live up to three hundred years as a third mark. You'll be their primary food source, the one who can do daylight things for them, watch over their sleeping spot. There are really so many things it is, and isn't, that it can't be fully described unless you know it firsthand."

"You made that choice with Anwyn. And maybe not just Anwyn?"

At his look, she proceeded hesitantly. "The other one, Scary Guy. The night Anwyn came back onto the floor fulltime, I saw him. I also saw the way he looked at her. But he looked at you the same way. So I figured he and Anwyn...share."

"Scary Guy." A flicker of humor and something else passed through his gaze. "Yeah. They've both marked me. Ella, do you know what Wolf's intentions are?"

She bit her lip. "He's made it pretty clear we're right now, and that's it. I can feel how much he wants me, but he didn't intend to second mark me. And he hasn't explained any of this to me. So that's pretty clear proof he doesn't intend us to go down this road, right?"

A few minutes ago, saying that aloud might have hurt worse, but now, thinking about what Gideon had described, she wondered if Wolf had been trying to protect her. Not wanting to draw her into such a brutal world. Odd how that didn't make her feel lots better, when it should. Twisted idiot that she was, it just focused her on how he didn't want to share everything about who he was with her.

"Intentions don't always pan out in any world, let alone the vampire ones." A sudden discomfort gripped Gideon's expression, as if he were trying to determine how much more to say. Then he spoke flatly, decision obviously made.

"How do you feel about murdering a schoolteacher, Ella? A Greenpeace worker? Some nine to five person who takes care of his family, does a lot of little good things that would add up to a great, valuable life, if he or she wasn't struck down at the peak of it?"

"What?" Her brow furrowed. "That would be awful, of course. I'd never do that. Are you saying..."

Gideon gave her a look that swept her with unease. "Yes. To maintain their full strength, vampires have to kill at least one human every year. They call it the annual kill. It can't be a serial killer or a pedophile. It has to be a good person, a person with the type of blood energy Wolf would want to ingest. If he doesn't do that once a year, he will start weakening, lose his mental faculties. Eventually another vampire would take advantage of that, kill him off, but before that, he would essentially start starving. Maybe even lose the will to live, walk into the sun."

"So...it's a survival thing." But her voice sounded weak, even to herself. Her heart had accelerated, and her palms felt damp.

"That kill, yes. But according to current Council law, a vampire can kill thirteen humans a year, including their annual, without repercussions. That limit isn't set because of compassion toward the human race. It's because the Council is hyperaware that too many human deaths draw attention, and keeping the vampire world from general human knowledge is their prime directive. A lot of other stuff revolves around that protection, including their treatment of their servants, and why they mark them fully to bind them. Human servants know about the existence of vampires. Being in their heads so deep ensures the servants have a slim-to-no-chance of betraying vampire kind."

Ella couldn't imagine Wolf harming anyone that way. Or Goddess...Anwyn. She wanted Gideon to stop talking. Instead, he reached out and touched her face, said what she didn't want to think in her own head. "How would you ever be okay with Wolf needing to kill a worthy human being while you stood on the sidelines, letting it happen? Ella, you're vegan. You don't like to harm an animal for food. My guess is, if he did third mark you, he would do his annual kill by himself, to spare you having a front row seat on it. But shit happens, and sometimes in this world you find yourself a part of things you'd never expect."

"How did you deal with it?" she asked, before she could pull back the question. She couldn't imagine it was an easy thing for Gideon to talk about, and it went beyond personal and need-to-know. But he gave her an answer.

"I don't," he said flatly. "I have that 'luxury' because of 'Scary Guy.'" A humorless smile crossed his lips. "He handles Anwyn's with her, and he...he doesn't need my help with his. He's been around and doing this vampire thing a whole lot longer. But just because I'm not involved, doesn't mean I don't wrestle with it. The night it happens, I'm somewhere they're not, maybe watching cable, or sleeping, or doing some shit, but I know a good person is out there dying while I... let it happen."

She swallowed hard. When she spoke, her voice was weaker than she'd intended. "I guess it's good I won't have to make a decision. That Wolf doesn't want me that way."

Gideon touched her knee, drawing her attention back to his serious expression. "What he says he wants and what he does may not be the same, Ella. Just like you said, you can feel that he really wants more than he's saying. That's why I'm telling you all this. I'm asking you to think it through, a lot, from every angle. That way, if things go in a deeper direction, you'll be able to make as informed a decision as is possible for this stuff."

They sat silently for a few moments, him finishing his Coke, her gazing pensively at her knees, not seeing them. There was nothing more to say on that. But she still had a few questions. She wasn't sure she wanted any more answers, but this one felt safe.

"You said he was born in 1946. How long has he been a vampire?"

"Since around the seventies."

So for decades. That many people killed... She closed her eyes. And yet, if that was a condition of her survival, what would she do? What would any of them do? Maybe that was why a made vampire started thinking differently from a human. Even more than the biology of it, if they didn't, they wouldn't survive. How else could a decent human, made into a vampire, handle killing an innocent person every year to survive?

She needed to get going. But before she moved to leave the dock, she pulled out of her own head enough to detect his tension. Gideon was very self-contained. He'd opened up to share a lot of information with her. He cared deeply for her, protected her. His relationship with her had always been like a big brother, with an intriguing sexual undercurrent. Not because he would ever do anything with another female other than Anwyn—unless she'd ordered it. Gideon's protectiveness toward women simply contained an overpowering sexual awareness.

She didn't want him to worry, especially about this. "Thank you, Gideon. You're a good friend."

He grimaced. "Ella, don't hesitate to come to me if ever you need to ask anything about this. All right?"

"Okay." And then, since she didn't want to leave him broody and concerned, she nudged him with her knee. "You know, if I tell Lars you have *ever* batted for the other team, even as a one-guy-only, gay-for-you thing, he will spontaneously orgasm."

"Which is why you won't tell him. Otherwise you will spontaneously be buried in the new concrete foundation over there."

The wry look he sent to her said he knew she was trying to make him feel better, but he accepted it. And gave her the same, since she was sure she still looked shell-shocked by his information. He shot her a mock frown.

"Why would you assume that Anwyn shares me with Scary Guy? Maybe it's only Anwyn who gets the benefit of my awesome sexual prowess."

She grinned. "I've only experienced a vampire through a second mark, but one thing I figured out without being told is they don't get close to anyone without sex being part of it. Anwyn always had this amazing sensual goddess energy, but afterward...she carries that low-level hum that tells anyone with a pulse if she turns up the volume, she'd take them down, with barely a whisper. Wolf has the same thing. I just didn't realize that it wasn't a human quality, but I should have figured it out. No human is that...overwhelming. They're living, breathing sex magnets, Gideon."

He chuckled dryly. "Tell me about it. There's a reason they have third mark, full servants. A regular human can't survive the things they want."

Though they were playing with one another now, the look he shot her with that statement told her he wasn't kidding.

She thought of Wolf and the belt, of how far he'd taken her past the edge she'd ever gone before. If she told Gideon about that and asked if that was what he meant, she suspected he'd give her a terrifying answer.

That's the kiddie end of the pool for them, Ella.

"Can I ask one more question?"

"Yeah."

"Do you ever regret binding yourself to either one of them, despite that dark side?"

His midnight blue gaze flickered. "No," he said.

"Because you love them both more than that darkness. You'll go to hell for them if they ask it."

"And even if they don't. But I've been to hell, Ella. Long before I met them."

So had she. But she didn't say that. She just wondered if it was a factor, what drew people like her and Gideon to vampires, brought them across their paths.

She scooted her butt to the edge of the dock, intending to hop down, but he closed his hand on her arm, made her give him her other hand, and lifted her down so she didn't have to worry about stumbling on the uneven asphalt below.

She snagged another bag of trail mix when he encouraged her to take it, and headed back to her car. Krista had an old Volkswagen bug straight gear that she didn't drive that much, so she let Ella borrow it whenever she wanted, to keep it in running shape.

It smelled like comfortable old car inside, and had seats that were ripped and broken in. A silk flower lei in multiple faded colors and Shelly's graduation cap tassel still hung from the mirror. Ella had kept them there, adding a little crystal she'd picked up at a secondhand store. It caught the light, swaying back and forth as she puttered along.

As she pulled away, she saw Gideon was still watching her. He was concerned. She was sorry about that, but not about talking to him.

He'd given her a lot to think about. She needed to digest it before she could figure out what it was all supposed to mean to her.

Or how to handle the fact her overwhelming desire to belong to Wolf fully hadn't abated at all, despite knowing far more about what that could mean.

Gideon said the third mark was past the point of no return. She couldn't help wondering if, for a human destined to be a full servant, that point was reached much earlier than the third marking.

CHAPTER TWENTY

Several nights later, it was time to go see Lonnie. Keeping her promise, somewhat, she reached out in her mind to Wolf. At seven o'clock, she told him she was going at eight, and if he wasn't available, that was okay. He was neck deep in working with Fort and his team on the security updates, after all.

She received an absent acknowledgment from him, telling her she'd likely dodged a bullet, which brought relief and perverse disappointment. Not about him accompanying her to Lonnie's; she was sure she could handle that on her own, and hated inconveniencing him to go with her. She just wanted to see him.

Or maybe not. She wasn't sure she could see Wolf without asking him the one question that had remained at the top of her mind after her discussion with Gideon. The one question that seemed to contain the answer to all the others.

She had no right to ask it except, if the answer wasn't what she hoped, she wasn't sure she could be with him at all. Even just as a second mark.

At quarter to eight, she was in the driveway, about to open the Volkswagen's door, when the rumbling of an engine drew her gaze to the road. Wolf's truck pulled up to the curb, blocking the driveway. He had the window down, his arm resting on the frame. His short sleeved blue shirt drew her gaze to his muscled arm, which saved her having to look directly into his reproving eyes.

"An hour's heads up? Thought we had a deal."

"We do," she said, though her cheeks colored. She walked to the end of the driveway, stopping a couple steps short of the open window. "I just wasn't going to hold you to it. You didn't really say anything when I told you. You didn't specifically tell me to wait."

"I thought I was very specific the other night."

She flushed, because yes, he had been. "Yes, sir."

"It's okay." He grunted. "You don't have expectations. I remember. It means I need to keep being pretty clear about my own until you understand. My fault."

He put the truck in park and got out. His lower body was clad in jeans that fit just right and boots, a look that had Mrs. Sweet, two doors down, severely overwatering her pansies.

When Ella stood there, obviously waffling, he lifted a brow. He offered her a hand, she assumed to guide her around to the passenger side. Not taking that hand was really hard, but she knew if she did, it would be even more difficult to keep her resolve. She shifted from one foot to another. Slipped her hands in her back pockets. She'd gone simple and functional tonight. Jeans and a lavender T-shirt. "I...I talked to Gideon. About things."

"Yeah?" He lowered the hand, studying her with his sharp eyes.

"I need to ask you a question. I get that I don't really have the right to pry into your life past a certain point. You've made that clear. So, if you don't want to answer, I'll accept that. But if you can't answer it, or if the answer is something I can't...accept, I can't be with you anymore. At all. I'm sorry, I just can't."

She'd started to quiver the second she said the words, her throat closing up as if to try and prevent them from escaping. But she hadn't seen any reason to wait. Best to get it over with, make the cut clean and brutal. Even now, every cell in her body was screaming in protest, wanting to be close to him. His scent and heat, those strong arms and warm chest. It shouldn't matter this much. She hadn't known him that long, she'd get over it fast, it was just hormones. All bullshit. Everything in her wanted to withdraw the question. But she couldn't. Not and be true to herself.

"Okay. Ask your question, Ella."

No one was close enough to hear, but she'd still keep it simple. "Thirteen a year...or just one? The one you have to have."

He adopted that expressionless mask she knew. Until recently, it was the face she saw most often. The loss of being able to know what lay behind it, the trust it implied she'd earned until this moment, hit her hard. She couldn't apologize, but suddenly, she didn't want to know. She'd rather just sever the relationship without ever knowing.

"It's okay," she said, backpedaling toward the Bug. "Don't worry about it. Please forget I asked. We can go back to the way we were at the club, before, and—"

Her voice broke. He reached out and clasped her arm. He drew her back, so she stood before him, staring a hole into his chest. She didn't struggle, not wanting Ms. Sweet to get the wrong idea, but she was rigid. "Please let me go."

"One, Ella. Look at me, and see the truth."

She lifted her gaze, met his eyes. His eyes usually had that silver lightning color, but in the evening darkness, lit only by streetlights, they were dark and smoky.

"If I do ever have a full servant, that's something I'll never ask them to do with or for me, Ella. Most of us...I don't know about born vampires, but most of us made ones know what that would cost our human servants, to help us do that."

She strongly suspected Scary Guy was a born vampire, and neither he nor Anwyn had Gideon help with their annual kill. Proof that at least one born *and* one made vampire felt as Wolf did. The relief was so strong, it made her sway into his touch. But she thought about his side of it.

"What does it cost you?"

His expression clouded. "Not as much as it costs them. I've been told it gets easier after the hundred-year point. Not that you ever feel good about it, but you manage it better. It's horrible, Ella. The first few years I did it, I thought...I can't do this. Even tried to do without. Made it two and a half years, and had to face that I needed to live. I couldn't...let myself die."

Those words seemed to pull something painful out of him, and her hands landed on his forearms. "Of course you couldn't." She laid her head on his chest. "I'm sorry I didn't call you until an hour before."

"You were trying to ditch me."

"Sort of. Maybe because I knew I had to ask the question, and I didn't really want an answer."

"But you did ask it. Is it better or worse now?"

"Better." She tipped her face up to him. "Though you really don't need to do this with me."

"Get in the truck before I spank you in front of your neighbor and she drowns her flowers."

Ella smiled and followed him around to the passenger side. When she stepped on the running board, she emitted a surprised yelp as Wolf helped her in with a healthy slap on her backside.

It told her he wasn't mad at her, a relief. Even better, when he returned to the driver's side, he didn't want her to stay in the passenger seat. He curled an arm around her and brought her over into his lap, his hand under her chin so he could possess her mouth.

Oh...she sank deep into that kiss, sank into his arms. The embrace reminded her how very much she'd missed him these past few days. His passion said he might feel the same about her. Her heart skipped rope, right in her chest.

He lifted his head after a time, but he didn't have her move. She remained cradled in his lap and arms as he put the car in gear, his forearm resting on her thighs. She'd never been happier to be with a tall, big man, who had plenty of room to keep her in his lap while he drove.

"That number may be two this year, because I'm going to beat Gideon to death," he commented, as he pulled back onto the road.

"Oh, no, don't do that. He was trying to help me understand. Dom/sub relationships are all about making informed choices, right? How is this different?"

He sent her an amused glance, and his stern mouth relaxed somewhat. "It's different. But I know he's looking out for your best interests. I just would have preferred him letting me know what you wanted to know before he planted all that in your head."

"Oh, I guess..." She bit her lip and his arm tightened on her, even as his gaze remained on traffic.

"What, Ella?"

"I guess I assumed you could read my mind. And you'd already know what I was going to ask, what I've been thinking about."

"Yeah. I could. Somewhat. If I'd been in your head these past several days."

"Oh." She squirmed. "Sorry, that was pretty self-centered,

believing you'd be keeping tabs on everything I was thinking and doing."

He hadn't spoken in her head during those days, she realized. Maybe it was just her romantic imaginings, thinking he was there, a constant presence. Now that she thought about it, there was a certain...feeling she got when he was in her head, even silently.

"It's not self-centered." A muscle flexed in his jaw. "You wouldn't know how to be self-centered. I've been clear about the limits I have to set on our relationship, Ella. I'm trying not to make that harder. Me being in your mind for no reason at all is a luxury that I think will only make things worse."

She wasn't sure she agreed, but she didn't say so. But she expected he understood, because he gave her a look and held her even closer. She put her head on his shoulder, mouth against his throat. Whether or not he held himself away from her, his loss would cut deep. But it was a wound she was prepared to bear.

Except for that somewhat awkward moment, it was a mostly relaxed drive. She asked about the status of the wall renovations and his work with the security team.

"I figured I would have seen you these past couple of days," he said, when they were idling at a stop light. He had the window down, his arm propped on it, his other hand resting on the gear shift, forearm still over her thighs. She was stroking that corded length, up and down, and he didn't seem to mind the contact. He felt good under her backside, his strong thighs and what was between them.

"I took a couple dinner shifts at the diner, with the understanding I might have to back out if you all needed me."

He frowned. "Anwyn is paying everyone for the time off."

"Oh, I know. Which is great. But I can use the extra money. You'll take another right up here. There's a little cut-through alley the GPS doesn't know."

"Ella, what do you use your money for? You don't seem to have a lot of expenses."

"I have a shoe fetish that's really out of control," she admitted. "I rent a warehouse for all of them."

He lifted a brow. "A shoe fetish?"

"Forty-three thousand, eight hundred and seventy-six pairs of shoes. I'm almost out of space."

She laughed at his expression. "Now you're giving me your stern Master face. You can just pull it out of my head, you know. Since we're together already, physically, it's okay to read my mind right now, right?" she added hastily.

"Yes and no. It's harder to do with a second mark when she's not thinking about it, and you're playing hide and seek with me with your thoughts while I'm driving in Atlanta traffic. So, if you want to live, you should tell me the truth."

"Can I show you, instead? Afterward? If you have time, I mean."

He looked at her again, at the next stoplight. "Yeah. I have time. They won't need me for the rest of the night. How about you?"

Her heart jumped a little, she couldn't help it, at the idea he was interested in spending the whole evening with her. She didn't care that she had to be at the diner by six a.m. tomorrow; he'd have her undivided attention as long as she could stay awake.

"I'll get you to bed at a reasonable hour, make sure you get your sleep. That way I know you're not out doing the bicycle courier thing half asleep tomorrow afternoon, in this godforsaken nightmare traffic."

She smiled. "You read my work schedule tomorrow clearly enough. However, you totally missed that I find you a total nuisance. Fort slipped me a hundred bucks to keep you out of their hair tonight."

He snorted. "That's Mr. Jones to you."

The rest of the trip continued along the same teasing, flirtatious vein. It had been a long time since she'd spent time with someone romantically, outside Club Atlantis's doors. When Wolf did dip into her head, she loved that feeling, that connection. She wished he'd do it all the time. She didn't care if it made the fallout worse, when and if he drew away from her in the future.

I care. I won't hurt you more than I can bear, Ella. I wish I was less of a bastard, so I wouldn't hurt you more than you can bear.

You won't. She put her face down against his shoulder again, brushed her lips there. *Please talk to me in my head, Master. I love the way that feels.*

So he did. Nothing all that significant, just a back and forth as he drove and held her, and she kept her head lying on his shoulder.

The sense of contentment helped counter the anxiety that built as they drew closer to their destination. When they turned into Lonnie's neighborhood, she asked Wolf to stop at the curb before the house.

"There it is," she said, with a calmness she didn't feel.

When he looked toward it, Wolf saw a house with vinyl siding so far past the need for a pressure washing the gray color had turned mottled brown and mint green on the northern side. The stretched and leaning panels of chain link fence surrounded a yard more field than lawn. Rusted yard implements leaned against the side of the house, and a pair of trashcans overflowed with garbage, primarily cheap beer bottles and fast food bags.

All the picture was missing was a neglected dog chained to the bumper of a junk car. Since he saw a chain snaking through the grass, one end attached to a few cinder blocks, he expected a canine had once been there. Hopefully the unlucky creature had run off and never looked back.

Several of the lights on the street had been knocked out, but fortunately the one over this house was still lit, providing some illumination for her. Wolf could see fine in the darkness without it. Since it was only about nine o'clock, most people on the street were on their porches. Saving money on their A/C or heat, if they had either.

"Do you mind staying here?" Ella asked.

He'd let her shift back into the passenger seat, so Wolf glanced at her pale face, clenched hands, and then at the dubious look of the house. "Yes," he said.

"Lonnie's not dangerous. He's just a jerk. He doesn't even have a gun."

"How long has it been since you saw him?"

"A couple years or so."

"He's had ample time to purchase one."

"He may not even live here anymore." But her expression said otherwise. "Please. I really feel I need to do this on my own. Kind of to prove to myself I can."

"One condition before I decide. I want a better explanation for why we're here than 'I need to pick up something.'"

She'd worn contacts today that gave her eyes the colors of a blue jay's wings; deep blue, punctuated by fathomless black and accented by soft white. She looked down at her lap, her expression brooding, then she fished in the small multi-colored bag with tassels and bells she had slung across her body. Removing her thin wallet, she flipped it open and dug behind a couple of folded papers, a driver's license, and removed a photo. She handed it over to him.

"That was me, with Lonnie."

At first glance, Wolf saw a man who looked big because he projected that attitude. His florid face was that of an aggressive drunk's. He had his arm wrapped like a bull hook around a colorless creature standing stiff and still next to him. She wore a white button-down shirt tucked into beige slacks. Her dark hair was pulled tight from a strained face with no makeup. Her lips were curved in the semblance of a smile for the camera.

Ella, he realized with a start. He was looking at Ella. She looked like a shadow, nothing like the vibrant, joyously girlish woman next to him. Seeing it in his expression, Ella nodded. "I keep this to remind myself of what I became with him, and what I really was underneath that. He didn't want me to wear makeup when I was at home, because he didn't want any of the neighbors to think I was easy and loose. He was...unkind."

Wolf understood just how much was in that word. Fuck this. She wasn't going in there alone, and whatever was behind that door wasn't getting off with less than three broken limbs. Maybe four.

Ella put her hand on his arm. "Lonnie was a very controlling person. Not hugely violent, really, just not a nice guy. I can say he emotionally abused me, made me think I couldn't do and be more, but there was a whole world of relationships around me showing me different. I could have said, 'Wait a second, this is bullshit.' But that submissive side, it can be a blessing or a curse, right? I thought I could figure out how to make it work. When I finally did realize that it wouldn't, I took myself away from it and became what I wanted to be, what I was meant to be. He didn't stop me. He just threw me out and wouldn't let me back into the house to get anything."

She took a breath. "I convinced myself what he had that still belonged to me didn't really matter. That I took what was important with me. My true self. And that's not wrong. But nearly dying made me realize there is one item that *does* matter, and I want it back. He's going to give it back."

She looked toward the house. "If he tries to stop me, I'm going to rip down the goddamn door. He's going to have to kill me to stop me from getting it."

It startled him, the sudden vehemence in her tone. She closed her eyes, and he saw her press the tips of her fingers together in her lap, her shoulders rising in a quick breath. Up, down. Once, twice. He didn't say anything, just watched. It was as if a blanket settled on her shoulders, the way they eased. Her head came up and she looked toward him. "Sorry about that. I have a temper sometimes."

"So I see." He gave her back the picture. "How about I go in as your backup? Then you won't have to push Lonnie to such extremes." And he could have the pleasure of dismembering him if he tried.

"Can I just call you if I need you? I really want to handle this one-on-one if I can."

He didn't like it. "First sign of trouble, I'm at your back. Non-negotiable. Even the police don't go into a domestic disturbance without backup."

"Okay, yes. That would be nice." Her smile was tentative, slightly surprised, as if a sexual partner had never tried to champion her. "Just keep in mind he's better if he's not dealing with anything that gets his hackles up."

"I'm far better dealing with something that does," Wolf said pleasantly. "So we'll see if he and I can meet in the middle. If he does anything toward you I don't like, I'm going to tear him to pieces. Keep that in mind, if you think his welfare is worth anything."

She didn't seem to know what to do with that, but from her flush, Wolf expected she knew he meant what he said. She put her hand on the door latch. "Unh-uh," he told her. "Stay put. I'm coming around."

"I thought you said—"

"I am going to let you go in on your own as you requested. But I'm handing you out of the car. Because I want everyone watching to know that you're not here alone. There has to be some benefit to being a big, badass-looking guy like myself."

Her grin, slightly less wan, made him feel better about her state of mind. As he exited the car, he scoped the area. In a neighborhood like this, they would be measured by the porch audience, or from behind drawn curtains. Several houses down, he saw a cluster of young males studying them and their intentions. From their clothing and markings, he identified them as gang members.

As he circled to the other side of the truck and opened the door, he glanced their way. Not a "come over here and try to kick my ass" look; he was savvy enough with testosterone dynamics not to go that route. Instead his even and steady look said, "you do your thing, I'll do mine, and we'll be fine," an expression less likely to encourage a pissing contest. He didn't have an aversion to a good brawl, but he didn't want Ella caught in the middle. Or anyone else in this neighborhood who'd be an innocent bystander.

He took her hand. When she stepped onto the running board, it put them a little closer eye-to-eye. She braced herself on his shoulder. "Okay?" he said.

"Yeah. I'm wanting to do this, so there's anticipation, while at the same time I feel like I want to throw up and be anywhere else. Know what I mean?"

"Perfectly. Maybe he's not home."

She gestured toward the left side of the house. He noted a window open and what looked like cigarette smoke curling out of it. "He's here. He got into drug dealing after I left, so I heard, which means he keeps an eye out for customers or cops."

Okay, he'd changed his mind about thinking this was a good idea. He was about to push her back into the truck, but she was staring at the house as if her eyes could shoot laser beams through it.

"Let's do ice cream after this," she said abruptly. Her jaw was tight, so he caressed it, made it soften as she looked up at him.

"If you're good," he said.

She dimpled, and then her chin set and she stepped down, giving his hand a light squeeze before she marched toward the house. He leaned against the truck, watching her and keeping an eye on anyone who might look ready to move off their porch toward her. So far, so good.

He didn't want her doing this, but she was determined, and if she was going to do it, she was safer with him. So that was that.

She went up the stairs, automatically moving left to avoid the sagging center of the middle one. He noticed a child's toy underneath the stairs. It looked like a bright red donut, one of the plastic ones that toddlers stacked on a stick. He wondered where the rest of the donuts had gone, or if it had belonged to the child of an earlier tenant. There was no other sign of the house being inhabited by children, thank God.

The door opened as she reached it. In a stroke of irony, the man who opened the door was a scrawny shadow of the robust image in her picture. He'd obviously graduated from alcohol into using way too much of his own product. His eyes were dark and a little too wild, the hands too twitchy for Wolf's peace of mind. He was still big enough to do damage to a woman Ella's size, no matter that she looked far healthier. Plus Wolf had never met a dealer who didn't keep a gun close to hand. Unless he'd pawned it off to buy more drugs, at which point he was likely no longer a dealer, because he'd lost the self-control to successfully pursue that career choice.

"Ella," Lonnie said in a rough voice, as if he'd just woken up. "What the fuck are you doing here?"

His voice held more curiosity than malevolence. He rubbed at his eyes as if to bring her into better focus.

"I left something here, and I came back to get it." Her voice was hard. A tense stillness had descended upon her from the time she walked from the truck to the front door.

Picking up on it, Lonnie woke up a little more. Bracing his foot in the bottom corner of the door, he situated his shoulder on the other side of the frame, forming a blockade as he crossed his arms. "Ain't shit here that belongs to you."

"Stop dicking me around." She stepped forward and, in one swift move, ducked into the opening he'd left between foot and upper arm, and elbowed him out of her way.

"Hey, what the fuck..." He spun around after her. In the same motion he slammed the door behind him.

Or would have, except it hit the flat of Wolf's palm. Lonnie stopped mid-lunge after Ella, who'd already slipped down the hallway. As he pivoted back toward the door, his gaze went straight out, then up, to meet Wolf's expression.

"We'll keep this open," Wolf said mildly. "I think it's best if you let her get what she wants."

"Fuck you," Lonnie sneered, already fumbling at his waistband. "I'm gonna—"

A blink later, he was up against the faded wallpaper of his front hallway. The gun he'd been reaching for was pointed at his nose, held in Wolf's steady hand.

"You're 'gonna' what?"

Lonnie whimpered, his eyes wide as dinner plates, an inch from the yawning barrel. Wolf cocked his head. "I have a steady finger. But struggle, and I might start squeezing."

"Who the hell are you, man? Get that the fuck out of my face."

"I'm her friend, and this is her show. I'm here to make sure you mind your manners."

Every vampire learned to avoid anger, particularly in the first century when bloodlust rode close to the surface and could break through with little provocation. He had better control than most, thanks to his military training and Nolan's reinforcement of that, but he couldn't stop himself from recalling Ella's sleepy, casual comment when she lay in his arms several days ago.

"You used to smack her around, did you?" he asked pleasantly.

"Bitches sometimes need to be taught their place, man. It didn't mean nothing."

"There's only one thing I see here that means nothing."

Lonnie flinched, biting back a yelp as Wolf de-cocked the gun, dropped out the magazine and racked it back, so the chambered bullet pinged to the floor. He tossed the gun, letting it bounce onto the ratty cushions of the couch. In the same motion, he swung Lonnie toward a distasteful-looking easy chair and shoved him into it.

"We'll hang out here and wait on her."

Lonnie opened his mouth, but Wolf shook his head, putting a finger to his lips. "It's far better for you to say nothing. Trust me."

Whatever he saw in Wolf's expression convinced him of the wisdom of that. Lonnie subsided into sullen, frightened silence, his leg jiggling fast, his eyes still darting around, marking the gun on one side of the room, the magazine on the other. The bullet had disappeared, likely underneath a piece of furniture. Wolf knew Lonnie wasn't likely to go for it, recognizing that whatever Ella was seeking wasn't worth the point of pride that might cost him his life. He was far more likely focused on the hit he was going to need as soon as they left and he cleaned his shorts.

As he thought of Lonnie's rough, large fists hitting Ella's delicate features, he wanted to turn the man's face into meat. Leave his body for the gang down the street to clean up. They'd toss him in a hole in back and take over the house as their second base of operations. The satisfaction he'd feel from that was enough to have his fangs pricking at his bottom lip, a warning sign. So he turned his attention to other things.

The interior of the house was worse than the exterior, every surface piled with trash. The floors and walls were covered with a layer of filth, exacerbating the smell of stale cigarettes and unwashed male. He hoped it hadn't been like this when Ella lived here, and assumed not, especially when he noted a framed print tacked up on the wall in the living room. It was one of those paintings with lots of soft, muted colors, showing a girl in a bonnet reading under a tree. It was possible another conquest of Lonnie's had put it up, but thinking of the photo Ella had shown him, Wolf knew it wasn't. The picture on the wall had been a cry in the dark, that strangled personality like a baby in the crib, begging to be noticed so she could become who she'd meant to be.

Wolf looked toward Lonnie, who'd been watching him. "She left it here," he said accusingly. "It's not like it's hers anymore."

"Do you like looking at it?" Wolf said.

Lonnie blinked. "Uh, yeah. Well, sometimes."

Wolf stepped closer to him. From the paling of Lonnie's features, he knew what his own looked like. "Would it have hurt you, to care about her even a little?" he growled.

"Hell, I was good to her," Lonnie whined. "She was the one who screwed me. She used to make me a lot of money, and then she just bailed."

"Pardon me?"

"She worked a corner up at Fulton. I didn't let her look slutty at home, cause I didn't want her whoring herself out to my friends, but it was different when she was working. She's a looker, pulled in good cash. Agreed to give me fifty percent when I said she could live here."

Wolf imagined breaking his neck. The effort it would take would be less than snapping a pretzel stick. A quiver went through his arms.

He could leave him here, lolling forward in the chair. Ella would think he'd nodded off.

Lonnie had lost his color, realizing he was once again staring looming death in the face. And he was.

"I got it," Ella crowed. She appeared at the opening to the living room, and was moving at a near skip. Seeing the two of them there, Wolf standing in such a forbidding pose over the cringing Lonnie, brought her to a halt. Whatever she'd come to get, she had it in a little velvet bag, cupped against her bosom.

As she took in the scene, she gave Wolf a censorious look that said, *I had this.*

His expression remained congenial, but he straightened, crossed his arms over his chest. She sighed.

"Men," she muttered.

Normally, he could have smiled. Not at the moment. He wanted her out of this place.

"Everything okay?" she ventured as he continued to look at her.

"No," Wolf said. "But I suspect that's the norm here."

She turned her attention to Lonnie. Apparently, it was the first time she'd really looked at him, because her brow creased. She went straight to the man. Though Wolf tensed in anticipation, Lonnie surprisingly stayed still when Ella leaned over him, tipped his face up, her hand gentle. "Oh, Lonnie," she murmured. "You got yourself hooked on that shit. I told you that you needed to kick the booze, or it would get so much worse."

He stared up at her, then grimaced uncertainly, an expression that made him look far younger. With some shock, Wolf realized he likely wasn't more than a year or two older than Ella. "Yeah, well. Shit happens. Money was good, and then it felt good, too."

"Get out of it," she told him. "There's the shelter on 5th. Go there, ask for Watt. He'll help you. Don't let this kill you. And for Heaven's sake, use some of that drug money and pay a couple ladies on the street to come shovel this place out. It's not a bad place to live when it's cleaned up."

"It needs a woman's touch," he grunted, pushing himself up, giving her a hopeful look. Wolf cleared his throat. Lonnie shot him a glance and hunched down again.

"Yes, it probably does," Ella said. "Clean up, and you might attract one that's worth something."

She straightened to put her hands on her hips, look at him with that same even stare. "You won't see me again, Lonnie. So I want to tell you something, and I mean it. If you're ever in the right place in your head, it will mean something. If it doesn't, well...it means something to me."

She leaned forward once more. Lonnie tipped his head up, an act of wild idealism or a death wish, but she forestalled both by laying her hand on the side of his face, bringing his chin down so she could press a kiss to his forehead instead of his thin lips. She eased back, so they were eye-to-eye.

"I forgive you," she said simply. "And thanks for giving me a place to stay."

CHAPTER TWENTY-ONE

Wolf's parents had kept him out of trouble as a teenager, but he'd grown up a short step above poor. Many of their immediate neighbors weren't as fortunate.

Two doors up, the family that lived in a house as shoddily maintained as Lonnie's had a dog they kept chained out. The pit bull was a gentle creature one of the kids had found. She wasn't vaccinated or spayed, so she was impregnated by stray males almost every heat cycle. They didn't feed her enough to keep up with the demands on her breeding body, so she was always scrawny looking. The puppies were given away or left loose to run off or be hit by cars.

One day, Wolf's mother had him accompany her up the road. She took the neighbors a pie and told them she had an elderly relative who needed a friendly, big dog as a pet and deterrent to troublemakers. She sweetened the deal with twenty-five dollars. Which explained to Wolf why she'd recently taken a couple extra shifts at the grocery store where she worked.

The family consisted of two parents, a daughter—the child who'd brought the dog home and now seemed indifferent to her fate—and a son. The adults had had their discussion on the porch, while Wolf and the two kids built highways in the dirt, around the roots of the big live oak in the front yard. Once the agreement was made, the tall, thin father had taken Wolf's mom inside to give her an open bag of greasy, cheap dog food.

Wolf had gone with his mother. He remembered the garbage was ankle deep in the five-room home. It smelled like a moldy, rancid dump. He didn't draw a deep breath until they were almost back home, his mother with the timid underfed dog on a leash and Wolf carrying the dog food. That night, Wolf overheard his father talking. His mother had settled the shivering dog in a corner, on a bed of blankets near the heater.

"People ought to be horse-whipped for treating an animal like that."

His mother's voice was quiet. "They didn't know any better, Craig. You should have seen the inside of the house. I've contacted the church to see if the pastor and outreach folks can stop by, see what they might need. People who don't treat themselves with kindness and respect have no idea how to treat an animal any better. That's the world they live in. Ours is just as alien to them as theirs is to us."

Lonnie had pimped Ella out, knocked her around. In return, she handled him like an exasperated big sister and offered him forgiveness. Ella's world had been far different from Wolf's. Almost as alien.

He thought of what Lonnie had let slip. His Ella, turning tricks on a street corner. A prostitute before she came to work at Club Atlantis.

He reminded himself there was nothing he could change about her life in the past. But he could affect her present. He wasn't going to think about the future, since he knew he likely could be no more useful to her there than the hapless Lonnie. That dug into his gut more than he wanted to admit.

She hadn't said much when he held the door, helped her in the truck. Once he sat in the driver's seat, he nodded to the velvet bag in her lap. "Care to show me?"

She seemed to pull herself out of a deep place in her head. "What? Oh, sure."

She offered a sheepish smile and handed it over, her fingers small against his large ones. The contrast never failed to give him pause, or make him remember the night on the loading dock. Black and white. *Contrasts are best.*

He opened the velvet bag and shook out the contents carefully, a small square box. It was plastic, but made to look like wood, with a face picture of two children under an umbrella. There was a wooden ball at the bottom of the box. As he studied it, Ella reached under his arm, pulling on the ball. It was attached to a string, and after she pulled it to its full length, music began to play, the string slowly retracting.

"'Raindrops Are Falling On My Head,'" she said. "The fireman who carried me out of the house came to see me once. He brought that to me. There was one bedroom that halfway survived the fire, a sewing room my mother had upstairs, and she had it tucked away in a box. I'd never seen it before, but she kept some stuff from her childhood up there.

"That's a Hummel music box. It's not worth much, but I kept it all these years, a reminder of my family. I didn't like to think of it still at Lonnie's, not honored or appreciated for what it was. I think the getting it back was the main thing, you know. Almost more important than the object itself. Reclaiming that part of myself, saying this is who I am now. That who I was with Lonnie has no hold on me anymore."

"I thought you might be there for the picture."

She looked puzzled, then her gaze cleared. "Oh, that. I cut that out of a magazine. It's one of Monet's Spring series. I didn't know that then. I just liked it because it was so pretty. I could stare at it, get lost in those purples and greens. I'd feel like I was sitting with that lady on the grass, the cool touch of spring wind on my face as I listened to it rustle through the tree overhead. Maybe Lonnie will find what I did in it. It kept reminding me there was something better."

He lifted his gaze, met hers. Held. After a few seconds, she broke the lock between them, turning her attention to the window. She swallowed. "He told you, didn't he?"

"Yeah."

She crossed her arms over her chest, tightened them. "Sorry I'm not what you thought I was."

"Brave? Beautiful? Kind-hearted beyond anything I've ever seen in my life? A survivor?"

Her surprised eyes came back to him. She studied him hard for a minute, as if she didn't believe that was his true opinion. Then he saw it in her mind, her recollection that he didn't say what he didn't mean, ever. Incredulity was replaced by deeper emotions. Emotions she kept corralled, not wanting to show him how much it meant to her.

He put his hand over hers. "You've told me, in several different ways, that you'll accept the pain of loss, if I give everything I can give to you freely. I can't always honor that, Ella, because I do care for your heart and your feelings, but don't hold back on me. Be as honest with me as you wish to be. Does it bother you that I know?"

She let out a breath. "Not now. It only would have if I saw it changed the way you think of me, in a bad way. But I guess I'd rather you know anyway. I don't want to be false to anyone."

"Ella, I don't think you would know how to be less than who you are."

She sent him a soft smile. "I showed you a picture that says otherwise. We can all be less than we are, if we doubt ourselves too much. If we let what others think creep in too deeply. If we forget how short life is, and wallow in stupid shit that doesn't mean anything. I tried really hard to be everything he wanted me to be, but I couldn't. It took me a while to figure out that I wasn't supposed to be what he wanted me to be, that he'd had no right to ask that of me."

"Good girl," he said, and won a small smile. "How did you end up with him? That's what I want to know."

"Desperation. Stupidity," she said baldly, with a half chuckle. "After the fire, I was an orphan. An orphan who barely said a word for three years. No one wanted that. Most people, if they even think of adopting, want a baby. Foster kids, older kids, come with too many problems. So I was passed around the system until I was eighteen. Didn't really have a lot of skills because I didn't do well in school. Didn't go that often. So through this or that, I ended up with a group on the street. One of the older girls fed herself by hooking. She got me into it, but I couldn't stay at her place because she already had too many roommates. Lonnie said I could move in with him if I gave him half of what I earned as rent."

She took a breath. "It was okay at first. I became his girlfriend because that was part of the deal. Then he wanted more of my money, all of it, accused me of not trusting him to take care of me when I wanted to keep my half as agreed. He smacked me around some, until I started giving more money to him. Which had more to do with me wanting to please him than him hitting me. But finally I had enough. The night I told him I was leaving, he threw me down the stairs. I'd learned to roll by then, so I was bruised but wasn't all that hurt, and made it to the sidewalk. He stood on the porch and told me not to come back, because I was an ungrateful whore. I had the clothes on my back and a twenty I'd managed to stuff in my bra."

Wolf looked across the street at the dilapidated house with the overgrown yard, so opposite of the whimsical beauty Ella surrounded herself with. "I'll be right back."

Ella's hand was on his arm, slim fingers tightening on muscles drawn tight as bow string. "Please don't," she said quietly.

When Wolf looked toward her, he knew she saw pure murder in his silver eyes. "That you care enough to want to break his legs, that's enough. It's not needed. You've seen him. He's pathetic, in trouble. Please, Wolf."

He pushed down the need to break the male, mainly because he couldn't push the image out of his mind she'd just so wisely planted there. Her colorful, healthy self, next to the scrawny, self-destructive Lonnie. The picture had reversed. Ella had survived and triumphed. All on her own. It gave him a peculiar feeling, not all bad, but complicated.

"Okay," he said.

Her shoulders eased, but the worry on her face was replaced by something more earnest. "I want to ask you something. Is that why you don't want me to be your full servant? Because you think I'd have to be something other than I am, and you won't ask that of me?"

He frowned, and she pushed on, before he could say anything.

"Would I have to be something other than what I am all the time, or just some of the time? With you, alone, could I still be who I am? I know it's a moot point, because you don't want me for that, but..."

"Ella."

"My point is, all of us, every day, have to be something other than what we are for a certain amount of time. Whether it's to hold down a job we don't really like but it pays the bills, or to do any one of a hundred things that don't feel like us. But as long as some of the time, with a person that matters, we can be who we are, life is good. You know what I mean? That's not a bad life."

She shook her head. "You haven't asked me to be your third mark. You didn't even want to make me your second mark. I know that. I just wanted to say that to you, so you know...if you did start thinking about it, about me or anyone, maybe you should think about it from that perspective, rather than an all-or-nothing kind of thing. Nothing is all or nothing. If you go down that road, you always end up with nothing."

She stopped. "Anyhow, hopefully now you understand."

He lifted a brow. "I understand plenty of things, but you're going to have to narrow it down."

Her expression sobered further. "Why I don't limit myself when I'm with people. I'm not ever going to restrain myself, make myself be something I'm not again, when it matters, when I'm with a person who matters. While that sometimes puts me in danger, I consider it far less a risk than becoming what I was with Lonnie. I know it sounds kind of contradictory, because I'll do most anything for a caring Dom, but that's because pleasing them makes me truly happy. The things they ask of me are things I want to give."

She gave him a searching look. "I do know the difference between that and doing something that's not me, not something I really want. Does that make better sense? Or do I still seem oblivious, a girl with a lack of common sense, crying out for attention?"

He bit back the wince, barely. "No, you don't seem like any of those things. But you take risks that worry the people you care about. You can expect them to grumble about it, give you hell."

"Okay. Deal." She smiled. "I can accept that."

"Only because you like spankings."

"Sometimes. That thing with the belt...it was harsh." She hesitated. "But you'd do it all again, wouldn't you?"

He put his hand over the one on his forearm and dipped his head close, brushing his lips over her brow, her nose, her cheek, before he spoke. "In a heartbeat. And enjoy every fucking minute of it, knowing the punishment was deserved and that it helps you let go, give all of yourself to me."

Her breath drew in. He saw the swirl of thoughts in her head, the images. The belting had been brutal, and feeling that heady mix of dread and longing in her, to embrace that edge again, where she couldn't hold any part of herself back, was hellishly distracting. He had to remember what he'd promised her.

She'd been very, very good.

"So..." He brushed a lock of hair from her face. "Ice cream?"

"Ice cream," she confirmed, though a little breathlessly. He cupped her breast because he could, brushed a thumb over the nipple he could feel taut against her bra.

"Where?"

Her gaze was unfocused. He had to lean in and speak against her ear, while he tightened his grip on the nipple. "Ella, I asked you a question. Where?"

She let out a breathy moan, but managed the words. "One of my favorite places. But..."

Her eyes had closed. Pure male satisfaction surged, because he saw she couldn't marshal an answer until he drew back, releasing her breast with a lingering touch. Slowly, she lifted her lashes, showing him eyes clouded with desire.

She cleared her throat. "We need to stop and get the ice cream first. A lot of it." Her lips slowly curved at his puzzled expression. "I promised to show you how I spend my money, right?"

He'd expected a park, a restaurant. A quaint café. He hadn't expected a homeless shelter run by a one-man church set in the most broken-down, drug and gang-infested area of the city. But in hindsight, he guessed he should have. This was Ella they were talking about.

She had him pull up to the back of the building and jumped out. Wolf moved fast to join her, since a trio of junkies were sitting on crates in the back. Then he realized, thanks to his enhanced senses, that the beverage they were sipping out of red cups was some kind of iced tea. One man had the shakes, but the second man was steadying the cup in his hand.

"Hey, Paul," Ella said, putting her hand on his bony shoulder. "Where's Watt? I know I missed dinner, but I've got ice cream. You can have your favorite flavor, as long as it's chocolate, vanilla, or strawberry. I brought hot fudge and some toppings."

She'd taken him to a twenty-four hour restaurant supply place for the ice cream, buying three giant tubs from the guys working the evening shift. Right before that she'd practically cleaned out the topping section of the all-night grocery store, since she knew the restaurant place didn't have them.

"I'm here, baby girl." The booming voice, the voice of a gospel preacher, belonged to a spare black man not much taller than Ella. Watt looked somewhere between forty and sixty, his ravaged face blurring the signs of youth. He didn't have any of his real teeth, replaced by a bridge. The spare build was likely permanent, but there was a healthy energy to the spry male that said his obvious past drug addiction no longer fueled him. It was a part of his past, not his present, except for a congregation populated with those fighting the same battle.

His eyes were shrewd, sharp and steady. The attitude he projected said he was willing to be fair, but he'd have no tolerance for bullshit. The moment he saw Ella, a smile took over his face, his arms already extended to take one of the tubs of ice cream.

"It's late, but that's just the way God planned it. An unexpected treat, staying up past bedtime to eat ice cream. We got a lot of kids in tonight, and adults needing to feel like kids. This will do the trick."

His gaze passed over Wolf, measured, assessed, but the man simply gave him a cordial nod. "We can catch up after we get this set up. Nothing more important than making sure ice cream gets eaten before it melts."

After they ferried the ice cream inside, Ella squeezed Wolf's hand, received his mental permission to leave his side. It did something to him, her taking the time to ask, treating him as her Master outside Atlantis.

He was such a fucking hypocrite.

As soon as he let her go, she took command of a group of volunteers like a pint-sized general, and began to set up an ice cream sundae buffet bar. There were about seventy people of varying ages and sexes hanging out in the converted warehouse. A small army of cots were set out in rows for sleeping. He saw a rec room, flanked with a wall of cheap shelves piled with books. Partitions showed there were other areas, maybe for therapy or health exams.

His gaze lifted to the big banner on the wall, and his brow lifted.

"Church of Watt. Yep." Watt was standing at his side.

"Modest," Wolf observed.

Watt grinned. "God is in me, he acts through me. So I tell people they're the same way. We're each of us a church, walking around, able to do good with God's help. We build that church under and around ourselves with everything we do, and we bring people to it and help them build a church of their own. Do you have a faith, young man?"

Wolf was likely twenty to thirty years older than Watt, but since most vampires looked in their thirties at full maturity, unless they were made at a later age, he was used to being called young man or son by those who perceived themselves as older than him. "My mother did. I lost my way during the war, but found my path eventually. Nothing formal, no doctrine bullshit."

"That's all right. Part of the reason I called this the Church of Watt. Otherwise people get caught up in that denomination nonsense. Baptist, Presbyterian, Methodist. Religion just gets in the way of what's between a man and the Almighty, however he views Him, whatever he calls Him."

Even in a normal tone, Watt had the relaxed singsong of the preachers Wolf remembered from church with his mother. It also recalled the church picnics afterward, fried chicken and ten different kinds of pies to choose from, laid out under the shade of wide canopied trees on a lazy Sunday afternoon. Kids playing, mothers calling, fathers laughing in deep voices.

So long ago. He swallowed.

"It still plagues you," Watt said quietly. "Whatever sins you carry, son, you're never alone. And God forgives you."

"It's not God's forgiveness that haunts me." Jesus, why was he talking to this guy?

"Yeah." Watt was looking at him with those perceptive dark eyes. "Easy enough to say God forgives you, because that's what the pamphlets say, right? He'll forgive any shit we do. But your family, your friends, yourself, all the people you let down? Yeah, that's not so easy. C'mon. Let's eat some ice cream."

Wolf blinked as Watt drew him toward the tables, where an eager line was forming. He noted, with a twist in his heart, that everyone let the kids go first. The adults took as much pleasure in watching them decide what toppings they wanted as getting a turn at the table themselves. Ella was right in the middle of it all, helping to scoop, leaning over to ask a child what he or she wanted, smiling and laughing.

When Wolf saw one of the kids hem and haw over the toppings the way Ella had done with the stuffed animals, and heard the kid's father scold him gently for it, hurrying him up, Ella shot a look his way. Her lips were pressed against a smile. She remembered, too.

"That child," Watt nodded to her, "is one of God's angels. She's paid our utilities three months this year. Scours the secondhand shops to come up with supplies, furniture for this place."

"How did you two meet?"

Watt slanted him a glance. "How much do you know about baby girl? Because I'm not going to give you info she hasn't volunteered. You obviously got some interest in her, but I don't know if you deserve her notice yet."

Wolf nodded. "Fair enough. I know she used to do what she had to do to make money, to feed herself."

"That she did. One night, she got herself beat up pretty good. She had a place to stay, but lost it. She bunked down temporarily with a friend, and the friend's pimp, a man with the devil in his heart, tried to get her strung out on junk. He wanted her to be another of his caged birds, who made him money until she OD'ed. He injected her against her will, she fought him, and he beat her up pretty bad."

Wolf's fingers had closed into half fists. He saw Watt notice it, but the man continued on, in the same placid tone. "She got away from him, but ended up in the alley next to this place. I found her, disoriented as hell, holding a piece of glass like a knife. She was half out of her mind hallucinating, but she had enough mind to be protecting herself."

With a grin, he lifted his shirt, showed Wolf a scar slashed over his rib cage like a shallow letter C. "That's what I got for my trouble, but I got my hands on her, calmed her down. She stayed here until she found a place. I got her hooked on books."

Watt waved at the shelves. "I keep as many as I can gather here. When I was at my lowest, a social worker gave me a book. Addicts, the mind is like a messed up kid, one who doesn't accept responsibility for their actions. She gave me an adventure story, called The Dragon and The George. Told me if I read the book cover to cover, and proved it, by answering her questions, she'd give me a hit. I did it, though reading it was hardest thing I'd done in a while. No concentration, you see." He tapped his forehead. "She offered me the hit, like she promised, but she said she could also give me a bed in rehab instead, and all the books I wanted to read. Most difficult decision I ever made, but I made the right one."

He gestured toward Ella. "She might be the hardest worker I've ever met in my life. She isn't happy if she isn't helping or making the world a brighter place. But she won't be pushed around, and she has a backbone like nothing I've ever seen, so if you've a mind to take advantage of her, I'd say you better sleep with one eye open. She also has a temper. Don't let it out often, but when it comes, woo-boy, stand back."

"I'll keep it in mind."

Ella looked up and saw them watching her. She struck a sassy pose, stuck her tongue out at Wolf, and then went back to what she was doing. Watt chuckled.

"Why don't you get yourself some ice cream and then go introduce yourself to those folks over there?" He nodded to a table of men, varying ages. When one of them looked toward Watt, Wolf saw he wore a Vietnam vet cap.

"They're a good group," Watt said. "All servicemen. Three of them recovering. Herb's the only one at the table who isn't homeless. He started here that way, but he's got his own place now, does monthly dinners for some of those guys."

"I don't...I'm different."

"We're all different, we're all the same. Go on, boy. Be rude not to say a hello when they already looked over here at you. They can tell you're one of them."

~

As Ella scooped ice cream, she saw Wolf move to one of the tables, taking a seat near Herb and his guys. She smiled at Watt. She should have known the shelter founder would figure out where Wolf fit best. It was Watt's particular gift.

She wondered if Wolf might be interested in doing some therapy here. Not BDSM therapy, obviously, but maybe a non-BDSM version of it. Or just hanging out and talking to the guys on occasion, which sometimes was good enough.

She was impressed by how he listened, the way he leaned forward, arms crossed on the table. Since she now knew he was a vampire, she remembered when she'd seen him eat, which wasn't often, it was usually only small bites of things. She deduced he might not be able to consume food the same way humans did. So when she turned over her place at the buffet to another volunteer, she made him a really small dish of ice cream and brought it to him, along with a cup of Watt's famous sweet tea. Deducing the overload of sugar might not put a vampire in a diabetic coma, she put both down at his elbow.

He drew her to his side, his arm around her hips and waist. Leaning in, he pressed a kiss high on her chest, above the rise of her breast and below her collar bone. It made her stomach tingle. Then he brought her down to sit on his knee, so she could listen in on the conversation. Her arm lay in a relaxed hook around his shoulder, his loosely around her hips.

Some of those at the table were normally sullen and quiet, but Wolf was good at bouncing off Herb's lead and drawing them out. They talked about a variety of things. Some innocuous stuff, like the ice cream. Then some more serious stuff, like what they were dealing with. They'd recognized he knew where they'd been. He was accepted.

It all felt normal, natural and easy. Like he was her guy and she was...his.

At length, it was time to get the kids ready for bed. She helped with that, tucking them into their cots. Most of the little ones wanted to sleep with their mothers, cling to them through the night to ensure they didn't disappear.

One young girl was in her own cot, though she'd pulled it frame to frame next to her mother, who was already half asleep, her face lined with exhaustion and worry, even in slumber. Ella squatted down before the child, after adjusting the blanket up over the mother's shoulder.

"You okay, Sal?" she asked.

The little girl nodded, but her eyes looked wet. "Don't cry," Ella crooned. "Look at this, how lovely this is."

She took the little music box from the small cloth purse slung across her body. She pulled the string, and the tune began to play. "Raindrops keep falling on my head," she sang, as the girl watched her wide-eyed. The mother's eyes opened a crack. Ella pointed out the picture of the boy and girl with the umbrella over them. "See, they don't care that it's raining. They have an umbrella and each other. They're happy. Do you know the song?"

The girl shook her head, taking the box from Ella's fingers and playing with the string, winding it over her fingers as it was slowly pulled back into the box. As Ella taught her the lyrics, and the mother picked them up, softly singing them, Wolf sank down on an empty cot, just listening.

He wasn't the only one watching Ella, though her attention was exclusively on the kid, one hand on her side, the other reaching out and clasping the mother's. "There's one thing I know, the blues they send to meet me, they won't defeat me..."

It won't be long till happiness steps up to greet me. He wondered if she'd held the music box after the fire, and thought of the words, wondering if they were mocking her. That was how he'd felt for so long; like every song about love and happiness was mocking him.

That is, until he pulled his head out of his ass and realized the truth. The world had moved on. Nothing was focused on his grief—except him.

~

They were both quiet after they left the shelter, but in a contented kind of way. It was after midnight, so traffic was light. Wolf drove with her leaning against him again, his arm around her. The evening had filled in a lot of pieces about Ella for him, but he wanted one more.

"How did you end up at Atlantis?"

She left her head on his shoulder, spoke drowsily. "When I was hooking, soon after I did the rope bunny thing I told you about, I ran into this woman who was a pro-Domme. She liked me, told me I could assist her, and she'd pay me some money, give me a place to sleep. She said I was a 'lovely little girl.' She'd purr it, almost like a cat. Mistress Sonya. The more I saw of her world, her friends, the more I realized I was close to finding a place I could call home. Then one night, she took me to Club Atlantis, and I knew. That was home. I started helping out there, and eventually Anwyn let me come on staff."

She fidgeted, a sudden tension to her body. He noted she'd adjusted her head to stare out the passenger window. "I haven't ever told Anwyn," she said. "That I was a prostitute. I know I should have. Clubs like hers have to be so careful, to make sure nothing illegal happens at them, because there's always somebody wanting to shut them down. I guess I was afraid if I told her I'd been a prostitute, she'd think I was looking to turn tricks in a safer place. Or if I was doing it for drugs, I'd bring in that element, you know. And I love it so much there. I loved it the first time I walked through the front doors."

He had, too. It was hard to explain why. He'd been to plenty of BDSM clubs across the world, but Club Atlantis was the first he'd visited run by a vampire, and one like Anwyn, who'd been in it as a human, and had a strong vision of what she wanted it to be—and didn't want it to be.

"You need to tell her," he said. "It bothers you, not being honest with her. Trust her. I'll be there with you when you tell her, if you want me to be. She knows you, Ella. She knows you would never do anything to harm her club. She'll just give you shit for not telling her sooner."

"I guess. I mean, I know you're right." Her hand rested on his thigh, and she drew idle, thoughtful circles there. "You were really good with them," she said at length. "The vets."

He made a noncommittal noise. Another pause. "Can you tell me...anything about it? Being one of them?"

He expected she wanted to know, to better relate to the men when she was there. But he knew she also wanted to know more about who he was. It surprised the shit out of him that he wanted to talk about it, just a little. Probably Watt's fault.

His voice echoed in the darkness when he spoke. "When you become a soldier, you have a vision of yourself. When you go to war, depending on the way that war is fought, and for what purpose, and what you do during it...it changes you. Scrambles your sense of self, who you are, who you were, wanted to be. Sometimes in good ways, sometimes in bad. Sometimes you see things you can't ever forget. After that, even when you have a good moment or good day, or whatever it is in life, you can't..."

He shook his head. "Have you seen The Untouchables? The Sean Connery, Kevin Costner film?"

"Of course. The fabulous train scene with Andy Garcia catching the carriage."

He squeezed her. "Yeah. That was a good scene. But it's like that line. 'Some part of the world still cares what color the kitchen is.' It's actually the most freaking important thing in the world, the only thing that matters. But sometimes by the time you figure that out, you can't feel it anymore, if that makes sense. You can't reach that feeling anymore."

"Yeah." Ella ran her fingertips up and down his thigh, thinking. "Wolf, will you tell me... Did you have a family?"

"Yeah. I did. A wife and son."

"What happened?"

Wolf stared out the windshield. He could tell her. Or not. "Another time. They're gone."

"I'm sorry." She paused. "You know what's so weird about the adoption or foster kid thing? These people who want to be parents, they don't know." She tipped her head up, looked at his profile. "They make a baby, and he comes out, mint brand new. The kid may love his parents the way they hope he will, or he may not. But deep inside every foster kid is this huge well of love. It's sometimes just buried under so much. We're buried alive by what's happened to us, the road we've had to walk, but under that, we want so, so, so badly to be loved in the way we imagine it was supposed to be."

She tucked her head down, laid it on his shoulder and continued, in a musing, quiet voice. "We already know half the chance of that ever happening is gone. Everyone wants their own kids, their own blood, like that alone guarantees the kid is going to love you, be something to be proud to call yours. I promised myself if ever anyone offered me love the way it was supposed to be, I would love them with three hundred percent of my heart, with every part of me. They would be so proud to call me theirs."

She lifted her face to him again, and now it was the face of a battle angel. "I wouldn't care if they had warts and a hundred extra pounds, or looked like you. It's their heart that matters. There are people who've said they loved me, like Lonnie, but I knew it wasn't the real thing. Some kids, they get mixed up, or let themselves believe because they want it so desperately, and I did that a couple times, but I always knew, so when it was time to go, it was time to go."

He didn't say anything to that, just ran his hand slowly up and down her arm, gripped. When she put her face against his shoulder, she pressed against it warmly to thank him for the affection.

"Thank you for spending the evening with me, Master. It was the best night I've had in awhile."

He felt the same way.

CHAPTER TWENTY-TWO

It was Burlesque Night. All the other events she'd planned had come with their challenges, but this one was the most significant, for several reasons. First, it was a celebration of the re-opening of Atlantis, the repairs done in record time. Second, each of her events had built on the popularity and success of the last, so that this one, combined with the re-opening hype, had drawn the biggest crowd yet. She'd heard people were already lining up outside the doors for opening.

"Lining the *fuck* up," Lars had crowed, giving her a high five. "You go, girl!"

Third...this was a performance situation, and not like being someone's rope bunny. She would be out front and in the spotlight, the first solo act of Burlesque Night.

Wolf was here tonight. For some absurd reason, that made her more nervous than the prospect of the crowds. He'd been busy since he'd arrived, though, only able to brush her mind with an affectionate greeting. This would be a challenging night for security, the first night they were "on" with all the new rules. While that would cause an expected amount of tension, she picked up on an additional note to it. As if something else was going on.

She didn't know what until she ran into Gideon, who had a grim look on his face. She was on her way to the lockers, but she laid a hand on his arm to stop him, shouldering her backpack and garment bag so they were out of her way. "Gideon, is everything okay?"

"Yeah." He gave her a decently reassuring look, but then he glanced around before he leaned in, spoke low. "The Region Master of this territory is coming to the opening tonight. A show of his support to Anwyn."

She assumed that meant a vampire of some kind of high rank. "Well, that's good, right? He's being supportive."

Gideon grimaced. "Yeah and no. Lord Richard isn't a complete asshole as vampire Region Masters go, but vamps can be unpredictable. Then there's a shit-ton of other pain in the ass protocols that happen when vampires congregate. I'll explain later. Main thing is, nothing for you to worry about. Just...Wolf's likely to make sure you steer way clear of him tonight, so you're not seen as connected to him. There are reasons for that. Just follow his lead, do whatever he tells you up here." He tapped his forehead. "Okay?"

"Sure."

He gave her an additional look. "I mean it, Ella. It's important."

"I promise. I'll do whatever my Master tells me to do." She showed him she meant it by meeting his eyes and tightening her hand on his arm. He had enough to worry about tonight.

His expression eased enough for the familiar devilish twinkle to enter his gaze. "Any truth to the rumor that you're going to sing a song dressed in nothing but a couple feathery fans?"

She narrowed her eyes. "That's Charlene. She's doing an homage to Gypsy Rose. I'm doing something different."

Gideon's radio beeped before he could goad her into revealing more. He glanced at it, then gave her a wink. "Saved by the bell. Guess I'll have to find out like everyone else. Go get 'em tonight."

He strode away, and she turned to watch him because, well, watching Gideon, coming or going, was always good for a woman's cardio check. He'd dressed up tonight, for him. Nice dark blue jeans, a Club Atlantis black placket shirt. She puzzled over his words, but there was so much about the vampire world she didn't know. She added another midday interrogation session with him to her to-do list. She'd bring cookies.

She could ask Wolf, but the way he was so deliberately staying out of her head most of the time, and the fact he was a vampire, not a servant, suggested he might not have the same perspective Gideon had. Well, Gideon had said servants were like a union, and watched out for each other. No matter how ephemeral her and Wolf's relationship might be, she was going to give him a hundred and twenty percent until it ended.

She planned to show him that, as part of her performance tonight. Another reason for her nervousness. However, the only way to fix that was to move forward. Which meant she better get her ass in gear and get ready.

An hour later, she stood in the shadows behind the black cloth partition that served as the stage wings. The whole performance part of the evening would last forty-five minutes, after which they'd clear the dance floor and let everyone break off into their preferred sessions or social activities.

People could do that now, but apparently most of them wanted to see the show. The tables arranged for an audience were overflowing, and it was standing room only at the walls, the bar and the upper level mezzanines. She glimpsed new people as well as regulars, in all manner of dress, from club and fetish wear to casual.

She closed her eyes, drew it in. Beneath it all, she found the heartbeat of Atlantis, that energy center that steadied her, told her she was home, no matter how many people were here. They were all connected, all wanting something marvelous that elevated them above the norm.

She'd chosen the right song. She knew it. Simple but powerful. Something straight from her heart. And the funny thing was, when she'd chosen it for Burlesque Night, it had been before she'd become closer to Wolf. Tonight, the words would mean so much more to her than when she'd made the selection.

She didn't need him to promise her forever to see the sparkle of this moment. The air was full of sparkles.

Wolf leaned against the back wall, watching the crowd. He knew Fort and Allan were on the outside perimeter, using their sharpened vampire senses to keep an eye on the crowd like bomb-sniffing dogs, detecting anything the least bit out of the ordinary. If they saw something, they'd signal the regular security team, who would pull the person out, question them, make sure they were legit. Saturnia and Hollow had the monitors and computer systems. All of them had their counterparts on Anwyn's regular security teams working with them, putting into application the new procedures they'd had drilled into them.

Anwyn had gone on radio shows over a week ago, taken out advertising spots there and in the Atlanta papers. "An explosion closed us down. We will open with a bang tonight, the kind that creates memories people don't ever want to lose. Half price cover for the floor show. If you want to stay later after that, then you're getting a deal, aren't you? We will be open to guests, but that guest must have a member with them, or have been vetted at least three days in advance.

"We've revamped our security, inside and out. Members will find entry is more complicated, but I hope they will understand why. I'd rather inconvenience someone for five minutes than risk harm to any of our people. And to anyone who thinks they will catch us off guard again? I'd reconsider that. You won't win outside your weight class with us again."

Then her dagger-sharp tone had reverted to Southern magnolia. "Anyone who comes tonight and thinks what we have to offer isn't worth the wait or price, I'll double the price of your refund. But I'll want to know why, so I can make your next trip to Club Atlantis more to your liking."

They'd received a slew of people to vet, Atlantis suddenly on the map as the hot place to be. They'd approved about a third of them, and had others in pending files for future consideration. Even with that whittling, they were going to be close to their maximum capacity. Anwyn anticipated, after a bit of gawking, the vanillas would head home or leave to take a late dinner at another Atlanta hot spot. The regular members and those interested in exploring their Dom/sub leanings would hang around. The latter were the new memberships she wanted.

She was a businesswoman, through and through. Earlier in the week, there'd been an editorial in the paper titled, "Jezebel has felt God's wrath." Wolf had been amused to see the sword-sharp gleam in Anwyn's gaze as she read it.

"I'm sending that jackass a bouquet of roses, with a thank you card signed by Jezebel," she decided.

Her tone on the radio stations had been confident and intimate at once. Despite the inevitable attempts by commentators to make adolescent jokes about sex clubs, she'd kept them on topic, elevating the dialogue to portray Club Atlantis as what it was. A sexy, glittery place of fantasy for mature adults interested in exploring the dynamics of the Dominant and submissive orientation. A safe, healthy way to embrace one's sexual power, on either side of the coin.

When Wolf had first come to Atlantis, he remembered considering a dalliance with Anwyn, some enjoyable bedroom gymnastics, no strings attached. In the vampire world, sex was right up there with enjoying a bite of a dessert. No commitment, pure pleasure, and the right hint of danger between predators to make it appealing to them both.

Gideon's presence hadn't deterred him. He'd considered ways they could involve her servant. Then Wolf learned that Anwyn had a different kind of bond going on, not just with Gideon, and that idea floated away. Particularly when she reinforced it with the same approach she'd used with the radio stations. Southern feminine charm combined with a steel core, to send the clear but friendly message. Not interested.

Wolf had respected it, and respected the hell out of her. As far as the message she'd sent to whoever had attacked Atlantis, he was in full agreement. He was a willing and deadly part of the army to enforce it.

A vampire hunter tried anything, now or in the future, he'd regret making Atlantis a target.

The lights dimmed, the spotlights sweeping the crowd, and everyone settled. At least until "Show Me How You Burlesque" started up. As the crowd whistled and cheered, the staff members participating in the musical number started flouncing through the crowd, jumping on the tables as others took the stage in a colorful burst of blazing energy.

Cheers turned into whoops of appreciation and stamps of feet as those on the stage drew back to reveal Anwyn, coming forth in a blue-green dress of sequins that flashed with the lights. The dress stopped high on the thigh to accommodate her boots. She had a single tail, lit up from the handle to the flicker at the end with tiny lights. She cracked it around her. When three muscular male subs dressed in nothing but leather shorts and glistening oil fell to their knees at her feet, she propped a boot on one broad shoulder. As she made an adjustment to it, she gave the cheering crowd a wink, blew them a kiss.

Wolf's lips curved as she took the hand of one of the subs who rose to his feet, escorting her to the back of the stage. Once there, her hand slipped from his and she tossed a look at the crowd over her bare shoulder.

A total, "we are open, and screw you assholes" look.

As she disappeared behind the curtain, the dance number took back over. It followed the Cher movie closely, and the volunteers with dance experience Elle had recruited from the staff and membership executed it impressively well. Ella had called in a favor with a friend and submissive who performed with an Atlanta dance troupe. The girl had given the volunteers pointers to bring the number up to par.

When "Show Me How To Burlesque" finished, Anwyn came out with everyone and took a bow. As she was handed a mic, she put a finger to her lips, a soft smile on her face while people settled back into their chairs.

"I am so glad you are all here," she said. Emotion and gratitude saturated every word, her expression, nothing more needed. No long speeches. She swept her gaze all around, and opened her arms. She pulled the mic away from her mouth because she didn't need it for the fierce declaration that followed. "We are *all* here."

The audience went wild, back on their feet, whistling and whooping their support. Then she settled them down again, that same finger to her curved lips. "Now, let's take it down into the quiet dark, where the things we love live and thrive...let's remember what we're about in the heart of Atlantis."

The club abruptly went dark, except for a moving spotlight that drifted here and there. After a bated pause, haunting string music came over the speakers, the volume drifting up and down, like a poignant wind moving through the crowd, quieting them. Then the music died away and a single voice sang the first notes of the song a cappella. They echoed through the now almost silent room.

"Sweet love, sweet love. Trapped in your love."

The first words in another *Burlesque* soundtrack song. "Bound to You." It couldn't be more perfect for a BDSM club, but that wasn't what had Wolf riveted.

That voice, rich and sultry, full and strong, belonged to his Ella.

The spotlight drifted to the back of the stage, gave the crowd a hint of her in the shadows, then left her. Now they heard the tap of her shoes across the wood floor, as she moved toward the front. Was it crazy that he felt a weird sort of pride, knowing it was his second mark giving her better eyesight in the dark? With a third mark, she would hardly have any problem at all doing that.

Shut up and watch the show, he admonished himself. Or rather, watch the fucking crowd to ensure there were no threats.

Three spotlights came together, revealing her to the audience. And then he forgot everything but her.

When he'd looked at her colorless image with Lonnie, he'd barely recognized her. Now he had the same unsettling experience, only in an entirely different direction.

He'd been born in the 1940s, too young to appreciate the vintage pinup girls painted on the noses of planes. However, as an adolescent, he'd seen the calendars in his uncle's garage, tucked in the back office. He was vividly reminded of those pictures now, the creamy skin and full glossed lips of women with the sex appeal of sirens.

Ella was dressed in white satin that molded and draped to accentuate every luscious curve in the most appealing way possible. It was a torch singer dress, cradling her high breasts and creating deep cleavage, while it bared her shoulders, coaxing the fingers and mouth to touch, taste.

She wrapped her fingers around the microphone in that slow fan of movement that looked like she was caressing it. The haunting strains of the song started again, and this time she attached the words to the yearning tune.

I've found a man I can trust...

Bound to you...

Terrified to love for the first time...

Bound to you...

Her thick hair had been straightened, and reflected the stage light like a raven's wing. It framed her visage, one dark shining lock falling close to an eye that was heavily mascaraed, bringing out the color. The natural color. She wasn't wearing contacts. All the rest, it was a costume, one she wore damn well, but he knew like a punch to the gut that the missing contacts were a message to him. He was seeing her real eyes, the real window to the soul, as she uttered the notes of the song with poignant need, powerful strength, yearning softness. The way the notes needed to be sung.

Look at me, he thought, and he'd never been so damn pleased to be able to speak in her mind. Command her attention.

Her gaze shifted right to him, telling him she'd known where he was in the shadows, and she hit a higher note.

Please don't tear us apart...

Another line to hit him in the gut.

The curtain had been pulled back, revealing a wide screen. Behind it, a woman was on her knees, reaching up and offering her arms to a male who was artistically and gracefully binding her in rope. The two of them twisted and turned together in a dance as elaborate as a tango and waltz mixed together. As Ella sang each lyric, revisited the chorus, their movements heightened the emotional strength of the song, if that was possible.

At the end of it, there was a brief hush, the audience realizing they'd just witnessed something so fucking real that it deserved a moment of respectful silence.

Ella kept her eyes on Wolf. Her mind had that curious emptiness she did when she had emotions so strong that she didn't want them to take her over, make her lose perspective, make the moment more than it was.

He wanted her to say the words. Goddamn it, he did, needed to hear them, and he had no right. No right at all. So he said what he could. With every fervent feeling in his heart.

Thank you.

Ella dipped her head, purportedly to the sudden burst of enthusiastic applause. Her eyes cleared as she reluctantly pulled herself out of the trance she'd created. When she surreptitiously touched her face, she was wiping away tears. He knew it, and so did the crowd. It only made her performance all the more powerful.

She drew their attention away from that, lifting her hand toward the back. The screen was taken away by discreet stagehands at the very moment the submissive was suspended in the air to spin, showing her naked, arched and posed body.

Des was a renowned rope artist, known throughout the national D/s community. Julie was his submissive. The couple was visiting from North Carolina, where Julie ran an erotic theater. Another favor called in. Wolf was beginning to think Ella had friends everywhere, something that didn't surprise him in the least.

The crowd gasped at the sight with pleasure. The next act would be Des's, where he'd untie and rebind Julie in another mesmerizing display of rope suspension. After that, there'd be a wax and fire show, complete with a closing dance number that would bring the show to an end. All while keeping everyone focused on the sexual possibilities, in the D/s framework the club provided.

But Wolf was still captured by the previous act, and he didn't think he was the only one. Ella had immediately stepped out of the way, giving the limelight to Des and Julie. While they deserved it, he thought the crowd had wanted to give Ella more of her due.

He didn't doubt she would have gotten a standing ovation, but this wasn't about that for her. It was all about creating a mood, a feeling. Just as she'd told him, for her, the reward was seeing people get wrapped up in it, carried away from whatever cares they had. If pleasure, bliss and imagination could capture them all so strongly in this moment, then how strong a hold could the bad things have on them, really?

He wanted her. God *damn*, he wanted her.

It was going so well. Ella couldn't be more pleased, though it took her a while to come out of the near subspace she'd somehow achieved, staring into Wolf's eyes during the song. Every note had been for him, every word.

Now the final number was drawing to a close. Chantal would step in and transition the attendees to the normal club activities. Ella had been told the show was her job tonight and she didn't have to work as staff when it was over, but she preferred to do that. She didn't want to be idle, and Wolf was going to be busy throughout the evening. However, with him here, she couldn't even think of subbing for someone, even as a staff member.

If she held onto that feeling, it could be problematic, particularly for her future income, but she'd be okay. She'd power through it. It was just the lingering effects of that song, and the connection she'd felt with him during it, the emotions that hung there between them.

She changed clothes, put on a knit skirt, sneakers and the baby-doll Club Atlantis tee that clung to her curves and gave her some nice cleavage. She'd help wait tables, pick up some tips and leads on future sessions.

Her mind was busy with that, trying so hard not to think of anything else, that she ran right into a pair of men as she emerged onto the main floor. Not a brushing glance, either. Instead, it was a full body smack and stumble that made her reach out and grab for the man she'd hit the most forcefully, in the event she'd unbalanced him. Unlikely, since he was built like an oak.

"Oh, I'm so sorry, sir," she said. "Are you all right? I apologize. I wasn't watching where I was going at all."

"No, you weren't."

The austere formality in the voice was touched with a reassuring dry humor, but that tone definitely said Dom. A quick glance revealed a male who looked as if he were in his forties. Silver was threaded through thick chestnut-colored hair. His gray eyes had some creased lines around them, which only added to his attractiveness.

But there was another component to that appeal, one she was starting to recognize. Oh holy crap. Vampire. Lord Richard.

"My apologies, my lord," she said quietly. And in the same breath, remembered she wasn't supposed to be anywhere near this visitor.

Lord Richard's gaze swept her thoroughly. The flicker in his gaze, the flare of his nostrils, said it might not be just the address that had given her away.

"Forgiven. Though others may not be as fortunate. Anwyn didn't advise me there was a marked servant here, other than Gideon and Holliman."

Her heart jumped. Shit, she really wished she'd asked Gideon more questions. But she did know how to comport herself around a Dom. Going with instinct, she knelt, lowering her eyes.

"Who is your master, child?" Richard asked, and his tone said she better not hesitate or lie. She wondered if she should have said "Anwyn," but in the next breath she knew honesty was best. Richard would have figured it out, and Ella's lie would have put Anwyn and Wolf in bigger trouble.

"Wolf, sir."

"Wolf?"

"Yes. Wolf." That came from the other male, the one she hadn't yet looked toward. "My apologies, my lord. I may have been aware peripherally of this situation. Allan mentioned that Ella was second marked by Wolf, when he was injured from the bombing. Since she belongs to the club and is under Anwyn's direct supervision, it was deemed acceptable for her to continue on as a second mark here, even when Wolf proceeds with making me his full servant. Ella is part of this environment already."

"Hmm. We'll still discuss it later tonight, Haru. While marking doesn't require my approval, leaving a marked servant without clear ownership is a situation I prefer to be aware of."

"Of course, my lord. I'm sure Allan expected to discuss it with you while you're here. He was more than willing to vouch for the girl. Said she is very service-oriented and loyal. Docile. Physically and emotionally incapable of topping."

How would Allan feel about her loyal foot planted halfway up his backside? But she set that aside, her mind rolling over the words, revisiting them, paring them down into bite-sized pieces. It didn't help them go down any better.

Lord Richard had turned away, dismissing her, as a waitress asked him about a drink order. Now Ella could lift her gaze and see who had spoken to Lord Richard.

The Club Atlantis Dommes had a "Top-the-Alpha Tea and Whiskey" party once a month. They gathered in the Club Atlantis social room, put on one of the subscription services, and chose popular TV series with a plethora of alpha male characters to choose from. In between tea or liquor libations that volunteer submissives like Ella helped serve, they'd come up with entertaining and colorful descriptions of how they'd top every alpha-presented male in the cast. They each had their favorites.

When Ella met Haru's eyes, she was reminded of Ian Anthony

Dale's character in the reprised Hawaii Five-O. Dark and slanted piercing eyes, strong chin and cheekbones, a confident and relaxed demeanor. His masculine, smooth tone had been a visual match for the rest of him. His suit looked expensive and fit his lean, strong body well.

He'd said he was a servant, but there was an alpha vibe there. Gideon was living proof the combination could exist, though no one would claim Gideon was the natural submissive that Ella was. Yet she suspected both he and Haru could top a fellow submissive, if the scene called for it.

Not her. *Incapable of topping.* She didn't disagree; she just would have preferred it put differently. He hadn't said it with disrespect; more of a dry wit, suggesting it wasn't considered a shortcoming at all. Yet she still felt as if he'd suggested she was a pet who didn't have the brain cells to think beyond her submission to her Master.

Noting Lord Richard's distraction, the male nodded to her, offered her a hand to help her up. "Haru," he said, introducing himself formally. "I've heard good things about you."

"Not that I could tell." She ignored his hand, and rose in one graceful lift, tightening her core. It helped her focus the swirl of emotions inside her. *Thank you*, Wolf had said. In a way that meant so many things. She didn't doubt his sincerity, but this was a face punch reminder of what he wouldn't give her.

She understood that; she did. It was open and above board between them. Her feelings were hers to express as she chose, without obligation or demand from his.

Even so, she couldn't help the way this felt. Like she was a pawn on a chess board among a species she couldn't begin to understand. She'd been pulled into the game by accident, hadn't she? That explosion.

Yet when Wolf had commanded her, speaking in her mind, saying *Look at me,* it was as if he'd really wanted her to look at him, see all of him, in a way he hadn't suggested before.

Haru's expression showed a flash of surprise, then caution. "No offense intended, Ella," he said, low. "Allan said you understood how things were between you and Wolf. That you knew you weren't part of the considerations for his full servant."

"Of course. Excuse me."

She skirted around him, ignoring his perplexed, slightly alarmed expression. She made a getaway before Lord Richard could engage her again. Her immediate game plan was to get to the locker room and do a fierce and fast meditation, to get her head right, to contain the dangerous waves of temper roiling in her gut. It was that song, that damn song, the connection she'd felt to Wolf, all of it. Meditate. She needed to meditate. Her temper was something she couldn't let loose like a normal person. It had to be channeled.

Then she saw Allan.

Allan was dressed in sweats, and headed toward the fitness room. She plowed through the crowds after him, for once not paying attention to anyone who called her name. Other words were filling her mind, pushing at the limits of her throbbing skull. *You weren't part of the considerations.*

Story of her life. *It won't be you.*

CHAPTER TWENTY-THREE

Gideon was in the middle of his third and final set with the punching bag. The successful reopening and Burlesque Night performance had everyone in good spirits. Anwyn was on track to recoup most of her lost time profits and cover the renovations. He couldn't wait to see Ella later in the evening when things were winding down. The little sprite was probably going to be floating in a cloud of pink champagne bubbles somewhere near the ceiling. If so, good. She deserved it.

"She's so damned accomplished," Anwyn had told Gideon, after they'd watched the entire club be riveted by that singing performance that none of them had seen coming. She'd rehearsed in the days leading up to this night, but not enough for them to know that voice had been hiding in that pocket Venus frame.

She had a good voice, but she wasn't a trained singer. It was the true emotion she put into it that captured everyone listening, carried them on that same journey. Especially those who knew what that kind of love felt like. Gideon had his hand curled on Anwyn's hip, his fingers stroking as she leaned against his side.

Every staff member with eyes in their head knew the depth and intensity Ella injected into each note was driven by the Dom whose eyes she held like a lifeline while she sang it.

I could walk up and stake him right now. He wouldn't even notice, Gideon said in Anwyn's mind.

No, he wouldn't. She's such a gift. All he has to do is love her back, and that gift will be his. He's such an idiot.

Anwyn hadn't explained further. Gideon suspected she knew more about Wolf's background than she let on, but since Anwyn shared pretty much everything with him, if she wasn't sharing it, it was because she was respecting a confidence with Wolf. He understood that.

He did another round with the bag, knocked it back. Again, and once more, pushing himself, making the muscles burn. He could have used the workout facilities in their private quarters, but he wanted to stay closer, in case security needed him. Plus, with Daegan still out on the hunt tonight and Gideon jonesing to be in on that kill, he would welcome an aggressive sparring partner. Sometimes the security guys came in here after their shift.

Careful what he wished for. There was someone headed for the workout room, but it wasn't one of the regular security guys. It was a vampire.

While third mark senses could detect vampire, he couldn't detect which vampire, unless it was Anwyn or Daegan. As a result, he'd been twitchy ever since Fort, Saturnia and Allan had arrived. Logically, he knew it had to be one of them headed his way, since they were all three here tonight, providing preternatural backup to the trained human security. But that knowledge didn't displace the memory burned in his brain, of the first night he and Anwyn had met. A trio of rogue vampires had showed up in the Atlantis lobby. She'd sent them on their way, but they'd come back. And now she was a fledgling vampire prone to seizures that gave her a severe handicap in the power-driven vampire world.

Plus, Lord Richard was here as well. Anwyn was with him right now. Seanna, Lord Richard's servant, was already enjoying some of the club amenities, scoping them out for her Master, while Anwyn played hostess to the Region Master. For parity, Anwyn had sent Gideon off for awhile. He had a feeling he'd be getting up close and personal with Seanna on some of that equipment later tonight, no telling whether as top or bottom. Whatever got Richard off.

He liked Seanna okay. She was the ultimate vampire servant pragmatist and a pure sensualist, but this kind of unpredictable shit wasn't his favorite thing. Vampires tended to initiate sexual games using their servants when they got together, and those games were sanctioned by the incessant power politics of their world.

Hence the workout, to settle his nerves.

Daegan, you out there? Can you give me a ping?

He felt Daegan's attention, and a brief pause while Daegan reached through Gideon, a feeling like a heated breeze in his bloodstream.

It is Allan.

Gideon grunted, not breaking form on the bag, though he did shift around so he had the best vantage point for the entrance to the workout room. *Got that job done yet? Dragging your ass, aren't you?*

Getting closer. There are layers to this I did not expect. Care for your Mistress.

Over and out, Gideon thought, and landed a fierce side kick on the bag that had it jerking away from him like a swatted balloon.

"Think you knocked that guy into the next room," Allan said. He put his security radio on a table and unzipped his jacket, shrugging out of it to reveal the trainer tank beneath, over his sweatpants. He had good muscle definition in his shoulders and arms. He didn't rely just on vampire strength to keep him sharp, his military discipline showing. "Got time and the balls for a sparring match?"

"Against one puny Ranger? I can handle it."

Allan flashed a smile that showed some fang. "Maybe not. Big, bad vampire hunter."

Gideon scoffed. "Had you in my sights one night."

He never knew when to leave enough alone. Allan arched a brow. "Really?"

"Yeah." Gideon shrugged. "Lost my window. All in all, glad it worked out, because you were a big help this week."

"Glad I could help," Allan responded after a brief pause, eyeing him with a wary look. "How were you going to take me down?"

Gideon met his gaze. "Trade secret. Never know when a vampire might get too full of himself."

Allan's lip curled. "You realize I could just ask your Mistress to pull it out of your head like a weed."

"You realize you just underscored my point."

Yeah, Allan was a vampire and a guest, but he'd also been a vampire barely a decade. Gideon wasn't going to play the kiss-ass servant with practically a newbie. He'd taken down vampires who were past multiple century marks.

With unconventional methods, months of planning and the luck of the gods. Do not challenge that luck, vampire hunter. Allan is a good male, and your Mistress needs you.

Just when he needed Daegan not to be paying attention, he was. Gideon cracked his neck. Yeah, he was spoiling for a fight because he wanted to be two places at once. He didn't want Anwyn to be on her own tonight, too much shit happening, but he didn't want Daegan hunting the guys that hurt her place without him.

I understand, but mind your temper.

He had a colorful response for that, to which Daegan shot him a pretty distracting image involving a woodshed and a belt. He did things like that just to mess Gideon up, knowing Gideon would claim not to get off on it. And he wouldn't...unless it was Daegan. Daegan ran the scene through Gideon's mind vividly, as if it was already happening. Daegan shoving Gideon against the rough boards of the shed, the heat of the enclosed space coating Gideon in sweat. He'd have Gideon's shirt pulled off his shoulders so he could bite him there, leave a track like needle marks on an addict.

Holding him with just the strength of his body forced against his, Daegan would strip the belt out of his own slacks and loop it around Gideon's throat. The strap would still be warm from Daegan's body. He'd hold the end looped over his fist while he took down Gideon's jeans and drove into him. Gideon would have to stay still and take it, or strangle himself on that thick strap.

Which was exactly why he'd do things to make Gideon struggle, so Gideon could feel that mix of violent desperation from not being able to breathe, and the euphoria the oxygen deprivation could cause. He was a third mark. The inability to breathe could make him pass out, but it couldn't kill him.

Daegan had to be somewhere he could indulge this moment, to help Gideon settle, but even so, he sent the warning. *Asshole. Focus, so you don't get yourself killed.*

Daegan's sensual chuckle was like fingers along his spine. *Take care of Seanna and Lord Richard as your Mistress directs, and I promise to give you everything I just showed you, and more.*

Gideon tuned back in to find Allan tugging on a pair of fingerless gloves. Only a blink of time had passed, so Allan was still giving him a narrow look, his answer to Gideon's smartass response. But then, proving what Daegan had said about the guy being a decent sort, a rueful smile tugged at Allan's lips.

"Okay, then. Let's go at it and see who's really too full of himself. I'll match your strength and speed to make it an even fight. I get a better workout that way and improve my skills."

Gideon grunted. He might not like it but, to spar equally, they needed to do as Allan said. Because Daegan was right about that much. A human couldn't fight a vampire toe-to-toe. Not if he wanted to do anything other than be looking at him from flat on his back on the mat.

They got into it. Truth, Gideon enjoyed sparring with a vampire, because he didn't have to hold back. At some point, he felt Daegan's attention, watching the way the other male fought, giving recommendations to Gideon on how to punch, kick, spin out of the way. He'd taught Daegan more about tactics; Daegan had increased the finesse of Gideon's fighting style, a win-win.

Be careful, vampire hunter. He's still young enough to get his bloodlust up as you spar with him.

I'm willing to bet he knows how to control it.

Yes, but he's likely used to sparring with Fort or Saturnia. I don't want Anwyn to have to give you blood because he breaks your neck.

Ye of little faith. Gideon ducked and shot a sharp jab in Allan's side as he spun away from him, but Allan was back in a blink, driving him back so he hit the bag. He slid off it and let Allan's fist hit that. Gideon used the momentum of the bag, dancing with it, around it, coming back and landing another side jab.

Allan scowled at him, and Gideon grinned.

A movement briefly caught their attention. Ella, entering the room. In addition to the fitness equipment, this area held some other recreational amenities, like a pool table and foosball, and a small breakroom, so she was probably snagging one of her healthy snacks from the fridge.

Gideon's attention came back to Allan immediately as Allan moved in again. Otherwise, Gideon would have taken a breath to congratulate her on her performance. She'd changed out of the slinky dress and was wearing the type of outfit she'd usually don to help out the wait staff. Cute mini, tit-enhancing baby-tee. Sometimes when she wore that, she might entertain picking up a session, but he had the feeling not so much tonight. Not after that total eye-fuck moment with Wolf.

My servant, the romantic. Anwyn's voice. She was no longer with Lord Richard, and was moving through the second level of the club. *He's browsing on his own now. You may not be called into service tonight. He and Seanna may find plenty of other entertainments to satisfy them.*

Gideon would respond to that bit of wishful thinking just as soon as he wasn't having to focus on Allan taking off his head. Allan was doing him the courtesy of pushing his limits as far as he could without doing him real harm. Mostly.

Ella had circled around them, moving toward the pool table. She must be meeting someone here on break to play a set. But then Gideon felt something else. Another vampire approaching. When Daegan gave him a terse, one-word warning of who it was, Gideon had a *damn it all to hell* moment. But it wasn't about the vampire coming down the hall.

Gideon called out a warning, lunging forward, but he was too late. Allan spun on the ball of his foot, only to have Ella hit him across the face with the broad end of the pool stick she swung like a club.

The totally unexpected attack, during a vital moment of distraction; that was what had made Gideon so successful as a hunter. They were just lucky that she wasn't trying to kill Allan. He hoped.

The pool stick broke from the impact. Allan's eyes flashed with pain. Bad, but not as hazardous as the inevitable reaction. Red fire shot through his brown irises and his fangs snapped into full view.

Fortunately, seeing it was Ella who'd hit him gave Allan a vital moment of surprise. That, and Gideon had a head start, his flash of pre-cog having warned him of impending calamity a critical second before it came to pass. Before Ella could complete the follow through, he'd snatched the broken pool stick out of her hand. In the same move, he grabbed and pulled her behind him, backing her to the wall so Allan had to come through him to get to her.

Gideon could handle Allan's rage. He was a third mark who could only be killed by metal driven through his heart. Or decapitation. A second mark was more resilient, but they could still be killed any way a normal human could.

The only thing that had saved her was his anticipation and Allan's hesitation. Allan might have his struggles with bloodlust, but they were backed by his still recent history as a human, with a value for human life. Plus, he had an ingrained reluctance to hit a woman. Unfortunately, Ella wasn't helping calm him down.

"Is that loyal enough for you?" she snapped at the stunned vampire, all while trying to reach around Gideon to grab the stick from his hand. "How about I impress you with my submissive nature by ramming that thing all the way up your ass?"

Gideon had no idea what the fuck was going on. Always contained, sweet Ella was snarling like a lioness. He was using his superior weight and fighting skills to keep her between him and the wall, but he was having to be rougher about it than he wanted, because the little she-demon was doing her best to climb her way over him. A glance showed her face suffused with cold fury, her fingers curved like claws. In hindsight—like that did him fuck-all any kind of good—he remembered there had been a peculiar stillness to her features when she'd entered the fitness area. Like a bomb about to blow.

But her temper, startling as it was, wasn't their biggest problem. It was the vampire who'd stepped in the room just as she'd cracked that stick over Allan's face.

Anwyn was on her way, but she wasn't coming alone. She'd already anticipated the urgent thought Gideon had.

We need Wolf. Like five minutes ago.

"What is going on here?" Lord Richard demanded.

As the haze of fury cleared from her mind, Ella finally stopped fighting Gideon. Then reason and horror set in. She'd done something terrible. After she'd seen Allan, she'd argued with herself, told herself over and over to go back to the locker room, meditate. She couldn't let herself get carried away by her emotions. How many years had passed since she'd lost her temper like this?

She'd almost stopped herself, then she'd foolishly thought of Haru's words again, the casual way he'd said them. She'd pivoted and made a beeline for the fitness area.

It didn't matter than Allan could handle it. It appalled her that she hadn't held back. This was why she worked so hard on her temper, those inexplicable fits of rage that had plagued her since she was young. She could have done him serious injury if he'd been human.

She was aware there were other people in the room, but her focus wasn't on them. She tried to move out from behind Gideon, but he wouldn't let her. "I'm sorry," she called around his shoulder. "I'm so sorry, Allan. I can't...I'm just...I didn't know about Haru, and I wasn't prepared. I just—"

Ella. Be quiet and listen. Wolf's voice in her head, urgent. *Kneel and do nothing else until I instruct you.*

But I want to—

Am I your Master or not?

I have no fucking idea, popped into her errant head. A thought that would have been totally private and safe, if she didn't have a vampire in there reading it.

Let's just assume for the moment and the preservation of your skin, that I am. You're in danger here, Ella. I need you to obey me so I can protect you, to the best of my ability.

Finally, she tuned into the energy of the room. She took in Gideon's grim expression, the rock-hard wall of his body between her and everyone else. Allan's tension. The fangs had retracted and he no longer had that feral look, but he didn't look pleased. Nor did the new arrival. His disapproval was palpable.

Oh, Goddess. Lord Richard. Haru stood at his shoulder, his expression chillingly unreadable. She didn't want him here. Why did he have to be here?

Ella. Wolf, bringing her back on point with the sharpness of his mind voice. She inhaled his scent, a startling combination, then she realized he was here, striding over the threshold. His expression was nearly as blank as Haru's, and that gave her another shiver. He didn't look at her at all. He executed a short bow to Lord Richard.

"My lord. Anwyn said there was a problem."

"Yes. There is." Richard nodded toward Ella. "She is your second mark, and she has struck a vampire with the intent to do harm. She must be punished for the transgression. If it is a flaw in her character that cannot be remedied, she must be dispatched."

For a moment she didn't think she'd heard him right. No one just walked into a situation and issued a sentence like that, on the spot. There were processes...

In the human world.

Richard didn't look at her, either. He didn't consider her a relevant voice. Just something to be punished or...killed.

A glimpse at Allan's face made her feel worse. The swelling on his cheek looked really painful. But now, in the absence of vampire aggression, she caught a flash of regret as he glanced toward her. Ella suspected he hadn't wanted Lord Richard involved in this.

If she had any doubt what the Region Master had meant, or whether it could actually go down the way he'd just laid it out, the increase in tension in the room reinforced it. Suddenly it felt like an oven in here, and a big source of that heat was coming from directly in front of her.

Lord Richard's steely expression was fixed on Gideon. "Step away from her."

She realized Gideon held the broken pool stick in a manner that reminded her of a martial artist's stance, right before he engaged the competition.

She had her hands on his back and waist, from when she'd last tried to scramble past him. When all this other had started to happen, she'd left her hands on him, a tense hold. Now she knew why he wouldn't let her past him.

She also knew if he lifted that broken stick in her defense, he wasn't going to be facing punishment.

He was going to face death.

Calling on that calm center she dearly wished she'd tapped five minutes ago, before she ever came in here, she relaxed her hands, sliding them along Gideon's back. A way to tell him she was okay, in control of herself. He shifted subtly, a warning to stay where she was.

Lord Richard's gaze turned from sharp to deadly.

"Gideon," Wolf said, his voice remarkably even, his usual command cadence, deep tones that reverberated authority. "I require my servant to attend me, and your Mistress requires you to be alive to feed her dinner. Step aside."

He met Gideon's gaze. At that moment, someone else joined them. Ella saw Anwyn at the doorway, out of Lord Richard's direct line of sight. Ella felt a strange buzzing, and saw something in Anwyn's eyes. Something that suggested she wasn't entirely stable. Which told Ella exactly how close to the edge they were all standing.

Why hadn't she gone to the locker room? Damn it, damn it, damn it.

Gideon muttered a curse. Ella had a feeling Anwyn had said something to him that was going to make him do what he didn't want to do. Let Ella step out from behind him. She also had a feeling that Anwyn wasn't the only voice in his head ordering him to go against his protective nature.

She trusted Anwyn and yes, though she was mad at him, she trusted Wolf. It would be okay.

"I'm all right," Ella whispered. She wiggled, made it out from behind him, though she had to gently push him to get him to shift, even now. His hand flexed on the pool stick, as if he was clenching his fist, but slowly he straightened, lowering it. She was pretty sure he kept his peripheral gaze trained on her, explaining why he didn't drop it. He needed to drop it.

Ella crossed the floor before Lord Richard's intent gaze and went to Wolf, kneeling at his feet.

"Please forgive me." The next words were bitter on her tongue, but she made herself say them, as much for herself as to defuse what was happening in the room. "I forgot my place."

The focus tonight had been on security, but sometime during the prep phase a couple days ago, Wolf had realized if Ella and Lord Richard crossed paths, they needed to be able to explain her situation. So he and Anwyn had talked, and agreed on their explanation to him, if needed.

They hadn't planned for Ella to go berserker on Allan.

While Wolf had no idea what had precipitated that, he noted Haru standing at Lord Richard's side, which gave him a good idea. If Ella had seen Wolf first, he expected he would have been the one fending off that pool stick.

Good guess.

She'd figured out shit had hit the fan, but the little idiot kneeling at his feet was still mad enough to goad him. In his agitation, he'd left the door to his mind open. He closed it firmly, though he did keep part of his mind following her thoughts and catching up on what was happening, a speed read, so he could head off any more foolish actions.

If he hadn't been so insistent on staying out of her head, to prove to himself he could, he could have stopped this before it ever happened. But there was no time for Monday morning quarterbacking.

"The fault is mine, my lord," Wolf said. "I have not appropriately informed her of the protocols of our world."

"But there are mitigating circumstances," Anwyn interjected before he could say more. "She was marked on the night of the explosion, and the subsequent days have been involved with the club's protection. We share blame, because either of us could have brought her up to speed."

"Gallant of you, Anwyn, but the responsibility was his," Lord Richard said. "He's been a vampire decades longer. He knew better. It is a problem with made vampires."

As Lord Richard pinned Wolf with a reproving look, Wolf acknowledged that at least the Region Master didn't say it in the snide way that born vampires usually did. Richard was made himself, so maybe that would help them in this situation. But Richard was the oldest vampire in this room, so it wasn't a foregone conclusion.

"You've not yet taken a full servant, Wolf," Richard continued. "Made vampires often make the mistake of approaching it like a romance, letting it unfold, rather than treating it as it is, a binding contract of expectations. From our previous meetings, I did not anticipate you having that difficulty. Especially since my understanding was you were contemplating a full marking of Haru, for practical reasons."

He really was going to murder Allan. Soon. Honesty was the best way out of this, but Ella wasn't going to appreciate it.

"Yes, my lord," he said courteously. "I have not instructed Ella on the realities of a vampire and servant's bond. She is a young woman whose view of relationships is framed by her human experience. But there was a reason I had not taken the time to correct that impression appropriately."

Time to use that explanation he and Anwyn had agreed upon. "The traumatic circumstances that resulted in her second marking didn't make a third marking a foregone conclusion. I was in negotiations with Anwyn on how to adapt her to being a second mark under Anwyn's protection going forward, once I made my third mark decision about Haru. I intended to apprise you of her circumstances once I could give you a full accounting of our plan.

"But you are correct. I have not kept her adequately informed or provided her the necessary indoctrination. It isn't an acceptable excuse, but our focus was on assessing the threat to the vampires here and putting the new security measures in place."

Richard pursed his lips. For several moments the room was silent, as he obviously deliberated the information he'd been given. Wolf didn't dare look toward Anwyn or Gideon, and especially not Ella.

"It appears there was a reasonable if not justifiable lack of attention to the matter," Richard said at last. "Bring her up to speed. Inform me of the proposed punishment and timeline to execute. I will approve and modify it if I feel more is required. Keep that in mind when you are determining it."

He turned to Anwyn, the matter done. "I've been very impressed by what I've seen so far of the facility. I would ask your company for a tour of the private rooms and their amenities.

"Absolutely, my lord." Anwyn inclined her head. "If you will give me a moment with Wolf and my servant, I will rejoin you in the VIP lounge and personally take you on that tour. We have some excellent new digital offerings in the VR room."

"I look forward to it." Richard glanced at Wolf. Wolf nodded in respectful acknowledgment, as did Allan and Anwyn, and then the Region Master departed.

Haru hung back a moment. He lowered his gaze, executed a short bow in Wolf's direction. "May I be of any service to you in this matter, sir? I can take the burden of instructing her before the punishment is decided so no further transgressions occur in the interim."

I will cut my own throat before I spend a moment in his company. I need to go, Wolf. I need to go.

He could feel it welling up in her. He needed to handle it, attend to it. He was her Master. But he'd said he'd take care of her, protect her. Instead, he was feeling her shattering with every word spoken in this room, hammering in what she'd known all along.

That she could expect nothing from him.

"Allan?" Anwyn said quietly. "Why don't you join me and Wolf in the private conference room down the hall in a few minutes?"

Allan, understanding the indirect request for privacy, inclined his head. His gaze swept briefly over Ella, then lifted to meet Wolf's eyes.

"Causing you a problem wasn't my intent," he said stiffly, but with true chagrin. "I was unaware your second mark was so ill-informed. I would have guarded my words with Haru otherwise."

He turned and left them. Wolf leaned down, gripped her arm to gently lift Ella to her feet.

She jerked away as if his hand was a brand. His reflexes and strength gave him the ability to hold her, but he saw her face and couldn't find it in him to press the issue. Her tears, the broken look in her eyes, snagged him, slowed him down. He let her pull away.

She ran out of the room, darting past Anwyn, and was gone, her feet pattering up the hallway. The hall shuddered as she hit a door, a side exit, and left the building.

"Punishment?" Gideon growled. "I think you pretty much just administered the worst fucking one you could. Do me a favor. Next time just rip her heart out of her chest and kick it across the floor. That would be easier to watch."

Wolf ignored him, leaving the room without a word, his face a stone mask. Unfortunately, he didn't turn to follow Ella. He went the opposite way. Gideon bit back a curse. Anwyn looked at him.

Go find her. Help her understand this however you can.

I'm worried about those gremlins in your head. They were getting pretty worked up.

They are calming, now that my servant is not holding a stake while standing before a Region Master. Daegan is going to want to discuss this with you.

Gideon kept his response in his head, knowing it was better not to be overheard. *I love you, Anwyn, but I don't have whatever it takes to step out from between a woman and a guy who think it's okay to 'dispatch her' because she broke a bullshit rule she didn't know.*

We know that, Gideon. Daegan's voice, strong and sure, settling both their nerves. *I'm still going to beat you for scaring your Mistress half to death.*

You're just looking for an excuse.

That is the pleasure of being your Master, Gideon. I don't have to have an excuse at all.

A ghost of a smile flitted across Anwyn's face as Gideon rolled his eyes. But it couldn't totally override his worry, or hers. Anwyn nodded to Gideon. *Go. She's hurting. Go help her. I'll see what I can do for Wolf. He's hurting too. He did what he had to do to protect her.*

Yeah. I know. It's a fucked-up world.

CHAPTER TWENTY-FOUR

One of the renovations Anwyn had incorporated involved the problematic and seemingly cursed alley way. So, more than any other repair or renovation, or even the triumphant re-opening tonight, the Alley Cat Café had become an unofficial symbol of overcoming adversity to the staff.

As if he served as both particularly good omen and blessing for the effort, Barnaby had made a reappearance the very day the café was completed. He had a few burned patches of fur, but otherwise seemed his normal indifferent self. He had suffered the indignity of Anwyn picking him up and rubbing his ears and head, giving him a hug and dousing him with a few happy tears. Then, being Barnaby, he'd stalked off to give himself a bath.

The café had bistro tables, potted plants and a stout iron fence at the opening to the alley. Cat shelters, towers and mazes were toward the back. While it had accesses for the ferals to come and go, there were no easy entrances for a human from the outside without a staff assigned gate code. If anyone tried, the fencing sensors would beep a warning on the security monitors. The security team could then determine if the interloper was human, cat or an overfed pigeon.

The dumpster had been placed at the opening of the alley, outside the fence, so the weekly trucks could get to it. However, in front of the fence on the alley side, a wooden screen had been built and painted to look like a white picket fence, with colorful flowers growing through the slats, butterflies flitting among them.

The whole area was enchanting and uplifting to anyone who visited it. As well as absurdly safe. At the moment, Ella couldn't appreciate any of it. She sat on her backside among the cats. Her face was still tear-streaked, eyes and nose red, but she petted the friendlier ones, talked to them in a soft, tremulous voice as she strove to calm down, get it together. Since a light misty rain was falling, she had the place to herself and the cats, for the moment.

"Yes, this is nice, isn't it? That explosion was terrible, but this is a pretty good housing upgrade, right? Like the penthouse version of a feral cat shelter. You might just get gentle enough that one day someone will take you home, give you a place that's all yours."

She looked at the black and white cat peering down at her from one of the towers. "Not you, Barnaby, don't worry. I know this is the only kind of home you want. You're a rolling stone, and the king of this particular castle. But some of these other guys, they might like to belong to someone, have someone belong to them. Have a window to sit in and gaze out at the rain when it's coming down, feel warmth when there's snow outside. Everyone's different, you know."

Gideon closed the outer door and walked past the table arrangements, choosing a nearby bench for his seat instead. Ella spoke in careful, even tones, without looking at him. "Anwyn was so worried they wouldn't come back, but they did."

"Cats are smart. They know a good deal when they see it. Since the explosion I think she has the kitchen staff giving this lot better cuts of meat than what they're putting in those fancy hors d'oeuvres."

Ella smiled weakly. "Yeah, that's true."

She was a mess of different emotions right now. Some of the fury was there, some hurt and confusion, some nerves and fear. But she wanted to figure out the right response for the situation, not just where her emotions wanted to take her. So she took a breath and lifted her chin. Gideon looked like he wanted another go at the punching bag.

"You remember the day you told me there was a darker side to them?" she asked.

"Yeah."

"I'm starting to understand. I need to know what's happening,

Gideon. And I don't want to hear it from Wolf. I want to hear it from another servant." She set her jaw, asking another question first, though. "Can a second mark be removed?"

"I don't know. They can remove third marks, but it's time consuming, expensive, and requires Council approval. This situation wouldn't be considered impor—big enough to warrant that."

"Easier to dispatch the unimportant person affected."

His face immediately hardened. "That's not going to happen. Older vampires, and born ones...they tend to be arrogant dicks in how they view humans."

"Like humans can be with animals," she said thoughtfully, tugging a striped tabby's tail as he turned and bumped his head against her shin. "If they cause a problem, the easiest, cheapest solution is to kill them. Or trap and dump them somewhere far from where they grew up or the world they know."

Her gaze slid to him. "I'm still in the world I know, but a part of me isn't, Gideon."

He rubbed a hand over his face. "This wouldn't have meant a damn thing if you didn't know about vampires. You would have hit some guy you were pissed at, and Allan would have blown it off, let it go, because you're not part of their world, didn't know he was a vampire. No vampire with any sense or self-control makes an issue of that. But you did know about vampires, you're second marked, and he's a guest vampire in the home of another vampire."

He sighed. "And it was witnessed by a Region Master, so there's no way Allan can let it go. If he does, Lord Richard would just pick it up, see it through. As it is, Allan has the right to ask for something. A compensation from the host vampire and the marking vampire, or to punish you personally. Or all three, depending."

She looked down at her hands, opening and closing on her knees now, because the tabby had wandered away. She tried to keep her voice steady, an absurd idea. "Am I...going to be executed?"

"No." Gideon leaned forward, propping his elbows on his knees. "Allan has the right to demand your life. Though Wolf is the senior, stronger vampire, Richard could decide that Allan's request is valid. But Allan doesn't want that, so Lord Richard has decided punishment makes more sense. Someone has to watch it happen, witness it."

His lip curled. "Then it's over and they move onto the next

thing. What's for dinner and what's on cable tonight. Wolf should never have pursued anything further with you without letting you know everything. But he keeps arguing with himself about it. As a result, he left you completely unprepared. The rest of us, like idiots, were letting him take the lead, like we thought we were still living in a human world, even though every damn one of us isn't."

Gideon was as furious with himself as anyone, she realized. It didn't make the situation any less precarious, but there were several things she knew.

Gideon cared about her. Anwyn cared about her. Wolf cared about her. They weren't going to let anyone harm her, even if they had to sacrifice something dear to protect her.

She had to figure out how to fix that.

"So you said servants are property," she said. "Literal property of their vampires."

"A third marked servant, yes. Second marks, it's more fluid, but they are bound to the vampire world and its laws."

"A third mark servant has no choices. Except whether he or she wants to be third mark," she recalled. "After that, all choices belong to the vampire master or mistress."

She stared at him and he stared back. "You belong to Anwyn. And to...him. If you hadn't wanted him to touch you...

He didn't flinch. "After agreeing to be his servant—hell, her servant, because he outranks her—I'd have had no goddamn say in that at all. Not in this world."

"Why would anyone sign up for that?"

But she knew. She knew even before he answered, confirming it.

"If you have to ask, then you're not ready for it." Gideon shook his head. "When I became a third mark, Anwyn needed my mind. Needed me, or she wouldn't have survived. And Daegan..." He shot her a glance. "Scary Guy. That name goes no further than the two of us. Or Wolf and Anwyn."

"Promise. I'll try to remember to keep calling him Scary Guy."

Gideon nodded, somber again. "Daegan loves her in a way I'd never encountered before. He was willing to let her hate him so that she could have me. Her heart was the bridge between him and me. He did...force me, in a way, but in that way you and I know. He saw in my head, and my heart, and knew where I wanted to go. He just didn't have the patience to wait for me to get there myself."

His lips tugged in a wry smile. "I can't fault him for that, because I'm a stubborn bastard. I might have taken two hundred and ninety-nine of my supposed three hundred years to make up my mind."

"Okay." She stood up.

"Okay?" Gideon's brow creased. "You going to tell me what that means?"

"It means a lot of things, but first I need to talk to Wolf."

"You don't need more information?"

"No," she said. "You told me there was no way to understand the reality of someone owning me and making all the decisions about my life until I was in it. It's why some decisions have to be made with the heart, not the head. Thank you, Gideon."

"Do you have a game plan?"

"We'll see." She stopped at the door leading back into the club. "But it isn't a game, is it? That's the point."

As she looked at Gideon over her shoulder, he saw her eyes were steady, not blinking. Earlier in the evening she'd had her makeup done up, a glittering dark blue liner that made her eyes look faintly exotic and tipped upward. Now she'd taken that off, but she wore a silver pentagram on her neck that showed a cat sitting on the horizontal bar of the star portion. It caught the light. A pair of tiny pewter dogs chased one another around the outer ring. Everything about her said *this is who I am. I will accept and follow the path I'm given, but on my own terms.*

She'd make a hell of a vampire's servant, Gideon realized with a start. Better than he'd ever be, but then he was as unconventional as the two vampires he served.

But Ella being a superlative submissive had never been her problem, had it? He wasn't the kind of man who gave a lot of credit to the hand of fate, gods, whatever, for things to turn out as they should. He'd seen too fucking much that turned out ass-backwards and horrifyingly wrong. But since bonding with Daegan and Anwyn, he grudgingly gave Fate more of its due. So it crossed his mind now that the track of Ella's life might have always been heading her toward an intersecting course with the vampire world.

The question was, would her heart survive it, or would that be the end of the story? Or of Ella herself?

~

Anwyn took the two ends of the pool stick with her, and laid them down on the conference room table. It felt better for her to have them far from where Lord Richard would have any reminder of them in the hands of her volatile male servant.

Gideon was in the alleyway with Ella, which was good, keeping him away from other vampires for awhile. She'd have sent him on an errand completely off property for the next couple hours, except she unfortunately needed him within close physical proximity.

Even while talking to Ella, his mind was warmly, intimately linked with Anwyn's, helping to keep her steady. When it came to this, he had an uncanny intuition for knowing when the full focus of their mind link was needed to keep a seizure at bay. Though he might give himself shit later for adding to her stress—even knowing he couldn't have done it differently, just as he'd told her—right now he kept even that out of the equation. Nothing but a full dose of support, and a rhythmic pulse of continuous strength.

She was well aware that often only two things kept Gideon alive. His brother was Jacob Green, the servant of Lady Lyssa, who happened to be the head of the Vampire Council. And Gideon was the servant of one of the most dangerous vampires in the vampire world other than Lady Lyssa—Daegan, of course, not Anwyn.

But vampires were well-known for asking for forgiveness rather than permission. Especially after they let their always ready-to-call bloodlust and stick-up-their-ass sense of proper servant behavior blend into an impulse execution.

Ssshhh... It was something she sometimes did with her gremlins, treating the vicious things like unruly children to calm them, soothe them. Rocking them in her mind. Didn't always work, but now that the immediate danger had passed, it was easier. It had been a near thing, right before she'd entered the break room. She'd had to stop, let Wolf go first, because she'd been so close to losing it.

Speaking of which, Wolf had just come into the conference room. Rather than talking to her, though, he was facing the wall, his head dipped as if he was thinking hard about something. On closer inspection, and because it was hitting her vampire senses like torpedo pings on radar, she had a feeling he was closing out all other input, trying to get a handle on something. The vibrating volatility to him made her think they might need to take a few extra minutes before they began discussion.

She opened her mouth to suggest Wolf go walk it off some more, and they'd reconvene after she gave Lord Richard his tour. Unfortunately, Allan stepped into the suddenly way too small meeting room. He'd taken a short break to go to the locker room, change back into street clothes. His face was already healed. He must have fed earlier in the evening, accelerating the already miraculously rapid process, when the injury wasn't too severe. Wolf's back had healed in a matter of a couple days, with Ella's blood, though the soreness had lingered somewhat longer.

"So I get she was second marked under violent circumstances," he said to Wolf. "But what the hell have you been doing these past few days that you couldn't bring her up to speed? Especially when you knew a fucking Region Master was going to be here tonight?"

Great. The perfect way to start off a calm conversation. But it wasn't the first time she'd had to deal with two males overflowing with testosterone, locked and loaded.

"I think we should focus on the problem at hand," she said. "Not how we got here."

"Why not?" Wolf spoke without turning, the muscles in his wide shoulders rippling as he jerked with a shrug. "You made me second mark her. I told you it was a mistake."

She'd wrestled with it herself since it had happened. Maybe what she'd seen growing between him and Ella before the attack had happened had made it easier to act on the split-second decision. Maybe she'd unconsciously thought of it as a way to give it a push, a vampire-servant matchmaker thing. She knew just how valuable and important it was for a vampire to have a third mark servant, and it was well past time for Wolf. But that hadn't been her call to make.

Since then, she'd watched what was growing between him and Ella with a mix of trepidation and hope for both of the people she cared about. Now she was second guessing herself again.

But in all fairness, when the second mark thing had happened, it had been a crazy fifteen minutes. A bomb going off, Wolf horribly injured in the alley. The first responders on scene, with only a few moments to keep Wolf from being taken to a hospital where his physiology would definitely raise eyebrows.

During all that stress, she'd been holding off an army of gremlins in her head, even with Gideon at her side, helping her keep it together.

It was that thought, all of it, that helped her rally. She was the Mistress of Atlantis and a vampire, and she wasn't going to take punches she hadn't earned.

"My top priority in the alley wasn't a philosophical debate on the pros and cons of giving Ella the second mark. I believe I told you shortly thereafter, if you considered it a mistake, it was a manageable one. Simply don't take advantage of that mark, keep the distance between you and her that you'd always so oddly and determinedly maintained—at least until a couple weeks before the attack happened."

His expression tightened and she nodded. "You chose to spend more time with her, get closer to her. I'm not the asshole who has been enjoying all the benefits, engaging her heart, head and soul, without taking stock of the cost, without bringing her fully into the loop."

She'd intended to keep this conversation calm, but her vampire side strengthened her annoyance as she spoke. Maybe that was what was needed. She'd made it around the table and stood before him, hands on her hips. His fists were clenched and his eyes were sparking dangerously, concerning Gideon, but she sent him a firm command to keep doing what he was doing.

Being a Mistress had uniquely prepared her for a world where she couldn't show weakness, particularly when a male vampire got snarly. If Wolf wanted to go a round, they'd go a round. She'd been sparring with Gideon and Daegan for months now. She was ready to test it out, and she had blood lust and violent impulses of her own.

Yes, you do, cher. Daegan's voice, telling her he'd been following things pretty closely. Damn it, she didn't want his attention divided.

You and Gideon worry needlessly for me, he responded. *Be a Mistress first and a vampire second. Something is coming off of him I do not like. He is hurting. Badly. You can see it if you push the rest aside and put the intuitive Mistress first. Ella's tears and what holds him from her have brought him close to breaking. Do not push him unnecessarily. He will not forgive himself for hurting you, and I will not be able to excuse it.*

Shit. She closed her eyes, stepped back. One, two. It was harder than she expected. Most of what she was pushing back was fledgling vampire bloodlust, not the gremlins that could throw her into a seizure. That was a relief, but the vampire side didn't want to back down. It was telling her she'd appear weak in front of Wolf and Allan.

But Daegan was telling her she wouldn't. She had to believe him, not some primal part of herself she couldn't yet adequately control.

"We can spend all day on this," she said shortly, opening her eyes and meeting Wolf's. "It's not helping."

"You're right," Allan said. He directed his next words to Wolf. "Maybe you should go ahead and mark Haru. It will tell Lord Richard your intentions, make Ella's transition to Anwyn's protection clearer."

Wolf swung toward him. "That serves your and Fort's purposes, doesn't it? Gets me hooked up with your hand-chosen servant."

Allan's eyes narrowed. "Sorry that everyone wants to see you happy, moving on, moving forward. We're getting damn tired of you denying your potential in this world because you can't get past how you got here, the choice *you* made. Focus, damn it. Richard isn't going to let it go. We have to come to a decision on a punishment that fits the crime, that satisfies Richard, while—"

Daegan had been right. That energy exploded off Wolf, and violence erupted. Everything happened so quickly. Before the gasp caught in Anwyn's throat, Wolf had Allan against the wall. Only the threat wasn't to Allan.

Wolf had picked up one of the broken pool stick pieces, and had that jagged end pressed against his own chest. His other hand clasped Allan's, forcing his friend to hold the shoving end of that stake.

"She committed no crime," Wolf snarled. "Except being exactly who she is, a soul incapable of failing another human being to the extent I did. If there's a punishment here, it is mine. Have my life as payment for her damaging your pretty face. The worst choices were mine, but you know damn well there was one thing that was not my choice. Finish what I should have had the balls to let be finished, decades ago."

"*No.*"

Before Anwyn could react, Ella flew into the room, shoving herself between the two men.

~

Ella had reached the conference room in time to see Wolf bare his fangs, growl something savage to Allan, obviously designed to escalate the fight. As the two men struggled, her eyes latched onto the pool stick. The broken end was pressed so forcefully against Wolf's chest it had cut through his shirt and drawn blood.

In an instant, she was wriggling in between the two males, pulling on Allan's clenched hand, pulling on Wolf's, terrifyingly unable to get either one to let go. Their rigid faces were inches apart, fangs bared, eyes like flame. Something evil and howling had broken loose in the dense energy in the room, something that wanted this to happen. All of it centered around the struggle between those two hard fists.

Then she realized Allan wasn't driving the stake *toward* Wolf's chest. He was fighting to pull it back.

"Stop, please. Stop, stop, *stop*. This is so stupid."

In her peripheral vision, she saw Fort and Saturnia barge into the room. Fort sized things up the quickest.

"For fuck's sake," Fort thundered. "Break it up, soldiers. Right this goddamn minute, or I'll stake both of you. Using the orifice that will do the most good."

They barely reacted, so even before Fort finished the command, he and Saturnia were in the mix, prying the two vampire males apart. Anwyn darted in, pulling Ella away. Haru had come with Fort and Saturnia, and reached out to take Ella's arm, she assumed so Anwyn could be free to join the fray. Ella recoiled from him, moving toward Gideon, who apparently had followed her from the alley.

Haru lifted both hands, respecting her desire, but positioned himself in her path to Wolf and Allan so she couldn't interfere again. She glared at him, even though Gideon laid a hand on her upper arm, probably for the same reason.

Fortunately, Fort made sure there was no need for her to figure out a way around him. He shoved Wolf hard, and the two vampires broke apart. The broken stick clattered to the ground. Anwyn darted in and took it, and two seconds later, neither piece of the pool stick was in the room, as if she'd simply flung them in the hall to get them out of sight, out of mind.

Fort put himself between Wolf and Allan as Wolf threw himself forward again. Fort shoved him backward a couple more times, pushing him toward the far corner.

"Damn it, this is not helping anything," Fort snapped at him. "You have better control than this. So does he."

"May I—" Ella started urgently.

Anwyn was back beside Ella and immediately clamped a restraining hand on her other arm. There was probably some rule here that said she wasn't supposed to interrupt vampires when they were talking. Like Doms, in certain situations.

Still, when Ella spoke those two words, they'd been high and sharp enough to capture Fort's attention. Even better, Wolf's eyes turned her way. The look on his face, an incomprehensible rage, almost froze the words in her throat, but she shoved them out.

Sometimes even when Doms ordered a sub not to speak unless given permission, it was necessary.

"I...I think I can help with the decision, if my Master will allow it. But I really need...may I speak to him first, just the two of us?" She kept her gaze on Wolf, showing that her appeal was going straight to him, that it had been spoken first to Fort merely as a formality. She added to it, sinking to her knees, easing herself out of Anwyn's hands. "Please, Master."

When she knelt, she brought the bulk of Wolf's attention to her. He was fighting for control, and she was the only one in the room he could look at right now without wanting to do all sorts of violence.

Allan and Haru exchanged a look. Ella steadfastly refused to look at Haru, though her tense body language telegraphed her awareness of his presence.

Fort and Saturnia stayed in between him and Allan, but they'd backed off some, giving him some space. Wolf spent a couple of long seconds gazing down at Ella. She had her head lifted, her gaze on his face, waiting on his decision. He cocked his head at her at last and she swept her gaze down. She knew his cues so well, knew what he needed before he needed it. That act of submission was like she'd gathered up the pieces of control he'd lost and handed them back to him. He was her Master. She expected him to act like it.

It almost made him smile, how horrified she'd be if he interpreted her behavior that way. She would never try to direct a Dom that way. Not consciously. She didn't recognize what it was about her that made a Master want to embrace that side of himself in every way possible. Fuck.

"Go to the entrance and wait for me there."

She lifted her gaze again, uncertain. He went to her, bent and lifted her to her feet by her elbows. He kept her so close she had to tilt her head up to meet his eyes. He made sure they possessed the vital elements of the Master she knew. Then he gave her the direction to reinforce it. *Obey me, little girl. Don't make me blister your ass.*

She gave him a searching look. As she did, another emotion gripped him. Regret so fierce it could double him over worse than a grenade shoved into his gut. He wished, he wanted, he yearned. And yet he'd accepted, so very long ago, what he could have and what he couldn't.

Was there any wonder, her acceptance and resignation about never finding, or being offered the love she deserved so much, had found an answering chord in him? The acceptance part, not the deserving part. She deserved everything good the world could give her. Instead, he was going to be just one more person who'd stopped short of offering it to her.

A fist clenched around his heart as she swallowed, the movement like a fragile bird egg in her slim throat, and nodded.

Yes, sir.

She turned away. He heard her footsteps receding up the hallway. He imagined her placing her feet so precisely, wearing the canvas sneakers she preferred, no laces or socks.

The doorway to the main floor opened and shut quietly. She was gone.

"Wolf," Fort began.

Wolf lifted a hand, shooting a hard look at him that made Fort's expression tighten, but there was no disrespect in Wolf's gesture. Just a harsh need for no one to say anything until he could get this out.

Wolf looked at Allan. "What I did in the past, I live and act as I do now because I know it's right to value the life I've been given. But there's a problem, and I've no idea how to make you understand it. There is something inside me that nothing in the universe can change or make me forget. I can only make sure nothing shines a light too bright on it."

He looked toward Anwyn. "You're right. You weren't at fault. It's all on me, for not being strong enough to resist."

He pointed toward the doorway where Ella had disappeared. When he spoke, there was a hoarseness to his voice he couldn't disguise, which he could tell startled all of them. He was trusting them with something a vampire wasn't supposed to, but if he couldn't trust the people in this room, then he was lost anyway.

"Every time I let her inside me, it's like sunlight, burning everything not worth her love to ash. You are not touching a fucking hair on her head. No one is, even if Richard kills me for it."

She was waiting for him at the entrance. When he offered her a hand, she took it, her hand small and tense inside his grasp, but given to him willingly enough.

Out in front of the building, they walked side by side in silence. She took him around the front of the vending machine warehouse to reach her favorite loading dock, the one where he'd sat with her a while ago. It made him wonder what she had in mind. He couldn't tell. She was doing that thing she did, her mind empty. He could dig for it, but he wouldn't. Not when it was clear she intended to tell him what she was thinking. He'd give her the right to organize her thoughts the way she wanted.

She walked up the short set of steps rather than asking him to lift her, as he would have. Wolf followed her as she walked, her on the dock, him on the ground. She moved to the yellow line painted along the dock edge, intended to catch the eye before someone stepped off into nothingness.

She put her arms out like wings to balance herself, and walked on that edge like a balance beam. When she tottered, Wolf clasped her hand, keeping her steady, and she sent him another smile. This one sadder.

She reached the mid-point and, still holding his hand, folded herself gracefully to a sitting position. Wolf drew closer, leaning against the dock edge, his hand on her thigh.

"It bugs me," he said abruptly. "That way you have of clearing your mind. Like clouds. But the weather changes. Sometimes it's like clouds on a rainy day. Sometimes clouds on a sunny day. Today, it's clouds over the ocean."

She grimaced. "I learned to do it to control my temper. I used to get really, really angry about certain things. A therapist at the homeless shelter said I had too many turbulent feelings, with no way to process or resolve them. I wouldn't take drugs, so she taught me the meditation." She sent him a wry look. "It's more effective when I actually do it. I didn't tonight."

He squeezed her hand. "You won't accept any blame for that. Besides, Allan won't admit it right now, but it impressed him. You're a hell of a stealth weapon. Though for future information, if you only want to beat up a vampire, it's best not to go after him with something that's considered a lethal weapon. Go with an aluminum bat next time."

"Oh. I guess I didn't think of that. That's why Lord Richard...why I'm in such trouble?"

Yes. He kept that thought to himself, though, and merely brushed a knuckle of his free hand along her cheek bone. He thought of what Gideon had said, about how Wolf had already delivered the worst punishment possible. He didn't want to make her feel any worse, didn't want to admonish her, though at another time, if they made it through this, he would enjoy punishing her in a far more sensual way for risking herself so recklessly. "You aren't in any trouble. You *are* trouble. The good kind."

She had her head down now, was watching his fingers move with hers as they twisted slowly together.

"Wolf, I need to ask you something. Will you answer?"

"If I can."

"Why is Haru auditioning to be your full servant, when you told me you can't third mark me?" Her voice trembled, but she lifted her chin. "I don't care about the punishment issue. I just...can you please tell me why? If I can know and understand why, I can bear it. You've said it's not me, so I need proof of that. So that I don't torture myself with it. Okay? Tell me what's really happening. Then, whatever needs to happen can happen. But I just want the simple truth. Please. If you feel that's something I deserve to hear."

No one deserved to have that shit dumped on them, but that wasn't what she was asking. She wanted to know if what she'd endured so far, what she'd endure after this night, was enough to deserve the truth.

It was. And yet opening his mouth and letting the words come out was still absurdly difficult.

He let go of her hand and turned, leaning against the dock. This was where she'd told him what happened to her family. Appropriate.

He was still close enough her dangling leg brushed his hip. He shifted so there were a few inches between them. Staying close, but he needed to keep a line in the sand, across which he couldn't invite her.

"No matter what I say, don't reach out and touch me until I say you can." He looked out into the night, looked for the words, even knowing the images would surge up from his gut the second he spoke them. They were always ready to be called, in maximum, hi-def color.

"Okay. I won't, Master. I promise."

She'd recognized it as a precaution, not a preference. Sweet, smart girl.

"In the 1960s, I was sent to Vietnam. I came back from the war messed up, mentally and physically."

He'd pretend he was talking about another vet, one he did sessions with, not him. "You've seen how Don is, the nights he comes to me in particularly bad shape. That was me, only maybe a lot worse, a lot further gone. Shell shock, PTSD, whatever the fuck they call it from generation to generation, they're just buzz words for finding out just how easy it is to kill one another. The ways to do it, experience it, they're limitless. And every one of them is a self-administered poison that gets in your system and never gets out. If they'd leave you in the thick of it, maybe you'd never realize it. But they don't. They send you back home, and you're trapped in your head, like you're inside a crate, watching your parents, your wife, your kid, your friends who were your friends before the war..."

"'Some part of the world still cares what color the kitchen is.'"

The bitter half laugh broke from his raw throat. He bit back unexpected tears. Fuck, she understood so much, listened so well.

He opened his mind a little, let her see a short montage of it. Blood, fire, screams. Another reason he was glad she wasn't his third mark, so there'd never be any chance he'd dump the whole of what was in his soul into hers, during some unguarded nightmare of his own. With a second mark, it was just words, some vague images. Which were bad enough, if her indrawn breath and the hand he felt rise and then close, short of touching his back, were any indication.

Time to move on. This wasn't a therapy session.

"Eventually, I couldn't hack it anymore. I talked myself into believing my family were better off without me." He stared into that darkness and had no idea if he was looking at the night or inside himself, the emptiness, the abyss that still beckoned whenever he thought of it.

"I killed myself."

CHAPTER TWENTY-FIVE

For a moment, Ella thought she'd misheard him. But from the corpse rigidity of his upright body, the way his gaze sought the night as if he were suddenly far away from her, she knew she hadn't.

"I'd put a bullet in my brain. I was drunk as hell when I did it. Though I'd entered brain death, my heart was still pumping. Nolan, soon to be my sire, was living in the basement of the shitty motel where I was staying on the first floor. I didn't know he'd been watching me, considering me as his next turning candidate. He heard the shot, came, and turned me before I could get away to the other side. A hospital would have pronounced me dead and unplugged me, but he had the juice to bring me back."

Wolf rubbed a heavy hand over his face. "When you become a vampire, something changes in your base makeup. I was still this fucked-up guy who'd killed himself, but I was also now the type of predator whose sense of self-preservation is so strong, suicide isn't an option. At least not in the first few centuries.

"Fuck, I hated him so much for it, for so long. It was a wonder he put up with me. In later years, I realized he'd been damn close to where I had been. It was the only thing that made sense, his patience. His damn stubbornness, because anyone else would have staked me after dealing with half of my self-wallowing shit."

He straightened and moved along the loading dock, trailing his hand on it, then made his way back. Not once did he look at her, and he stopped a foot away. His long dark fingers tapped the yellow safety line, a restless movement.

Ella had seen Don do tics like that. Her heart tightened with the desire to reach out, but she didn't. She waited, and listened.

"When I killed myself, I was married." He swallowed. "I had a son."

As she clutched her hands in her lap, she closed her eyes. This was the crux of it.

"You saw that scar on my body. The war...I was injured in a bad firefight, an explosion..." He shook his head. "The day in the alley, that was a bad moment for a lot of reasons, but it took me back there. When I saw your face over me, for this insane second, I actually felt so much relief, realizing it had been a bomb in the here and now. That I wasn't back there again, only with the knowledge about what it would mean already injected into my head.

"I was too badly injured to return to combat. I could move, but not really well. So many muscles had been severed, destroyed. I should have died from those wounds. But I was the team leader, a stubborn, strong son of a bitch who thought he was some kind of invincible hero. Death wasn't going to take me from my family. When I was shipped back home, it never entered my mind that I couldn't heal from anything I survived.

"The injury...I couldn't have sex with my wife. I never would be able to again. I couldn't play ball with my little boy because I could barely lift my arms. They talked about wheelchairs, walkers. I wasn't thirty years old yet. I discovered drugs and alcohol, lost myself in them. My inability to get myself back a hundred percent dragged me down into other things, things I'd seen and done in Vietnam that I couldn't forget."

He was tapping more rapidly now, uneven notes, and then abruptly, he just stopped, staring into the night as if he'd bore a hole into that darkness. His body was so stiff there was a vibration of energy around it. When he spoke, his deep voice was higher, hoarse.

"Sheila. My wife. She wouldn't give up on me. Month after month, into two years. Maybe three. Can't remember now, which fucking pisses me off, because I deserve to remember every minute of what she endured. She was so strong. And yet I found the way to break her.

You know how I couldn't contemplate being less than I was? She couldn't believe that love wouldn't be enough to save our family. She put her money on the wrong horse, the wrong love."

Ella had tears running down her face. She was hurting so much for him. The knot of her hands in her lap had become painful as she dug in her nails, to keep them there and honor what he'd requested, not to touch him. He kept looking anywhere but at her, yet she felt his full focus on her, revolving around her.

"When I woke up as a vampire, Nolan told me I couldn't go back to them. If it had just been Sheila...maybe. But not Ross. He was a kid. You can't bring a kid into our world, for obvious reasons. But beyond that, I was in no fit state. For the next five years I was more raging, wounded beast than anything resembling a civilized human. Wasn't much of a change from the piece of useless shit I'd been since I'd been wounded, to tell the truth. I was the same asshole, just in perfect, superhuman health."

He took a breath. "Didn't matter. I still couldn't wrap my head around it, the guilt of leaving them, until Nolan pointed out, rather ruthlessly, that was exactly what I'd done when I killed myself. I'd believed to my marrow they'd be better off without me. I couldn't handle the shame of being what I was, failing them, breaking her heart all the damn time. I'd lost my chance. It was done."

His voice broke, but he snapped himself to attention like he was on a parade field, as if he'd admonished himself for showing weakness. The next words were said in a flat tone.

"I missed something, though. Nolan didn't point it out because I was such a mess, and he knew I wasn't up to it. It took me a decade to get my shit together, and I didn't make any attempt to see them for all that time, because it was as hard as kicking an addiction. The more I wanted to see them, reach out, the farther away I went. I saw more of the ass-end corners of the world in those ten years than I can remember. I spent time with Fort and Nolan, helped them with things, things they could do with their special skillset to make the world a better place, even as vampires."

A grim smile touched his mouth. "There are special ops guys out there who don't know how close their night missions came to being fucked. We were three shadows, making sure they achieved their objectives and got home safe. And somewhere during that eleventh year, I had my head together, and made the connection. I couldn't be part of their lives anymore; I accepted that. But I sure as hell should be checking in, seeing if there were things I could be doing, unseen, to help make their lives better. It would be tough, but I owed them that. I owed them everything. I was the head of the family."

That strangled, bitter chuckle came from him again. "I was steeled for the worst. You know what I imagined that was? That they'd moved on, that Sheila had remarried, and I'd have to see some other guy in her bed, raising my son, playing catch with him."

He paused. Ella heard a cricket start up somewhere, that *chirrup, chirrup* noise. Wolf looked up, and she followed his gaze. Only a scattering of stars penetrated Atlanta's urban sky.

As the silence drew out, and that stiffness in his shoulders didn't ease, she realized, with a terrible dread, that there was more.

"Sheila hadn't handled my suicide well. She'd gotten hooked on prescription drugs. My strong girl, so strong for me and my son, reached her breaking point. She'd OD'ed, three years into my turning."

"Oh, Wolf."

Now he looked toward her. The pain in his face had vanished, back behind the impassive mask. Yet she didn't see the mask anymore. She felt everything from him as he pivoted and walked toward her. Three steps, every heavy footfall precise, as if he were walking that yellow line she'd been following along the dock edge. When he reached her, he cupped her face and brushed her tears away with his thumbs. Slow. When she twitched, she heard it in her head, a reminder.

Don't touch me, baby girl.

His hands were cold, and she suspected the rest of him was too, as if all his heat and life had gone somewhere else. He was turning into the marble statue he needed to become to tell the story that broke him, and kept breaking him, with every retelling.

"My son had practically raised himself, while taking care of her, best he knew how," he said flatly. "He'd been put into foster care."

"No." She thought distantly what a strange picture they must make. Her back hunched against the sobs, hands knotted in her lap, her tear-stained face cupped in his hands, while he stood straight and unmoved, at least to those who didn't know where to look. Her eyes were on his, and she saw past the flat exterior to the ravaged depths. But his thumbs never stopped moving over her cheeks and lips in that slow caress, taking away tears.

"Now do you understand?" he asked. "It's never been you, Ella."

He saw himself as a stone, one that had landed in the pond of their lives, his wife, his son. The ripples that he'd caused had kept expanding outward, drowning them in the consequences of his actions. Until only he was left on the banks, howling his pain.

She lifted her arms, a mute plea and offer, and Wolf moved into them. He couldn't unbend, couldn't let it all spill out, but now he wanted her arms, her hands on him, like he hadn't wanted anything in a very long time. So he clasped her hard to him, almost bruising, and spoke the harsh truth into her hair.

"Sheila and Ross, they were gifts in my life. And I pissed those gifts away, so I don't get anymore."

She nodded, held him, ran her hands over his back, his shoulders, wept some more for him. "I understand."

She spoke it, thought it. Her heart broke for him, while her arms held him as if she'd never let go.

Nolan, Fort, everyone else who'd known him since he'd become a vampire, they'd understood parts of it, but they hadn't understood enough not to get impatient with him, feel like he should move on. When Ella looked at him, he saw she did understand. She understood. And she accepted.

"You've are the best damn gift I've ever received, since Sheila and Ross," he said gruffly.

Her gaze flickered with pain, but she nodded, with that resolute set to her chin that told him just how tough she was. He wished he didn't know how fragile she was as well, but Sheila had taught him that, and it was a lesson he'd never, ever forget. They all had their breaking point.

Actually, the first one who'd tried to teach him that was himself. Allan had said it, right? *For not being the superhero you believed you were, that nobody is, not a hundred percent of the time.* Unfortunately, Sheila had to be the one who drove the truth home.

Ella had another question for him.

Your son...do you know what happened to him?

"Yeah." On that at least, his heart could ease, even though it was accompanied by the bitter knowledge Ross had come out on the other side in spite of his dad, not because of him.

He eased back, but let her keep her hands resting on his chest, kneading, kitten movements of reassurance for them both, a reminder of her presence.

"He landed in a good foster home, and then he was adopted. The dad's a travel writer, the mom a cooking expert. My son's been all over the world, knows about four languages. He works with diplomats, has even been a translator at peace talks. He looks like me, though he's a bit slimmer, fine-boned like his mother. He's gay."

Wolf gave a deprecating half-chuckle. "I probably would have given him a hard time about that, since like most straight men of my era I thought being gay was the most fucked up thing that a son could be. I like to think if I'd stuck around, been his dad, love would have taken me past that, helped me figure it out and know that it was okay. But since I was so clueless about so much, maybe not. His adopted parents...Joan and Rob, they saved my boy."

His lips twisted. "The irony is that, for years, I've put most of my sexual focus on men, because it was safer. A vampire's nature is to enjoy men and women, so it was easy to make that transition. I know I can enjoy sex with a man, but I can never feel for a man the way I could feel for a woman. If I was going to fall in love again, it would be with a woman. So I've stayed away from them, or gone only with the really safe situations, a woman I know I'm not in danger of that with."

He took a breath, met her gaze. "Until you. You are extra ordinary, Ella."

He said it as two words, which made a puzzled frown pucker her brows, so he explained it to her.

"When I was in Vietnam, in the thick of things, I'd get this despair. It seemed our brutal souls and dull minds were beyond hope. Everything around me was fire, blood, hatred, violence. It coated me, hardened upon me. But every time I was close to losing my mind, I thought of ordinary things. A bowl of cereal in the morning, sitting on the back stoop of my house. Listening to the cicadas in the early morning, telling me it would be a hot day. But it was never that bad early in the morning, because we had an old oak that spread its arms over the house.

"When I was a kid, my friend, Newt, he'd be coming down the road, and when he got to me, he'd already be yammering about what we should do with our day. That was the kind of kid he was, always with a plan. Telling me how he'd found a quarter and maybe we could split a moon pie down at Myrtle's, the lady who ran the general store. My mother, she'd come out with a basket of laundry, fuss at us for blocking the stoop. 'Boys, don't you have nothing better to do than plant yourselves here? Get off with you now, before I find something for you to do.'"

A painful smile touched his lips, reflected in the faint quiver on Ella's mouth.

"But she'd smile at me," he said. "That distracted way mamas do when they have lots on their minds. It was...ordinary, Ella. Extra ordinary. In the middle of death, blood and despair, it was those extra ordinary moments I held to me like the greatest treasure that's ever been and ever was. If I lost those moments, I'd lose everything, everything that might make my existence mean something. When I'm with you, it returns me to those extra ordinary moments of life, reminds me they exist. So if I call you extra ordinary, I mean it, with all my heart."

His little girl had a limitless amount of tears. He brushed each one away again, kissed the tracks, lingered on her lips. And he kept going. He knew every word would tear her open, but he also knew he couldn't not tell her.

You will never tell yourself I didn't choose you because you weren't enough. It was because you were far more than I deserved. You were the answer to the emptiness inside me that I've wanted to fill for decades, but never thought I would. That's how you made it in—I didn't think someone like you existed.

She opened eagerly to the kiss he couldn't hold back any longer. She showed him her desperation, her heart pounding with the ache of his truths. He gave her the same emotions in that kiss, bringing her up tight against him, holding her so close as he kissed her, kissed her into oblivion.

When he finally drew back, his body was heated by the need in hers. "Please," she whispered. "Master."

They were on a loading dock. While this place wasn't Atlantis, it had to have at least one camera in the back. No way was she going to be some security guard's masturbation fantasy. He hooked an arm around her waist. With a flash of vampire speed, he had them in the shadows between buildings. They'd think it was a blip on the screen.

She'd gasped as he'd done it. When he pressed her up against the wall, he saw her eyes shining through her tears, her lips curved in a smile. She could experience joy and laughter through pain. She had a limitless ability to gather to her what life had to offer. If he didn't immerse himself in that in the next breath, by being inside her, he wouldn't be able to bear it.

"Yes," she whispered, telling him he'd given her that thought, and she'd answered, telling him not to wait.

He opened his jeans, hooked her underwear beneath the skirt in one finger and tore it. In the next second, he'd sheathed himself. She was ready for him, his desire and hers matching pace. She groaned as he hit the root, and he growled, holding her hard against the wall with one arm, his other palm slapped to the brick as he dug as deep as he could into her. "This'll be a rough ride, babygirl. Your Master needs you."

Her answer was to wrap her arms around his shoulders, put her face to his neck and bite him. Hard. She kept clamping down, as if she was trying to break skin. Nothing turned a vampire on more.

He thrust as if his life depended on it, savoring every second of her slick heat squeezing him, her short breaths and little groans as he shoved into her. The only restraint he showed was not using his full strength. He could be much rougher if she was his third mark. But that was resolved and done. He took what he could get, the same way she did.

He came within seconds, one of the most animal-like fucks he'd allowed himself in forever. He kept thrusting until she tightened around him and screamed her release, a strangled sound against his flesh he helped muffle by cupping the back of her skull. He kept his other arm tight around her waist and hips, pushing into her, working her until the end.

When at last she was done, he held her against the wall, his weight pinning her, his face against her disheveled hair. Her hands moved over his shoulders and neck, stroking, as their hearts pounded against one another, separated only by an inconsequential amount of flesh and bone.

"It's going to be all right," he promised her. "I'll watch after you always."

When everything was resolved at Atlantis—fuck, the damn punishment issue—he'd eventually take them back to who they were to one another before. He wouldn't talk in her head anymore, but he would be there for her, if ever she needed him.

"You are one of the most remarkable women I've ever met," he muttered. "I wish I could be with you. I wish I could make you my third mark. I just...can't."

Tell me once more you understand.

A long pause, as her arms stilled, but then tightened over him again, her lips brushing where she'd bitten him. Her mind cleared, that stillness of a stormy sky.

Yes, Master. I understand.

Ella gave it a lot of thought after he left her. He saw her safely home, but he didn't stay. He told her he'd keep her posted on the Lord Richard matter, but not to worry about it. He'd handle it.

She didn't know what that meant, but it definitely made her worry.

A couple minutes after he saw her safely into her little cottage, she heard his truck pull away. She'd changed into her nightshirt—Wolf's shirt, which he'd never asked to have back—and sat in her bed, listening to the crickets and frogs, the sounds of the night, and wondering where he was.

When she finally lay down, she still didn't sleep much. She drifted in and out. Finally, at a precious, sweet moment of that night, he entered her mind and let her know. He was driving. Just driving, miles and miles of back rural roads, out of Atlanta, all the way to Savannah. It reminded him of where he'd grown up, oak trees dripping with moss, fierce summers, fishing in creeks with his friend Newt. They'd once discovered a nest of baby copperheads Wolf had thought were worms, which Newt had thought was terribly funny. After they were far away from the venomous snakes.

She smiled at that, and he told her a couple more stories about his friend, who she also learned had died in Vietnam. He had a lot of pain over that, too. She realized he was very alone, her Master. He had plenty of people around him who cared for him, but she thought he'd moored himself on a deserted island, within view of the mainland, but with no desire to ever rejoin the people there.

The bitch of it was, she did understand why he felt the way he did, and just how impossible it would be to change his mind. Only he could do that. Unfortunately, that might happen well after her lifespan. That truth was a jagged ache in her heart, her stomach.

Eventually, her Master sat out on the beach at Tybee Island, watched the surf come and go. He didn't talk much to her directly, but he kept letting her see his thoughts, of home, of the past. Then, near dawn, he told her he was going to find a place to go to ground and ordered her to go to sleep.

She was finally tired, so she slept deep and hard. She should have been bruised all to hell from the rough fucking against the brick wall, and she did wake up sore, but nowhere as much as she'd expected. That second mark was good stuff.

She went to her waitress job, still thinking, only this time about other things. From his thoughts, she knew Wolf planned to stay in Savannah at least another day. He said he was going to return to Club Atlantis in twenty-four hours and offer Lord Richard his decision about "her punishment." That worked because Richard was staying in Atlanta for the week to visit other vampires in his territory. He'd be coming back to Atlantis two nights hence to enjoy the entertainments once more, before returning to his home base in Alabama.

As night closed in, she waited to see if Wolf would talk to her, or she'd feel that sense of him in her mind. She didn't. That was when she came to a decision.

She was going to do the unthinkable. She was going to handle something, but definitely not the way Wolf wanted it handled.

She wasn't doing it impulsively, however. She had her reasons, and if he gave her the chance to tell them, she would. But first she was proceeding the way her heart dictated. She headed for Club Atlantis.

~

Sometimes fate lined things up so well she knew she had to be on the right track. Or it made it easier for her to tell herself that.

She found Allan in the small conference room with Fort, Anwyn and Saturnia. Gideon wasn't there. She considered that fortunate, since Gideon would strongly oppose what she was trying to do.

The only human present was Hollow, but he was reviewing info on a tablet while he sat at a corner table. Ella had done her best to draw him out since he'd arrived, but other than yes and no answers to most questions, he was so uncommunicative she would have believed he was mute. In every way, he projected a complete lack of interest in engaging with anyone.

From what she'd learned about Saturnia and Hollow's CIA backgrounds, Ella thought Hollow might suffer from some kind of condition that severely detached him from the rest of the world. Except Saturnia.

Toward her, he had an entirely different body language. The way he positioned himself toward her, minute changes in his behavior when she moved or spoke, showed how hyperaware he was of his Mistress. Ella found it odd that Saturnia rarely touched him. Even when she leaned over his chair to look at what he was doing, she'd brace her hand on the table, or on the back of his chair. If he leaned back, where there'd be contact between her hand and his body, she'd remove it. It was like they were more co-workers than vampire and servant. But then Ella had a front row seat to only one vampire-servant relationship, Anwyn and Gideon. She expected everyone was different.

As Ella entered the meeting room, it was obvious how non-human their vampire visitors were. Three sets of vibrant and unnaturally steady eyes were focused on the door as she came into view. It made her moisten her lips, a nervous gesture. She acknowledged Anwyn with a nod, but went straight to Allan.

He was pushed back from the table, his jean-clad legs stretched out and crossed at the ankles, his hand resting on the table. She could see the smooth curve of biceps stretching the sleeve of his T-shirt and pushed away the thought of how much strength he could wield with that vampire-power enhanced arm.

In her hours of thinking, she'd forced herself to acknowledge what consequences in the vampire world meant. This wasn't going to be a

Dom/sub session at Club Atlantis, where pain might happen, but within the structure of limits, safe words, under the watchful eye of a Dungeon Master. It would be an actual punitive sentence, like in the days of public whippings.

But her decision was made. No sense getting butterflies over it now. She knelt before Allan. "Forgive me, sir," she said. "I'm here to submit to whatever punishment you and Lord Richard deem fair. I accept whatever you wish to do."

A significant pause gripped those at the table. She expected some WTF looks were being exchanged over her bowed head. Maybe some more thoughtful deliberations. The chair creaked as Allan pulled in his feet. She tensed when he leaned forward, but he simply touched her head, her temple, a cue to look up and meet his steady gaze. He had strong features, a handsome male. Though she remembered the violence that flashed through his gaze when she'd struck him, she remembered how he'd restrained himself. If Gideon's analysis of vampire strength was to be believed, Allan could have killed her with nothing more than a punch to the face.

Lonnie would have hit her for nothing more than irritating him. She would have carried bruises for a week if she'd hit him with a pool stick the way she had Allan.

"You can't accept anything, little one," Allan said, not unkindly. "Only your Master can, on your behalf."

She swallowed. She could try lying to them, say Wolf had said it was okay for her to handle this in his absence, but that sounded so lame, even to her, she'd destroy any credibility she had unless she went for the whole truth.

"I...I want to prove to him that he can require this of me." *That I can be his full servant, capable of existing in his world, even if he can't choose me. Because maybe, sometime in the future, he'll change his mind.*

"I know that's not the way things are done. But I think...you've all been human. Perhaps, in this case, you'd understand and accept my offer, to help him. I don't want him to be in trouble with Lord Richard. You all made that sound like it's a really bad thing. Wolf is in Savannah, at least until tomorrow night and he doesn't...he doesn't really listen in, like I'm his servant."

She stopped there. First, because it hurt a little bit to say that aloud. Second and more importantly, because years of embracing a submissive nature had taught her when to be silent. It was a Master or Mistress's decision, not hers. Just as Allan had said. Third? Though she thought she was doing the right thing, acting so deceptively behind her Master's back gave her a heavy feeling in her chest.

Fort at last spoke. "Your decision, boy," he said gruffly. "He'll do his level best to kill you if you do it."

"Well, it's been a few hours since that's happened," Allan responded dryly. "I was starting to feel he didn't love me anymore."

Saturnia chuckled. When Allan looked toward her, she shrugged. "You know Wolf. He's a team player until he stumbles over a point of honor. I think it's our only option, unless we want to wait for him to tell Richard what he told us. To go fuck himself, because nobody is touching her."

"Then Richard will be forced to decide whether to kill him, or worse," Fort added.

Ella bit back an automatic protest, hearing Wolf might come to harm. But if Wolf had said that, he meant it. She knew he did. Which meant being here was doubly the right thing to do.

Then she understood what Fort meant by "worse." Richard likely wouldn't kill a vampire over a human servant, but he *would* kill the human servant. Wolf wouldn't be able to stop him. With all the other deaths on his heart, Wolf would be destroyed anyway.

You were the answer to the emptiness inside me that I've wanted to fill for decades, but never thought I would...

She'd thought about those words, over and over. Held them close to her heart, filled with an almost giddy joy, while she wept over what she wished could be, for both of them.

"You think Richard will be fine with Wolf not being present?" Saturnia asked. "Or himself?"

"He left Seanna here until his return," Fort said. "We can run it through her. I'm guessing he doesn't care all that much about being present. To him, it's a minor matter. He'll watch through her eyes. His priority is ensuring the punishment is severe enough and carried out."

"What punishment is being considered?" Anwyn spoke at last. Ella could feel her employer's eyes upon her, and heard the tension in Anwyn's voice. She didn't want to do anything to upset Anwyn, and did her best to look completely accepting, the calm submissive. Not one scared down to the bone to be doing this without her Master present.

She returned her gaze to Allan's feet and imagined they were Wolf's instead, in his thick tread shoes. He also had a pair of laced knee-high boots. One night he'd worn those with a pair of slick latex pants that fit his thighs and ass so mouthwateringly well, it felt like a transgression to indulge even the quickest look without his permission.

"I'm thinking the standard punishment," Allan said. "Nothing too creative. Which reinforces that it's simply a procedural matter, handled and done, no more attention to it needed. She's a second mark, and a relatively new one, and Richard already knows she was given that second mark under unusual circumstances."

"On that note, he'll likely want an update on her ownership status," Saturnia pointed out.

Ownership status. Unsettling words in the world outside these walls. Even inside them, those involved knew, deep down, that ownership was a consensual thing that met mutual cravings. The way Saturnia said it, the way they treated it, the way Gideon had spoken of it...it was real. If she carried two marks from a vampire, she had to belong to someone.

Fort spoke gruffly. "Wolf has made it clear he's not retaining her as his full servant. I believe you agreed to become her permanent Mistress."

Though Ella's head was still down, she knew that was directed toward Anwyn. "Yes," Anwyn said quietly. "Which means technically my being present for the execution of the punishment should be sufficient. But it feels wrong to me. As I expect it does to you, too, Ella."

"We do it any other way, Wolf is going to get himself in deep shit with Lord Richard," Allan said.

"Which is his choice," Anwyn responded. "Look at me, Ella."

When Ella complied, the Mistress of Atlantis was as serious as she'd ever seen her. "You understand what you're doing here is overriding your Master's will."

There were lines of tension around Anwyn's mouth, in the set of her delicate chin and swanlike throat, that told Ella how stressful agreeing to this might be. Ella didn't know how to fix that, other than to assure Anwyn that whatever happened had her full consent.

Even if her consent wasn't required.

Ella swallowed. "He's made it clear he's not going to be my Master. Not that way."

He couldn't be. She understood, Goddess, she did. Because of what he'd done to his family, he'd passed sentence on himself, and was committed to that sentence, because he was a man of honor. No one could commute that punishment but Wolf. No matter how much Ella wished it was otherwise.

"That's not my question and you know it. Look at me."

Anwyn leaned forward, bringing that penetrating stare closer. Yeah, Anwyn might be upset, but she was still a hundred percent the Domme who could tear a sub a new one, if they didn't give her, and themselves, total honesty.

"I've looked into the eyes of hundreds of submissives, Ella," Anwyn said. "The shape of their souls can be so different, the level of devotion and self-sacrifice. As well as how much of themselves they're willing to give to their Master or Mistress to nourish that need inside them. So, you answer me. Is he your Master or isn't he?"

He was. Him not being able to commit himself to that wouldn't stop her loving him and serving him like he was her Master, now and forever.

"He is," Ella responded, her throat aching. "That's why I'm doing this. If I'm not going to be his, I at least can do this. The act was mine. I struck Allan. Let me clear the slate. Please...Mistress. If, in this world, I am considered yours, then the choice would be yours, but I don't want him angry with you, either. I'm not anyone's fully marked servant. I want him to know this choice is mine."

"I don't think Wolf is going to see it that way." Anwyn's smile was tight. "But thank you for trying to protect all of us."

There was another half-chuckle from Saturnia, equally grim smiles from Allan and Fort. Ella wished they would decide, so she could get on with it. There was a dread in her belly, perhaps because if Wolf tuned in and figured out what was happening, he might start talking in her head, ordering her not to do this, and then she wasn't sure if she'd be able to refuse him.

She needed reinforcement. Unstoppable resolve.

"If Wolf doesn't obey, I know Lord Richard will kill me." What a surreal thing to say aloud. She tried to ignore that and focused on her question. "But what would happen to Wolf? Is it all right to ask?"

She looked toward Anwyn, but it was Fort who answered. "Depends on the Region Master. There are standard punishments for vampires who don't fall into line. Usually starts with 'milder' things, like being shut up in a coffin and buried for a couple months. If the vampire is really a problem, they might break a couple of limbs and tie them in the wrong direction before putting him in there."

Ella had paled. She noticed Anwyn had as well, and realized Anwyn hadn't known that, either. "Christ, Fort," Saturnia said. "What the hell."

Fort's expression hardened. "I expect the girl had a good reason for asking. She wanted to confirm that an hour's worth of punishment was a good trade for what he'd endure. And she'd still be punished, because she has no choice in that. This way, she gets ahead of it. Smart, and it means she cares about Wolf. That kind of backbone deserves honesty."

"Yes," Ella managed. "Thank you, sir."

She cleared her throat, looked toward Allan. "Is it all right to ask... what is the standard punishment for what I did?"

"You don't get to know that until it happens," Allan said. "But as long as Lord Richard doesn't have an objection, I don't see any reason not to get on with it. Do you?"

She shook her head and he glanced at the others. "Are we all in agreement on our course of action?"

Just like a PTA meeting or something. She had to stifle a giggle because she knew it might come out like a hysterical sob. There was so much wrong with all this, wasn't there? But this was Wolf's world. Knowing it didn't make her want to be with him any less. Maybe she'd feel differently after her punishment, and maybe that would help her deal with his resolve not to make her his full servant.

While she'd been going over that in her head, Anwyn had picked up the club phone and murmured into it. Ella focused on the slim, tense line of her back. She knew Anwyn didn't want this. That helped, as did the hint of kindness in Allan's eyes when he'd told her they'd move forward. If Gideon was to be believed, that consideration wasn't always a given.

She thought of the way Wolf had punished her that unforgettable night. It had been a hint of the extreme power balance of the vampire world. Like his response about safewords.

Vampires don't believe in them.

Yes, their world was ruthless and had a lot of strict rules. And the inequity factor between vampires and humans was over the moon. But beneath that...there was something Ella recognized, and still craved. She couldn't explain it, or put words to it, but the answer to it had been in Gideon's simple answer to that final question.

"Do you ever regret binding yourself to either one of them, despite that dark side?"

"No."

"You requested my presence?"

She looked toward the door. The woman who stood there emanated a velvet sexual vibe that reminded Ella of an old-world bordello, populated by women with long curling hair. Their lips curved in secret, promising smiles behind lace fans as they trailed scarlet-painted nails along the smooth surfaces of dark, ornate furniture upholstered in silk brocade.

This woman's features looked carved out of creamy mocha-colored soap. She had dark eyes and a curtain of long, slim braids that framed prominent cheek bones, drawing attention to full glossy lips and a delicate chin. Her impossible to overlook body was highlighted by a classy black wraparound dress that cinched at the waist with a belt made up of lots of straps tipped with fleur-de-lis charms. Ella realized it was a cat-o-nine, designed as an accessory. It accentuated the curves above and below. Her tall skinny heels made the most of her legs, the fragile anklet on one glittering with a diamond fleur-de-lis charm.

"Seanna." Allan rose from the chair. "I need you to convey a message to your Master."

CHAPTER TWENTY-SIX

Allan left the room, out of Ella's earshot, to handle that. Ella had stayed where she was, on her knees, head down. The submissive posture centered her, and she kept her mind empty. Anwyn shifted to Allan's chair. As she quietly discussed other matters with the two vampires remaining, she put her hand on Ella's shoulder, a simple, firm contact.

Ella turned her cheek to it, a light brush that she hoped reassured Anwyn. She accepted this. She was okay.

Allan returned. "Richard approved the punishment. Seanna will witness for her Master, and Anwyn's presence is acceptable to Richard as the party responsible for Ella. We can do it now."

He looked toward Anwyn. "We need a sound-proof room with a drain. I want a cold and sterile place, no props to soften it up. Something like a prison cell would be best."

Ella's heart accelerated. She relaxed her shoulders, closed her eyes. It would be more difficult to meditate with adrenaline surging through her, but she'd learned how to zone out when needed. But she was jerked out of that state when a rough hand gripped her hair and yanked her head back.

Allan stood over her. Anwyn was still in the chair, her long, slim leg extended so her foot almost touched Ella's knee, but she did not move, her body language tense again. Ella could see Seanna standing behind him. As he did what he was doing, he adjusted so she had a more direct view of Ella's reaction.

She was on camera. She got it. Lord Richard was watching. But it wasn't an act, none of it. The look on Allan's face was as deadly as the one she'd seen when she'd struck him, but this was scarier, because it was cold, controlled. The tips of his fangs showed as his gaze coursed over her thoroughly. A sexual appraisal, an appraisal, period. For the duration of this punishment, she was his, to do with as he wished. He might not have sex with her, but what he would do to her would feed the sadist in his Dominant side. She felt that in the heat of his regard, the danger of it.

"You will not detach from this, little one," he said. "You remain fully present, from beginning to end. If I suspect otherwise, I start my count over. The punishment is a hundred strikes with the object of my choice. I'm fond of the cane."

Stinging pain. Of course. She should have expected it would be the kind she disliked most, though she was capable of handling it. But a hundred...Goddess. Never had she taken that much in one session.

Allan released her and stepped aside, nodded to Seanna. "Prepare her."

"Ella, show Seanna to the room we use for prison scenes," Anwyn said, her expression stiff. "Prepare it accordingly. We'll be there shortly."

"Yes, ma'am." Ella rose. Seanna executed a slight bow toward the vampires in the room. As she circled behind the table to move toward the door, she passed Hollow at his corner table. She trailed fingers playfully along his shoulder. The expressionless male didn't react to her touch, but when she would have continued on, that changed.

He surged up from his chair. His knee hit the table, making a jarring thunk against the wall. It didn't stop him from putting himself between Richard's servant and Saturnia. Since Saturnia had been sitting with her back to him, Seanna would have been passing behind Saturnia, between her and her servant, to leave the room.

Hollow's position was so close to Saturnia he was pressed to her chair. He gestured with wooden courtesy to Seanna. Now she could continue on her way.

Seanna didn't seem perturbed, but her distracting mouth deepened that sensual curve. It made Ella wonder if she'd done it on purpose, to tease or test Hollow for his overprotectiveness. But she lifted her hands, a pacific gesture, and passed before him.

Saturnia didn't pay any attention to the exchange. She was discussing something with Fort about the security system. Ella's punishment was just part of the day's to-do list, apparently, and now that a course of action was set, they'd moved on.

Ella met Seanna at the door. The woman's eyes were expressive. Sharp and intrigued by the entire situation, the different players in this room, but not unsettled by it a bit. Ella didn't know if she should find that comforting.

As they left the room, Ella stole a sidelong look at her. How did it feel to Seanna, to have Lord Richard's third mark? Have him soul-deep in her consciousness, like Gideon had described. Maybe the second mark was a lot like a gateway drug. It planted the yearning for more.

Maybe this punishment would be so wretched that it would stop that ache.

"That Holliman is an odd one," Seanna said. She had a cultured Southern drawl, and was as casually friendly as if she and Ella had met at a social event. "Has Saturnia used any of the public facilities, let you see a scene between them?"

Ella shook her head. Chantal had mentioned that Saturnia and Hollow had used one of the private rooms once, no camera engaged, but they'd been back out in fifteen minutes. Ella's assumption was they'd done it for Saturnia to feed. Or it had been a very functional sexual encounter, understandable with so much needing to be done to get the security up to speed for reopening.

When they entered the stark room Allan had designated, Seanna's gaze swept the cinder block wall with rings embedded in the rough surface. She also registered the concrete floor with a built-in drain, and the hose coiled on a hook in the corner. "I expect many fantasies have played out here. There's an energy to this room. You could feed on it." She closed her eyes, drew in a deep breath. "Yes. There it is."

She opened them again, looked toward Ella. "Where are your restraints?"

Ella nodded toward the cabinet. This room was the one most likely to be used for extreme scenes where blood play was approved, or the submissive might lose control of bodily functions. However, while Seanna rummaged among the restraints, murmuring in pleased approval at the wide range of options, Ella verified the right supplies were in the room for a "session" of that intensity.

Seanna spoke, her back to Ella.

"I admire your resolve, though I do not envy you your Master's wrath when he finds you acted without his consent."

"I'm not his full servant. This will be my last duty as his second-mark before I'm considered fully Anwyn's." At least, that was what Ella assumed. Regardless, she figured it was best to remind Richard she was securely under vampire control.

"Perhaps. Our Masters and Mistresses have their own ideas about where the lines of ownership begin and end."

The response fueled Ella's hope *and* trepidation, but the time for conversation was apparently over. Seanna nodded to the scattering of rings in the cinderblock wall. "Go there, face the wall. Put your palms flat upon the stone. I'll chain your arms and legs. Keep your clothes on."

Ella complied. Her legs were starting to shake. "Do you think I'm doing the wrong thing?"

"It is always wrong to go against your Master's will," Seanna said promptly. But as she came to stand beside Ella, her expression was unexpectedly understanding. "Yet sometimes what must be done, is done. And we can bear anything because we know, as much as they enjoy seeing us become aroused at pain, there is a part of them that feeds on the pleasure of the kind of pain we fear. Especially when we face it because we belong to them. We are theirs to do with as they wish, and our desire to embrace that pleases them like nothing else."

Ella was sure there were those who would find it twisted that her body roused at those words, but her shaking increased. She did yearn to serve her Master's will. Truth, she could bear so much, if it was Wolf's command. But Wolf's will wasn't part of this, so that arousal gave way to a coldness she tried to ignore. A vital ingredient was missing, to handle this moment the way she should.

She'd figure it out. She would.

Seanna caressed her arms before lifting the restraints she'd chosen. Ella's dread increased, her shaking. This room was all about edge play, so no surprise, the restraint options reflected the theme. The cuffs were lined with metal studs, so the more fiercely the submissive struggled, the more the studs would dig into flesh, abrade it.

Seanna tightened them on her wrists. They weren't cutting off circulation, but couldn't be slipped, either. Then she did the same to Ella's ankles, leaving her legs shoulder width apart. Once done, the woman ran a familiar hand over Ella's arm, to her back, and down, over her ass, giving it a squeeze. "You are a lovely handful," she said. "Now, for a little something extra."

She'd had a black tote on her shoulder when she'd come to the conference room, as if she'd known why she was being summoned. Now she went to it, and withdrew a jar of what looked like pale green lotion.

"Is it okay to ask what that is?" Ella said, sure she probably didn't want to know.

"You can ask me anything you want, *ma chatounette*," Seanna responded simply. "I'm a servant, not a vampire. I'll tell you if I can't answer." She held up the jar for Ella's inspection. "There is a version of this that, when smoothed on the skin, feels so soft and creamy, so healing. It smells so good, and tastes the same. Made of a very rare combination of flowers and herbs. Your Master would bury his face in your cunt to taste it. The barest touch of his lips would have you fighting not to release, because it makes the skin so sensitive to arousal. But my lord had a chemist work with it, change the composition, so now there is a before version and an after version. This is the before version. It makes the skin sensitive, too, but in a different way. A pin prick becomes the stab of a knife blade."

"Oh," Ella said faintly. Her hands curled in the bonds. "What does *ma chatounette* mean?"

Seanna smiled. "My little kitten. Lord Richard commands you to be silent now. Until the punishment is done, you say nothing, do as you're told, and endure."

Ella put her cheek to the stone. Seanna reached under Ella's knit skirt with brisk, efficient fingers and slid her panties down to mid-thigh, then ripped the seams to remove them fully. She unhooked her bra, threaded the straps out of Ella's T-shirt before she broke them as well, so she could remove the undergarment without unchaining Ella.

Ella understood this was part of the lesson being applied. It was why Seanna hadn't told her to undress before being bound. Nothing she owned was sacred. It could be destroyed and cast aside. Just like Ella herself.

Stop it. Stop thinking that way. This is for Wolf. You do this for your Master.

Even if he wasn't here to steady her, to approve of her obedience, to give her that core of strength she so desperately needed. She focused on her submissive instincts, which had never failed her. A weak spiral of arousal had happened the second the first cuff closed around her wrist. She held onto that feeling with both mental hands, trying desperately not to let it slip away.

Seanna at least was willing to help with that. When she began to apply the lotion underneath Ella's T-shirt and skirt, she applied the mixture with an efficient, firm and thorough rubbing. She worked the lotion into Ella's back and shoulders, her ass and thighs, and then against her labia and the tender pocket between them and her thighs, rubbing with extra thoroughness.

Ella tried to focus on the touch, not on what the lotion was doing to her skin, but it was impossible. The nerves were coming to life, prickling against her skin.

"Beautiful ass," Seanna murmured. "I wouldn't mind strapping on a nice big shaft like your Master has and seeing how you handle that. Would you cry pretty tears for me, *ma chatounette*?"

Seanna coiled strong fingers in her hair, lifting Ella's head and sucking on her neck briefly, giving her a brief bite with her human teeth.

"How long have you and Lord Richard..." Ella stopped herself, biting back the words. She'd forgotten Lord Richard's mandate so quickly. Perhaps because her mind was scrambling for how she was going to get through this in a way that would make Wolf proud.

Except she really didn't know what would make him proud in a situation where she was going behind his back to do something he didn't want her to do. Damn it.

"He says I can answer your question. Since the beginning. Since he heard a nightingale singing in the window of a New Orleans brothel and found a child-whore who wanted to see the world."

Ella remembered the pictures Chantal had brought back from her trip to New Orleans, and how she'd described the city to James, giving him recommendations on where to go, what to see. Graceful gardens, dancing and music everywhere, the aroma of wonderful food. Second story balconies with wrought iron railings painted different colors.

She could easily see Seanna there. And she'd been right about the bordello. Wow. A small way to bolster her faith in her instincts.

"I've been with him for decades," Seanna continued. "He is my home now, and always. Oh, look at your hips, dancing against my fingers as I rub your rim. Such a sweet, responsive thing. My Master looks forward to hearing you scream."

It wasn't malicious. It was...sexual. She could feel Seanna feeding on the power of having her here at her mercy, her Master in her head feeding on it as well.

"Now, speaking of shafts..." Seanna removed a soft-sided cooler from the bag, and opened it, expelling a cool mist. She removed two ice dildos. The frost-covered, translucent phallic shapes were both sizeable.

"There we go. The lotion has lubricant in it. So versatile."

Ella bit her lip as the first one was inserted into her rectum. Hell, it was cold. So cold. But the moment it came in contact with the nerves on her rim that had been treated with the lotion, it started to burn. Burn like someone had forced a much bigger thing into her backside without any lubricant at all. *Oh...Oh Goddess, that hurts.*

"It will become very painful, but not leave any damage. And the lasting effects...even if I removed it this very minute, the pain you are feeling will continue for quite a while. There is a special wash in my bag that eases the effect, makes it bearable. Only one substance, other than time, eradicates it completely. I will not tell you what that is. That is a surprise, one you might not experience."

Ella had to choke back a whimper as Seanna efficiently parted her labia and worked in the other curved ice dildo. "It's all a lesson, isn't it? Teaching you your place in the vampire world. It is very important you learn it. You attack one of them again, my sweet pussy, your life will be forfeit."

Ella was focusing on breathing. In, out, in, out. Fuck, fuck, fuck, this hurt. Rise above the pain. Rise above it. She needed her Master. Needed him so much. She could bear anything with him, if it was his punishment. This was making her feel so isolated, so alone. Where was Anwyn? She was getting scared. She didn't want to be scared.

The door opened, bringing her head around. Her heart plummeted as her stomach twisted. It was Allan. He'd stripped down to his jeans. And he already had his weapon of choice in hand.

An intense impact cane, with rubber grip handle and wrist strap to make it easier for the Dom to hold during a prolonged caning session.

She'd received very pleasurable canings from Mistresses or Masters who knew how to warm her up, find her sweet spot, where even with the pain, she'd still want more. A caning was typically a slow build, deep tissue pain, but once it reached a certain point, it could be shudderingly memorable. She'd been at the mercy of those who knew how to make it hurt, make her cry, because that was the kind of scene they wanted. She remembered one Dom who held her afterward, dried her tears, and told her how very pleased he was with her, which had made it all worth it. But each time he came back to do that scene, she'd still dreaded it.

She had a feeling that was going to be a picnic compared to this.

Seanna stepped back as Allan took her place. He stared down into Ella's face, tipping up her chin.

"If you cry out, we start over," Allan said quietly. "Do you understand?"

There was no way she wouldn't cry out from a hundred strikes from a cane. Her voice shook. "Yes, sir."

Allan gripped the collar of her shirt with both hands and ripped it off her shoulders, tearing it down the middle of her back. He left it hanging that way, in tatters. He tore the waistband of the skirt, down the seam. The fabric fell around her ankles. She still wore her sneakers, no socks.

He'd done it brutally, a deliberate lack of sexual finesse, matching the stark bleakness of the room. All of it screamed *this is not a fantasy.* Yet that didn't mean every bit of it wasn't arousing to the vampire watching through his servant, or to the vampire executing the punishment.

She saw it in Allan's face, in the way he touched her as he checked the security of the restraints, discovered the studded lining. But she also saw something else. He was reining it back. Which suggested he wouldn't be having sex with her as part of this, a relief that almost balanced her fear about everything else.

He was still human enough to respect his friend, to try not to get off on hurting his servant. Or think about taking her, even in this situation where Ella suspected it was entirely permitted, if Lord Richard sanctioned it.

Ella's heart hammered against her chest, her mouth dry. She really, really, really wished Wolf was here. *Don't talk to him, don't try to talk to him...*

She'd hoped Anwyn would be in the room, but there was a camera. She expected Anwyn was watching from there, so if she revealed any discomfort about this, Richard wouldn't see that. Or maybe Richard had required she view it through a camera, rather than being physically present.

Ella wished at least Gideon was here, but she understood why he wasn't. It was possible Anwyn hadn't even told him about this, knowing it would be very difficult for him not to interfere. She was protecting her servant.

As Ella was protecting her vampire. It was all she wanted, though a close second was her desire for this to be over.

Seanna, now positioned at the wall where Ella could see her, was moistening her lips, her eyes glittering. She wanted to be where Ella was, Ella realized. With her Master wielding the cane.

Goddess help her, Ella understood that. Just as she knew her Master's absence was going to make this even more unbearable than the pain itself.

Though that was saying a lot, because those ice dildos were pushing her even now to start screaming, and keep doing so, until the echoes reached all the corners of Atlantis.

Maybe, since he didn't listen in on her mind the way other vampires did, she could talk to him during this. The knowledge that he *could* listen in might be enough of a substitute to help her.

I'm so sorry, Master. This is so wrong, but I don't know what to do.

That's my fault. Because I haven't taught you to trust me the way you should.

Goddess. The flood of feeling was instant, breaking through every flimsy wall she'd been trying to build to get her through this. She closed her eyes, hating herself for the weak-kneed relief she felt at the sound of his mind-voice. Would he be willing to stay there in her head throughout, despite her doing what he hadn't wanted her to do? She imagined him sitting on a bench in Savannah, watching the boats come and go as she was caned. Could he let her watch the boats with him? Or would he be so angry with her, he'd leave her closed in the darkness of her head. But he was here with her, even in that darkness. She could get through it.

Allan had stopped circling her. He'd turned toward the door. Then she felt him, her Master, coming down the hallway. Her stomach lurched.

You were in Savannah.

Yes, I was. Then I started thinking about my girl, and how her mind works. I thought of my friends and what they might do if my friends and my girl got together and decided to try and protect me. And I knew nothing but my actual presence could stop this from happening.

He was angry, but a cold, controlled anger that she knew didn't bode well. Even so, that relief didn't abate. He'd be here during her punishment.

There will be no punishment. This is not happening.

He entered the room, stood on the threshold. Seanna had put her in the center of the wall, so she had to crane her neck to a straining angle just to see him in her peripheral vision. Whoever had designed the room had had a wicked understanding of how to make a sub feel even more helpless.

But she saw enough to see he wore a long-sleeved dark shirt, loose over his jeans, with a pair of boots under the denim. He looked so good, smelled so good. She inhaled him and his heat through all her senses.

But the thunderous look on his face was unmistakable. He was going to order Allan out of the room, take her out of the cuffs. Seanna was watching—Lord Richard was watching.

Please, Master. If you aren't going to be with me, please don't let the last thing I remember between us be this. That I did something that got you hurt, in trouble. Please...I couldn't bear to think of it, if you were trapped in a coffin for months as a punishment, if someone was hurting you...please, this is just a moment.

He moved fully into her view, standing at her side. She bit back a sob of pure relief. Closing his hand on her throat, he tipped up her chin.

"I've been too gentle with you, Ella," he said. "Too much of a Daddy and not enough of a Master. You don't make decisions about punishment, when you deserve it, how you ask for it. Do you?"

She wet her lips, but before she could say anything, he barked it, making her jump as if he'd struck her with a single tail. "*Do you?*"

He was right. She'd forgotten just how scary he could be. There were rules about things, like contracts and consent and all that, and he followed them in the expected, reasonable ways with his session guests and within Atlantis's walls. But the face she was seeing now said that, once a submissive was under his care, there was no civilized world and contracts about things like this. There was only His Will, and hell to pay if she didn't obey him.

"I fucking own you. Don't I?"

He'd said that one night to a sub he'd reduced to jelly. The woman who'd asked for a more extreme scene had quavered, "Yes, sir." Then she looked into his face. Three breaths later, she safe worded to end the scene. She'd reached a limit she hadn't expected to have, and Wolf had pushed her to that understanding, knowing she'd needed it.

Ella understood that, because that expression was inches from her own. But unlike that woman, she wanted his large body looming over her, whether like this or in tenderness. She'd take him however she could get him. But oh Goddess, she was trying her best not to writhe. The ice had to melt, right? It should be melting now, yet the agony didn't abate. Just as Seanna had warned.

But there were more important things. Wolf was more important.

It took an effort of will she hadn't known she had, but her gaze lifted, locked with his, so he'd see the truth of her thoughts. *If the punishment is at your hands, the pain is nothing. Let me prove to you just how worth it I think you are. You've told me what you did, what happened. And it's okay. You believe I have a pure heart. A pure heart sees true. You are a good man, Wolf. I don't need a third mark to feel your soul, to give you mine. You deserve goodness. Please...just please. I don't know the right combination of words...I need you. I need my Master to get me through this.*

His gaze flickered, his features tightened. She couldn't say anything aloud, and neither did he, the both of them cognizant Richard was watching through Seanna's eyes.

If you want Allan to do it, I accept that. I know you don't want to hurt me like this. But please, please stay here. Stay in my mind. I need you.

~

He was going to fucking kill Fort for telling her the consequences of him saying *hell no* to this.

It didn't matter, though. When he walked into this room, he'd been resolved, knowing what needed to be done. It had terrified her, the idea of Allan caning her. Then she'd spoken in his mind. Yes, it scared her, in all the wrong ways. Yet knowing she'd be facing the same kind of pain, the same punishment, if Wolf was doing it, she wasn't afraid. Just fiercely determined to prove to him how much, how deeply she was willing to serve him. That she trusted him, even if the pain frightened her.

Fucking hell, all those months he'd avoided any kind of intimate interaction with her, it was because his mind had told him he'd find her too appealing. Now he knew it was his very soul that had avoided her, understanding the truth. He simply couldn't resist her. He had to have her, possess her, even if it damned him. Even if it damned her. That was the fucking tragedy of it.

The difference in her reaction to him administering the punishment, and Allan doing it, triggered Wolf's Dominant sadist side in a very tempting way.

I don't need a third mark to feel your soul, to give you mine. She'd said that to him.

Damn right. She was his.

He'd lifted his hand, palmed her skull. She pressed her cheek hard into his hand. She was shuddering. She was in serious pain. What was happening?

He saw the open cooler, the foam forms inside that were meant to hold two dildos, and put it together. He also saw the green lotion sitting on the side bar. He'd observed its use at the first overlord dinner he'd attended. A vampire who operated a lotion and scents kind of place had brought it as a gift to Lord Richard—and to promote it to the gathered vampires, of course.

She was doing everything she could not to writhe, not to cry out.

"Lord Richard approved a hundred cane strikes," Allan said, filling in the gap. "While impaled on ice and her skin coated with a nerve stimulant. She is not allowed to cry out, or the count starts over."

There was no fucking way a second mark was going to get through all that without crying out, and every one of them, including Ella, knew it.

Wolf kept his hand on Ella, his eyes on her. He heard the words, but acknowledged no one in the room but her. He set aside everything, even the turbulent emotions storming inside him. She needed her Master, and he needed to be rational, steady, cool. Think all this through.

Allan would understand, give him the time to do it, uninterrupted. Ella did, too. Her head dipped, and he shifted forward so her forehead could rest on his chest. She emitted a little sigh at the contact. He kept his hand curved around her head, fingers in her disheveled hair. He didn't stroke. He couldn't appear too reassuring or tender, too attached, even as every vampire, even the one watching, knew in their gut what a fucking lie that was.

If he refused to let any of them do it, Richard would default to the idea that it was best to neutralize Ella. While she'd kept her cool so far, there was no doubt in his mind what Anwyn's response to that would be. And Daegan would not tolerate anyone raising a hand to Anwyn. Wolf had the distinct impression that Daegan obeyed his own laws, not the Council's.

But if Daegan came to Anwyn's defense for refusing Ella's execution, that would force Lyssa's hand. She'd have to act against her servant's brother and his vampires. Fuck, a mini-civil war could be started right here, right now. Lady Lyssa might figure out some phenomenally clever way around it, because it was rumored she preferred not to take human life when other options were available. But it left a lot to chance.

Worse, Anwyn's response would be reactive, because she couldn't prevent Ella's execution. Within certain parameters—and this fell within them—Richard had the authority to kill a human without consulting the Council. He was in Atlanta now, and there were vampires under his jurisdiction who would not hesitate to join him at Atlantis to handle a matter like this. So Wolf could potentially be overwhelmed, bound, placed below ground as punishment. When he was finally allowed out of the horror of his living grave, Ella would already be gone.

It took so little time to take a human life. While it was the last thing he wanted at this moment, his flashbacks were rarely convenient. In an indrawn breath, he was back in Vietnam. His team, slipping through the jungle, had had the bad luck to run into a Charlie out foraging. A young girl. She'd been carrying a grenade and had tried to pull the pin. They'd been faster. They'd disarmed her, then put her on the ground on her stomach, gagged and bound, while they evaluated their options.

They had to complete the mission. They couldn't leave her tied up in the jungle, because she could be found and the mission compromised. They couldn't take her with them.

They'd all known what needed to be done. He was team leader. The longer they dicked about it, the more frightened she became, though she was doing her best to hide it. But by that time, Wolf knew every mask fear and hate could wear.

He remembered Smitty, his boot pressed to her bound hands, resting against the small of her back. A reminder that she was under someone's direct view, and shouldn't move. Wolf met Smitty's gaze, then drew his knife. Smitty inclined his head, his gaze flickering, and backed up, giving Wolf room.

Wolf dropped to one knee, put his hand on the back of her shoulder to hold her steady, and stabbed. Quick, fast, just as he'd been trained, severing the spine at the base of the brain. Her body went limp.

He'd wiped the blade, risen. "Weight her body and drop it in the water."

He picked up her basket, saw the greens she'd been collecting. Tucked into the weave on the inside was a dog-eared fashion magazine. He couldn't imagine where she'd gotten it, but she'd probably planned to take a break and sneak a look at it while doing her chores. It had been in there with the grenade. He also found a pistol she hadn't had time to draw.

He pocketed the gun and handed off the basket to another of his guys to hide or destroy. He'd held onto the magazine, pushing it into his pack, because things like that could be useful. When at last they'd returned to base, mission accomplished, he'd offered it to a teenage hooker at one of the bars they frequented. He'd watched her slim fingers close on it, saw her smile. Two different girls, both wanting to look at pretty pictures about makeup tips and the best dresses to wear for the winter season. Christ.

All that went through his head in a blink, but he felt the light sheen of sweat that popped up when he damn well didn't want it to do so. He reminded himself where he was, using the proximity of Ella's trembling body to ground him, but the memory intertwined with the present in a way he couldn't ignore.

If he refused to carry out the punishment, would they make it quick like he had? A blink, and the light that was Ella, who loved carnivals, gardens, laughter and music, who had the sultry singing voice of a siren, whose appetite for submissive sexual play seemed limitless, whose parents had died in a fire... Her story would be over, past, present and future.

A soldier did what needed to be done. One person extinguished was like extinguishing one flower in a field of them. But there would never be another flower like that one. That was the part a soldier couldn't think about. Until war was over and it hit him like a ton of bricks at unexpected times.

Weighing all the variables, Ella's logic was despicably hard to argue. The little pest was still working on him in her head, perhaps sensing he hadn't yet made the decision.

It's one caning. An hour of our lives. Then we can move on. Please, Wolf.

She was wishing she was free, so she could drop to her knees at his feet, press her cheek hard against his thigh. *I know how very much you don't want to do this. That you don't want to hurt me. But there's some part of you...it enjoys the fact it can take everything from me I can bear to give and even beyond that. Just like some part of me craves you to take that much...and more.*

Which was pretty much the fucking definition of the vampire-servant relationship, when it was done right.

Showing just how deep in his head he'd been, Fort was now somehow in the room, and Saturnia was at the door, her expression still. Fort stopped parallel with Wolf's shoulder, facing away from Seanna and the others. "So what's it to be?" he said, low. "Do you do this, or do we start a shitstorm?"

He turned his head to meet Wolf's gaze, and the look in his eyes reminded Wolf of one of the great truths in life. The loyalty of brothers-in-arms trumped pretty much everything, including common sense. "I'm thinking there's another question you're not asking," Wolf said.

Fort's lips twisted. "Okay. Question two. One I haven't had to ask you in a good long time. Are you man or vampire, Leroy?"

Ella lifted her face. Her fingers were tight around the rings holding her manacles, her brown eyes on him. Pleading. Needing him to take charge. To make this work.

Wolf held her gaze a long moment, then he turned to Allan and held his hand out for the cane.

"I'm her Master."

CHAPTER TWENTY-SEVEN

Ella let out a relieved breath. She didn't know a tenth of what she suspected she needed to know about vampires and servants, but she'd been pretty sure that things were going to be really bad if this didn't happen.

Now, that worry had been removed. There was just the nervousness that came with facing something she wasn't sure she could handle. But no safe word could stop this, so there was no other choice but to handle it. In a not-funny-at-all, laughable way, it made it easier.

Wolf's fingers dug into her hair, twisted, and pulled her head back. She saw that demonic face again. This time the shudder that went through her was the kind that a lesser minion felt at the feet of Satan. Knowing she faced her absolute Master, and his approval and disapproval were everything that governed her life.

She didn't want it any other way. Though she quaked at the words he said.

"You think I don't want to hurt you? Think again, little girl. You've gone so far over the line, it's going to take every stripe of this cane to bring you back to the right side of it. And when it's all over, I'm going to be inside you. You'll make me come while you bleed, and remember who you serve."

His eyes were sharp, slicing to her core. His face was rigid tight, all the muscles defined, making him look even more formidable. The hand coiled in her hair reminded her he could break her neck with the strength in it.

It wasn't an act. That was what made it so terrifying and impressive. Gideon had promised her she had no idea how deep it could go. Wolf was showing her, up close and personal. It served the right purpose. Even Seanna had edged a little further away along the wall.

Wolf shifted back. He removed her ripped T-shirt and picked up the skirt, tossed it out of his way.

He moved her hands from the fixed rings in the wall to one with a chain running through it, then had Seanna go to the wall and draw up the slack. After the cuffs were attached to the chain and her arms were stretched above her head, Wolf slid an arm around her waist. "Keep your muscles tight around those ice dicks," he ordered. "They better be toothpicks before they fall out."

He tightened his arm, lifting her off the floor as the chain continued to retract. "Toe off your shoes."

She complied and he kicked the small set of sneakers out of their way. When she was about a foot off the floor, Wolf nodded toward something else, which Allan brought him. A wooden stool was placed beneath her toes. Just her toes. Her body was stretched upward like a taut cord.

Wolf had modified the setup. Without changing anything proscribed by Lord Richard, he'd made it a bigger challenge than it already was.

He backed up a step, put his hand on the juncture of her shoulder and neck. "As Lord Richard has ordered, you will not cry out, or we start over. You will keep your toes on this stool. You won't struggle or twitch in a way that takes you off it. Do you understand?"

"Yes, Master." Her voice was garbled, tearful.

"Does the ice hurt?"

"Yes, sir. It really, really does."

"And yet, water is dripping down your legs. The heat of your cunt and eager little ass is melting it."

She bit back a whimper that would have been a wail if she could let it out. He feathered his fingers over her clit and she nearly choked on the sound she wanted to make. When she blinked up at him, she was certain her eyes reflected the unbearable surplus of what was within. Agony and need.

"Lord Richard is punishing you for striking a vampire with malice. I am punishing you for taking matters into your own hands. As such, your punishment at my hands will be far worse than what he has designated."

I don't care. It feels better, having you do it. I want you to punish me, however you desire.

"Why are you being punished?" he barked.

"For overriding your will. For striking Allan, another vampire and Master."

"You will tell him you are sorry with the first twenty-five strikes. Then Anwyn, since Allan was a guest in her home. Then Lord Richard, as the Region Master of this territory. The final twenty-five strikes you will apologize to me, for not controlling yourself and not relying on your Master's guidance. Tell me you understand."

"I understand, sir," Ella stammered. He closed the distance between them again and ran the cane along her flank, slow, caressing.

"Tell me you understand again." He struck her thigh with it, a tap, but even a faint sting sent a tingle of burning electricity over her leg. The lotion. She'd forgotten.

"Yes, Master, I understand." Her voice was high and tight. "I welcome your punishment."

He tightened his hand on her throat in reproof. "Not if I do it right."

~

Wolf stepped back, and not just physically. He would have to stay mindful that she wasn't third marked, because all of her reactions matched a third mark's. Able to take anything from her Master and still be aroused. Even as she suffered, all for him.

Staying in that mind frame, he let himself appreciate, savor, and let her feel that in him. She was gorgeous and all his. Her pert round backside, stretched back muscles, straining legs and calves, her whole body reaching. As he moved around her, he caressed a quivering breast, flicked a nipple. The dildos continued to melt, making him think of her honey running down her thighs after she came. He played with her clit some more, running the cane up and down her legs as he did.

There was no rush to this now. Vampires were the ultimate voyeurs, and he could take the time he would have if he'd been here from the beginning, getting her in the right mindset.

By telling her to call out her apology, he'd given her a way to respond to the pain without incurring more strikes. A screamed apology was still an apology, not an involuntary cry.

Richard could easily call him on it, but he intended to put the right amount of detail and effort into this. He'd bring to life that amazing part of Ella that mesmerized anyone with a Dominant bone in their body. Let alone vampires, whose entire skeletal system vibrated with that orientation.

"We're missing one more thing." He went to the cabinet that held additional supplies and returned with a ball gag, a large one. He fitted it into her mouth. The size of the gag filled her mouth, stretching her jaw. He Velcro'd the straps securely around her head. "Don't want you biting through your tongue."

It would also help her not scream out the apologies so loudly. As he looked at her profile, her wide eyes, stretched mouth, her body strained and bound, Wolf knew he could come just by looking at her, helpless like this, all for him. It didn't matter how much pain she was in, how agonizing the punishment was—when this was over, he could shove his cock into her and find wet, dripping heat. She'd know she'd pleased him, and that was what she needed, more than anything.

That level of giving and receiving tore a person open, down to the quick. She *was* giving him her soul.

He trailed the tip of the cane down her back, saw her body ripple, the lotion increasing the sensation.

After every apology, Ella, I will tell you how much you have pleased me. You will earn my approval with every strike, sweet girl. Can you do that?

She nodded, vehemently, a muffled whimper coming around the gag. He pressed a kiss to the back of her head, his arm coming around to hold her against him for one moment, then he stepped back.

And landed the first blow.

Wolf administered the blows exactly as he would as a Master of Club Atlantis. A pause after each one, holding the cane against her flesh, letting the sensation build and roll. Amateurs hit fast and sharp, never realizing how much was felt if there was a pause for the brain to process the strike. To let the pain radiate out.

Ella said she was sorry as he'd instructed, on every strike. Identified to whom she was apologizing. She made it through twenty-five for Allan, and then the same for Anwyn. Earned her Master's approval. He not only told her he was pleased, in their shared minds, but added in some comments, at unexpected moments.

That's my girl. Allan's face needed the improvement. He was too pretty.

It almost startled a hysterical chuckle out of her. She thought her cunt and ass might have caught fire by now. He kept reminding her to hold the phalluses tight, tighter, which made her thigh and backside muscles more rigid, increasing the pain. The cane fell again and again. The welts began to rise, and there was no way Wolf couldn't hit them again, with the number of blows that had been mandated.

Halfway through Lord Richard's twenty-five, the cane struck one particularly sensitive part. She screamed against the gag before she could get the apology out. The wave of pain was too much to suppress the sound.

Oh Goddess. She just couldn't. She couldn't bear starting over.

Gideon's words rolled through her head. *Their darkness... Property... You belong to your Master and Mistress entirely...*

She was going to know exactly what that meant before this was over.

There was a significant pause. Then Wolf began at one again. He made her say she was sorry again. The next involuntary shriek happened somewhere during Allan's count. She hadn't made it as far.

She was failing him. Failing her Master.

You aren't failing me, Ella. Not crying out was Lord Richard's requirement, not mine. He intended you to fail. I love the beauty of your sweet cries. I'm looking forward to unchaining you, taking care of you, tending your wounds. I'll make you lie on your stomach, and I'll look at the marks you accepted from your Master.

I know you are strong. Strong enough to obey me, when I tell you I don't want to hear another sound from your beautiful lips. But I do want to hear you sing for me in your head, talk to me, say whatever you wish.

She tried to obey, until she was sure she was talking gibberish in her head. Inside that contained space, she was crying. She was saying she was sorry. She was singing to him, calling to him, trying to remember poems she hadn't remembered since childhood. She eventually went with pictures, images of things she liked. A garden statue of a pig with a laughing mouth and floppy ears. Wolf's body, stretched out on her tiny bed, his powerful thigh muscles flexing as she followed them with her fingertips...

The cane fell again and again, and the pain was never ending. Things felt sticky and wet, and she knew she was bleeding. The welts had broken open and now fire swept up her legs, sickly, excruciating pain.

In a haze, disoriented, she wouldn't know until later that Richard stopped Wolf at a hundred and seventy-two strikes. But she vaguely heard Wolf's words, directed toward Seanna, and the vampire who had witnessed this through her eyes.

"Lord Richard, Ella desires only to serve. Her actions came from her lack of understanding of our world. She will be an exemplary servant for Anwyn, because she is one of Atlantis's most exceptional submissives. She will be a credit to our world. Are you satisfied?"

Seanna's response was almost instant. "More than satisfied. You may tend to her now as she well deserves."

Seanna left the room. A blink later, Wolf was with her, touching her, his voice filling her mind. "That's it. It's done. Sssh."

She was somewhere between subspace and unconsciousness, she was sure. It wasn't a bad place to be, but that burning. Goddess, she hated the burning. The ice had melted away sometime during the punishment, but as Seanna had foretold, her sensitive tissues remained on fire.

Oh no... She hadn't realized until now, and was mortified. With great levels of pain and stress, the body reacted. She'd thrown up at some point. She'd barely been aware when it had happened, but now she remembered Wolf had removed her gag right before, his attention to her state of mind and body saving her from choking on her own vomit.

Which was good, because ever since that bad night on the stretcher wheel, vomiting kind of scared her. But she was still embarrassed by the condition she was in.

If you'll free me, Master, I'll care for myself.

"No, you won't. Taking care of you is my job tonight."

The chain was lowered, stool removed, so she could stand fully on the soles of her feet. She sagged against the wall, the manacles bearing her weight because she was unable to hold herself up. Her arches and calf muscles wept in relief, even as they cramped, but Wolf's strong hands were there, massaging. He knelt by her, guiding her so her hip and thigh rested against his broad shoulder. It relieved the pressure on her shoulders and wrists.

He eased her back against the wall when he was done with the massage, but he didn't go far. He turned on the room hose, rewarding her with blissfully warm water. He rinsed Ella thoroughly, then used that fragrant wash Seanna had mentioned. As promised, it eased the exacerbated pain wherever it was applied, made it more bearable. He held her as much as possible, banding one arm around her waist while he gently cleaned her with his free hand. Ella nearly sobbed with bliss when he injected the wash into her backside.

She phased out for some of it, but throughout, she was aware of Wolf whispering to her, out loud, in her head, with savage satisfaction. He was so pleased with her. It was in every gesture, the light in his eyes, when she found the strength to look at his face. She'd exceeded his expectations. She could die happy.

You don't have my permission to die. I have other things I want from you.

Though he'd cleaned her painfully throbbing pussy with thorough fingers, he hadn't used that wash there. Instead, now, he goaded that discomfort, teasing her clit and labia with his fingers, making her bite back pitiful whimpers.

"I'm not done with you yet, little girl. You owe your Master one more thing, don't you?"

She fought through the confusion in her mind, trying to understand. And then she did. "You're going to take me now, aren't you, sweet servant?"

She whimpered again, but he'd guided her legs up off the floor and around his waist. He made her look at him, a hand to her face, and she saw the glittering eyes, the set expression. Seanna hadn't stayed to make sure Wolf delivered on his last threat. But almost before Wolf said it, Ella knew why. The same reason Wolf was doing what he was doing now.

"He didn't have to see it. He knows a vampire's nature. He demanded the punishment to satisfy protocol. This is me, reclaiming what's mine. Mine to fuck and punish, however and whenever I wish, aren't you?"

She couldn't get her mouth to work, but she could tell him with her eyes, her mind, that yes, no matter the circumstances, she would never think of denying him. Never.

That feeling of wrongness she'd had, about doing something he didn't want her to do? He was going to take it away with this act, this demand. She considered that wrong feeling worse than the worst burning lotion in the world.

His eyes darkened. He had his hand cradling her skull in that way he did that made her feel so small and protected. As he pushed into her, she moaned.

That one last spot seemed worse now that it was the only one, as if everything was concentrated there, screaming for relief. It was so painful, and yet she needed him there, filling the emptiness. He seated himself to the hilt, his gaze remaining locked on hers. Then he gripped both her buttocks in his hands.

"You can scream all you want now." And he squeezed her welted flesh.

She obeyed, and then some. She screamed, moaned, shrieked, wailed, as he thrust into her. She knew he must have restrained himself somewhat, because she was so close to breaking she was like a cracked window on the verge of shattering from the pressure, but it didn't seem as if he held back. He fucked her strong and thoroughly, her breasts quivering against his chest, her ass held firmly in his hands until he climaxed, bathing her with his seed.

Which was the exact moment she knew the "substance" Seanna had hinted at. Whatever was in semen counteracted what had been in the lotion, bringing almost instant, blissful, slick coolness to her cunt.

Now she did weep, with the utter relief and wonder of it. A lotion designed to give pain, a pain that could be taken away by her Master's release. A diabolical thing, designed by someone who understood the dark beauty of what could lie between a Dom and sub.

"That's my baby," he said, with fierce approval in his gaze.

Just those few words, and that one place, filled by him and no longer throbbing and in agony, helped everything else feel better. She gazed at him, mindless, trusting him with all of herself.

He unhooked her cuffs, so her hands dropped around his neck.

She managed to curl her fingers, hold onto his shoulders. She'd satisfied Lord Richard's requirements, but that was not her concern. Her Master was in charge of that.

Correct. Keep that in mind, and next time you think you should take a decision out of my hands, perhaps the punishment won't be as severe.

I couldn't let you suffer.

I know, sweet girl. Sshhh. Just relax. I'm handling everything right now.

Wolf lifted her so she could wrap her limbs around him, arms and legs, rest her head on his shoulder. He folded his arms around her, holding her. Murmured, "It's all right. I'm going to make everything all right."

She squeezed her eyes shut. Listening to him in the dark, everything had a better chance of being believed. It would be so nice if what he said were true.

"For tonight, it is."

Gideon stood in the control room with Anwyn. He hadn't been able to watch most of it. Daegan had arrived right before it started, which at some point in the far future Gideon might consider good timing, because Gideon had tried to go through him to get out the door. He wouldn't let Anwyn watch it alone, but she'd watched it with calm stoicism while Gideon basically wanted to kill the whole roomful of people tormenting Ella.

Ultimately, he just couldn't look. He stood to the side, staring at the wall, focused only on Anwyn's state of mind while she didn't give him a window in her head to watch. Until she put her hand on his arm. *You will want to see this part, Gideon.*

In the monitor, he saw Wolf holding Ella, wrapped around him like a little kid, while he sat down in the room's single plastic chair and rocked her back and forth, slow, gentle movements. He kept his thighs spread so her tender backside wasn't coming in contact with anything. His jeans and upper body were wet where he'd gotten up close and personal to care for her.

He was kissing her, humming. Gideon picked it up in his head, the words of the .38 Special song playing in the slow-mo way Wolf was uttering it, making it into a lullaby.

...so caught up in you, little girl. You're the one that's got me down on my knees...

Daegan stood in the shadows by the door. Things had gotten pretty ugly between them for a few minutes, but Daegan had kept him in this room without breaking any limbs. Gideon might owe him a grudging apology for some of the things he'd called him. Maybe.

"Gideon. Look at her, resting in her Master's arms, and somehow it makes sense," Anwyn said softly. "Though I defy anyone to explain it."

"No." He shook his head. "I'm not seeing it."

"Aren't you?" She cocked her head. "Right before the punishment you endured before Council, I told you something. Do you remember what you thought back at me?"

He did, but he didn't care for where this was going. "That was different."

"Gideon," Anwyn said softly. She reached toward his face and he didn't deny her the contact, though he gripped her wrist, tightened on it. "I require an answer to my question. Do you remember what we said to one another?"

This isn't what it's about, Gideon, she'd said. *Not what it's supposed to be.*

Then make it what it's supposed to be, he'd responded. *I don't fear any pain at your hands, Anwyn. A weird part of me... Well, you already know, right?*

"Before you looked away," she nodded at the monitor, "You saw the transformation in her expression, her body language, when she knew Wolf would be wielding the cane, not Allan."

Anwyn gave Gideon a knowing look. "In the right circumstances, you will crave the most brutal punishments at my hands, to prove your worth to me, to prove your strength can serve me through anything. That you can be a servant I can always depend upon."

She turned her attention to Wolf and Ella again. "Now, if only you had an equal level of dedication toward keeping your chip crumbs off my couch..."

He couldn't let the humor in. Not yet, while Ella was a bloody mess, but as he saw her arms tighten over Wolf, and the gentle way he was holding her, pressing his mouth to her temple, disgust and anger gave way to other things.

She is all right, vampire hunter. Daegan's voice. *She is with her Master, and he will be all she needs.*

At least for right now, Gideon thought. He had the security of knowing the two vampires in this room were committed to him. Ella didn't have that. Wolf wasn't going to give her that.

"Maybe. Maybe not," Anwyn said quietly. "But Ella will have us. Always. No matter what."

Damn straight.

CHAPTER TWENTY-EIGHT

Wolf took her to one of the recovery rooms. Aftercare often happened on the main floor, in cozy little nooks which provided semi-privacy but allowed a Dom social time with other Doms while caring for their subs. But for the extreme scenes or a Dom who wanted to dedicate his full attention to the aftercare, there were the recovery rooms.

The one he chose was one of Ella's favorites. The scene projected onto one wall, covering it from ceiling to floor, made it look as if the viewer was standing on a beach. The ocean spread before them, complete with the rushing sound of waves coming in and out. A pair of beach loungers were in the room, positioned under a cabana, canopied with gauzy fabric. The fabric drifted in the air, thanks to a manufactured breeze that had that humid, salt smell to it like the ocean did.

A hot tub was also provided, nested in a rock façade. It gave the beach goers the impression they'd found a hot spring, hidden in a cave near the surf. Wolf turned the jets on low churn. He took off his clothes and got in with her, turning her so she was once again facing him, folded into his arms, her thighs spread over his lap, all of her limp, and yet quivering from the aftermath and pain. He dropped something into the water, something that made it slippery and soft, and eased the pain even more. A healing topical, applied by the bath jets. She blessed the designers of Atlantis, all the attention to detail and the needs of those who might play here.

He'd given her pain, and taken it away. That worked so well in her mind, her feelings about having a Master who controlled everything for her, and who could look to her for love and support in return. It wasn't fair. She could be so good for him.

"I know, baby. I'm sorry." He stroked her hair.

She nodded, and knew only some of the moisture she was feeling on her cheeks was mist from the bath.

She understood there was a struggle happening within him, against an enemy he'd made clear was only his to fight. Usually she'd try to figure out the face of that enemy, to see if she could help him fight it, but she'd had a sinking feeling from the beginning it wasn't that kind of fight. Learning his truth had confirmed it. But she had right now.

"You said, after we got Atlantis up and running again, we'd have to go back to how we were before. Do you think, before we make it official, we could...do something?" Her voice was rough, shaky.

"Something like what?"

She lifted a shoulder, and he understood. "Show me in your mind," he suggested in a low rumble. "You're not telling me what to do that way."

"Well, before you could read my mind, that might have been true."

He smiled. "Show me anyway. That's an order."

She wanted to go somewhere with him for a couple days. Somewhere that they could be whatever they wanted to be to one another, a timeout place from everything that had to be faced and accepted. She didn't really care where. A beach, an interstate hotel. The main thing she wanted was him as her Master, no holds barred.

"Won't that make it harder, afterward?"

"Yes. I don't care about that either. Afterward, you can mark Haru, or do whatever you need to do. You'll go back to being Wolf, this fabulous Dom who's not my Dom...but in my head, I'll feel you, know you're my Master, and that will be enough for me."

"Why? Why is that enough for you?"

Because it has to be. The simplest answer, but that was the other irritating thing about the best Doms. They didn't ever let you get away with the simplest answers.

"No," he said, lifting her so she was facing him, meeting his eyes.

"How can that be enough without it breaking you, Ella? Not that I think anything can break you."

"I've been broken plenty of times," she said. "I mend."

His hands tightened on her, and he repeated himself, that Master's edge coming into his voice. "Tell me. How can it be enough for you?"

"Because life is abundant," she said, tears in her throat. "There is so much we're given, Wolf. I was given you for these few days. If you tell me you love me, and that you would give me all of yourself if you could, I believe it. That's the gift. Not having it after a certain day will hurt like hell, but I'll know it was mine, those feelings.

"You know how I told you most people don't get me, think I trust too much, and why that is? Well, this is like that, too. Everything that comes my way...I don't have low expectations. I have a highly developed sense of gratitude. Because if I focus on what I don't have, parents, siblings, a love of my life that I can grow old with...I would miss so much, wouldn't I?"

He let her slide back down, put her head on his chest. The water lapped against her back, soothing. She felt bruised, so bruised. A heavy caning did that, bruised the muscles beneath the skin. Bruised the soul. He ran his hand along her arm, down to her hip. He skirted around all the areas he'd hit, never coming in contact with one of them, telling her he was aware of her wellbeing, her condition, every inch of her. A good Dom did that, too.

She was lying between his splayed thighs, his cock pressed to her belly. Remembering him inside her, at the height of the pain, the way his seed had taken away the pain in that channel, made her move against him now. A soft questing stroke of flesh against flesh, her fingers curling into his shoulders. She wanted him inside her again. Truth, she could lie beneath him, his sex hard and full inside her, and she might not ever need to be anywhere else in the world.

"You like me on top of you, do you? Pressing you down, holding you there?"

"Yes, sir." She imagined his hands on her wrists, holding them pinned as he thrust. He didn't need to do so. He could order her to keep her hands where he put them, and that would bring a similar charge to her lower belly, a deepening need as he triggered the submissive side of her.

"But you like that feeling. Sometimes, you'd like to fight a little, wouldn't you? Struggle."

He spoke to her drifting thoughts, making the hazy cloud of feelings into coherent words.

"Not to get away," he added thoughtfully. "Just to remind yourself how much stronger I am, how I can hold you down. That you have to submit. That you're safe under my control."

A little sigh, another nod. *Yes, Master.* When he was inside her, on top, she felt like he was taking over everything.

"All right. I'll think about it. The couple of days together when we reach that point."

She swallowed, closed her eyes. He saw the feeling in her mind, swelling up strong from her heart.

Soon. Please, soon. I can't bear to have you much longer, and then not have you. If that makes sense. If you don't want to do it, the couple of days, then okay. Just tell me, and that will be okay, too. It was just a wish. I can handle not having it come true.

She could imagine how it would have been, and that would be enough. It wasn't his fault. It was no one's fault. Life was hard, and complicated. That was all.

Somewhere, someday, it wouldn't be.

~

A highly developed sense of gratitude.

Wolf thought of that after he tucked her into the bed they had in the recovery room, and left her under Anwyn's watchful eye. He bypassed his truck and started walking. Once he started walking, he just kept going, mile after mile, through parts of Atlanta where other, lesser predators watched him and drew back in the shadows, recognizing a man whose thoughts they would regret disturbing.

Until he met one who didn't give a shit.

He'd made a big circle, and saw Gideon leaning against the bumper of his truck when he returned to the Club Atlantis parking lot. He wondered how long the male had been standing there waiting on him, or maybe he'd asked security to give him a heads up when he came back.

The midnight blue eyes were inscrutable, the jaw set, but Wolf had been around Gideon long enough to know when the male was ready to throw down. He could get his own hackles up about it, play the vampire card, but all he could feel was sadness, and a resigned gladness that Ella had strong friends in her corner. Ones who could stand by her.

He was going to need to leave. She knew it; he knew it. It was what wasn't being said, and what that request for two days with him was about. He would likely come back a couple years down the road, when they'd both had space and time. Or he wouldn't. A vampire's life was hard to predict. The one thing he wouldn't do was force her to be the one to withdraw and stay away from Club Atlantis. She needed the sanctuary, its protection. He would make sure she had ready access to it, always.

Which would also make it possible for him to check in with Anwyn and see how Ella was doing.

He stopped a few feet from the truck, braced his feet. Gideon didn't straighten. He appeared to be looking up at the sky, his arms crossed over his broad chest.

"Good news and bad news," he said. "Good news is Daegan found the cell that engineered the alley bombing."

"Okay." Wolf's brow creased. It seemed pretty momentous news to be sharing out in the parking lot. "Get any info before he killed them?"

"No. That's the bad news. All three of them killed themselves before he could. Last one laughed at him while he chewed on the cyanide pill." Gideon's gaze flicked to Wolf as Wolf frowned.

"Shit."

"Yeah. Left us all with an uneasy feeling. Didn't find a damn thing where they were holed up. Completely scrubbed of anything useful. Fort will give you all the details, which aren't much more than what I gave you."

"Which he could have done, without you waiting for me here in the parking lot."

"True enough." Gideon looked back toward the sky. "You know, most vampires gravitate toward the big cities. I've had to spend a lot of time in them. Makes it hard to see the stars."

"Yeah. Harder to find places to go to ground outside the city, though. Did you check on her?"

"Yeah."

"You need to take a swing at me, get it out of your system?" Because Wolf figured that was the real reason Gideon was here. "I'll give you a free shot. Just you and me out here. No Lord Richard."

"Tempting." Gideon kept on with his star-gazing. "You know, when Anwyn made me her servant, she and Daegan had to take me for an audience with the Council."

"Jesus." Wolf considered that. "And you walked out alive."

"They were in a mellow mood. Well, after they made Anwyn carve up my back with a bull whip. She nearly refused, just as you did."

Gideon brought his gaze down, met Wolf's. "I wanted to kill you tonight. Wanted to rip your fucking heart out for hurting Ella. I'm bound to Daegan and Anwyn, but there's a part of me that still fucking hates how the vampire world works. Still pretty much despise most of them. Doesn't make a lot of sense, does it?"

"Tonight wasn't one of my favorite nights either, Gideon." Wolf found his cigarettes, tapped one out, lit it, cupping his hands over the flame. "But I suspect you're heading toward a particular point. Or you're hiding a spear gun and waiting for the right moment."

"Naw." Gideon shrugged. "Spear guns ruin the line of my jacket. For this scenario, a wide-open parking lot, an explosive with a fifteen-foot range is sufficient. You pack it in something you can throw at the vampire like a baseball, only it hooks onto them, sticks. They can pull it away in an instant, but there's that moment where they look down to see what it is. If the detonation is less than three seconds, you've got them. Trick is being out of range yourself and throwing with accuracy. I played football in high school. Long time ago, but who knew it would be a useful skill for anything other than attracting girls?"

Wolf blinked. "How'd you figure out the sticking thing?"

The corner of Gideon's mouth curled. "That game where you throw the Velcro balls at a target and try to get them to stick to the bulls-eye? I compared that to the engineering of butterfly grenades and figured out how to bring the two ideas together."

"Would have been better for Perry if he'd figured that out."

Gideon shrugged. "Don't think it would have mattered. He was looking for a way out. He found it. And those other guys killing themselves? It suggests they all knew there was only one end for them and this particular plan. It's bugging the shit out of me. You don't sacrifice four hunters for nothing."

"Yeah. Good thing we've beefed up security. Maybe they'll move on to an easier target. Not that that will make any of us feel any better."

Wolf opened his door, pulled a cooler out from behind his front seat. Tilting his head toward the bed of the truck, he moved there himself. He lowered the tailgate and took a seat on it. Offered Gideon a soda from the cooler.

Gideon raised a brow. "Coke?"

"It's a classic, right?"

"Hmm." Gideon sat down on the tailgate next to him, listening to the creak. "Can it handle both our weights?"

"And then some. This truck was built when vehicles were supposed to last beyond a five-year lease."

They drank in silence. Wolf didn't see any point in fishing for where Gideon was going. Not when it was obvious the male would get there in his own time.

"I think what helped Anwyn handle the Council's sentence was I was okay with it," Gideon said, returning to that topic. "Because no matter what I thought of those Council assholes, part of it felt like penance, for lives I took that maybe didn't deserve it. For not being fast enough to save others I cared about, wanted to protect. But I can't think of a fucking thing Ella needs to seek redemption for. There's only one thing she wants, wants so badly, and I've been thinking a lot about why you won't give that to her."

"I don't see how that's your business," Wolf said.

Gideon ignored him. "Most of us come to the servant thing by accident or circumstances. But some gut deep part of us knows it's where we're meant to be. That's written all over you and Ella. You get that. I know you do."

"Gideon."

"Really wasn't a question, man. No need to argue it." Gideon squinted at the sky again. "You know, I don't know what your deal is, exactly. If Anwyn knows, she's not saying. She respects you that much. But I do know there are certain fuckups that don't come with a punishment to fit the crime. There's nothing big enough, not even death. So, you have to come to terms with them a different way. I'm guessing the whole BDSM therapy thing, that's what that is for you."

Allan's words flashed through his mind. His immersion in therapy for others against his personal rejection of it for himself. They got better, in spite of what he truly believed, whereas he...stayed the same.

Gideon glanced at him. "I eventually realized the only balm to make it bearable is someone you trust to say, 'you're forgiven,' or, if not totally forgiven, they accept. But that's not what makes things change. Amid all the darkness, they *see* something worth loving, and *you believe them*. Finding someone you can believe when they say *I love you*? That's the person you can't do without. They see who you are, all your dark and light. They get past all your insecurities and bullshit, and you believe in their love, because it's a gift from something way bigger than your puny ass.

"If you turn your back on it, even if you can't figure out the why or what the hell happened to bring you to that spot, the powers that be are going to do a number on your ass, totally deserved." Gideon pushed himself up from Wolf's truck. "Anyway, Anwyn's coming. She had me keeping lookout for you."

At Wolf's expression, Gideon gave him an arch look. "What, you think, me, a lowly servant, was going to be the one to read you the riot act on this? I'm just the opening act. The lookout."

Wolf snorted, but looked toward the entrance. Anwyn was headed their way. She was no longer wearing club garb, but instead was in a pair of belted jeans, heeled boots and a T-shirt that clung to her curves. Even casually dressed, she looked like a woman who could bring anyone to their knees.

"I didn't—" Wolf turned back toward Gideon.

Son of a bitch. The fist had the propulsion of a battering ram and took him solidly across the jaw. The force bounced him off the tailgate and had him stumbling down to one knee on the asphalt. For a second, Wolf was pretty sure Gideon had busted the hinge of his jaw. He sprang back to his feet and spun, ready to meet the next attack. Gideon was sitting on the tailgate again, sipping his soda. Despite his apparent calm, the offending fist was curled on his knee, his knuckles turning red, and the midnight blue eyes were filled with fire.

"So," he said. "You going to welch on that whole 'free shot' thing and take my head off?"

Despite the mild comment, Gideon had his feet braced flat on the ground, body coiled and ready to spring out of the way. Though Wolf doubted he would get very far. The man was as reckless as he was courageous. A vampire might strike in retaliation first and consider whether that was the best course of action later.

Fortunately for Gideon's sake, Wolf called to mind the young woman asleep in the recesses of the darkened club, and how she had looked after her punishment. He also remembered watching her and Gideon on the main floor little more than a day ago. Gideon had been teasing her, making her laugh, as he leaned against the ladder she was on. He'd been steadying it while she hung decorations for Burlesque Night.

He cared about Ella. So Wolf had the sucker punch coming. But for form's sake, he shot Gideon a warning look. "I said I'd give you one shot. But just the one."

He ignored Gideon's chuckle. Instead he took a swallow of his Coke and twitched his jaw, trying to determine if it was working properly.

Gideon rose and left him, moving toward his Mistress. As she passed him, Anwyn twined her fingers briefly with his, stopped to press her face into his neck, something he responded to by turning his mouth to hers and holding still as she took her fill. Then she released him with a smile and strode toward Wolf. He already had a Coke Zero out next to him, knowing that was her preference. He'd had time to fish a towel out of the back seat of the truck and spread it out, so she didn't get her superior ass dirty.

She took a seat next to him. Her dark hair gleamed in the parking lot lights, and her blue-green eyes considered him as she lifted the drink to her lips.

"It was a lucky shot," he said in his defense, and earned a faint smile.

"They'd never admit it, but at the overlord gatherings, I think some of the younger vampires are afraid of him. His legend expands with time, but it's actually not far off the mark. He's one never to underestimate."

Wolf wanted to ask Anwyn how Ella was doing, even knowing he didn't need to do so. His mind had never been farther from her than her bedside. She was still sleeping. He should take her home before he had to go to ground. She loved Atlantis, but home was where she wanted to be tonight. Where she could remind herself that her life had to have balance.

It was an additional perspective, seeing someone through the eyes of a friend, who knew her differently. So he asked.

"She doing okay?"

"Ella is okay until she's not okay. I honestly don't know her threshold. She lets herself break, then puts herself back together again."

I mend. He recalled the simple words.

"Yeah." They sat in silence a few moments. He told himself not to ask anything else, but the girl had endured the mother of all canings for him. He could ask a few questions.

"Tell me something..."

Anwyn glanced at him as he let the words trail off. He shook his head at himself, and finished it. "Tell me the things that matter, that you want me to know about her, Anwyn. The things I should know. Don't be cryptic and female. Just say them straight out."

"Women are not cryptic. Men are just thick-headed." Anwyn nudged him with her elbow, softening the tartness of the comment. "But all right."

She set down the soda, and met his gaze. "Ella has never realized she's beautiful, Wolf. She thinks she's pretty in a nice sort of way, and knows she has a body that attracts men and women alike. But she has no clue how genuinely beautiful she is. She has no idea how others react to her."

"What?" He thought of her on Burlesque Night, when everyone in the room was mesmerized by her voice, the way the lights shimmered over her thick, dark hair, the satin over her curves. The intensity of her eyes.

Or maybe it had just been him who was mesmerized.

"Why?"

"Ella didn't have a normal childhood. High school, proms, first dances, first dates. A mother or father, to see herself through their eyes. A hooker is going to routinely hear that she's attractive, but that's hardly the same thing, is it? Nowhere near the same as hearing it from a man who thinks you are uniquely his, who tells you how beautiful you truly are to him. People can tell you you're sexy, pretty, beautiful, whatever, all they wish, but until someone who loves you says it, and you feel the love behind it, you don't realize it. Not in that way that's so beyond vanity, so much deeper than that, such that you'd never have to look at a mirror again. The truth of your appearance is in that person's eyes, no matter your age, weight, or anything else the world defines as beauty."

He cocked his head. "So you knew she was a prostitute."

"Of course I knew." Anwyn gave him a *yes, dumbass* look that he decided to let pass in favor of further information. "I vet everyone who works at my place thoroughly. People who walk through my doors entrust their privacy and sometimes their very lives and emotional wellbeing to me and my staff. I want to be sure Atlantis deserves that trust."

"But you've never told her you knew."

"She will tell me when she's ready. When she trusts our friendship enough. I want that knowledge as a gift."

"She worries about it," he confided. "Feels bad about lying to you."

"I know. But I never saw it as a lie. It was an omission, an understandable one. It made sense, that she covered it, to give her a chance to prove herself to me. How many legitimate employers will hire someone who has turned tricks? Especially in the legal adult entertainment industry, which is always under a microscope. We know the trouble that can follow them, or the bad habits that they might bring to a legal business. One of these days, I hope it will be a legal profession, one that can have the same protections as any other job, and won't have to walk so closely to the criminal element. But until then, every employer has to be understandably cautious."

"What made you decide to keep her on anyway?"

"Have you met her?" Anwyn asked wryly, and Wolf smiled. "She'd come as a Domme's guest a couple times, but one day she came on her own. Brought me a loaf of bread from that little organic place where she now delivers groceries. Told me she could work as a paid submissive, waitress, janitor, whatever I needed. 'It's not my job' wasn't in her vocabulary, and I didn't need to pay her for the first couple weeks, if I wanted to see how she worked out. She was healthy, lovely, earnest. Sincere. Her gaze reminded me of the Grand Canyon."

She shot him an ironic glance, a reminder of his earlier comment, about taking a left turn at the Grand Canyon, the first time she'd suggested Ella become his servant. "Carved out by time, marked by every natural catastrophe that could hit the planet, but still there. Enduring, something immutable under the softness."

"Yeah." It was a good description. He lapsed back into silence, which stretched out into five minutes before Anwyn spoke again.

"You've been a vampire long enough to lose some of the human qualities and sentiment, but you're not that far gone. Tell me you know the not loving your servant thing is a crock of shit that we're all supposed to pretend is true."

He glanced at her. "I served in the military, Anwyn. There are rules that are put in place for good reason. If we break them, we better have a damn better reason for doing so."

"Being in love with someone seems about the best reason I can imagine."

He frowned. "Maybe so, but let's think about that. How could anyone bring someone they love into our world? Lord Richard could have decided to kill her. Quick neck snap and done. Did you think about that?"

Her eyes darkened and she looked away. "Gideon came to me under traumatic circumstances, Wolf. The most successful vampire hunter who'd ever pitted himself against vampire kind. During my transition, when so many things were up in the air? His life or death never really crossed his mind, because he'd accepted that one day his luck would run out. When he bound himself to me, he was pretty sure that clock was winding down. He'd set up camp in the middle of the species he'd dedicated his life to killing. So I really don't need you to tell me the risks of bringing someone you care about into our world."

She shot him an exasperated look. "And are you under the impression that whoever came up with love designed it only to handle the easy scenarios? It's the most precious gift we've ever been given. It can withstand fire, flood, despair."

He shook his head. "It also involves self-sacrifice and denial, to protect those you love."

Or to pay for wasted chances. But he didn't say that part aloud.

"Where would she be a better fit, Wolf? Yes, she can belong here at Atlantis as long as she wishes, but that might not be her destiny.

Atlantis may have been part of the path leading her right to where she is. Kneeling at your feet, offering her whole self to you."

She stood, gestured with the soda. "I won't beat a dead horse. I've said my piece. Ella is ready to go home, but she asked me to take her. She didn't want to impose on you."

He thought about it, wrestled with it, but then nodded, despite the effort it took. "Okay."

Anwyn gazed at him, then turned without a word, walking toward her club. A few feet away, she stopped, looked back at him. "At a certain point, self-flagellation and noble self-sacrifice becomes nothing more than a screen for cowardice, Wolf. Or an ego stroke, to hold yourself apart and above others. You're an arrogant ass, like most uber-Doms, but you're a good man. Don't become that guy."

He bit back the defensive retort. Instead, he asked one last question. "Back when Ella stabbed that Dom with his own scalpel. What was the hard limit he didn't respect?"

Anwyn blinked. "Fire play."

~

He walked some more. And he thought about all of it. The war, the death and blood. His family.

Wolf agreed with Anwyn's assessment of Gideon and younger vampires. Gideon still had the look of someone who'd been neck deep in violence so long, that was where he felt most at home. Wolf knew about that.

He also knew how despair and darkness could take over. He remembered how lost he'd gotten. So lost he couldn't respond to his wife anymore. The war had taken his ability to have sex with her, but the darkness in his heart and soul had taken his ability to make love. He'd hurt her so badly they'd both gotten lost. She'd OD'ed, and he'd become a vampire, and they'd both abandoned their son. Who, thanks to good adopted parents and a will inside him greater than his birth parents', had found a life worth living.

His son had found his well of gratitude, just as Ella had.

When Wolf stood at the edge of his own well, he'd always seen a shallow coat of water, barely covering the dry dirt beneath. But as he thought of Ella, he realized her well overflowed because she continually filled it. It wasn't some easy, rainbow and flowers thing, either. Now he understood the meditation, the rare flashes of astonishingly violent temper. She lived her life with an apparent recklessness that wasn't reckless at all.

It was fucking brave.

I will love my life and who I am, she said, with every action she took. *I will forgive myself when I stumble, pick myself up and keep going. I will make sure that everyone in my life gets value from my presence in it, to thank them for their friendship and the experiences they provide me.*

He thought of Don, and the many faces of the men he'd...he'd helped. He'd helped them, because he'd understood the depth of that darkness, just how horrible it could be. It was a living coffin, the lid weighed down by overwhelming emotions and hopelessness. Day after day, no light, no hope capable of penetrating the void.

To get back out, they had to do one thing. Something that sounded so easy, almost self-serving. Yet his inability to do it was what had compelled him to take his own life.

He helped his therapy clients find that path, yet he remained behind, in the darkness. He'd rationalized that staying there helped him help them, but now he wondered if that was a crock of shit. How much further could he take a person like Don, if Wolf himself finally found his way? Filled that hole with abundance, so it became a well instead of a grave, lifting him up and out.

He needed to keep walking.

When Ella had woken, she'd still had the warmth of Wolf's body around her, but he was gone. It reminded her that he wasn't hers to hold onto, which meant she had to get herself out of bed, move onward. He'd said he'd take her somewhere for a couple days before it was official, but that wasn't right now. She'd look forward to that, but she needed to get home, recuperate so she could work tomorrow afternoon. They'd said the second mark would heal her decently in about twenty-four hours, though she had no illusions that it wouldn't be a tough day, a lot of the bruising needing more time to heal.

Anwyn told her she'd drive her home. She wouldn't take no for an answer, and made Ella wait another half hour while she attended to some things. It gave Ella time to get dressed, and realize the Mistress was right about the driving thing. Her mind was still spinning, drifting, the aftereffects of the trauma and then her Master's unforgettable attention.

When they arrived in front of her landlord's house, Krista was home, thankfully. Ella reminded Anwyn she'd have someone nearby if she needed help.

Anwyn gave her a searching look, but maybe because she was a woman as well as a Domme, she picked up on Ella's need to have some alone time. But as Ella moved through the back gate, she sensed Anwyn watching her closely.

She made sure she didn't stumble or show any sign of the heavy fatigue she was carrying, the emotional turmoil. In most respects, Atlantis was home, but when she felt like this, she needed her very own space so she could shower, meditate. Eat a peanut butter and jelly sandwich.

She managed all of that, slowly. And eventually found herself curled in her bed, tears drifting down her face as she thought of every moment she'd shared with Wolf, and the things she wouldn't be able to share with him after they reverted back to the relationship they'd had before all this other had started.

Technically, he hadn't said tonight was the end of it, but somehow, she knew. This was the turning point. Those couple days she'd requested? It was probably best to let them both off the hook on that.

She drifted off to sleep, thinking of him, his expressions, his scent, the strength of his hands. The way he called her baby, or little girl. When she lifted her lids again, it was still dark. Her eyes felt red and tired. But that was okay. Cathartic crying was the perfect way to reboot, start the day fresh.

Then she realized she wasn't alone.

Ella pushed herself up on an arm, squinting at the silhouette leaning in her doorway.

"Master?"

Ella.

He didn't speak it aloud, but there was so much pain in that one thought. Her heart leaped as he took a step toward her, but stumbled over her threshold. In an instant, she'd pushed out of the covers, scooted across them to the end of the mattress.

Her first thought was that he was hurt. But he gripped her hands, held them hard against his forehead. He was shaking, and cold, which scared her. He only wore his jeans, the rest of him shirtless and barefoot. As he dropped heavily to his knees, she pulled the blanket from the bed with one free hand and went to the floor with him. She wrapped the quilt around him, around them both.

"Talk to me," she whispered, trying to put as much of her arms around him as she could. "What's happening? Are you all right?"

His head was down, her fingers still sandwiched between it and the tight grip of his hands. He shifted abruptly, so he was sitting, his back against her bed, his knees drawn up, and his intense gaze on her face, his fists on his knees. Since she'd had the blanket wrapped around them, he pulled her with him. She was leaning against one of his bent knees, her hand there and on his shoulder to brace herself.

"Do you really understand what happened tonight?" he said roughly. "If you were a full servant, my servant, that could happen weekly, daily. If you thought I was treating you cruelly, you'd have no one to champion you."

"That punishment wasn't you. You did it tonight only because Lord Richard ordered it."

"When I punished you with my belt, that was a taste of how I would punish you, when I thought you needed it. Or just because I wanted to do it."

"I wanted that, Master. You know I did."

He closed his eyes, his face tightening. "Vampires have to attend at least one overlord event a year. Sometimes more. Any vampire get-together...requires things. The overlord might want you to be fucked by every male servant at dinner, while we all watched."

His gaze pinned her again. "I would have to order you to do it, because to refuse would be refusing a senior vampire, and I'm not allowed to do that."

"Okay." She nodded. "You'd order me to do it. But you'd be in my head, wouldn't you? Talking me through it, telling me it was your will. You'd see how aroused it makes me, doing what you want. Knowing that everything is your command, your will. The overlord might order it, but for me, it would be your mind, your heart, that I would be obeying. And that would pleasure you, too."

She gripped his hand at the anguish that crossed his face. "What is it, Master? Please, tell me. I understand those things."

He stared at her. *I want you, Ella. I want to give myself that. I want to be the selfish bastard who makes you his, keeps you forever.*

Her heart leaped. "Yes. Please. I want that, too."

"I've been alone a long time, Ella. I might be insufferable to be around, except in small doses."

"I've been alone a long time, too. I can be pretty stubborn. I like bed sheets with cute animals printed on them, and I don't dust. I dance naked in the rain on moonlit nights, and I don't care who might see me."

He put his head down in his hands, pulling the one away from her, and scrubbed his face ferociously, raking his nails over his shaved head, leaving red scrapes. When he spoke, there was an additional fierceness to his voice, as if the words were scraping him just as raw inside.

"Vampires rarely have children, Ella. And the only way a third mark gets pregnant is by their vampire. It's likely you'd never have children."

"There are a whole world of children already here who need someone's love, remember? That doesn't worry me." She wrapped her hands around his calf, put her cheek on his knees, so she could gaze at his face. "Please, Master. What do *you* need?" *Tell me. Please tell me.*

He jerked his head up abruptly, gripping her chin in the same motion, so their gazes were locked, inches apart.

Love me, Ella. Love me with everything you are. I want you to be mine. I want you as my servant, for three hundred years, for the eternity that follows. And...please forgive me. Help me find forgiveness, so I don't have this tearing pain anymore, for Ross and Sheila, for the people I killed, for the life I lived, the way I died...I don't know how...

"You have it," she assured him, her voice cracking. "You have it. You have my forgiveness, and my love." *Remember? I told you. I need a Master who can get so deep inside my head, my soul, that he can surround and possess everything I am. I've been lonely and empty for so long, looking for that, needing that.*

"All I want is to be yours," she said, a whispered entreaty. "Everything you do to me, everything you let me do for you...it will tell me that I am. Please...use me as you need me, Master."

His expression had changed as she spoke. Become more intense, dangerous. Another woman would be afraid, but she wasn't. She was overjoyed, because she saw she'd touched the dark place within him that wanted to possess her exactly that way, beyond reason or rationale.

Beyond choice.

In one swift move he was off the floor, had scooped her up and put her down on the bed, on her hands and knees. He kept one hand curved over her shoulder to hold her like that. His other hand slid down the middle of her back, palm flat, fingers spread. Slow. Then he made a circle, came back to rest in the middle of her back.

She heard him taking off his jeans, doing it one-handed so he could keep that contact with her.

Then he put a knee on the bed and was over her, pressing her down to her elbows, his large hands moving to cover hers. Her knees were already spread and she lifted to him, sucking in a breath that trembled through her as he slowly pushed inside, easing but not stopping, all the way in, until he was curved over her. He banded one arm above her breasts, his other staying braced next to her, large fingers overlapping her spread ones.

"I want to fill all your emptiness," he said. "Am I there? In every corner?"

"Almost. It hurts."

"Where? Show me."

She clutched his hand, guided it over her heart. He flattened his palm there, supported her with its strong breadth. "Okay, now?"

She nodded, her throat tight, body quivering and liquid, heart pounding against his hand. In his hand.

"Take my life, Wolf. Please. It's yours. I give it to you."

He was nuzzling her throat, his fangs lengthening, just like his cock, pushing against her flesh with every word she whispered. "Do it, please. I'll never be empty again."

And maybe not just her.

Wolf heard the thought in his head. Knew the danger of it. But in the end, all his self-control, his denial, all the bullshit—it just deserted him, and he became the animal again. No, not an animal. A vampire. The one who had to have what he desired the most, no matter what.

He bit down, found her blood and made her his.

Ella felt his fangs penetrate her throat and tipped her head to the side further, wanting to give him as much access as he needed. His large body was pressing against her backside, cock thrusting deep, a slow, undeniable rhythm while he held her as if he'd never let go. Then his fingers were in her hair, tightening the grip so he lifted her head. He kept lifting it as he drank, so her neck arched and she was staring at her ceiling. And yet he took it even further, one more straining inch. A reminder she was under his control.

She almost cried out in protest when he lifted his mouth from her, but it was for a bare second. He'd put his wrist to his lips to puncture a vein, because suddenly it was at her lips, before the welling blood could fall anywhere but upon them.

Drink, Ella.

It smelled...appetizing. She licked at it tentatively, and then her mouth was over the wound entirely. He pressed her cheek into his large palm, giving her a cradle as she drank from the wrist below. He returned to her own throat, puncturing her anew, the pain shooting through her, but headed straight down to her core.

Then he did something else. She felt something burn out from that bite mark, sizzle like fireworks through her blood, spiraling so her body jerked under his hold.

She was falling, falling deep, but he had her, a swirling descent in their shared minds. No, they weren't falling at all. He was drawing her down.

I am descending to the very bottom of your soul, so you know I am there, that I will always be there. There is nothing you ever need to hide from me. Nothing you can hide from me. No thought, no feeling. You are all mine, in every way.

Goddess...she could feel it. She could feel him inside of her. Had she said he'd filled her emptiness? He had, filled her heart and mind with his. But this. The only thing that could do what he was doing was his own soul, which meant...their souls were linked.

She belonged to him. She belonged to someone. Not just for a moment, or until they tired of her, or until they no longer needed what she provided.

More than that. She belonged to someone she wanted as her Master, more than she'd ever wanted anyone.

The fireman had carried her body out of the fire, but it was Wolf who now brought her soul out of that pyre, telling her that there was someone who wanted to be connected to her, that didn't want her left alone in the flames.

She held him tighter as he thrust, withdrew, thrust. He was no longer biting her, but he kept his mouth on her throat, teasing, licking. She wanted him to take her this way, then she wanted him to turn her over, lie upon her. She'd lock her legs high over his flexing ass, as he drove deeper, dug in, like he never intended to leave her body or any other part of her.

Count on it. You belong to me from here out, Ella. Do you really think you understand what that means? A lifetime of what a vampire master will demand from you?

No. But I'm willing to find out.

CHAPTER TWENTY-NINE

"Have you ever noticed, when you listen to 'Queen of the Night' by Whitney Houston, on the chorus, there's a drum beat that sounds just like a flogger hitting flesh? It was playing one night when my Mistress went after me, and she kept perfect time to it. Every time Whitney belts out that song and hits that beat, I feel the impact. By the end of it, I'm ready to spew like a teenager."

"I'll ask Lucille for a demonstration tonight." Madelyn shot Tex, the burly submissive who'd spoken, a teasing look. "I'm pretty sure we can work a Whitney song or two into our theme. Come get these decorations and put them up where we discussed."

Madelyn leaned against the ladder and tossed a grin up at Ella as the young man, dressed in a Dungeons and Dragons T-shirt and faded jeans, headed off under the weight of a full box of disco ball string lights and eighties album covers. "I can't believe we're doing Disco Night."

"People love retro stuff," Ella said, her gaze on the disco ball she was adjusting over the main stage. Maintenance had hung it, but it wasn't straight, requiring a minor adjustment. "Especially when you put some modern twists on it. Ed, that great DJ we had a few weeks back, he's already here. He's worked up some great mashups between disco music and modern stuff. Including Whitney." She sent Maddie a smile. "We're going to dance our asses off."

"Good. I can have a piece of that chocolate cake they're serving on the bar menu tonight."

"You might want to get yours early. They ran out of it last time." Ella headed back down the ladder, Madelyn moving out of the way so Ella could view her handiwork. "There. That's better."

"Looks perfect." Madelyn looped an arm around her waist and pressed a moist kiss to Ella's smiling lips.

"What was that for?" Ella asked.

"You look like a small, shining sun. I just wanted to take in some of that sunshine." Madelyn gave her a wink. "And the sun blushes."

Ella pushed at her, but couldn't help smiling at the Domme's lusty laugh.

Since Wolf had third marked her, she'd seen him every night, and he was in her head. Often. She guessed her reaction to that showed in ways she couldn't hide, especially not from the close-knit Club Atlantis community.

Fort and Allan had departed a few days after the opening, James and the security team now up to speed on the new set up. Saturnia and Hollow would be in and out for the next couple days, finalizing and troubleshooting the tech stuff. Well, Saturnia would. Hollow was leaving later today, headed back to Washington to handle a contract job there.

Construction was finished, no evidence a bomb had ever happened. Except now there were no more vulnerable approaches to Atlantis. As long as security stayed on top of things, and the staff followed the training they'd been given, the club would be far harder to attack than some of the most secure locations imaginable. Though Ella had picked up that Gideon, James and Wolf all had some lingering concerns about whether those involved had a more long-range plan, they'd done what they could to shore up defenses for now.

Ed was testing his equipment, because Andy Gibb's "I Just Want to Be Your Everything," started playing. Ella couldn't think of a song that better fit her feelings of the moment. It made her wish Wolf was here already. To distract herself, she went back to what she'd been doing before she'd noted the disco ball needed straightening. She had a bunch of papers spread out on two six-foot tables in front of her. She wanted to lead some line dances, and was going over the steps of the Hustle. Her feet twitched and lips moved as she murmured the instructions.

If only you knew someone who'd admit to knowing how to do those dances. Someone who actually hung out at disco clubs in the seventies.

Warmth filled her. It was seven o'clock, earlier than she'd expected him. He wasn't just in her head; he was here. She realized that a breath before his shadow loomed over her, his solid heat pressing against her back as his hands settled low on her waist. "I'm liking this look," he growled.

The glittery purple top fit sleekly over her breasts and nipped into points at her waist and the small of her back. The shirt fluttered over a pair of skin-tight pants that flared at the knee and were a mind-boggling swirl of purple and orange. She'd added a belt of wide white links and tied a purple scarf around her hair. She wiggled her hips and did a little turn for him.

At her first look, she laughed out loud in delight. With a wry smile, he backed off so she could get the full effect, though he retained her hand.

Wolf was rocking the disco era look in black polyester slacks and a silk, dark red and black patterned shirt. It was open at the throat, revealing a gold chain with two charms—a peace symbol and a Christian cross. He made the whole ensemble seriously sexy.

"You look...wow. Hey, were you serious? Do you know the Hustle?"

"It's been awhile." He pulled her away from the pages. He didn't even look at them. Instead, he took her hands, shifting her to his side so they were hip to hip, ready for the opening step. "Have you figured out the basics?"

"Pretty much. You lead and I'll follow."

"What every Master likes to hear."

He took the lead with confidence. The man could work it. She couldn't take her eyes off the relaxed movements of his hips, waist and shoulders. He had the rhythm of a natural dancer. As he spun her around, she heard whistles and cheers from the bar area.

Wolf grinned before he turned her so she was facing outward, her backside against him as he folded his arms over her and bent his head to kiss her throat. He gave her a discreet, thrilling brush with his fangs.

Are you hungry, Master? She ventured shyly.

For a variety of things. Blood, your sweet cunt, your mouth, your scent, the feel of your hands. I'm going to start taking you home with me so I can fall asleep inside your body, hold you pinned underneath me as long as the sun is in the sky.

Her breath caught. She didn't know all the rules of being fully marked, but she'd had a feeling part of it was her being where he was. Like living together. But until this very moment, Wolf hadn't indicated that was part of his immediate plan. The past week had been full of enough changes, so she'd been waiting for him to let her know how they'd proceed. She'd deduced maybe he was just getting used to the idea, like she was.

She loved the idea of them having a place together, even as she cautioned herself against thinking of it like any other couple setting up house. He was in her head, her very soul, so trying to play it cool was no longer an option. But being a servant likely came with the expectation that the vampire wouldn't have to keep reminding his servant what the relationship was and wasn't.

So she drew in that breath, let it out, and smiled up at him. "I'm waiting for the trademark John Travolta pose."

He rolled his eyes. "Total white boy move. I'm way too groovy for that, baby."

"I don't know, he looked pretty hot doing it. Maybe black men just can't pull it off as well."

You're angling for a walloping with Daddy's belt.

My night just gets better and better.

He shot her a look and spun her around again. When he brought her up to him this time, he kept her there, sliding a strong arm around her waist to take her off her feet. He held her firmly against his body, and she felt the pressure of his arousal against her thighs. "You don't know how to behave, do you?" he demanded.

Before she could answer, he'd cupped her head to give her a heated kiss, then he let her slide down to her feet. He was pretty good at misbehaving himself, since he made sure her clit rubbed against his erection with a slow, tempting stroke before she reached the floor.

A Dom doesn't misbehave. He shows a sub what she can have, when he wants her to have it. If *she behaves.*

At her impish smile, he sighed, a quirk to his lips, but resumed dancing with her. They moved together, so fluidly. How he spun her around, guided her feet with the direction of his own, it was like she was floating within the circle of his arms.

His words had her thinking, though. "You were really there. Is anything we've done tonight like it?"

He looked around at the decorations, the outfits that staff members had put together. "Echoes," he said. "But an atmosphere, a time period, it can't be duplicated. For all the drugs and sex of that time, there was an innocence and lack of self-awareness then. We're far more jaded and self-conscious now. This is a nice homage to the best parts of it, though."

She was pleased by his praise. He'd slowed them to a simple swaying back and forth beneath the disco ball. As he gazed down at her, he opened his mind, and let images of that past time flood into hers.

He hadn't done that before, and it startled and delighted her at once. Though she liked nothing better than looking at him, she closed her eyes so she could shut out all other input, fully step into the memories he was offering.

She saw a dance club he'd been in decades ago. There was a haze of smoke she was glad not to be inhaling, but it added to the surreal, glittering atmosphere. Glittering because of all the sparkles on the outfits, the rotation of the disco ball. The hairstyles and make up were like what would be represented here tonight, but yet different, as he'd said. It was similar to viewing a movie shot in the seventies, versus a current day film emulating the look of those decades. The original view was grainy, more real, unpolished.

Then, as if there was a spotlight on her, she saw a woman on the dance floor, her arms and hips moving with sensual grace and an earthy sexuality. She turned her head toward Ella and smiled, her whole heart in her eyes.

The image winked out, as if the camera had been shut off to end a scene. A second later, it started up again, in a different part of the club.

She opened her eyes, and registered the brief storm clouds in Wolf's gaze, the tension in his jaw. He hadn't meant to include the woman in the memory, but Ella expected she had been so much a part of it, it would have been impossible to excise her.

"Is that..."

"Yes. That was Sheila."

Ella held the image in her mind, thinking of the details she'd been able to absorb.

She'd been so beautiful. A cloud of soft dark hair around a youthful, rounded face, full lips, laughing eyes. She was wearing a pants suit in a rich salmon color, tied in the back, low in the front. Large gold hoops at her ears. Around her neck, on a decorative chain, she wore Wolf's dog tags. On her finger glittered a wedding ring.

"It was on a leave," he said. "Before everything."

Just that brief look, and she'd seen in Sheila's eyes what Wolf had realized, too late. Sheila had been a strong woman who loved him with everything she was. Him giving up on their love, their family...it had broken something in her she couldn't fix.

Oh Goddess, she wished she hadn't had that thought.

"It's only the truth, little girl," Wolf murmured. "Don't worry about it."

She looked up at him, her hands on his rigid biceps. His hand was curled hard into her waist. She lifted herself up on her toes, brushed her lips against the base of his jaw.

"She was wonderful, Wolf. I'm so sorry."

"How Deep Is Your Love" started up, with its dreamy soft quality. The disco ball was active, its dim snowfall of lights rotating over the floor, over their skin.

Wolf drew Ella closer, moving her in a slow four-step waltz to the tune, holding onto her. She didn't say anything more, letting him feel whatever that image had brought to him. But she didn't want him to go too far into that dark place.

I missed you today," she whispered, pressing her face to his chest. "I don't know if it's okay for a servant to feel that way. I'm not yet sure what all a servant does or doesn't do."

"There's no rule against a servant being head over heels about her Master or Mistress."

"Just against the vampire feeling the same."

He made a noncommittal noise and she left it there. Accepting the bounty of what she had in the here and now.

"You teach others that, little girl. In so many ways." He eased her back after a few more rotations. When he spoke again, his more practical tone reassured her that she'd tuned him back into the here and now.

"For the day-to-day, our relationship can be what we want it to be," he told her. "It's only when we're around other vampires that more of the protocol stuff kicks in."

"Like not hitting a vampire in the head with a pool stick?" She couldn't resist the tease.

"Yes." His hands tightened on her. "You ever put me through something like that again, I will dish out a punishment ten times worse."

She shuddered at the thought. Another type of person might have had the indignant thought "Put *you* through it?" since she'd been the recipient of all those cane strikes, but she knew what he meant. She'd much rather take someone else's pain than watch them go through it. Or worse, be the one dishing it out. While the Dom in him had cherished what she was willing to endure for him, she understood the line past which he had most definitely not liked it.

"I'm not talking about being around vampires like Fort, Allan and Saturnia in the situation we've been in here," he continued. "Though technically, as senior vampire, Fort could have initiated something with you and Hollow on our off times, we don't really have that kind of relationship. But when the Georgia overlord has his annual event, all vampires in his territory are required to attend."

"I get to go?"

The skin around his eyes crinkled with amusement. "You do. Does that scare you?"

"Not if you're going to be there." She looked up at him. "Do we get to dress up?"

The amusement deepened, but there was a far more serious note to the explanation he offered, in her head this time. *Remember what I said. You may be required to have sex with other servants as part of the entertainment. Vampires can be very creative sexually, and the games keep the cutthroat politics to a low simmer.*

"Wow." She rolled that over in her mind. "Okay. So a lot like orgy night in the private back room. I can do that. As long as that's what you need from me."

At his look, she shrugged. "Sex is sex, Master. I learned that when I...was working the streets."

His hands tightened on her, his expression darkening, but she shook her head. "It can be awful, but I was lucky. The girl who got me into it, she and her friends, we watched out for one another. I could choose my clients and yeah, sometimes I was hungry enough to be a little less choosy, but it was giving the client something he wanted. That satisfied my submissive side, while I earned money to eat."

"Ella." He held her tighter as she took a breath, rushed on.

"Sometimes sex is viewed as this tremendous treasure and gift, a be all, end all. Normal sex is just sex. It's just a really good meal, or an okay meal. Not spiritual or earthshattering, not good or bad. But sex with someone I care about or love? That can become the meal of all meals."

She smiled up at him. "So what I'm saying is, the sex isn't the important thing to me. There are other, more important things I only want to give to you. As long as I don't have to give those things to anyone else, I don't have any issues."

His eyes flickered and his lips parted, as if he might ask her what those things were, but Ed segued to "You Should Be Dancing" by the Bee Gees. It brought more staff members to the floor. Wolf transitioned to a medley of dances. Before long, he wasn't only teaching her, though he kept her close, using her as his demo partner for the couples' dances. He worked them through the Bump, the Bus Stop, the Electric Slide, and made them all laugh when he introduced the very simple Sprinkler for those like Tex, who didn't have a dancing bone in his body. After that, they all just free styled it, a mix of every dance from every era, the rowdy fun egged on by Ed's subsequent choice of "Disco Inferno."

When Wolf initiated a sexy bump and grind with her, it got way more into the grind part of things, fast, with his large hands clamped on her backside. The other staff members shouted encouragement. Ella simply looped her arms around his neck and held on. It was arousing, and so, so much fun.

She loved seeing him smile, and she thought everyone else did as well. They were seeing a different side of Wolf, too. And they were all carrying on like kids, having a good time dancing. Even with all the vampire stuff, this could be part of her life from here forward. Enjoying this with him.

Now Wolf slid his hands from her ass. He rested one palm against her lower back beneath the point of the shirt. The intimate touch made her shiver, because it was also a reminder of what was now imprinted on her flesh there.

She'd noticed it that night he'd third marked her, but he'd noticed it first. They'd been getting dressed in her small cottage and abruptly he'd gripped her arm, keeping her facing away from him, her shirt gathered in her hands. After a bated pause, he'd dropped to one knee, caressing it with his fingertips, much as he was doing now—and had been doing, with welcome frequency, during the time in between.

"Right after a third marking, a new mark shows up on a servant's flesh," he'd murmured. "The shape always has a special significance. Though I've seen it on other servants, I guess I didn't believe the part about the symbolism."

He'd let her see it through his eyes, explaining with a picture, instead of further words. It was a cross between a tattoo and a brand. The instantly recognizable shape had brought a peculiar tightness to her chest.

A phoenix. A mythical creature reborn from the fire. The raised mark was a dark crimson color, with the bold lines of a tribal tattoo. The phoenix's lifted wings almost met in a circle above its head.

The first time some of the Atlantis staff had seen it, she'd had to come up with some crazy story about having it done at the carnival and forgetting to tell them about it. She hadn't wanted them asking who had done it and seeking that person out for similar work, since the curious blend could only be duplicated by a third marking.

But as she'd rattled off the awkward explanation to Chantal, she'd glanced across the room at Anwyn and seen the knowledge in her eyes. In that moment, Ella had realized the significance of the trinity of teardrops—or drops of blood—in a circular pattern on Gideon's chest, over his heart. And now she knew what the "D" on his wrist brand meant.

Another delicious secret for their exclusive club within a club.

Returning to the present, Ella gazed up at Wolf, her heart in her eyes. The mark didn't just represent who she was, but that she was bound to him. Forever.

And then some, little girl.

"Ella, Ella." Charlene was waving to catch her attention. Seeing it, Wolf backed her over there, putting her in a dip in front of Charlene, making her laugh. She cupped Ella's head playfully, tousling her loose hair.

"You had a message from Master Gregor. He'll be held up tonight. He asked if you could move your session with him to eleven-thirty instead of eleven."

"Sure. All the theme night stuff I have to oversee will be done by then. Oh, crap. I need to make sure the props he wanted have been pulled from inventory and prepared." She put her hands on Wolf's formidable biceps as he helped her back onto both feet. She beamed up at him. "To be continued."

She started to move away, but abruptly found her arm in his very firm grasp. Wolf turned her to face him squarely.

"I think you better rewind and explain to me what you're doing, having a session with another Dom," he said.

The look on his face, the tension in his hands, a vibrating energy that was more vampire than human, focused her immediately. Charlene registered it, discreetly withdrawing, though she gave Ella a pleased wink that said, like the rest of the staff, she was playfully enjoying seeing the two of them as a couple.

So was Ella, but this was an unexpected wrinkle. Her Master was waiting for an answer, and didn't look pleased. "He's trying out some new wax play techniques and wants to demo them on me first. A paid session...no sex."

"Paid sessions involve sexual interaction. Touching, orgasms, oral."

"Yeah. But what we were just talking about, vampire get-togethers, it's less than what can happen at those."

"Those are under my supervision. At my direction."

She was glad of that, because she didn't want to do anything that wasn't approved by him first. But she'd assumed the things she did here, under the auspices of her job, that he already knew about, fell in that category.

More storm clouds gathered in his narrowed eyes. His attitude was giving her not-unpleasant butterflies in her lower belly, but she reminded herself she had to be practical, not dreamy about her Master's possessiveness.

"Okay, maybe not. We really haven't talked about it." She moistened her lips. "I don't want to do anything that upsets you, but...I have to do my job, Wolf. Paid sessions make up a good chunk of my monthly income. Plus tips. So what do you need from me on this?"

He stared at her, then let her go. "You're fine," he said. "You're right. You have to take care of yourself, pay your bills."

"Right." So why did she feel like something was off, like he was saying words he didn't want to believe? "If you want me to approach something differently, I just need to know. I'm figuring all this out, trying to understand how it works."

"Yeah. Me too." He sighed and curled a lock of her hair over her ear before he tugged on the strand. His gaze dipped, swept over her colorful, sexy outfit again. The heat in his expression suggested he was about to take her to a hidden corner to feed him, in a couple different ways.

She thought about being there first thing in the evening when he woke, so he could hold her against him. His fangs would puncture her neck as he thrust an impressively thick "morning" erection in her, stretching her, demanding more from her, growling as she dug her nails into his back...

His silver eyes grew more vibrant. "Go do what you need to do for your session tonight. You'll feed me later. When I call for you."

And then he was gone, leaving her on the floor with her hands closed on emptiness.

She wasn't sure if she'd offended him or not. Even with being able to talk in one another's heads, some of the more frustrating things about a new relationship persevered. She suspected a request for full access to what was going on in his head would be met with a flat *no*, especially in the vampire world.

After she took care of what would be needed for Master Gregor, she took her dinner break, and ran a quick errand she'd promised to do for Krista. When she returned, rather than heading right back into Club Atlantis, she decided to take a few minutes to clear her head before Disco Night was in full swing. So she headed to her loading dock, walking around the long ways.

Yeah, she knew nobody liked her to go there, but it was still her best thinking spot. And now she had a vampire in her head she could call if she got into trouble, right?

The number of soda can mobiles had increased. As she took a seat on the dock and tilted her head up to look at them, she wondered about the person who worked there and made them. They fluttered above her head, creating a hollow clunk-clank sound with the breeze.

"They're beautiful, aren't they?"

She started at the even male tone, then saw a slim man wearing slacks and a placket shirt with the logo of the company whose dock she was sitting on. "Oh, hi. I'm sorry, I don't mean to be trespassing."

He shook his head, waving an affable hand. "You're fine. I'm Bill. I handle the night shift security here. I see you've been enjoying my handiwork." He gestured to the mobiles, making Ella's mouth crease in delight.

"I love these. You made them?"

"Yep. We do recycling, so I make all sorts of things out of the trash. Origami out of the paper goods, mobiles out of the cans. I've seen you out here before, enjoying them. On the monitors inside."

She chuckled. "I'll have to tell our people you guys have a good eye on things. I get a lot of shit about coming out here by myself." She beamed at him. "Now I know I'm not alone at all."

"Sounds like you have good people who want you to be safe. I have a sister and I'd probably feel the same way." Bill ambled past a stack of pallets, a barrel trashcan roped to one of the covered loading dock pillars, and came to sit down next to her. "So what's going on at that fancy club of yours tonight?"

"Disco night," she pronounced. "Hence the crazy outfit."

"Looks good on you," he said, without any hint of creepy come-on. His blue eyes were friendly, and familiar. He'd probably gone by the alley some nights on his way to his job. Since they were neighbors, she wondered if she should invite him back to the club as a guest, if he would be interested.

"I saw you come in on that side," he nodded toward it. "You must have come from the street, rather than taking your usual short cut."

"Oh, yeah." She looked that way and gestured. "I usually cut through, but—"

And then all was darkness.

~

She'd fallen off her bike once, her helmeted head smacking the curb. When she woke from the blackout, it was like struggling to the surface of murky water, with weights tied to her.

She had the same feeling now. She was aware something bad had happened, that she needed to be afraid, but that uneasiness couldn't push her to consciousness yet. So she drifted. Then, somewhere deep inside, far away but getting closer, was a voice. Someone was calling her. And he was very, very angry.

Wolf.

He was connected to her. He was going to find her.

"Don't worry, Ella." Bill spoke. "He knows where you are. Just rest. He's coming. Hey, you know, I came to that club of yours a couple times as a guest of a buddy of mine. Well, he used to be a buddy. We don't get along much anymore. He thought I had the wrong 'mindset' for it." Bill shrugged. "But it was a nice place. I applied for membership on my own, but was turned down, probably because of him. Whatever. Though it definitely had a better layout than the place I used to go in Florida—"

No... Ella was only halfway listening. Even though she knew she needed to pay closer attention, the fear that had seized her mind took priority. This wasn't about her. It was about Wolf. He wanted Wolf to come. *Don't come here... Stay away.*

Even through that haze, she tried to give him a picture of what was happening, so he'd know. But she was under again, time passing. Yet now she knew Wolf was in danger. In her consciousness, she thrashed, she screamed at herself, she visualized catapulting herself out of the muck of her concussion into full awareness.

In the end, she succeeded, but rather than bouncing out of that torpor, she surfaced like a drowning swimmer, floundering, except one who could barely move. Oh, Goddess.

In a very different situation, it would have amused her, how quickly she realized why she couldn't move. She'd been restrained in so many creative ways, by so many Doms.

But always in session, where there was a safe word, rules to protect her. Where the Dom put her wellbeing first. That thought brought a fear she fought not to let take her over.

Her arms were folded in front of her, forearms taped to one another all the way past the wrists. Ankles and legs taped to the knees. She was in an incredibly uncomfortable chair. Her mouth was stuffed with something, a thick piece of tape over it. Bill stood in front of her. The affable expression had been replaced by a far different, far less friendly attentiveness.

A thundering crash. In her disoriented state, it was so much like the sound of the alley explosion she flinched.

But the noise was not a bomb. The loud noise had reverberated through the walls, making it seem louder than it was. She was in a small space, like a storeroom. Her third mark let her see Bill, but there was no light except what was coming from a dim source somewhere.

Her head was aching, her neck. Her entire spine felt like it was vibrating. Someone was beating on something. Ripping something free. Advancing toward their location like a stampede of rabid bears.

Bill picked up a hood and dropped it over her head. She tried to shake it free, no matter the illogic of resisting with her arms bound. He pulled it down to her shoulders, ran a strap around it that tightened on her throat, closed her in. She instantly felt like she couldn't breathe, and had to tell herself that she could, that the fabric was porous, but it was dense, enough to make her feel like her air had been reduced significantly, especially with her mouth already gagged.

Bill swiveled her office chair prison slowly around toward the wall. He put his knee between her spread ones, his fisted knuckles against her chest. He had bones that dug in, sharp and hard.

She'd done deprivation play before, but that was different. Not being able to see what was going on, in a situation like this, wasn't something she liked at all.

"I know you're listening in, vampire," Bill said. "You don't have to break through this door when you get to it. It's unlocked. But here's the sitrep. I'm wearing a gauntlet loaded with three steel spikes, six inches in length and a half inch in diameter. They will shred her heart when they pierce it. The back of this chair is a two-inch thick board. The barbed head of the spikes will lodge into the wood, keeping the shaft firmly penetrating her heart. If you come through that door intending to use your speed and strength to snatch her away from me, she'll be dead. So I suggest you come in at a far more courteous pace."

She heard the squeak, a doorknob turning, and the waft of air as a door was opened, slow, cautious.

She inhaled his heat, his scent, and was thankful for the third mark sense enhancement that allowed her to detect that, even through the hood.

I'm here, Ella. Wolf's voice, in her mind. *It's okay.*

She wanted to agree, but the relief that flooded her was matched by fear, a remembrance of her dream state, or whatever it was. Wolf was being drawn here on purpose. Ella was the bait.

"Wolf," Bill said, by way of greeting.

"Do I know you?" Wolf's voice was cold as death. She could almost see the lethal steadiness of his eyes. If Bill made one false move, Wolf would take him apart.

Bill cleared his throat. The slight quaver said he was all too aware of it. "Flip the switch in that light box hanging in front of you, Wolf. It will drop a net over you. Do it now, or I kill her in front of you."

Please, Wolf. Don't. I have a really bad feeling about this. Go get help, backup, something.

"You have five seconds. Five, four, three, two..." The pressure of Bill's knuckles increased, sending shards of pain through her chest.

Air rushed against her face as the net was released, as it fell from above. *No...*

It's all right. We'll figure this out, Ella. Just—

A crackle of heat and electricity, a sharp hum. The impression of white-hot pain shot through her head, not hurting her directly, yet letting her know just what he was experiencing. She heard his grunts, felt the vibration of the floor as he went down, his body rolling or jerking.

"Wolf." She cried out against the gag.

Bill yanked away her hood. She saw Wolf on the ground, under the net. The covering was a mesh of twisted metal. Once it had fallen upon him, Bill had activated an electrical current. It sparked along the lines of the mesh, burning into Wolf's flesh, making him jerk. His lips were stretched back in an agonized grimace, his eyes wild. What tore her heart from her chest was how hard she could tell he was fighting to regain control. To help her.

No, no, no.

"There's no point fighting," Bill said. "When that level of voltage is running through you, even a vampire is incapable of directing his own movements. You're helpless, and in a great deal of pain."

Several other people entered the storeroom. Serious looking people, in slacks and blouses, dress shirts with ties. Which made the gray rat eye masks they were wearing all the more surreal, complete with feral, pointed faces, whiskers, and rounded ears.

They flipped on the lights in another part of the room and she saw a large metal cage there. As Ella screamed against the tape over her mouth, they used some kind of pincers with rubber handles to clamp onto Wolf's limbs and drag him and the live charged net into the cage, dumping him there. His hand flailed, latched onto one of the bars, and electricity crackled there, pinning him between it and the net, his body arched up.

Goddess, how much could he take? With sudden horror, she realized what it meant, that a vampire could only be killed by a couple things. It meant he could be tortured like this forever, without dying. But what could it do to his mind?

Stop it, stop it, stop it.

She wished she had the hood back on so she didn't have to watch this, even as she needed to let her gaze cling to Wolf, to let him know she was there.

The people, other than Bill, reminded her of scientists. One had even pulled out a tablet and it looked like he was inputting data.

"It doesn't yet prove it conclusively," he said to Bill in an annoyed voice.

"Not my department, bro. Take it up with your egghead boss. I'm in the homestretch here. Can't wait to see this place and this shitass cover job in the rearview mirror." Bill had straightened, removing the immediate threat from Ella, and he was keying something on his phone. A communication to someone?

Or a program being deactivated.

The electrical charge stopped. Wolf's hand fell from the cage bars, leaving him in a crumpled heap on the floor. Two of the masked scientists pulled the net away, through the bars. Wolf was still conscious, rage-filled eyes on Bill, every muscle bunched with the desire to do violence, no matter the agony those muscles must have been feeling only moments ago, that were likely still feeling.

"Stand back," Bill said. "I'm activating the cage."

She heard a hum, saw Wolf's gaze course around him. The floor of the cage was covered with thick rubber, so it didn't take her long to figure it out. The bars had been charged with the same debilitating voltage as the net. As long as he stayed seated in the cramped cage and kept his legs drawn up to stay away from any contact with the sides, he could be all right.

Then Bill pointed a closed fist at her abdomen and pressed a trigger on the gauntlet.

"No!"

Wolf's thunderous roar vibrated through her as the steel shafts went through her stomach. Adrenaline protected her for half a second, the shock of it, and then pain like she'd never felt before in her life took over. Nausea, pain, dizziness. She was suffocating from the pain.

She vaguely heard the clang of the bars as Wolf threw himself against the cage, with enough force he ripped loose the bolts holding it to the floor. Unfortunately, that turned the cage onto its side, which put him on the fully charged bars, not the rubber flooring.

She smelled that horrible chemical smell again as electricity met flesh. Wolf was knocked back, into the opposing side of bars, so the cage continued to electrocute him as his limbs flailed.

She was screaming against the gag, telling them to stop, even as the pain made her feel like she was being sawed in half.

He couldn't speak in her mind while that was going on, but neither could he block his mind, so it was like tumbling in a jar of nails, stabbing her with words and cries and nothing but chaotic feeling.

The scientists used those pincer things to right the cage, with effort. They pushed him back into a position away from the bars, holding him there while Wolf regained his senses. Somewhere amid a thicket of agony, she felt a horrifying gratitude to them for that.

Bill looked merely satisfied that the cage was holding. It had been a test, she realized.

Now he rose and came back to her. He gripped Ella's hair and tipped her head back, looking into her tear-stained face thoughtfully. His thumb passed over a tiny track of saliva that had escaped around the tape, caused by her screams and sobs, her pain-wracked gasps. He leaned in, spoke against her ear. As he did, he tilted his head to meet her gaze. With his next whispered words, she knew why his eyes seemed so familiar.

"Run, little pussy. Try to run."

Her blood went cold and he straightened, giving her a satisfied look. "Perry didn't die for nothing," he said. "But you likely will."

He jerked his head at the others. "Get them into the truck. He may have called someone as backup when she regained consciousness and he knew she was in trouble. We need to get where we're going. Far beyond where anyone can help them."

CHAPTER THIRTY

Pain. So much pain. She figured she'd eventually die, because her mind still didn't really believe what she'd been told, about a steel shaft through the heart being the only thing that could kill a full servant. But that was what Bill had threatened, before he shot three bolts into her abdomen instead.

They'd been removed by a woman wearing purple latex gloves. She'd wrapped Ella's stomach up tight in bandages to staunch the blood. She was given a handful of pain pills. They were neither cruel nor compassionate about the bandaging or drug administration. Just executing brisk, functional steps to ensure she didn't slow them down.

She'd been loaded into a truck container, dumped on a cot and strapped down on it, even with the taped bindings still in place on her arms and legs. Wolf's cage was put in the roomy space. Even as they did that, he kept throwing himself against the electrified bars, trying to get to her.

It was tearing her apart, watching it. She understood something animalistic had taken him over, his eyes red, fangs lengthening. She wanted to do something to help, to calm him, but she could barely think through the pain. Her blood was all over her purple glittery shirt. The throbbing was relentless. Having her body laid out flat and bound made it worse.

Three of the male scientists in the rat masks approached the cage. Wolf moved back to the center, staring at them with those feral eyes.

They reached through the bars with the clamps, seized Wolf around a wrist, forearm and biceps. It allowed them to pull his arm between one set of bars, hold it immobile so it wasn't touching the electrified part. Though he could have struggled, now he'd gone deadly still, watching while another man wearing latex gloves approached, supplies to draw blood in hand.

"You reach in there with that needle, he will remove your arm," a familiar voice said. Bill, sitting on a stack of boxes, turned his head toward the recesses of the truck.

"Hey, boss," he said. "Everything you told us worked, like clockwork. Though this monster gave me some worries for a minute."

"I have employed you, Bill. It does not make me your boss. I expect you to do the job exactly as I laid it out, so you can earn payment. Go up front with the driver and keep a lookout."

It had taken her a mind a moment to wrap around it. She could see it hitting Wolf as well, the incredulity.

Hollow stopped near Ella's chair and frowned. "Now, as to the blood draw..."

The three scientists looked at him blankly and he shook his head.

"Waste of effort," Hollow muttered, the first show of emotion she'd seen from him—irritation. "Just think."

"Wolf," he said. "Ella needs your blood to heal and to ease her pain. Let Paul set up the line. No one in this room has any intrinsic value. Everyone is replaceable, so if you tear off his head, it won't mean anything to us but a delay. She's hurting badly, your servant. Help her."

Wolf fixed that glare on him, but some of the wildness died back as the words penetrated. His expression remained like fury-carved-in-granite, but he nodded, a short movement. "Reach in and get it," Hollow said to the one he was calling Paul, a tall, thin rat-masked man. "Keep in mind, Wolf, Ella's wound isn't fatal. Misbehave, and I have no problem letting her suffer until we get where we're going. We're going to hit a lot of potholes along the way."

Wolf... She wanted to tell him not to do it, not to cooperate in any way, because they had no idea what the endgame was here, but Wolf sent her a look.

Better chance of escape if we keep strong.

Logical, though she still didn't like it. Yet she was filled with relief to hear the coherent thought, clipped and rough though it was. *Are you okay?*

Not even close. When you are safe and I tear everyone in this room into raw, bleeding meat, I will be okay.

Fair enough. She had no argument with that plan.

Paul cleared his throat. He looked a little pale and a lot diminutive next to Wolf, like a white mouse next to a crouching panther. "Make a fist," he ventured.

"Gladly," Wolf said, showing his fangs.

Would they offer juice and cookies afterward, like the Red Cross? Ella knew she was a little punchy, but anything to distract her from the pain would help. Had Wolf been able to alert anyone, or had he merely come to the loading dock when he couldn't get a response from her, and followed her trail? She'd been pretty instantly unconscious, so he might not have seen she was in distress. Just suddenly radio silent and full dark.

She bet the storeroom had been inside the loading dock warehouse, which meant he'd been far more likely to come in to find her, rather than going back to give anyone a heads up. But Disco Night. She'd be missed. They'd know something was up.

A sudden ice-cold fear grabbed her gut. Saturnia. Oh Goddess. Was she part of this? She must be, because Hollow was third-marked. How could she not know he was doing this? What did they want?

"No," Hollow said to the woman who took the blood bag from Paul. She was picking up a needle, intending to set up a transfusion with Ella. "She can drink it. Film it, and keep your camera on the progression of her stomach wound. Document how drinking the blood heals her."

One of the masked men came and stood next to Hollow. From the color of his hands and his accent, he appeared to be Asian Indian. He had a good physique and thoughtful, intelligent eyes behind the mask. "She seems like a normal young woman. Disturbingly so."

"Yes. She's new to the servant thing," Hollow explained. "A sweet girl, not a fighter. Not that kind of fighter. If we condition her properly, she can become an ally. If we torture him enough, she may be able to read things out of his head, because he won't be able to maintain his mind shields."

Like fucking hell.

Hollow read it from her expression, and shook his head. "I'm not insulting you, Ella. Everyone breaks. I spent a lifetime learning how, from my own experiments and the techniques of others in my profession. You will give us everything we are seeking, and there will be no blame to it. It's simply a matter of understanding human nature, how it responds under duress."

The tape was taken away, the gag removed from her mouth. She could see Wolf crouched on his heels in the electrified cage, his eyes on her. She wanted the Asian guy to move, because he was partly blocking her view of Wolf.

Drink, Ella. He's right about needing to keep up our strength. It's okay.

They are filming it. If I don't drink, I won't heal as fast and it won't prove anything. At least not as effectively.

They will not live to do whatever it is they intend to do. I need you to drink. I can bear my pain. Yours I can't tolerate.

Wolf. Master. Oh, Goddess.

It's okay, baby girl. Hang onto me. It's okay.

He was trying to orient his mind after the trauma of the electrocution, she could tell. He didn't have the energy to block her out of it like he normally did, and she could see him rolling around contingencies, ideas, knowing they would have to wait this out and see when an opportunity presented itself. They'd have to stay alert for it. And he was worried as hell about her.

I'm all right, Master. I'm here. I'll keep alert, too.

Part of the blood was drained into a cup. The woman who brought it watched her closely, the blue eyes behind the rat mask moving in a stilted, horror-movie kind of way.

There were hands on her, cutting away her bloody shirt, the leggings, leaving her just in her underwear and the bandages. She writhed, but she was ignored, and the bindings wouldn't let her resist them. The bed could be cranked to an upright position. Once they did that, the woman put the cup to her lips while Paul held up a phone, filming.

During the third marking, she'd learned the taste of Wolf's blood was appealing to her, obviously an effect of being marked. Now she craved it, hatefully proving what Hollow said, that it was something her body could use to heal her. As she drank, her fervor for it increased. It was as if her body knew what it needed, and latched onto it like mother's milk. She would have gulped it, if the woman hadn't given it to her in measured draughts.

She started to feel better. Not cartwheel great, but the pain died back, enough to have her determined to finish every drop so she could recuperate and be a help to Wolf, face whatever was coming their way.

"Look at that," the woman said in a marveling tone. "The wound. It's knitting before our eyes."

"The Master or Mistress's blood can heal the servant from almost anything," Hollow said. "Her blood can help restore his strength as well, even right after he's given her blood for the same. Some of the timing depends on the age of the vampire, but Wolf is a remarkably strong made vampire for his age."

"What the hell is this, Hollow?" Wolf said in that same hard voice. "Are you going to tell me, or is it need-to-know?"

Hollow shrugged. "You won't leave a lab again, until your usefulness is over, and they stake you to end it. But the answer why is straightforward enough. To figure out how to overwhelm and eradicate the vampire race."

At Wolf's stunned look, he shook his head.

"I served my country most my adult human life, Wolf. Same as you. Vampires are a threat to humans."

He swept a flat gaze over the scientists enthralled with Ella's healing. Ella wanted to scream at them to get away from her, particularly when one of them shifted so she couldn't see Wolf's face. She could feel his fury, though. She was the vessel catching the overflow of his lethal rage, helping him contain it. She welcomed it, because the heat kept her fear from overcoming her.

Hollow continued. His voice rarely rose or fell, an odd monotone cadence. "The vampire hunters that are out there, they're romantic and emotional, like comic book heroes. Even Gideon Green, considered the smartest of them all. It was about vengeance, about protecting people. They would be far more effective if they thought like the villains. It's about the end game, the big picture. Villains don't pick off one person at a time. They look for the weapon of mass destruction. One of them did that some years back. Introduced the Delilah virus. Hell of a chemist, until the Council figured it out and sent their assassin after him. Took him out, destroyed all his work. And then the Council's scientist figured out a cure."

He tapped his temple. "I'm not a chemist, but a strategic thinker. Put Saturnia and me in a room and we can come up with the way to bring down every government, the largest corporate entities. But the answer was so simple. To end vampire kind, reveal their existence to humans in a way that can't be denied. Humans won't suffer anything to survive they think has any power over them. And the worst insult of all, vampires are immortal. You all have the golden egg all humans want. To live forever."

The scientist in Ella's field of vision had shifted. She could see Wolf studying Hollow, his stern mouth a flat line. "So these people here," her Master said. "You found someone in government to sanction this."

"Of course. But not in government. Not directly. You look for the right kind of humans, with the right kind of government connections. The ones who might be called paranoid or off, because they won't dismiss any threat out of hand, no matter how outlandish it sounds. They will evaluate anything for risk, whether it be a baby in its stroller, or someone's claim that vampires exist.

"You find that kind of group, one that runs a private company that supports the needs of our military, and suddenly you have tremendous resources to support your goal. There are only about five thousand vampires. If humans know enough about their weaknesses to exterminate them, in the quickest and most efficient ways...mission accomplished."

Hollow nodded to the scientists, who were mostly ignoring his dialogue with Wolf as they entered data on their tablets and conferred with one another. Ella noticed none of them made eye contact with her, as if she weren't something real, living, capable of pain or fear.

"They will log their data to prove you are what I've told them you are. When they have enough, they'll take it to their superiors. At that point we transport you to an official facility, where you'll go through all the grueling tests we're going to put you through at our temporary lab, because you'll have to prove what you are to the next group of higher-ups. Then they'll get the government on board to finance the extermination. They'll likely keep it all on the down low, using private companies like this one to do the dirty work. But once they understand more about you, your weaknesses and strengths, hunting vampire kind to extinction will be possible within a relatively short timeframe."

A muscle flexed in Wolf's jaw. "No. I'm not buying it."

Hollow looked puzzled. "It all makes logical sense. You led teams in battle. You understand tactics."

Wolf shook his head. "Not that. I'm not buying your reasons. We all sign up to serve. But in the end, it's about the guy next to you. This is about Saturnia."

Hollow's gaze darkened. He took a step toward Wolf, his voice going as sharp as a thin blade. "You won't talk about her."

An emotion. Ella didn't know if the leap in her own blood stream came from her or Wolf, but her Master latched onto that cue the way the best Doms did.

"So that's it." Wolf nodded. "You're too fucked up to have a normal relationship. But while you're working for the CIA, you meet Saturnia, and you finally click with someone. But then she gets cancer, and is phased out. You're about to lose the one person who could stand to have you around. You go to find her, only to realize, fuck, she's no longer dying. She's become something else entirely...something not human. And guess what? She likes you, wants you in the club, so she makes you her servant. Maybe you can bridge that last hurdle, finally discover what seems to come so easily, too easily, to others. Real emotions."

Whatever emotional reaction Saturnia's name had triggered, its effect was gone. Now Hollow was processing the information, rather than getting more defensive. It was as if Wolf had presented him with an intriguing math problem to solve.

Ella wondered if Hollow was like a cat, with fewer facial muscles so he looked impassive all the time. She'd thought Wolf was good at that, but now that she knew him better, she could discern the subtle tells of emotions beneath that steely eyed surface. She couldn't with Hollow.

During the time Hollow had been working at Atlantis, she'd found it interesting, fascinating, trying to determine what he was feeling or thinking. Now that lack of emotion in his eyes made her cold.

"But that was the rub, wasn't it?" Wolf persisted. "Saturnia didn't help you break down that final wall. She can't fix what's broken in you. You're incapable of real feeling, have always been incapable of it, so now you decided to get rid of all evidence of how supremely fucked up you are. Somewhere deep inside that fortress of logic is a little kid, lashing out."

As she'd said, Wolf was a good Dom. Too good. And he wasn't done. He gave Hollow a considering look. "Because it runs even deeper than that. She made you her *servant*. She didn't make you her equal. She didn't offer you the vampire prize, did she? She knew that immortality would be a bad idea for something like you."

Hollow's face had closed down, his shoulders stiffening. *No...* Ella could see it coming. She was sure Wolf could, too, and didn't know if he'd pushed it deliberately, to figure something out that would be worth it to help them survive. Or maybe the bloodlust and rage still so obviously close to the surface had played a part too, the "come on, asshole, do your worst" gauntlet thrown down.

"Cuff him to the bars," Hollow said.

When they reached their destination, she was hooded and gagged again. The cot in the truck transitioned into a gurney, so they wheeled her out. She cried and begged to stay, begged them to stop doing what they were doing. Her last glimpse of Wolf was the stuff of nightmares. Hollow had activated the cage's electrical field as soon as they had Wolf cuffed to it with steel manacles. His body jerked like a puppet, his eyes rolled back in his head, a strangled cry frozen on his stretched lips, his arched throat.

Hollow had sat down to work on his laptop only a few feet away. She expected he'd leave the electricity on for hours if he could. The only thing that would end Wolf's torment was the obvious impatience of the scientists, wanting to get started on the other terrible things they wanted to do to him.

The blood had rejuvenated her, so her strength was returning. Though full healing might take longer, if the aching tenderness beneath the skin was any indication, the wound in her stomach was almost completely closed. Any other time, she'd marvel at it. Now it didn't matter.

After what felt like a maze of hallways, she was in a room, where the hood was removed again. Her surroundings were not reassuring.

The equipment and sterile environment suggested she was in some sort of lab, and the cage with a chair bolted in the center of it struck terror into the pit of her belly.

Even worse, they hadn't brought Wolf here, and at the moment, she couldn't feel him. She should be able to hear him in her mind. Yet she didn't. Which meant he'd found a way, even during that terrible, horrible agony, to keep that door shut between their minds, so she wasn't being shredded by his torment.

They cut the tape bindings off of her to do what they wanted to do next. The hands that held her were detached, those rat faces expressionless, except for the eyes. All of them wanted to touch the wound, prod it, check the healing. None of them asking to touch. She'd never thought about how terrifying it would feel, to realize she was at the mercy of those to whom her emotional state, her reactions to pain, were irrelevant, except for what information it gave them.

When she survived this, she was donating as much as possible to whatever organizations opposed the use of animals in a lab, whether mouse or chimpanzee. Nothing living should be treated like this. Her belief in life, her innate spirituality, recoiled from all of it. Shut her down, made her hate them. Want to fight them, spit at them.

Especially when they cut off the rest of her clothes, stripping her naked, and put her in a cage, too. She wanted to curl up, hide herself from them, but they took that chance away. They strapped her to the metal chair in the cage. The chair had no seat or back, the frame pressing uncomfortably into her shoulders and thighs. Her arms were bound behind her, her ankles spread and attached to the chair legs.

She closed her eyes, tried to close it all out, center herself. Take herself to that meditative state where she could figure this out. If Wolf was keeping that door shut, it wasn't just to cushion her from his pain. Stay alert, look for an opportunity. She needed to collect information. To listen.

Her stomach jumped as Hollow entered the room. Had he turned it off? She doubted it, because she still couldn't sense Wolf. Surely he'd speak in her head if he could. Focus, she told herself. Focus on the here and now.

The other rat-faced scientists were busy with their equipment, except for a female standing next to Hollow.

"I'll start the first phase of her conditioning," he said. She'll be more forthcoming that way."

The woman nodded. "How long do you need?"

"For the first phase, not too long. She's not that resilient. Continue with your prep. I'll let you know when you can start your first battery of questions with her."

The woman left him and Hollow turned to Ella. For the first time in some minutes, someone met her gaze, but she found no comfort in his dead eyes. She thought the others didn't meet her eyes because if they did, some deep down part of them would recognize what they were doing, and it would give them a sense of unease. Hollow could look at her directly without any concerns about that. Just as Wolf had said.

"What would you do to get me to turn off the electricity, Ella?" he asked. Conversational. He pressed a button on a panel and the wide screen on the wall flickered to life. It showed another room, a lab space similar to this one. Sound filled the room. The stress of the electricity didn't allow Wolf to scream, but it forced sounds from his throat, an awful, strangled noise like a dying animal, deep in a dark forest, beyond reach of help.

She knew what Hollow was doing, but awareness didn't block her recoil from such purposeful cruelty.

"Over the years, I kept one thing from each person I had to interrogate and break. A recording of their cries. It will provide a background to Wolf's."

Hollow picked up a pair of headphones with the kind of cushioned earpieces that shut out all other sound. He came into her cage, fitted them over her throbbing skull. He strapped the device tightly across her forehead and around her neck so she couldn't shake them loose. Then he removed her gag. It surprised her.

At least until she deduced, with a sick feeling, that he was likely planning to add her screams to his sick collection.

He returned to his computer, began tapping the keys. Sound flooded in. Turning his attention to her, he watched her carefully as he started turning up the volume. Up and up and up, until her eardrums felt the pain. He stopped just one click short of bursting them, she was sure. And now her head was full of those cries.

He picked up a black marker, wrote on a pad of paper the female scientist brought to him. Then he propped it up on the counter where Ella could see it. The neat block letters were too easy to read.

We stop when I know you're ready. Not a moment before. You are powerless here. Can you tell which voice is Wolf's?

Wailing, sobbing, shrieks. A cacophony of people begging for a mercy that never came, begging to die, screaming out what they knew, information that would get people they cared about killed, but they couldn't stop themselves...it was all there. Maybe it was on a loop, but anguish was never repetitious. It hit all her senses, over and over. And through it all, Wolf. His wasn't a recording. It was live. Those strangled noises got weaker and weaker, and then died away. When she couldn't hear him anymore was when she was pleading for it to stop.

It did. Her heart was hammering, yet her body was exhausted, everything exhausted. Hollow came and removed the earphones. Stroked her hair back from her sweaty, tear-stained face. Her mind was so chaotic, she could only be grateful for a gentle touch, even from an enemy. She'd bitten through her tongue and lip, and he wiped away the blood, the saliva, collected it all on his fingers. Her mouth was so dry.

Then he reached down and put his fingers inside her, lubricated with her spit and blood. She hadn't been expecting it. Nothing about Hollow suggested a sexual sadist, or that sex even remotely interested him.

It didn't now. He had a purpose. He was a vampire's servant. He knew how to arouse a body, no matter how repelled the mind within it.

No. please, no... As he dispassionately probed and thrust, played with her clit, she wanted to cry, but this was beyond tears. Her eyes sought Wolf on the screen, though she didn't know if she could bear to see him writhing in pain. But he wasn't. Hollow had finally turned off the electricity so that someone could remove Wolf's cuffs, let him struggle back to the center of the cage before activating the bars again, keeping him contained but no longer actively shocked.

He was staring at something before him. Hollow was letting Wolf see what he was doing to her, on a screen just like the one she had in here.

Ella's thighs trembled. She wanted to close them, but she couldn't. She knew the body would respond to the right stimulus, no matter what. It still felt shameful, like she should be able to stop it. Her nipples had grown tauter, and Hollow was flicking them gently.

No. Please don't watch this, Wolf. Please.

She didn't think she could bear to hear her Master speak in her head when Hollow was doing this, but when he did, she found she was wrong. He gave her a lifeline to seize.

I'm not looking at a single damn thing he's doing, Ella. Because it doesn't matter. It's not you he's touching. He's touching a shell you've built around yourself. That shell will do anything he wants, because it's plastic, a toy. You're inside, hunkered down, safe, and thinking. Thinking just as hard as I am about how we get out of this. Right?

He sounded strained, exhausted. But his thoughts were fierce, a warrior ready to fight to the last. And he turned his head away from the screen he was viewing. Instead, he gazed straight into the camera, so he was meeting her eyes.

Is Saturnia part of this? It was the question she still couldn't answer.

I don't think so. He and she...there's not enough time to explain, but they never had that kind of relationship. Saturnia communicates mind-to-mind, but she doesn't dig, or drift, or play around in there, except for a quiet room he keeps for her, a compartmentalized spot to escape her own demons. It has to do with their history together in the CIA, why they do it that way.

But soon he's going to remember that you and I are different. He'll cut off our ability to look at one another. He'll try to do things to separate our minds, so I'm going to say it now. Use that focused mind of yours. Every corner of it, including the part that contains that rage inside of you. Everything that helps you see the world in a way no one else does.

Her body was building to a release point, her hips twitching. She cut herself off from it, like Wolf said. Focused just on him and made herself believe his words as she climaxed under Hollow's touch, as her stomach heaved and she ended up throwing up on herself right afterward. Hollow jumped back quickly, another move that didn't look calculated.

He doesn't like to get dirty. Not like that. Another piece of information.

Good girl. Keep collecting them, Ella. We'll get out of here, baby. It might be a long road, but we'll do it. And no matter what happens, I love you. I love you so damn much, with everything I am. That's the truth, no matter how he'll try to twist things. Beat him at his own game. I got him revved up, you calm him down. He thinks he's conditioning us. We condition him right the fuck back.

She couldn't take her eyes from the screen, from Wolf looking at her through the camera. If Hollow was going to take that away, she'd get as much as she could out of it first.

He thinks he can break you. He can. He can break you because you've been broken before. Plenty of times. You know how to break, but still embrace who you are and the life you've been given. That abundance.

Use it to beat his fucking ass, and then I'll tear him apart for hurting you.

Wolf staring at her in the camera strengthened her. Unfortunately, Hollow noticed.

It had not been easy to cuff him to the bars, and now they implemented a plan that made that unnecessary. The scientists inserted a grid in front of Wolf and behind him, and secured it to the bars of the cage, locking him into the middle of the cage, the bars pressed up against his flesh in front and behind. They made him hand over his clothes, too. Ella saw the looks a couple of the female scientists gave his genitalia. One of them made a joke about them that caused the other to laugh.

On the surface, it looked like her and Charlene, whispering and giggling about a handsome Dom or sub in a club session. Whereas the scientists' behavior appalled her, she and Charlene had been having flirtatious, harmless fun, earning grins from the sub or a mock reproof from the amused Dom. Context and consent were everything. But it made the surface similarities no less horrifying.

The earphones and electricity were activated once again, effectively destroying any mental conversation between them. Just as Wolf predicted.

Another...how long? Ten minutes? An hour? She wasn't sure how one measured time when going through something like that. All she knew was when it stopped, she was slumped in the chair. She wasn't sure, but she might have blacked out, because for awhile she couldn't see Wolf, though the screen hadn't been darkened. Not until the earphones were shut off. She felt so weak.

The cage opened, and a woman in a rat mask was there, making her sip water. When she asked Ella a question, Ella just looked at her blankly. She couldn't tell if the woman was new, or someone she'd seen before. She hated those masks. Her ears were ringing. And when she spoke, her voice didn't work. At some point, she'd started screaming, too. Her vocal cords hurt.

More fluid put to her lips. Blood this time. More of Wolf's blood. She didn't want them weakening him. He needed her blood, she was sure of it. How long had Hollow kept the electricity on this time? She wanted to reach out to Wolf, but if he was resting, unconscious, she wanted him to stay that way as long as possible. He'd reach out to her when he could. She didn't want to rouse him from the bliss of unconsciousness.

The whole idea was ludicrous, that she could do anything against a seasoned, sociopathic CIA operative that he wouldn't see coming a mile off. So she'd be herself, wouldn't she?

He thinks he can break you. He can. But you know how to break...

Hollow was saying something to the woman. She left, and it was just Ella and Hollow now. She didn't want to think about what the others were doing, because if they weren't here, they were with Wolf. Hollow was staring at his laptop, working on something. He glanced her way, spoke every once in awhile. Eventually, she started to hear him.

"...told her your ears and voice needed to have time to heal after the administering of the blood."

"Yeah," Ella said, clearing her throat. His head came around, eyes narrowing. She tried to straighten up. Tried to dispel the immediate memory of his fingers inside her.

"Is Wolf going to break my heart, the way Saturnia did you?" she asked quietly. "Do you really think that? I'm still human, Hollow. I want to know."

He looked at her for so long she figured he would just ignore her, turn back to his computer. Instinctively she knew trying to make him believe she wanted an answer to the question wasn't the right tactic. She had to make herself believe she wanted the answer. It had to be as close to authentic as possible to fool him.

"Yes," he said at last. "It's too late for you, though. You're already third marked."

"So are you, and it's not too late for you."

"That's because she doesn't look into my mind to figure out what I'm doing. She just asks me where I am, what I'm doing, and takes it at face value. Saturnia can't handle more white noise in her head than she already has. Communication with her is direct give and take."

"Sounds lonely," Ella mumbled. "No meandering, no picnics together in the hallway of your mind. I like having Wolf in my head."

"Sounds clean," Hollow disagreed. "Simple. Quiet. No messages exchanged, except what's functional. That's why she thinks I'm in Washington. She won't be looking for me. If she asks me to come back to help look for you and Wolf, I'll give her a reason I can't get there, or tell her I'm doing something from my location that appears to be helping."

Messages. A phone. That was it.

She needed access to a phone. If she could let anyone know that Hollow was the key...then Saturnia could figure out what he'd done, where he was...

A vampire could scour a servant down to the soul. Hadn't Gideon said that, as bluntly as possible?

Sometimes the strategy was so simple, it was staring you straight in the face.

Her gaze scanned the room, fixed on a glitter of purple. They'd put her belongings in a little cubby hole at the back of the temporary lab, along with the tiny purse she'd had slung across her body. That didn't bring her any hope, because she'd left her phone at the club, like an idiot.

No, not an idiot, she realized. Because while she didn't know many phone numbers by heart, being like everyone else, overly dependent on the address book in her phone, she knew her own damn number. Someone at the club would be smart enough to track her phone's whereabouts first, and would have it in their keeping.

She was surrounded by people with phones, tablets, laptops. She just needed to get her hands on one for a minute...

"I don't get it," she said. "How you can remain that...separate from her. I couldn't be that way with Wolf."

"Because you think you love him, and he is attached to you." Hollow's mind was apparently agile enough to work on what he was doing and keep up a conversation with her. That meant he wasn't assigning much significance to her questions, or his mind needed additional diversion while he worked. She'd noticed he preferred to listen to tapes while he worked. Saturnia had said he was always learning new things. Languages, history, politics. His mind never stopped devouring knowledge.

"Ours is a practical arrangement," he said. "The work..."

He stopped, and the look that crossed his face was what she expected most men looked like when considering sex with a really good lover. "When we worked together, everything made sense. So I wasn't surprised when she recruited me the same way she used to recruit assets for the CIA. She was up front about being a vampire. She knew I wasn't happy without her, and she wanted an easy blood source. Working with Fort, she figured I'd appreciate a three-hundred-year life span to do more of what I was already good at."

"So killing off vampires wasn't the grand plan from the beginning. Which means she was your focus, like Wolf said."

Whatever button Wolf had pushed with his question about Saturnia, apparently didn't rouse Hollow the same way when the subject was raised by Ella. But then, Ella was a servant.

At Hollow's bemused look, Ella met his expression head on. "Wolf is the first one who wanted to keep me. I hoped..." Her voice caught. "I thought he really cared about me, but the way you're making it sound, it's about blood and convenience."

"For me and Saturnia. I think Wolf does genuinely feel something for you. At least right now. That worked out well for us. A flaw in the plan resulted in a better plan and avoided complete failure. It's why you have to be fluid, adaptable, in this business."

He lifted a shoulder, paused to make a change, and then kept going, his fingers always smoothly moving over the keys.

"Our planned target was Anwyn, because her attachment to Gideon is obvious. The hunters would blow up the alley, take out Wolf, so we didn't have to contend with him. I would conveniently hear about the tragedy, alert Allan, Fort and Saturnia. Because of the friendship between him and Wolf, Fort would have automatically reached out to Anwyn, offered the team's help. If necessary, I would have made the right suggestions to land us where we ended up, revamping security. Which would put me in the right position to set up Anwyn for capture the way I did Wolf."

"But Wolf...didn't die."

"No, he didn't." Hollow shrugged again. He might have been discussing chess strategy. "We thought we would have to cut our losses. Especially when we recognized that Anwyn had an active sire. We never met him, but Wolf made it clear there was another vampire bound to her. Which meant he could track her if she disappeared, regardless of our precautions. So another plan was needed.

"This time, it was the best one possible, better than the first, actually. Spending time in Atlantis, it was clear how much you'd come to mean to the heretofore 'lone Wolf.'" A strange smile crossed Hollow's face, as if he wasn't used to making jokes. "He's far too human, right now at least, to let you die. So we decided to realign our capture target to him."

Ella's mind was whirling. So much had been going on, all of it so undetectable to the security measures that had been stringent, even before the revamp. And Bill...Bill had been a guest of a member. The vetting would have still been there, but he said he'd been at the cover job a while. Just the same way Perry had been homeless.

She went back to her earlier angle. "What did you mean about Wolf...being far too human 'right now at least' to let me die?"

"Caught that, did you? You may not have drunk the Kool-Aid yet." He gave her a serious look as if the word choice was not meant as a joke, not even slightly. "Over time, they all relegate their human servants to a compartmentalized part of their lives. The inequities in their world make having too much emotion for them problematic."

She'd become Atlantis's most in demand submissive for her ability to listen and anticipate, and she did that by being genuinely interested in the Dom, connecting to what he or she wanted. Not just what they said they wanted, but what they felt beneath that. Sometimes, especially with the less experienced ones, she knew what experience and result they were seeking before they did.

She tuned out everything but Hollow. There was no Wolf, no Atlantis, no life or death situation. There was just her and Hollow, talking.

"You haven't really mentioned sex. Do you and Saturnia not..."

Hollow shrugged, apparently unfazed by the revelation that would make most men defensive. "Either one of us can perform upon demand. It's how we're trained. We become what we need to be."

"Why would you want her dead? Don't you love her?"

Hollow's jaw flexed, his fingers pausing on the keys as he stared at the screen without seeing it. "Love is just a social construct," he said.

Ella laughed, gaining a startled look from him. "Oh, ow, I shouldn't have done that." Her middle ached like fire. Since her arms were bound, all she could do to lessen it was press her chin to her chest, which did almost nothing. "Sorry, I shouldn't have laughed, but I mean, really? How can something that's affected so much of the world and so many people and decisions, be 'just a construct'? That doesn't make sense to me. That's the first time you've sounded defensive. You do love her, but love is unfamiliar and unknown. Uncontrollable."

Hollow stood up, took a drink from his water bottle. Pointed at her. "Being a good undercover agent is about becoming the role you're playing, so you're no longer playing. Everything you do is motivated by who you are, the ultimate goal only in the peripheral vision, almost out of the picture entirely, so it isn't detected by your target."

He put down the bottle and closed the screen on the laptop. When his gaze met hers, Ella's heart sank at the knowing look. "You would have made a good agent."

He moved for the door. "The techs will be coming in to do some diagnostics on you. Don't struggle; it will only waste time and make things worse. They've turned off the grid on Wolf for now, but they will turn it back on if needed to make you behave."

He stopped at the door, looking back at her. "None of this is personal, Ella. I know what you were trying to do, but you are human, and not completely under their control yet, so you deserve an answer. I was born detached from humans. Outside, looking in. The usual cliché for someone recruited to the CIA. But then, I learned about this vampire-servant relationship, all this overwhelming intimacy. We could be in one another's minds. The possibilities were overwhelming. And yet...Saturnia told me she would give me the privacy of my mind, would stay out of it unless we were in a clandestine situation. I told her it didn't bother me, but she said it bothered her."

He stared down at his hands. "This is the way she wanted it. Bad things happened to her, in our service. She needs four impenetrable walls in her mind. She comes to the safety of mine when the noise gets to be too much, but the only one inside her head is her."

A thoughtful look crossed his face. "I suppose you're right. I expected the ability to connect as vampire and servant would mean more to her. It didn't. That's when I understood. It really is just functional to them. Humans are always seeking connection, intimacy, even someone like me, after a fashion. Vampires have no humanity, and made ones leave it behind quickly. None of them are like us. They see themselves as superior, and I can't argue the logic of it. If a vampire dies, the servant dies. Not the other way around. So if push comes to shove, they will sacrifice the servant to spare their own skin. No point in both dying."

He raised his gaze to her. "Wolf's a vampire and yet, despite that, he thinks he loves you, Ella. Maybe he even told you that. You're this sweet, gentle little thing. It's understandable. Who wouldn't love you, want to protect you? But it's his arrogance that was his true undoing. He thought he could save you and still preserve his own life. His feelings for you, temporary though they are, contributed to that miscalculation."

He pursed his lips. "I had nothing that would inspire such tender, protective feelings from a lover. But to answer your question, yes. At the end of the day, you are just a servant to him. He will never put you before himself. You are the help, the buffet table, the sex object. But I guess someone like you is okay with that. You've accepted it, as the closest thing you'll get to what you truly want."

The door opened, a trio of masked scientists returning. Hollow moved past them, leaving the room without further instruction, telling her everyone knew what they were supposed to be doing. As they gathered around her prison, there was a low hum of excitement about them as they considered her and what questions they were going to ask her. Their talking among themselves added to her torment. They would record all of this, prove evidence of the vampire bond. How much had already been logged and transferred to the places that would spread the knowledge?

They'd used Wolf's feelings for her to trap him. Love between a vampire and a human would destroy an entire race.

"If you don't answer our questions, we turn the electricity back on," one of the women reminded her in a firm, no-nonsense tone.

"So?" Ella said in a subdued voice. "He just told me that Wolf's love is only temporary. That it will go away." She lifted her lashes. "You don't have to threaten me. I just want out of here. Can I at least sit at that table over there and have a soda or something?" She nodded toward it. "And clothes?"

"No clothes," one of the men said brusquely.

"Come on," she said plaintively. "I answer twenty of your bazillion questions, and you give me time at the table with a soda. And maybe some crackers. I know I can keep going forever and not die, but third marks still need food. Check with Hollow, see if he's okay with it, but please let me out of here for a couple minutes. It'd be nice to go to the bathroom."

"Non-negotiable," the other male said. She realized then that, at least for one of them, there was more to this than a scientist's detached fascination with the data to be learned. The gleam in his eye as he ran his gaze over her made her feel a little sick. He was enjoying the whole planet Gor dynamic, holding power over a naked female, binding her so she could hide nothing, have no dignity.

Yes, it made her feel sick, but it was something else that could be used. She filed that away. She might have just found her weak link.

The laptop Hollow had left on the counter beeped. The scientist leaned over, tapped it. "Yeah."

Hollow's voice came through the audio, sharp and clear. "She's playing you. Another hour of conditioning. When she comes out of it, she speaks only when asked a question. Any requests, any questions, any comments or conversation, except in response to what we're asking, and conditioning re-commences."

The scientists didn't like it. They were obviously impatient to start their questions, but they deferred to Hollow. Dread gathered in the pit of her belly, and fear. *No. No, no, no...*

She tried not to shrink away, but there was no use. The headphones were strapped back in place. Something else was said and responded to by the man at the keyboard, but she couldn't hear it. One of the women, still in the cage with her, squatted next to her, ran an impersonal finger over the mark on Ella's back. Ella wanted to spit at her and jerked away before she remembered she was supposed to be acting cooperative and docile. But she didn't want them touching that mark, tainting it with their evil.

Wolf...

But there was nothing. She suddenly realized why they were all in here, but he wasn't responding, despite the indications from the team that he wasn't being tortured. It must be past sunrise. The strain they'd put on Wolf would have depleted any energy reserves he had to stay awake to reach out to her. Oh, Goddess.

She was relieved he could get away from them for awhile, but she was terrified, because for the next few hours, she was truly alone.

The woman left the cage, and the wailing cries poured through the headphones again. But now there was a new horror to face. The male scientist, the tall one with the creepy eyes, took off his lab coat and rolled up his sleeves. He spoke a word to the others, and they left. To her credit, one of the women hung back a second, gave him a hard look, said something, and he shrugged her off, pointed to the computer as if to say, "Holliman ordered it."

All while people in torment screamed in her head, as if she was in the midst of hell. And she guessed she was. The scientist calmly fished in a supply cabinet and came back out with a jar of oil.

When she'd been a prostitute, there'd been nights she hadn't been in the mood to work but, as she'd told Wolf, she'd needed to eat more. She'd made it work. Hollow had made his first serious mistake if he thought a guy shoving his dick inside her without her enthusiastic endorsement was something that would traumatize her, help her "conditioning" move along faster. The only thing she felt when she saw what the Gor guy intended was relief that he'd decided to use lubricant. She preferred that to him trying to arouse her, turning her body against her the way Hollow did.

But she made her expression appropriately pleading, shaking her head as he came toward her. Though he tried to look "professional," she knew the signs. He was getting off on her powerlessness.

All she had to do was find her moment. Send a one-word text to her phone. It became the goal of all goals, and she held it to her when her cell door opened.

She thought of Wolf. For the next few hours, she had to figure out ways to help them both. But oh, Goddess, she missed hearing him in her head. If she could have meditated, maybe she could find that thread of connection between them, even when he was sleeping. She would wrap it around her like ropes during a suspension session, let it keep her spinning above all this.

But now all she heard was screaming.

CHAPTER THIRTY-ONE

Twice more she went through "conditioning." She cried, vomited, passed out, was brought back with buckets of ice water. The scientists came and went, but for most of them it was too much. They eventually left and stayed gone, indicating they would only be present for the actual "scientific" part of things.

But her Gor-fan and the cold-eyed woman scientist persevered. The woman checked her phone a lot, sending texts back and forth with the other team members.

So Ella had her target. If she could hold onto enough of her mind to get an opportunity to strike.

This latest time, she'd fallen forward, slumped over. She was slick with sweat, and she'd soiled herself.

"We need to hose her down," the woman said. "Fuck, I'm tired of this mask."

"Take it off," the male said. "It's not to protect our identities."

"Holliman said it was important for the conditioning." Though she sounded edgy about that.

They'd moved inside the cell. She mumbled something, her head down.

"Now, now, be quiet," the woman said, almost kindly. "Speak only if spoken to. We've wasted enough time waiting on you not to be stubborn or deceptive. I think Holliman's being a little overly paranoid." That to the other scientist. "She's barely more than a child. That's what's making the others so uncomfortable with all this."

She unlatched the wrist restraints while the other scientist squatted to distastefully unlatch her ankles, since the chair was in a pool of her own waste. Ella whimpered, shrank back.

"It's okay," the woman said in her authoritative voice. "If you cooperate with us from here forward, there's no reason for any other conditioning. Hell, hold on. Got her?"

"Yeah. She's out of it."

The woman's pocket had vibrated. Now she withdrew the phone, tapped in the password and viewed the text. "They've downloaded some interesting results on his bloodwork. We'll take a look at it in a minute."

She pocketed the phone and bent to Ella again. "Remember what I said. Cooperate, and no more pain."

Goddess help her, it almost swayed Ella from her course. Because what she was about to do would start it all over again. She couldn't bear it. She couldn't.

Then she thought of Wolf, the things they might do to him or had done. She'd thought he'd get a respite at sunrise, but what if they'd figured out a way to torment him, even during daylight?

She put aside everything else. She moaned a little as the woman started to help her up. She concentrated on making her every movement docile, submissive, disoriented. The laptop started beeping, and she vaguely saw a bubble onscreen, a message.

"He's warning us to be careful," Gor-scientist said. "Said she might not be as out of it as she seems. The third mark, even with the conditioning, still makes her dangerous."

"Good God," the woman snapped. "She's barely moving on her own. She's lost control of her bladder and bowels. We'll be lucky if we can get any useful data out of her today."

"We've acquired some proof from simple observation. Her eardrums should have ruptured from the headphone treatment. We also should have seen far more physical neurological degradation from the conditioning thus far. I think it's best that we take his advice. Let's cuff her to her cage bars while we clean her up, clean the cell. We need to bring more support staff here. I'm not a damn janitor."

"We can't bring in lower level staff until we get the data we need.

We have to prove these aren't delusional humans pretending to be vampires. Here, turn her, I'm losing my grip. Ah shit, I don't want her leaning against me. She's filthy."

Ella stumbled against her, almost went to her knees. Then she wrapped her arms around the woman and bulled forward, slamming them both into the cage door. She rolled to the ground outside it, hitting the counter that held the computer. It teetered and fell on them, striking Ella on the back. She punched at the woman, screaming, and then stumbled to her feet, throwing herself at the male.

He'd been right about one thing. She was like a floundering fish, but the added strength the marks gave her meant she managed to land a pretty solid hit to his face, busting his lip below the rat mask. If the mask hadn't been rubber, she would have broken it, revealed his face fully. Instead, he grabbed her, threw her toward the cage door. She caught the frame, launched herself forward and tried to scramble past him, but he shoved her back once more. She tripped over her own feet, landing inside, then screamed in frustration when he slammed the door.

"Christ, Robert," the woman swore.

"It's fine. She's back in."

Ella had scrambled to the back corner, her eyes wild and angry upon them, her lip curled in a snarl, knees pulled to her chest.

"Damn, Syd, he was right." Robert rubbed the back of his hand on his bloody lips and glanced at himself. "Fuck. C'mon. Let's go over here to the bathroom. I'll stand in the doorway and keep watch on her while you clean up, then we can swap and you do the same."

They moved to do that. Robert stood at the threshold and kept glancing at Ella, as he'd said. However, as she kept rocking, her head down, he would look back at the other scientist for a longer stretch of time. The computer was on the ground, but she didn't discount the possibility there were other cameras focused on her, the same way they were watching Wolf. So Ella turned away, curled in a fetal ball, but sitting up, her forehead pressed to the bars, one arm up against her face, hiding it, with the other curled protectively in toward her chest.

A position that allowed her to cup the woman's cell phone close against her chest, unseen by anyone else. The password screen came up, and she typed the four-number code the woman had been close enough to reveal to Ella, several times. She prayed she'd seen it right.

She had. Slowly, so slowly, not wanting to reveal anything suspicious about her movements, she entered her phone number, and then the one-word text.

Holliman.

Send.

She shuddered, said a mindless prayer that someone had her phone, that it was in Anwyn's hand, or Gideon's. Chantal knew her password, as did Lars.

She had her arms folded before herself, her head down and body cringing against those back bars. It was a good clamshell position which gave her the ability to hold the phone between both her concealed hands. She thanked all the powers that be for the third mark strength, depleted though it was, that allowed her to twist the phone in her hand, break it, so the woman wouldn't be able to check her texts.

Now to the rest of it. She actually was hurting everywhere, so it wasn't too much of an act to crawl forward in a hunching, halting manner, holding her ribs. When she reached the cage door, she had the device under her as she sat on the ground and grasped the bars.

"Let me out of here," she said. Then she screamed it, shaking the bars back and forth. As she moved so violently, she shifted her feet, sent the phone spinning across the floor so it ended up under the counter, beside the upended computer.

With any luck, anyone viewing the cameras had been focused on her behavior, not the phone. They would think it had been lying next to the computer the whole time, thrown there during the scuffle. Or they would think the phone had been lying next to the bars and Ella had sent it spinning away with her actions, oblivious to its presence because of her wild state of mind.

Robert returned. He kicked at the bars, sending her scrambling back to the chair. She wanted to glare at him, but she'd just used up the last energy she had. She'd done what she could think of right now, and she had to hope...to hope...

She laid her head against the frame of chair. I *can't do anymore right now. Oh, Goddess, I can't bear anymore. I'm going to answer their questions. I don't know if that's the right thing.*

They put her through another "conditioning." This time they added electric shock, running it through the chair where they bound her again. However, when the Gor scientist tried to take her again—after they cleaned her up of course—she spit in his face. He hit her several times, until her lip and nose bled, and she dropped her head back, dazed, while he did what he wanted to do.

She wanted to tune out. Needed to tune out. When she phased in again, Hollow was back. He brought a new laptop, telling her the other had been damaged.

"Nighttime at last, Ella," he said absently. He spoke as if they were just at the club, her cleaning the bar area while he worked on the computer systems, rather than her naked, bleeding, half out of her mind, him the director of her torment.

"Wolf is a tougher bastard than I gave him credit for," he continued. "We took him to a second-floor room with windows. We kept him out of the direct sunlight, but it's hell for a vampire his age to be that far above ground during daylight."

"You're a monster," she said hoarsely.

He shot her a puzzled look. "Not at all. A monster tortures for the pleasure of it. All of this serves a purpose. They had to do the tests they needed to prove what you and I already know about him."

He shot Ella a look, as if they were actually sharing a moment of commiseration. "Every time he passed out, we brought him back with the right level of stimulation, but he passed out a lot less than I expected."

She was supposed to make Hollow think she was doubting hers and Wolf's bond. If the text didn't work, they had to have a plan B. But she was so tired, her body so battered, and now her heart cried out, wondering if that was why she hadn't heard Wolf's voice in her mind. How far past sundown was it? He was alive, but in what condition?

Wolf, I'm here. I'm okay. Even though she wasn't. But she wanted him to know... *I sent a text to my phone. I left it at the club. It might get found.*

Or it might not. She closed her eyes as the tapping of Hollow's fingers on the keys continued on. She was beginning to hate that sound, a symbol of his horrific apathy.

Syd came back in. "Can we finally question her now?"

Hollow looked at Ella, his gaze steady. Soulless. "Ella, are you ready to answer questions? Or should we continue on the course we've been on? The choice is yours, of course."

So reasonable, so calm. He could do this endlessly, because he knew there would be an end.

Yes, she would answer questions. She would. She couldn't handle anymore.

But then, she thought of this moment and what later moments would look like. If there was a good end to all this, but she had to face her weakness, her capitulation, and how it might have hurt those she cared about. Wolf, Anwyn. Gideon. Could she live with that? Anything was better than this moment, right?

She knew better.

"I—"

The building rumbled, a low roar like a distant animal. The light fixtures vibrated.

Gor-guy's face came popping up in the corner of Hollow's screen. "We have a breach. We—"

The screen went dark and Hollow surged up from his seat, slapping the laptop closed. "They've found us. Initiate burn protocol. Get out."

"The test subjects." Syd gestured toward Ella.

"Leave them. Fire will kill them both. There's..."

Hollow stopped abruptly, mid-sentence. His gaze slid to Ella, slow, painfully. "What..." His lips formed the word, but no sound came out.

Syd didn't notice. She'd already started rushing around when Hollow issued the order. They'd been prepared for this eventuality, lighter fluid and other quick burn materials tucked under the counter. She stuffed the tinder in strategic places, not in a random way. She knew what she was doing. Their own weird form of fire drill, Ella realized, as terror flooded her.

Not fire. Please not fire. Ella was still strapped to the chair, in her cage. She couldn't handle it, seeing the flame close in around her.

Even knowing they'd pay no more attention to her distress than before, fear compelled her to cry out. "Please, don't leave me here. Please."

Syd barely gave her or Hollow a glance as she lit the materials in the corner. As flame shot up quickly, she was already striding from the room. "I'll meet you at the rendezvous, Holliman."

Hollow didn't acknowledge her. He had his eyes locked on Ella, but he didn't see her. He put his hands in front of him as if he couldn't see anything. He turned, stumbled into the table, crashed to his knees in a shower of papers and equipment. He put his hands to his head and started to moan.

"Help me," Ella said desperately. "Please, *help me*."

The flames were licking along the countertops, the papers on the floor, now moving up along the walls. Coming closer. Way too fast. Hollow paid no attention, though he was right in the path of the oncoming flames.

Fire. She was back inside a house of fire. There was no one to be brave for, no way out. She couldn't get loose from the chair, out of the cage. The utter helplessness of it, in the face of what was bearing down on her, had her heart thundering in her chest so painfully, as if the fear would make it explode.

Screaming filled her head, filled her mind, the pain and terror taking her over. The screams were hers. She was pulling against her bonds, not caring that muscles were tearing, the cuffs becoming like wire, digging into flesh and making her bleed. Then one voice thundered in her head, overpowering and silencing all the others.

Ella. I'm here. I'm coming. You're not alone, little girl.

A sob burst from her. For a moment, she was sure she was manufacturing him in her head to give herself a futile scrap of comfort. Except nothing could imitate the stern timbre of her Master's voice when he was commanding her. When it was vibrating with a rage and urgency that told her if anyone could get to her in time, it was him.

Hollow crashed against the side of her cage, startling her. She'd forgotten about him entirely. Blood was coming from his mouth... from his eyes? He was scratching his face, digging, as if trying to claw something out of his head. He was howling. All the helplessness and terror Ella was feeling about the element rushing down on her; Hollow seemed to be facing that inside himself.

Then a shadow moved behind him, distorted through the flames, a giant hawk, with great wide, flapping wings.

Wolf burst through the tongues of fire, the wet blanket he was wearing swirling around his shoulders. He kicked Hollow out of his way as if he was trash on the floor, gripped the cage door, and that was the end of that. It burst off its hinges as he ripped it loose, tossed it aside. Then he was in the cell with her, tearing off her restraints so quickly, she couldn't follow it. He was there, and she was free.

To stave off her terror at the encroaching flames, her Master knew exactly what thought to give her. The hope she'd clung to as a child, wanting to be saved from the fire.

Daddy's here.

She wrapped her shaking arms around his neck as he lifted her, held her curled up in his arms. He swathed her in that wet blanket. As he did, she glimpsed someone else at the door to the lab. Saturnia.

The flame wreathed her, but the female vampire didn't seem to notice. Her face was terrible to look upon, her eyes fastened on her servant, writhing on the floor.

Whatever was happening to Hollow, it was Saturnia doing it, destroying his mind from the inside out, tearing into his soul like he'd torn at his flesh, trying to get her out of his head, but he couldn't. He had no eyes left, huge gouges in his face, and he was still screeching. Saturnia's face was as terrifyingly expressionless now as his had been while torturing Ella.

"A vampire who third marks you could strip your mind, your soul. Hollow you out if he or she wanted to do so."

Gideon's words echoed in her head. Hollow's nickname had become prophetic.

Wolf passed Saturnia, shouted something. The female vampire gave him a bare nod. Unexpectedly, she put her hand on Ella, a gesture of reassurance, or even brief affection. Somehow, she had Ella's purse, the little beaded one Ella liked so much. Saturnia pressed it into Ella's hands, then stepped out of the way so Wolf could pass.

Wolf took them through several rooms, then doubled back with a curse when he encountered a wall of fire. Ella saw it, ducked her face back against his chest. Her head was mostly buried in the blanket, because he had his hand cupped over her skull to keep her that way, but she felt the heat. He forced the lock on one door and suddenly they were in a dark, quiet space, cooler. They were out of it for the moment. A maintenance closet, she realized.

He set her down on a worktable, and cupped her chin. His fingers gently caressed the bruises and cuts where she'd been struck. His eyes blazed like an angel of death's, but his voice was her Master's, at his most tender. "Ella," he murmured.

It almost broke her, to hear him say her name. She was crying again, her hands over his, as she pressed her mouth to his knuckles, his wrists and then his face. He found her lips with his own and kissed her, deep, strong, like a current moving through her, carrying her away from this, even though they were still in it. He pulled back too soon.

When he looked up, she followed his gaze. There was an air conditioning panel above them.

"This building is an old community college," he spoke brusquely. "Abandoned when a newer structure was built. We were in the basement interior rooms, outfitted as a temporary laboratory. We're on the third floor now, top level. I'll get you to a room with an outer wall and windows. You'll be able to get out. We've got reinforcements outside."

"I'm not leaving you," she said, her fingers curling over his. "Not ever again, not for any reason. But particularly not now."

The cold death in his eyes warmed slightly, and his thumb caressed her lips. "My brave girl. Ella, I can get through the fire on my own. I promise. Especially if I know there's someone out there who can give me blood to heal my injuries. But I move faster if I get you out first."

She stared up at him. "Are you lying to me, to protect me?"

"No." *I intend to be holding you again as soon as possible, demanding everything from my servant.*

He opened his mind to her so she could see, understanding she needed to be sure. A whole lot swirled around in there, but she saw his intent was true.

Which just left her childish fear of being away from him again, so soon after having the security of his arms.

That infused even more warmth into his eyes, into the firm touch on her chin. She could do this. It would help both of them. Her Master was telling her what she needed to do.

She blinked, looking down at her beaded purse. A thought hit her, and she dug into it, found what she was seeking. She quelled a hysterical laugh. Wolf looked down as she withdrew the piece of dark chocolate she usually kept in there for when she needed an emotional pick-me-up. Carefully she opened the silver wrapper, spreading it out in the center of her palm, since the contents were a little melted, no surprise. She lifted it toward him.

"Would you like half? If we die, it might be our last chance to have chocolate."

He gazed at her, his expression unfathomable, yet just as mesmerizing to her as it always was. She expected if he kept looking at her like that, she wouldn't mind sitting here until the flames arrived. Theoretically.

He gripped the wrist of the hand that had opened the candy. She'd gotten chocolate on her fingertips, and that was how he chose to sample it, licking the melted part off her flesh. She curled her fingers over his face, caressing any part she could reach as he did it. Then he lifted her palm, cupping his hand under it, encouraging her to take the rest.

"Right then." She let the sweetness melt on her tongue, and put the now empty wrapper back in her purse. When she slid off the table, she was much weaker than she'd realized, but she managed, with his help. He gripped her shoulders.

"The fire is moving quickly. You're going to have to pass over some rooms already on fire, so things might get hot in places, smoky. Don't stop, don't overthink it. Keep moving."

He lifted her onto his shoulders, and she reached up without prompting, removing the vented ceiling panel and tossing it to the table she'd just vacated.

"Here you go." He hoisted her up so she could scramble into the ducts. Crap, it was close quarters. She was on her stomach, the space just wide and tall enough for her to wriggle through, but not turn around. Which meant she had no excuse not to get a move on, particularly with Wolf encouraging her in her head. No time for good-byes.

No good-byes necessary, little girl. Move your ass.

If you were lying to me about you being able to get out of here, I will be so mad at you.

She was okay at first, moving forward, taking a dog leg when he told her to turn, keeping going, trying not to look at the array of dead bugs, the occasional mouse carcass. Then the metal started to heat, and she realized the darkness had a smokiness to it. Dim, flickering light came through the vent opening just ahead, telling her the room below was on fire. She recoiled as sparks abruptly speared up through the grate.

Go. The barked order in her head was fierce enough to launch her past her fear. She scuttled forward, trying not to feel the heat burning her knees. Sparks swirled over her hands. Everything in her wanted to freeze, balk.

Keep moving, or I swear to God, you won't sit for a month.

She knew what he was doing, but it didn't matter. He meant it, even if he had to follow her to the afterlife to deliver the punishment. She'd never felt so reassured and terrified at the same time. She kept moving. It seemed to take forever, though she was sure it hadn't been more than a few minutes before she reached a slatted vent that looked down into an empty room with no fire. The smoke here was like a white, acrid mist.

You're at the outer wall. That room should have a window. Kick the vent loose, drop down and get out of the building.

Though Wolf said the building was abandoned, Hollow and the others must have used the below as a makeshift office. There was a desk within her view with some printouts on it, a scattering of office supplies. It made sense, if Hollow had set this up weeks ago.

The desk wasn't close enough to help her get to the floor, so she just lowered herself out of the vent and let go, awkwardly. She landed on her feet, but one knee buckled and she went down, rolling across the floor.

Her grunt of pain choked in her throat as she came to a stop in front of a pair of feet.

Her gaze flew upward and met a pair of eyes she wasn't likely ever to forget, even if they had a look of startled surprise in them.

Gor-guy, or Robert, wasn't wearing the rat mask anymore. He had an attractive face, but it was one that would never be appealing to her, because she saw the monster moving under the flesh. The last time he'd violated her, he'd put his other hand down, driven his fingers into her with his cock, wanting to hurt her, wanting to see pain on her face.

He bent down, grabbing for her.

She rolled away and kicked out, striking his knee. She was barefoot and no martial artist, so she couldn't break it, but she did have enough strength to set him off balance and let her scramble away, turning the mist of smoke into chaotic whorls around her.

She could feel the heat increasing, knew the floor beneath them had to be engulfed. This one would go soon. She could hear something in her head, a distant voice. Wolf, ordering her to get away, break the window, jump. She would.

I will, I promise. In a minute.

Robert had been like all the rest. Willing to leave her and Wolf to die.

Her mind was going a hundred miles a minute and slow like a turtle at the same time. She was terrified, and yet there was an adrenaline surging through her veins, hot and fast, that she recognized.

Fury. She let it loose, because it vanquished the terror and told her she had something to fight.

She made it to her feet, looked around wildly. As Gor-guy rushed her, she'd found what she wanted. He seized her arm and she whipped around in his grasp, using his brutal hold to add to her momentum. She screamed something, she didn't know what. It didn't matter. It was just a focus for the rage. She jammed the sharp end of the letter opener she'd clutched from the desk into his abdomen, up under his rib cage, and twisted.

He howled, trying to push away from her. She followed him down as he fell back against the desk. He shoved at her, trying to get away. He was afraid, and the fear in his eyes delighted the darkest part of her soul. She was still screaming her rage. Wolf's voice had gone silent, or maybe it was just lost in all the rest. She wanted Hollow to have *this* scream on his fucking tape. Her scream of defiance, a primal sound that translated into one message.

You will not fuck with me and the people I love.

She had him down, his blood on her hands, and suddenly the wall crumbled. A roar, and a wall of fire replaced it, an avalanche of flame.

The heat rolled toward her, sure death. In that half blink of time while the scientist died beneath her, and she clutched the letter opener in her hand, rage was swallowed whole by terror. She was being consigned to the flames with her family. It had just taken Fate a while to catch back up to her. She even saw a dark angel in the fire, black wings spread, fathomless eyes focused on her, hand outstretched. Ready to take her.

She was jerked off Robert's body, tucked against a strong torso she knew. A dark angel in truth. Her Master. As the flames enveloped her and Wolf, she closed her eyes and pressed her face to his chest. At least she wouldn't die alone.

We're not dying at all. Hold on.

He had his large hand covering her skull, pressing her face to his chest, as he leaped through the window.

CHAPTER THIRTY-TWO

Glass shattered, spinning Gideon around. The fire had already broken through the first and second level windows, but it wasn't only the bursts of heat and flame shattering the glass this time. A large form hurtled out into space.

Gideon broke into a run, Fort and Allan close on his heels.

Wolf landed heavily. He did nothing to cushion his fall, and the reason was evident as soon as they were close enough to see who he was curved around so protectively. Gideon saw blood and burns. The vampire's skin was a torn, bloody mess, but not as bad as the day he'd been blown up. Didn't mean Gideon's heart wasn't in his throat, because he didn't yet know Ella's condition.

He and Fort coaxed the disoriented male to loosen his hold. Allan jerked Gideon back as a sharp blade whipped through the air a hair away from his nose. Ella stumbled to her feet, gripping a letter opener that appeared to be covered with blood. Her eyes were wild, and she was screaming something at him he couldn't understand, though her voice was so hoarse and broken that it was barely more than a whisper over the roar of the burning building.

Before any of them could decide how to disarm her the gentlest way possible, Wolf pushed his upper body from the ground, a large hand closing over her wrist. As she collapsed to her knees, he spoke to her, head bent over hers when he gathered her into the shelter of his body. She trembled, and then the letter opener dropped. Allan smoothly moved it out of reach, but all was good. Ella had started to cry, and Wolf was holding her close. Neither one of them was wearing a stitch of clothing. Gideon suspected most the damage he saw on both of them hadn't had a thing to do with the fire. Which made him hope fervently those responsible were burning alive in there, in agony.

But the important thing was they were both alive.

They're all right, Anwyn. We have them.

She hadn't been pleased—a major understatement—when Daegan had said she needed to stay behind. She was so worried about Ella and Wolf, she hadn't been diplomatic in the least about her going, so in the end Daegan had to be brutally blunt.

"We are going into a combat situation, cher. What happens if you have a seizure that makes you vulnerable at the wrong time—which, since they are triggered by excess stress, is possible—and endangers the very ones we're trying to help, because we must focus on you?"

Gideon was her servant. He could get bullish and protective with her, too, but with her being a vampire, sometimes Daegan had to be the one to step in and put his foot down. Though Gideon knew he didn't like doing it, Daegan never turned away from moments when he had to be the bad guy and lay down the law as head of their unorthodox household. Particularly when Anwyn's wellbeing was on the line.

As a vampire and a Mistress, Anwyn didn't always capitulate gracefully. Fortunately, two things had helped it not evolve into an even uglier fight. First was the pressing need to go save Wolf and Ella, every minute vital. The second was the arrival of someone who agreed to stay with Anwyn, thereby reinforcing the confidence that Daegan, Fort, Allan, Saturnia and Gideon would get the job done.

Good. Anwyn replied at last. Gideon expected she'd taken a moment to draw a relieved breath, same as he had when he'd seen Ella alive. *Is Daegan with you?*

No. He's taking care of Holliman's team. And making sure Saturnia gets Holliman out.

Which had been done, because as he and Fort helped Wolf and Ella to the front of the building, Allan following behind, Gideon saw Holliman lying on the broken asphalt of the parking lot. Saturnia was standing over him. She appeared to be watching the building burn, but the unnatural stillness of her body told Gideon she was actually deep in her servant's head, mining every bit of data she would need to determine just how much he'd compromised the vampire world. Holliman was in a fetal ball, rocking, while the female vampire stood a couple feet away, seemingly indifferent to his distress. Gideon found himself glad he couldn't see the guy's face as his Mistress stripped what she needed out of every corner of his being.

They'd reached one of the vehicles. As Gideon opened the second seat doors of the SUV, a terrified cry brought all four males around as one, a quartet of hypervigilance.

A woman stumbled out from the hedges on the other side of the building. She must have gotten out through the back and just now worked her way to the parking lot, where all the vehicles were parked, including those that had belonged to Holliman and his minions.

Her black slacks and pink blouse were torn and burned, her hair mostly gone. As she fell to her hands and knees, coughing, Allan started forward. Gideon put out a hand, stopping him.

Out of the smoke billowing behind the woman came a tall, dark figure. He had his katana held out to his side in the ready position, which told Gideon he'd been using it. However, as Gideon watched, Daegan sheathed the now clean blade.

Allan shot Gideon a sidelong glance. "What—"

"He won't soil the blade with the blood of someone who isn't a warrior," Gideon said quietly. "Not if he can help it. That's what he carries other weapons for."

One part of Gideon's mind had things to say about what was about to happen. This was a human woman, not a vampire. But then Gideon thought again of Ella. Naked, wounded, that crazy light in her eyes. He pressed his lips together and didn't look away. Daegan would know if he did. He knew Anwyn watched through his eyes for the very same reason. Daegan would never ask them to look, never say a word if they didn't. They looked so he knew they accepted everything he was.

Daegan bent, put a hand on the woman's back. He lifted her up onto her knees, firm, not unkind. Gideon felt the tightness in his chest, a quick hitch in his breath. In that space of time, it was done. Daegan broke her neck.

The movies made it look so easy, a run-of-the-mill action hero move, but in the real world it was very difficult to break the cerebral vertebrae. But the strength in Daegan's hands made snapping that column of bones away from the skull, severing the spine's connection to the brain stem, as simple as a hawk doing it to a pigeon.

The woman slumped. He'd done it so smoothly, Gideon didn't see a flash of fear in her eyes. She likely deserved to feel a whole lot of fear, but Daegan didn't let his emotions factor into his kills. Not usually. His job was execution, not punishment.

He picked her up, carried her to one of the broken windows, and tossed the corpse back into the flames. Then he was striding in their direction, his expression hard to read. But not his mind.

"We've got to get them out of here," Fort said, drawing Gideon's attention. "This place is surrounded by forest and farmland, but even in the dead of night, it won't be long before someone nearby smells the smoke and calls the fire department to get it checked out."

Wolf had already tucked Ella into the vehicle, and now Fort gave him a helping hand to duck in after her. He'd pulled a couple blankets from the back, part of the first aid supplies they'd assembled, and Wolf wrapped them around him and Ella.

Fort went to the driver's seat and Gideon took shotgun, watching as Daegan stopped beside Saturnia. He would stand guard over her, take her and Holliman wherever was necessary in his vehicle.

As Fort backed the SUV, Gideon heard Daegan's message to Anwyn, since the vampire assassin shared it with them both.

It's done. Everyone involved in Wolf and Ella's capture at this facility has been dispatched. With the exception of Holliman, who Saturnia has effectively neutralized. She will terminate him once she determines how much further this goes outside these walls.

Gideon focused on Daegan, silhouetted by the flames, as long as he could, before Fort turned the vehicle onto the main road. Then he brought his attention back to Wolf and Ella. Ella was slumped and curved into her Master's body, his arms wrapped around her as if they were one melded creature. Allan was in the third row seat, watching their backs.

Gideon let out another steadying breath, met Fort's gaze. The vampire gave him a satisfied, grim nod. The most immediate concern was handled.

The next steps would depend on what the bastard had done.

Daegan's message had not been only for Anwyn. It had also been a relay to the vampire with her.

Lady Lyssa, the head of the Vampire Council, last royal member of the Far East clan, was waiting for them at Club Atlantis.

CHAPTER THIRTY-THREE

Wolf held Ella in his arms for the whole car trip to Atlantis. She held him back as much as she could, thinking he might need it, until he spoke in her head, a soothing caress.

Let me take care of you, Ella. For once, I don't want you to think about what you need to do for me, or anyone else. That's an order from your Master.

She couldn't think of a time he hadn't taken care of her, but she understood what he was saying. After not being able to get to her, stop what was being done to her, the ability to hold her, protect her, care for her, would give him back the balance he needed. By letting him do that, she was helping.

While her thought process didn't reflect full compliance with what he'd ordered, it was as close to it as she could get, since she hadn't been able to get to him, help him, either. If she closed her eyes, she saw him being electrocuted relentlessly, heard the strangled anguish in his voice over those headphones. She was glad they'd burned up in the fire. But now that her mind had turned in that direction, she couldn't shut it off. She couldn't hear anything else but that discordant symphony of screams. It was making her lose her mind more than a bit.

"Sing, little girl," Wolf, murmured. "Like on Burlesque Night. Sing me a song."

Since her mind didn't have any room to think of another song, she sang that same one to him, albeit in halting, broken tones where she drifted in and out of speech and sang it to him in her head. *Bound to you... I am bound to you...*

At some point, she wasn't singing the song, but chanting the words, as if the simple truth would hold her to him, keep her from being sucked into the nightmare of fire and pain.

"It's all right," he murmured, holding her closer. She was sobbing, shivering. "I've got you. We're all right. We're okay. The fire can't have you, Ella. It knows you're mine."

"Blood," she whispered, tipping her head back to look at him, even as she lifted her arm, her hand dropped back to fully expose the tender underside of her wrist. *Please...drink. I need to feel you gaining strength from me. You'll take care of me, I know it. Please take what I'm offering. Let me feel what I am to you...*

He didn't want to make her weaker, but the plea in her voice, the way she was struggling to hold her arm up, told Wolf this was a request that went beyond her compulsive need to care for him. She wanted, needed the reminder of what she was to him.

Everything.

She might not phrase it that way, but he would. He gripped her wrist, lifted it to his mouth. He closed his eyes as her other hand lifted, rested on his head, his nape, and he remembered the night she'd asked permission to do that. He'd granted it, as long as she could bear the pain he'd inflicted on her. She'd struggled through it beautifully, arousing him with that intense, tightly-coiled anticipation that told him he was going to have that beautiful, intriguing sub, fuck her deep, feel the grip of her sweet little pussy around his cock, hear her cries and gasps as he took her over the edge.

It had been mostly physical that night, but with the deeper emotions fully realized, he couldn't see it any way but how he felt it now. He wanted to be inside her with the same urgent need she wanted him to take his blood, their wounds and dirt notwithstanding. But he knew how to exercise control. And take sips of what he knew he was going to consume like the last water on earth, as soon as the time was right.

He put his mouth on her wrist, registered the beat of the pulse. He rubbed his temple against her hand, felt her fingers curl against his bare scalp. "Count to five for me," he murmured.

She made it to three and he bit, when she'd settled into the count and wasn't expecting it. She drew in a breath, rocked against him, her fingers tightening against his skull. Tears seeped out of the corners of her eyes as she mouthed "Thank you," to him.

He had to put a tight rein on himself, because they'd given him no blood, while doing their best to prove nothing could kill him but a stake through the heart. His body was screaming for full strength, vitality. While logically he knew once he reached that goal he could give her the same, by the same method, he didn't like seeing her so weary while he took from her.

Yet he was also in her heart. When he took what she freely offered, needed him to take, he was nourishing and strengthening her soul, in a way just as vital as healing her body.

So he drank, felt her fingers slide over his head and nape, making caressing circles and figure eights. She was still humming the song, sometimes saying a word or two of it.

Even though the vehicle was populated by those he trusted, his sense of danger was still elevated to the point he became aware of a thread of tension—directed toward him.

In the front seat, Gideon was watching him. He had his back propped against the car door, providing him an angle where he didn't have his back to anyone. Wolf knew it was mainly to help Allan, sitting behind Wolf, keep tabs on him and Ella, in case they needed anything. Neither he nor Allan could be seen in a rearview mirror. However, like many warriors, Gideon rarely chose to have a blind spot in his visual radius.

Wolf had no problem with the keeping tabs thing. Gideon loved Ella with a big brother protectiveness. However, after being through what he'd just been through with her, the dark, savage soul of a predator was too close to the surface. Gideon's obvious concern about him drinking from Ella when she was wounded and weak triggered it in the blink it took Wolf to notice it.

Wolf withdrew from Ella's throat, but left his fangs unsheathed. A hissing growl rumbled from his throat. Fort glanced back, at the same moment Gideon's expression hardened. The senior vampire spoke a low, firm word to Anwyn's servant.

"Don't."

Wolf issued his own warning in the same breath.

"Back off."

Ella's eyes were half slits, her body loose in his arms now. She was no longer trembling with pain. Her mind drifted inside his with soft images, quiet things that soothed him as much as her blood nourished him. Only that kept him from lunging over the seat at Gideon, and even that bond was tentative. Especially when Gideon's body language remained stiff, his jaw tight. Fuck, the man had a death wish.

"Get him out of the car," Wolf said. "Now."

He had no idea where they were, but it didn't matter. It was a warning, not a threat. Gideon's reaction to being challenged over the protection he felt Ella needed was goading Wolf to dangerous levels.

Allan brought the SUV to a halt. Fort spoke a quiet word to Gideon. Gideon shook off his hand, his gaze fastened to Wolf's, still challenging. The bloodlust bloomed red hot, and a shudder ran through Wolf's limbs, a preparation to attack, tear, rend anything that tried to get between him and Ella. And feed on the interloper's gloriously hot, pumping fresh blood.

The SUV door opened, and Gideon left the car, somewhat forcefully. Wolf was aware that someone had jerked him out of the vehicle, slammed the door and then tapped the roof, a non-verbal cue to get going.

He knew it had to be Daegan, who had been following not far behind in a van carrying Saturnia and Hollow. Wolf would let him explain to Gideon the finer points of not interfering between a vampire and a servant, before Gideon got his throat ripped out.

Ella was moving, her hand cupping his jaw, fingertips sliding along his throat, a vampire's most erogenous zone. She made a noise, almost soothing. Even as weak and out of it as she was, she was picking up on his agitation, offering calm.

Wolf closed his hand around her fragile wrist and dipped his head. This time he bit her neck, though not to drink or break skin. Just to hold her, tell her she was his.

A shudder went through her, a soft exhalation of breath. She fumbled, urgent, found his hand, and put it between her legs, beneath the blanket wrapped around them. Christ. He laid his other hand alongside her face, and she pressed into that touch. Her lips parted, latching onto his thumb like a horse's bit, using it to hold back her whimpers as her cunt spasmed against his hand.

A small rippling only, given how weak her body was, but she'd climaxed, just the way she had when he bit her on the dance floor. Odd as it sounded, it wasn't exactly sexual. It was an emotional response, one that overwhelmed him, her reaction to him, even now, wounded and exhausted.

Sweet, sweet, girl. All mine. He savored her blood, the strength and vitality it brought to his body, and held her close again. He was suddenly impatient to reach their destination, where he could turn his full attention to restoring her fully—body, heart, mind and soul.

~

"Get off me," Gideon snapped, throwing off Daegan's touch. When Daegan complied, he knew it was because that was Daegan's decision, since the vampire had about fifty times Gideon's strength. He threw a punch at him anyway, which Daegan sidestepped and caught, twisting his arm and shoving him away. Gideon whirled on him again, fists clenched, but he'd found enough control to stop there.

Daegan stood, silent and dark in his black clothes, with the katana sheathed, and his other weapons hidden. Except his eyes, which were a lethal weapon by themselves. The van engine was running. Gideon couldn't see Saturnia or Hollow through the dark windows, but knew they had to be riding in the back.

"Fuck." Gideon paced in a circle. "He's drinking her blood after she just went through all that. What's he thinking?"

"He will be able to use his blood to strengthen her once he is strong. He can protect her better if he's strong."

"Able to read his fucking mind?"

"No. It is what a warrior would do. Plus, Ella needs service to feel centered. He is giving her that as well. Think, Gideon. I could see through your eyes what you refused to see. She wanted to give her Master strength. It is what servants do, when their vampire Master or Mistress is harmed. You have done it for me, and for Anwyn."

"But she just..."

Gideon stopped, hands on hips, and tipped his head back, restraining the desire to snarl. Daegan came and stood before Gideon, put a hand on his shoulder.

"You are angry about what occurred before we could find them.

You also had to channel your Mistress's agitation at not being able to accompany us. It was a bad situation, Gideon. We could have lost them both, and what they were doing to them...it was monstrous."

"So you're saying I'm out of my right mind?" Gideon barked a laugh. Daegan didn't crack a smile.

"Yes. Wolf is not fully himself, either, for much the same reasons. She's his first full servant, and their bond is new. It brings out territorial responses from a vampire best not challenged, whether by a servant or another vampire. In a physically stressful situation like now, that response increases tenfold."

Gideon paced in a wider circle, muttering, kicking the dirt.

You've just managed to piss everyone off today, haven't you?

Anwyn's dry observation. Daegan was glad to hear the teasing purr in her mind-voice. She was done being mad at him.

I do not think it is my doing, he responded. *I just have the privilege and curse of being bonded to two of the most stubborn people ever created.*

He felt her quiet amusement, and then a shift as she directed her next thought to their servant, helping him. *Gideon. You know Daegan is right. Ella has made her choice. So has Wolf. Do you think I would do nothing if I thought Wolf didn't have Ella's best interests at heart? You feel protective toward her. You always have, because she brings that out in any male who sees her. But because of that, you overlook her strengths. You are also ignoring how Wolf feels about her.*

"I still don't like it," Gideon muttered.

"Hmm. Then perhaps put yourself in her shoes," Daegan pointed out. "What if Anwyn or I were hurt, and you were as well? You could give us blood to restore us. Or we could give you blood to restore you first. Which makes more sense to you as a warrior? Which one would you prefer to have happen first, as a servant?"

Gideon heaved out a breath and stalked away, headed down the rural road on foot. "If you're going to spout sense and logic, I'm walking home."

Despite the set of the other male's shoulders, the attempt at wry humor told him Gideon was balancing out. It gave Daegan a painful smile.

I'll get us both home, cher. *Never fear.*

~

Once they arrived at Club Atlantis, Ella was a little more awake. Wolf carried her down to the basement, where Anwyn had prepared a guest room for them. Those rooms were relatively new, additions she'd had renovated out of storage space in the past year. Now Ella knew it had been to handle the occasional vampire visitor.

Anwyn had met them at the private elevator. Though Wolf still held her, Anwyn enveloped her in a tight hug that Ella cherished, the Mistress of Atlantis kissing her face, stroking back her hair, giving her a thorough looking over. She was more reserved with Wolf, but her relief and affection for him were obvious, as she lightly embraced him and asked what he needed.

"Just the room. Thank you for your kindness. For everything. But for now, we just need the room and a bath."

He was already moving better, she realized hazily, and the way he'd spoken to Anwyn was steady, his voice strong. Her blood had done that.

Anwyn let them go, and a few strides later, Ella opened her eyes to see he'd brought them into a comfortable room, bathed in warm lamplight. The king-sized canopy bed, the frame a dark wood, had a white coverlet scattered with pale gold embroidered flowers, and a wealth of pillows. A long burnished gold scarf wound around the top frame and draped down the bottom pillars.

It was all so comfortable and normal, it almost brought on a fresh wave of tears.

She was aware of easy chairs, a TV, but Wolf took them straight to the bathroom. At the sight of the gleaming white tub, the bronze fixtures of the adjacent shower, a small pearlescent army of body washes and shampoos waiting, something broke loose in Ella. She could be clean. She could wash everything away.

She reached out toward the shower like it was a person, ready to embrace and welcome her home. She only did that with one arm, though. She had the other firmly crooked around Wolf's neck. When he started to let her down, her body automatically drew up like a caterpillar in its cocoon, coiling around him.

He cupped her head in one hand, holding her face to his strong throat. "Easy," he murmured. "I'm not going anywhere."

She understood that, but she thought nothing short of a Master's command, uttered at its sharpest, could loosen her grip. Apparently,

Wolf wasn't ready to speak that way to her right now. For once, she was willing to take advantage of that and press her suit.

With a tender sigh, he carried her to the shower. He started the water and stepped in, but turned his back to it, sheltering her and taking the brunt of the brief, initially cold spray, until it became warmer. The simple consideration gripped her heart, spilled tears out of her eyes.

He murmured soothingly to her and put her under the hot spray. She moaned in relief, a weight lifted off her soul. As she sagged in his arms, he eased her feet down, though she practically stood on his while he ran his fingers through her hair, got it wet.

For the next time span, there was only this. Cleaning and caring for one another. He rinsed everything out of her hair she didn't want to remember. Blood, filth, smoke. That hated sterile laboratory smell. Her own vomit and waste. They'd hosed that off, but she could still feel it.

At some point, she was feeling better, more aware, and the thought tapped her on a mental shoulder. What was she doing? Wolf needed care and cleaning, too. She should—

"Do exactly what you're doing. Just drift, sweet girl. Like I told you. You're not going to do anything for anyone until you've had some of my blood. Argue with me, and I'll remember it when you're strong enough for me to make the punishment fit the crime."

His voice stayed low, but she could hear the steel, knew he meant it. It meant the world to her, to hear that Master's certainty in that distant-thunder rumble of his deep voice.

He put shampoo in her hair and started to work it in. Oh Goddess, bliss. Total bliss. She leaned against him, her head tipped back and eyes closed. When he dipped down to brush her mouth with his, her lips curved. Things were quivering, though, telling her tears were running down her face among the shower water. Her fingers curled into his skin, the firm, brown muscles. She tried to keep everything out of her head but this moment. If she thought of what they'd been through, the images of him being tortured, of those horrible people, of Hollow's dispassion...

Those images dissolved, because another image came in. How she looked, her head tipped back from the massaging touch of his fingers, the weight of her wet hair. Her closed eyes emphasized the sable thickness of her soft lashes. Her mouth was soft and easy as she surrendered everything to her Master's care. He soaped her shoulders and arms, lifting one then the other before letting them return to hold him. He covered every inch of her with his touch. Her shoulders and back, inside and outside of shoulder blades, the valley of her spine, rise of her buttocks, upper thighs.

His mind. He'd put his mind inside of hers, crowded out her thoughts, made her join him inside a far different room.

"The outer grime is gone. I'm moving us to the tub."

He'd started the water running before they stepped into the shower. She hadn't remembered it, but apparently she was still weak enough to be zoning in and out some.

He bent and lifted her once more, carrying her out of the shower and over to the tub. The water was almost to the top, and a fragrant scent hit her nose. She recognized it as a restorative oil she and Brownie both used in the massage room. Atlantis stocked it in their gift shop.

He sat down on the edge of the tub, putting his feet in the water. It reached his knees. Since she wasn't inclined to let go of him, he adjusted to cradle her in his arms. She could see the burns healing on his flesh, the bruises and cuts. Another bolstering reminder that her blood had helped him.

"It did. Now it's time for mine to help you." He tightened the arm around her back, which allowed him to bring his wrist to his mouth. He sliced the vein with one sharp fang and took the welling blood to her mouth, cupping her head with his broad palm. Her hands, trembling again, curled over his forearm, holding onto it.

As she put her lips over the wound, his taste filled her mouth. She wondered if this was how blood smelled and tasted to wild animal carnivores, who ate their food raw with such eager pleasure. She was glad for it, because a long time ago when such things mattered, she'd worried that the taste would repulse her.

Instead, the aroma of her Master's blood was like a favorite memory, triggered by scent. Or like when she smelled vanilla and it made her want to eat cake.

A couple times in her life, she'd been so hungry, the need for food had actually shut down so it didn't overwhelm other survival priorities. But then a shelter volunteer had offered her a peanut butter sandwich. She'd fallen on it like the proverbial wolf, almost swallowing it whole, the hunger surging up like a bear coming out of hibernation. This was like that. She suddenly couldn't drink fast enough. When his hand tightened on her hair, trying to slow her down, she was shocked to hear a small growl come from her lips.

"Easy, fierce kitten. Don't make your Master get rough with you. Slow it down, or you'll make yourself sick. You've had all you need. I promise."

She reluctantly let him go, licking her lips as he brought his wrist back to his mouth, passed his tongue over the puncture wounds a couple times, which apparently helped speed the clotting and kept him from dripping into the tub. However, he missed one drop, which splashed high on his chest. When he put his arm back around her, she put her mouth there, licking, scraping him with her teeth.

She was weak, but suddenly something else was raging up in her. Needing him...but not until...oh Goddess...

It flooded into her, Robert on top of her, shoving into her, the cruel look in his eyes. More than being forced to have sex with him against her will, it was that look that twisted her insides, made her feel dirty. His darkness had infected her. What if it never left?

She was hyperventilating. Wolf eased her into the heated waters of the tub, turned her so she had her arms hooked over the edge, her forehead pressed to the coolness as she tried to get her breath. His hand was on her back, rubbing. Dropping to caress her third mark, that phoenix, reminding her that she was alive. That she was with her Master.

I'm here. He's not. You killed him, Ella.

She had killed the man, but not what he'd left inside her soul.

"I'll take care of that," Wolf said, with a dangerous note to his voice that told her if she hadn't killed the man, her Master would have. Three times over if he could. He gave her that reaction, surrounded her scattered, fragile feelings about it, gathered them up. Outside that boundary, she sensed his deep rage, something he was protecting her from as much as anything else. It reminded her of what Anwyn had said, about Wolf having an exceptional level of control for a vampire. She suspected it was possible because when the right moment called for it, he could unleash and vent it in terrible, terrifying ways.

He stepped into the tub behind her, knelt over her, sheltering her, putting his face against her hair, crossing his arms in front of her, another form of cocoon. "Sweet girl. I'm here."

A stack of washcloths and towels had been left on the wide edge, and when her face pressed there, absorbing her tears, she felt how plush-soft they were.

Anwyn had done all this. Anwyn was a Mistress who understood that delegation gave submissives the chance to exercise that deep service yearning. But when something happened to one of her people, she cared for them herself. A reminder that she was there, and she would do whatever she could to fix it, make it better.

She wasn't the only Dom who had shown that side to Ella. And both of them were vampires.

Ella was just free-flow crying now. *Please, Wolf. I need you, Master. I need you now. Before anything else. Please?*

"There will be many times in our life together where I will take deep pleasure in hearing you beg, and beg hard, baby girl. Not right now. You don't need to beg for anything from me tonight. It's all yours."

She was so glad they were in the sleeping quarters of a BDSM club, because one of those bottles held an oil that allowed lubrication in bath water. In her peripheral vision, she saw Wolf pick it up. But she wanted to see more, even as she knew he wanted her to stay in the position she was in. So she ventured shyly to the doorway of his mind.

May I...see what you're doing?

A blink, and a window opened. Her heart accelerated as she watched him stand behind her, grip his cock, work the oil on it as the shaft stiffened, thickened, grew. She drank in every detail. Her heart constricted over the healing wounds on his body. Someone had harmed him. But they couldn't change the beauty of his form, the muscled long limbs, the graceful curves of back, shoulder, chest.

As he grew even more aroused, he let her feel how that reaction was feeding not only on the physical stimulation and anticipation of being inside her, but the hunger he felt growing within her.

Her cunt contracted, her lower belly tightened, and she gripped the edge of the tub to make herself wait on her Master's pleasure. Now that she knew he would take her, she needed him before another breath passed. She pressed her forehead to her knuckles, squeezed her eyes shut. Would he understand what she was feeling now, something that lived close to that rage that was always within her?

"Say it, Ella," he said. "Don't be afraid to be everything you are with me."

Please don't be gentle, Wolf. Remind me that I'm yours, and no male touches what's yours.

She was remembering how he'd taken her after the punishment Lord Richard had required. It had been another Master's punishment, which translated into a claim that Wolf had erased, by taking her so thoroughly, almost brutally.

If he hadn't been in her mind seeing that was what she genuinely, urgently needed, she doubted he would do it, since up until now he'd been handling her like a cracked egg in danger of losing structural integrity.

But he saw the need, the scream inside her head that was so close to ripping loose from her. All of it was crowding in, and she needed it driven away, to restore order and balance, serenity within her again.

He dropped to one knee behind her with a ripple of water that lapped against her buttocks and thighs. His powerful hand curled in her hair. She felt the pull against his fist as he leaned in and spoke against her ear with quiet menace.

"Who's been in this pussy, little girl?"

"Someone...not you." Her voice was choked up. "I'm sorry. I didn't want them there. Didn't invite them."

"Then you're not to blame, are you? Tell me." He sharpened his voice, and she heard something beneath it, an ache that told her they were sharing this pain together, no matter that he was dealing with it as a Master, while she handled it as a submissive.

"No, sir. I'm not to blame. But it all belongs to you. So I'm still ashamed."

"I'd expect nothing less of a submissive as precious as you are. Lift your ass out of the water. Show me what's mine to fuck. Show me that mark that says you belong to me."

She did, leaning further over the edge of the tub. A moan vibrated out of her as he fitted the oiled head of his cock to the mouth of her sex. He folded his body over hers, once more taking a tight grip on her hair. "Careful what you wish for, little girl. Because you just unleashed the monster inside your Master that wants the same thing. To pummel him away so even his memory is driven out of your head."

"Please." Please, Goddess, yes. That was what she wanted, too.

He thrust in, hard enough to wrench a cry from her. She grabbed the pain with both hands, the way she held the tub wall, and embraced it, making pitiful whimpers as her Master hammered into her.

He also put his mouth down to her throat as he fucked her. She cried out as he drove his fangs into her as well. Not to drink, but to pin her there, like he was doing with his cock.

"Please..." She kept saying it. Never demanding, but the harder and deeper he went, the more she needed.

He was rough, as she craved, but he refused to be as cruel as she thought she needed. He had other ideas, a decision that proved why he was her Master. The one she'd wanted for so long. The only one she'd ever want.

He was in her head, then her heart, then farther. Spiraling down, down and down, twisting, weaving, tangling with and surrounding every part of her soul. She could feel the clasp of his will around it, a tight binding more welcome than any she'd ever experienced.

I've got you, Ella. Always. Never doubt it.

He had one arm across her chest and now he adjusted so his hand was over her heart, the way he'd done that night when she'd told him that was where it hurt. He'd filled that first, and then expanded to all corners, driving out anything that didn't serve him. She was crying again, damn it, but it was okay. One climax. Two. He didn't stop, and he didn't release himself. He just kept working that steel cock into her, pushing her past her physical limits. As he did, he drove away everything on the inside that didn't serve him, leaving only her. His property, his submissive, his slave, his little girl.

His servant.

Another climax roared up on her, this one more intense than all the others. It took her by surprise, but he had his hand on her clit, was rubbing it in an irresistible rhythm with the thrusts. It swamped her with desperate power, rushing her forward on the wave of pleasure. She screamed as he kept thrusting, and then he was bucking, shoving her against the side of the tub forcefully as he came, bathing her inside with the hot jet of his semen, the final cleansing, burning out anything else.

They slowed together, her heart thundering in her chest. Somewhere along the way he'd given her his hand. She'd locked it against her chest with the help of both sets of fingers fisted around it. She was still curved forward, her breasts quivering over the lip of the tub. It was a good position for him to grip one with his free hand, lazily fondle it, while she shuddered with the aftershock that the stimulation rocketed through her, her pussy clenching him tighter.

"Good baby," he muttered in that voice that made her think of deep caves in the earth, rich brown earth and fiery lava flows. His breath was ragged, his mouth against her ear. "When they were hurting you, I would have sold out the universe to get you away from them."

She thought of the indifference of the scientists as they'd left the voltage rocketing through his body. The agonized arch of his spine, the rigidity of his muscles, his eyes rolling up in his head, his fangs jerking jagged wounds across his sensual mouth. "I never want to see anyone hurt you again, either," she said.

"Sssh. Don't go there. I have a better place for you to go."

"Where?" She'd learned how to handle putting away bad memories on her own, but right now she didn't have the strength.

"That's why you can rely on your Master's will entirely right now. Yours is resting." He paused. "You remember when you said if you ever had someone love you, the way you longed to be loved, you would make that Master proud to call you his?"

She nodded.

"Good. Then listen. I am very, very proud to call you mine."

He was telling her he loved her. Not in the heat of the moment in the lab when he thought they were going to die. Now, when everything was going to be okay, he was telling her. In a way she believed, all the way to her soul.

He loved her.

CHAPTER THIRTY-FOUR

They lay in the tub for a long while. She found that vampires didn't get pruny toes, but servants did. Then Wolf toweled her off, took her to the king-sized bed. They rested, slept together. As dawn approached, he kept his arms firmly around her, making it clear she wasn't to leave the bed until he gave her that permission. She was okay with that. She was content to lie quietly in his arms while he slept.

However, before dawn claimed him, he asked her a question.

"Do you remember, the first night you asked to touch me, and I started claiming each part of you?"

Her nipple ached in Pavlovian response, her answer. She felt his surge of male satisfaction. He passed his fingers over it, a gentle flick. "You seemed almost hesitant to approach me that night."

"You're Wolf. One of the most intimidating male Doms at Atlantis. No one approaches you without invitation."

"That's general Dom/sub 101. Your response was personal."

She smiled. It still felt weak, not her usual wattage, but that was okay, too. It would get there. "When you let me touch you, I felt like the nerd freshman being asked to dance by the hottest guy at the prom. There had to be a mistake."

He played with the nipple, toying, stroking, making her body start to quiver. It didn't matter how exhausted she was. If he wanted her again, she would take him, however he wanted her.

"My sweet servant. All mine. You're right. I'll want to be in you once more before I go to sleep, and I plan to thoroughly fuck you when I wake up, which is why you'll keep your ass in this bed, resting with me, throughout the daylight. But back to that night..."

Sure, now that he'd scattered her concentration entirely.

He chuckled, but then his tone became more serious. "Your reaction that night suggests you don't know how remarkable you are. Another trait the most precious of subs has."

"There are plenty like me."

"No." He shifted, gripped her under both of her arms and lifted her with that impressive strength she thought might be as much Wolf as vampire. He guided her to straddle him so he could more easily cradle her breasts in his hands, look at her intently.

"We were trapped in that maintenance closet," he said. "With fire all around us, something that terrifies you. We'd been tortured for hours, and in that moment, we weren't sure if we'd get out. You offered me half of the last chocolate you might ever have."

"Well...yes. Of course." Not sure where he was going with that, she spread her fingers out on his chest and upper abdomen. To balance herself, of course. Though there was no harm in stroking the firm muscle beneath her touch. Her Master didn't seem to mind. "If you'd had a can of your favorite beer on you, you would have offered me half," she pointed out.

"You don't like beer. Why would I have wasted half of a perfectly good brew?"

At her mock offended expression, he chuckled, a sound as soothing as the bath water they'd just shared. But she sniffed. "All right, bad example. But you would have given me something vital to you. Like your middle name."

"Nope. I would have died with that one."

It should have made her laugh, but just the opposite happened. Why was everything making her overflow like a fountain?

"Oh baby." His voice broke a little, too, a sound she hadn't expected. She had a brief glimpse of his face, the tight jaw and eyes full of emotions. He brought her back down to lie upon him. She rested between his thighs, his cock and testicles nested intimately against her abdomen. He kept his arms around her, and she had both her hands laced with one of his, her head tucked down over it. It was like she was the yolk of a boiled egg, wanting to stay surrounded by the protective outer white. Or...brown, in this case.

He chuckled again, held her tighter. "Ella, I will never tire of listening to your mind. My mother would have loved you."

A lump grew in her throat. Maybe that was another thing that connected her and Wolf. That all these years later, he still remembered the pull of home, the familiar sense of it. And to say his mother would have loved her...

"Would it have mattered to her? That I'm not black?"

She sensed he was surprised by the question. Then he considered. "Maybe at first. But she'd have gotten past that quick, especially these days. It's been so long since I thought of skin color that way. With vampires, superiority is based entirely in power, the brain behind it. If you can fight your way up the ladder, then your place is respected, as long as you maintain that strength. Probably the closest thing we have to discrimination in our own species is between born and made vampires." He smiled against her temple. "Born vampires can be snooty about that sometimes."

"Is she one of those?"

"Who?"

"Lady Lyssa."

"Oh, Christ. I forgot about her being here. Other priorities." He tightened his grip on her. "I've only met her once, when she was visiting my overlord during his annual meet with vampires in his territory. It was a few years back, when she still had a monk as a servant, and she was married to another Council member, Lord Rex. I'd only been a vampire for a few years at that point. She's not snooty...not that way. But anyone with any sense doesn't disrespect her. Even though we're not under a monarchy anymore, she's the last of us with full royal blood, a queen, supposedly over a thousand years old. She's also the first to do something that no other vampire has. Not one of her rank."

"What's that?" She tilted her head up as he remained quiet. He traced her lips with his thumb, her chin, the curve of her cheek. She stilled, because the way he was looking at her, she didn't want to do anything to make him stop.

"She publicly declared her love for her servant," he said, his eyes on her face. "In the past, a vampire who did that faced severe punishment. And the servant was put to death."

She swallowed. "Oh my God. Why?"

But she thought she knew. Everything she'd just endured, coupled to what Gideon had told her, what she'd pieced together about the relationship of vampires to humans, gave her a sense of the terrible truth. But she wanted to hear Wolf's version of it. His view of it.

Which might have worried her far more if she still wasn't holding those words to her heart. *I am very, very proud to call you mine.*

He brushed his lips over her forehead, a confirmation, but then looked pensively down at their hands, loosely linked on his chest. "There are very few of us, Ella. About five thousand. We don't reproduce enough to grow that number. Made vampires often have impulse problems that mean they don't make it to their first century. Sometimes not to their first decade. As a result, any sort of perceived vulnerability to vampires, born or made, is squashed harshly or regulated to keep it from being a liability to our survival. To many vampires and most of the Council, letting yourself love your servant, a human, is a liability."

"But..." She frowned. "There's another side to that, isn't there? Your servant can be your greatest strength. Someone to give you blood, watch over you while you sleep, be someone you can trust, because your minds are so close..."

She trailed off, her heart thumping hard as she remembered Bill telling Wolf to drop the net over himself. "Oh Goddess. They're right. If you hadn't felt the way you had about me..."

"No." Wolf gave her a firm squeeze. "There are some who will see it that way, but the truth is how you just said it. A vampire's greatest strength, their greatest weakness. Loving a servant, that can be both. But the same thing could be said about loving anyone. If I loved another vampire, that vampire could sabotage me, or be used to sabotage me."

"Yes, but that's going to be viewed differently, because vampires see one another as...equals."

He was silent, which she knew acknowledged the uneasy truth to that. His fingers slid up her spine, then back down, over the rise of her buttock, a caress meant to reassure, but she sensed he was also thinking. "What?"

He sighed. "There were some recent protocols approved by Council to give servants more...consideration. I'm wondering how Hollow's actions are going to affect that."

He tipped up her chin then, so their eyes could meet once more. "Ella, there are ways to separate a vampire and a servant. Erase the three marks. It isn't approved lightly, but with everything that has happened these past few days, I could likely get it." He hesitated. "It comes with a memory wipe. You won't remember what I am."

"Or who you are to me," she realized. Maybe he had his mind closed to her, but some things had nothing to do with mind reading. She felt it in the way he held her, looked at her. *Or who I am to you.*

It went back to her thought about what pleasure her surrender gave him, how her willingness to belong to him filled his soul. If she forgot who he was, if she even believed such a powerful feeling could forever be erased, she would be taking that from him as well.

She gripped his hand, flattened her fingers in the spaces between his, and didn't look away. "You can see down into my soul. Surely you know I don't want that."

No matter how difficult, morally or physically, she was going to be with him. Because she couldn't imagine it otherwise.

Wherever this takes us, whatever we face, it doesn't change what I am to you, Master. Whatever you need, I'm here to serve.

He was silent a long moment, and then he spoke in her head.

It's Dauntless. Leroy Dauntless Wolfram.

She would have loved his mother.

~

Her own mother used to say a good night's sleep helped everything. With a vampire, she guessed that would be a good day's sleep, but the same maxim held true. Once they woke, the evening started off with fairly normal expectations. Wolf had to go off for a thorough briefing with the vampires in residence. He told Ella not to leave Atlantis.

I don't even want you in that cat alley without me. Not for a decade or so at least.

Last time I was in the alley with *you, I got blown up. Maybe we should both stay away from it for awhile.*

He'd had a threatening response to that which warmed her, head to toe. Since he'd started his "day" exactly as he'd warned, by taking her thoroughly, she should be sated for the time being, but maybe third marks received an elevated libido to keep up with the expansive vampire one.

Left to her own devices and looking for a place to be useful, she sought out Gideon first. Their escape was coming back to her in more detail. She remembered Gideon's reaction to Wolf drinking from her. She wanted to assure him she was okay.

He was on the first level at the bar, sharing a beer with Allan. There was a tension to both males, as if they were killing time, waiting for the next step in what needed to be handled.

"Do third marks want to have sex all the time? Like rabbits on Viagra?"

At her cheerfully delivered question, Gideon nearly fumbled the beer, eliciting a chuckle from Allan. Gideon rose, scowling, but it wasn't a real scowl. His gaze swept her quickly, taking stock of her condition. She propped a hip against a table, her arms crossed. She'd donned her spare set of clothes from her locker, a worn pair of jeans and a pink T-shirt. On the shirt was a pen and ink drawing of a variety of insects, beneath which was written "Don't Bug Me."

"You look better," he said.

"I feel better." She came to him, gave him a hug. She made a little noise as his arms tightened around her, harder than she'd expected.

"I had your phone," he said gruffly. "I've never been so damn glad to see a text message in my life."

Her heart overflowed. She ran her hands up his broad back in reassurance, even as she baptized his shoulder with a couple more of her endless tears. "I'm okay," she whispered. "Thank you."

When she was a little more composed, she turned her face toward Allan, including him in that statement. "Thank you for rescuing me and my Master. I'm glad I didn't stake you with a pool stick."

Allan grinned. "Me too. But watch the smart mouth, young one. One wiseass around here is enough."

"I've no idea who you're talking about," Gideon said.

Since he seemed recovered from the emotional moment as well, Ella cocked a brow. "You didn't answer my question."

"I think you already know the answer. You were just trying to lighten the mood."

"Did it work?"

"Brat." He pulled her hair.

"That's a yes."

Allan's attention moved abruptly away from them. When Ella turned, she saw another male headed their way, striding through the public area.

"Wow. Oh wow."

"He's not that good-looking," Gideon grumbled.

"It's not that," she elbowed him. "Though he is. It's..."

It was the delight one felt at meeting a family member of a good friend, and she considered Gideon one of her best.

During her drowsy pillow talk with Wolf, she'd learned Lady Lyssa's servant was Jacob Green. Gideon's brother. She would have known it without being told.

The two men had matching midnight blue eyes, though Gideon's hair was black and Jacob's was brown, with traces of reddish-copper. Gideon had a bigger build, while Jacob was all tensile strength. But the set of the face, the way they moved, the eyes—they were obviously related.

It could give anyone some pretty serious threesome-with-two-brothers fantasies. She hid a smile, knowing for sure she'd hear that thought echoed by most the female staff, if they had the chance to see the two men together.

Her teasing of Gideon wasn't an act. She'd woken in an almost ebullient mood. They'd survived the unsurvivable, and Wolf was now her permanent, forever Master. But the serious look on Jacob's face, the concern it created on Gideon and Allan's faces, put a cloud in that blue sky.

Gideon touched her shoulder, drawing her attention. "Lady Lyssa wants to talk to you, Ella."

Could he and Jacob communicate without words? Or was someone like Daegan or Anwyn with Lyssa, able to relate it to him?

Less than twenty-four hours ago she'd been tortured in a lab, expecting herself or Wolf to die. Or be burned to death. Her nerves hadn't settled as much as she thought.

Wolf...

She had the thought before she could quell it. She didn't want to seem needy, but she felt that humming connection with him, and wanted to know what she should expect, what was going on.

I'm on my way. After he'd finished the general briefing, he'd headed to the security office, directed there by Lady Lyssa to work with Fort and Saturnia. They'd been discussing the technical mop-up steps to handle Hollow's mess. But Wolf left them now, headed toward her.

And not at a casual pace. He appeared behind Jacob so quickly, she knew he'd used vampire speed to get there.

Jacob pivoted. "Lady Lyssa will interview your servant now. Alone."

Wolf's lips tightened. "You should have come directly to me with that request. Not to my servant."

Jacob inclined his head. He didn't have the edge Gideon had in his tone, but an interesting mix of formality and easy amiability that she expected could be sharpened to match the cut of a sword blade when needed. But right now he was all neutral deference. "Of course. I was on my way to you when I saw her with my brother. I was going to ask her to accompany me to where you were. Your work with Fort and Saturnia is considered a priority, since my lady will be awaiting the final threat assessment report before dawn."

"He hadn't said a word yet," Allan confirmed. "Easy, Wolf."

There was a warning in his tone, and Wolf's gaze flickered to him. Ella remembered how Lord Richard had reacted to Gideon holding the pool sticks and not putting them down when a higher-ranking vampire demanded he do so. By his lack of immediate compliance, Wolf was signaling a resistance to Lady Lyssa's wishes. And that couldn't be good.

She has to protect the whole vampire world, doesn't she? So a few questions to everyone involved, on their own, makes sense.

It does. Doesn't mean I like it. His jaw stayed tight, but Wolf inclined his head to Jacob. "My apologies. The things that have happened over the past few days have put me on edge toward those who do not deserve it. I have nothing but the highest regard for your lady. My servant will answer any questions she has."

Ella understood that response was for Lyssa, not Jacob. Lyssa was very likely watching the exchange from Jacob's mind. The slight head nod from Allan, subtle approval, and relaxing of Gideon's shoulders, confirmed it. Until Jacob, whose expression remained more fixed, spoke.

"My lady says your regard, while appreciated, does not excuse the need for prompt and obedient response to a requirement from a Vampire Council member. She will question your servant without you providing her any direction. If she senses you speaking in Ella's mind, influencing her answers, she will be displeased."

Not "very displeased" or "excessively displeased;" just "displeased." A woman who didn't see the need to embellish. Displeased could run the gamut from mild dismemberment to death, because if Ella's interpretation of the tone was correct, Lady Lyssa was already in a bitch of a mood.

Wolf's expression was set in stone, but he inclined his head. "My apologies, my lady. You are correct."

To his credit, Jacob almost winced, but relayed the response without hesitation. "Actions speak far louder than words."

Even delivered in a flat, even tone, the edge was sharp enough to cut. Wolf wisely seemed to conclude no other words were advisable. He glanced at Ella.

I won't be far, Ella. Just be truthful, as you always are. She will know a lie, regardless.

Despite the reassurance, she sensed his concern. As she accompanied Jacob through the club, headed toward the meeting rooms, she determined what it was. If humans had no status in vampire society, there was only one reason that Lady Lyssa would want to question her without Wolf. She thought something inappropriate had caused the situation with Hollow.

But Lyssa had openly declared her love for her own servant. That had to temper such thoughts, right? But was she queen or woman first?

"My lady is fair, but she requires complete honesty," Jacob said, as they turned down the hallway which held the meeting room.

Ella looked at him. He was tall, like his sibling. "Was Gideon a good big brother?"

"Except when we were young, when he wouldn't let me use his Legos," Jacob responded promptly. A smile touched his firm mouth. "I asked my mother if we could give him away so I could have his toys. I told her she could give me a sister instead, one who only wanted to play with dolls."

As they reached the closed door of the meeting room, she looked up at him. His faint smile hadn't changed the seriousness in his eyes, or the tension around his mouth that told her things were no laughing matter right now, but she interpreted his direct look, the slight nod of reassurance, in the way she thought it was meant. She'd take it, along with Wolf's advice, and hope for the best.

Play it straight and be herself.

Jacob opened the door and held it open, gesturing her to precede him.

The power emanating from Lady Lyssa was unmistakable. It pushed against the walls of the conference room, making it seem far too small. When the door opened, it hit Ella like a wall. She needed Jacob's firm hand on her lower back, easing her farther into the room.

In marked contrast to that energy blast, Lyssa was a petite female. Dark, straight hair and almond-shaped eyes of a jade green, vivid as an exotic bird's breast. She wore a silk blouse, visible over the table edge, since Lyssa sat at the head of it, at the far end of the room.

Jacob gestured Ella to one of the chairs. While Ella gave him a courteous nod of acknowledgement, she moved to the right of the table, so Lady Lyssa had a clear view of her. The Council head wore flowing slacks, and her shoes would have made Madelyn salivate. The four figure designer heels would add several inches to the vampire queen's stature. Ella could tell she wasn't tall, probably no more than five feet in her bare soles.

Ella absorbed all that in one deferential sweep of her glance, headed to the floor. In the same motion, she sank to her knees, assuming a submissive posture, head dipped down, though back straight, hands on her knees.

"How may I be of service, my lady?"

A pause, then Lyssa proved she didn't care to waste time with games or pleasantries, either.

"How deeply does Wolf enter your mind, Ella?" She had a fluid, sensual voice Ella suspected never had to increase in volume to be heard or obeyed. It brought gooseflesh up on her skin and made that swirling energy vibrate around them. She had to struggle to remember the question.

"As deeply as he wishes, my lady."

"When was the last time he was soul deep?"

"Right after our rescue. I was empty, and it made me feel so much better, having him there. I wish he was that deeply inside me all the time."

Too late, she thought that might show too much emotion. But the brief glimpse she snatched showed Lyssa simply nodding.

"How was Wolf captured?"

"When Wolf arrived, a metal net was dropped over him and electrified to incapacitate him."

"Wolf didn't see the net? Hear it coming down? He has exceedingly quick reflexes, I have been informed."

Madelyn's lawyerly advice in any precarious situation was, "Avoid nervous talking; answer a question in the fewest words possible. Never volunteer information." Ella had a feeling that wasn't going to fly with Lady Lyssa. She knew exactly which question to ask that Ella didn't want to answer.

Be truthful. Her Master had told her that, and she would obey.

"He does, my lady. A man had a weapon against my chest, with three steel spikes in it. He told Wolf to drop the net over himself or he would kill me."

The significant pause was telling. Ella threw Maddie's advice to the wind. "He would have done it for Anwyn just as quickly as he did it for me. Because he's honorable and good, and strong. I know maybe vampires aren't supposed to do the same things for humans they would do for another vampire, but life isn't easy to split up that way."

She took a breath, ostensibly to give Lady Lyssa a chance to talk, but then rushed onward. "I know Wolf would have burned down that whole building and killed Holliman and all his people to protect vampire kind, too. He didn't know what Holliman was planning when he came to get me. He saw the net thing as him sacrificing himself, not endangering vampire kind. And maybe that's not forward thinking enough, but..."

What was wrong with her? She was babbling. She shut down, and the palpable silence was damning. She had fucked this up totally. She swallowed, hard. As the quiet drew out, she could hear her heart hammering against her chest, and closed her fingers into balls on her knees. Everything had been going so well...but things didn't always turn out well. Sometimes you had to take the moments of bliss you were given.

"Wolf was considering third marking another servant," she said in the pregnant silence, every word cutting into her heart. "Circumstances changed, but if you think I'm the wrong servant for him, I can...not be." Her voice trembled, but she firmed it. "I can be with Anwyn instead, so I'm not a security risk."

Wolf's opinion on that exploded in her mind, telling her she was in a lot of trouble with him for saying it, but Lyssa wanted Ella's honest reactions, not those of her Master. And since Lyssa was still sitting there like a statue, Jacob another unfathomable wall of silence at her back, Ella might as well throw in something else, for what her opinion was worth.

"I think any race would want Wolf in a leadership role, looking out for the good of everyone."

Lyssa shifted at last, those glossy shoes changing position as she uncrossed and re-crossed her legs. Her hand rested on the arm of the chair. She had a beautiful manicure, the nails done in deep green color with a feathery black brush mark on the three center fingers.

"He's giving you hell for your opinion, isn't he?" Lyssa's tone was pleasant, but Ella heard the coolness beneath.

How on earth... With despair, Ella acknowledged her face was far too expressive. When her gaze darted toward Jacob, he confirmed it.

"Your right eye is twitching," he said courteously.

"The child will give me honest answers, from the heart, without your interference, Wolf. You can deal with your reaction to them as you wish with her, after this questioning is complete." Lyssa's tone chilled considerably, sending a shiver over Ella's skin. "But if you make me come out into that hallway where you are presently hovering, you will regret it."

Christ, she's a nightmare version of my mother.

Ella kept her face as blank as possible. "Yes, my lady. That was his response."

"I'm sure." Lyssa studied her a long moment, then glanced to her right. For the first time, Ella noticed there was a third person in the room. Daegan, so still against the wall he blended, as if he could stay there a hundred years and not have to move. He reminded her of a fallen angel statue on the corner of a towering church, in one of Tex's

Gothic-style video games. Ella had played it with him in the breakroom one slow night.

"A good servant has a value beyond measure," Lyssa said. "A smart vampire recognizes that, at the same time he recognizes a threat that needs to be contained. Where they are not in conflict, he strives to protect the one and neutralize the other. That was the end result of this situation, with help. While that has raised concerns that need to be addressed, I am pleased to see that Wolf has finally found a servant worthy of his intelligence and courage."

It took a few minutes for the words to sink in. Ella wasn't entirely sure they meant what she thought until she noted the curve of Jacob's lips. He gave her a subtle nod. Things were okay.

Ella didn't realize she'd been holding her breath until she let it out in a surge of relief. She almost toppled from the dizziness.

"My lady, may I approach, on my knees?"

Lyssa's brow rose. "You may."

Ella inched forward until she was a foot away from the strappy black heels. Then she leaned in and wrapped her arms around Lyssa's calves in a careful but extremely heartfelt hug. "Thank you," she whispered.

She immediately withdrew and put her forehead to the floor in front of the pointed, silver-tipped toes. An apology if she'd overstepped. After a long moment, Lyssa leaned over so her long hair brushed Ella's back. She touched her head.

"This one is a keeper. If you decide otherwise, I have obviously overestimated your intelligence."

The queen was talking to Wolf, Ella realized. It was going to take a while for her to get used to being utilized as a communications conduit, without any preamble or cue. But she was okay with that.

She was ready to learn anything that would help her care for her Master.

~

If Wolf doesn't want her, can we keep her? Kane would love her.

Lyssa waited until Ella had slipped from the room to shoot Jacob an arch look. "Our son has more than enough toys already," she said. "And if you're suggesting you don't, I'd reconsider that."

Jacob grinned, but executed a half-bow toward her. "Of course, my lady."

"Anwyn may now join us, with her servant."

Daegan nodded. A few seconds later, Anwyn slipped in through another door. Gideon entered behind her, closing it and moving to the wall to stand by Jacob.

"Thank you, my lady," Anwyn said immediately, taking a seat at the conference table. She put a roll of papers in front of her. "I think it would have torn her to shreds if Wolf had been punished for this."

"Hmm." Lyssa sat back in her chair, her long nails tapping the arm in an asymmetric fashion. One tap. Three. Four. "Saturnia and Holliman. What is the status there?"

"Saturnia executed him yesterday," Daegan said. "I offered, but she indicated it was her mess, and she would clean it up. She also said she would accept whatever punishment the Council meted out for her oversight, including death. She'll stay here until you tell her otherwise."

"Execution will certainly be on the table," Lyssa said, her expression going flat. "I may not be able to save her from that if the Council puts it to a vote. But Saturnia is a very accomplished made vampire. It is my hope we can determine something severe enough to underscore the point to others, and yet preserve her value to us."

Lyssa looked at everyone in the room. "The Council is going to receive a full report on what has transpired here. Unfortunately, the information is damning enough to give the Council members who oppose the new servant protocols the fuel they need to push for revocation or amendment. I can likely prevent the former, but not the latter. Depending on what amendments are proposed, I may or may not oppose them. This situation has brought to light some legitimate concerns. Holliman very nearly succeeded in exposing our kind completely. And likely would have, if not for one remarkably brave female human figuring out how to get her hands on a phone and send a one-word text."

She sighed irritably. "This never should have happened. Every vampire is responsible for ensuring their servant's loyalty. No one should be allowing their servant the kind of mental privacy Saturnia permitted Holliman. Lord Belizar will say that allowing vampires to cultivate more intimate, emotionally equitable relationships with their servants is leading to this kind of situation. Respecting their privacy and self-determination increases the danger to our world."

"My lady, if I can be so bold, may I make a point for the Council's consideration?"

Lyssa turned her gaze to Anwyn. "You may."

Anwyn took a breath. "I love Gideon, love him and Daegan with my whole soul. Which means I accept nothing less than being in the depths of Gideon's soul, not as an invasion, but as a natural expression of who I am, as his Mistress and the woman—and vampire—who loves him."

She looked toward Gideon, held his gaze a moment before she returned hers to the queen. "With that kind of bond, there's no way any servant could conceal something as complicated as what Holliman had planned. In the handful of situations where servants have betrayed their Masters, there was a distinct lack of that emotional connection, that craving to be deep inside the soul of one's servant, for the right reasons. So an argument could be made that it's the vampires who think of their servants as less who are creating these problems. Not those who don't."

Lyssa pursed her lips, but her jade eyes flickered with approval. "A compelling argument for Council. For the members receptive to anything other than doing things the way they have always been done, it might help mitigate some of the more punitive responses. Thank you, Anwyn. I will consider it.

"That said, if the choice before us becomes the extinction of our species, or stripping every hint of freedom a servant has, I will choose the latter. I am the last of the royals of my kind, and head of the Vampire Council. I can do no less to preserve our species. Gideon, I am curious as to your reaction to that."

The line of his shoulders had grown taut as she spoke, and now Gideon lifted a surprised gaze to the queen. However, he spoke after only a short pause. "It is what it is, my lady. I get it. Billions of us, five thousand of you. I'm never good with humans being treated as less important than a vampire. But I stand with Daegan and Anwyn. That's not ever going to change, and it's what guides me now."

He looked at the two of them, then came back to Lyssa. "Plus...I trust you, my lady."

A ripple of surprise crossed Lyssa's face, here then gone. She inclined her head. "Thank you."

"But I'm not hugging your legs."

A fine brow arched. "A wise decision. Ella is far more adorable than you, and therefore was spared having her arms removed."

Lyssa's attention went to the roll of paper in front of Anwyn. "You had another issue you wished to discuss with me, on Atlantis's security?"

"Yes, my lady. Fort, Saturnia and Allan are tweaking the security setup, in case Holliman gave anyone still living any inside info on the system. However, I want to take it further, and I think we're already headed in that direction. You're aware that, a few months ago, Lord Uthe discussed placing the Fae Lord Keldwyn's ward here? The girl prefers to be in our world, rather than the Fae one."

"I am aware," Lyssa said.

Anwyn continued. "My understanding is that, in order to shelter a Fae, the club would have to become some sort of magical nexus. A portal, a nourishment or energy point, some combination of that. We're still figuring that out. However, a few months ago, before all this went down, we had a guest member. Lady Yvette. She seemed to think you know one another?"

Lyssa blinked once. "Yes. We met some years ago."

"Are you aware of her current circumstances?"

"That she runs a circus slash carnival of sensual delights and talents, and she mainly operates outside this dimension, using portals to show up in different towns to perform."

"That's the one. She and I hit it off, and she's contracting for a couple takeover events at Atlantis annually. She mentioned if that becomes a regular thing, they'd pin down a portal foot at Atlantis, which feeds into my same idea."

"And that idea is?" Lyssa prompted.

Anwyn met her gaze. "I want this place to become inviolate, a safe haven for anyone. For the vampires, Fae, and whoever else deserves its shelter. A fortress, if need be."

Anwyn tapped the blueprint. "This plan increases the contact between vampires and other magical worlds. Reinforcements if ever... if something like what Holliman attempted is ever successful. If vampires ever become fugitives in their own world."

Lyssa considered that. "How will you handle the employees unaware of our worlds?"

"It might not impact peripheral staff, if we have the right rules in place. For the more integral staff, I relocate the ones who don't know and shouldn't know, and keep the ones I trust, who are willing to be second marked. There will be policies at the door, telling everyone how they can and can't behave. My place, my rules. I'll have Yvette's backup on that...and Daegan's."

"What if your wishes conflict with Council's?" Lyssa asked.

"Then I bring it to Council to resolve, figure out the best compromise. If this is presented as something that can be beneficial to our world, I think they'll be on board."

Lyssa pursed her lips. "And if Council doesn't accept this idea, thinking it is putting too much power in the hands of a fledgling, and more importantly, a vampire of near limitless power they are not entirely sure they control?"

Her gaze went directly to Daegan.

Anwyn hadn't anticipated that direction to the conversation, and her heart speeded up, her hands closing on the blueprints. Daegan met Lyssa's gaze squarely, however. He leaned forward, lacing his hands on the table. "Do you fear that outcome, my lady?" he asked in a mild voice.

"I do not. But there are those on the Council who might."

"If that's a worry, then I withdraw the idea," Anwyn said quickly into the seemingly tense silence. "The Lady Yvette comes twice a year to do a takeover event at Club Atlantis, and that's the end of it. Her friendship remains beneficial to those of us here only."

"And why do you not worry about it, Lady Lyssa?" Daegan asked. He lifted a hand toward Anwyn, acknowledging her comment but counseling silence, a firm suggestion, until Lyssa responded.

"Because you have pledged your loyalty to me, Daegan Rei," the queen said quietly, meeting his gaze. "And as your servant said to me, I trust you."

Daegan blinked, then inclined his head, a muscle flexing in his jaw. "Thank you, my lady. Your faith is not misplaced."

"Hmm." Lyssa adjusted her attention back to Anwyn. "If you are this ambitious in your goals, then you will present the idea to them yourself."

Anwyn blanched, but only for a second. She looked at Daegan, caught his hint of a smile, and recovered. "It would be my honor, my lady."

"Is your fledgling up to the task, Lord Daegan?" Lyssa asked, though Anwyn suspected that was just a formality.

"More than, my lady. She is formidable."

"We shall see, but I have seen nothing that makes me believe otherwise." Lyssa rose, indicating the meeting was at an end. "I will depart tomorrow night for Savannah, where the Council will meet me. You and Anwyn will come with me."

"Of course, my lady."

Lyssa looked toward Jacob. Moving away from the wall, he dropped to a knee at her feet. She laid a hand on his shoulder, gazed at him a long moment. Then she brushed her fingertips along his face, and nodded, as if to herself.

"Navigating a world like ours is never easy. But it is easier when you can trust the one closest to you. No matter the dysfunctionality of their relationship, that person was Holliman for Saturnia. She may never heal from that blow. Death may be a mercy she seeks."

A tight smile appeared on her face. "Fortunately for the preservation of her life, mercy is not a trait that vampires embrace often."

CHAPTER THIRTY-FIVE

Ella went to find Wolf. She thought he might have returned to Fort and Saturnia, but he showed her he was waiting for her on the second level dance floor. Seeing him there reminded her of that night when she'd hoped against hope that he was beginning to see her as his.

He opened his arms and she went into them, holding on and making a noise of contentment as he lifted her off her feet.

"You did well," he murmured.

"I thought Lyssa was going to come out in the hall and give you a spanking." She smiled against his chest. He harrumphed at that.

"I expect she doesn't waste her time on those kinds of punishments. If she lives up to her reputation, she could make what we went through these past few days feel like a picnic."

"Oh Goddess. Now you tell me. I gave her a hug. Well, her legs. She didn't seem mad at the time."

"You enchant everyone you meet, little girl. It's your special gift. If she was mad, she'd just kill me, and get two for the effort of one."

Ella blinked. She was going to have to get used to vampire humor, since they liked to joke about things that were not yet a laughing matter to her. She tightened her arms around his neck. "I have a lot to learn about all this stuff. I'll come up to speed as fast as I can."

"You never disappoint. But right now, you only have one job. Do you know what it is?"

She dropped her head back, gazed at him with love in her eyes. "Whatever you tell me?"

His gaze heated. "Exactly."

~

Wolf took her to her home. She still had no idea where he kept his belongings, where he slept, but she liked that he seemed to enjoy her small house so much. He opened the door and window so the breeze could flirt through, and leaned in the doorway, a dark silhouette. She'd knelt on the floor at his feet, and had stayed that way awhile. It had brought her peace, and she suspected that steady thread between them, Master and servant, did the same for him.

At length, he crooked a finger at her. She rose and stood before him. For a long moment they just stood like that, her facing him, her gaze on his chest. Though they didn't touch, there was so much density of feeling between them, it felt like they did.

He put his hands on her shoulders. He removed her shirt and unhooked her bra, bringing her in close to lean against him as he pulled the garment free. He'd taken off his shirt, so her breasts brushed his hard chest. He took care of her jeans and panties, and had her step out of her canvas sneakers.

He lifted her under the arms, so she could wrap arms and legs around him, and he carried her to the bed. Laid her down on her back, putting his knee on the bed so he was over her, looking down. He'd laid her perpendicular to the headboard, so her head rested on the mattress, not pillows, and her feet came to the opposite edge. At least until he started commanding her otherwise.

"Hands above your head," he said quietly. "Eyes closed, no matter what."

She obeyed, her arms draping over the edge of the coverlet, then they trembled as he spoke again. "Feet flat on the mattress, knees bent and spread open."

As she complied, the aching pulse between her legs increased exponentially. And kept increasing, for she sensed him moving back to the doorway, leaning in it once again. It was such a small space, it wasn't difficult to know where anyone was, even with eyes closed.

With Wolf, she could literally feel the heat of his gaze when it passed over her.

"One-word answers, Ella. How does this make you feel?"

"Aroused. Helpless. Afraid. Good afraid."

"That's two words," he said, but he wasn't disapproving. "You know how I feel?"

She shook her head.

"Savage. Content. Hungry. Aroused. I'm a lion in his den, Ella, everything here mine to enjoy, tear apart and taste as I wish. Isn't that correct?"

"Yes, sir."

"Good. Be still and quiet unless I tell you otherwise." Then he fell silent. Her arousal built with every ticking moment, for she knew she had his attention. Not just her. Her total submission.

He moved to where her arms were. His thighs brushed her knuckles. His legs were bare, telling her he'd removed his clothes. He put his hands beneath her, pulled her further in his direction, so her head dropped back. Her stomach leaped in anticipation. When he leaned over her, guided his cock in her mouth, her lips were already parted.

"Get me nice and slippery. Got a bigger than usual erection, probably because it goes into caveman mode the more you show me how much you're mine."

She sucked on him, licked, making noises in her throat to tell him how much she wanted him there. She'd suck him off completely if that was what he desired, swallowing his seed down.

"Not now. But later." He drew his shaft from her eager mouth and moved to the other side of the bed. Her knees were still bent, feet still flat as he'd ordered.

"You keep them that way. Stay completely still. No movement at all."

She bit her lip on a soft moan when he pressed inside her. Her saliva had helped, as had her natural lubrication, a result of the anticipation he'd built, but he was right. He was even larger than usual.

Once he was fully seated, he put his hands on her shins, pushing her knees back toward her. Then he gripped both her ankles, bringing her legs together and straight, holding them against his shoulder, her hips off the bed. The position made her an even tighter fit, and with her hips lifted up, he went even deeper. He controlled all her movements as he pumped in and out of her, slow glides full of heat and friction that built the arousal to a wild, mindless tornado. The more he controlled her, the wilder she felt.

Then he made it worse.

He placed her legs back where they'd been and then lowered himself between them, spreading her thighs wider so she had to adjust her feet out. Bending down, he captured a nipple in his mouth, started sucking. She was getting so worked up, gasping between her teeth, trying so hard to stay still.

"Master, please..."

Stay still, little girl. Or else.

She heard the ruthless vampire, the Master who would be obeyed. He moved to the other nipple, left it aching and taut at once. When he at last lifted his upper body and clasped her throat, she was shuddering from his full assault on her senses.

As he held her that way, his fingers over her galloping pulse, he placed two fingers against her clit, just a faint pressure.

No, no...

She couldn't stop it. She came, even as she tried her best to stay all rigid as he'd required. Her cunt spasmed over the thick rigidity of his cock. He enjoyed making small movements that increased her response, even as he didn't lift the command for her to stay still. She couldn't move, and it was overwhelming.

The orgasm seemed to go on forever as a result, tiny, excruciating ripples that had her whimpering. His lightning-gaze rested on her, logging every reaction.

When she was still shuddering, he withdrew, but he didn't leave her empty for long. He lay down on her bed and put her on top of him, sitting up, facing his feet. He brought her down on his cock with a decisive, full sheathing that had her drawing in a breath.

She was leaning back toward him to take that penetration, but her Master had other ideas. "Pick up the two pillows next to you. Put them on my thighs, one on top of the other. Lean forward onto those pillows."

With the angle they provided, she could manage it and keep him inside of her. His hands spread over her back, stroking, gripping, dropping to her waist and hips to grip.

"Good. You'll stay still until I come. And then, when I'm done, I'm going to put you on your back again. I'll make you close your eyes, and I'll show you in your head what I'm going to do to you before dawn. When I think you're ready, I will lean down and start breathing on your cunt, just soft, moist breezes, blowing sweet ripples over your clit. I'm going to watch you come just from the touch of my breath."

A spasm went through her, and he slapped her buttock. It made her flex inside, no help for it, and he grunted his approval.

"I think I'll need to keep your backside a bit bruised up on a regular basis. Now," he trailed a fingertip down her spine, making her shiver. "Tell me why you don't like my smoking."

It was an unexpected topic. She couldn't marshal the right thoughts for it, so she went with what was safe. "I don't dislike it. It's—"

She bit back another yelp as he slapped her buttock again. "I don't like the smell," she admitted. "It gives me headaches."

"All right." He grunted. "I guess I'll have to quit. I think every time I want a cigarette, I'll just paddle your beautiful ass."

She chewed on her lip as he caressed her backside, teased her rim with a fingertip. He hadn't taken her there yet. She wanted him to. She wanted him everywhere.

But her mind couldn't help going back to his plan. And since she *was* Atlantis's cruise director...

"Um...with that kind of incentive, we could start a quit smoking program at Club Atlantis. I think that would work...I'll talk to Anwyn...maybe I should call her now..."

She was laughing when he hit her the next time, but she knew he was biting back a chuckle. Then he became more serious. He moved his hands up the curve of her spine, found her nape, one hand gripping her there as the other coiled in her hair. He began to move inside of her, holding her still as he did deep, short thrusts. Another moan caught in her throat. Her nipples brushed the pillows, still throbbing from the bite of his fangs, the strong suction of his mouth.

"There's my sweet girl. Be quiet now. I need your obedience. Your submission is my drug of choice. Be warned—no matter how much you give, it will never be enough. I will always want more."

She hoped so. Goddess, she hoped so.

~

WANT MORE OF THE VAMPIRE QUEEN SERIES? Adan has nothing but hatred for the Fae. But when the vampire sorcerer comes to Club Atlantis to set up a portal for magic users, he discovers it's a haven for a Fae female. Even her scent sets off his bloodlust.

Catriona can't put down roots anywhere. For a tree nymph, that's a serious problem. One that calls for a solution that will appall the Fae world – and risk her life and heart to a vampire who may not be able to forgive what her kind took from him.

CLICK HERE TO READ NOW
VAMPIRE GUARDIAN

Reading this in print format?
Look for it at your favorite book vendor!

ABOUT THE AUTHOR

Having penned over fifty acclaimed BDSM contemporary and paranormal titles, which includes six award-winning series, *Joey W. Hill* has been awarded the RT Book Reviews Career Achievement Award for Erotic Romance. A submissive herself, Hill brings authenticity to her intensely emotional love stories.

She is grateful for the support of a wonderful and enthusiastic readership, which allows her to live on her beloved Carolina coast with her even more beloved husband and menagerie of animals.

- On the Web: https://storywitch.com
- Twitter: https://twitter.com/JoeyWHill
- Facebook: https://facebook.com/JoeyWHillAuthor
- Facebook Fan Forum: https://facebook.com/groups/JWHMembersOnly
- MeWe: https://mewe.com/i/joeywhill
- GoodReads: https://www.goodreads.com/author/show/103359.Joey_W_Hill
- BookBub: https://bookbub.com/authors/joey-w-hill
- Amazon: https://amazon.com/Joey-W-Hill/e/B001JSCIW0

ALSO BY JOEY W. HILL

Arcane Shot Series

Arcane Shot

Arcane Madame

Arcane Chaos

Arcane Knight

Daughters of Arianne Series

A Mermaid's Kiss

A Witch's Beauty

A Mermaid's Ransom

Knights of the Board Room Seri

Board Resolution

Controlled Response

Honor Bound

Afterlife

Hostile Takeover

Willing Sacrifice

Soul Rest

Knight Nostalgia *(Antho*

Mistresses of the Board Ro

At Her Comman

At Her Service

At Her Call

At Her Pleasu

Nature of Desir

Holding the (

Natural L

Ice Que

Mirror of My Soul

Mistress of Redemption

Rough Canvas

Branded Sanctuary

Divine Solace

Worth The Wait

Truly Helpless

In His Arms

Ignition Sequence

Naughty Bits Series

Naughty Bits

Naughty Wishes

Vampire Queen Series

Vampire Queen's Servant

Mark of the Vampire Queen

Vampire's Claim

Beloved Vampire

Vampire Mistress *(VQS: Club Atlantis)*

Vampire Trinity *(VQS: Club Atlantis)*

Vampire Instinct

Bound by the Vampire Queen

Taken by a Vampire

The Scientific Method

Nightfall

Elusive Hero

Night's Templar

Vampire's Soul

Vampire's Embrace

Vampire Master *(VQS: Club Atlantis)*

Vampire Guardian *(VQS: Club Atlantis)*

Vampire's Choice

ALSO BY JOEY W. HILL

Arcane Shot Series

Arcane Shot

Arcane Madame

Arcane Chaos

Arcane Knight

Daughters of Arianne Series

A Mermaid's Kiss

A Witch's Beauty

A Mermaid's Ransom

Knights of the Board Room Series

Board Resolution

Controlled Response

Honor Bound

Afterlife

Hostile Takeover

Willing Sacrifice

Soul Rest

Knight Nostalgia *(Anthology)*

Mistresses of the Board Room Series

At Her Command

At Her Service

At Her Call

At Her Pleasure

Nature of Desire Series

Holding the Cards

Natural Law

Ice Queen